exhausted, leaned for support against the wall. Her features, which were delicately beautiful, had gained from distress an expression of captivating sweetness: she had

An eye

As when the blue sky trembles through a cloud

Of purest white.

A habit of gray camlet, with short slashed sleeves, showed, but did not adorn, her figure: it was thrown open at the bosom, upon which part of her hair had fallen in disorder, while the light veil hastily thrown on, had, in her confusion, been suffered to fall back. Every moment of further observation heightened the surprise of La Motte, and interested him more warmly in her favour. Such elegance and apparent refinement, contrasted with the desolation of the house, and the savage manners of its inhabitants, seemed to him like a romance of imagination, rather than an occurrence of real life. He endeavoured to comfort her, and his sense of compassion was too sincere to be misunderstood. Her terror gradually subsided into gratitude and grief. Ah, Sir, said she, Heaven has sent you to my relief, and will surely reward you for your protection: I have no friend in the world, if do not find one in you.

La Motte assured her of his kindness, when he was interrupted by the entrance of the ruffian. He desired to be conducted to his family. All in good time, replied the latter; I have taken care of one of them, and will of you, please St. Peter; so be comforted. These comfortable words renewed the terror of La Motte, who now earnestly begged to know if his family were safe. O! as for that matter they are safe enough, and you will be with them presently; but don't stand parlying here all night. Do you choose to go or stay? you know the conditions. They now bound the eyes of La Motte and of the young lady, whom terror had hitherto kept silent, and then placing them on two horses, a man mounted behind each, and they immediately galloped off. They had proceeded in this way near half an hour, when La Motte entreated to know whither he was going? You will know that by and by, said the ruffian, so be at peace. Finding interrogatories useless, La Motte resumed silence till the horses stopped. His conductor then hallooed, and being answered by voices at some distance, in a few moments the sound of carriage wheels was heard, and, presently after, the words of a man directing Peter which way to drive. As the carriage approached, La Motte called, and, to his inexpressible joy, was answered by his wife.

The Ghastly Gothic Tomes

Vol. 2

Published by NRM Books.

ISBN: 978-1-965179-05-5

CREDITS
Cover Art by: Nathan Reese Maher

COPYRIGHT

Table of Contents

The Romance of the Forest

By Ann Radcliffe

CHAPTER I

I am a man,

So weary with disasters, tugg'd with fortune,

That I would set my life on any chance,

To mend it, or be rid ou't.

When once sordid interest seizes on the heart, it freezes up
the source of every warm and liberal feeling; it is an enemy
alike to virtue and to taste—this it perverts, and that it
annihilates. The time may come, my friend, when death shall
dissolve the sinews of avarice, and justice be permitted to
resume her rights.

Such were the words of the Advocate Nemours to Pierre de
la Motte, as the latter stept at midnight into the carriage which
was to bear him far from Paris, from his creditors and the
persecution of the laws. De la Motte thanked him for this last
instance of his kindness; the assistance he had given him in
escape; and, when the carriage drove away, uttered a sad adieu!
The gloom of the hour, and the peculiar emergency of his
circumstances, sunk him in silent reverie.

Whoever has read Gayot de Pitaval, the most faithful of
those writers who record the proceedings in the Parliamentary
Courts of Paris during the seventeenth century, must surely
remember the striking story of Pierre de la Motte and the
Marquess Philippe de Montalt: let all such, therefore, be
informed, that the person here introduced to their notice was
that individual Pierre de la Motte.

As Madame de la Motte leaned from the coach window, and
gave a last look to the walls of Paris—Paris, the scene of her
former happiness, and the residence of many dear friends—the
fortitude, which had till now supported her, yielding to the

force of grief—Farewell all! sighed she, this last look and we are separated for ever! Tears followed her words, and, sinking back, she resigned herself to the stillness of sorrow. The recollection of former times pressed heavily upon her heart; a few months before and she was surrounded by friends, fortune, and consequence; now she was deprived of all, a miserable exile from her native place, without home, without comfort—almost without hope. It was not the least of her afflictions that she had been obliged to quit Paris without bidding adieu to her only son, who was now on duty with his regiment in Germany; and such had been the precipitancy of this removal, that had she even known where he was stationed, she had no time to inform him of it, or of the alteration in his father's circumstances.

Pierre de la Motte was a gentleman, descended from an ancient house of France. He was a man whose passions often overcame his reason, and, for a time, silenced his conscience; but though the image of virtue, which nature had impressed upon his heart, was sometimes obscured by the passing influence of vice, it was never wholly obliterated. With strength of mind sufficient to have withstood temptation, he would have been a good man; as it was, he was always a weak, and sometimes a vicious member of society; yet his mind was active, and his imagination vivid, which co-operating with the force of passion, often dazzled his judgment and subdued principle. Thus he was a man, infirm in purpose and visionary in virtue:— in a word, his conduct was suggested by feeling, rather than principle; and his virtue, such as it was, could not stand the pressure of occasion.

Early in life he had married Constance Valentia, a beautiful and elegant woman, attached to her family and beloved by them. Her birth was equal, her fortune superior to his; and their nuptials had been celebrated under the auspices of an approving and flattering world. Her heart was devoted to La Motte, and, for some time, she found in him an affectionate husband; but, allured by the gaieties of Paris, he was soon devoted to its luxuries, and in a few years his fortune and affection were equally lost in dissipation. A false pride had still operated against his interest, and withheld him from honourable retreat while it was yet in his power: the habits which he had acquired, enchained him to the scene of his former pleasure; and thus he had continued an expensive style of life till the means of prolonging it were exhausted. He at length awoke from this lethargy of security; but it was only to plunge into new error, and to attempt schemes for the reparation of his fortune, which served to sink him deeper in destruction. The consequence of a transaction, in which he thus engaged, now drove him, with the small wreck of his property, into dangerous and ignominious exile.

It was his design to pass into one of the southern provinces, and there seek, near the borders of the kingdom, an asylum in some obscure village. His family consisted of a wife and two faithful domestics, a man and woman, who had followed the fortune of their master.

The night was dark and tempestuous, and at about the distance of three leagues from Paris, Peter, who now acted as postillion, having driven for some time over a wild heath where many ways crossed, stopped, and acquainted De la Motte with his perplexity. The sudden stopping of the carriage roused the latter from his reverie, and filled the whole party with the terror of pursuit; he was unable to supply the necessary direction, and the extreme darkness made it dangerous to proceed without one. During this period of distress, a light was perceived at some distance, and after much doubt and hesitation, La Motte, in the hope of obtaining assistance, alighted and advanced towards it; he proceeded slowly, from the fear of unknown pits. The light issued from the window of a small and ancient house, which stood alone on the heath, at the distance of half a mile.

Having reached the door, he stopped for some moments, listening in apprehensive anxiety — no sound was heard but that of the wind, which swept in hollow gusts over the waste. At length he ventured to knock, and having waited for some time, during which he indistinctly heard several voices in conversation, some one within inquired what he wanted? La Motte answered, that he was a traveller who had lost his way, and desired to be directed to the nearest town. That, said the person, is seven miles off, and the road bad enough, even if you could see it; if you only want a bed, you may have it here, and had better stay.

The "pitiless pelting" of the storm, which at this time beat with increasing fury upon La Motte, inclined him to give up the attempt of proceeding further till daylight; but, desirous of seeing the person with whom he conversed, before he ventured to expose his family by calling up the carriage, he asked to be admitted. The door was now opened by a tall figure with a light, who invited La Motte to enter. He followed the man through a passage into a room almost unfurnished, in one corner of which a bed was spread upon the floor. The forlorn and desolate aspect of this apartment made La Motte shrink involuntarily, and he was turning to go out when the man suddenly pushed him back, and he heard the door locked upon him; his heart failed, yet he made a desperate, though vain, effort to force the door, and called loudly for release. No answer was returned; but he distinguished the voices of men in the room above, and, not doubting but their intention was to rob and murder him, his agitation, at first, overcame his reason. By the light of some almost-expiring embers, he perceived a window, but the hope which this discovery revived was quickly lost, when he found the aperture guarded by strong iron bars. Such preparation for security surprised him, and confirmed his worst apprehensions. Alone, unarmed — beyond the chance of assistance, he saw himself in the power of people whose trade was apparently rapine! — murder their means! — After revolving every possibility of escape, he endeavoured to await the event with fortitude; but La Motte could boast of no such virtue.

The voices had ceased, and all remained still for a quarter of an hour, when, between the pauses of the wind, he thought he distinguished the sobs and moaning of a female; he listened attentively, and became confirmed in his conjecture; it was too evidently the accent of distress. At this conviction the remains of his courage forsook him, and a terrible surmise darted, with the rapidity of lightning, across his brain. It was probable that his carriage had been discovered by the people of the house, who, with a design of plunder, had secured his servant, and brought hither Madame de la Motte. He was the more inclined to believe this, by the stillness which had for some time reigned in the house, previous to the sounds he now heard. Or it was possible that the inhabitants were not robbers, but persons to whom he had been betrayed by his friend or servant, and who were appointed to deliver him into the hands of justice. Yet he hardly dared to doubt the integrity of his friend, who had been intrusted with the secret of his flight and the plan of his route, and had procured him the carriage in which he had escaped. Such depravity, exclaimed La Motte, cannot surely exist in human nature; much less in the heart of Nemours!

This ejaculation was interrupted by a noise in the passage leading to the room: it approached — the door was unlocked — and the man who had admitted La Motte into the house entered, leading, or rather forcibly dragging along, a beautiful girl, who appeared to be about eighteen. Her features were bathed in tears, and she seemed to suffer the utmost distress. The man fastened the lock and put the key in his pocket. He then advanced to La Motte, who had before observed other persons in the passage, and pointing a pistol to his breast, You are wholly in our power, said he, no assistance can reach you: if you wish to save your life, swear that you will convey this girl where I may never see her more; or rather consent to take her with you, for your oath I would not believe, and I can take care you shall not find me again. — Answer quickly, you have no time to lose.

He now seized the trembling hand of the girl, who shrunk aghast with terror, and hurried her towards La Motte, whom surprise still kept silent. She sunk at his feet, and with supplicating eyes, that streamed with tears, implored him to have pity on her. Notwithstanding his present agitation, he found it impossible to contemplate the beauty and distress of the object before him with indifference. Her youth, her apparent innocence — the artless energy of her manner forcibly assailed his heart, and he was going to speak, when the ruffian, who mistook the silence of astonishment for that of hesitation, prevented him, I have a horse ready to take you from hence, said he, and I will direct you over the heath. If you return within an hour, you die: after then, you are at liberty to come here when you please.

La Motte, without answering, raised the lovely girl from the floor, and was so much relieved from his own apprehensions, that he had leisure to attempt dissipating hers. Let us be gone, said the ruffian, and have no more of this nonsense; you may think yourself well off it's no worse. I'll go and get the horse ready.

The last words roused La Motte, and perplexed him with new fears; he dreaded to discover his carriage, lest its appearance might tempt the banditti to plunder; and to depart on horseback with this man might reduce a consequence yet more to be dreaded, Madame la Motte, wearied with apprehension, would, probably, send for her husband to the house, when all the former danger would be incurred, with the additional evil of being separated from his family, and the chance of being detected by the emissaries of justice in endeavouring to recover them. As these reflections passed over his mind in tumultuous rapidity, a noise was again heard in the passage, an uproar and scuffle ensued, and in the same moment he could distinguish the voice of his servant, who had been sent by Madame La Motte in search of him. Being now determined to disclose what could not long be concealed, he exclaimed aloud, that a horse was unnecessary, that he had a carriage at some distance, which would convey them from the heath, the man who was seized being his servant.

The ruffian, speaking through the door, bade him be patient a while and he should hear more from him. La Motte now turned his eyes upon his unfortunate companion, who, pale and exhausted, leaned for support against the wall. Her features, which were delicately beautiful, had gained from distress an expression of captivating sweetness: she had

An eye

As when the blue sky trembles through a cloud

Of purest white.

A habit of gray camlet, with short slashed sleeves, showed, but did not adorn, her figure: it was thrown open at the bosom, upon which part of her hair had fallen in disorder, while the light veil hastily thrown on, had, in her confusion, been suffered to fall back. Every moment of further observation heightened the surprise of La Motte, and interested him more warmly in her favour. Such elegance and apparent refinement, contrasted with the desolation of the house, and the savage manners of its inhabitants, seemed to him like a romance of imagination, rather than an occurrence of real life. He endeavoured to comfort her, and his sense of compassion was too sincere to be misunderstood. Her terror gradually subsided into gratitude and grief. Ah, Sir, said she, Heaven has sent you to my relief, and will surely reward you for your protection: I have no friend in the world, if do not find one in you.

La Motte assured her of his kindness, when he was interrupted by the entrance of the ruffian. He desired to be conducted to his family. All in good time, replied the latter; I have taken care of one of them, and will of you, please St. Peter; so be comforted. These comfortable words renewed the terror of La Motte, who now earnestly begged to know if his family were safe. O! as for that matter they are safe enough, and you will be with them presently; but don't stand parlying here all night. Do you choose to go or stay? you know the conditions. They now bound the eyes of La Motte and of the young lady, whom terror had hitherto kept silent, and then placing them on two horses, a man mounted behind each, and they immediately galloped off. They had proceeded in this way near half an hour, when La Motte entreated to know whither he was going? You will know that by and by, said the ruffian, so be at peace. Finding interrogatories useless, La Motte resumed silence till the horses stopped. His conductor then hallooed, and being answered by voices at some distance, in a few moments the sound of carriage wheels was heard, and, presently after, the words of a man directing Peter which way to drive. As the carriage approached, La Motte called, and, to his inexpressible joy, was answered by his wife.

You are now beyond the borders of the heath, and may go which way you will, said the ruffian; if you return within an hour, you will be welcomed by a brace of bullets. This was a very unnecessary caution to La Motte, whom they now released. The young stranger sighed deeply, as she entered the carriage; and the ruffian, having bestowed upon Peter some directions and more threats, waited to see him drive off. They did not wait long.

La Motte immediately gave a short relation of what passed at the house, including account of the manner in which the young stranger had been introduced to him. During this narrative, her deep convulsive sighs frequently drew the attention of Madame La Motte, whose compassion became gradually interested in her behalf, and who now endeavoured to tranquillize her spirits. The unhappy girl answered her kindness in artless and simple expressions, and then relapsed into tears and silence. Madame forbore for the present to ask any questions that might lead to a discovery of her connexions, or seem to require an explanation of the late adventure, which now furnishing her with a new subject of reflection, the sense of her own misfortunes pressed less heavily upon her mind. The distress of La Motte was even for a while suspended; he ruminated on the late scene, and it appeared like a vision, or one of those improbable fictions that sometimes are exhibited in a romance: he could reduce it to no principles of probability, nor render it comprehensible by any endeavour to analyze it. The present charge, and the chance of future trouble brought upon him by this adventure, occasioned some dissatisfaction; but the beauty and seeming innocence of Adeline united with the pleadings of humanity in her favor, and he determined to protect her.

The tumult of emotions which had passed in the bosom of Adeline began now to subside; terror was softened into anxiety, and despair into grief. The sympathy so evident in the manners of her companions, particularly in those of Madame La Motte, soothed her heart, and encouraged her to hope for better days.

Dismally and silently the night passed on, for the minds of the travellers were too much occupied by their several sufferings to admit of conversation.

The dawn, so anxiously watched for, at length appeared, and introduced the strangers more fully to each other. Adeline derived comfort from the looks of Madame La Motte, who gazed frequently and attentively at her, and thought she had seldom seen a countenance so interesting, or a form so striking.

The languor of sorrow threw a melancholy grace upon her features, that appealed immediately to the heart; and there was a penetrating sweetness in her blue eyes, which indicated an intelligent and amiable mind.

La Motte now looked anxiously from the coach window, that he might judge of their situation, and observe whether he was followed. The obscurity of the dawn confined his views, but no person appeared. The sun at length tinted the eastern clouds and the tops of the highest hills, and soon after burst in full splendour on the scene. The terrors of La Motte began to subside, and the griefs of Adeline to soften. They entered upon a lane confined by high banks and overarched by trees, on whose branches appeared the first green buds of spring glittering with dews. The fresh breeze of the morning animated the spirits of Adeline, whose mind was delicately sensible to the beauties of nature. As she viewed the flowery luxuriance of the turf, and the tender green of the trees, or caught, between the opening banks, a glimpse of the varied landscape, rich with wood, and fading into blue and distant mountains, her heart expanded in momentary joy. With Adeline the charms of external nature were heightened by those of novelty: she had seldom seen the grandeur of an extensive prospect, or the magnificence of a wide horizon — and not often the picturesque beauties of more confined scenery. Her mind had not lost by long oppression that elastic energy, which resists calamity; else, however, susceptible might have been her original taste, the beauties of nature would no longer have charmed her thus easily even to temporary repose.

The road, at length, wound down the side of a hill, and La Motte, again looking anxiously from the window, saw before him an open champaign country, through which the road, wholly unsheltered from observation, extended almost in a direct line. The danger of these circumstances alarmed him, for his flight might, without difficulty, be traced for many leagues from the hills he was now descending. Of the first peasant that passed, he inquired for a road among the hills, but heard of none. La Motte now sunk into his former terrors. Madame, notwithstanding her own apprehensions, endeavoured to reassure him; but finding her efforts ineffectual, she also retired to the contemplation of her misfortunes. Often, as they went on, did La Motte look back upon the country they had passed, and often did imagination suggest to him the sounds of distant pursuit.

The travellers stopped to breakfast in a village, where the road was at length obscured by woods, and La Motte's spirits again revived. Adeline appeared more tranquil than she had yet been, and La Motte now asked for an explanation of the scene he had witnessed on the preceding night. The inquiry renewed all her distress, and with tears she entreated for the present to be spared on the subject. La Motte pressed it no farther, but he observed that for the greater part of the day she seemed to remember it in melancholy and dejection. They now travelled among the hills, and were, therefore, in less danger of observation; but La Motte avoided the great towns, and stopped in obscure ones no longer than to refresh the horses. About two hours after noon, the road wound into a deep valley, watered by a rivulet and overhung with wood. La Motte called to Peter, and ordered him to drive to a thickly embowered spot, that appeared on the left. Here he alighted with his family; and Peter having spread the provisions on the turf, they seated themselves and partook of a repast, which, in other circumstances, would have been thought delicious. Adeline endeavoured to smile, but the languor of grief was now heightened by indisposition. The violent agitation of mind and fatigue of body which she had suffered for the last twenty-four hours, had overpowed her strength, and when La Motte led her back to the carriage, her whole frame trembled with illness. But she uttered no complaint, and, having long observed the dejection of her companions, she made a feeble effort to enliven them.

They continued to travel throughout the day without any accident or interruption, and about three hours after sunset arrived at Monville, a small town where La Motte determined to pass the night. Repose was, indeed, necessary to the whole party, whose pale and haggard looks, as they alighted from the carriage, were but too obvious to pass unobserved by the people of the inn. As soon as beds could be prepared, Adeline withdrew to her chamber, accompanied by Madame La Motte, whose concern for the fair stranger made her exert every effort to soothe and console her. Adeline wept in silence, and taking the hand of Madame, pressed it to her bosom. These were not merely tears of grief — they were mingled with those which flow from the grateful heart, when, unexpectedly, it meets with sympathy. Madame La Motte understood them. After some momentary silence, she renewed her assurances of kindness, and entreated Adeline to confide in her friendship; but she carefully avoided any mention of the subject which had before so much affected her. Adeline at length found words to express her sense of this goodness, which she did in a manner so natural and sincere, that Madame, finding herself much affected, took leave of her for the night.

In the morning, La Motte rose at an early hour, impatient to be gone. Every thing was prepared for his departure, and the breakfast had been waiting some time, but Adeline did not appear. Madame La Motte went to her chamber, and found her sunk in a disturbed slumber. Her breathing was short and irregular — she frequently started, or sighed, and sometimes she muttered an incoherent sentence. While Madame gazed with concern upon her languid countenance, she awoke, and, looking up, gave her hand to Madame La Motte, who found it burning with fever. She had passed a restless night, and, as she now attempted to rise, her head, which beat with intense pain, grew giddy, her strength failed, and she sunk back.

Madame was much alarmed, being at once convinced that it was impossible she could travel, and that a delay might prove fatal to her husband. She went to inform him of the truth, and his distress may be more easily imagined than described. He saw all the inconvenience and danger of delay, yet he could not so far divest himself of humanity as to abandon Adeline to the care, or rather to the neglect, of strangers. He sent immediately for a physician, who pronounced her to be in a high fever, and said a removal in her present state must be fatal. La Motte now determined to wait the event, and endeavour to calm the transports of terror which at times assailed him. In the mean while he took such precautions as his situation admitted of, passing the greater part of the day out of the village, in a spot from whence he had a view of the road for some distance; yet to be exposed to destruction by the illness of a girl whom he did not know, and who had actually been forced upon him, was a misfortune to which La Motte had not philosophy enough to submit with composure.

Adeline's fever continued to increase during the whole day, and at night, when the physician took his leave, he told La Motte the event would very soon be decided. La Motte received this intelligence with real concern. The beauty and innocence of Adeline had overcome the disadvantageous circumstances under which she had been introduced to him, and he now gave less consideration to the inconvenience she might hereafter occasion him, than to the hope of her recovery.

Madame La Motte watched over her with tender anxiety, and observed with admiration her patient sweetness and mild resignation. Adeline amply repaid her, though she thought she could not. — Young as I am, she would say, and deserted by those upon whom I have a claim for protection, I can remember no connexion to make me regret life so much, as that I hoped to form with you. If I live, my conduct will best express my sense of your goodness;—words are but feeble testimonies.

The sweetness of her manners so much attracted Madame La Motte, that she watched the crisis of her disorder with a solicitude which precluded every other interest. Adeline passed a very disturbed night, and, when the physician appeared in the morning, he gave orders that she should be indulged with whatever she liked, and answered the inquiries of La Motte with a frankness that left him nothing to hope.

In the mean time, his patient, after drinking profusely of some mild liquids, fell asleep, in which she continued for several hours, and so profound was her repose, that her breath alone gave sign of existence. She awoke free from fever, and with no other disorder than weakness, which in a few days she overcame so well as to be able to set out with La Motte for B——, a village out of the great road, which he thought it prudent to quit. There they passed the following night, and early the next morning commenced their journey upon a wild and woody tract of country. They stopped about noon at a solitary village, where they took refreshments, and obtained directions for passing the vast forest of Fontanville, upon the borders of which they now were. La Motte wished at first to take a guide, but he apprehended more evil from the discovery he might make of his route, than he hoped for benefit from assistance in the wilds of this uncultivated tract.

La Motte now designed to pass on to Lyons, where he could either seek concealment in its neighbourhood, or embark on the Rhone for Geneva, should the emergency of his circumstances hereafter require him to leave France. It was about twelve o'clock at noon, and he was desirous to hasten forward, that he might pass the forest of Fontanville, and reach the town on its opposite borders, before night-fall. Having deposited a fresh stock of provisions in the carriage, and received such directions as were necessary concerning the roads, they again set forward, and in a short time entered upon the forest. It was now the latter end of April, and the weather was remarkably temperate and fine. The balmy freshness of the air, which breathed the first pure essence of vegetation; and the gentle warmth of the sun, whose beams vivified every hue of nature, and opened every floweret of spring, revived Adeline and inspired her with life and health. As she inhaled the breeze, her strength seemed to return, and as her eyes wandered through the romantic glades that opened into the forest, her heart was gladdened with complacent delight: but when from these objects she turned her regard upon Monsieur and Madame La Motte, to whose tender attentions she owed her life, and in whose looks she now read esteem and kindness, her bosom glowed with sweet affections, and she experienced a force of gratitude which might be called sublime.

For the remainder of the day they continued to travel, without seeing a hut or meeting a human being. It was now near sunset, and the prospect being closed on all sides by the forest, La Motte began to have apprehensions that his servant had mistaken the way. The road, if a road it could be called, which afforded only a slight track upon the grass, was sometimes over-run by luxuriant vegetation, and sometimes obscured by the deep shades, and Peter at length stopped uncertain of the way. La Motte, who dreaded being benighted in a scene so wild and solitary as this forest, and whose apprehensions of banditti were very sanguine, ordered him to proceed at any rate, and, if he found no track, to endeavour to gain a more open part of the forest. With these orders Peter again set forwards; but having proceeded some way, and his views being still confined by woody glades and forest walks, he began to despair of extricating himself, and stopped for further orders. The sun was now set; but as La Motte looked anxiously from the window, he observed upon the vivid glow of the western horizon some dark towers rising from among the trees at a little distance, and ordered Peter to drive towards them. — If they belong to a monastery, said he, we may probably gain admittance for the night.

The carriage drove along under the shade of "melancholy boughs," through which the evening twilight, which yet coloured the air, diffused a solemnity that vibrated in thrilling sensations upon the hearts of the travellers. Expectation kept them silent. The present scene recalled to Adeline a remembrance of the late terrific circumstances, and her mind responded but too easily to the apprehension of new misfortunes. La Motte alighted at the foot of a green knoll, where the trees again opening to light, permitted a nearer though imperfect view of the edifice.

CHAPTER II

..........how these antique towers

And vacant courts chill the suspended soul!

Till expectation wears the face of fear:

And fear, half ready to become devotion,

Mutters a kind of mental orison

It knows not wherefore! What a kind of being

Is circumstance!

HORACE WALPOLE.

He approached, and perceived the Gothic remains of an abbey: it stood on a kind of rude lawn, overshadowed by high and spreading trees which seemed coeval with the building, and diffused a romantic gloom around. The greater part of the pile appeared to be sinking into ruins, and that which had withstood the ravages of time, showed the remaining features of the fabric more awful in decay. The lofty battlements, thickly enwreathed with ivy, were half demolished, and become the residence of birds of prey. Huge fragments of the eastern tower, which was almost demolished, lay scattered amid the high grass, that waved slowly to the breeze. "The thistle shook its lonely head; the moss whistled to the wind." A Gothic gate, richly ornamented with fret-work, which opened into the main body of the edifice, but which was now obstructed with brush-wood, remained entire. Above the vast and magnificent portal of this gate arose a window of the same order, whose pointed arches still exhibited fragments of stained glass, once the pride of monkish devotion. La Motte, thinking it possible it might yet shelter some human being, advanced to the gate and lifted a massy knocker. The hollow sounds rung through the emptiness of the place. After waiting a few minutes, he forced back the gate, which was heavy with iron work and creaked harshly on its hinges.

He entered what appeared to have been the chapel of the abbey, where the hymn of devotion had once been raised, and the tear of penitence had once been shed; sounds, which could now only be recalled by imagination—tears of penitence, which had been long since fixed in fate. La Motte paused a moment, for he felt a sensation of sublimity rising into terror—a

14

suspension of mingled astonishment and awe! He surveyed the vastness of the place, and as he contemplated its ruins, fancy bore him back to past ages. — And these walls, said he, where once superstition lurked, and austerity anticipated an earthly purgatory, now tremble over the mortal remains of the beings who reared them!

The deepening gloom now reminded La Motte that he had no time to lose; but curiosity prompted him to explore further, and he obeyed the impulse. As he walked over the broken pavement, the sound of his steps ran in echoes through the place, and seemed like the mysterious accents of the dead reproving the sacrilegious mortal who thus dared to disturb their precincts.

From this chapel he passed into the nave of the great church, of which one window, more perfect than the rest, opened upon a long vista of the forest, through which was seen the rich colouring of evening, melting by imperceptible gradations into the solemn gray of upper air. Dark hills, whose outline appeared distinct upon the vivid glow of the horizon, closed the perspective. Several of the pillars, which had once supported the roof, remained the proud effigies of sinking greatness, and seemed to nod at every murmur of the blast over the fragments of those that had fallen a little before them. La Motte sighed. The comparison between himself and the gradation of decay which these columns exhibited, was but too obvious and affecting. A few years, said he, and I shall become like the mortals on whose relicks I now gaze, and, like them too, I may be the subject of meditation to a succeeding generation, which shall totter but a little while over the object they contemplate ere they also sink into the dust.

Retiring from the scene, he walked through the cloisters, till a door, which communicated with the lofty part of the building, attracted his curiosity. He opened this, and perceived across the foot of the staircase another door; — but now, partly checked by fear, and partly by the recollection of the surprise his family might feel in his absence, he returned with hasty steps to his carriage, having wasted some of the precious moments of twilight and gained no information.

Some slight answer to Madame La Motte's inquiries, and a general direction to Peter to drive carefully on and look for a road, was all that his anxiety would permit him to utter. The night shade fell thick around, which, deepened by the gloom of the forest, soon rendered it dangerous to proceed. Peter stopped; but La Motte, persisting in his first determination, ordered him to go on. Peter ventured to remonstrate, Madame La Motte entreated, but La Motte reproved — commanded, and at length repented; for the hind wheel rising upon the stump of an old tree, which the darkness had prevented Peter from observing, the carriage was in an instant overturned.

The party, as may be supposed, were much terrified, but no one was materially hurt; and having disengaged themselves from their perilous situation, La Motte and Peter endeavoured to raise the carriage. The extent of this misfortune was now discovered, for they perceived that the wheel was broke. Their distress was reasonably great, for not only was the coach disabled from proceeding, but it could not even afford a shelter from the cold dews of the night, it being impossible to preserve it in an upright situation. After a few moments' silence, La Motte proposed that they should return to the ruins which they had just quitted, which lay at a very short distance, and pass the night in the most habitable part of them: that, when morning dawned, Peter should take one of the coach horses, and endeavour to find a road and a town, from whence assistance could be procured for repairing the carriage. This proposal was opposed by Madame La Motte, who shuddered at the idea of passing so many hours of darkness in a place so forlorn as the monastery. Terrors, which she neither endeavoured to examine or combat, overcame her, and she told La Motte she had rather remain exposed to the unwholesome dews of night, than encounter the desolation of the ruins. La Motte had at first felt an equal reluctance to return to this spot; but having subdued his own feelings, he resolved not to yield to those of his wife.

The horses being now disengaged from the carriage, the party moved towards the edifice. As they proceeded, Peter, who followed them, struck a light, and they entered the ruins by the flame of sticks which he had collected. The partial gleams thrown across the fabric seemed to make its desolation more solemn, while the obscurity of the greater part of the pile heightened its sublimity, and led fancy on to scenes of horror. Adeline, who had hitherto remained in silence, now uttered an exclamation of mingled admiration and fear. A kind of pleasing dread thrilled her bosom, and filled all her soul. Tears started into her eyes: — she wished yet feared to go on; — she hung upon the arm of La Motte, and looked at him with a sort of hesitating interrogation.

He opened the door of the great hall, and they entered: its extent was lost in gloom. — Let us stay here, said Madame de La Motte, I will go no further. La Motte pointed to the broken roof, and was proceeding, when he was interrupted by an uncommon noise, which passed along the hall. They were all silent — it was the silence of terror. Madame La Motte spoke first. Let us quit this spot, said she, any evil is preferable to the feeling which now oppresses me. Let us retire instantly. The stillness had for some time remained undisturbed, and La Motte, ashamed of the fear he had involuntarily betrayed, now thought it necessary to affect a boldness which he did not feel. He therefore opposed ridicule to the terror of Madame, and insisted upon proceeding. Thus compelled to acquiesce, she traversed the hall with trembling steps. They came to a narrow passage, and Peter's sticks being nearly exhausted, they awaited here, while he went in search of more.

The almost expiring light flashed faintly upon the walls of the passage, showing the recess more horrible. Across the hall, the greater part of which was concealed in shadow, the feeble ray spread a tremulous gleam, exhibiting the chasm in the roof, while many nameless objects were seen imperfectly through the dusk. Adeline with a smile inquired of La Motte if he believed in spirits. The question was ill-timed; for the present scene impressed its terrors upon La Motte, and, in spite of endeavour, he felt a superstitious dread stealing upon him. He was now, perhaps, standing over the ashes of the dead. If spirits were ever permitted to revisit the earth, this seemed the hour and the place most suitable for their appearance. La Motte remaining silent, Adeline said, Were I inclined to superstition — she was interrupted by a return of the noise which had been lately heard. It sounded down the passage, at whose entrance they stood, and sunk gradually away. Every heart palpitated, and they remained listening in silence. A new subject of apprehension seized La Motte: — the noise might proceed from banditti, and he hesitated whether it would be safe to proceed. Peter now came with the light: Madame refused to enter the passage — La Motte was not much inclined to it; but Peter, in whom curiosity was more prevalent than fear, readily offered his services. La Motte, after some hesitation, suffered him to go, while he awaited at the entrance the result of the inquiry. The extent of the passage soon concealed Peter from view, and the echoes of his footsteps were lost in a sound which rushed along the avenue, and became fainter and fainter till it sunk into silence. La Motte now called aloud to Peter, but no answer was returned; at length, they heard the sound of a distant footstep, and Peter soon after appeared, breathless, and pale with fear.

When he came within hearing of La Motte, he called out, An please your honour, I've done for them, I believe, but I've had a hard bout. I thought I was fighting with the devil. — What are you speaking of? said La Motte.

They were nothing but owls and rooks after all, continued Peter; but the light brought them all about my ears, and they made such a confounded clapping with their wings, that I thought at first I had been beset with a legion of devils. But I have driven them all out, master, and you have nothing to fear now.

The latter part of the sentence, intimating a suspicion of his courage, La Motte, could have dispensed with, and to retrieve in some degree his reputation, he made a point of proceeding through the passage. They now moved on with alacrity, for, as Peter said, they had nothing to fear.

The passage led into a large area, on one side of which, over a range of cloisters, appeared the west tower, and a lofty part of the edifice; the other side was open to the woods. La Motte led the way to a door of the tower, which he now perceived was the same he had formerly entered; but he found some difficulty in advancing, for the area was overgrown with brambles and nettles, and the light which Peter carried afforded only an uncertain gleam. When he unclosed the door, the dismal aspect of the place revived the apprehensions of Madame La Motte, and extorted from Adeline an inquiry whither they were going. Peter held up the light to show the narrow staircase that wound round the tower; but La Motte, observing the second door, drew back the rusty bolts, and entered a spacious apartment, which, from its style and condition, was evidently of a much later date than the other part of the structure: though desolate and forlorn, it was very little impaired by time; the walls were damp, but not decayed; and the glass was yet firm in the windows.

They passed on to a suit of apartments resembling the first they had seen, and expressed their surprise at the incongruous appearance of this part of the edifice with the mouldering walls they had left behind. These apartments conducted them to a winding passage, that received light and air through narrow cavities placed high in the wall; and was at length closed by a door barred with iron, which being with some difficulty opened, they entered a vaulted room. La Motte surveyed it with a scrutinizing eye, and endeavoured to conjecture for what purpose it had been guarded by a door of such strength; but he saw little within to assist his curiosity. The room appeared to have been built in modern times upon a Gothic plan. Adeline approached a large window that formed a kind of recess raised by one step over the level of the floor; she observed to La Motte that the whole floor was inlaid with Mosaic work; which drew from him a remark, that the style of this apartment was not strictly Gothic. He passed on to a door which appeared on the opposite side of the apartment, and, unlocking it, found himself in the great ball by which he had entered the fabric.

He now perceived, what the gloom had before concealed, a spiral staircase which led to a gallery above, and which, from its present condition, seemed to have been built with the more modern part of the fabric, though this also affected the Gothic mode of architecture: La Motte had little doubt that these stairs led to apartments corresponding with those he had passed below, and hesitated whether to explore them; but the entreaties of Madame, who was much fatigued, prevailed with him to defer all further examination. After some deliberation in which of the rooms they should pass the night, they determined to return to that which opened from the tower.

A fire was kindled on a hearth, which it is probable had not for many years before afforded the warmth of hospitality; and Peter having spread the provision he had brought from the coach, La Motte and his family, encircled round the fire, partook of a repast which hunger and fatigue made delicious. Apprehension gradually gave way to confidence, for they now found themselves in something like a human habitation, and they had leisure to laugh at their late terrors; but, as the blasts shook the doors, Adeline often started, and threw a fearful glance around. They continued to laugh and talk cheerfully for a time; yet their merriment was transient, if not affected; for a sense of their peculiar and distressed circumstances pressed upon their recollection, and sunk each individual into languor and pensive silence. Adeline felt the forlornness of her condition with energy; she reflected upon the past with astonishment, and anticipated the future with fear. She found herself wholly dependent upon strangers, with no other claim than what distress demands from the common sympathy of kindred beings; sighs swelled her heart, and the frequent tear started to her eye; but she checked it, ere it betrayed on her check the sorrow which she thought it would be ungrateful to reveal.

La Motte at length broke this meditative silence, by directing the fire to be renewed for the night, and the door to be secured: this seemed a necessary precaution, even in this solitude, and was effected by means of large stones piled against it, for other fastening there was none. It had frequently occurred to La Motte, that this apparently forsaken edifice might be a place of refuge to banditti. Here was solitude to conceal them; and a wild and extensive forest to assist their schemes of rapine, and to perplex with its labyrinths those who might be bold enough to attempt pursuit. These apprehensions, however, he hid within his own bosom, saving his companions from a share of the uneasiness they occasioned. Peter was ordered to watch at the door; and having given the fire a rousing stir, our desolate party drew round it, and sought in sleep a short oblivion of care.

The night passed on without disturbance. Adeline slept, but uneasy dreams fleeted before her fancy, and she awoke at an early hour: the recollection of her sorrows arose upon her mind, and yielding to their pressure, her tears flowed silently and fast. That she might indulge them without restraint, she went to a window that looked upon an open part of the forest: all was gloom and silence; she stood for some time viewing the shadowy scene.

The first tender tints of morning now appeared on the verge of the horizon, stealing upon the darkness; — so pure, so fine, so ethereal! it seemed as if heaven was opening to the view. The dark mists were seen to roll off to the west, as the tints of light grew stronger, deepening the obscurity of that part of the hemisphere, and involving the features of the country below; meanwhile, in the east, the hues became more vivid, darting a trembling lustre far around, till a ruddy glow, which fired all that part of the heavens, announced the rising sun. At first, a small line of inconceivable splendour emerged on the horizon, which quickly expanding, the sun appeared in all his glory, unveiling the whole face of nature, vivifying every colour of the landscape, and sprinkling the dewy earth with glittering light. The low and gentle responses of birds, awakened by the morning ray, now broke the silence of the hour; their soft warblings rising by degrees till they swelled the chorus of universal gladness. Adeline's heart swelled too with gratitude and adoration.

The scene before her soothed her mind, and exalted her thoughts to the great Author of Nature; she uttered an involuntary prayer: Father of good, who made this glorious scene! I resign myself to thy hands: thou wilt support me under my present sorrows, and to protect me from future evil.

Thus confiding in the benevolence of God, she wiped the tears from her eyes, while the sweet union of conscience and reflection rewarded her trust; and her mind, losing the feelings which had lately oppressed it, became tranquil and composed.

La Motte awoke soon after, and Peter prepared to set out on his expedition. As he mounted his horse. An' please you, master, said he, I think we had as good look no further for a habitation till better times turn up; for nobody will think of looking for us here; and when one sees the place by daylight, it's none so bad, but what a little patching up would make it comfortable enough. La Motte made no reply, but he thought of Peter's words. During the intervals of the night, when anxiety had kept him waking, the same idea had occurred to him; concealment was his only security, and this place afforded it. The desolation of the spot was repulsive to his wishes; but he had only a choice of evils—a forest with liberty was not a bad home for one who had too much reason to expect a prison. As he walked through the apartments, and examined their condition more attentively, he perceived they might easily be made habitable; and now surveying them under the cheerfulness of morning, his design strengthened; and he mused upon the means of accomplishing it, which nothing seemed so much to obstruct as the apparent difficulty of procuring food.

He communicated his thoughts to Madame La Motte, who felt repugnance to the scheme. La Motte, however, seldom consulted his wife till he had determined how to act; and he had already resolved to be guided in this affair by the report of Peter. If he could discover a town in the neighbourhood of the forest, where provisions and other necessaries could be procured, he would seek no further for a place of rest.

In the mean time he spent the anxious interval of Peter's absence in examining the ruin, and walking over the environs; they were sweetly romantic, and the luxuriant woods with which they abounded, seemed to sequester this spot from the rest of the world. Frequently a natural vista would yield a view of the country, terminated by hills, which retiring in distance faded into the blue horizon. A stream, various and musical in its course, wound at the foot of the lawn on which stood the abbey; here it silently glided beneath the shades, feeding the flowers that bloomed on its banks, and diffusing dewy freshness around; there it spread in broad expanse to day, reflecting the sylvan scene, and the wild deer that tasted its waves. La Motte observed every where a profusion of game; the pheasants scarcely flew from his approach, and the deer gazed mildly at him as he passed. They were strangers to man!

On his return to the abbey, La Motte ascended the stairs that led to the tower. About half way up, a door appeared in the wall; it yielded, without resistance, to his hand; but a sudden noise within, accompanied by a cloud of dust, made him step back and close the door. After waiting a few minutes, he again opened it, and perceived a large room of the more modern building. The remains of tapestry hung in tatters upon the walls, which were become the residence of birds of prey, whose sudden flight on the opening of the door had brought down a quantity of dust, and occasioned the noise. The windows were shattered, and almost without glass; but he was surprised to observe some remains of furniture; chairs, whose fashion and condition bore the date of their antiquity; a broken table, and an iron grate almost consumed by rust.

On the opposite side of the room was a door which led to another apartment, proportioned like the first, but hung with arras somewhat less tattered. In one corner stood a small bedstead, and a few shattered chairs were placed round the walls. La Motte gazed with a mixture of wonder and curiosity. 'Tis strange, said he, that these rooms, and these alone, should bear the marks of inhabitation; perhaps, some wretched wanderer like myself, may have here sought refuge from a persecuting world; and here, perhaps, laid down the load of existence; perhaps, too, I have followed his footsteps, but to mingle my dust with his! He turned suddenly, and was about to quit the room, when he perceived a small door near the bed; it opened into a closet, which was lighted by one small window, and was in the same condition as the apartments he had passed, except that it was destitute even of the remains of furniture. As he walked over the floor, he thought he felt one part of it shake beneath his steps, and, examining, found a trap-door. Curiosity prompted him to explore further, and with some difficulty he opened it. It disclosed a staircase which terminated in darkness. La Motte descended a few steps, but was unwilling to trust the abyss; and, after wondering for what purpose it was so secretly constructed, he closed the trap, and quitted this suit of apartments.

The stairs in the tower above were so much decayed, that he did not attempt to ascend them: he returned to the hall, and by the spiral staircase which he had observed the evening before, reached the gallery, and found another suit of apartments entirely furnished, very much like those below.

He renewed with Madame La Motte his former conversation respecting the abbey, and she exerted all her endeavours to dissuade him from his purpose, acknowledging the solitary security of the spot, but pleading that other places might be found equally well adapted for concealment and more for comfort. This La Motte doubted: besides, the forest abounded with game, which would, at once, afford him amusement and food, a circumstance, considering his small stock of money, by no means to be overlooked; and he had suffered his mind to dwell so much upon the scheme, that it was become a favourite one. Adeline listened in anxiety to the discourse, and waited the issue of Peter's report.

The morning passed but Peter did not return. Our solitary party took their dinner of the provision they had fortunately brought with them, and afterwards walked forth into the woods. Adeline, who never suffered any good to pass unnoticed because it came attended with evil, forgot for a while the desolation of the abbey in the beauty of the adjacent scenery. The pleasantness of the shades soothed her heart, and the varied features of the landscape amused her fancy; she almost thought she could be contented to live here. Already she began to feel an interest in the concerns of her companions, and for Madame La Motte she felt more; it was the warm emotion of gratitude and affection.

The afternoon wore away, and they returned to the abbey. Peter was still absent, and his absence now began to excite surprise and apprehension. The approach of darkness also threw a gloom upon the hopes of the wanderers: another night must be passed under the same forlorn circumstances as the preceding one! and, what was still worse, with a very scanty stock of provisions. The fortitude of Madame La Motte now entirely forsook her, and she wept bitterly. Adeline's heart was as mournful as Madame's, but she rallied her drooping spirits, and gave the first instance of her kindness by endeavouring to revive those of her friend.

La Motte was restless and uneasy, and, leaving the abbey, he walked alone the way which Peter had taken. He had not gone far, when he perceived him between the trees, leading his horse. —What news, Peter? hallooed La Motte. Peter came on, panting for breath, and said not a word, till La Motte repeated the question in a tone of somewhat more authority. Ah, bless you, master! said he, when he had taken breath to answer, I am glad to see you; I thought I should never have got back again: I've met with a world of misfortunes.

Well, you may relate them hereafter; let me hear whether you have discovered —

Discovered? interrupted Peter, yes, I am discovered with a vengeance! if your honour will look at my arms, you'll see how I am discovered.

Discoloured! I suppose you mean, said La Motte. But how came you in this condition!

Why I tell you how it was, Sir; your honour knows I learnt a smack of boxing of that Englishman that used to come with his master to our house.

Well, well—tell me where you have been.

I scarcely know myself, master; I've been where I got a sound drubbing, but then it was in your business, and so I don't mind. But if ever I meet with that rascal again!—

You seem to like your first drubbing so well, that you want another, and unless you speak more to the purpose, you shall soon have one.

Peter was now frightened into method, and endeavoured to proceed: When I left the old abbey, said he, I followed the way you directed, and turning to the right of that grove of trees yonder, I looked this way and that to see if I could see a house or a cottage, or even a man, but not a soul of them was to be seen, and so I jogged on near the value of a league, I warrant, and then I came to a track; Oh! oh! says I, we have you now; this will do—paths can't be made without feet. However, I was out in my reckoning, for the devil a bit of a soul could I see, and after following the track this way and that way, for the third of a league, I lost it, and had to find out another.

Is it impossible for you to speak to the point? said La Motte; omit these foolish particulars, and tell whether you have succeeded.

Well, then, master, to be short, for that's the nearest way after all, I wandered a long while at random, I did not know where, all through a forest like this, and I took special care to note how the trees stood, that I might find my way back. At last I came to another path, and was sure I should find something now, though I had found nothing before, for I could not be mistaken twice; so, peeping between the trees, I spied a cottage, and I gave my horse a lash that sounded through the forest, and I was at the door in a minute. They told me there was a town about half a league off, and bade me follow the track and it would bring me there,—so it did; and my horse, I believe, smelt the corn in the manger by the rate he went at. I inquired for a wheel-wright, and was told there was but one in the place, and he could not be found. I waited and waited, for I knew it was in vain to think of returning without doing my business. The man at last came home from the country, and I told him how long I had waited; for, says I, I knew it was in vain to return without my business.

Do be less tedious, said La Motte, if it is in thy nature.

It is in my nature, answered Peter, and if it was more in my nature your honour should have it all. Would you think it, Sir, the fellow had the impudence to ask a louis-d'or for mending the coach-wheel! I believe in my conscience he saw I was in a hurry and could not do without him. A louis-d'or! says I, my master shall give no such price, he sha'n't be imposed upon by no such rascal as you. Whereupon, the fellow looked glum, and gave me a douse o'the chops: with this, I up with my fist and gave him another, and should have beat him presently, if another man had not come in, and then I was obliged to give up.

And so you are returned as wise as you went?

Why, master, I hope I have too much spirit to submit to a rascal, or let you submit, to one either: besides, I have bought some nails to try if I can't mend the wheel myself — I had always a hand at carpentry.

Well, I commend your zeal in my cause, but on this occasion it was rather ill-timed. And what have you got in that basket?

Why, master, I bethought me that we could not get away from this place till the carriage was ready to draw us, and in the mean time, says I, nobody can live without victuals, so I'll e'en lay out the little money I have and take a basket with me.

That's the only wise thing you have done yet, and this, indeed, redeems your blunders.

Why now, master, it does my heart good to hear you speak; I knew I was doing for the best all the while: but I've had a hard job to find my way back; and here's another piece of ill luck, for the horse has got a thorn in his foot.

La Motte made inquiries concerning the town, and found it was capable of supplying him with provision, and what little furniture was necessary to render the abbey habitable. This intelligence almost settled his plans, and he ordered Peter to return on the following morning and make inquiries concerning the abbey. If the answers were favourable to his wishes, he commissioned him to buy a cart and load it with some furniture, and some materials necessary for repairing the modern apartments. Peter stared: What, does your honour mean to live here?

Why, suppose I do?

Why, then your honour has made a wise determination, according to my hint; for your honour knows I said—

Well, Peter, it is not necessary to repeat what you said; perhaps I had determined on the subject before.

Egad, master, you're in the right, and I'm glad of it, for I believe we shall not quickly be disturbed here, except by the rooks and owls. Yes, yes—I warrant I'll make it a place fit for a king; and as for the town, one may get any thing, I'm sure of that; though they think no more about this place than they do about India or England, or any of those places.

They now reached the abbey; where Peter was received with great joy: but the hopes of his mistress and Adeline were repressed, when they learned that he returned without having executed his commission, and heard his account of the town. La Motte's orders to Peter were heard with almost equal concern by Madame and Adeline; but the latter concealed her uneasiness, and used all her efforts to overcome that of her friend. The sweetness of her behaviour, and the air of satisfaction she assumed, sensibly affected Madame, and discovered to her a source of comfort which she had hitherto overlooked. The affectionate attentions of her young friend promised to console her for the want of other society, and her conversation to enliven the hours which might otherwise be passed in painful regret.

The observations and general behaviour of Adeline already bespoke a good understanding and an amiable heart; but she had yet more—she had genius. She was now in her nineteenth year; her figure of the middling size, and turned to the most exquisite proportion; her hair was dark auburn, her eyes blue, and whether they sparkled with intelligence, or melted with tenderness, they were equally attractive: her form had the airy lightness of a nymph, and when she smiled, her countenance might have been drawn for the younger sister of Hebe: the captivations of her beauty were heightened by the grace and simplicity of her manners, and confirmed by the intrinsic value of a heart.

That might be shrined in chrystal,

And have all its movements scann'd.

Annette now kindled the fire for the night: Peter's basket

was opened, and supper prepared. Madame La Motte was still pensive and silent. — There is scarcely any condition so bad, said Adeline, but we may one time or the other wish we had not quitted it. Honest Peter, when he was bewildered in the forest, or had two enemies to encounter instead of one, confesses he wished himself at the abbey. And I am certain, there is no situation so destitute, but comfort may be extracted from it. The blaze of this fire shines yet more cheerfully from the contrasted dreariness of the place; and this plentiful repast is made yet more delicious from the temporary want we have suffered. Let us enjoy the good and forget the evil.

You speak, my dear, replied Madame La Motte, like one whose spirits have not been often depressed by misfortune (Adeline sighed), and whose hopes are therefore vigorous. Long suffering, said La Motte, has subdued in our minds that elastic energy which repels the pressure of evil and dances to the bound of joy. But I speak in raphsody, though only from the remembrance of such a time. I once, like you, Adeline, could extract comfort from most situations.

And may now, my dear Sir, said Adeline. Still believe it possible, and you will find it is so.

The illusion is gone — I can no longer deceive myself.

Pardon me, Sir, if I say, it is now only you deceive yourself, by suffering the cloud of sorrow to tinge every object you look upon.

It may be so, said La Motte, but let us leave the subject.

After supper, the doors were secured, as before, for the night, and the wanderers resigned themselves to repose.

On the following morning, Peter again set out for the little town of Auboine, and the hours of his absence were again spent by Madame La Motte and Adeline in much anxiety and some hope, for the intelligence he might bring concerning the abbey might yet release them from the plans of La Motte. Towards the close of the day he was descried coming slowly on; and the cart, which accompanied him, too certainly confirmed their fears. He brought materials for repairing the place, and some furniture.

Of the abbey he gave an account, of which the following is the substance: — It belonged, together with a large part of the adjacent forest, to a nobleman, who now resided with his family on a remote estate. He inherited it, in right of his wife, from his father-in-law, who had caused the more modern apartments to be erected, and had resided in them some part of every year, for the purpose of shooting and hunting. It was reported, that some person was, soon after it came to the present possessor, brought secretly to the abbey and confined in these apartments; who, or what he was, had never been conjectured, and what became of him nobody knew. The report died gradually away, and many persons entirely disbelieved the whole of it. But however this affair might be, certain it was, the present owner had visited the abbey only two summers since his succeeding to it; and the furniture after some time, was removed.

This circumstance had at first excited surprise, and various reports rose in consequence, but it was difficult to know what ought to be believed. Among the rest, it was said that strange appearances had been observed at the abbey, and uncommon noises heard; and though this report had been ridiculed by sensible persons as the idle superstition of ignorance, it had fastened so strongly upon the minds of the common people, that for the last seventeen years none of the peasantry had ventured to approach the spot. The abbey was now, therefore, abandoned to decay.

La Motte ruminated upon this account. At first it called up unpleasant ideas, but they were soon dismissed, and considerations more interesting to his welfare took place: he congratulated himself that he had now found a spot where he was not likely to be either discovered or disturbed; yet it could not escape him that there was a strange coincidence between one part of Peter's narrative, and the condition of the chambers that opened from the tower above stairs. The remains of furniture, of which the other apartments were void—the solitary bed—the number and connexion of the rooms, were circumstances that united to confirm his opinion. This, however, he concealed in his own breast, for he already perceived that Peter's account had not assisted in reconciling his family to the necessity of dwelling at the abbey.

But they had only to submit in silence, and whatever disagreeable apprehension might intrude upon them, they now appeared willing to suppress the expression of it. Peter, indeed, was exempt from any evil of this kind; he knew no fear, and his mind was now wholly occupied with his approaching business. Madame La Motte, with a placid kind of despair, endeavoured to reconcile herself to that which no effort of understanding could teach her to avoid, and which an indulgence in lamentation could only make more intolerable. Indeed, though a sense of the immediate inconveniences to be endured at the abbey had made her oppose the scheme of living there, she did not really know how their situation could be improved by removal: yet her thoughts often wandered towards Paris, and reflected the retrospect of past times, with the images of weeping friends left, perhaps, for ever. The affectionate endearments of her only son, whom, from the danger of his situation, and the obscurity of hers, she might reasonably fear never to see again, arose upon her memory and overcame her fortitude. Why—why was I reserved for this hour? would she say, and what will be my years to come?

Adeline had no retrospect of past delight to give emphasis to present calamity—no weeping friends—no dear regretted objects to point the edge of sorrow, and throw a sickly hue upon her future prospects: she knew not yet the pangs of disappointed hope, or the acuter sting of self-accusation; she had no misery but what patience could assuage, or fortitude overcome.

At the dawn of the following day Peter arose to his labour: he proceeded with alacrity, and in a few days two of the lower apartments were so much altered for the better that La Motte began to exult, and his family to perceive that their situation would not be so miserable as they had imagined. The furniture Peter had already brought was disposed in these rooms, one of which was the vaulted apartment. Madame La Motte furnished this as a sitting-room, preferring it for its large Gothic window, that descended almost to the floor, admitting a prospect of the lawn, and the picturesque scenery of the surrounding woods.

Peter having returned to Auboine for a further supply, all the lower apartments were in a few weeks not only habitable, but comfortable. These, however, being insufficient for the accommodation of the family, a room above stairs was prepared for Adeline: it was the chamber that opened immediately from the tower, and she preferred it to those beyond, because it was less distant from the family, and the windows fronting an avenue of the forest afforded a more extensive prospect. The tapestry, that was decayed, and hung loosely from the walls, was now nailed up, and made to look less desolate; and though the room had still a solemn aspect, from its spaciousness and the narrowness of the windows, it was not uncomfortable.

The first night that Adeline retired hither, she slept little: the solitary air of the place affected her spirits; the more so, perhaps, because she had, with friendly consideration, endeavoured to support them in the presence of Madame La Motte. She remembered the narrative of Peter, several circumstances of which had impressed her imagination in spite of her reason, and she found it difficult wholly to subdue apprehension. At one time, terror so strongly seized her mind, that she had even opened the door with an intention of calling Madame La Motte; but, listening for a moment on the stairs of the tower, every thing seemed still: at length, she heard the voice of La Motte speaking cheerfully, and the absurdity of her fears struck her forcibly; she blushed that she had for a moment submitted to them, and returned to her chamber wondering at herself.

CHAPTER III

Are not these woods

More free from peril than the envious court?

Here feel we but the penalty of Adam,

The season's difference, as the icy fang

And churlish chiding of the winter's wind.

SHAKSPEARE.

La Motte arranged his little plan of living. His mornings were usually spent in shooting or fishing, and the dinner, thus provided by his industry, he relished with a keener appetite than had ever attended him at the luxurious tables of Paris. The afternoons he passed with his family: sometimes he would select a book from the few he had brought with him, and endeavoured to fix his attention to the words his lips repeated: —but his mind suffered little abstraction from its own cares, and the sentiment he pronounced left no trace behind it. Sometimes he conversed, but oftener sat in gloomy silence, musing upon the past, or anticipating the future.

At these moments, Adeline, with a sweetness almost irresistible, endeavoured to enliven his spirits, and to withdraw him from himself. Seldom she succeeded; but when she did, the grateful looks of Madame La Motte, and the benevolent feelings of her own bosom, realized the cheerfulness she had at first only assumed. Adeline's mind had the happy art, or, perhaps, it were more just to say, the happy nature, of accommodating itself to her situation. Her present condition, though forlorn, was not devoid of comfort, and this comfort was confirmed by her virtues. So much she won upon the affections of her protectors, that Madame La Motte loved her as her child, and La Motte himself, though a man little susceptible of tenderness, could not be insensible to her solicitudes. Whenever he relaxed from the sullenness of misery, it was at the influence of Adeline.

Peter regularly brought a weekly supply of provisions from Auboine, and, on those occasions, always quitted the town by a route contrary to that leading to the abbey. Several weeks having passed without molestation, La Motte dismissed all apprehension of pursuit, and at length became tolerably reconciled to the complexion of his circumstances.

As habit and effort strengthened the fortitude of Madame La Motte, the features of misfortune appeared to soften. The forest, which at first seemed to her a frightful solitude, had lost its terrific aspect; and that edifice, whose half demolished walls and gloomy desolation had struck her mind with the force of melancholy and dismay, was now beheld as a domestic asylum, and a safe refuge from the storms of power.

She was a sensible and highly accomplished woman, and it became her chief delight to form the rising graces of Adeline, who had, as has been already shown, a sweetness of disposition, which made her quick to repay instruction with improvement, and indulgence with love. Never was Adeline so pleased as when she anticipated her wishes, and never so diligent as when she was employed in her business. The little affairs of the household she overlooked and managed with such admirable exactness, that Madame La Motte had neither anxiety nor care concerning them. And Adeline formed for herself in this barren situation, many amusements that occasionally banished the remembrance of her misfortunes. La Motte's books were her chief consolation. With one of these she would frequently ramble into the forest, where the river, winding through a glade, diffused coolness, and with its murmuring accents invited repose: there she would seat herself, and, resigned to the illusions of the page, pass many hours in oblivion of sorrow.

Here too, when her mind was tranquillized by the surrounding scenery, she wooed the gentle muse, and indulged in ideal happiness. The delight of these moments she commemorated in the following address:

TO THE VISIONS OF FANCY.

Dear, wild illusions of creative mind!

Whose varying hues arise to Fancy's art,

And by her magic force are swift combined

In forms that please, and scenes that touch the heart:

Oh! whether at her voice ye soft assume

The pensive grace of sorrow drooping low;

Or rise sublime on terror's lofty plume,

And shake the soul with wildly thrilling woe;

Or, sweetly bright, your gayer tints ye spread,

Bid scenes of pleasures steal upon my view,

Love wave his purple pinions o'er my head,

And wake the tender thought to passion true.

O! still — — ye shadowy forms! attend my lonely hours,

Still chase my real cares with your illusive powers!

Madame La Motte had frequently expressed curiosity concerning the events of Adeline's life, and by what circumstances she had been thrown into a situation so perilous and mysterious as that in which La Motte had found her. Adeline had given a brief account of the manner in which she had been brought thither, but had always with tears entreated to be spared for that time from a particular relation of her history. Her spirits were not then equal to retrospection; but now that they were soothed by quiet, and strengthened by confidence, she one day gave Madame La Motte the following narration.

* * * * * * * * * * * * * * *

I am the only child, said Adeline, Of Louis de St. Pierre, a chevalier of reputable family, but of small fortune, who for many years resided at Paris. Of my mother I have a faint remembrance: I lost her when I was only seven years old, and this was my first misfortune. At her death, my father gave up housekeeping, boarded me in a convent, and quitted Paris. Thus was I, at this early period of my life, abandoned to strangers. My father came sometimes to Paris; he then visited me, and I well remember the grief I used to feel when he bade me farewell. On these occasions, which wrung my heart with grief, he appeared unmoved; so that I often thought he had little tenderness for me. But he was my father, and the only person to whom I could lookup for protection and love.

In this convent I continued till I was twelve years old. A thousand times I had entreated my father to take me home; but at first, motives of prudence, and afterwards of avarice, prevented him. I was now removed from this convent, and placed in another, where I learned my father intended I should take the veil. I will not attempt to express my surprise and grief on this occasion. Too long I had been immured in the walls of a cloister, and too much had I seen of the sullen misery of its votaries, not to feel horror and disgust at the prospect of being added to their number.

The Lady Abbess was a woman of rigid decorum and severe devotion: exact in the observance of every detail of form, and never forgave an offence against ceremony. It was her method, when she wanted to make converts to her order, to denounce and terrify, rather than to persuade and allure. Hers were the arts of cunning practised upon fear, not those of sophistication upon reason. She employed numberless stratagems to gain me to her purpose, and they all wore the complexion of her character. But in the life to which she would have devoted me, I saw too many forms of real terror, to be overcome by the influence of her ideal host, and was resolute in rejecting the veil. Here I passed several years of miserable resistance against cruelty and superstition. My father I seldom saw; when I did, I entreated him to alter my destination; but he objected that his fortune was insufficient to support me in the world, and at length denounced vengeance on my head if I persisted in disobedience.

You, my dear Madam, can form little idea of the wretchedness of my situation, condemned to perpetual imprisonment, and imprisonment of the most dreadful kind, or to the vengeance of a father, from whom I had no appeal. My resolution relaxed — for some time I paused upon the choice of evils — but at length the horrors of the monastic life rose so fully to my view, that fortitude gave way before them. Excluded from the cheerful intercourse of society — from the pleasant view of nature — almost from the light of day — condemned to silence — rigid formality — abstinence and penance — condemned to forgo the delights of a world which imagination painted in the gayest and most alluring colours, and whose hues were, perhaps, not the less captivating because they were only ideal — such was the sate to which I was destined. Again my resolution was invigorated: my father's cruelty subdued tenderness, and roused indignation. Since he can forget, said I, the affection of a parent, and condemn his child without remorse to wretchedness and despair — the bond of filial and parental duty no longer subsists between us — he has himself dissolved it, and I will yet struggle for liberty and life.

Finding me unmoved by menace, the Lady Abbess had now recourse to more subtle measures: she condescended to smile, and even to flatter; but hers was the distorted smile of cunning, not the gracious emblem of kindness; it provoked disgust, instead of inspiring affection. She painted the character of a vestal in the most beautiful tints of art — its holy innocence — its mild dignity — its sublime devotion. I sighed as she spoke. This she regarded as a favourable symptom, and proceeded on her picture with more animation. She described the serenity of a monastic life—its security from the seductive charms, restless passions, and sorrowful vicissitudes of the world—the rapturous delights of religion, and the sweet reciprocal affection of the sisterhood.

So highly she finished the piece, that the lurking lines of cunning would, to an inexperienced eye, have escaped detection. Mine was too sorrowfully informed. Too often had I witnessed the secret tear and bursting sigh of vain regret, the sullen pinings of discontent, and the mute anguish of despair. My silence and my manner assured her of my incredulity, and it was with difficulty that she preserved a decent composure.

My father, as may be imagined, was highly incensed at my perseverance, which he called obstinacy; but, what will not be so easily believed, he soon after relented, and appointed a day to take me from the convent. O! judge of my feelings when I received this intelligence. The joy it occasioned awakened all my gratitude; I forgot the former cruelty of my father, and that the present indulgence was less the effect of his kindness than of my resolution. I wept that I could not indulge his every wish.

What days of blissful expectation were those that preceded my departure! The world, from which I had been hitherto secluded—the world, in which my fancy had been so often delighted to roam—whose paths were strewn with fadeless roses—whose every scene smiled in beauty and invited to delight—where all the people were good, and all the good happy—Ah! then that world was bursting upon my view. Let me catch the rapturous remembrance before it vanish! It is like the passing lights of autumn, that gleam for a moment on a hill, and then leave it to darkness. I counted the days and hours that withheld me from this fairy land. It was in the convent only that people were deceitful and cruel; it was there only that misery dwelt. I was quitting it all! How I pitied the poor nuns that were to be left behind! I would have given half that world I prized so much, had it been mine, to have taken them out with me.

The long wished for day at last arrived. My father came, and for a moment my joy was lost in the sorrow of bidding farewell to my poor companions, for whom I had never felt such warmth of kindness as at this instant. I was soon beyond the gates of the convent. I looked around me, and viewed the vast vault of heaven no longer bounded by monastic walls, and the green earth extended in hill and dale to the round verge of the horizon! My heart danced with delight, tears swelled in my eyes, and for some moments I was unable to speak. My thoughts rose to heaven in sentiments of gratitude to the Giver of all good!

At length I returned to my father: Dear Sir, said I, how I thank you for my deliverance, and how I wish I could do every thing to oblige you!

Return, then, to your convent, said he in a harsh accent. I shuddered: his look and manner jarred the tone of my feelings; they struck discord upon my heart! which had before responded only to harmony. The ardour of joy was in a moment repressed, and every object around me was saddened with the gloom of disappointment. It was not that I suspected my father would take me back to the convent; but that his feelings seemed so very dissonant to the joy and gratitude which I had but a moment before felt and expressed to him. — Pardon, Madam, a relation of these trivial circumstances; the strong vicissitudes of feeling which they impressed upon my heart, make me think them important, when they are, perhaps, only disgusting.

No, my dear, said Madame La Motte, they are interesting to me; they illustrate little traits of character, which I love to observe. You are worthy of all my regards, and from this moment I give my tenderest pity to your misfortunes, and my affection to your goodness.

These words melted the heart of Adeline; she kissed the hand which Madame held out, and remained a few minutes silent. At length she said, May I deserve this goodness! and may I ever be thankful to God, who, in giving me such a friend, has raised me to comfort and hope!

My father's house was situated a few leagues on the other side of Paris, and in our way to it we passed through that city. What a novel scene! Where were now the solemn faces, the demure manners I had been accustomed to see in the convent? Every countenance was here animated, either by business or pleasure; every step was airy, and every smile was gay. All the people appeared like friends; they looked and smiled at me; I smiled again, and wished to have told them how pleased I was. How delightful, said I, to live surrounded by friends!

What crowded streets! what magnificent hotels! what splendid equipages! I scarcely observed that the streets were narrow, or the way dangerous. What bustle, what tumult, what delight! I could never be sufficiently thankful that I was removed from the convent. Again I was going to express my gratitude to my father, but his looks forbad me, and I was silent. I am too diffuse; even the faint forms which memory reflects of passed delight are grateful to the heart. The shadow of pleasure is still gazed upon with a melancholy enjoyment, though the substance is fled beyond our reach.

Having quitted Paris, which I left with many sighs, and gazed upon till the towers of every church dissolved in distance from my view, we entered upon a gloomy and unfrequented road. It was evening when we reached a wild heath; I looked round in search of a human dwelling, but could find none; and not a human being was to be seen. I experienced something of what I used to feel in the convent; my heart had not been so sad since I left it. Of my father, who still sat in silence, I inquired if we were near home; he answered in the affirmative. Night came on, however, before we reached the place of our destination; it was a lone house on the waste; but I need not describe it to you, Madam. When the carriage stopped, two men appeared at the door, and assisted us to alight: so gloomy were their countenances, and so few their words, I almost fancied myself again in the convent; certain it is, I had not seen such melancholy faces since I quitted it. Is this a part of the world I have so fondly contemplated? said I.

The interior appearance of the house was desolate and mean; I was surprised that my father had chosen such a place for his habitation, and also that no woman was to be seen; but I knew that inquiry would only produce a reproof, and was therefore silent. At supper, the two men I had before seen sat down with us; they said little, but seemed to observe me much. I was confused and displeased; which my father noticing, frowned at them with a look which convinced me he meant more than I comprehended. When the cloth was drawn, my father took my hand and conducted me to the door of my chamber; having set down the candle, and wished me good night, he left me to my own solitary thoughts.

How different were they from those I had indulged a few hours before! then expectation, hope, delight, danced before me; now melancholy and disappointment chilled the ardour of my mind, and discoloured my future prospect. The appearance of every thing around conduced to depress me. On the floor lay a small bed without curtains or hangings; two old chairs and a table were all the remaining furniture in the room. I went to the window, with an intention of looking out upon the surrounding scene, and found it was grated. I was shocked at this circumstance, and comparing it with the lonely situation and the strange appearance of the house, together with the countenances and behaviour of the men who had supped with us, I was lost in a labyrinth of conjecture.

At length I lay down to sleep; but the anxiety of my mind prevented repose; gloomy unpleasing images flitted before my fancy, and I fell into a sort of waking dream: I thought that I was in a lonely forest with my father; his looks were severe, and his gestures menacing: he upbraided me for leaving the convent, and while he spoke, drew from his pocket a mirror, which he held before my face; I looked in it and saw, (my blood now thrills as I repeat it) I saw myself wounded, and bleeding profusely. Then I thought myself in the house again; and suddenly heard these words, in accents so distinct, that for some time after I awoke I could scarcely believe them ideal, Depart this house, destruction hovers here.

I was awakened by a footstep on the stairs; it was my father retiring to his chamber; the lateness of the hour surprised me, for it was past midnight.

On the following morning, the party of the preceding evening assembled at breakfast, and were as gloomy and silent as before. The table was spread by a boy of my father's; but the cook and the housemaid, whatever they might be, were invisible.

The next morning I was surprised, on attempting to leave my chamber, to find the door locked; I waited a considerable time before I ventured to call; when I did, no answer was returned; I then went to the window, and called more loudly, but my own voice was still the only sound I heard. Near an hour I passed in a state of surprise and terror not to be described: at length I heard a person coming up stairs, and I renewed the call; I was answered, that my father had that morning set off for Paris, whence he would return in a few days; in the meanwhile he had ordered me to be confined in my chamber. On my expressing surprise and apprehension at this circumstance, I was assured I had nothing to fear, and that I should live as well as if I was at liberty.

The latter part of this speech seemed to contain an odd kind of comfort; I made little reply, but submitted to necessity. Once more I was abandoned to sorrowful reflection: what a day was the one I now passed! alone, and agitated with grief and apprehension. I endeavoured to conjecture the cause of this harsh treatment; and at length concluded it was designed by my father, as a punishment for my former disobedience. But why abandon me to the power of strangers, to men, whose countenances bore the stamp of villainy so strongly as to impress even my inexperienced mind with terror! Surmise involved me only deeper in perplexity, yet I found it impossible to forbear pursuing the subject; and the day was divided between lamentation and conjecture. Night at length came, and such a night! Darkness brought new terrors: I looked round the chamber for some means of fastening my door on the inside, but could perceive none; at last I contrived to place the back of a chair in an oblique direction, so as to render it secure.

I had scarcely done this, and lain down upon my bed in my clothes, not to sleep, but to watch, when I heard a rap at the door of the house, which was opened and shut so quickly, that the person who had knocked, seemed only to deliver a letter or message. Soon after, I heard voices at intervals in a room below stairs, sometimes speaking very low, and sometimes rising all together, as if in dispute. Something more excusable than curiosity made me endeavour to distinguish what was said, but in vain; now and then a word or two reached me, and once I heard my name repeated, but no more.

Thus passed the hours till midnight, when all became still. I had lain for some time in a state between fear and hope, when I heard the lock of my door gently moved backward and forward; I started up and listened; for a moment it was still, then the noise returned, and I heard a whispering without; my spirits died away, but I was yet sensible. Presently an effort was made at the door, as if to force it; I shrieked aloud, and immediately heard the voices of the men I had seen at my father's table: they called loudly for the door to be opened, and on my returning no answer, uttered dreadful execrations. I had just strength sufficient to move to the window, in the desperate hope of escaping thence; but my feeble efforts could not even shake the bars. O! how can I recollect these moments of horror, and be sufficiently thankful that I am now in safety and comfort!

They remained some time at the door, then they quitted it, and went down stairs. How my heart revived at every step of their departure! I fell upon my knees, thanked God that he had preserved me this time, and implored his further protection. I was rising from this short prayer, when suddenly I heard a noise in a different part of the room, and on looking round, I perceived the door of a small closet open, and two men enter the chamber.

They seized me, and I sunk senseless in their arms; how long I remained in this condition I know not; but on reviving, I perceived myself again alone, and heard several voices from below stairs. I had presence of mind to run to the door of the closet, my only chance of escape; but it was locked! I then recollected it was possible that the ruffians might have forgot to turn the key of the chamber door, which was held by the chair; but here, also, I was disappointed. I clasped my hands in an agony of despair, and stood for some time immoveable.

A violent noise from below roused me, and soon after I heard people ascending the stairs: I now gave myself up for lost. The steps approached, the door of the closet was again unlocked. I stood calmly, and again saw the men enter the chamber; I neither spoke, nor resisted: the faculties of my soul were wrought up beyond the power of feeling; as a violent blow on the body stuns for awhile the sense of pain. They led me down stairs; the door of a room below was thrown open, and I beheld a stranger; it was then that my senses returned; I shrieked and resisted, but was forced along. It is unnecessary to say that this stranger was Monsieur La Motte, or to add, that I shall for ever bless him as my deliverer.

Adeline ceased to speak; Madame La Motte remained silent. There were some circumstances in Adeline's narrative, which raised all her curiosity. She asked if Adeline believed her father to be a party in this mysterious affair. Adeline, though it was impossible to doubt that he had been principally and materially concerned in some part of it, thought, or said she thought, he was innocent of any intention against her life. Yet, what motive, said Madame La Motte, could there be for a degree of cruelty so apparently unprofitable?—Here the inquiry ended; and Adeline confessed she had pursued it till her mind shrunk from all further research.

The sympathy which such uncommon misfortune excited, Madame La Motte now expressed without reserve, and this expression of it strengthened the tie of mutual friendship. Adeline felt her spirits relieved by the disclosure she had made to Madame La Motte; and the latter acknowledged the value of the confidence, by an increase of affectionate attentions.

CHAPTER IV

...... My May of life

Is fall'n into the sear, the yellow leaf.

MACBETH.

Full oft, unknowing and unknown,

He wore his endless noons alone,

Amid th' autumnal wood:

Oft was he wont in hasty fit,

Abrupt the social board to quit.

WHARTON.

La Motte had now passed above a month in this seclusion; and his wife had the pleasure to see him recover tranquillity and even cheerfulness. In this pleasure Adeline warmly participated; and she might justly have congratulated herself as one cause of his restoration; her cheerfulness and delicate attention had effected what Madame La Motte's greater anxiety had failed to accomplish. La Motte did not seem regardless of her amiable disposition, and sometimes thanked her in a manner more earnest than was usual with him. She, in her turn, considered him as her only protector and now felt towards him the affection of a daughter.

The time she had spent in this peaceful retirement had softened the remembrance of past events, and restored her mind to its natural tone: and when memory brought back to her view the former short and romantic expectations of happiness, though she gave a sigh to the rapturous illusion, she less lamented the disappointment, than rejoiced in her present security and comfort.

But the satisfaction which La Motte's cheerfulness diffused around him was of short continuance; he became suddenly gloomy and reserved; the society of his family was no longer grateful to him; and he would spend whole hours in the most secluded parts of the forest, devoted to melancholy and secret grief. He did not, as formerly, indulge the humour of his sadness, without restraint, in the presence of others; he now evidently endeavoured to conceal it, and affected a cheerfulness that was too artificial to escape detection.

His servant Peter, either impelled by curiosity or kindness, sometimes followed him unseen, into the forest. He observed him frequently retire to one particular spot, in a remote part, which having gained, he always disappeared, before Peter, who was obliged to follow at a distance, could exactly notice where. All his endeavours, now prompted by wonder and invigorated by disappointment, were unsuccessful, and he was at length compelled to endure the tortures of unsatisfied curiosity.

This change in the manners and habits of her husband was too conspicuous to pass unobserved by Madame La Motte, who endeavoured, by all the stratagems which affection could suggest, or female invention supply, to win him to her confidence. He seemed insensible to the influence of the first, and withstood the wiles of the latter. Finding all her efforts insufficient to dissipate the glooms which overhung his mind, or to penetrate their secret cause, she desisted from further attempt, and endeavoured to submit to this mysterious distress.

Week after week elapsed, and the same unknown cause sealed the lips and corroded the heart of La Motte. The place of his visitation in the forest had not been traced. Peter had frequently examined round the spot where his master disappeared, but had never discovered any recess which could be supposed to conceal him. The astonishment of the servant was at length raised to an insupportable degree, and he communicated to his mistress the subject of it.

The emotion which this information excited, she disguised from Peter, and reproved him for the means he had taken to gratify his curiosity. But she revolved this circumstance in her thoughts, and comparing it with the late alteration in his temper, her uneasiness was renewed, and her perplexity considerably increased. After much consideration, being unable to assign any other motive for his conduct, she began to attribute it to the influence of illicit passion; and her heart, which now out-ran her judgment, confirmed the supposition, and roused all the torturing pangs of jealousy.

Comparatively speaking, she had never known affliction till now: she had abandoned her dearest friends and connexions — had relinquished the gaieties, the luxuries, and almost the necessaries of life; — fled with her family into exile, an exile the most dreary and comfortless; experiencing the evils of reality, and those of apprehension, united: all these she had patiently endured, supported by the affection of him for whose sake she suffered. Though that affection, indeed, had for some time appeared to be abated, she had borne its decrease with fortitude; but the last stroke of calamity, hitherto withheld, now came with irresistible force — the love, of which she lamented the loss, she now believed was transferred to another.

The operation of strong passion confuses the powers of reason, and warps them to its own particular direction. Her usual degree of judgment, unopposed by the influence of her heart, would probably have pointed out to Madame La Motte some circumstances upon the subject of her distress, equivocal, if not contradictory to her suspicions. No such circumstances appeared to her, and she did not long hesitate to decide, that Adeline was the object of her husband's attachment. Her beauty out of the question, who else, indeed, could it be in a spot thus secluded from the world?

The same cause destroyed, almost at the same moment, her only remaining comfort; and when she wept that she could no longer look for happiness in the affection of La Motte, she wept also, that she could no longer seek solace in the friendship of Adeline. She had too great an esteem for her, to doubt, at first, the integrity of her conduct; but, in spite of reason, her heart no longer expanded to her with its usual warmth of kindness. She shrunk from her confidence; and as the secret broodings of jealousy cherished her suspicions, she became less kind to her, even in manner.

Adeline, observing the change, at first attributed it to accident, and afterwards to a temporary displeasure arising from some little inadvertency in her conduct. She, therefore, increased her assiduities; but perceiving, contrary to all expectation, that her efforts to please failed of their usual consequence, and that the reserve of Madame's manner rather increased than abated, she became seriously uneasy, and resolved to seek an explanation. This Madame La Motte as sedulously avoided, and was for some time able to prevent. Adeline, however, too much interested in the event to yield to delicate scruples, pressed the subject so closely, that Madame, at first agitated and confused, at length invented some idle excuse, and laughed off the affair.

She now saw the necessity of subduing all appearance of reserve towards Adeline; and though her art could not conquer the prejudices of passion, it taught her to assume, with tolerable success, the aspect of kindness. Adeline was deceived, and was again at peace. Indeed, confidence in the sincerity and goodness of others was her weakness. But the pangs of stifled jealousy struck deeper to the heart of Madame La Motte, and she resolved, at all events, to obtain some certainty upon the subject of her suspicions.

She now condescended to a meanness which she had before despised, and ordered Peter to watch the steps of his master, in order to discover, if possible, the place of his visitation! So much did passion win upon her judgment, by time and indulgence, that she sometimes ventured even to doubt the integrity of Adeline, and afterwards proceeded to believe it possible that the object of La Motte's rambles might be an assignation with her. What suggested this conjecture was, that Adeline frequently took long walks alone in the forest, and sometimes was absent from the abbey for many hours. This circumstance, which Madame La Motte had at first attributed to Adeline's fondness for the picturesque beauties of nature, now operated forcibly upon her imagination, and she could view it in no other light, than as affording an opportunity for secret conversation with her husband.

Peter obeyed the orders of his mistress with alacrity, for they were warmly seconded by his own curiosity. All his endeavours were, however, fruitless; he never dared to follow La Motte near enough to observe the place of his last retreat. Her impatience thus heightened by delay, and her passion stimulated by difficulty, Madame La Motte now resolved to apply to her husband for an explanation of his conduct.

After some consideration concerning the manner most likely to succeed with him, she went to La Motte; but when she entered the room where he sat, forgetting all her concerted address, she fell at his feet, and was for some moments lost in tears. Surprised at her attitude and distress, he inquired the occasion of it, and was answered, that it was caused by his own conduct. My conduct! What part of it, pray? inquired he.

Your reserve, your secret sorrow, and frequent absence from the abbey.

Is it then so wonderful, that a man who has lost almost every thing should sometimes lament his misfortunes? or so criminal to attempt concealing his grief, that he must be blamed for it by those whom he would save from the pain of sharing it?

Having uttered these words, he quitted the room, leaving Madame La Motte lost in surprise, but somewhat relieved from the pressure of her former suspicions. Still however, she pursued Adeline with an eye of scrutiny; and the mask of kindness would sometimes fall off, and discover the features of distrust. Adeline, without exactly knowing why, felt less at ease and less happy in her presence than formerly; her spirits drooped, and she would often, when alone, weep at the forlornness of her condition. Formerly, her remembrance of past sufferings was lost in the friendship of Madame La Motte; now, though her behaviour was too guarded to betray any striking instances of unkindness, there was something in her manner which chilled the hopes of Adeline, unable as she was to analyze it. But a circumstance which soon occurred, suspended for a while the jealousy of Madame La Motte, and roused her husband from his state of gloomy stupefaction.

Peter, having been one day to Auboine for the weekly supply of provisions, returned with intelligence that awakened in La Motte new apprehension and anxiety.

Oh, Sir! I have heard something that has astonished me, as well it may, cried Peter, and so it will you when you come to know it. As I was standing in the blacksmith's shop, while the smith was driving a nail into the horse's shoe (by the by, the horse lost it in an odd way, I'll tell you, Sir, how it was) —

Nay, prithee leave it till another time, and go on with your story.

Why then, Sir, as I was standing in the blacksmith's shop, comes in a man with a pipe in his mouth, and a large pouch of tobacco in his hand —

Well — what has the pipe to do with the story?

Nay, Sir, you put me out; I can't go on, unless you let me tell it my own way. As I was saying — with a pipe in his mouth — I think I was there your honour!

Yes, yes.

He sets himself down on the bench, and, taking the pipe from his mouth, says to the blacksmith — Neighbour, do you know any body of the Name of La Motte hereabouts! — Bless your honour, I turned all of a cold sweat in a minute! — Is not your honour well! shall I fetch you any thing?

No — but be short in your narrative.

La Motte! La Motte! said the blacksmith, I think I've heard the name. — Have you? said I, you're cunning then, for there's no such person hereabouts, to my knowledge.

45

Fool!—why did you say that?

Because I did not want them to know your honour was here; and if I had not managed very cleverly, they would have found me out. There is no such person hereabouts, to my knowledge, says I.—Indeed! says the blacksmith, you know more of the neighbourhood than I do then.—Aye, says the man with the pipe, that's very true. How came you to know so much of the neighbourhood? I came here twenty-six years ago, come next St. Michael, and you know more than I do. How came you to know so much?

With that he put his pipe in his mouth, and gave a whiff full in my face. Lord! your honour, I trembled from head to foot. Nay, as for that matter says I, I don't know more than other people, but I'm sure I never heard of such a man as that.—Pray, says the blacksmith, staring me full in the face, an't you the man that was inquiring some time since about St. Clair's abbey?—Well, what of that? says I, what does that prove?—Why they say somebody lives in the abbey now, said the man, turning to the other; and, for aught I know, it may be this same La Motte.—Aye, or for aught I know either, says the man with the pipe, getting up from the bench, and you know more of this than you'll own. I'll lay my life on't, this Monsieur La Motte lives at the abbey.—Aye, says I, you are out there, for he does not live at the abbey now.

Confound your folly! cried La Motte; but be quick—how did the matter end?

My master does not live there now, said I.—Oh! oh! said the man with the pipe; he is your master then? And pray how long has he left the abbey—and where does he live now?—Hold, said I, not so fast—I know when to speak and when to hold my tongue—but who has been inquiring for him?

What! he expected somebody to inquire for him? says the man.—No, says I, he did not, but if he did, what does that prove?—that argues nothing. With that he looked at the blacksmith, and they went out of the shop together, leaving my horse's shoe undone. But I never minded that, for the moment they were gone, I mounted and rode away as fast as I could. But in my fright, your honour, I forgot to take the round about way, and so came straight home.

La Motte, extremely shocked at Peter's intelligence, made no other reply than by cursing his folly, and immediately went in search of Madame, who was walking with Adeline on the banks

46

of the river. La Motte was too much agitated to soften his information by preface. We are discovered! said he, the king's officers have been inquiring for me at Auboine, and Peter has blundered upon my ruin. He then informed her of what Peter had related, and bade her prepare to quit the abbey.

But whither can we fly? said Madame La Motte, scarcely able to support herself. Any where! said he: to stay here is certain destruction. We must take refuge in Switzerland, I think. If any part of France would have concealed me, surely it had been this!

Alas, how are we persecuted! rejoined Madame. This spot is scarcely made comfortable, before we are obliged to leave it, and go we know not whither.

I wish we may not yet know whither, replied La Motte, that is the least evil that threatens us. Let us escape a prison, and I care not whither we go. But return to the abbey immediately, and pack up what moveables you can. — A flood of tears came to the relief of Madame La Motte, and she hung upon Adeline's arm, silent and trembling. Adeline, though she had no comfort to bestow, endeavoured to command her feelings and appear composed. Come, said La Motte, we waste time; let us lament hereafter, but at present prepare for flight; exert a little of that fortitude which is so necessary for our preservation. Adeline does not weep, yet her state is as wretched as your own, for I know not how long I shall be able to protect her.

Notwithstanding her terror, this reproof touched the pride of Madame La Motte, who dried her tears, but disdained to reply, and looked at Adeline with a strong expression of displeasure. As they moved silently toward the abbey, Adeline asked La Motte if he was sure they were the king's officers who inquired for him. I cannot doubt it, he replied, who else could possibly inquire for me? Besides, the behaviour of the man, who mentioned my name, puts the matter beyond a question.

Perhaps not, said Madame La Motte: let us wait till morning ere we set off. We may then find it will be unnecessary to go.

We may, indeed; the king's officers would probably by that time have told us as much. La Motte went to give orders to Peter. Set off in an hour! said Peter, Lord bless you, master! only consider the coach wheel; it would take me a day at least to mend it, for your honour knows I never mended one in my life.

This was a circumstance which La Motte had entirely overlooked. When they settled at the abbey, Peter had at first been too busy in repairing the apartments, to remember the carriage; and afterwards, believing it would not quickly be wanted, he had neglected to do it. La Motte's temper now entirely forsook him, and with many execrations he ordered Peter to go to work immediately: but on searching for the materials formerly bought, they were no where to be found; and Peter at length remembered, though he was prudent enough to conceal this circumstance, that he had used the nails in repairing the abbey.

It was now, therefore, impossible to quit the forest that night, and La Motte had only to consider the most probable plan of concealment, should the officers of justice visit the ruin before the morning; a circumstance which the thoughtlessness of Peter, in returning from Auboine by the straight way, made not unlikely.

At first, indeed, it occurred to him, that, though his family could not be removed, he might himself take one of the horses, and escape from the forest before night. But he thought there would still be some danger of detection in the towns through which he must pass, and he could not well bear the idea of leaving his family unprotected, without knowing when he could return to them, or whither he could direct them to follow him. La Motte was not a man of very vigorous resolution, and he was, perhaps, rather more willing to suffer in company than alone.

After much consideration, he recollected the trap-door of the closet belonging to the chambers above. It was invisible to the eye and whatever might be its direction, it would securely shelter him, at least, from discovery. Having deliberated further upon the subject he determined to explore the recess to which the stairs led, and thought it possible that for a short time his whole family might be concealed within it. There was little time between the suggestion of the plan and the execution of his purpose, for darkness was spreading around, and in every murmur of the wind he thought he heard the voices of his enemies.

He called for a light, and ascended alone to the chamber. When he came to the closet, it was some time before he could find the trap-door, so exactly did it correspond with the boards of the floor. At length, he found and raised it. The chill damps of long confined air rushed from the aperture, and he stood for a moment to let them pass, ere he descended. As he stood looking down the abyss, he recollected the report which Peter had brought concerning the abbey, and it gave him an uneasy sensation. But this soon yielded to more pressing interests.

The stairs were steep, and in many places trembled beneath his weight. Having continued to descend for some time, his feet touched the ground, and he found himself in a narrow passage; but as he turned to pursue it, the damp vapours curled round him and extinguished the light. He called aloud for Peter, but could make nobody hear, and after some time he endeavoured to find his way up the stairs. In this, with difficulty, he succeeded, and passing the chambers with cautious steps descended the tower.

The security which the place he had just quitted seemed to promise, was of too much importance to be slightly rejected, and he determined immediately to make another experiment with the light:—having now fixed it in a lantern, he descended a second time to the passage. The current of vapours occasioned by the opening of the trap-door was abated, and the fresh air thence admitted had begun to circulate: La Motte passed on unmolested.

The passage was of considerable length, and led him to a door which was fastened. He placed the lantern at some distance, to avoid the current of air, and applied his strength to the door. It shook under his hands, but did not yield. Upon examining it more closely, he perceived the wood round the lock was decayed, probably by the damps, and this encouraged him to proceed. After some time it gave way to his effort, and he found himself in a square stone room.

He stood for some time to survey it. The walls, which were dripping with unwholesome dews, were entirely bare, and afforded not even a window. A small iron grate alone admitted the air. At the further end, near a low recess, was another door. La Motte went towards it, and, as he passed, looked into the recess. Upon the ground within it stood a large chest, which he went forward to examine; and, lifting the lid, he saw the remains of a human skeleton. Horror struck upon his heart, and he involuntarily stepped back. During a pause of some moments, his first emotion subsided. That thrilling curiosity, which objects of terror often excite in the human mind, impelled him to take a second view of this dismal spectacle.

La Motte stood motionless as he gazed; the object before him seemed to confirm the report that some person had formerly been murdered in the abbey. At length he closed the chest, and advanced to the second door, which also was fastened, but the key was in the lock. He turned it with difficulty, and then found the door was held by two strong bolts. Having undrawn these, it disclosed a flight of steps, which he descended. They terminated in a chain of low vaults, or rather cells, that, from the manner of their construction and present condition, seemed to be coeval with the most ancient parts of the abbey. La Motte, in his then depressed state of mind, thought them the burial places of the monks, who formerly inhabited the pile above; but they were more calculated for places of penance for the living, than of rest for the dead.

Having reached the extremity of these cells, the way was again closed by a door. La Motte now hesitated whether he should attempt to proceed any further. The present spot seemed to afford the security he sought. Here he might pass the night unmolested by apprehension of discovery; and it was most probable, that if the officers arrived in the night, and found the abbey vacated, they would quit it before morning, or, at least, before he could have any occasion to emerge from concealment. These considerations restored his mind to a state of greater composure. His only immediate care was to bring his family, as soon as possible, to this place of security, lest the officers should come unawares upon them; and while he stood thus musing, he blamed himself for delay.

But an irresistible desire of knowing to what this door led, arrested his steps, and he turned to open it. The door, however, was fastened; and as he attempted to force it, he suddenly thought he heard a noice above. It now occurred to him that the officers might already have arrived, and he quitted the cells with precipitation, intending to listen at the trap-door.

There, said he, I may wait in security, and perhaps hear something of what passes. My family will not be known, or at least not hurt, and their uneasiness on my account they must learn to endure.

These were the arguments of La Motte, in which, it must be owned, selfish prudence was more conspicuous than tender anxiety for his wife. He had by this time reached the bottom of the stairs, when, on looking up, he perceived the trap-door was left open; and ascending in haste to close it, he heard footsteps advancing through the chambers above. Before he could descend entirely out of sight, he again looked up, and perceived through the aperture the face of a man looking down, upon him. Master, cried Peter. — La Motte was somewhat relieved at the sound of his voice, though angry that he had occasioned, him so much terror.

What brings you here, and what is the matter below?

Nothing, Sir, nothing's the matter, only my mistress sent me to see after your honour.

There's nobody there then? said La Motte, setting his foot upon the step.

Yes, Sir, there is my mistress and Mademoiselle Adeline, and —

Well — well — said La Motte briskly, go your ways, I am coming.

He informed Madame La Motte where he had been, and of his intention of secreting himself, and deliberated upon the means of convincing the officers, should they arrive, that he had quitted the abbey. For this purpose he ordered all the moveable furniture to be conveyed to the cells below. La Motte himself assisted in this business, and every hand was employed for dispatch. In a very short time the habitable part of the fabric was left almost as desolate as he had found it. He then bade Peter take the horses to a distance from the abbey and turn them loose. After further consideration, he thought it might contribute to mislead them, if he placed in some conspicuous part of the fabric an inscription, signifying his condition, and mentioning the date of his departure from the abbey. Over the door of the tower which led to the habitable part of the structure, he therefore cut the following lines:

O ye! whom misfortune may lead to this spot,

Learn that there are others as miserable as yourselves.

P— —L—M— —a wretched exile, sought within these walls a refuge from persecution on the 27th of April, 1658, and quitted them on the 12th of July in the same year, in search of a more convenient asylum.

After engraving these words with a knife, the small stock of provisions remaining from the week's supply (for Peter, in his fright, had returned unloaded from his last journey) was put into a basket; and La Motte having assembled his family, they all ascended the stairs of the tower, and passed through the chambers to the closet. Peter went first with a light, and with some difficulty found the trap-door. Madame La Motte shuddered as she surveyed the gloomy abyss; but they were all silent.

La Motte now took the light and led the way; Madame followed, and then Adeline. These old monks loved good wine as well as other people, said Peter, who brought up the rear; I warrant your honour, now, this was their cellar; I smell the casks already.

Peace, said La Motte, reserve your jokes for a proper occasion.

There is no harm in loving good wine, as your honour knows.

Have done with this buffoonery, said La Motte in a tone more authoritative, and go first. Peter obeyed.

They came to the vaulted room. The dismal spectacle he had seen here, deterred La Motte from passing a night in this chamber; and the furniture had, by his own order, been conveyed to the cells below. He was anxious that his family should not perceive the skeleton; an object which would probably excite a degree of horror not to be overcome during their stay. La Motte now passed the chest in haste; and Madame La Motte and Adeline were too much engrossed by their own thoughts, to give minute attention to external circumstances.

When they reached the cells, Madame La Motte wept at the necessity which condemned her to a spot so dismal. Alas, said she, are we indeed thus reduced! The apartments above formerly appeared to me a deplorable habitation; but they are a palace compared to these.

True, my dear, said La Motte, and let the remembrance of what you once thought them soothe your discontent now; these cells are also a palace compared to the Bicêtre, or the Bastille, and to the terrors of further punishment which would accompany them: let the apprehension of the greater evil teach you to endure the less: I am contented if we find here the refuge I seek.

Madame La Motte was silent, and Adeline, forgetting her late unkindness, endeavoured as much as she could to console her; while her heart was sinking with the misfortunes which she could not but anticipate, she appeared composed, and even cheerful. She attended Madame La Motte with the most watchful solicitude, and felt so thankful that La Motte was now secreted within this recess, that she almost lost her perception of its glooms and inconveniences.

This she artlessly expressed to him, who could not be insensible to the tenderness it discovered. Madame La Motte was also sensible of it, and it renewed a painful sensation. The effusions of gratitude she mistook for those of tenderness.

La Motte returned frequently to the trap-door to listen if any body was in the abbey; but no sound disturbed the stillness of night: at length they sat down to supper; the repast was a melancholy one. If the officers do not come hither to-night, said Madame La Motte, sighing, suppose, my dear, Peter returns to Auboine to-morrow? He may there learn something more of this affair; or, at least, he might procure a carriage to convey us hence.

To be sure he might, said La Motte peevishly, and people to attend it also. Peter would be an excellent person to show the officers the way to the abbey, and to inform them of what they might else be in doubt about, my concealment here.

How cruel is this irony! replied Madame La Motte. I proposed only what I thought would be for our mutual good; my judgment was, perhaps, wrong, but my intention was certainly right. Tears swelled into her eyes as she spoke these words. Adeline wished to relieve her; but delicacy kept her silent. La Motte observed the effect of his speech, and something like remorse touched his heart. He approached, and taking her hand, You must allow for the perturbation of my mind, said he, I did not mean to afflict you thus. The idea of sending Peter to Auboine, where he has already done so much harm by his blunders, teased me, and I could not let it pass unnoticed. No, my dear, our only chance of safety is to remain where we are while our provisions last. If the officers do not come here to-night, they probably will to-morrow, or, perhaps, the next day. When they have searched the abbey, without finding me, they will depart; we may then emerge from this recess, and take measures for removing to a distant country.

Madame La Motte acknowledged the justice of his words; and her mind being relieved by the little apology he had made, she became tolerably cheerful. Supper being ended, La Motte stationed the faithful though simple Peter at the foot of the steps that ascended to the closet, there to keep watch during the night. Having done this, he returned to the lower cells, where he had left his little family. The beds were spread; and having mournfully bidden each other good night, they lay down, and implored rest.

Adeline's thoughts were too busy to suffer her to repose, and when she believed her companions were sunk in slumbers, she indulged the sorrow which reflection brought. She also looked forward to the future with the most mournful apprehension. Should La Motte be seized, what was to become of her. She would then be a wanderer in the wide world; without friends to protect, or money to support her. The prospect was gloomy — was terrible! She surveyed it, and shuddered! The distresses too of Monsieur and Madame La Motte, whom she loved with the most lively affection, formed no inconsiderable part of hers.

Sometimes she looked back to her father; but in him she only saw an enemy from whom she must fly: this remembrance heightened her sorrow; yet it was not the recollection of the suffering he had occasioned her, by which she was so much afflicted, as by the sense of his unkindness: she wept bitterly. At length, with that artless piety which innocence only knows, she addressed the Supreme Being, and resigned herself to his care. Her mind then gradually became peaceful and reassured, and soon after she sunk to repose.

CHAPTER V

A SURPRISE — AN ADVENTURE — A

MYSTERY.

The night passed without any alarm; Peter had remained upon his post, and heard nothing that prevented his sleeping. La Motte heard him, long before he saw him, most musically snoring; though it must be owned there was more of the bass than of any other part of the gamut in his performance. He was soon roused by the bravura of La Motte, whose notes sounded discord to his ears, and destroyed the torpor of his tranquillity.

God bless you, master! what's the matter? cried Peter, waking, are they come?

Yes, for aught you care, they might be come. Did I place you here to sleep, sirrah? Bless you, master, returned Peter, sleep is the only comfort to be had here; I'm sure I would not deny it to a dog in such a place as this.

La Motte sternly questioned him concerning any noise he might have heard in the night; and Peter full as solemnly protested he had heard none; an assertion which was strictly true, for he had enjoyed the comfort of being asleep the whole time.

La Motte ascended to the trap-door and listened attentively. No sounds were heard, and as he ventured to lift it, the full light of the sun burst upon his sight, the morning being now far advanced: he walked softly along the chambers, and looked through a window — no person was to be seen. Encouraged by this apparent security, he ventured down the stairs of the tower, and entered the first apartment. He was proceeding towards the second, when suddenly recollecting himself, he first peeped through the crevice of the door, which stood half open. He looked, and distinctly saw a person sitting near the window, upon which his arm rested.

The discovery so much shocked him, that for a moment he lost all presence of mind, and was utterly unable to move from the spot. The person, whose back was towards him, arose, and turned his head: La Motte now recovered himself, and quitting the apartment as quickly and at the same time as silently as possible, ascended to the closet. He raised the trap-door, but, before he closed it, heard the footsteps of a person entering the outward chamber. Bolts or other fastening to the trap there was none; and his security depended solely upon the exact correspondence of the boards. The outer door of the stone room had no means of defence, and the fastenings of the inner one were on the wrong side to afford security even till some means of escape could be found.

When he reached this room he paused, and heard distinctly persons walking in the closet above. While he was listening, he heard a voice call him by name, and he instantly fled to the cells below, expecting every moment to hear the trap lifted and the footsteps of pursuit; but he was fled beyond the reach of hearing either. Having thrown himself on the ground at the furthest extremity of the vaults, he lay for some time breathless with agitation. Madame La Motte and Adeline, in the utmost terror, inquired what had happened. It was some time before he could speak; when he did, it was almost unnecessary, for the distant noises which sounded from above, informed his family of a part of the truth.

The sounds did not seem to approach; but Madame La Motte, unable to command her terror, shrieked aloud: this redoubled the distress of La Motte. You have already destroyed me, cried he; that shriek has informed them where I am. He traversed the cells with clasped hands and quick steps. Adeline stood pale and still as death, supporting Madame La Motte, whom with difficulty she prevented from fainting. O! Dupras! Dupras! you are already avenged! said he in a voice that seemed to burst from his heart: there was a pause of silence. But why should I deceive myself with a hope of escaping? he resumed; why do I wait here for their coming? Let me rather end those torturing pangs by throwing myself into their hands at once.

As he spoke, he moved towards the door; but the distress of Madame La Motte arrested his steps. Stay, said she, for my sake, stay; do not leave me thus, nor throw yourself voluntarily into destruction!

Surely, Sir, said Adeline, you are too precipitate; this despair is useless, as it is ill-founded. We hear no person approaching; if the officers had discovered the trap-door, they would certainly have been here before now. The words of Adeline stilled the tumult of his mind: the agitation of terror subsided; and reason beamed a feeble ray upon his hopes. He listened attentively; and perceiving that all was silent, advanced with caution to the stone room, and thence to the foot of the stairs that led to the trap-door. It was closed: no sound was heard above.

He watched a long time, and the silence continuing, his hopes strengthened; and at length he began to believe that the officers had quitted the abbey; the day, however, was spent in anxious watchfulness. He did not dare to unclose the trap-door; and he frequently thought he heard distant noises. It was evident, however, that the secret of the closet had escaped discovery; and on this circumstance he justly founded his security. The following night was passed, like the day, in trembling hope and incessant watching.

But the necessities of hunger now threatened them. The provisions, which had been distributed with the nicest economy, were nearly exhausted, and the most deplorable consequences might be expected from their remaining longer in concealment. Thus circumstanced, La Motte deliberated upon the most prudent method of proceeding. There appeared no other alternative, than to send Peter to Auboine, the only town from which he could return within the time prescribed by their necessities. There was game, indeed, in the forest; but Peter could neither handle a gun nor use a fishing rod to any advantage.

It was therefore agreed he should go to Auboine for a supply of provisions, and at the same time bring materials for mending the coach-wheel, that they might have some ready conveyance from the forest. La Motte forbade Peter to ask any questions concerning the people who had inquired for him, or take any methods for discovering whether they had quitted the country, lest his blunders should again betray him. He ordered him to be entirely silent as to these subjects, and to finish his business and leave the place with all possible dispatch.

A difficulty yet remained to be overcome—Who should first venture abroad into the abbey, to learn whether it was vacated by the officers of justice? La Motte considered that if he was again seen, he should be effectually betrayed; which would not be so certain if one of his family was observed, for they were all unknown to the officers. It was necessary, however, that the person he sent should have courage enough to go through with the inquiry, and wit enough to conduct it with caution. Peter, perhaps, had the first; but was certainly destitute of the last. Annette had neither. La Motte looked at his wife, and asked her if, for his sake, she dared to venture. Her heart shrunk from the proposal, yet she was unwilling to refuse, or appear indifferent upon a point so essential to the safety of her husband. Adeline observed in her countenance the agitation of her mind, and, surmounting the fears which had hitherto kept her silent, she offered herself to go.

57

They will be less likely to offend me, said she, than a man—Shame would not suffer La Motte to accept her offer; and Madame, touched with the magnanimity of her conduct, felt a momentary renewal of all her former kindness. Adeline pressed her proposal so warmly, and seemed so much in earnest, that La Motte began to hesitate. You, Sir, said she, once preserved me from the most imminent danger, and your kindness has since protected me: do not refuse me the satisfaction of deserving your goodness by a grateful return of it. Let me go into the abbey; and if, by so doing, I should preserve you from evil, I shall be sufficiently rewarded for what little danger I may incur, for my pleasure will be at least equal to yours.

Madame La Motte could scarcely refrain from tears as Adeline spoke; and La Motte sighing deeply, said, Well, be it so; go, Adeline, and from this moment consider me as your debtor. Adeline staid not to reply, but taking a light, quitted the cells. La Motte following to raise the trap-door, and cautioning her to look, if possible, into every apartment before she entered it. If you should be seen, said he, you must account for your appearance so as not to discover me. Your own presence of mind may assist you, I cannot—God bless you!

When she was gone, Madame La Motte's admiration of her conduct began to yield to other emotions. Distrust gradually undermined kindness, and jealousy raised suspicions. It must be a sentiment more powerful than gratitude, thought she, that could teach Adeline to subdue her fears. What, but love, could influence her to a conduct so generous! Madame La Motte, when she found it impossible to account for Adeline's conduct without alleging some interested motives for it, however her suspicions might agree with the practice of the world, had surely forgotten how much she once admired the purity and disinterestedness of her young friend.

Adeline, mean while, ascended to the chambers: the cheerful beams of the sun played once more upon her sight, and reanimated her spirits; she walked lightly through the apartments, nor stopped till she came to the stairs of the tower. Here she stood for some time, but no sounds met her ear, save the sighing of the wind among the trees, and at length she descended. She passed the apartments below without seeing any person, and the little furniture that remained seemed to stand exactly as she had left it. She now ventured to look out from the tower: the only animate objects that appeared were the deer quietly grazing under the shade of the woods. Her favourite little fawn distinguished Adeline, and came bounding towards her with strong marks of joy. She was somewhat

58

alarmed lest the animal, being observed, should betray her, and walked swiftly away through the cloisters.

She opened the door that lead to the great hall of the abbey, but the passage was so gloomy and dark that she feared to enter it, and started back. It was necessary, however, that she should examine further, particularly on the opposite side of the ruin, of which she had hitherto had no view: but her fears returned when she recollected how far it would lead her from her only place of refuge, and how difficult it would be to retreat. She hesitated what to do; but when she recollected her obligations to La Motte, and considered this as perhaps her only opportunity of doing him a service, she determined to proceed.

As these thoughts passed rapidly over her mind, she raised her innocent looks to heaven, and breathed a silent prayer. With trembling steps she proceeded over fragments of the ruin, looking anxiously around, and often starting as the breeze rustled among the trees, mistaking it for the whisperings of men. She came to the lawn which fronted the fabric, but no person was to be seen, and her spirits revived. The great door of the hall she now endeavoured to open; but suddenly remembering that it was fastened by La Motte's orders, she proceeded to the north end of the abbey, and, having surveyed the prospect around as far as the thick foliage of the trees would permit, without perceiving any person, she turned her steps to the tower from which she had issued.

Adeline was now light of heart, and returned with impatience to inform La Motte of his security. In the cloisters she was again met by her little favourite, and stopped for a moment to caress it. The fawn seemed sensible to the sound of her voice, and discovered new joy; but while she spoke, it suddenly started from her hand, and looking up, she perceived the door of the passage, leading to the great hall, open, and a man in the habit of a soldier issue forth.

With the swiftness of an arrow she fled along the cloisters, nor once ventured to look back; but a voice called to her to stop, and she heard steps advancing quick in pursuit. Before she could reach the tower, her breath failed her, and she leaned against a pillar of the ruin, pale and exhausted. The man came up, and gazing at her with a strong expression of surprise and curiosity, he assumed a gentle manner, assured her she had nothing to fear, and inquired if she belonged to La Motte. Observing that she still looked terrified and remained silent, he repeated his assurances and his question.

I know that he is concealed within the ruin, said the stranger; the occasion of his concealment I also know; but it is of the utmost importance I should see him, and he will then be convinced he has nothing to fear from me. Adeline trembled so excessively, that it was with difficulty she could support herself—she hesitated, and knew not what to reply. Her manner seemed to confirm the suspicions of the stranger, and her consciousness of this increased her embarrassment: he took advantage of it to press her further. Adeline at length, replied that La Motte had some time since resided at the abbey. And does still. Madam, said the stranger; lead me to where he may be found—I must see him, and—

Never, Sir, replied Adeline; and I solemnly assure you it will be in vain to search for him.

That I must try, resumed he, since you, Madam, will not assist me. I have already followed him to some chambers above, where I suddenly lost him; thereabouts he must be concealed, and it's plain therefore they afford some secret passage.

Without waiting Adeline's reply, he sprung to the door of the tower. She now thought it would betray a consciousness of the truth of his conjecture to follow him, and resolved to remain below. But upon further consideration, it occurred to her that he might steal silently into the closet, and possibly surprise La Motte at the door of the trap. She therefore hastened after him, that her voice might prevent the danger she apprehended. He was already in the second chamber when she overtook him: she immediately began to speak aloud.

This room he searched with the most scrupulous care; but finding no private door, or other outlet, he proceeded to the closet: then it was that it required all her fortitude to conceal her agitation. He continued the search. Within these chambers I know he is concealed, said he, though hitherto I have not been able to discover how. It was hither I followed a man, whom I believe to be him, and he could not escape without a passage; I shall not quit the place till I have found it.

He examined the walls and the boards, but without discovering the division of the floor, which indeed so exactly corresponded, that La Motte himself had not perceived it by the eye, but by the trembling of the floor beneath his feet. Here is some mystery, said the stranger, which I cannot comprehend, and perhaps never shall. He was turning to quit the closet, when, who can paint the distress of Adeline, upon seeing the trap-door gently raised, and La Motte himself appeared! Hah!

cried the stranger, advancing eagerly to him. La Motte sprang forward, and they were locked in each other's arms.

The astonishment of Adeline, for a moment, surpassed even her former distress; but a remembrance darted across her mind, which explained the present scene, and before La Motte could exclaim My son! she knew the stranger as such. Peter, who stood at the foot of the stairs, and heard what passed above, flew to acquaint his mistress with the joyful discovery, and in a few moments she was folded in the embrace of her son. This spot, so lately the mansion of despair, seemed metamorphosed into the palace of pleasure, and the walls echoed only to the accents of joy and congratulation.

The joy of Peter on this occasion was beyond expression: he acted a perfect pantomime — he capered about, clasped his hands — ran to his young master — shook him by the hand, in spite of the frowns of La Motte; ran every where, without knowing for what, and gave no rational answer to any thing that was said to him.

After their first emotions were subsided, La Motte, as if suddenly recollecting himself, resumed his wanted solemnity: I am to blame, said he, thus to give way to joy, when I am still, perhaps surrounded by danger. Let us secure a retreat while it is yet in our power, continued he; in a few hours the king's officers may search for me again.

Louis comprehended his father's words, and immediately relieved his apprehensions by the following relation: —

A letter from Monsieur Nemours, containing an account of your flight from Paris, reached me at Peronne, where I was then upon duty with my regiment. He mentioned that you were gone towards the south of France, but as he had not since heard from you, he was ignorant of the place of your refuge. It was about this time that I was dispatched into Flanders; and being unable to obtain further intelligence of you, I passed some weeks of very painful solicitude. At the conclusion of the campaign I obtained leave of absence, and immediately set out for Paris, hoping to learn from Nemours where you had found an asylum.

Of this, however, he was equally ignorant with myself. He informed me that you had once before written to him from D— —, upon your second day's journey from Paris, under an assumed name, as had been agreed upon; and that you then said the fear of discovery would prevent your hazarding another letter. He therefore remained ignorant of your abode, but said he had no doubt you had continued your journey to the southward. Upon this slender information I quitted Paris in search of you, and proceeded immediately to V— —, where my inquiries concerning your further progress were successful as far as M— —. There they told me you had staid some time, on account of the illness of a young lady; a circumstance which perplexed me much, as I could not imagine what young lady would accompany you. I proceeded, however, to L— —; but there all traces of you seemed to be lost. As I sat musing at the window of the inn, I observed some scribbling on the glass, and the curiosity of idleness prompted me to read it. I thought I knew the characters, and the lines I read confirmed my conjectures, for I remembered to have heard you often repeat them.

Here I renewed my inquiries concerning your route, and at length I made the people of the inn recollect you, and traced you as far as Auboine. There I again lost you, till upon my return from a fruitless inquiry in the neighbourhood, the landlord of the little inn where I lodged, told me he believed he had heard news of you, and immediately recounted what had happened at a blacksmith's shop a few hours before.

His description of Peter was so exact, that I had not a doubt it was you who inhabited the abbey; and as I knew your necessity for concealment, Peter's denial did not shake my confidence. The next morning, with the assistance of my landlord, I found my way hither, and having searched every visible part of the fabric, I began to credit Peter's assertion: your appearance, however, destroyed this fear, by proving that the place was still inhabited, for you disappeared so instantaneously that I was not certain it was you whom I had seen. I continued seeking you till near the close of day, and till then scarcely quitted the chambers whence you had disappeared. I called on you repeatedly, believing that my voice might convince you of your mistake. At length I retired to pass the night at a cottage near the border of the forest.

I came early this morning to renew my inquiries, and hoped that, believing yourself safe, you would emerge from concealment. But how was I disappointed to find the abbey as silent and solitary as I had left it the preceding evening! I was returning once more from the great hall, when the voice of this young lady caught my ear, and effected the discovery I had so anxiously sought.

This little narrative entirely dissipated the late apprehensions of La Motte; but he now dreaded that the inquiries of his son, and his own obvious desire of concealment, might excite a curiosity amongst the people of Auboine, and lead to a discovery of his true circumstances. However, for the present he determined to dismiss all painful thoughts, and endeavour to enjoy the comfort which the presence of his son had brought him. The furniture was removed to a more habitable part of the abbey, and the cells were again abandoned to their own glooms.

The arrival of her son seemed to have animated Madame La Motte with new life, and all her afflictions were, for the present, absorbed in joy. She often gazed silently on him with a mother's fondness, and her partiality heightened every improvement which time had wrought in his person and manner. He was now in his twenty-third year; his person was manly and his air military; his manners were unaffected and graceful, rather than dignified; and though his features were irregular, they composed a countenance which, having seen it once, you would seek it again.

She made eager inquiries after the friends she had left at Paris, and learned that within the few months of her absence some had died and others quitted the place. La Motte also learned that a very strenuous search for him had been prosecuted at Paris; and, though this intelligence was only what he had before expected, it shocked him so much, that he now declared it would be expedient to remove to a distant country. Louis did not scruple to say that he thought he would be as safe at the abbey as at any other place; and repeated what Nemours had said, that the king's officers had been unable to trace any part of his route from Paris.

Besides, resumed Louis, this abbey is protected by a supernatural power, and none of the country people dare approach it.

Please you, my young master, said Peter, who was waiting in the room, we were frightened enough the first night we came here, and I myself, God forgive me! thought the place was inhabited by devils, but they were only owls, and such like, after all.

Your opinion was not asked, said La Motte, learn to be silent.

Peter was abashed. When he had quitted the room, La Motte asked his son with seeming carelessness, what were the reports circulated by the country people? O! Sir, replies Louis, I cannot recollect half of them: I remember, however, they said that, many years ago, a person (but nobody had ever seen him, so we may judge how far the report ought to be credited)—a person was privately brought to this abbey, and confined in some part of it, and that there was strong reasons to believe he came unfairly to his end.

La Motte sighed. They further said, continued Louis, that the spectre of the deceased had ever since watched nightly among the ruins: and to make the story more wonderful, for the marvellous is the delight of the vulgar, they added, that there was a certain part of the ruin from whence no person that had dared to explore it, had ever returned. Thus people, who have few objects of real interest to engage their thoughts, conjure up for themselves imaginary ones.

La Motte sat musing. And what were the reasons, said he, at length awaking from his reverie, they pretended to assign for believing the person confined here was murdered?

They did not use a term so positive as that, replied Louis.

True, said La Motte, recollecting himself, they only said he came unfairly to his end.

That is a nice distinction, said Adeline.

Why I could not well comprehend what these reasons were, resumed Louis; the people indeed say, that the person who was brought here, was never known to depart; but I do not find it certain that he ever arrived: that there was strange privacy and mystery observed, while he was here, and that the abbey has never since been inhabited by its owner. There seems, however, to be nothing in all this that deserves to be remembered.—La Motte raised his head, as if to reply, when the entrance of Madame turned the discourse upon a new subject, and it was not resumed that day.

Peter was now dispatched for provisions, while La Motte and Louis retired to consider how far it was safe for them to continue at the abbey. La Motte, notwithstanding the assurances lately given him, could not but think that Peter's blunders and his son's inquiries might lead to a discovery of his residence. He revolved this in his mind for some time; but at length a thought struck him, that the latter of these circumstances might considerably contribute to his security. If you, said he to Louis, return to the inn at Auboine, from whence you were directed here, and without seeming to intend giving intelligence, do give the landlord an account of your having found the abbey uninhabited, and then add, that you had discovered the residence of the person you sought in some distant town, it would suppress any reports that may at present exist, and prevent the belief of any in future. And if, after all this, you can trust yourself for presence of mind and command of countenance, so far as to describe some dreadful apparition, I think these circumstances, together with the distance of the abbey and the intricacies of the forest, could entitle me to consider this place as my castle.

Louis agreed to all that his father had proposed, and on the following day executed his commission with such success, that the tranquillity of the abbey might be then said to have been entirely restored.

Thus ended this adventure, the only one that had occurred to disturb the family during their residence in the forest. Adeline, removed from the apprehension of those evils with which the late situation of La Motte had threatened her, and from the depression which her interest in his occasioned her, now experienced a more than usual complacency of mind. She thought, too, that she observed in Madame La Motte a renewal of her former kindness; and this circumstance awakened all her gratitude, and imparted to her a pleasure as lively as it was innocent. The satisfaction with which the presence of her son inspired Madame La Motte, Adeline mistook for kindness to herself, and she exerted her whole attention in an endeavour to become worthy of it.

But the joy which his unexpected arrival had given to La Motte quickly began to evaporate, and the gloom of despondency again settled on his countenance. He returned frequently to his haunt in the forest—the same mysterious sadness tinctured his manner, and revived the anxiety of Madame La Motte, who was resolved to acquaint her son with this subject of distress, and solicit his assistance to penetrate its source.

Her jealousy of Adeline, however, she could not communicate, though it again tormented her, and taught her to misconstrue with wonderful ingenuity every look and word of La Motte, and often to mistake the artless expressions of Adeline's gratitude and regard for those of warmer tenderness. Adeline had formerly accustomed herself to long walks in the forest, and the design Madame had formed of watching her steps, had been frustrated by the late circumstances, and was now entirely overcome by her sense of its difficulty and danger. To employ Peter in the affair, would be to acquaint him with her fears; and to follow her herself, would most probably betray her scheme, by making Adeline aware of her jealousy. Being thus restrained by pride and delicacy, she was obliged to endure the pangs of uncertainty concerning the greatest part of her suspicions.

To Louis, however, she related the mysterious change in his father's temper. He listened to her account with very earnest attention, and the surprise and concern impressed upon his countenance spoke how much his heart was interested. He was, however, involved in equal perplexity with herself upon this subject, and readily undertook to observe the motions of La Motte, believing his interference likely to be of equal service, both to his father and his mother. He saw, in some degree, the suspicions of his mother; but as he thought she wished to disguise her feelings, he suffered her to believe that she succeeded.

He now inquired concerning Adeline; and listened to her little history, of which his mother gave a brief relation, with great apparent interest. So much pity did he express for her condition, and so much indignation at the unnatural conduct of her father, that the apprehensions which Madame La Motte began to form, of his having discovered her jealousy, yielded to those of a different kind. She perceived that the beauty of Adeline had already fascinated his imagination, and she feared that her amiable manners would soon impress his heart. Had her first fondness for Adeline continued, she would still have looked with displeasure upon their attachment, as an obstacle to the promotion and the fortune she hoped to see one day enjoyed by her son. On these she rested all her future hopes of prosperity, and regarded the matrimonial alliance which he might form as the only means of extricating his family from their present difficulties. She therefore touched lightly upon Adeline's merit, joined coolly with Louis, in compassionating her misfortunes, and with her censure of the father's conduct mixed an implied suspicion of that of Adeline's. The means she employed to repress the passions of her son had a contrary effect. The indifference which she repressed towards Adeline, increased his pity for her destitute condition; and the tenderness with which she affected to judge the father, heightened his honest indignation at his character.

As he quitted Madame La Motte, he saw his father cross the lawn and enter the deep shade of the forest on the left. He judged this to be a good opportunity of commencing his plan, and quitting the abbey, slowly followed at a distance. La Motte continued to walk straight forward, and seemed so deeply wrapt in thought, that he looked neither to the right nor left, and scarcely lifted his head from the ground. Louis had followed him near half a mile, when he saw him suddenly strike into an avenue of the forest, which took a different direction from the way he had hitherto gone. He quickened his steps that he might not lose sight of him, but, having reached the avenue, found the trees so thickly interwoven that La Motte was already hid from his view.

He continued, however, to pursue the way before him: it conducted him through the most gloomy part of the forest he had yet seen, till at length it terminated in an obscure recess, over-arched with high trees, whose interwoven branches secluded the direct rays of the sun, and admitted only a sort of solemn twilight. Louis looked around in search of La Motte, but he was no where to be seen. While he stood surveying the place, and considering what further should be done, he observed, through the gloom, an object at some distance, but the deep shadow that fell around prevented his distinguishing what it was.

In advancing, he perceived the ruins of a small building, which, from the traces that remained, appeared to have been a tomb. As he gazed upon it, Here, said he, are probably deposited the ashes of some ancient monk, once an inhabitant of the abbey; perhaps, of the founder, who, after having spent a life of abstinence and prayer, sought in heaven the reward of his forbearance upon earth. Peace be to his soul! but did he think a life of mere negative virtue deserved an eternal reward? Mistaken man! reason, had you trusted to its dictates, would have informed you, that the active virtues, the adherence to the golden rule, Do as you would be done unto, could alone deserve the favour of a Deity whose glory is benevolence.

He remained with his eyes fixed upon the spot, and presently saw a figure arise under the arch of the sepulchre. It started, as if on perceiving him, and immediately disappeared. Louis, though unused to fear, felt at that moment an uneasy sensation, but it almost immediately struck him that this was La Motte himself. He advanced to the ruin and called him. No answer was returned; and he repeated the call, but all was yet still as the grave. He then went up to the archway and endeavoured to examine the place where he had disappeared, but the shadowy obscurity rendered the attempt fruitless. He observed, however, a little to the right, an entrance to the ruin, and advanced some steps down a kind of dark passage, when, recollecting that this place might be the haunt of banditti, his danger alarmed him, and he retreated with precipitation.

He walked towards the abbey by the way he came; and finding no person followed him, and believing himself again in safety, his former surmise returned, and he thought it was La Motte he had seen. He mused upon this strange possibility, and endeavoured to assign a reason for so mysterious a conduct, but in vain. Notwithstanding this, his belief of it strengthened, and he entered the abbey under as full a conviction as the circumstances would admit of, that it was his father who had appeared in the sepulchre. On entering what was now used as a parlour, he was much surprised to find him quietly seated there with Madame La Motte and Adeline, and conversing as if he had been returned some time.

He took the first opportunity of acquainting his mother with his late adventure, and of inquiring how long La Motte had been returned before him; when, learning that it was near half an hour, his surprise increased, and he knew not what to conclude.

Meanwhile, a perception of the growing partiality of Louis co-operated with the canker of suspicion to destroy in Madame La Motte that affection which pity and esteem had formerly excited for Adeline. Her unkindness was now too obvious to escape the notice of her to whom it was directed, and, being noticed, it occasioned an anguish which Adeline found it very difficult to endure. With the warmth and candour of youth, she sought an explanation of this change of behaviour, and an opportunity of exculpating herself from any intention of provoking it. But this Madame La Motte artfully evaded; while at the same time she threw out hints that involved Adeline in deeper perplexity, and served to make her present affliction more intolerable.

I have lost that affection, she would say, which was my all. It was my only comfort — yet I have lost it — and this without even knowing my offence. But I am thankful that I have not merited unkindness, and, though she has abandoned me, I shall always love her.

Thus distressed, she would frequently leave the parlour, and, retiring to her chamber, would yield to a despondency which she had never known till now.

One morning, being unable to sleep, she arose at a very early hour. The faint light of day now trembled through the clouds, and gradually spreading from the horizon, announced the rising sun. Every feature of the landscape was slowly unveiled, moist with the dews of night and brightening with the dawn, till at length the sun appeared and shed the full flood of day. The beauty of the hour invited her to walk, and she went forth into the forest to taste the sweets of morning. The carols of new-waked birds saluted her as she passed, and the fresh gale came scented with the breath of flowers, whose tints glowed more vivid through the dew drops that hung on their leaves.

She wandered on without noticing the distance, and, following the windings of the river, came to a dewy glade, whose woods, sweeping down to the very edge of the water, formed a scene so sweetly romantic, that she sealed herself at the foot of a tree, to contemplate its beauty. These images insensibly soothed her sorrow, and inspired her with that soft and pleasing melancholy so dear to the feeling mind. For some time she sat lost in a reverie, while the flowers that grew on the banks beside her seemed to smile in new life, and drew from her a comparison with her own condition. She mused and sighed, and then, in a voice whose charming melody was modulated by the tenderness of her heart, she sung the following words:

SONNET,

TO THE LILY.

Soft silken flower! that in the dewy vale

Unfold'st thy modest beauties to the morn,

And breath'st thy fragrance on her wandering gale,

O'er earth's green hills and shadowy valley borne.

When day has closed his dazzling eye,

And dying gales sink soft away;

When eve steals down the western sky,

And mountains, woods, and vales decay.

Thy tender cups, that graceful swell,

Droop sad beneath her chilly dew;

Thy odours seek their silken cell,

And twilight veils their languid hue.

But soon fair flower! the morn shall rise,

And rear again thy pensive head;

Again unveil thy snowy dyes,

Again thy velvet foliage spread.

Sweet child of Spring! like thee, in sorrow's shade,

Full oft I mourn in tears, and droop forlorn:

And O! like thine, may light my glooms pervade,

And Sorrow fly before Joy's living morn!

A distant echo lengthened out her tones, and she sat listening to the soft response, till repeating the last stanza of the sonnet she was answered by a voice almost as tender, and less distant. She looked round in surprise, and saw a young man in a hunter's dress leaning against a tree, and gazing on her with that deep attention which marks an enraptured mind.

A thousand apprehensions shot athwart her busy thought; and she now first remembered her distance from the abbey. She rose in haste to be gone, when the stranger respectfully advanced; but, observing her timid looks and retiring steps, he paused. She pursued her way towards the abbey; and though many reasons made her anxious to know whether she was followed, delicacy forbade her to look back. When she reached the abbey, finding the family was not yet assembled to breakfast, she retired to her chamber, where her whole thoughts were employed in conjectures concerning the stranger. Believing that she was interested on this point no further than as it concerned the safety of La Motte, she indulged without scruple the remembrance of that dignified air and manner which so much distinguished the youth she had seen. After revolving the circumstance more deeply, she believed it impossible that a person of his appearance should be engaged in a stratagem to betray a fellow-creature; and though she was destitute of a single circumstance that might assist her surmises of who he was, or what was his business in an unfrequented forest, she rejected, unconsciously, every suspicion injurious to his character. Upon further deliberation, therefore, she resolved not to mention this little circumstance to La Motte; well knowing, that though his danger might be imaginary, his apprehensions would be real, and would renew all the sufferings and perplexity from which he was but just released. She resolved, however, to refrain, for some time walking in the forest.

When she came down to breakfast, she observed Madame La Motte to be more than usually reserved. La Motte entered the room soon after her, and made some trifling observations on the weather; and, having endeavoured to support an effort at cheerfulness, sunk into his usual melancholy. Adeline watched the countenance of Madame with anxiety; and when there appeared in it a gleam of kindness, it was as sunshine to her soul: but she very seldom suffered Adeline thus to flatter herself. Her conversation was restrained, and often pointed at something more than could be understood. The entrance of Louis was a very seasonable relief to Adeline, who almost feared to trust her voice with a sentence, lest its trembling accents should betray her uneasiness.

This charming morning drew you early from your chamber? said Louis, addressing Adeline. You had, no doubt, a pleasant companion too? said Madame La Motte, a solitary walk is seldom agreeable.

I was alone, Madam, replied Adeline.

Indeed! your own thoughts must be highly pleasing then.

Alas! returned Adeline, a tear spite of her efforts starting to her eye, there are now few subjects of pleasure left for them.

That is very surprising, pursued Madame La Motte.

Is it, indeed, surprising, Madam, for those who have lost their last friend to be unhappy?

Madame La Motte's conscience acknowledged the rebuke, and she blushed.

Well, resumed she, after a short pause, that is not your situation, Adeline, looking earnestly at La Motte. Adeline, whose innocence protected her from suspicion, did not regard this circumstance; but, smiling through her tears, said, she rejoiced to hear her say so. During this conversation, La Motte had remained absorbed in his own thoughts; and Louis, unable to guess at what it pointed, looked alternately at his mother and Adeline for an explanation. The latter he regarded with an expression so full of tender compassion, that it revealed at once to Madame La Motte the sentiments of his soul; and she immediately replied to the last words of Adeline with a very serious air: A friend is only estimable when our conduct deserves one; the friendship that survives the merit of its object is a disgrace, instead of an honour, to both parties.

The manner and emphasis with which she delivered these words, again alarmed Adeline, who mildly said, she hoped she should never deserve such censure. Madame was silent; but Adeline was so much shocked by what had already passed, that tears sprung from her eyes, and she hid her face with her handkerchief.

Louis now rose with some emotion; and La Motte, roused from his reverie, inquired what was the matter: but before he could receive an answer he seemed to have forgotten that he had asked the question. Adeline may give you her own account, said Madame La Motte. I have not deserved this, said Adeline rising; but since my presence is displeasing, I will retire.

She moved towards the door; when Louis, who was pacing the room in apparent agitation, gently took her hand, saying, Here is some unhappy mistake—and would have led her to the seat: but her spirits were too much depressed to endure longer restraint; and, withdrawing her hand, Suffer me to go, said she; if there is any mistake, I am unable to explain it. Saying this, she quitted the room. Louis followed her with his eyes to the door; when turning to his mother, Surely, Madam, said he, you are to blame: my life on it she deserves your warmest tenderness.

You are very eloquent in her cause, Sir, said Madame, may I presume to ask what interested you thus in her favour.

Her own amiable manners, rejoined Louis, which no one can observe without esteeming them.

But you may presume too much on your own observations; it is possible these amiable manners may deceive you.

Your pardon Madam; I may, without presumption, affirm they cannot deceive me.

You have, no doubt, good reasons for this assertion, and I perceive, by your admiration of this artless innocence, she has succeeded in her design of entrapping your heart.

Without designing it, she has won my admiration, which would not have been the case, had she been capable of the conduct you mention.

Madame La Motte was going to reply, but was prevented by her husband, who, again roused from his reverie, inquired into the cause of dispute. Away with this ridiculous behaviour, said he in a voice of displeasure; Adeline has omitted some household duty, I suppose; and an offence so heinous deserves severe punishment, no doubt: but let me be no more disturbed with your petty quarrels; if you must be tyrannical, Madam, indulge your humour in private.

Saying this, he abruptly quitted the room; and Louis immediately following, Madame was left to her own unpleasant reflections. Her ill-humour proceeded from the usual cause. She had heard of Adeline's walk; and La Motte having gone forth into the forest at an early hour, her imagination, heated by the broodings of jealousy, suggested that they had appointed a meeting. This was confirmed to her by the entrance of Adeline, quickly followed by La Motte; and her perceptions thus jaundiced by passion, neither the presence of her son, nor her usual attention to good manners, had been able to restrain her emotions. The behaviour of Adeline in the late scene she considered as a refined piece of art, and the indifference of La Motte as affected. So true is it that:

...... Trifles, light as air,

Are, to the jealous, confirmations strong

As proofs of Holy Writ;

and so ingenious was she 'to twist the true cause the wrong way.'

Adeline had retired to her chamber to weep. When her first agitations were subsided, she took an ample view of her conduct; and perceiving nothing of which she could accuse herself, she became more satisfied, deriving her best comfort from the integrity of her intentions. In the moment of accusation, innocence may sometimes be oppressed with the punishment due only to guilt; but reflection dissolves the illusion of terror, and brings to the aching bosom the consolations of virtue.

When La Motte quitted the room, he had gone into the forest; which Louis observing, he followed and joined him, with an intention of touching upon the subject of his melancholy. It is a fine morning, Sir, said Louis; if you will give me leave, I will walk with you. La Motte, though dissatisfied, did not object; and after they had proceeded some way, he changed the course of his walk, striking into a path contrary to that which Louis had observed him take on the foregoing day.

Louis remarked that the avenue they had quitted was more shady, and therefore more pleasant. La Motte not seeming to notice this remark, It leads to a singular spot, continued he, which I discovered yesterday. La Motte raised his head: Louis proceeded to describe the tomb, and the adventure he had met with. During this relation, La Motte regarded him with attention, while his own countenance suffered various changes. When he had concluded, You were very daring, said La Motte, to examine that place, particularly when you ventured down the passage: I would advise you to be more cautious how you penetrate the depths of this forest. I myself have not ventured beyond a certain boundary and am therefore uninformed what inhabitants it may harbour. Your account has alarmed me, continued he; for if banditti are in the neighbourhood, I am not safe from their depredations: — 'tis true, I have but little to lose, except my life.

And the lives of your family, rejoined Louis. — Of course, said La Motte.

It would be well to have more certainty upon that head, rejoined Louis; I am considering how we may obtain it.

'Tis useless to consider that, said La Motte; the inquiry itself brings danger with it; your life would perhaps be paid for the indulgence of your curiosity; our only chance of safety is by endeavouring to remain undiscovered. Let us move towards the abbey.

Louis knew not what to think, but said no more upon the subject. La Motte soon after relapsed into a fit of musing; and his son now took occasion to lament that depression of spirits which he had lately observed in him. Rather lament the cause of it, said La Motte with a sigh. That I do most sincerely, whatever it may be. May I venture to inquire, Sir, what is this cause?

Are then my misfortunes so little known to you, rejoined La Motte, as to make that question necessary? Am I not driven from my home, from my friends, and almost from my country? And shall it be asked why I am afflicted? Louis felt the justice of this reproof, and was a moment silent. That you are afflicted, Sir, does not excite my surprise, resumed he; it would indeed be strange, were you not.

What then does excite your surprise?

The air of cheerfulness you wore when I first came hither.

You lately lamented that I was afflicted, said La Motte, and now seem not very well pleased that I once was cheerful. What is the meaning of this?

You much mistake me, said his son; nothing could give me so much satisfaction as to see that cheerfulness renewed; the same cause of sorrow existed at that time, yet you was then cheerful.

That I was then cheerful, said La Motte, you might, without flattery, have attributed to yourself; your presence revived me, and I was relieved at the same time from a load of apprehensions.

Why then, as the same cause exists, are you not still cheerful?

And why do you not recollect that it is your father you thus speak to?

I do, Sir, and nothing but anxiety for my father could have urged me thus far: it is with inexpressible concern I perceive you have some secret cause of uneasiness; reveal it, Sir, to those who claim a share in all your affliction, and suffer them, by participation to soften its severity. Louis looked up, and observed the countenance of his father pale as death: his lips trembled while he spoke. Your penetration, however, you may rely upon it, has, in the present instance, deceived you: I have no subject of distress, but what you are already acquainted with, and I desire this conversation may never be renewed.

If it is your desire, of course I obey, said Louis; but, pardon me, Sir, if —

I will not pardon you, Sir, interrupted La Motte; let the discourse end here. Saying this, he quickened his steps; and Louis, not daring to pursue, walked quietly on till he reached the abbey.

Adeline passed the greatest part of the day alone in her chamber, where, having examined her conduct, she endeavoured to fortify her heart against the unmerited displeasure of Madame La Motte. This was a task more difficult than that of self-acquittance. She loved her, and had relied on her friendship, which, notwithstanding the conduct of Madame, still appeared valuable to her. It was true, she had not deserved to lose it; but Madame was so averse to explanation, that there was little probability of recovering it, however ill-founded might be the cause of her dislike. At length she reasoned, or rather perhaps persuaded herself into tolerable composure; for to resign a real good with contentment is less an effort of reason than of temper.

For many hours she busied herself upon a piece of work which she had undertaken for Madame La Motte; and this she did without the least intention of conciliating her favour, but because she felt there was something in thus repaying unkindness, which was suitable to her own temper, her sentiments, and her pride. Self-love may be the centre round which the human affections move; for whatever motive conduces to self-gratification may be resolved into self-love; yet some of these affections are in their nature so refined, that though we cannot deny their origin, they almost deserve the name of virtue. Of this species was that of Adeline.

In this employment, and in reading, Adeline passed as much of the day as possible. From books, indeed, she had constantly derived her chief information and amusement: those belonging to La Motte were few, but well chosen; and Adeline could find pleasure in reading them more than once. When her mind was discomposed by the behaviour of Madame La Motte, or by a retrospection of her early misfortunes, a book was the opiate that lulled it to repose. La Motte had several of the best English poets, a language which Adeline had learned in the convent; their beauties, therefore, she was capable of tasting, and they often inspired her with enthusiastic delight.

At the decline of day she quitted her chamber to enjoy the sweet evening hour, but strayed no further than an avenue near the abbey, which fronted the west. She read a little; but finding it impossible any longer to abstract her attention from the scene around; she closed the book, and yielded to the sweet complacent melancholy which the hour inspired. The air was still; the sun sinking below the distant hill, spread a purple glow over the landscape, and touched the forest glades with softer light. A dewy freshness was diffused upon the air. As the sun descended, the dusk came silently on, and the scene assumed a solemn grandeur. As she mused, she recollected and repeated the following stanzas:

NIGHT.

Now Evening fades! her pensive step retires,
And Night leads on the dews and shadowy hours:
Her awful pomp of planetary fires,
And all her train of visionary powers.

These paint with fleeting shapes the dream of sleep,
These swell the waking soul with pleasing dread;
These through the glooms in forms terrific sweep,
And rouse the thrilling horrors of the dead!

Queen of the solemn thought—mysterious Night!
Whose step is darkness, and whose voice is fear!
Thy shades I welcome with severe delight,
And hail thy hollow gales, that sigh so drear!

When wrapt in clouds, and riding in the blast,
Thou roll'st the storm along the sounding shore,
I love to watch the whelming billows cast
On rocks below, and listen to the roar.

Thy milder terrors, Night, I frequent woo
Thy silent lightnings, and thy meteors' glare,
Thy northern fires, bright with ensanguine hue,
That light in heaven's high vault the fervid air.

But chief I love thee, when thy hold car
Sheds through the fleecy clouds a trembling gleam,
And shows the misty mountain from afar,
The nearer forest, and the valley's stream:

And nameless objects in the vale below,
That, floating dimly to the musing eye,
Assume, at Fancy's touch, fantastic show,
And raise her sweet romantic visions high.

Then let me stand amidst thy glooms profound,

On some wide woody steep, and hear the breeze

That swells in mournful melody around,

And faintly dies upon the distant trees.

What melancholy charm steals o'er the mind!

What hallow'd tears the rising rapture greet!

While many a viewless spirit in the wind

Sighs to the lonely hour in accents sweet!

Ah! who the dear illusions pleased would yield,

Which Fancy wakes from silence and from shades,

For all the sober forms of Truth reveal'd,

For all the scenes that Day's bright eye pervades!

On her return to the abbey she was joined by Louis, who, after some conversation, said, I am much grieved by the scene to which I was witness this morning, and have longed for an opportunity of telling you so. My mother's behaviour is too mysterious to be accounted for, but it is not difficult to perceive she labours under some mistake. What I have to request is, that whenever I can be of service to you, you will command me.

Adeline thanked him for this friendly offer, which she felt more sensibly than she chose to express. I am unconscious, said she, of any offence that may have deserved Madame La Motte's displeasure, and am therefore totally unable to account for it. I have repeatedly sought an explanation, which she has as anxiously avoided; it is better, therefore, to press the subject no farther. At the same time, Sir, suffer me to assure you, I have a just sense of your goodness. Louis sighed, and was silent. At length, I wish you would permit me, resumed he, to speak with my mother upon this subject; I am sure I could convince her of her error.

By no means, replied Adeline: Madame La Motte's displeasure has given me inexpressible concern; but to compel her to an explanation, would only increase this displeasure, instead of removing it. Let me beg of you not to attempt it.

I submit to your judgment, said Louis, but, for once, it is with reluctance. I should esteem myself most happy if I could be of service to you. He spoke this with an accent so tender, that Adeline, for the first time, perceived the sentiments of his heart. A mind more fraught with vanity than hers would have taught her long ago to regard the attentions of Louis as the result of something more than well-bred gallantry. She did not appear to notice his last words, but remained silent, and involuntarily quickened her pace. Louis said no more, but seemed sunk in thought; and this silence remained uninterrupted till they entered the abbey.

CHAPTER VI

Hence, horrible shadow!

Unreal mockery, hence!

MACBETH.

Near a month elapsed without any remarkable occurrence: the melancholy of La Motte suffered little abatement; and the behaviour of Madame to Adeline, though somewhat softened, was still far from kind. Louis by numberless little attentions testified his growing affection for Adeline, who continued to treat them as passing civilities.

It happened, one stormy night, as they were preparing for rest, that they were alarmed by the trampling of horses near the abbey. The sound of several voices succeeded, and a loud knocking at the great gate of the hall soon after confirmed the alarm. La Motte had little doubt that the officers of justice had at length discovered his retreat, and the perturbation of fear almost confounded his senses: he, however, ordered the lights to be extinguished, and a profound silence to be observed, unwilling to neglect even the slightest possibility of security. There was a chance, he thought, that the persons might suppose the place uninhabited, and believe they had mistaken the object of their search. His orders were scarcely obeyed, when the knocking was renewed, and with increased violence. La Motte now repaired to a small grated window in the portal of the gate, that he might observe the number and appearance of the strangers.

The darkness of the night baffled his purpose, he could only perceive a group of men on horseback; but listening attentively, he distinguished part of their discourse. Several of the men contended that they had mistaken the place; till a person, who, from his authoritative voice, appeared to be their leader, affirmed that the lights had issued from this spot, and he was positive there were persons within. Having said this, he again knocked loudly at the gate, and was answered only by hollow echoes. La Motte's heart trembled at the sound, and he was unable to move.

After waiting some time, the strangers seemed as if in consultation; but their discourse was conducted in such a low tone of voice, that La Motte was unable to distinguish its purport. They withdrew from the gate, as if to depart; but he presently thought he heard them amongst the trees on the other side of the fabric, and soon became convinced they had not left the abbey. A few minutes held La Motte in a state of torturing suspense; he quitted the grate, where Louis now stationed himself, for that part of the edifice which overlooked the spot where he supposed them to be waiting.

The storm was now loud, and the hollow blasts which rushed among the trees prevented his distinguishing any other sound. Once, in the pauses of the wind, he thought he heard distinct voices; but he was not long left to conjecture, for the renewed knocking at the gate again appalled him; and regardless of the terrors of Madame La Motte and Adeline, he ran to try his last chance of concealment by means of the trap-door.

Soon after, the violence of the assailants seeming to increase with every gust of the tempest, the gate, which was old and decayed, burst from its hinges, and admitted them to the hall. At the moment of their entrance, a scream from Madame La Motte, who stood at the door of an adjoining apartment, confirmed the suspicions of the principal stranger, who continued to advance as fast as the darkness would permit him.

Adeline had fainted, and Madame La Motte was calling loudly for assistance, when Peter entered with lights, and discovered the hall filled with men, and his young mistress senseless upon the floor. A chevalier now advanced, and, soliciting pardon of Madame for the rudeness of his conduct, was attempting an apology, when, perceiving Adeline, he hastened to raise her from the ground; but Louis, who now returned, caught her in his arms, and desired the stranger not to interfere.

The person to whom he spoke this, wore the star of one of the first orders in France, and had an air of dignity which declared him to be of superior rank. He appeared to be about forty, but perhaps the spirit and fire of his countenance made the impression of time upon his features less perceptible. His softened aspect and insinuating manners, while, regardless of himself, he seemed attentive only to the condition of Adeline, gradually dissipated the apprehensions of Madame La Motte, and subdued the sudden resentment of Louis. Upon Adeline, who was yet insensible, he gazed with an eager admiration, which seemed to absorb all the faculties of his mind. She was indeed an object not to be contemplated with indifference.

Her beauty, touched with the languid delicacy of illness, gained from sentiment what it lost in bloom. The negligence of her dress, loosened for the purpose of freer respiration, discovered those glowing charms, which her auburn tresses, that fell in profusion over her bosom, shaded, but could not conceal.

There now entered another stranger, a young chevalier, who having spoke hastily to the elder, joined the general group that surrounded Adeline. He was of a person in which elegance was happily blended with strength, and had a countenance animated, but not haughty; noble, yet expressive of peculiar sweetness. What rendered it at present more interesting, was the compassion, he seemed to feel for Adeline, who now revived and saw him, the first object that met her eyes, bending over her in silent anxiety.

On perceiving him, a blush of quick surprise passed over her cheek, for she knew him to be the stranger she had seen in the forest. Her countenance instantly changed to the paleness of terror when she observed the room crowded with people. Louis now supported her into another apartment, where the two chevaliers, who followed her, again apologized for the alarm they had occasioned. The elder, turning to Madame La Motte, said, You are, no doubt, Madam, ignorant that I am the proprietor of this abbey. She started. Be not alarmed, Madam, you are safe and welcome. This ruinous spot has been long abandoned by me, and if it has afforded you a shelter I am happy. Madame La Motte expressed her gratitude for this condescension, and Louis declared his sense of the politeness of the Marquis de Montalt, for that was the name of the noble stranger.

My chief residence, said the Marquis, is in a distant province, but I have a chateau near the borders of the forest, and in returning from an excursion I have been benighted and lost my way. A light which gleamed through the trees attracted me hither; and such was the darkness without, that I did not know it proceeded from the abbey till I came to the door. The noble deportment of the strangers, the splendour of their apparel, and above all, this speech dissipated every remaining doubt of Madame's, and she was giving orders for refreshments to be set before them, when La Motte, who had listened, and was now convinced he had nothing to fear, entered the apartment.

He advanced towards the Marquis with a complacent air; but as he would have spoke, the words of welcome faltered on his lips, his limbs trembled, and a ghastly paleness overspread his countenance.

The Marquis was little less agitated, and in the first moment of surprise put his hand upon his sword; but recollecting himself, he withdrew it, and endeavoured to obtain a command of features. A pause of agonizing silence ensued. La Motte made some motion towards the door, but his agitated frame refused to support him, and he sunk into a chair, silent and exhausted. The horror of his countenance, together with his whole behaviour, excited the utmost surprise in Madame, whose eyes inquired of the Marquis more than he thought proper to answer: his look increased instead of explaining the mystery, and expressed a mixture of emotions which she could not analyze. Meanwhile she endeavoured to soothe and revive her husband; but he repressed her efforts, and, averting his face, covered it with his hands.

The Marquis seeming to recover his presence of mind, stepped to the door of the hall where his people were assembled, when La Motte, starting from his seat with a frantic air, called on him to return. The Marquis looked back and stopped: but still hesitating whether to proceed, the supplications of Adeline, who was now returned, added to those of La Motte, determined him, and he sat down. I request of you, my Lord, said La Motte, that we may converse for a few moments by ourselves.

The request is bold, and the indulgence perhaps dangerous, said the Marquis: it is more also than I will grant. You can have nothing to say with which your family are not acquainted — speak your purpose and be brief. La Motte's complexion varied to every sentence of this speech. Impossible, my Lord, said he; my lips shall close for ever, ere they pronounced before another human being the words reserved for you alone. I entreat — I supplicate of you a few moments' private discourse. As he pronounced these words, tears swelled into his eyes; and the Marquis, softened by his distress, consented, though with evident emotion and reluctance, to his request.

La Motte took a light and led the Marquis to a small room in a remote part of the edifice, where they remained near an hour. Madame, alarmed by the length of their absence, went in quest of them: as she drew near, a curiosity in such circumstances perhaps not unjustifiable, prompted her to listen. La Motte just then exclaimed — The phrensy of despair! — some words followed, delivered in a low tone, which she could not understand. I have suffered more than I can express, continued he; the same image has pursued me in my midnight dream and in my daily wanderings. There is no punishment, short of death, which I would not have endured to regain the state of mind with which I entered this forest. I again address myself to your compassion.

A loud gust of wind that burst along the passage where Madame La Motte stood, overpowered his voice and that of the Marquis, who spoke in reply: but she soon after distinguished these words,—To-morrow, my Lord, if you return to these ruins, I will lead you to the spot.

That is scarcely necessary, and may be dangerous, said the Marquis. From you, my Lord, I can excuse these doubts, resumed La Motte; but I will swear whatever you shall propose. Yes, continued he, whatever may be the consequence, I will swear to submit to your decree! The rising tempest again drowned the sound of their voices, and Madame La Motte vainly endeavoured to hear those words upon which probably hung the explanation of this mysterious conduct. They now moved towards the door, and she retreated with precipitation to the apartment where she had left Adeline with Louis and the young chevalier.

Hither the Marquis and La Motte soon followed, the first haughty and cool, the latter somewhat more composed than before, though the impression of horror was not yet faded from his countenance. The Marquis passed on to the hall where his retinue awaited; the storm was not yet subsided, but he seemed impatient to be gone, and ordered his people to be in readiness. La Motte observed a sullen silence, frequently pacing the room with hasty steps, and sometimes lost in reverie. Meanwhile the Marquis, seating himself by Adeline, directed to her his whole attention, except when sudden fits of absence came over his mind and suspended him in silence: at these times the young chevalier addressed Adeline, who with diffidence and some agitation shrunk from the observance of both.

The Marquis had been near two hours at the abbey, and the tempest still continuing, Madame La Motte offered him a bed. A look from her husband made her tremble for the consequence. Her offer was however politely declined, the Marquis being evidently as impatient to be gone, as his tenant appeared distressed by his presence. He often returned to the hall, and from the gates raised a look of impatience to the clouds. Nothing was to be seen through the darkness of night—nothing heard but the howlings of the storm.

The morning dawned before he departed. As he was preparing to leave the abbey, La Motte again drew him aside, and held him for a few moments in close conversation. His impassioned gestures, which Madame La Motte observed from a remote part of the room, added to her curiosity a degree of wild apprehension, derived from the obscurity of the subject. Her endeavour to distinguish the corresponding words was baffled by the low voice in which they were uttered.

The Marquis and his retinue at length departed; and La Motte, having himself fastened the gates, silently and dejectedly withdrew to his chamber. The moment they were alone, Madame seized the opportunity of entreating her husband to explain the scene she had witnessed. Ask me no questions, said La Motte sternly, for I will answer none. I have already forbidden your speaking to me on this subject.

What subject? said his wife. La Motte seemed to recollect himself — No matter — I was mistaken — I thought you had repeated these questions before.

Ah! said Madame La Motte, it is then as I suspected; your former melancholy and the distress of this night have the same cause.

And why should you either suspect or inquire? Am I always to be persecuted with conjectures?

Pardon me, I meant not to persecute you; but my anxiety for your welfare will not suffer me to rest under this dreadful uncertainty. Let me claim the privilege of a wife, and share the affliction which oppresses you. Deny me not. — La Motte interrupted her, Whatever may be the cause of the emotions which you have witnessed, I swear that I will not now reveal it. A time may come when I shall no longer judge concealment necessary; till then be silent, and desist from importunity; above all, forbear to remark to any one what you may have seen uncommon in me, bury your surmise in your own bosom, as you would avoid my curse and my destruction. The determined air with which he spoke this, while his countenance was overspread with a livid hue, made his wife shudder; and she forbore all reply.

Madame La Motte retired to bed, but not to rest. She ruminated on the past occurrence; and her surprise and curiosity concerning the words and behaviour of her husband were but more strongly stimulated by reflection. One truth, however, appeared: she could not doubt but the mysterious conduct of La Motte, which had for so many months oppressed her with anxiety, and the late scene with the Marquis, originated from the same cause. This belief, which seemed to prove how unjustly she had suspected Adeline, brought with it a pang of self-accusation. She looked forward to the morrow, which would lead the Marquis again to the abbey, with impatience. Wearied nature at length resumed her rights, and yielded a short oblivion of care.

At a late hour the next day the family assembled to breakfast. Each individual of the party appeared silent and abstracted; but very different was the aspect of their features, and still more the complexion of their thoughts. La Motte seemed agitated by impatient fear, yet the sullenness of despair overspread his countenance; a certain wildness in his eye at times expressed the sudden start of horror, and again his features would sink into the gloom of despondency.

Madame La Motte seemed harassed with anxiety; she watched every turn of her husband's countenance, and impatiently awaited the arrival of the Marquis. Louis was composed and thoughtful. Adeline seemed to feel her full share of uneasiness; she had observed the behaviour of La Motte the preceding night with much surprise, and the happy confidence she had hitherto reposed in him was shaken. She feared also, lest the exigency of his circumstances should precipitate him again into the world, and that he would be either unable or unwilling to afford her a shelter beneath his roof.

During breakfast La Motte frequently rose to the window, from whence he cast many an anxious look. His wife understood too well the cause of his impatience, and endeavoured to repress her own. In these intervals Louis attempted by whispers to obtain some information from his father; but La Motte always returned to the table, where the presence of Adeline prevented further discourse.

After breakfast, as he walked upon the lawn, Louis would have joined him, but La Motte peremptorily declared he intended to be alone; and soon after, the Marquis having not yet arrived, proceeded to a greater distance from the abbey.

Adeline retired into their usual working room with Madame La Motte, who affected an air of cheerfulness and even of kindness. Feeling the necessity of offering some reason for the striking agitation of La Motte, and of preventing the surprise which the unexpected appearance of the Marquis would occasion Adeline, if she was left to connect it with his behaviour of the preceding night, she mentioned that the Marquis and La Motte had long been known to each other, and that this unexpected meeting, after an absence of many years, and under circumstances so altered and humiliating on the part of the latter, had occasioned him much painful emotion. This had been heightened by a consciousness that the Marquis had formerly misinterpreted some circumstances in his conduct towards him, which had caused a suspension of their intimacy.

This account did not bring conviction to the mind of Adeline, for it seemed inadequate to the degree of emotion which the Marquis and La Motte had mutually betrayed. Her surprise was excited, and her curiosity awakened by the words, which were meant to delude them both. But she forbore to express her thoughts.

Madame proceeding with her plan, said, the Marquis was now expected, and she hoped whatever differences remained would be perfectly adjusted. Adeline blushed, and endeavouring to reply, her lips faltered. Conscious of this agitation, and of the observance of Madame La Motte, her confusion increased, and her endeavours to suppress served only to heighten it. Still she tried to renew the discourse, and still she found it impossible to collect her thoughts. Shocked lest Madame should apprehend the sentiment which had till this moment been concealed almost from herself, her colour fled, she fixed her eyes on the ground, and for some time found it difficult to respire. Madame La Motte inquired if she was ill; when Adeline, glad of the excuse, withdrew to the indulgence of her own thoughts, which were now wholly engrossed by the expectation of seeing again the young chevalier who had accompanied the Marquis.

As she looked from her room, she saw the Marquis on horseback, with several attendants, advancing at a distance, and she hastened to apprize Madame La Motte of his approach. In a short time, he arrived at the gates, and Madame and Louis went out to receive him, La Motte being not yet returned. He entered the hall, followed by the young chevalier, and accosting Madame with a sort of stately politeness, inquired for La Motte, whom Louis now went to seek.

The Marquis remained for a few minutes silent, and then asked of Madame La Motte how her fair daughter did? Madame understood it was Adeline he meant; and having answered his inquiry, and slightly said that she was not related to them, Adeline, upon some indication of the Marquis's wish, was sent for. She entered the room with a modest blush and a timid air, which seemed to engage all his attention. His compliments she received with a sweet grace; but when the young chevalier approached, the warmth of his manner rendered hers involuntarily more reserved, and she scarcely dared to raise her eyes from the ground, lest they should encounter his.

La Motte now entered and apologized for his absence, which the Marquis noticed only by a slight inclination of his head, expressing at the same time by his looks both distrust and pride. They immediately quitted the abbey together, and the Marquis beckoned his attendants to follow at a distance. La Motte forbad his son to accompany him, but Louis observed he took the way into the thickest part of the forest. He was lost in a chaos of conjecture concerning this affair, but curiosity and anxiety for his father induced him to follow at some distance.

In the mean time the young stranger, whom the Marquis addressed by the name of Theodore, remained at the abbey with Madame La Motte and Adeline. The former, with all her address, could scarcely conceal her agitation during this interval. She moved involuntary to the door whenever she heard a footstep, and several times she went to the hall door, in order to look into the forest, but as often returned, checked by disappointment; no person appeared. Theodore seemed to address as much of his attention to Adeline as politeness would allow him to withdraw from Madame La Motte. His manners so gentle, yet dignified, insensibly subdued her timidity, and banished her reserve. Her conversation no longer suffered a painful constraint, but gradually disclosed the beauties of her mind, and seemed to produce a mutual confidence. A similarity of sentiment soon appeared; and Theodore, by the impatient pleasure which animated his countenance, seemed frequently to anticipate the thought of Adeline.

To them the absence of the Marquis was short, though long to Madame La Motte, whose countenance brightened when she heard the trampling of horses at the gate.

The Marquis appeared but for a moment, and passed on with La Motte to a private room, where they remained for some time in conference; immediately after which he departed. Theodore took leave of Adeline—who, as well as La Motte and Madame, attended them to the gates—with an expression of tender regret, and often, as he went, looked back upon the abbey, till the intervening branches entirely excluded it from his view.

The transient glow of pleasure diffused over the cheek of Adeline disappeared with the young stranger, and she sighed as she turned into the hall. The image of Theodore pursued her to her chamber; she recollected with exactness every particular of his late conversation — his sentiments so congenial with her own — his manners so engaging — his countenance so animated — so ingenious and so noble, in which manly dignity was blended with the sweetness of benevolence; these, and every other grace, she recollected, and a soft melancholy stole upon her heart. I shall see him no more, said she. A sigh that followed, told her more of her heart than she wished to know. She blushed, and sighed again; and then suddenly recollecting herself, she endeavoured to divert her thoughts to a different subject. La Motte's connection with the Marquis for sometime engaged her attention; but, unable to develop the mystery that attended it, she sought a refuge from her own reflections in the more pleasing ones to be derived from books.

During this time, Louis, shocked and surprised at the extreme distress which his father had manifested upon the first appearance of the Marquis, addressed him upon the subject. He had no doubt that the Marquis was intimately concerned in the event which made it necessary for La Motte to leave Paris, and he spoke his thoughts without disguise, lamenting at the same time the unlucky chance, which had brought him to seek refuge in a place, of all others, the least capable of affording it — the estate of his enemy. La Motte did not contradict this opinion of his son's, and joined in lamenting the evil fate which had conducted him thither.

The term of Louis's absence from his regiment was now nearly expired, and he took occasion to express his sorrow that he must soon be obliged to leave his father in circumstances so dangerous as the present. I should leave you, Sir, with less pain, continued he, was I sure I knew the full extent of your misfortunes; at present I am left to conjecture evils which perhaps do not exist. Relieve me, Sir, from this state of painful uncertainty, and suffer me to prove myself worthy of your confidence.

I have already answered you on this subject, said La Motte, and forbad you to renew it: I am now obliged to tell you, I care not how soon you depart, if I am to be subjected to these inquiries. La Motte walked abruptly away, and left his son to doubt and concern.

The arrival of the Marquis had dissipated the jealous fears of Madame La Motte, and she awoke to a sense of her cruelty towards Adeline. When she considered her orphan state — the uniform affection which had appeared in her behaviour — the mildness and patience with which she had borne her injurious treatment, she was shocked, and took an early opportunity of renewing her former kindness. But she could not explain this seeming inconsistency of conduct, without betraying her late suspicions, which she now blushed to remember, nor could she apologize for her former behaviour, without giving this explanation.

She contented herself, therefore, with expressing in her manner the regard which was thus revived. Adeline was at first surprised, but she felt too much pleasure at the change to be scrupulous in inquiring its cause.

But notwithstanding the satisfaction which Adeline received from the revival of Madame La Motte's kindness, her thoughts frequently recurred to the peculiar and forlorn circumstances of her condition. She could not help feeling less confidence than she had formerly done in the friendship of Madame La Motte, whose character now appeared less amiable than her imagination had represented it, and seemed strongly tinctured with caprice. Her thoughts often dwelt upon the strange introduction of the Marquis at the abbey, and on the mutual emotions and apparent dislike of La Motte and himself; and under these circumstances, it equally excited her surprise that La Motte should choose, and that the Marquis should permit him, to remain in his territory.

Her mind returned the oftener, perhaps, to this subject, because it was connected with Theodore; but it returned unconscious of the idea which attracted it. She attributed the interest she felt in the affair to her anxiety for the welfare of La Motte, and for her own future destination, which was now so deeply involved in his. Sometimes, indeed, she caught herself busy in conjecture as to the degree of relationship in which Theodore stood to the Marquis; but she immediately checked her thoughts, and severely blamed herself for having suffered them to stray to an object which she perceived was too dangerous to her peace.

CHAPTER VII

Present fears

Are less than horrible imaginings.

A few days after the occurrence related in the preceding chapter, as Adeline was alone in her chamber, she was roused from a reverie by a trampling of horses near the gate; and on looking from the casement she saw the Marquis de Montalt enter the abbey. This circumstance surprised her, and an emotion, whose cause she did not trouble herself to inquire for, made her instantly retreat from the window. The same cause, however, led her thither again as hastily; but the object of her search did not appear, and she was in no haste to retire.

As she stood musing and disappointed, the Marquis came out with La Motte, and immediately looking up, saw Adeline and bowed. She returned his compliment respectfully, and withdrew from the window, vexed at having been seen there. They went into the forest, but the Marquis's attendants did not, as before, follow them thither. When they returned, which was not till after a considerable time, the Marquis immediately mounted his horse and rode away.

For the remainder of the day La Motte appeared gloomy and silent, and was frequently lost in thought. Adeline observed him with particular attention and concern: she perceived that he was always more melancholy after an interview with the Marquis, and was now surprised to hear that the latter had appointed to dine the next day at the abbey.

When La Motte mentioned this, he added some high eulogiums on the character of the Marquis, and particularly praised his generosity and nobleness of soul. At this instant, Adeline recollected the anecdotes she had formerly heard concerning the abbey, and they threw a shadow over the brightness of that excellence which La Motte now celebrated. The account, however, did not appear to deserve much credit; a part of it, as far as a negative will admit of demonstration, having been already proved false; for it had been reported that the abbey was haunted, and no supernatural appearance had ever been observed by the present inhabitants.

Adeline, however, ventured to inquire whether it was the present Marquis of whom those injurious reports had been raised? La Motte answered her with a smile of ridicule: Stories of ghosts and hobgoblins have always been admired and cherished by the vulgar, said he: I am inclined to rely upon my own experience, at least as much as upon the accounts of these peasants; if you have seen any thing to corroborate these accounts, pray inform me of it, that I may establish my faith.

You mistake me, Sir, said she, it was not concerning supernatural agency that I would inquire; I alluded to a different part of the report, which hinted that some person had been confined here by order of the Marquis, who was said to have died unfairly; this was alleged as a reason for the Marquis's having abandoned the abbey.

All the mere coinage of idleness, said La Motte; a romantic tale to excite wonder: to see the Marquis is alone sufficient to refute this; and if we credit half the number of those stories that spring from the same source, we prove ourselves little superior to the simpletons who invent them. Your good sense, Adeline, I think, will teach you the merit of disbelief.

Adeline blushed and was silent; but La Motte's defence of the Marquis appeared much warmer and more diffuse than was consistent with his own disposition, or required by the occasion: his former conversation with Louis occurred to her, and she was the more surprised at what passed at present.

She looked forward to the morrow with a mixture of pain and pleasure: the expectation of seeing again the young chevalier occupying her thoughts, and agitating them with a various emotion: — now she feared his presence, and now she doubted whether he would come. At length she observed this, and blushed to find how much he engaged her attention. The morrow arrived — the Marquis came — but he came alone; and the sunshine of Adeline's mind was clouded, though she was able to wear her usual air of cheerfulness. The Marquis was polite, affable, and attentive: to manners the most easy and elegant, was added the last refinement of polished life. His conversation was lively, amusing, sometimes even witty, and discovered great knowledge of the world; or, what is often mistaken for it, an acquaintance with the higher circles, and with the topics of the day.

Here La Motte was also qualified to converse with him, and they entered into a discussion of the characters and manners of the age with great spirit and some humour. Madame La Motte had not seen her husband so cheerful since they left Paris, and sometimes she could almost fancy she was there. Adeline listened, till the cheerfulness which she had at first only assumed became real. The address of the Marquis was so insinuating and affable, that her reserve insensibly gave way before it, and her natural vivacity resumed its long-lost empire.

At parting, the Marquis told La Motte he rejoiced at having found so agreeable a neighbour. La Motte bowed. I shall sometimes visit you, continued he, and I lament that I cannot at present invite Madame La Motte and her fair friend to my chateau; but it is undergoing some repairs, which make it but an uncomfortable residence.

The vivacity of La Motte disappeared with his guest, and he soon relapsed into fits of silence and abstraction. The Marquis is a very agreeable man, said Madame La Motte. Very agreeable, replied he. And seems to have an excellent heart, she resumed. An excellent one, said La Motte.

You seem discomposed, my dear; what has disturbed you?

Not in the least — I was only thinking, that with such agreeable talents and such an excellent heart, it was a pity the Marquis should —

What? my dear, said Madame with impatience. That the Marquis should — should suffer this abbey to fall into ruins, replied La Motte.

Is that all? said Madame with disappointment. — That is all, upon my honour, said La Motte, and left the room.

Adeline's spirits, no longer supported by the animated conversation of the Marquis, sunk into languor, and when he departed she walked pensively into the forest. She followed a little romantic path that wound along the margin of the stream and was overhung with deep shades. The tranquillity of the scenes which autumn now touched with her sweetest tints, softened her mind to a tender kind of melancholy; and she suffered a tear, which she knew not wherefore had stolen into her eye, to tremble there unchecked. She came to a little lonely recess formed by high trees; the wind sighed mournfully among the branches, and as it waved their lofty heads scattered their leaves to the ground. She seated herself on a bank beneath, and indulged the melancholy reflections that pressed on her mind.

O! could I dive into futurity and behold the events which await me! said she; I should perhaps, by constant contemplation, be enabled to meet them with fortitude. An orphan in this wide world — thrown upon the friendship of strangers for comfort, and upon their bounty for the very means of existence, what but evil have I to expect? Alas, my father! how could you thus abandon your child — how leave her to the storms of life — to sink, perhaps, beneath them? alas, I have no friend!

She was interrupted by a rustling among the fallen leaves; she turned her head, and perceiving the Marquis's young friend, arose to depart. Pardon this intrusion, said he, your voice attracted me hither, and your words detained me: my offence, however, brings with it its own punishment; having learned your sorrows — how can I help feeling them myself? would that my sympathy or my suffering could rescue you from them! — He hesitated. — Would that I could deserve the title of your friend, and be thought worthy of it by yourself!

The confusion of Adeline's thoughts could scarcely permit her to reply; she trembled, and gently withdrew her hand, which he had taken while he spoke. You have perhaps heard, Sir, more than is true: I am indeed not happy; but a moment of dejection has made me unjust, and I am less unfortunate than I have represented. When I said I had no friend, I was ungrateful to the kindness of Monsieur and Madame La Motte, who have been more than friends — have been as parents to me.

If so, I honour them, cried Theodore with warmth; and if I did not feel it to be presumption, I would ask why you are unhappy? — But — he paused. Adeline, raising her eyes, saw him gazing upon her with intense and eager anxiety, and her looks were again fixed upon the ground. I have pained you, said Theodore, by an improper request. Can you forgive me, and also when I add, that it was an interest in your welfare which urged my inquiry?

Forgiveness, Sir, it is unnecessary to ask; I am certainly obliged by the compassion you express. But the evening is cold, if you please we will walk towards the abbey. As they moved on, Theodore was for some time silent. At length, It was but lately that I solicited your pardon, said he, and I shall now perhaps have need of it again; but you will do me the justice to believe that I have a strong and indeed a pressing reason to inquire how nearly you are related to Monsieur La Motte.

We are not at all related, said Adeline; but the service he has done me I can never repay, and I hope my gratitude will teach me never to forget it.

Indeed! said Theodore, surprised: and may I ask how long you have known him?

Rather, Sir, let me ask why these questions should be necessary.

You are just, said he, with an air of self-condemnation, my conduct has deserved this reproof; I should have been more explicit. He looked as if his mind was labouring with something which he was unwilling to express. But you know not how delicately I am circumstanced, continued he; yet I will aver that my questions are prompted by the tenderest interest in your happiness — and even by my fears for your safety. Adeline started. I fear you are deceived, said he, I fear there's danger near you.

Adeline stopped, and looking earnestly at him, begged he would explain himself. She suspected that some mischief threatened La Motte; and Theodore continuing silent, she repeated her request. If La Motte is concerned in this danger, said she, let me entreat you to acquaint him with it immediately; he has but too many misfortunes to apprehend.

Excellent Adeline! cried Theodore, that heart must be adamant that would injure you. How shall I hint what I fear is too true, and how forbear to warn you of your danger without — He was interrupted by a step among the trees, and presently after saw La Motte cross into the path they were in. Adeline felt confused at being thus seen with the chevalier, and was hastening to join La Motte; but Theodore detained her, and entreated a moment's attention. There is now no time to explain myself, said he; yet what I would say is of the utmost consequence to yourself.

Promise, therefore, to meet me in some part of the forest at about this time to-morrow evening; you will then, I hope, be convinced that my conduct is directed neither by common circumstances nor common regard. Adeline shuddered at the idea of making an appointment; she hesitated, and at length entreated Theodore not to delay till to-morrow an explanation which appeared to be so important, but to follow La Motte and inform him of his danger immediately. It is not with La Motte I would speak, replied Theodore; I know of no danger that threatens him — but he approaches, be quick, lovely Adeline, and promise to meet me.

I do promise, said Adeline, with a faltering voice; I will come to the spot where you found me this evening, an hour earlier to-morrow. Saying this, she withdrew her trembling hand, which Theodore had pressed to his lips in token of acknowledgement, and he immediately disappeared.

La Motte now approached Adeline, who, fearing that he had seen Theodore, was in some confusion. Whither is Louis gone so fast? said La Motte. She rejoiced to find his mistake, and suffered him to remain in it. They walked pensively towards the abbey, where Adeline, too much occupied by her own thoughts to bear company, retired to her chamber. She ruminated upon the words of Theodore; and the more she considered them, the more she was perplexed. Sometimes she blamed herself for having made an appointment, doubting whether he had not solicited it for the purpose of pleading a passion; and now delicacy checked this thought, and made her vexed that she had presumed upon having inspired one. She recollected the serious earnestness of his voice and manner when he entreated her to meet him; and as they convinced her of the importance of the subject, she shuddered at a danger which she could not comprehend, looking forward to the morrow with anxious impatience.

Sometimes too a remembrance of the tender interest he had expressed for her welfare, and of his correspondent look and air, would steal across her memory, awakening a pleasing emotion and a latent hope that she was not indifferent to him. From reflections like these she was roused by a summons to supper: — the repast was a melancholy one, it being the last evening of Louis's stay at the abbey. Adeline, who esteemed him, regretted his departure, while his eyes were often bent on her with a look which seemed to express that he was about to leave the object of his affection. She endeavoured by her cheerfulness to reanimate the whole party, and especially Madame La Motte, who frequently shed tears. We shall soon meet again, said Adeline, I trust in happier circumstances. La Motte sighed. The countenance of Louis brightened at her words. Do you wish it? said he with peculiar emphasis. Most certainly I do, she replied: can you doubt my regard for my best friends?

I cannot doubt any thing that is good of you, said he.

You forget you have left Paris, said La Motte to his son, while a faint smile crossed his face; such a compliment would there be in character with the place — in these solitary woods it is quite outre.

The language of admiration is not always that of compliment, Sir, said Louis. Adeline, willing to change the discourse, asked to what part of France he was going. He replied that his regiment was now at Peronne, and he should go immediately thither. After some mention of indifferent subjects, the family withdrew for the night to their several chambers.

The approaching departure of her son occupied the thoughts of Madame La Motte, and she appeared at breakfast with eyes swollen with weeping. The pale countenance of Louis seemed to indicate that he had rested no better than his mother. When breakfast was over, Adeline retired for a while, that she might not interrupt by her presence their last conversation. As she walked on the lawn before the abbey, she returned in thought to the occurrence of yesterday evening, and her impatience for the appointed interview increased. She was soon joined by Louis. It was unkind of you to leave us, said he, in the last moments of my stay. Could I hope that you would sometimes remember me when I am far away, I should depart with less sorrow. He then expressed his concern at leaving her: and though he had hitherto armed himself with resolution to forbear a direct avowal of an attachment, which must be fruitless, his heart now yielded to the force of passion, and he told what Adeline every moment feared to hear.

This declaration, said Adeline, endeavouring to overcome the agitation it excited, gives me inexpressible concern.

O, say not so! interrupted Louis, but give me some slender hope to support me in the miseries of absence. Say that you do not hate me — Say —

That I do most readily say, replied Adeline in a tremulous voice; if it will give you pleasure to be assured of my esteem and friendship — receive this assurance: — as the son of my best benefactors, you are entitled to — —

Name not benefits, said Louis, your merits outrun them all: and suffer me to hope for a sentiment less cool than that of friendship, as well as to believe that I do not owe your approbation of me to the actions of others. I have long borne my passion in silence, because I foresaw the difficulties that would attend it; nay, I have even dared to endeavour to overcome it: I have dared to believe it possible — forgive the supposition, that I could forget you — and — —

You distress me, interrupted Adeline; this is a conversation which I ought not to hear. I am above disguise, and therefore assure you that, though your virtues will always command my esteem, you have nothing to hope from my love. Were it even otherwise, our circumstances would effectually decide for us. If you are really my friend, you will rejoice that I am spared this struggle between affection and prudence. Let me hope, also, that time will teach you to reduce love within the limits of friendship.

Never, cried Louis vehemently: were this possible, my passion would be unworthy of its object. While he spoke, Adeline's favourite fawn came bounding towards her. This circumstance affected Louis even to tears. This little animal, said he, after a short pause, first conducted me to you: it was witness to that happy moment when I first saw you surrounded by attractions too powerful for my heart; that moment is now fresh in my memory, and the creature comes even to witness this sad one of my departure. Grief interrupted his utterance.

When he recovered his voice, he said, Adeline! when you look upon your little favourite and caress it, remember the unhappy Louis, who will then be far — far from you. Do not deny me the poor consolation of believing this!

I shall not require such a monitor to remind me of you, said Adeline with a smile; your excellent parents and your own merits have sufficient claim upon my remembrance. Could I see your natural good sense resume its influence over passion, my satisfaction would equal my esteem for you.

Do not hope it, said Louis, nor will I wish it; for passion here is virtue. As he spoke he saw La Motte turning round an angle of the abbey. The moments are precious, said he, I am interrupted. O! Adeline, farewell! and say that you will sometimes think of me.

Farewell, said Adeline, who was affected by his distress — farewell! and peace attend you. I will think of you with the affection of a sister. — He sighed deeply and pressed her hand; when La Motte, winding round another projection of the ruin, again appeared. Adeline left them together, and withdrew to her chamber, oppressed by the scene. Louis's passion and her esteem were too sincere not to inspire her with a strong degree of pity for his unhappy attachment. She remained in her chamber till he had quitted the abbey, unwilling to subject him or herself to the pain of a formal parting.

As evening and the hour of appointment drew nigh, Adeline's impatience increased; yet when the time arrived, her resolution failed, and she faltered from her purpose. There was something of indelicacy and dissimulation in an appointed interview on her part, that shocked her. She recollected the tenderness of Theodore's manner, and several little circumstances which seemed to indicate that his heart was not unconcerned in the event. Again she was inclined to doubt whether he had not obtained her consent to this meeting upon some groundless suspicion; and she almost determined not to go: yet it was possible Theodore's assertion might be sincere, and her danger real; the chance of this made her delicate scruples appear ridiculous; she wondered that she had for a moment suffered them to weigh against so serious an interest, and blaming herself for the delay they had occasioned, hastened to the place of appointment.

The little path which led to this spot, was silent and solitary, and when she reached the recess Theodore had not arrived. A transient pride made her unwilling he should find that she was more punctual to his appointment than himself; and she turned from the recess into a track which wound among the trees to the right. Having walked some way without seeing any person or hearing a footstep, she returned; but he was not come, and she again left the place. A second time she came back, and Theodore was still absent. Recollecting the time at which she had quitted the abbey, she grew uneasy, and calculated that the hour appointed was now much exceeded. She was offended and perplexed; but she seated herself on the turf, and was resolved to wait the event. After remaining here till the fall of twilight in fruitless expectation, her pride became more alarmed; she feared that he had discovered something of the partiality he had inspired; and believing that he now treated her with purposed neglect, she quitted the place with disgust and self-accusation.

When these emotions subsided, and reason resumed its influence, she blushed for what she termed this childish effervescence of self-love. She recollected, as if for the first time, these words of Theodore: I fear you are deceived, and that some danger is near you. Her judgment now acquitted the offender, and she saw only the friend. The import of these words, whose truth she no longer doubted, again alarmed her. Why did he trouble himself to come from the chateau, on purpose to hint her danger, if he did not wish to preserve her? And if he wished to preserve her, what but necessity could have withheld him from the appointment?

These reflections decided her at once. She resolved to repair on the following day at the same hour to the recess, whither the interest which she believed him to take in her fate would no doubt conduct him in the hope of meeting her. That some evil hovered over her she could not disbelieve, but what it might be she was unable to guess. Monsieur and Madame La Motte were her friends, and who else, removed as she now thought herself, beyond the reach of her father, could injure her? But why did

Theodore say she was deceived? She found it impossible to extricate herself from the labyrinth of conjecture, but endeavoured to command her anxiety till the following evening. In the mean time she engaged herself in efforts to amuse Madame La Motte, who required some relief after the departure of her son.

Thus oppressed by her own cares and interested by those of Madame La Motte, Adeline retired to rest. She soon lost her recollection: but it was only to fall into harassed slumbers, such as but too often haunt the couch of the unhappy. At length her perturbed fancy suggested the following dream.

She thought she was in a large old chamber belonging to the abbey, more ancient and desolate, though in part furnished, than any she had yet seen. It was strongly barricadoed, yet no person appeared. While she stood musing and surveying the apartment, she heard a low voice call her; and looking towards the place whence it came, she perceived by the dim light of a lamp a figure stretched on a bed that lay on the floor. The Voice called again; and approaching the bed, she distinctly saw the features of a man who appeared to be dying. A ghastly paleness overspread his countenance, yet there was an expression of mildness and dignity in it, which strongly interested her.

While she looked on him his features changed, and seemed convulsed in the agonies of death. The spectacle shocked her, and she started back; but he suddenly stretched forth his hand, and seizing hers, grasped it with violence: she struggled in terror to disengage herself; and again looking on his face, saw a man who appeared to be about thirty, with the same features, but in full health, and of a most benign countenance. He smiled tenderly upon her, and moved his lips as if to speak, when the floor of the chamber suddenly opened and he sunk from her view. The effort she made to save herself from following awoke her. —This dream had so strongly impressed her fancy, that it was some time before she could overcome the terror it occasioned, or even be perfectly convinced she was in her own apartment. At length, however, she composed herself to sleep; again she fell into a dream.

She thought she was bewildered in some winding passages of the abbey; that it was almost dark, and that she wandered about a considerable time without being able to find a door. Suddenly she heard a bell toll from above, and soon after a confusion of distant voices. She redoubled her efforts to extricate herself. Presently all was still; and at length wearied with the search, she sat down on a step that crossed the passage.

100

She had not been long here when she saw a light glimmer at a distance on the walls; but a turn in the passage, which was very long, prevented her seeing from what it proceeded. It continued to glimmer faintly for some time and then grew stronger, when she saw a man enter the passage habited in a long black cloak like those usually worn by attendants at funerals, and bearing a torch. He called to her to follow him, and led her through a long passage to the foot of a staircase. Here she feared to proceed, and was running back, when the man suddenly turned to pursue her, and with the terror which this occasioned she awoke.

Shocked by these visions, and more so by their seeming connection, which now struck her, she endeavoured to continue awake, lest their terrific images should again haunt her mind: after some time, however, her harassed spirits again sunk into slumber, though not to repose.

She now thought herself in a large old gallery, and saw at one end of it a chamber door standing a little open and a light within: she went towards it, and perceived the man she had before seen, standing at the door and beckoning her towards him. With the inconsistency so common in dreams, she no longer endeavoured to avoid him, but advancing, followed him into a suit of very ancient apartments hung with black and lighted up as if for a funeral. Still he led her on, till she found herself in the same chamber she remembered to have seen in her former dream: a coffin covered with a pall stood at the further end of the room; some lights and several persons surrounded it, who appeared to be in great distress.

Suddenly she thought these persons were all gone, and that she was left alone; that she went up to the coffin, and while she gazed upon it, she heard a voice speak, as if from within, but saw nobody. The man she had before seen, soon after stood by the coffin, and lifting the pall, she saw beneath it a dead person, whom she thought to be the dying chevalier she had seen in her former dream; his features were sunk in death, but they were yet serene. While she looked at him, a stream of blood gushed from his side, and descending to the floor the whole chamber was overflowed; at the same time some words were uttered in a voice she heard before; but the horror of the scene so entirely overcame her, that she started and awoke.

When she had recovered her recollection, she raised herself in the bed, to be convinced it was a dream she had witnessed; and the agitation of her spirits was so great, that she feared to be alone, and almost determined to call Annette. The features of the deceased person, and the chamber where he lay, were strongly impressed upon her memory, and she still thought she heard the voice and saw the countenance which her dream represented. The longer she considered these dreams, the more she was surprised; they were so very terrible, returned so often, and seemed to be so connected with each other, that she could scarcely think them accidental; yet why they should be supernatural, she could not tell. She slept no more that night.

CHAPTER VIII

...... When these prodigies

Do so conjointly meet, let not men say,

These are their reasons; they are natural;

For I believe they are portentous things.

JULIUS CÆSAR.

When Adeline appeared at breakfast, her harassed and languid countenance struck Madame La Motte, who inquired if she was ill. Adeline, forcing a smile upon her features, said she had not rested well, for that she had had very disturbed dreams: she was about to describe them, but a strong and involuntary impulse prevented her. At the same time La Motte ridiculed her concern so unmercifully, that she was almost ashamed to have mentioned it, and tried to overcome the remembrance of its cause.

After breakfast, she endeavoured to employ her thoughts by conversing with Madame La Motte; but they were really engaged by the incidents of the last two days, the circumstance of her dreams, and her conjectures concerning the information to be communicated to her by Theodore. They had thus sat for some time, when a sound of voices arose from the great gate of the abbey; and on going to the casement, Adeline saw the Marquis and his attendants on the lawn below. The portal of the abbey concealed several people from her view, and among these it was possible might be Theodore, who had not yet appeared: she continued to look for him with great anxiety, till the Marquis entered the hall with La Motte and some other persons, soon after which Madame went to receive him, and Adeline retired to her own apartment.

A message from La Motte, however, soon called her to join the party, where she vainly hoped to find Theodore. The Marquis arose as she approached, and, having paid her some general compliments, the conversation took a very lively turn. Adeline, finding it impossible to counterfeit cheerfulness while her heart was sinking with anxiety and disappointment, took little part in it: Theodore was not once named. She would have asked concerning him, had it been possible to inquire with propriety; but she was obliged to content herself with hoping, first, that he would arrive before dinner, and then before the departure of the Marquis.

Thus the day passed in expectation and disappointment. The evening was now approaching, and she was condemned to remain in the presence of the Marquis, apparently listening to a conversation which, in truth, she scarcely heard, while the opportunity was perhaps escaping that would decide her fate. She was suddenly relieved from this state of torture, and thrown into one, if possible, still more distressing.

The Marquis inquired for Louis, and being informed of his departure, mentioned that Theodore Peyrou had that morning set out for his regiment in a distant province. He lamented the loss he should sustain by his absence; and expressed some very flattering praise of his talents. The shock of this intelligence overpowered the long-agitated spirits of Adeline: the blood forsook her cheeks, and a sudden faintness came over her, from which she recovered only to a consciousness of having discovered her emotion, and the danger of relapsing into a second fit.

She retired to her chamber, where being once more alone, her oppressed heart found relief from tears, in which she freely indulged. Ideas crowded so fast upon her mind, that it was long ere she could arrange them so as to produce any thing like reasoning. She endeavoured to account for the abrupt departure of Theodore. Is it possible, said she, that he should take an interest in my welfare, and yet leave me exposed to the full force of a danger which he himself foresaw? Or am I to believe that he has trifled with my simplicity for an idle frolic, and has now left me to the wondering apprehension he has raised? Impossible! a countenance so noble, and a manner so amiable, could never disguise a heart capable of forming so despicable a design. No!—whatever is reserved for me, let me not relinquish the pleasure of believing that he is worthy of my esteem.

She was awakened from thoughts like these by a peal of distant thunder, and now perceived that the gloominess of evening was deepened by the coming storm; it rolled onward, and soon after the lightning began to flash along the chamber. Adeline was superior to the affectation of fear, and was not apt to be terrified; but she now felt it unpleasant to be alone, and hoping that the Marquis might have left the abby, she went down to the sitting-room: but the threatening aspect of the heavens had hitherto detained him, and now the evening tempest made him rejoice that he had not quitted a shelter. The storm continued, and night came on. La Motte pressed his guest to take a bed at the abbey, and he at length consented; a circumstance which threw Madame La Motte into some perplexity as to the accommodation to be afforded him. After some time she arranged the affair to her satisfaction; resigning her own apartment to the Marquis, and that of Louis to two of his superior attendants; Adeline, it was further settled, should give up her room to Monsieur and Madame La Motte, and to remove to an inner chamber, where a small bed, usually occupied by Annette, was placed for her.

At supper the Marquis was less gay than usual; he frequently addressed Adeline, and his look and manner seemed to express the tender interest which her indisposition, for she still appeared pale and languid, had excited. Adeline, as usual, made an effort to forget her anxiety and appear happy: but the veil of assumed cheerfulness was too thin to conceal the features of sorrow; and her feeble smiles only added a peculiar softness to her air. The Marquis conversed with her on a variety of subjects, and displayed an elegant mind. The observations of Adeline, which, when called upon, she gave with reluctant modesty, in words at once simple and forceful, seemed to excite his admiration, which he sometimes betrayed by an inadvertent expression.

Adeline retired early to her room, which adjoined on one side to Madame La Motte's, and on the other to the closet formerly mentioned. It was spacious and lofty, and what little furniture it contained was falling to decay; but perhaps the present tone of her spirits might contribute more than these circumstances to give that air of melancholy which seemed to reign in it. She was unwilling to go to bed, lest the dreams that had lately pursued her should return; and determined to sit up till she found herself oppressed by sleep, when it was probable her rest would be profound. She placed the light on a small table, and taking a book, continued to read for above an hour, till her mind refused any longer to abstract itself from its own cares, and she sat for some time leaning pensively on her arm.

The wind was high, and as it whistled through the desolate apartment, and shook the feeble doors, she often started, and sometimes even thought she heard sighs between the pauses of the gust; but she checked these illusions, which the hour of the night and her own melancholy imagination conspired to raise. As she sat musing, her eyes fixed on the opposite wall, she perceived the arras, with which the room was hung, wave backwards and forwards; she continued to observe it for some minutes, and then rose to examine it further. It was moved by the wind; and she blushed at the momentary fear it had excited; but she observed that the tapestry was more strongly agitated in one particular place than elsewhere, and a noise that seemed something more than that of the wind issued thence. The old bedstead, which La Motte had found in this apartment, had been removed to accommodate Adeline, and it was behind the place where this had stood, that the wind seemed to rush with particular force: curiosity prompted her to examine still further; she felt about the tapestry, and perceiving the wall behind shake under her hand, she lifted the arras, and discovered a small door, whose loosened hinges admitted the wind, and occasioned the noise she had heard.

The door was held only by a bolt, having undrawn which, and brought the light, she descended by a few steps into another chamber; she instantly remembered her dreams. The chamber was not much like that in which she had seen the dying chevalier, and afterwards the bier; but it gave her a confused remembrance of one through which she had passed. Holding up the light to examine it more fully, she was convinced by its structure that it was part of the ancient foundation. A shattered casement, placed high from the floor, seemed to be the only opening to admit light. She observed a door on the opposite side of the apartment; and after some moments of hesitation gained courage, and determined to pursue the inquiry. A mystery seems to hang over these chambers, said she, which it is perhaps my lot to develop; I will at least see to what that door leads.

She stepped forward, and having unclosed it, proceeded with faltering steps along a suite of apartments, resembling the first in style and condition, and terminating in one exactly like that where her dream had represented the dying person; the remembrance struck so forcibly upon her imagination, that she was in danger of fainting; and looking round the room, almost expected to see the phantom of her dream.

Unable to quit the place, she sat down on some old lumber to recover herself, while her spirits were nearly overcome by a superstitious dread, such as she had never felt before. She wondered to what part of the abbey these chambers belonged, and that they had so long escaped detection. The casements were all too high to afford any information from without. When she was sufficiently composed to consider the direction of the rooms and the situation of the abbey, there appeared not a doubt that they formed an interior part of the original building.

As these reflections passed over her mind, a sudden gleam of moonlight fell upon some object without the casement. Being now sufficiently composed to wish to pursue the inquiry, and believing this object might afford her some means of learning the situation of these rooms, she combated her remaining terrors; and in order to distinguish it more clearly, removed the light to an outer chamber; but before she could return, a heavy cloud was driven over the face of the moon, and all without was perfectly dark; she stood for some moments waiting a returning gleam, but the obscurity continued. As she went softly back for the light, her foot stumbled over something on the floor; and while she stooped to examine it, the moon again shone, so that she could distinguish through the casement, the eastern towers of the abbey. This discovery confirmed her former conjectures concerning the interior situation of these apartments. The obscurity of the place prevented her discovering what it was that had impeded her steps, but having brought the light forward, she perceived on the floor an old dagger: with a trembling hand she took it up, and upon a closer view perceived that it was spotted and stained with rust.

Shocked and surprised, she looked round the room for some object that might confirm or destroy the dreadful suspicion which now rushed upon her mind; but she saw only a great chair with broken arms, that stood in one corner of the room, and a table in a condition equally shattered, except that in another part lay a confused heap of things, which appeared to be old lumber. She went up to it, and perceived a broken bedstead, with some decayed remnants of furniture, covered with dust and cobwebs, and which seemed indeed as if they had not been moved for many years. Desirous, however, of examining further, she attempted to raise what appeared to have been part of the bedstead; but it slipped from her hand, and, rolling to the floor, brought with it some of the remaining lumber. Adeline started aside and saved herself; and when the noise it made had ceased, she heard a small rustling sound, and as she was about to leave the chamber, saw something falling gently among the lumber.

It was a small roll of paper, tied with a string, and covered with dust. Adeline took it up, and on opening it perceived a hand writing. She attempted to read it, but the part of the manuscript she looked at was so much obliterated, that she found this difficult, though what few words were legible impressed her with curiosity and terror, and induced her to return with it immediately to her chamber.

Having reached her own room, she fastened the private door, and let the arras fall over it as before. It was now midnight. The stillness of the hour, interrupted only at intervals by the hollow sighings of the blast, heightened the solemnity of

Adeline's feelings. She wished she was not alone, and before she proceeded to look into the manuscript, listened whether Madame La Motte was yet in her chamber: — not the least sound was heard, and she gently opened the door. The profound silence within almost convinced her that no person was there; but willing to be further satisfied, she brought the light and found the room empty. The lateness of the hour made her wonder that Madame La Motte was not in her chamber, and she proceeded to the top of the tower stairs, to hearken if any person was stirring.

She heard the sound of voices from below, and, amongst the rest, that of La Motte speaking in his usual tone. Being now satisfied that all was well, she turned towards her room, when she heard the Marquis pronounce her name with very unusual emphasis. She paused. I adore her, pursued he, and by Heaven — He was interrupted by La Motte, my Lord, remember your promise.

I do, replied the Marquis, and I will abide by it. But we trifle. To-morrow I will declare myself, and I shall then know both what to hope and how to act. Adeline trembled so excessively, that she could scarcely support herself: she wished to return to her chamber; yet she was too much interested in the words she had heard, not to be anxious to have them more fully explained. There was an interval of silence, after which they conversed in a lower tone. Adeline remembered the hints of Theodore, and determined, if possible, to be relieved from the terrible suspense she now suffered. She stole softly down a few steps, that she might catch the accents of the speakers, but they were so low that she could only now and then distinguish a few words. Her father, say you? said the Marquis. Yes, my Lord, her father. I am well informed of what I say. Adeline shuddered at the mention of her father, a new terror seized her, and with increasing eagerness she endeavoured to distinguish their words, but for some time found this to be impossible. Here is no time to be lost, said the Marquis, to-morrow then. — She heard La Motte rise, and believing it was to leave the room, she hurried up the steps, and having reached her chamber, sunk almost lifeless in a chair.

It was her father only of whom she thought. She doubted not that he had pursued and discovered her retreat; and though this conduct appeared very inconsistent with his former behaviour in abandoning her to strangers, her fears suggested that it would terminate in some new cruelty. She did not hesitate to pronounce this the danger of which Theodore had warned her; but it was impossible to surmise how he had gained his knowledge of it, or how he had become sufficiently acquainted with her story, except through La Motte, her apparent friend and protector, whom she was thus, though unwillingly, led to suspect of treachery. Why, indeed, should La Motte conceal from her only his knowledge of her father's intention, unless he designed to deliver her into his hands? Yet it was long ere she could bring herself to believe this conclusion possible. To discover depravity in those whom we have loved, is one of the most exquisite tortures to a virtuous mind, and the conviction is often rejected before it is finally admitted.

The words of Theodore, which told her he was fearful she was deceived, confirmed this most painful apprehension of La Motte, with another yet more distressing, that Madame La Motte was also united against her. This thought, for a moment, subdued terror and left her only grief; she wept bitterly. Is this human nature? cried she. Am I doomed to find every body deceitful? An unexpected discovery of vice in those whom we have admired, inclines us to extend our censure of the individual to the species; we henceforth contemn appearances, and too hastily conclude that no person is to be trusted.

Adeline determined to throw herself at the feet of La Motte on the following morning, and implore his pity and protection. Her mind was now too much agitated by her own interests to permit her to examine the manuscripts, and she sat musing in her chair till she heard the steps of Madame La Motte, when she retired to bed. La Motte soon after came up to his chamber; and Adeline, the mild, persecuted Adeline, who had now passed two days of torturing anxiety, and one night of terrific visions, endeavoured to compose her mind to sleep. In the present state of her spirits she quickly caught alarm, and she had scarcely fallen into a slumber when she was roused by a loud and uncommon noise. She listened, and thought the sound came from the apartments below, but in a few minutes there was a hasty knocking at the door of La Motte's chamber.

La Motte, who had just fallen asleep, was not easily to be roused; but the knocking increased with such violence, that Adeline, extremely terrified, arose and went to the door that opened from her chamber into his, with a design to call him. She was stopped by the voice of the Marquis, which she now clearly distinguished at the door. He called to La Motte to rise immediately; and Madame La Motte endeavoured at the same time to rouse her husband, who at length awoke in much alarm, and soon after joining the Marquis, they went down stairs together. Adeline now dressed herself, as well as her trembling hands would permit, and went into the adjoining chamber, where she found Madame La Motte extremely surprised and terrified.

The Marquis in the mean time told La Motte, with great agitation, that he recollected having appointed some persons to meet him upon business of importance early in the morning, and it was therefore necessary for him to set off for his chateau immediately. As he said this, and desired that his servants might be called, La Motte could not help observing the ashy paleness of his countenance, or expressing some apprehension that his Lordship was ill. The Marquis assured him he was perfectly well, but desired that he might set out immediately. Peter was now ordered to call the other servants, and the Marquis having refused to take any refreshment, bade La Motte a hasty adieu, and as soon as his people were ready left the abbey.

La Motte returned to his chamber, musing on the abrupt departure of his guest, whose emotion appeared much too strong to proceed from the cause assigned. He appeased the anxiety of Madame La Motte, and at the same time excited her surprise by acquainting her with the occasion of the late disturbance. Adeline, who had retired from the chamber on the approach of La Motte, looked out from her window on hearing the trampling of horses. It was the Marquis and his people, who just then passed at a little distance. Unable to distinguish who the persons were, she was alarmed at observing such a party about the abbey at that hour, and calling to inform La Motte of the circumstance, was made acquainted with what had passed.

At length she retired to her bed, and her slumbers were this night undisturbed by dreams.

When she arose in the morning, she observed La Motte walking alone in the avenue below, and she hastened to seize the opportunity which now offered of pleading her cause. She approached him with faltering steps, while the paleness and timidity of her countenance discovered the disorder of her mind. Her first words, without entering upon any explanation, implored his compassion. La Motte stopped, and looking earnestly in her face, inquired whether any part of his conduct towards her merited the suspicion which her request implied. Adeline for a moment blushed that she had doubted his integrity, but the words she had overheard returned to her memory.

Your behaviour, Sir, said she, I acknowledge to have been kind and generous, beyond what I had a right to expect, but—

and she paused. She knew not how to mention what she blushed to believe. La Motte continued to gaze on her in silent expectation, and at length desired her to proceed and explain her meaning. She entreated that he would protect her from her father. La Motte looked surprised and confused. Your father! said he. Yes, Sir, replied Adeline; I am not ignorant that he has discovered my retreat: I have every thing to dread from a parent who has treated me with such cruelty as you was witness of; and I again implore that you will save me from his hands.

La Motte stood fixed in thought, and Adeline continued her endeavours to interest his pity. What reason have you to suppose, or rather how have you learned, that your father pursues you? The question confused Adeline, who blushed to acknowledge that she had overheard his discourse, and disdained to invent or utter a falsity: at length she confessed the truth. The countenance of La Motte instantly changed to a savage fierceness, and, sharply rebuking her for a conduct to which she had been rather tempted by chance than prompted by design, he inquired what she had overheard that could so much alarm her. She faithfully repeated the substance of the incoherent sentences that had met her ear; — while she spoke, he regarded her with a fixed attention. And was this all you heard? Is it from these few words that you draw such a positive conclusion? Examine them, and you will find they do not justify it.

She now perceived, what the fervour of her fears had not permitted her to observe before, that the words, unconnectedly as she heard them, imported little, and that her imagination had filled up the void in the sentences, so as to suggest the evil apprehended. Notwithstanding this, her fears were little abated. Your apprehensions are, doubtless, now removed, resumed La Motte; but to give you a proof of the sincerity which you have ventured to question, I will tell you they were just. You seem alarmed, and with reason. Your father has discovered your residence, and has already demanded you. It is true, that from a motive of compassion I have refused to resign you, but I have neither authority to withhold nor means to defend you. When he comes to enforce his demand, you will perceive this. Prepare yourself, therefore, for the evil, which you see is inevitable.

Adeline for some time could speak only by her tears. At length, with a fortitude which despair had roused, she said, I resign myself to the will of Heaven! La Motte gazed on her in silence, and a strong emotion appeared in his countenance. He forbore, however, to renew the discourse, and withdrew to the abbey, leaving Adeline in the avenue, absorbed in grief.

A summons to breakfast hastened her to the parlour, where she passed the morning in conversation with Madame La Motte, to whom she told all her apprehensions, and expressed all her sorrow. Pity and superficial consolation were all that Madame La Motte could offer, though apparently much affected by Adeline's discourse. Thus the hours passed heavily away, while the anxiety of Adeline continued to increase, and the moment of her fate seemed fast approaching. Dinner was scarcely over, when Adeline was surprised to see the Marquis arrive. He entered the room with his usual ease, and apologizing for the disturbance he had occasioned on the preceding night, repeated what he had before told La Motte.

The remembrance of the conversation she had overheard at first gave Adeline some confusion, and withdrew her mind from a sense of the evils to be apprehended from her father. The Marquis, who was, as usual, attentive to Adeline, seemed affected by her apparent indisposition, and expressed much concern for that dejection of spirits which, notwithstanding every effort, her manner betrayed. When Madame La Motte withdrew, Adeline would have followed her; but the Marquis entreated a few moments' attention, and led her back to her seat. La Motte immediately disappeared.

Adeline knew too well what would be the purport of the Marquis's discourse, and his words soon increased the confusion which her fears had occasioned. While he was declaring the ardour of his passion in such terms as but too often make vehemence pass for sincerity, Adeline, to whom this declaration, if honourable, was distressing, and if dishonourable, was shocking, interrupted him and thanked him for the offer of a distinction which, with a modest but determined air, she said she must refuse. She rose to withdraw. Stay, too lovely Adeline! said he, and if compassion for my sufferings will not interest you in my favour, allow a consideration of your own dangers to do so. Monsieur La Motte has informed me of your misfortunes, and of the evil that now threatens you; accept from me the protection which he cannot afford.

Adeline continued to move towards the door, when the Marquis threw himself at her feet, and seizing her hand, impressed it with kisses. She struggled to disengage herself. Hear me, charming Adeline! hear me, cried the Marquis; I exist but for you. Listen to my entreaties, and my fortune shall be yours. Do not drive me to despair by ill-judged rigour, or, because—

My Lord, interrupted Adeline with an air of ineffable dignity, and still affecting to believe his proposal honourable, I am sensible of the generosity of your conduct, and also flattered by the distinction you offer me; I will therefore say something more than is necessary to a bare expression of the denial which I must continue to give. I can not bestow my heart. You can not obtain more than my esteem, to which, indeed, nothing can so much contribute as a forbearance from any similar offers in future.

She again attempted to go, but the Marquis prevented her; and, after some hesitation, again urged his suit, though in terms that would no longer allow her to misunderstand him. Tears swelled into her eyes, but she endeavoured to check them; and with a look in which grief and indignation seemed to struggle for pre-eminence, she said, My Lord, this is unworthy of reply; let me pass.

For a moment he was awed by the dignity of her manner, and he threw himself at her feet to implore forgiveness. But she waved her hand in silence, and hurried from the room. When she reached her chamber she locked the door, and, sinking into a chair, yielded to the sorrow that pressed at her heart. And it was not the least of her sorrow to suspect that La Motte was unworthy of her confidence; for it was almost impossible that he could be ignorant of the real designs of the Marquis. Madame La Motte, she believed, was imposed upon by a specious pretence of honourable attachment; and thus was she spared the pang which a doubt of her integrity would have added.

She threw a trembling glance upon the prospect around her. On one side was her father, whose cruelty had already been but too plainly manifested; and on the other, the Marquis pursuing her with insult and vicious passion. She resolved to acquaint Madame La Motte with the purport of the late conversation; and, in the hope of her protection and sympathy, she wiped away her tears, and was leaving the room just as Madame La Motte entered it. While Adeline related what had passed, her friend wept, and appeared to suffer great agitation. She endeavoured to comfort her, and promised to use her influence in persuading La Motte to prohibit the addressee of the Marquis. You know, my dear, added Madame, that our present circumstances oblige us to preserve terms with the Marquis, and you will therefore suffer as little resentment to appear in your manner towards him as possible; conduct yourself with your usual ease in his presence, and I doubt not this affair will pass over without subjecting you to further solicitation.

Ah, Madam! said Adeline, how hard is the task you assign me! I entreat you that I may never more be subjected to the humiliation of being in his presence, — that, whenever he visits the abbey, I may be suffered to remain in my chamber.

This, said Madame La Motte, I would most readily consent to, would our situation permit it. But you well know our asylum in this abbey depends upon the good-will of the Marquis, which we must not wantonly lose; and surely such a conduct as you propose would endanger this. Let us use milder measures, and we shall preserve his friendship without subjecting you to any serious evil. Appear with your usual complaisance: the task is not so difficult as you imagine.

Adeline sighed. I obey you, Madam, said she; it is my duty to do so: but I may be pardoned for saying — it is with extreme reluctance. Madame La Motte promised to go immediately to her husband; and Adeline departed, though not convinced of her safety, yet somewhat more at ease.

She soon after saw the Marquis depart; and as there now appeared to be no obstacle to the return of Madame La Motte, she expected her with extreme impatience. After thus waiting near an hour in her chamber, she was at length summoned to the parlour, and there found Monsieur La Motte alone. He arose upon her entrance, and for some minutes paced the room in silence. He then seated himself, and addressed her: What you have mentioned to Madame La Motte, said he, would give me much concern, did I consider the behaviour of the Marquis in a light so serious as she does. I know that young ladies are apt to misconstrue the unmeaning gallantry of fashionable manners; and you, Adeline, can never be too cautious in distinguishing between a levity of this kind and a more serious address.

Adeline was surprised and offended that La Motte should think so lightly both of her understanding and disposition as his speech implied. Is it possible, Sir, said she, that you have been apprized of the Marquis's conduct?

It is very possible, and very certain, replied La Motte with some asperity; and very possible, also, that I may see this affair with a judgment less discoloured by prejudice than you do. But, however, I shall not dispute this point; I shall only request that, since you are acquainted with the emergency of my circumstances, you will conform to them, and not, by an ill-timed resentment, expose me to the enmity of the Marquis. He is now my friend, and it is necessary to my safety that he should continue such; but if I suffer any part of my family to treat him

114

with rudeness, I must expect to see him my enemy. You may surely treat him with complaisance. Adeline thought the term rudeness a harsh one as La Motte applied it, but she forbore from any expression of displeasure. I could have wished, Sir, said she, for the privilege of retiring whenever the Marquis appeared; but since you believe this conduct would affect your interest, I ought to submit.

This prudence and good-will delights me, said La Motte; and since you wish to serve me, know that you cannot more effectually do it than by treating the Marquis as a friend. The word friend, as it stood connected with the Marquis, sounded dissonantly to Adeline's ear; she hesitated, and looked at La Motte. As your friend, Sir, said she, I will endeavour to—treat him as mine, she would have said, but she found it impossible to finish the sentence. She entreated his protection from the power of her father.

What protection I can afford is yours, said La Motte; but you know how destitute I am both of the right and the means of resisting him, and also how much I require protection myself. Since he has discovered your retreat, he is probably not ignorant of the circumstances which detain me here; and if I oppose him, he may betray me to the officers of the law, as the surest method of obtaining possession of you. We are encompassed with dangers, continued La Motte; would I could see any method of extricating ourselves!

Quit this abbey, said Adeline, and seek an asylum in Switzerland or Germany; you will then be freed from further obligation to the Marquis, and from the persecution you dread. Pardon me for thus offering advice, which is certainly in some degree prompted by a sense of my own safety, but which, at the same time, seems to afford the only means of ensuring yours.

Your plan is reasonable, said La Motte, had I money to execute it. As it is, I must be contented to remain here as little known as possible, and defend myself by making those who know me my friends. Chiefly I must endeavour to preserve the favour of the Marquis: he may do much, should your father even pursue desperate measures. But why do I talk thus? your father may ere this have commenced these measures, and the effects of his vengeance may now be hanging over my head. My regard for you, Adeline, has exposed me to this; had I resigned you to his will, I should have remained secure.

Adeline was so much affected by this instance of La Motte's kindness, which she could not doubt, that she was unable to express her sense of it. When she could speak, she uttered her gratitude in the most lively terms. — Are you sincere in these expressions? said La Motte.

Is it possible I can be less than sincere? replied Adeline, weeping at the idea of ingratitude. — Sentiments are easily pronounced, said La Motte, though they may have no connection with the heart; I believe them to be sincere so far only as they influence our actions.

What mean you, Sir? said Adeline with surprise.

I mean to inquire whether, if an opportunity should ever offer of thus proving your gratitude, you would adhere to your sentiments?

Name one that I shall refuse, said Adeline with energy.

If, for instance, the Marquis should hereafter avow a serious passion for you, and offer you his hand, would no petty resentment, no lurking prepossession for some more happy lover prompt you to refuse it?

Adeline blushed, and fixed her eyes on the ground. You have, indeed, Sir, named the only means I should reject of evincing my sincerity. The Marquis I can never love, nor, to speak sincerely, ever esteem. I confess the peace of one's whole life is too much to sacrifice even to gratitude. — La Motte looked displeased. 'Tis as I thought, said he; these delicate sentiments make a fine appearance in speech, and render the person who utters them infinitely amiable; but bring them to the test of action, and they dissolve into air, leaving only the wreck of vanity behind.

This unjust sarcasm brought tears to her eyes. Since your safety, Sir, depends upon my conduct, said she, resign me to my father: I am willing to return to him, since my stay here must involve you in new misfortune: let me not prove myself unworthy of the protection I have hitherto experienced, by preferring my own welfare to yours. When I am gone, you will have no reason to apprehend the Marquis's displeasure, which you may probably incur if I stay here; for I feel it impossible that I could even consent to receive his addresses, however honourable were his views.

La Motte seemed hurt and alarmed. This must not be, said he; let us not harass ourselves by stating possible evils, and then, to avoid them, fly to those which are certain. No, Adeline, though you are ready to sacrifice yourself to my safety, I will not suffer you to do so;—I will not yield you to your father but upon compulsion. Be satisfied, therefore, upon this point. The only return I ask, is a civil deportment towards the Marquis.

I will endeavour to obey you, Sir, said Adeline.—Madame La Motte now entered the room, and this conversation ceased. Adeline passed the evening in melancholy thoughts, and retired as soon as possible to her chamber, eager to seek in sleep a refuge from sorrow.

CHAPTER IX

Full many a melancholy night

He watch'd the slow return of light,

And sought the powers of sleep;

To spread a momentary calm

O'er his sad couch, and in the balm

Of bland oblivion's dews his burning eyes to steep.

WARTON.

The MS. found by Adeline the preceding night had several times occurred to her recollection in the course of the day; but she had then been either too much interested by the events of the moment, or too apprehensive of interruption, to attempt a perusal of it. She now took it from the drawer in which it had been deposited, and, intending only to look cursorily over the few first pages, sat down with it by her bed-side.

She opened it with an eagerness of inquiry which the discoloured and almost obliterated ink but slowly gratified. The first words on the page were entirely lost, but those that appeared to commence the narrative were as follows:

O! ye, whoever ye are, whom chance or misfortune may hereafter conduct to this spot—to you I speak—to you reveal the story of my wrongs, and ask you to avenge them. Vain hope! yet it imparts some comfort to believe it possible that what I now write may one day meet the eye of a fellow-creature; that the words which tell my sufferings may one day draw pity from the feeling heart.

Yet stay your tears—your pity now is useless: lone since have the pangs of misery ceased; the voice of complaining is passed away. It is weakness to wish for compassion which cannot be felt till I shall sink in the repose of death, and taste, I hope, the happiness of eternity!

Know, then, that on the night of the twelfth of October, in the year 1642, I was arrested on the road to Caux,—and on the very spot where a column is erected to the memory of the immortal Henry,—by four ruffians, who, after disabling my servant, bore me through wilds and woods to this abbey. Their demeanour was not that of common banditti, and I soon perceived they were employed by a superior power to perpetrate some dreadful purpose. Entreaties and bribes were vainly offered them to discover their employer and abandon their design; they would not reveal even the least circumstance of their intentions.

But when, after a long journey, they arrived at this edifice, their base employer was at once revealed, and his horrid scheme but too well understood. What a moment was that! All the thunders of heaven seemed launched at this defenceless head! O! fortitude! nerve my heart to— —

Adeline's light was now expiring in the socket, and the paleness of the ink, so feebly shone upon, baffled her efforts to discriminate the letters: it was impossible to procure a light from below, without discovering that she was yet up; a circumstance which would excite surprise, and lead to explanations such as she did not wish to enter upon. Thus compelled to suspend the inquiry, which so many attendant circumstances had rendered awfully interesting, she retired to her humble bed.

What she had read of the MS. awakened a dreadful interest in the fate of the writer, and called up terrific images to her mind. In these apartments!—said she; and she shuddered and closed her eyes. At length she heard Madame La Motte enter her chamber, and the phantoms of fear beginning to dissipate, left her to repose.

In the morning she was awakened by Madame La Motte, and found to her disappointment that she had slept so much beyond her usual time as to be unable to renew the perusal of the MS.—La Motte appeared uncommonly gloomy, and Madame wore an air of melancholy, which Adeline attributed to the concern she felt for her. Breakfast was scarcely over, when the sound of horses' feet announced the arrival of a stranger; and Adeline from the oriel recess of the hall saw the Marquis alight. She retreated with precipitation, and, forgetting the request of La Motte, was hastening to her chamber: but the Marquis was already in the hall; and seeing her leaving it, turned to La Motte with a look of inquiry. La Motte called her back, and by a frown too intelligent reminded her of her promise. She summoned all her spirits to her aid, but advanced, notwithstanding, in visible emotion; while the Marquis addressed her as usual, the same easy gaiety playing upon his countenance and directing his manner.

Adeline was surprised and shocked at this careless confidence; which, however, by awakening her pride, communicated to her an air of dignity that abashed him. He spoke with hesitation, and frequently appeared abstracted from the subject of discourse. At length arising, he begged Adeline would favour him with a few moments' conversation. Monsieur and Madame La Motte were now leaving the room, when Adeline, turning to the Marquis, told him she would not hear any conversation except in the presence of her friends. But she said it in vain, for they were gone; and La Motte, as he withdrew, expressed by his looks how much an attempt to follow would displease him.

She sat for some time in silence and trembling expectation. I am sensible, said the Marquis at length, that the conduct to which the ardour of my passion lately betrayed me, has injured me in your opinion, and that you will not easily restore me to your esteem; but I trust the offer which I now make you, both of my title and fortune, will sufficiently prove the sincerity of my attachment, and atone for the transgression which love only prompted.

After this specimen of common-place verbosity, which the Marquis seemed to consider as a prelude to triumph, he attempted to impress a kiss upon the hand of Adeline, who, withdrawing it hastily, said, You are already, my Lord, acquainted with my sentiments upon this subject, and it is almost unnecessary for me now to repeat that I cannot accept the honour you offer me.

Explain yourself, lovely Adeline! I am ignorant that till now I ever made you this offer.

Most true, Sir, said Adeline; and you do well to remind me of this, since, after having heard your former proposal, I cannot listen for a moment to any other. She rose to quit the room. Stay, Madam, said the Marquis, with a look in which offended pride struggled to conceal itself; do not suffer an extravagant resentment to operate against your true interests; recollect the dangers that surround you, and consider the value of an offer which may afford you at least an honourable asylum.

My misfortunes, my Lord, whatever they are, I have never obtruded upon you; you will, therefore, excuse my observing, that your present mention of them conveys a much greater appearance of insult than compassion. The Marquis, though with evident confusion, was going to reply; but Adeline would not be detained, and retired to her chamber. Destitute as she was, her heart revolted from the proposal of the Marquis, and she determined never to accept it. To her dislike of his general disposition, and the aversion excited by his late offer, was added, indeed, the influence of a prior attachment, and of a remembrance which she found it impossible to erase from her heart.

The Marquis staid to dine, and in consideration of La Motte, Adeline appeared at table, where the former gazed upon her with such frequent and silent earnestness, that her distress became insupportable; and when the cloth was drawn, she instantly retired. Madame La Motte soon followed, and it was not till evening that she had an opportunity of returning to the MS. When Monsieur and Madame La Motte were in their chamber, and all was still, she drew forth the narrative, and trimming her lamp, sat down to read as follows:

The ruffians unbound me from my horse, and led me through the hall up the spiral staircase of the abbey: resistance was useless; but I looked around in the hope of seeing some person less obdurate than the men who brought me hither; some one who might be sensible to pity, and capable at least of civil treatment. I looked in vain; no person appeared: and this circumstance confirmed my worst apprehensions. The secrecy of the business foretold a horrible conclusion. Having passed some chambers, they stopped in one hung with old tapestry. I inquired why we did not go on, and was told I should soon know.

At that moment I expected to see the instrument of death uplifted, and silently recommended myself to God. But death was not then designed for me; they raised the arras, and discovered a door, which they then opened. Seizing my arms, they led me through a suite of dismal chambers beyond. Having reached the furthest of these, they again stopped: the horrid gloom of the place seemed congenial to murder, and inspired deadly thoughts. Again I looked round for the instrument of destruction, and again I was respited. I supplicated to know what was designed me; it was now unnecessary to ask who was the author of the design. They were silent to my question, but at length told me this chamber was my prison. Having said this, and set down a jug of water, they left the room, and I heard the door barred upon me.

O sound of despair! O moment of unutterable anguish! The pang of death itself is surely not superior to that I then suffered. Shut out from day, from friends, from life—for such I must foretell it—in the prime of my years, in the height of my transgressions, and left to imagine horrors more terrible than any, perhaps, which certainty could give—I sink beneath the—

Here several pages of the manuscript were decayed with damp, and totally illegible. With much difficulty Adeline made out the following lines:

Three days have now passed in solitude and silence: the horrors of death are ever before my eyes, let me endeavour to prepare for the dreadful change! When I awake in the morning I think I shall not live to see another night; and when night returns, that I must never more unclose my eyes on morning. Why am I brought hither—why confined thus rigorously—but for death! Yet what action of my life has deserved this at the hand of a fellow-creature?—Of——

* * * * * * * * * * * * *

* * * * * * * * * * * *

* * * * * * * * * * * *

O my children! O friends far distant! I shall never see you more—never more receive the parting look of kindness—never bestow a parting blessing!—Ye know not my wretched state—alas! ye cannot know it by human means. Ye believe me happy, or ye would fly to my relief. I know that what I now write cannot avail me, yet there is comfort in pouring forth my griefs; and I bless that man, less savage than his fellows, who has supplied me these means of recording them. Alas! he knows full well, that from this indulgence he has nothing to fear. My pen can call no friends to succour me, nor reveal my danger ere it is too late. O! ye, who may hereafter read what I now write, give a tear to my sufferings: I have wept often for the distresses of my fellow-creatures!

Adeline paused. Here the wretched writer appealed directly to her heart; he spoke in the energy of truth, and, by a strong illusion of fancy, it seemed as if his past suffering were at this moment present. She was for some time unable to proceed, and sat in musing sorrow. In these very apartments, said she, this poor sufferer was confined—here he—Adeline started, and thought she heard a sound; but the stillness of the night was undisturbed.—In these very chambers, said she, these lines were written—these lines, from which he then derived a comfort in believing they would hereafter be read by some pitying eye: this time is now come. Your miseries, O injured being! are lamented where they were endured. Here, where you suffered, I weep for your sufferings!

Her imagination was now strongly impressed, and to her distempered senses the suggestions of a bewildered mind appeared with the force of reality. Again she started and listened, and thought she heard Here distinctly repeated by a whisper immediately behind her. The terror of the thought, however, was but momentary, she knew it could not be; convinced that her fancy had deceived her, she took up the MS. and again began to read.

For what am I reserved? Why this delay? If I am to die — why not quickly? Three weeks have I now passed within these walls, during which time no look of pity has softened my afflictions; no voice, save my own, has met my ear. The countenances of the ruffians who attend me are stern and inflexible, and their silence is obstinate. This stillness is dreadful! O! ye, who have known what it is to live in the depths of solitude, who have passed your dreary days without one sound to cheer you; ye, and ye only, can tell what now I feel; and ye may know how much I would endure to hear the accents of a human voice.

O dire extremity! O state of living death! What dreadful stillness! All around me is dead; and do I really exist, or am I but a statue? Is this a vision? Are these things real? Alas, I am bewildered! — this death-like and perpetual silence — this dismal chamber — the dread of further sufferings have disturbed my fancy. O for some friendly breast to lay my weary head on! some cordial accents to revive my soul!

* * * * * * * * * * * * * *

* * * * * * * * * * * * * *

* * * * * * * * * * * * * *

I write by stealth. He who furnished me with the means, I fear, has suffered for some symptoms of pity he may have discovered for me; I have not seen him for several days: perhaps he is inclined to help me, and for that reason is forbid to come. O that hope! but how vain! Never more must I quit these walls while life remains. Another day is gone, and yet I live; at this time to-morrow night my sufferings may be sealed in death. I will continue my journal nightly, till the hand that writes shall be stopped by death: when the journal ceases, the reader will know I am no more. Perhaps these are the last lines I shall ever write.

* * * * * * * * * * * * * *

* * * * * * * * * * * * * *

* * * * * * * * * * * * * *

Adeline paused, while her tears fell fast. Unhappy man! she exclaimed: and was here no pitying soul to save thee! Great God! thy ways are wonderful! While she sat musing, her fancy, which now wandered in the regions of terror, gradually subdued reason. There was a glass before her upon the table, and she feared to raise her looks towards it, lest some other face than her own should meet her eyes: other dreadful ideas and strange images of fantastic thought now crossed her mind.

A hollow sigh seemed to pass near her. Holy Virgin, protect me! cried she, and threw a fearful glance round the room; — this is surely something more than fancy. Her fears so far overcame her, that she was several times upon the point of calling up a part of the family; but, unwillingness to disturb them, and a dread of ridicule, withheld her. She was also afraid to move, and almost to breathe. As she listened to the wind, that murmured at the casement of her lonely chamber, she again thought she heard a sigh. Her imagination refused any longer the control of reason, and, turning her eyes, a figure, whose exact form she could not distinguish, appeared to pass along an obscure part of the chamber: a dreadful chillness came over her, and she sat fixed in her chair. At length a deep sigh somewhat relieved her oppressed spirits, and her senses seemed to return.

All remaining quiet, after some time she began to question whether her fancy had not deceived her, and she so far conquered her terror as to desist from calling Madame La Motte: her mind was, however, so much disturbed, that she did not venture to trust herself that night again with the MS.; but having spent some time in prayer, and in endeavouring to compose her spirits, she retired to bed.

When she awoke in the morning, the cheerful sun-beams played upon the casements, and dispelled the illusions of darkness: her mind soothed and invigorated by sleep, rejected the mystic and turbulent promptings of imagination. She arose refreshed and thankful; but upon going down to breakfast, this transient gleam of peace fled upon the appearance of the Marquis, whose frequent visits at the abbey, after what had passed, not only displeased, but alarmed her. She saw that he was determined to persevere in addressing her: and the boldness and insensibility of this conduct, while it excited her indignation, increased her disgust. In pity to La Motte, she endeavoured to conceal these emotions, though she now thought that he required too much from her complaisance, and began seriously to consider how she might avoid the necessity of continuing it. The Marquis behaved to her with the most respectful attention; but Adeline was silent and reserved, and seized the first opportunity of withdrawing.

As she passed up the spiral staircase, Peter entered the hall below, and seeing Adeline, he stopped and looked earnestly at her: she did not observe him, but he called her softly, and she then saw him make a signal, as if he had something to communicate. In the next instant, La Motte opened the door of the vaulted room, and Peter hastily disappeared. She proceeded to her chamber, ruminating upon this signal, and the cautious manner in which Peter had given it.

But her thoughts soon returned to their wonted subjects. Three days were now passed, and she heard no intelligence of her father; she began to hope that he had relented from the violent measures hinted at by La Motte, and that he meant to pursue a milder plan: but when she considered his character, this appeared improbable, and she relapsed into her former fears. Her residence at the abbey was now become painful, from the perseverance of the Marquis and the conduct which La Motte obliged her to adopt; yet she could not think without dread of quitting it to return to her father.

The image of Theodore often intruded upon her busy thoughts, and brought with it a pang which his strange departure occasioned. She had a confused notion that his fate was somehow connected with her own; and her struggles to prevent the remembrance of him served only to show how much her heart was his.

To divert her thoughts from these subjects, and gratify the curiosity so strongly excited on the preceding night, she now took up the MS. but was hindered from opening it by the entrance of Madame La Motte, who came to tell her the Marquis was gone. They passed their morning together in work and general conversation; La Motte not appearing till dinner, when he said little, and Adeline less. She asked him, however, if he had heard from her father? I have not heard from him, said La Motte; but there is good reason, as I am informed by the Marquis, to believe he is not far off.

Adeline was shocked, yet she was able to reply with becoming firmness. I have already, Sir, involved you too much in my distress, and now see that resistance will destroy you, without serving me; I am therefore contented to return to my father, and thus spare you further calamity.

This is a rash determination, replied La Motte; and if you pursue it, I fear you will severely repent. I speak to you as a friend, Adeline, and desire you will endeavour to listen to me without prejudice. The Marquis, I find, has offered you his hand. I know not which circumstance most excites my surprise, that a man of his rank and consequence should solicit a marriage with a person without fortune or ostensible connexions, or that a person so circumstanced should even for a moment reject the advantages just offered her. You weep, Adeline; let me hope that you are convinced of the absurdity of this conduct, and will no longer trifle with your good fortune. The kindness I have shown you must convince you of my regard, and that I have no motive for offering you this advice but your advantage. It is necessary, however, to say, that should your father not insist upon your removal, I know not how long my circumstances may enable me to afford even the humble pittance you receive here. Still you are silent.

The anguish which this speech excited, suppressed her utterance, and she continued to weep. At length she said, Suffer me, Sir, to go back to my father; I should indeed make an ill return for the kindness you mention, could I wish to stay after what you now tell me; and to accept the Marquis, I feel to be impossible. The remembrance of Theodore arose to her mind, and she wept aloud.

La Motte sat for some time musing. Strange infatuation! said he; is it possible that you can persist in this heroism of romance, and prefer a father so inhuman as yours, to the Marquis de Montalt! a destiny so full of danger, to a life of splendour and delight!

Pardon me, said Adeline; a marriage with the Marquis would be splendid, but never happy. His character excites my aversion, and I entreat, Sir, that he may no more be mentioned.

CHAPTER X

Nor are those empty hearted, whose low sound

Reverbs no hollowness.

LEAR.

The conversation related in the last chapter was interrupted by the entrance of Peter, who, as he left the room, looked significantly at Adeline, and almost beckoned. She was anxious to know what he meant, and soon after went into the hall, where she found him loitering. The moment he saw her, he made a sign of silence, and beckoned her into the recess. Well, Peter, what is it you would say? said Adeline.

Hush, Ma'mselle; for heaven's sake speak lower; if we should be overheard, we are all blown up. — Adeline begged him to explain what he meant Yes, Ma'mselle, that is what I have wanted all day long: I have watched and watched for an opportunity, and looked and looked till I was afraid my master himself would see me; but all would not do, you would not understand.

Adeline entreated he would be quick. Yes Ma'm, but I'm so afraid we shall be seen; but I would do much to serve such a good young lady, for I could not bear to think of what threatened you, without telling you of it.

For God's sake, said Adeline, speak quickly, or we shall be interrupted.

Well then; — but you must first promise by the Holy Virgin never to say it was I that told you; my master would —

I do, I do, said Adeline.

Well, then — on Monday evening as I — hark! did not I hear a step? do, Ma'mselle, just step this way to the cloisters: I would not for the world we should be seen: I'll go out at the hall door, and you can go through the passage. I would not for the world we should be seen. — Adeline was much alarmed by Peter's words, and hurried to the cloisters. He quickly appeared, and, looking cautiously round, resumed his discourse. As I was saying, Ma'mselle, Monday night, when the Marquis slept here, you know he sat up very late, and I can guess, perhaps, the reason of that. Strange things came out, but it is not my business

127

to tell all I think.

Pray do speak to the purpose, said Adeline impatiently; what is this danger which you say threatens me? Be quick, or we shall be observed.

Danger enough, Ma'mselle, replied Peter, if you knew all; and when you do, what will it signify? for you can't help yourself. But that's neither here nor there; I was resolved to tell you, though I may repent it.

Or rather, you are resolved not to tell me, said Adeline; for you have made no progress towards it. But what do you mean? You was speaking of the Marquis.

Hush, Ma'am, not so loud. The Marquis, as I said, sat up very late, and my master sat up with him. One of his men went to bed in the oak room, and the other staid to undress his lord. So as we were sitting together. Lord have mercy! it made my hair stand on end! I tremble yet. So as we were sitting together—but as sure as I live, yonder is my master: I caught a glimpse of him between the trees; if he sees me it is all over with us. I'll tell you another time. So saying, he hurried into the abbey, leaving Adeline in a state of alarm, curiosity, and vexation. She walked out into the forest ruminating upon Peter's words, and endeavouring to guess to what they alluded: there Madame La Motte joined her, and they conversed on various topics till they reached the abbey.

Adeline watched in vain through that day for an opportunity of speaking with Peter. While he waited at supper, she occasionally observed his countenance with great anxiety, hoping it might afford her some degree of intelligence on the subject of her fears. When she retired, Madame La Motte accompanied her to her chamber, and continued to converse with her for a considerable time, so that she had no means of obtaining an interview with Peter.—Madame La Motte appeared to labour under some great affliction; and when Adeline, noticing this, entreated to know the cause of her dejection, tears started into her eyes, and she abruptly left the room.

This behaviour of Madame La Motte concurred with Peter's discourse to alarm Adeline, who sat pensively upon her bed, giving up to reflection, till she was roused by the sound of a clock, which stood in the room below, and which now struck twelve. She was preparing for rest, when she recollected the MS. and was unable to conclude the night without reading it. The first words she could distinguish were the following:

Again I return to this poor consolation—again I have been permitted to see another day. It is now midnight! My solitary lamp burns beside me; the time is awful, but to me the silence of noon is as the silence of midnight; a deeper gloom is all in which they differ. The still, unvarying hours are numbered only by my sufferings; Great God! when shall I be released:

* * * * * * * * * * * * * *

* * * * * * * * * * * * * *

But whence this strange confinement? I have never injured him. If death is designed me, why this delay; and for what but death am I brought hither? This abbey—alas!—Here the MS. was again illegible, and for several pages Adeline could only make out disjointed sentences.

O bitter draught! when, when shall I have rest? O my friends! will none of ye fly to aid me; will none of ye avenge my sufferings? Ah! when it is too late—when I am gone for ever, ye will endeavour to avenge them.

* * * * * * * * * * * * * *

* * * * * * * * * * * * * *

Once more is night returned to me. Another day has passed in solitude and misery. I have climbed to the casement, thinking the view of nature would refresh my soul, and somewhat enable me to support these afflictions. Alas! even this small comfort is denied me, the windows open towards other parts of this abbey, and admit only a portion of that day which I must never more fully behold. Last night! last night! O scene of horror!

Adeline shuddered. She feared to read the coming sentence, yet curiosity prompted her to proceed. Still she paused: an unaccountable dread came over her. Some horrid deed has been done here, said she; the reports of the peasants are true: murder has been committed. The idea thrilled her with horror. She recollected the dagger which had impeded her steps in the secret chamber, and this circumstance served to confirm her most terrible conjectures. She wished to examine it, but it lay in one of these chambers, and she feared to go in quest of it.

Wretched, wretched victim! she exclaimed, could no friend rescue thee from destruction! O that I had been near! Yet what could I have done to save thee? Alas! nothing. I forget that even now, perhaps, I am, like thee, abandoned to dangers from which I have no friend to succour me. Too surely I guess the author of thy miseries! She stopped, and thought she heard a sigh, such as on the preceding night had passed along the chamber. Her blood was chilled, and she sat motionless. The lonely situation of her room, remote from the rest of the family, (for she was now in her old apartment, from which Madame La Motte had removed,) who were almost beyond call, struck so forcibly upon her imagination, that she with difficulty preserved herself from fainting. She sat for a considerable time, and all was still. When she was somewhat recovered, her first design was to alarm the family; but further reflection again withheld her.

She endeavoured to compose her spirits, and addressed a short prayer to that Being, who had hitherto protected her in every danger. While she was thus employed, her mind gradually became elevated and reassured; a sublime complacency filled her heart, and she sat down once more to pursue the narrative.

Several lines that immediately followed, were obliterated. —

* * * * * * * * * * * * *

* * * * * * * * * * * * *

He had told me I should not be permitted to live long, not more than three days, and bade me choose whether I would die by poison or the sword. O the agonies of that moment! Great God! thou seest my sufferings! I often viewed, with a momentary hope of escaping, the high grated windows of my prison—all things within the compass of possibility I was resolved to try, and with an eager desperation I climbed towards the casements, but my foot slipped, and falling back to the floor, I was stunned by the blow. On recovering, the first sounds I heard, were the steps of a person entering my prison. A recollection of the past returned, and deplorable was my condition. I shuddered at what was to come. The same man approached; he looked at me at first with pity, but his countenance soon recovered its natural ferocity. Yet he did not then come to execute the purposes of his employer: I am reserved to another day—Great God, thy will be done!

Adeline could not go on. All the circumstances that seemed to corroborate the fate of this unhappy man, crowded upon her mind the reports concerning the abbey — the dreams which had forerun her discovery of the private apartments — the singular manner in which she had found the MS — and the apparition, which she now believed she had really seen. She blamed herself for not having yet mentioned the discovery of the manuscript and chambers to La Motte, and resolved to delay the disclosure no longer than the following morning. The immediate cares that had occupied her mind, and a fear of losing the manuscript before she had read it, had hitherto kept her silent.

Such a combination of circumstances, she believed, could only be produced by some supernatural power, operating for the retribution of the guilty. These reflections filled her mind with a degree of awe, which the loneliness of the large old chamber in which she sat, and the hour of the night, soon heightened into terror. She had never been superstitious, but circumstances so uncommon had hitherto conspired in this affair, that she could not believe them accidental. Her imagination, wrought upon by these reflections, again became sensible to every impression; she feared to look round, lest she should again see some dreadful phantom, and she almost fancied she heard voices swell in the storm which now shook the fabric.

Still she tried to command her feelings so as to avoid disturbing the family; but they became so painful, that even the dread of La Motte's ridicule had hardly power to prevent her quitting the chamber. Her mind was now in such a state, that she found it impossible to pursue the story in the MS. though, to avoid the tortures of suspense, she had attempted it. She laid it down again, and tried to argue herself into composure. What have I to fear? said she; I am at least innocent, and I shall not be punished for the crime of another.

The violent gust of wind that now rushed through the whole suite of apartments, shook the door that led from her late bedchamber to the private rooms so forcibly, that Adeline, unable to remain longer in doubt, ran to see from whence the noise issued. The arras which concealed the door was violently agitated, and she stood for a moment observing it in indescribable terror; till believing it was swayed by the wind, she made a sudden effort to overcome her feelings, and was stooping to raise it. At that instant she thought she heard a voice. She stopped and listened, but every thing was still; yet apprehension so far overcame her, that she had no power either to examine or to leave the chamber.

In a few moments the voice returned: she was now convinced she had not been deceived, for, though low, she heard it distinctly, and was almost sure it repeated her own name. So much was her fancy affected, that she even thought it was the same voice she had heard in her dreams. This conviction entirely subdued the small remains of her courage, and sinking into a chair she lost all recollection.

How long she remained in this state she knew not; but when she recovered, she exerted all her strength, and reached the winding staircase, where she called aloud. No one heard her; and she hastened, as fast as her feebleness would permit, to the chamber of Madame La Motte. She tapped gently at the door, and was answered by Madame, who was alarmed at being awakened at so unusual an hour, and believed that some danger threatened her husband. When she understood that it was Adeline, and that she was unwell, she quickly came to her relief. The terror that was yet visible in Adeline's countenance excited her inquiries, and the occasion of it was explained to her.

Madame was so much discomposed by the relation, that she called La Motte from his bed, who, more angry at being disturbed than interested for the agitation he witnessed, reproved Adeline for suffering her fancies to overcome her reason. She now mentioned the discovery she had made of the inner chamber and the manuscript, circumstances which roused the attention of La Motte so much, that he desired to see the MS. and resolved to go immediately to the apartments described by Adeline.

Madame La Motte endeavoured to dissuade him from his purpose; but La Motte, with whom opposition had always an effect contrary to the one designed, and who wished to throw further ridicule upon the terrors of Adeline, persisted in his intention. He called to Peter to attend with a light, and insisted that Madame La Motte and Adeline should accompany him. Madame La Motte desired to be excused, and Adeline at first declared she could not go; but he would be obeyed.

They ascended the tower, and entered the first chambers together, for each of the party was reluctant to be the last; in the second chamber all was quiet and in order. Adeline presented the MS. and pointed to the arras which concealed the door. La Motte lifted the arras, and opened the door; but Madame La Motte and Adeline entreated to go no further—again he called to them to follow. All was quiet in the first chamber: he expressed his surprise that the rooms should so long have remained undiscovered, and was proceeding to the second, but suddenly stopped. We will defer our examination till to-morrow, said he, the damps of these apartments are unwholesome at any time; but they strike one more sensibly at night. I am chilled. Peter, remember to throw open the windows early in the morning, that the air may circulate.

Lord bless your honour, said Peter, don't you see I can't reach them; besides, I don't believe they are made to open; see what strong iron bars there are; the room looks for all the world like a prison: I suppose this is the place the people meant, when they said nobody that had been in ever came out. La Motte, who during this speech had been looking attentively at the high windows, which if he had seen them at first he had certainly not observed, now interrupted the eloquence of Peter, and bade him carry the light before them. They all willingly quitted these chambers, and returned to the room below, where a fire was lighted, and the party remained together for some time.

La Motte for reasons best known to himself, attempted to ridicule the discovery and fears of Adeline, till she with a seriousness that checked him, entreated he would desist. He was silent; and soon after, Adeline, encouraged by the return of daylight, ventured to her chamber, and for some hours experienced the blessing of undisturbed repose.

On the following day, Adeline's first care was to obtain an interview with Peter, whom she had some hopes of seeing as she went downstairs: he, however, did not appear; and she proceeded to the sitting-room, where she found La Motte apparently much disturbed. Adeline asked him if he had looked at the MS. I have run my eye over it, said he, but it is so much obscured by time that it can scarcely be deciphered. It appears to exhibit a strange romantic story; and I do not wonder that after you had suffered its terrors to impress your imagination, you fancied you saw spectres and heard wondrous noises.

Adeline thought La Motte did not choose to be convinced, and she therefore forbore reply. During breakfast she often looked at Peter (who waited) with anxious inquiry; and from his countenance was still more assured that he had something of importance to communicate. In the hope of some conversation with him, she left the room as soon as possible, and repaired to her favourite avenue, where she had not long remained when he appeared.

God bless you! Ma'mselle, said he, I'm sorry I frighted you so last night.

Frighted me, said Adeline; how was you concerned in that?

He then informed her that when he thought Monsieur and Madame La Motte were asleep, he had stolen to her chamber door, with an intention of giving her the sequel of what he had begun in the morning; that he had called several times as loudly as he dared; but receiving no answer, he believed she was asleep, or did not choose to speak with him, and he had therefore left the door. This account of the voice she had heard, relieved Adeline's spirits; she was even surprised that she did not know it, till remembering the perturbation of her mind for some time preceding, this surprise disappeared.

She entreated Peter to be brief in explaining the danger with which she was threatened. If you'll let me go on my own way, Ma'am, you'll soon know it; but if you hurry me, and ask me questions here and there, out of their places, I don't know what I am saying.

Be it so, said Adeline; only, remember that we may be observed.

Yes. Ma'mselle, I'm as much afraid of that as you are, for I believe I should be almost as ill off; however, that is neither here nor there, but I'm sure if you stay in this old abbey another night it will be worse for you; for, as I said before, I know all about it.

What mean you, Peter?

Why, about this scheme that's going on.

What then, is my father — —? — Your father! interrupted Peter; Lord bless you, that is all fudge, to frighten you: your father, nor nobody else has ever sent after you; I dare say he knows no more of you than the Pope does — not he. Adeline looked displeased. You trifle, said she; if you have any thing to tell, say it quickly; I am in haste.

Bless you, young lady, I meant no harm, I hope you're not angry; but I'm sure you can't deny that your father is cruel. But as I was saying, the Marquis de Montalt likes you; and he and my master (Peter looked round) have been laying their heads together about you. Adeline turned pale; she comprehended a part of the truth, and eagerly entreated him to proceed.

They have been laying their heads together about you. This is what Jaques the Marquis's man tells me: Says he, Peter, you little know what is going on: I could tell all if I chose it; but it is not for those who are trusted to tell again. I warrant now your master is close enough with you. Upon which I was piqued, and resolved to make him believe I could be trusted as well as he. Perhaps not says I; perhaps I know as much as you, though I do not choose to brag on't; and I winked. — Do you so? says he, then you are closer than I thought for. She is a fine girl, says he, — meaning you Ma'mselle; but she is nothing but a poor foundling after all, so it does not much signify. I had a mind to know further what he meant — so I did not knock him down. By seeming to know as much as he, I at last made him discover all; and he told me — but you look pale, Ma'mselle, are you ill?

No, said Adeline in a tremulous accent, and scarcely able to support herself; pray proceed.

And he told me that the Marquis had been courting you a good while, but you would not listen to him, and had even pretended he would marry you, and all would not do. As for marriage, says I, I suppose she knows the Marchioness is alive; and I'm sure she is not one for his turn upon other terms.

The Marchioness is really living then! said Adeline.

O yes, Ma'mselle! we all know that, and I thought you had known it too. — We shall see that, replies Jaques; at least, I believe that our master will outwit her. — I stared; I could not help it. — Aye, says he, you know your master has agreed to give her up to my Lord.

Good God! what will become of me? exclaimed Adeline.

Aye, Ma'mselle, I am sorry for you; but hear me out. When Jaques said this, I quite forgot myself: I'll never believe it, said I, I'll never believe my master would be guilty of such a base action; he'll not give her up, or I'm no Christian. — Oh! said, Jaques, for that matter, I thought you'd known all, else I should not have said a word about it. However, you may soon satisfy yourself by going to the parlour door, as I have done; they're in consultation about it now, I dare say.

You need not repeat any more of this conversation, said Adeline; but tell me the result of what you heard from the parlour.

Why, Ma'mselle, when he said this, I took him at his word, and went to the door, where, sure enough, I heard my master and the Marquis talking about you. They said a great deal which I could make nothing of; but, at last, I heard the Marquis say, You know the terms; on these terms only will I consent to bury the past in ob—ob—oblivion——that was the word. Monsieur La Motte then told the Marquis, if he would return to the abbey upon such a night, meaning this very night, Ma'mselle, every thing should be prepared according to his wishes;—Adeline shall then be yours, my Lord, said he—you are already acquainted with her chamber.

At these words Adeline clasped her hands, and raised her eyes to heaven in silent despair.—Peter went on. When I heard this, I could not doubt what Jaques had said.—Well, said he, what do you think of it now?—Why, that my master's a rascal, says I.—It's well you don't think mine one too, says he.—Why, as for that matter, says I——Adeline, interrupting him, inquired if he had heard any thing further. Just then, said Peter, we heard Madame La Motte come out from another room, and so we made haste back to the kitchen.

She was not present at this conversation then? said Adeline. No, Ma'mselle; but my master has told her of it, I warrant. Adeline was almost as much shocked by this apparent perfidy of Madame La Motte, as by a knowledge of the destruction that threatened her. After musing a few moments in extreme agitation, Peter, said she, you have a good heart, and feel a just indignation at your master's treachery—will you assist me to escape?

Ah, Ma'mselle! said he, how can I assist you? besides, where can we go? I have no friends about here, no more than yourself.

O! replied Adeline in extreme emotion, we fly from enemies; strangers may prove friends: assist me but to escape from this forest, and you will claim my eternal gratitude; I have no fears beyond it.

Why as for this forest, replied Peter, I am weary of it myself; though when we first came I thought it would be fine living here, at least, I thought it was very different from any life I had ever lived before. But these ghosts that haunt the abbey—I am no more a coward than other men, but I don't like them; and then there is so many strange reports abroad; and my master—I thought I could have served him to the end of the world, but now I care not how soon I leave him, for his behaviour to you, Ma'mselle.

You consent then to assist me in escaping? said Adeline with eagerness.

Why as to that, Ma'mselle, I would willingly, if I knew where to go. To be sure I have a sister lives in Savoy, but that is a great way off; and I have saved a little money out of my wages, but that won't carry us such a long journey.

Regard not that, said Adeline; if I was once beyond this forest, I would then endeavour to take care of myself, and repay you for your kindness.

O! as for that, Madam——Well, well, Peter, let us consider how we may escape. This night—say you this night—the Marquis is to return? Yes, Ma'mselle, to-night about dark. I have just thought of a scheme:—my master's horses are grazing in the forest; we may take one of them, and send it back from the first stage: but how shall we avoid being seen? besides if we go off in the daylight, he will soon pursue and overtake us; and if you stay till night, the Marquis will be come, and then there is no chance. If they miss us both at the same time too, they'll guess how it is, and set off directly. Could not you contrive to go first, and wait for me till the hurly-burly's over? Then, while they're searching in the place under ground for you, I can slip away, and we should be out of their reach before they thought of pursuing us.

Adeline agreed to the truth of all this, and was somewhat surprised at Peter's sagacity. She inquired if he knew of any place in the neighbourhood of the abbey, where she could remain concealed, till he came with a horse. Why yes, Madam, there is a place, now I think of it, where you may be safe enough, for nobody goes near; but they say it's haunted, and perhaps you would not like to go there. Adeline, remembering the last night, was somewhat startled at this intelligence; but a sense of her present danger pressed again upon her mind, and overcame every other apprehension. Where is this place? said she; if it will conceal me, I shall not hesitate to go.

It is an old tomb that stands in the thickest part of the forest, about a quarter of a mile off the nearest way and almost a mile the other. When my master used to hide himself so much in the forest, I have followed him somewhere thereabouts, but I did not find out the tomb till t'other day. However, that's neither here nor there; if you dare venture to it, Ma'mselle, I'll show you the nearest way. So saying he pointed to a winding path on the right. Adeline, having looked round without perceiving any person near, directed Peter to lead her to the tomb: they pursued the path, till turning into a gloomy romantic part of the forest, almost impervious to the rays of the sun, they came to the spot whither Louis had formerly traced his father.

The stillness and solemnity of the scene struck awe upon the heart of Adeline, who paused and surveyed it for some time in silence. At length Peter led her into the interior part of the ruin, to which they descended by several steps. Some old abbot, said he, was formerly buried here, as the Marquis's people say; and it's like enough that he belonged to the abbey yonder. But I don't see why he should take it in his head to walk; he was not murdered, surely!

I hope not, said Adeline.

That's more than can be said for all that lies buried at the abbey though, and — — Adeline interrupted him: Hark! surely I hear a noise, said she; Heaven protect us from discovery! They listened, but all was still; and they went on. Peter opened a low door, and they entered upon a dark passage, frequently obstructed by loose fragments of stone, and along which they moved with caution. Whither are we going? said Adeline. — I scarcely know myself, said Peter, for I never was so far before, but the place seems quiet enough. Something obstructed his way; it was a door which yielded to his hand, and discovered a kind of cell obscurely seen by the twilight admitted through a grate above. A partial gleam shot athwart the place, leaving the greatest part of it in shadow.

Adeline sighed as she surveyed it. This is a frightful spot, said she: but if it will afford me a shelter, it is a palace. Remember, Peter, that my peace and honour depend upon your faithfulness; be both discreet and resolute. In the dusk of the evening, I can pass from the abbey with least danger of being observed, and in this cell I will wait your arrival. As soon as Monsieur and Madame La Motte are engaged in searching the vaults, you will bring here a horse; three knocks upon the tomb shall inform me of your arrival. For Heaven's sake be cautious, and be punctual!

I will, Ma'mselle, let come what may.

They re-ascended to the forest; and Adeline fearful of observation, directed Peter, to run first to the abbey, and invent some excuse for his absence, if he had been missed. When she was again alone, she yielded to a flood of tears, and indulged the excess of her distress. She saw herself without friends, without relations, destitute, forlorn, and abandoned to the worst of evils; betrayed by the very persons to whose comfort she had so long administered, whom she had loved as her protectors, and revered as her parents! These reflections touched her heart with the most afflicting sensations, and the sense of her immediate danger was for a while absorbed in the grief occasioned by a discovery of such guilt in others.

At length she roused all her fortitude, and turning towards the abbey endeavoured to await with patience the hour of evening, and to sustain an appearance of composure in the presence of Monsieur and Madame La Motte. For the present she wished to avoid seeing either of them, doubting her ability to disguise her emotions: having reached the abbey, she therefore passed on to her chamber. Here she endeavoured to direct her attention to indifferent subjects, but in vain; the danger of her situation, and the severe disappointment she had received in the character of those whom she had so much esteemed and even loved, pressed hard upon her thoughts. To a generous mind few circumstances are more afflicting than a discovery of perfidy in those whom we have trusted, even though it may fail of any absolute inconvenience to ourselves. The behaviour of Madame La Motte in thus, by concealment, conspiring to her destruction, particularly shocked her.

How has my imagination deceived me! said she; what a picture did it draw of the goodness of the world! And must I then believe that every body is cruel and deceitful? No—let me still be deceived, and still suffer, rather than be condemned to a state of such wretched suspicion. She now endeavoured to extenuate the conduct of Madame La Motte, by attributing it to a fear of her husband. She dares not oppose his will, said she, else she would warn me of my danger, and assist me to escape from it. No—I will never believe her capable of conspiring my ruin; terror alone keeps her silent.

Adeline was somewhat comforted by this thought. The benevolence of her heart taught her, in this instance to sophisticate. She perceived not, that by ascribing the conduct of Madame La Motte to terror, she only softened the degree of her guilt, imputing it to a motive less depraved but not less selfish. She remained in her chamber till summoned to dinner, when, drying her tears, she descended with faltering steps and a palpitating heart to the parlour. When she saw La Motte, in spite of all her efforts she trembled and grew pale; she could not behold even with apparent indifference the man who she knew had destined her to destruction. He observed her emotion, and inquiring if she was ill, she saw the danger to which her agitation exposed her. Fearful lest La Motte should suspect its true cause, she rallied all her spirits, and with a look of complacency answered she was well.

During dinner she preserved a degree of composure that effectually concealed the varied anguish of her heart. When she looked at La Motte, terror and indignation were her predominant feelings; but when she regarded Madame La Motte, it was otherwise: gratitude for her former tenderness had long been confirmed into affection, and her heart now swelled with the bitterness of grief and disappointment. Madame La Motte appeared depressed and said little. La Motte seemed anxious to prevent thought, by assuming a fictitious and unnatural gaiety: he laughed and talked, and threw off frequent bumpers of wine: it was the mirth of desperation. Madame became alarmed, and would have restrained him; but he persisted in his libations to Bacchus till reflection seemed to be almost overcome.

Madame La Motte, fearful that in the carelessness of the present moment he might betray himself, withdrew with Adeline to another room. Adeline recollected the happy hours she once passed with her, when confidence banished reserve, and sympathy and esteem dictated the sentiments of friendship: now those hours were gone for ever; she could no longer unbosom her griefs to Madame La Motte, no longer even esteem her. Yet, notwithstanding all the danger to which she was exposed by the criminal silence of the latter, she could not converse with her, consciously for the last time, without feeling a degree of sorrow which wisdom may call weakness, but to which benevolence will allow a softer name.

Madame La Motte in her conversation appeared to labour under an almost equal oppression with Adeline: her thoughts were abstracted from the subject of discourse, and there were long and frequent intervals of silence. Adeline more than once caught her gazing with a look of tenderness upon her, and saw her eyes fill with tears. By this circumstance she was so much affected, that she was several times upon the point of throwing herself at her feet, and imploring her pity and protection. Cooler reflection showed her the extravagance and danger of this conduct: she suppressed her emotions, but they at length compelled her to withdraw from the presence of Madame La Motte.

CHAPTER XI

Thou! to whom the world unknown

With all its shadowy shapes is shown;

Who seest appall'd th' unreal scene,

While fancy lifts the veil between;

Ah, Fear! ah, frantic Fear!

I see, I see thee near!

I know thy hurry'd step, thy haggard eye

Like thee I start, like thee disorder'd fly!

COLLINS.

Adeline anxiously watched from her chamber window the sun set behind the distant hills, and the time of her departure draw nigh: it set with uncommon splendour, and threw a fiery gleam athwart the woods and upon some scattered fragments of the ruins, which she could not gaze upon with indifference. Never, probably, again shall I see the sun sink below those hills, said she, or illumine this scene! Where shall I be when next it sets — where this time to-morrow? sunk perhaps in misery! She wept at the thought. A few hours, resumed Adeline, and the Marquis will arrive — a few hours, and this abbey will be a scene of confusion and tumult: every eye will be in search of me, every recess will be explored. These reflections inspired her with new terror, and increased her impatience to be gone.

Twilight gradually came on, and she now thought it sufficiently dark to venture forth: but before she went, she kneeled down and addressed herself to Heaven. She implored support and protection, and committed herself to the care of the God of mercies. Having done this, she quitted her chamber, and passed with cautious steps down the winding staircase. No person appeared, and she proceeded through the door of the tower into the forest. She looked around; the gloom of the evening obscured every object.

With a trembling heart she sought the path pointed out by Peter, which led to the tomb: having found it, she passed along forlorn and terrified. Often did she start as the breeze shook the light leaves of the trees, or as the bat flitted by gamboling in the twilight; and often, as she looked back towards the abbey,

141

thought she distinguished amid the deepening gloom the figures of men. Having proceeded some way, she suddenly heard the feet of horses, and soon after a sound of voices, among which she distinguished that of the Marquis; they seemed to come from the quarter she was approaching, and evidently advanced. Terror for some minutes arrested her steps; she stood in a state of dreadful hesitation: to proceed was to run into the hands of the Marquis; to return was to fall into the power of La Motte.

After remaining for some time uncertain whither to fly, the sounds suddenly took a different direction, and wheeled towards the abbey. Adeline had a short cessation of terror; she now understood that the Marquis had passed this spot only in his way to the abbey, and she hastened to secrete herself in the ruin. At length, after much difficulty, she reached it, the deep shades almost concealing it from her search. She paused at the entrance, awed by the solemnity that reigned within, and the utter darkness of the place; at length she determined to watch without till Peter should arrive. If any person approaches, said she, I can hear them before they can see me, and I can then secrete myself in the cell.

She leaned against a fragment of the tomb in trembling expectation, and as she listened, no sound broke the silence of the hour. The state of her mind can only be imagined by considering that upon the present time turned the crisis of her fate. They have now, thought she, discovered my flight; even now they are seeking me in every part of the abbey. I hear their dreadful voices call me; I see their eager looks. The power of imagination almost overcame her. While she yet looked around, she saw lights moving at a distance; sometimes they glimmered between the trees, and sometimes they totally disappeared.

They seemed to be in a direction with the abbey; and she now remembered that in the morning she had seen a part of the fabric through an opening in the forest. She had therefore no doubt that the lights she saw proceeded from people in search of her: who, she feared, not finding her at the abbey, might direct their steps towards the tomb. Her place of refuge now seemed too near her enemies to be safe, and she would have fled to a more distant part of the forest, but recollected that Peter would not know where to find her.

While these thoughts passed over her mind, she heard distant voices in the wind, and was hastening to conceal herself in the cell, when she observed the lights suddenly disappear. All was soon after hushed in silence and darkness, yet she endeavoured to find the way to the cell. She remembered the situation of the outward door and of the passage, and having passed these, she unclosed the door of the cell. Within it was utterly dark. She trembled violently, but entered; and having felt about the walls, at length seated herself on a projection of stone.

She here again addressed herself to Heaven, and endeavoured to reanimate her spirits till Peter should arrive. Above half an hour elapsed in this gloomy recess, and no sound foretold his approach. Her spirits sunk; she feared some part of their plan was discovered or interrupted, and that he was detained by La Motte. This conviction operated sometimes so strongly upon her fears, as to urge her to quit the cell alone, and seek in flight her only chance of escape.

While this design was fluctuating in her mind, she distinguished through the grate above a clattering of hoofs. The noise approached, and at length stopped at the tomb. In the succeeding moment she heard three strokes of a whip; her heart beat, and for some moments her agitation was such, that she made no effort to quit the cell. The strokes were repeated: she now roused her spirits, and stepping forward, ascended to the forest. She called Peter; for the deep gloom would not permit her to distinguish either man or horse. She was quickly answered, Hush! Ma'mselle, our voices will betray us.

They mounted and rode off as fast as the darkness would permit. Adeline's heart revived at every step they took. She inquired what had passed at the abbey, and how he had contrived to get away. Speak softly, Ma'mselle; you'll know all by and by, but I can't tell you now. He had scarcely spoke ere they saw lights move along at a distance; and coming now to a more open part of the forest, he set off on a full gallop, and continued the pace till the horse could hold it no longer. They looked back, and no lights appearing, Adeline's terror subsided. She inquired again what had passed at the abbey when her flight was discovered. You may speak without fear of being heard, said she, we are gone beyond their reach, I hope.

Why, Ma'mselle, said he, you had not been gone long before the Marquis arrived, and Monsieur La Motte then found out you was fled. Upon this a great rout there was, and he talked a great deal with the Marquis.

Speak louder, said Adeline, I cannot hear you.

I will, Ma'mselle —

Oh! heavens! interrupted Adeline, What voice is this? It is not Peter's. For God's sake tell me who you are, and whither I am going?

You'll know that soon enough, young lady, answered the stranger, for it was indeed not Peter; I am taking you where my master ordered. Adeline, not doubting he was the Marquis's servant, attempted to leap to the ground; but the man, dismounting, bound her to the horse. One feeble ray of hope at length beamed upon her mind; she endeavoured to soften the man to pity, and pleaded with all the genuine eloquence of distress; but he understood his interest too well to yield even for a moment to the compassion which, in spite of himself, her artless supplication inspired.

She now resigned herself to despair, and in passive silence submitted to her fate. They continued thus to travel, till a storm of rain accompanied by thunder and lightning drove them to the covert of a thick grove. The man believed this a safe situation, and Adeline was now too careless of life to attempt convincing him of his error. The storm was violent and long, but as soon as it abated they set off on full gallop; and having continued to travel for about two hours, they came to the borders of the forest, and soon after to a high lonely wall, which Adeline could just distinguish by the moonlight, which now streamed through the parting clouds.

Here they stopped: the man dismounted, and having opened a small door in the wall, he unbound Adeline, who shrieked, though involuntarily and in vain, as he took her from the horse. The door opened upon a narrow passage, dimly lighted by a lamp, which hung at the further end. He led her on; they came to another door; it opened, and disclosed a magnificent saloon splendidly illuminated, and fitted up in the most airy and elegant taste.

The walls were painted in fresco, representing scenes from Ovid, and hung above with silk, drawn up in festoons, and richly fringed. The sofas were of a silk to suit the hangings. From the centre of the ceiling, which exhibited a scene from the Armida of Tasso, descended a silver lamp of Etruscan form; it diffused a blaze of light that, reflected from large pier glasses, completely illuminated the saloon. Busts of Horace, Ovid, Anacreon, Tibullus, and Petronius Arbiter, adorned the recesses, and stands of flowers placed in Etruscan vases breathed the most delicious perfume. In the middle of the apartment stood a small table spread with a collation of fruits, ices, and liqueurs. No person appeared. The whole seemed the works of enchantment, and rather resembled the palace of a fairy than any thing of human conformation.

Adeline was astonished, and inquired where she was; but the man refused to answer her questions; and having desired her to take some refreshment, left her. She walked to the windows, from which a gleam of moonlight discovered to her an extensive garden, where groves and lawns, and water glittering in the moonbeam, composed a scenery of varied and romantic beauty. What can this mean! said she: Is this a charm to lure me to destruction? She endeavoured, with a hope of escaping, to open the windows, but they were all fastened; she next attempted several doors, and found them also secured.

Perceiving all chance of escape was removed, she remained for some time given up to sorrow and reflection; but was at length drawn from her reverie by the notes of soft music, breathing such dulcet and entrancing sounds as suspended grief and awaked the soul to tenderness and pensive pleasure. Adeline listened in surprise, and insensibly became soothed and interested; a tender melancholy stole upon her heart, and subdued every harsher feeling: but the moment the strain ceased, the enchantment dissolved, and she returned to a sense of her situation.

Again the music sounded — music such as charmeth sleep — and again she gradually yielded to its sweet magic. A female voice, accompanied by a lute, a hautboy, and a few other instruments, now gradually swelled into a tone so exquisite as raised attention into ecstasy. It sunk by degrees, and touched a few simple notes with pathetic softness, when the measure was suddenly changed, and in a gay and airy melody Adeline distinguished the following words:

SONG.

Life's a varied, bright illusion,

Joy and sorrow — light and shade;

Turn from sorrow's dark suffusion,

Catch the pleasures ere they fade.

Fancy paints with hues unreal,

Smile of bliss, and sorrow's mood;

If they both are but ideal,

Why reject the seeming good?

Hence! no more! 'tis Wisdom calls ye,

Bids ye court Time's present aid;

The future trust not — Hope enthralls ye,

"Catch the pleasures ere they fade."

The music ceased; but the sounds still vibrated on her imagination, and she was sunk in the pleasing languor they had inspired, when the door opened, and the Marquis de Montalt appeared. He approached the sofa where Adeline sat, and addressed her, but she heard not his voice — she had fainted. He endeavoured to recover her, and at length succeeded; but when she unclosed her eyes, and again beheld him, she relapsed into a state of insensibility; and having in vain tried various methods to restore her, he was obliged to call assistance. Two young women entered; and when she began to revive, he left them to prepare her for his reappearance. When Adeline perceived that the Marquis was gone, and that she was in the care of women, her spirits gradually returned; she looked at her attendants, and was surprised to see so much elegance and beauty.

Some endeavour she made to interest their pity; but they seemed wholly insensible to her distress, and began to talk of the Marquis in terms of the highest admiration. They assured her it would be her own fault if she was not happy, and advised her to appear so in his presence. It was with the utmost difficulty that Adeline forbore to express the disdain which was rising to her lips, and that she listened to their discourse in silence. But she saw the inconvenience and fruitlessness of opposition, and she commanded her feelings.

They were thus proceeding in their praises of the Marquis, when he himself appeared; and waving his hand, they immediately quitted the apartment. Adeline beheld him with a kind of mute despair while he approached and took her hand, which she hastily withdrew; and turning from him with a look of unutterable distress, burst into tears. He was for some time silent, and appeared softened by her anguish: but again approaching and addressing her in a gentle voice, he entreated her pardon for the step which despair, and, as he called it, love had prompted. She was too much absorbed in grief to reply, till he solicited a return of his love; when her sorrow yielded to indignation, and she reproached him with his conduct. He pleaded that he had long loved and sought her upon honourable terms, and his offer of those terms he began to repeat; but raising his eyes towards Adeline, he saw in her looks the contempt which he was conscious he deserved.

For a moment he was confused, and seemed to understand both that his plan was discovered and his person despised; but soon resuming his usual command of feature, he again pressed his suit, and solicited her love. A little reflection showed Adeline the danger of exasperating his pride by an avowal of the contempt which his pretended offer of marriage excited; and she thought it not improper, upon an occasion in which the honour and peace of her life was concerned, to yield somewhat to the policy of dissimulation. She saw that her only chance of escaping his designs depended upon delaying them, and she now wished him to believe her ignorant that the Marchioness was living, and that his offers were delusive.

He observed her pause; and in the eagerness to turn her hesitation to his advantage, renewed his proposal with increased vehemence—To-morrow shall unite us, lovely Adeline; to-morrow you shall consent to become the Marchioness de Montalt. You will then return my love and— —

You must first deserve my esteem, my Lord.

I will—I do deserve it. Are you not now in my power, and do I not forbear to take advantage of your situation? Do I not make you the most honourable proposals?—Adeline shuddered: If you wish I should esteem you, my Lord, endeavour, if possible, to make me forget by what means I came into your power; if your views are indeed honourable, prove them so by releasing me from my confinement.

Can you then wish, lovely Adeline, to fly from him who adores you? replied the Marquis with a studied air of tenderness. Why will you exact so severe a proof of my disinterestedness, a disinterestedness which is not consistent with love? No, charming Adeline! let me at least have the pleasure of beholding you till the bonds of the church shall remove every obstacle to my love. To-morrow— —

Adeline saw the danger to which she was now exposed, and interrupted him. Deserve my esteem, Sir, and then you will obtain it: as a first step towards which, liberate me from a confinement that obliges me to look on you only with terror and aversion. How can I believe your professions of love, while you show that you have no interest in my happiness?—Thus did Adeline, to whom the arts and the practice of dissimulation were hitherto equally unknown, condescend to make use of them in disguising her indignation and contempt. But though these arts were adopted only for the purpose of self-preservation, she used them with reluctance, and almost with abhorrence; for her mind was habitually impregnated with the love of virtue, in thought, word, and action; and while her end in using them was certainly good, she scarcely thought that end could justify the means.

The Marquis persisted in his sophistry. Can you doubt the reality of that love, which to obtain you has urged me to risk your displeasure? But have I not consulted your happiness, even in the very conduct which you condemn? I have removed you from a solitary and desolate ruin to a gay and splendid villa, where every luxury is at your command, and where every person shall be obedient to your wishes.

My first wish is to go hence, said Adeline; I entreat, I conjure you, my Lord, no longer to detain me. I am a friendless and wretched orphan, exposed to many evils, and I fear abandoned to misfortune: I do not wish to be rude; but allow me to say, that no misery can exceed that I shall feel in remaining here, or indeed in being any where pursued by the offers you make me. Adeline had now forgot her policy: tears prevented her from proceeding, and she turned away her face to hide her emotion.

By Heaven! Adeline, you do me wrong, said the Marquis, rising from his seat and seizing her hand; I love, I adore you; yet you doubt my passion, and are insensible to my vows. Every pleasure possible to be enjoyed within these walls you shall partake, — but beyond them you shall not go. She disengaged her hand, and in silent anguish walked to a distant part of the saloon: deep sighs burst from her heart, and almost fainting she leaned on a window-frame for support.

The Marquis followed her: Why thus obstinately persist in refusing to be happy? said he: recollect the proposal I have made you, and accept it while it is yet in your power. To-morrow a priest shall join our hands—Surely, being, as you are, in my power, it must be your interest to consent to this? Adeline could answer only by tears; she despaired of softening his heart to pity, and feared to exasperate his pride by disdain. He now led her, and she suffered him, to a seat near the banquet, at which he pressed her to partake of a variety of confectionaries, particularly of some liqueurs of which he himself drank freely: Adeline accepted only of a peach.

And now the Marquis, who interrupted her silence into a secret compliance with his proposal, resumed all his gaiety and spirit, while the long and ardent regards he bestowed on Adeline overcame her with confusion and indignation. In the midst of the banquet, soft music again sounded the most tender and impassioned airs; but its effect on Adeline was now lost, her mind being too much embarrassed and distressed by the presence of the Marquis to admit even the soothings of harmony. A song was now heard, written with that sort of impotent art by which some voluptuous poets believe they can at once conceal and recommend the principles of vice. Adeline received it with contempt and displeasure; and the Marquis perceiving its effect, presently made a sign for another composition, which, adding the force of poetry to the charms of music, might withdraw her mind from the present scene, and enchant it in sweet delirium.

SONG OF A SPIRIT.

In the sightless air I dwell,

On the sloping sun-beams play;

Delve the cavern's inmost cell,

Where never yet did daylight stray.

Dive beneath the green sea waves,

And gambol in the briny deeps;

Skim every shore that Neptune laves,

From Lapland's plains to India's steeps.

Oft I mount with rapid force

Above the wide earth's shadowy zone;

Follow the day-star's flaming course

Through realms of space to thought unknown:

And listen oft celestial sounds

That swell the air unheard of men,

As I watch my nightly rounds

O'er woody steep and silent glen.

Under the shade of waving trees,

On the green bank of fountain clear,

At pensive eve I sit at ease,

While dying music murmurs near.

And oft on point of airy clift,

That hangs upon the western main,

I watch the gay tints passing swift,

And twilight veil the liquid plain.

Then, when the breeze has sunk away,

And ocean scarce is heard to lave,

For me the sea-nymphs softly play

Their dulcet shells beneath the wave.

Their dulcet shells! I hear them now,

Slow swells the strain upon mine ear

Now faintly falls—now warbles low,

Till rapture melts into a tear.

The ray that silvers o'er the dew,

And trembles through the leafy shade,

And tints the scene with softer hue,

Calls me to rove the lonely glade;

Or hie me to some ruin'd tower,

Faintly shewn by moonlight gleam,

Where the lone wanderer owns my power

In shadows dire that substance seem.

In thrilling sounds that murmur woe,

And pausing silence makes more dread;

In music breathing from below

Sad, solemn strains, that wake the dead.

Unseen I move—unknown am fear'd!

Fancy's wildest dreams I weave;

And oft by bards my voice is heard

To die along the gales of eve.

When the voice ceased, a mournful strain, played with exquisite expression, sounded from a distant horn; sometimes the notes floated on the air in soft undulations — now they swelled into full and sweeping melody, and now died faintly into silence, when again they rose and trembled in sounds so sweetly tender, as drew tears from Adeline, and exclamations of rapture from the Marquis: he threw his arm round her, and would have pressed her towards him; but she liberated herself from his embrace, and with a look, on which was impressed the firm dignity of virtue, yet touched with sorrow, she awed him to forbearance. Conscious of a superiority which he was ashamed to acknowledge, and endeavouring to despise the influence which he could not resist, he stood for a moment the slave of virtue, though the votary of vice. Soon, however, he recovered his confidence, and began to plead his love; when Adeline, no longer animated by the spirit she had lately shown, and sinking beneath the languor and fatigue which the various and violent agitations of her mind produced, entreated he would leave her to repose.

The paleness of her countenance and the tremulous tone of her voice were too expressive to be misunderstood; and the Marquis, bidding her remember to-morrow, with some hesitation withdrew. The moment she was alone she yielded to the bursting anguish of her heart; and was so absorbed in grief, that it was some time before she perceived she was in the presence of the young women who had lately attended her, and had entered the saloon soon after the Marquis quitted it; they came to conduct her to her chamber. She followed them for some time in silence, till, prompted by desperation, she again endeavoured to awaken their compassion: but again the praises of the Marquis were repeated: and perceiving that all attempts to interest them in her favour were in vain she dismissed them. She secured the door through which they had departed, and then, in the languid hope of discovering some means of escape, she surveyed her chamber. The airy elegance with which it was fitted up, and the luxurious accommodations with which it abounded, seemed designed to fascinate the imagination and to seduce the heart. The hangings were of straw-coloured silk, adorned with a variety of landscapes and historical paintings, the subjects of which partook of the voluptuous character of the owner; the chimney-piece, of Parian marble, was ornamented with several reposing figures from the antique. The bed was of silk, the colour of the hangings, richly fringed with purple and silver, and the head made in form of a canopy. The steps which were placed near the bed to assist in ascending it, were supported by cupids apparently of solid silver. China vases filled with perfume stood in several of the recesses, upon stands of the same structure as the toilet, which was magnificent, and ornamented with a variety of trinkets.

Adeline threw a transient look upon these various objects, and proceeded to examine the windows, which descended to the floor and opened into balconies towards the garden she had seen from the saloon. They were now fastened, and her efforts to move them were ineffectual: at length she gave up the attempt. A door next attracted her notice, which she found was not fastened; it opened upon a dressing-closet, to which she descended by a few steps: two windows appeared, she hastened towards them; one refused to yield, but her heart beat with sudden joy when the other opened to her touch.

In the transport of the moment, she forgot that its distance from the ground might yet deny the escape she meditated. She returned to lock the door of the closet, to prevent a surprise, which, however, was unnecessary, that of the bed-room being already secured. She now looked out from the window; the garden lay before her, and she perceived that the window, which descended to the floor, was so near the ground, that she might jump from it with ease: almost in the same moment she perceived this, she sprang forward and alighted safely in an extensive garden, resembling more an English pleasure ground, than a series of French parterres.

Thence she had little doubt of escaping, either by some broken fence, or low part of the wall; she tripped lightly along, for hope played round her heart. The clouds of the late storm were now dispersed, and the moonlight, which slept on the lawns and spangled the flowerets yet heavy with rain drops, afforded her a distinct view of the surrounding scenery; she followed the direction of the high wall that adjoined the chateau, till it was concealed from her sight by a thick wilderness, so entangled with boughs and obscured by darkness, that she feared to enter, and turned aside into a walk on the right; it conducted her to the margin of a lake overhung with lofty trees.

The moonbeams dancing upon the waters, that with gentle undulation played along the shore, exhibited a scene of tranquil beauty, which would have soothed a heart less agitated than was that of Adeline: she sighed as she transiently surveyed it, and passed hastily on in search of the garden wall, from which she had now strayed a considerable way. After wandering for some time through alleys and over lawns, without meeting with any thing like a boundary to the grounds, she again found herself at the lake, and now traversed its border with the footsteps of despair:—tears rolled down her cheeks. The scene around exhibited only images of peace and delight; every object seemed to repose; not a breath waved the foliage, not a sound stole through the air: it was in her bosom only that tumult and distress prevailed. She still pursued the windings of the shore, till an opening in the woods conducted her up a gentle ascent: the path now wound along the side of a hill where the gloom was so deep, that it was with some difficulty she found her way: suddenly, however, the avenue opened to a lofty grove, and she perceived a light issue from a recess at some distance.

She paused, and her first impulse was to retreat; but listening, and hearing no sound, a faint hope beamed upon her mind, that the person to whom the light belonged, might be won to favour her escape. She advanced, with trembling and cautious steps, towards the recess, that she might secretly observe the person, before she ventured to enter it. Her emotion increased as she approached; and, having reached the bower, she beheld, through an open window, the Marquis reclining on a sofa, near which stood a table, covered with fruit and wine. He was alone, and his countenance was flushed with drinking.

While she gazed, fixed to the spot by terror, he looked up towards the casement; the light gleamed full upon her face, but she stayed not to learn whether he had observed her, for, with the swiftness of sound, she left the place and ran, without knowing whether she was pursued. Having gone a considerable way, fatigue at length compelled her to stop, and she threw herself upon the turf, almost fainting with fear and languor. She knew, if the Marquis detected her in an attempt to escape, he would, probably, burst the bounds which she had hitherto prescribed to himself, and that she had the most dreadful evils to expect. The palpitations of terror were so strong, that she could with difficulty breathe.

She watched and listened in trembling expectation, but no form met her eye, no sound her ear; in this state she remained a considerable time. She wept, and the tears she shed relieved her oppressed heart. O my father! said she, why did you abandon your child? If you knew the dangers to which you have exposed her, you would, surely, pity and relieve her. Alas! shall I never find a friend! am I destined still to trust and be deceived?— Peter too, could he be treacherous? She wept again, and then returned to a sense of her present danger, and to a consideration of the means of escaping it—but no means appeared.

To her imagination the grounds were boundless; she had wandered from lawn to lawn, and from grove to grove, without perceiving any termination to the place; the garden-wall she could not find, but she resolved neither to return to the chateau, nor to relinquish her search. As she was rising to depart, she perceived a shadow move along at some distance: she stood still to observe it. It slowly advanced and then disappeared; but presently she saw a person emerge from the gloom, and approach the spot where she stood. She had no doubt that the Marquis had observed her, and she ran with all possible speed to the shade of some woods on the left. Footsteps pursued her, and she heard her name repeated, while she in vain endeavoured to quicken her pace.

Suddenly the sound of pursuit turned, and sunk away in a different direction: she paused to take breath; she looked around, and no person appeared. She now proceeded slowly along the avenue, and had almost reached its termination, when she saw the same figure emerge from the woods and dart across the avenue: it instantly pursued her and approached. A voice called her, but she was gone beyond its reach, for she had sunk senseless upon the ground: it was long before she revived: when she did, she found herself in the arms of a stranger, and made an effort to disengage herself.

Fear nothing, lovely Adeline, said he, fear nothing: you are in the arms of a friend, who will encounter any hazard for your sake; who will protect you with his life. He pressed her gently to his heart. Have you then forgot me? continued he. She looked earnestly at him, and was now convinced that it was Theodore who spoke. Joy was her first emotion; but, recollecting his former abrupt departure, at a time so critical to her safety and that he was the friend of the Marquis, a thousand mingled sensations struggled in her breast, and overwhelmed her with mistrust, apprehension, and disappointment.

Theodore raised her from the ground, and while he yet supported her, let us fly from this place, said he; a carriage waits to receive us; it shall go wherever you direct, and convey you to your friends. This last sentence touched her heart: Alas, I have no friends! said she, nor do I know whither to go. Theodore gently pressed her hand between his, and, in a voice of the softest compassion, said, My friends then shall be yours; suffer me to lead you to them. But I am in agony while you remain in this place; let us hasten to quit it. Adeline was going to reply, when voices were heard among the trees, and Theodore, supporting her with his arm, hurried her along the avenue; they continued their flight till Adeline, panting for breath, could go no further.

Having paused a while, and heard no footsteps in pursuit, they renewed their course: Theodore knew that they were now not far from the garden wall; but he was also aware, that in the intermediate space several paths wound from remote parts of the grounds into the walk he was to pass, from whence the Marquis's people might issue and intercept him. He, however, concealed his apprehensions from Adeline, and endeavoured to soothe and support her spirits.

At length they reached the wall, and Theodore was leading her towards a low part of it, near which stood the carriage, when again they heard voices in the air. Adeline's spirits and strength were nearly exhausted, but she made a last effort to proceed and she now saw the ladder at some distance by which Theodore had descended to the garden. Exert yourself yet a little longer, said he, and you will be in safety. He held the ladder while she ascended; the top of the wall was broad and level, and Adeline, having reached it, remained there till Theodore followed and drew the ladder to the other side.

When they had descended, the carriage appeared in waiting, but without the driver. Theodore feared to call, lest his voice should betray him; he, therefore, put Adeline into the carriage, and went in search of the postillion, whom he found asleep under a tree at some distance: having awakened him, they returned to the vehicle, which soon drove furiously away. Adeline did not yet dare to believe herself safe; but, after proceeding a considerable time without interruption, joy burst upon her heart, and she thanked her deliverer in terms of the warmest gratitude. The sympathy expressed in the tone of his voice and manner, proved that his happiness, on this occasion, almost equalled her own.

As reflection gradually stole upon her mind, anxiety superseded joy: in the tumult of the late moments, she thought only of escape; but the circumstances of her present situation now appeared to her, and she became silent and pensive: she had no friends to whom she could fly, and was going with a young chevalier, almost a stranger to her, she knew not whither. She remembered how often she had been deceived and betrayed where she trusted most, and her spirits sunk: she remembered also the former attention which Theodore had shown her, and dreaded lest his conduct might be prompted by a selfish passion. She saw this to be possible, but she disdained to believe it probable, and felt that nothing could give her greater pain than to doubt the integrity of Theodore.

155

He interrupted her reverie, by recurring to her late situation at the abbey. You would be much surprised, said he, and, I fear, offended that I did not attend my appointment at the abbey, after the alarming hints I had given you in our last interview. That circumstance has, perhaps, injured me in your esteem, if, indeed, I was ever so happy as to possess it: but my designs were overruled by those of the Marquis de Montalt; and I think I may venture to assert, that my distress upon this occasion was, at least, equal to your apprehensions.

Adeline said, she had been much alarmed by the hints he had given her, and by his failing to afford further information concerning the subject of her danger; and—She checked the sentence that hung upon her lips, for she perceived that she was unwarily betraying the interest he held in her heart. There were a few moments of silence, and neither party seemed perfectly at ease. Theodore, at length, renewed the conversation: Suffer me to acquaint you, said he, with the circumstances that withheld me from the interview I solicited; I am anxious to exculpate myself. Without waiting her reply, he proceeded to inform her, that the Marquis had, by some inexplicable means, learned or suspected the subject of their last conversation, and, perceiving his designs were in danger of being counteracted, had taken effectual means to prevent her obtaining further intelligence of them. Adeline immediately recollected that Theodore and herself had been seen in the forest by La Motte, who had, no doubt, suspected their growing intimacy, and had taken care to inform the Marquis how likely he was to find a rival in his friend.

On the day following that on which I last saw you, said Theodore, the Marquis, who is my colonel, commanded me to prepare to attend my regiment, and appointed the following morning for my journey. This sudden order gave me some surprise, but I was not long in doubt concerning the motive for it: a servant of the Marquis, who had been long attached to me, entered my room soon after I had left his lord, and expressing concern at my abrupt departure, dropped some hints respecting it, which excited my surprise. I inquired further, and was confirmed in the suspicions I had for some time entertained of the Marquis's designs upon you.

Jaques further informed me, that our late interview had been noticed and communicated to the Marquis. His information had been obtained from a fellow-servant, and it alarmed me so much, that I engaged him to send me intelligence from time to time, concerning the proceedings of the Marquis. I now looked forward to the evening which would bring me again to your presence with increased impatience: but the ingenuity of the Marquis effectually counteracted my endeavours and wishes; he had made an engagement to pass the day at the villa of a nobleman some leagues distant, and, notwithstanding all the excuses I could offer, I was obliged to attend him. Thus compelled to obey, I passed a day of more agitation and anxiety than I had ever before experienced. It was midnight before we returned to the Marquis's chateau. I arose early in the morning to commence my journey, and resolved to seek an interview with you before I left the province.

When I entered the breakfast room, I was much surprised to find the Marquis there already, who, commending the beauty of the morning, declared his intention of accompanying me as far as Chineau. Thus unexpectedly deprived of my last hope, my countenance, I believe, expressed what I felt, for the scrutinizing eye of the Marquis instantly changed from seeming carelessness to displeasure. The distance from Chineau to the abbey was at least twelve leagues; yet I had once some intention of returning from thence, when the Marquis should leave me, till I recollected the very remote chance there would even then be of seeing you alone, and also, that if I was observed by La Motte, it would awaken all his suspicions, and caution him against any future plan I might see it expedient to attempt; I therefore proceeded to join my regiment.

Jaques sent me frequent accounts of the operations of the Marquis; but his manner of relating them was so very confused, that they only served to perplex and distress me. His last letter, however, alarmed me so much, that my residence in quarters became intolerable; and, as I found it impossible to obtain leave of absence, I secretly left the regiment, and concealed myself in a cottage about a mile from the chateau, that I might obtain the earliest intelligence of the Marquis's plans. Jaques brought me daily information, and, at last, an account of the horrible plot which was laid for the following night.

I saw little probability of warning you of your danger. If I ventured near the abbey, La Motte might discover me, and frustrate every attempt on my part to save you; yet I determined to encounter this risk for the chance of seeing you, and towards evening I was preparing to set out for the forest, when Jaques arrived, and informed me that you was to be brought to the chateau. My plan was thus rendered less difficult. I learned also, that the Marquis, by means of those refinements in luxury, with which he is but too well acquainted, designed, now that his apprehension of losing you was no more, to seduce you to his wishes, and impose upon you by a fictitious marriage. Having obtained information concerning the situation of the room allotted you, I ordered a chaise to be in waiting, and with a design of scaling your window, and conducting you thence, I entered the garden at midnight.

Theodore having ceased to speak:—I know not how words can express my sense of the obligations I owe you, said Adeline, or my gratitude for your generosity.

Ah! call it not generosity, he replied, it was love. He paused. Adeline was silent. After some moments of expressive emotion, he resumed; But pardon this abrupt declaration; yet why do I call it abrupt, since my actions have already disclosed what my lips have never, till this instant, ventured to acknowledge. He paused again. Adeline was still silent. Yet do me the justice to believe, that I am sensible of the impropriety of pleading my love at present, and have been surprised into this confession. I promise also to forbear from a renewal of the subject, till you are placed in a situation where you may freely accept, or refuse, the sincere regards I offer you. If I could, however, now be certain that I possess your esteem, it would relieve me from much anxiety.

Adeline felt surprised that he should doubt her esteem for him, after the signal and generous service he had rendered her; but she was not yet acquainted with the timidity of love. Do you then, said she in a tremulous voice, believe me ungrateful? It is impossible I can consider your friendly interference in my behalf without esteeming you. Theodore immediately took her hand and pressed it to his lips in silence. They were both too much agitated to converse, and continued to travel for some miles without exchanging a word.

CHAPTER XII

And hope enchanted smiled and waved her golden

hair,

And longer had she sung — but, with a frown,

Revenge impatient rose.

ODE TO THE PASSIONS.

The dawn of morning now trembled through the clouds, when the travellers stopped at a small town to change horses. Theodore entreated Adeline to alight and take some refreshment, and to this she at length consented. But the people of the inn were not yet up, and it was some time before the knocking and the roaring of the postillion could rouse them.

Having taken some slight refreshment, Theodore and Adeline returned to the carriage. The only subject upon which Theodore could have spoke with interest, delicacy forbade him at this time to notice; and after pointing out some beautiful scenery on the road, and making other efforts to support a conversation, he relapsed into silence. His mind, though still anxious, was now relieved from the apprehension that had long oppressed it. When he first saw Adeline, her loveliness made a deep impression on his heart: there was a sentiment in her beauty, which his mind immediately acknowledged, and the effect of which, her manners and conversation had afterwards confirmed. Her charms appeared to him like those since so finely described by an English poet:

Oh! have you seen, bathed in the morning dew,

The budding rose its infant bloom display?

When first its virgin tints unfold to view.

It shrinks, and scarcely trusts the blaze of day.

So soft, so delicate, so sweet she came,

Youth's damask glow just dawning on her cheek.

I gaz'd, I sigh'd, I caught the tender flame,

Felt the fond pang, and droop'd with passion weak.

A knowledge of her destitute condition and of the dangers with which she was environed, had awakened in his heart the tenderest touch of pity, and assisted the change of admiration into love. The distress he suffered, when compelled to leave her exposed to these dangers, without being able to warn her of them, can only be imagined. During his residence with his regiment, his mind was the constant prey of terrors, which he saw no means of combating but by returning to the neighbourhood of the abbey where he might obtain early intelligence of the Marquis's schemes, and be ready to give his assistance to Adeline.

Leave of absence he could not request, without betraying his design where most he dreaded it should be known; and at length with a generous rashness, which though it defied law was impelled by virtue, he secretly quitted his regiment. The progress of the Marquis's plan he had observed with trembling anxiety, till the night that was to decide the fate of Adeline and himself roused all his mind to action, and involved him in a tumult of hope and fear, horror and expectation.

Never till the present hour had he ventured to believe she was in safety. Now the distance they had gained from the chateau without perceiving any pursuit, increased his best hopes. It was impossible he could sit by the side of his beloved Adeline, and receive assurances of her gratitude and esteem, without venturing to hope for her love. He congratulated himself as her preserver, and anticipated scenes of happiness when she should be under the protection of his family. The clouds of misery and apprehension disappeared from his mind, and left it to the sunshine of joy. When a shadow of fear would sometimes return, or when he recollected with compunction the circumstances under which he had left his regiment, stationed as it was upon the frontiers, and in a time of war, he looked at Adeline, and her countenance with instantaneous magic beamed peace upon his heart.

But Adeline had a subject of anxiety from which Theodore was exempt: the prospect of her future days was involved in darkness and uncertainty. Again she was going to claim the bounty of strangers—again going to encounter the uncertainty of their kindness; exposed to the hardships of dependance, or to the difficulty of earning a precarious livelihood. These anticipations obscured the joy occasioned by her escape, and by the affection which the conduct and avowal of Theodore had exhibited. The delicacy of his behaviour, in forbearing to take advantage of her present situation to plead his love, increased her esteem and flattered her pride.

Adeline was lost in meditation upon subjects like these, when the postillion stopped the carriage, and pointing to part of a road which wound down the side of a hill they had passed, said there were several horsemen in pursuit! Theodore immediately ordered him to proceed with all possible speed, and to strike out of the great road into the first obscure way that offered. The postillion cracked his whip in the air, and set off as if he was flying for life. In the meanwhile Theodore endeavoured to reanimate Adeline, who was sinking with terror, and who now thought, if she could only escape from the Marquis, she could defy the future.

Presently they struck into a by lane screened and overshadowed by thick trees. Theodore again looked from the window, but the closing boughs prevented his seeing far enough to determine whether the pursuit continued. For his sake Adeline endeavoured to disguise her emotions. This lane, said Theodore, will certainly lead to a town or village, and then we have nothing to apprehend: for, though my single arm could not defend you against the number of our pursuers, I nave no doubt of being able to interest some of the inhabitants in our behalf.

Adeline appeared to be comforted by the hope this reflection suggested: and Theodore again looked back: but the windings of the road closed his view, and the rattling of the wheels overcame every other sound. At length he called to the postillion to stop; and having listened attentively without perceiving any sound of horses, he began to hope they were now in safety. Do you know whither this road leads? said he. The postillion answered that he did not, but he saw some houses through the trees at a distance, and believed that it led to them. This was most welcome intelligence to Theodore, who looked forward and perceived the houses. The postillion set off. Fear nothing, my adored Adeline, said he, you are now safe; I will part with you but with life. Adeline sighed, not for herself only, but for the danger to which Theodore might be exposed.

They had continued to travel in this manner for near half an hour, when they arrived at a small village, and soon after stopped at an inn, the best the place afforded. As Theodore lifted Adeline from the chaise, he again entreated her to dismiss her apprehensions, and spoke with a tenderness to which she could reply only by a smile that ill concealed her anxiety. After ordering refreshments, he went out to speak with the landlord; but had scarcely left the room when Adeline observed a party of horsemen enter the inn yard, and she had no doubt these were the persons from whom they fled. The faces of two of them only were turned towards her, but she thought the figure of one of the others not unlike that of the Marquis.

Her heart was chilled, and for some moments the powers of reason forsook her. Her first design was to seek concealments but while she considered the means, one of the horsemen looked up to the window near, which she stood, and speaking to his companions they entered the inn. To quit the room without being observed was impossible; to remain there, alone and unprotected as she was, would almost be equally dangerous. She paced the room in an agony of terror, often secretly calling on Theodore, and often wondering he did not return. These were moments of indescribable suffering. A loud and tumultuous sound of voices now arose from a distant part of the house, and she soon, distinguished the words of the disputants. I arrest you in the king's name, said one; and bid you, at your peril, attempt to go from hence, except under a guard.

The next minute Adeline heard the voice of Theodore in reply. I do not mean to dispute the king's orders, said he, and give you my word of honour not to go without you; but first unhand me, that I may return to that room; I have a friend there whom I wish to speak with. To this proposal they at first objected, considering it merely as an excuse to obtain an opportunity of escaping; but after much altercation and entreaty his request was granted. He sprang forward towards the room where Adeline remained; and while a sergeant and corporal followed him to the door, the two soldiers went out into the yard of the inn to watch the windows of the apartment.

With an eager hand he unclosed the door; but Adeline hastened not to meet him, for she had fainted almost at the beginning of the dispute. Theodore called loudly for assistance; and the mistress of the inn soon appeared with her stock of remedies, which were administered in vain to Adeline, who remained insensible, and by breathing alone gave signs of her existence. The distress of Theodore was in the mean time heightened by the appearance of the officers, who, laughing at the discovery of his pretended friend, declared they could wait no longer. Saying this, they would have forced him from the inanimate form of Adeline, over whom he hung in unutterable anguish, when fiercely turning upon them he drew his sword, and swore no power on earth should force him away before the lady recovered.

The men, enraged by the action and the determined air of Theodore, exclaimed, Do you oppose the king's orders? and advanced to seize him: but he presented the point of his sword, and bade them at their peril approach. One of them immediately drew. Theodore kept his guard, but did not advance. I demand only to wait here till the lady recovers, said he; — you understand the alternative. The man already exasperated by the opposition of Theodore, regarded the latter part of his speech as a threat, and became determined not to give up the point: he pressed forward; and while his comrade called the men from the yard, Theodore wounded him slightly in the shoulder, and received himself the stroke of a sabre on his head.

The blood gushed furiously from the wound: Theodore, staggering to a chair, sunk into it, just as the remainder of the party entered the room; and Adeline unclosed her eyes to see him ghastly pale, and covered with blood. She uttered an involuntary scream, and exclaiming, They have murdered him, nearly relapsed. At the sound of her voice he raised his head, and smiling held out his hand to her. I am not much hurt said he faintly, and shall soon be better, if indeed you are recovered. She hastened towards him, and gave her hand. Is nobody gone for a surgeon? said she with a look of agony. Do not be alarmed, said Theodore, I am not so ill as you imagine. The room was now crowded with people, whom the report of the affray had now brought together; among these was a man who acted as physician, apothecary, and surgeon to the village, and who now stepped forward to the assistance of Theodore.

Having examined the wound, he declined giving his opinion, but ordered the patient to be immediately put to bed; to which the officers objected, alleging that it was their duty to carry him to the regiment. That cannot be done without great danger to his life, replied the doctor; and —

Oh; his life, said the sergeant; we have nothing to do with that, we must do our duty. Adeline, who had hitherto stood in trembling anxiety, could now no longer be silent. Since the surgeon, said she, has declared it his opinion that this gentleman cannot be removed in his present condition without endangering his life, you will remember that if he dies, yours will probably answer it.

Yes, rejoined the surgeon, who was unwilling to relinquish his patient; I declare before these witnesses, that he cannot be removed with safety: you will do well therefore to consider the consequences. He has received a very dangerous wound, which requires the most careful treatment, and the event is even then doubtful; but if he travels, a fever may ensue, and the wound will then be mortal. Theodore heard this sentence with composure, but Adeline could with difficulty conceal the anguish of her heart: she roused all her fortitude to suppress the tears that struggled in her eyes; and though she wished to interest the humanity or to awaken the fears of the men in behalf of their unfortunate prisoner, she dared not to trust her voice with utterance.

From this internal struggle she was relieved by the compassion of the people who filled the room, and becoming clamorous in the cause of Theodore, declared the officers would be guilty of murder if they removed him. Why he must die at any rate, said the sergeant, for quitting his post, and drawing upon me in the execution of the king's orders. A faint sickness seized the heart of Adeline, and she leaned for support against Theodore's chair, whose concern for himself was for a while suspended in his anxiety for her. He supported her with his arm, and forcing a smile, said in a low voice, which she only could hear. This is a misrepresentation; I doubt not, when the affair is inquired into, it will be settled without any serious consequences.

Adeline knew these words were uttered only to console her, and therefore did not give much credit to them, though Theodore continued to give her similar assurances of his safety. Meanwhile the mob, whose compassion for him had been gradually excited by the obduracy of the officer, were now roused to pity and indignation by the seeming certainty of his punishment, and the unfeeling manner in which it had been denounced. In a short time they became so much enraged that, partly from a dread of further consequences, and partly from the shame which their charges of cruelty occasioned, the sergeant consented that he should be put to bed, till his commanding officer might direct what was to be done. Adeline's joy at this circumstance overcame for a moment the sense of her misfortunes and of her situation.

She waited in an adjoining room the sentence of the surgeon, who was now engaged in examining the wound; and though the accident would in any other circumstances have severely afflicted her, she now lamented it the more, because she considered herself as the cause of it, and because the misfortune by illustrating more fully the affection of her lover, drew him closer to her heart, and seemed therefore to sharpen the poignancy of her affliction. The dreadful assertion that Theodore, should he recover, would be punished with death, she scarcely dared to consider, but endeavoured to believe that it was no more than a cruel exaggeration of his antagonist.

Upon the whole, Theodore's present danger, together with the attendant circumstances, awakened all her tenderness, and discovered to her the true state of her affections. The graceful form, the noble, intelligent, countenance, and the engaging manners which she had at first admired in Theodore, became afterwards more interesting by that strength of thought and elegance of sentiment exhibited in his conversation. His conduct, since her escape, had excited her warmest gratitude; and the danger which he had now encountered in her behalf, called forth her tenderness, and heightened it into love. The veil was removed from her heart, and she saw for the first time its genuine emotions.

The surgeon at length came out of Theodore's chamber into the room where Adeline was waiting to speak with him. She inquired concerning the state of his wound. You are a relation of the gentleman's, I presume, Madam; his sister, perhaps? The question vexed and embarrassed her, and without answering it she repeated her inquiry. Perhaps, Madam, you are more nearly related, pursued the surgeon, seeming also to disregard her question, — perhaps you are his wife? Adeline blushed, and was about to reply, but he continued his speech. The interest you take in his welfare is at least very flattering, and I would almost consent to exchange conditions with him, were I sure of receiving such tender compassion from so charming a lady. Saying this, he bowed to the ground. Adeline assuming a very reserved air, said, Now, Sir, that you have concluded your compliment, you will perhaps attend to my question; I have inquired how you have left your patient.

That, Madam, is perhaps a question very difficult to be resolved; and it is likewise a very disagreeable office to pronounce ill news — I fear he will die. The surgeon opened his snuff-box and presented it to Adeline. Die! she exclaimed in a faint voice, die!

Do not be alarmed, Madam, resumed the surgeon, observing her grow pale, do not be alarmed. It is possible that the wound may not have reached the — —, he stammered, in that case the — —, stammering again, is not affected; and if so, the interior membranes of the brain are not touched: in this case the wound may perhaps escape inflammation, and the patient may possibly recover. But if, on the other hand — —

I beseech you, Sir, to speak intelligibly, interrupted Adeline, and not to trifle with my anxiety. Do you really believe him in danger?

In danger, Madam, exclaimed the surgeon, in danger! yes, certainly, in very great danger. Saying this, he walked away with an air of chagrin and displeasure. Adeline remained for some moments in the room, in an excess of sorrow, which she found it impossible to restrain; and then drying her tears, and endeavouring to compose her countenance, she went to inquire for the mistress of the inn, to whom she sent a waiter. After expecting her in vain for some time, she rang the bell, and sent another message somewhat more pressing. Still the hostess did not appear; and Adeline at length went herself down stairs, where she found her, surrounded by a number of people, relating, with a loud voice and various gesticulations, the particulars of the late accident. Perceiving Adeline, she called out, Oh! here is Mademoiselle herself; and the eyes of the assembly were immediately turned upon her. Adeline, whom the crowd prevented from approaching the hostess, now beckoned her, and was going to withdraw; but the landlady, eager in the pursuit of her story, disregarded the signal. In vain did Adeline endeavour to catch her eye; it glanced every where but upon her, who was unwilling to attract the further notice of the crowd by calling out.

It is a great pity, to be sure, that he should be shot, said the landlady, he's such a handsome man; but they say he certainly will if he recovers. Poor gentleman! he will very likely not suffer though, for the doctor says he will never go out of this house alive. Adeline now spoke to a man who stood near, and desiring he would tell the hostess she wished to speak with her, left the place.

In about ten minutes the landlady appeared. Alas! Mademoiselle, said she, your brother is in a sad condition; they fear he won't get over. Adeline inquired whether there was any other medical person in the town than the surgeon whom she had seen. Lord, Madam, this is a rare healthy place; we have little need of medicine people here; such an accident never happened in it before. The doctor has been here ten years, but there's very bad encouragement for his trade, and I believe he's poor enough himself. One of the sort's quite enough for us. Adeline interrupted her to ask some questions concerning Theodore, whom the hostess had attended to his chamber. She inquired how he had borne the dressing of the wound, and whether he appeared to be easier after the operation; questions to which the hostess gave no very satisfactory answers. She now inquired whether there was any surgeon in the neighbourhood of the town, and was told there was not.

The distress visible in Adeline's countenance seemed to excite the compassion of the landlady, who now endeavoured to console her in the best manner she was able. She advised her to send for her friends, and offered to procure a messenger. Adeline sighed, and said it was unnecessary. I don't know, Ma'mselle, what you may think necessary, continued the hostess; but I know I should think it very hard to die in a strange place, with no relations near me, and I dare say the poor gentleman thinks so himself; and besides, who is to pay for his funeral if he dies? Adeline begged she would be silent; and desiring that every proper attention might be given, she promised her a reward for her trouble, and requested pen and ink immediately. Ay, to be sure, Ma'mselle, that is the proper way; why your friends would never forgive you if you did not acquaint them; I know it by myself. And as for taking care of him, he shall have every thing the house affords; and I warrant there is never a better inn in the province, though the town is none of the biggest. Adeline was obliged to repeat her request for pen and ink, before the loquacious hostess would quit the room.

The thought of sending for Theodore's friends had, in the tumult of the late scenes, never occurred to her, and she was now somewhat consoled by the prospect of comfort which it opened for him. When the pen and ink were brought, she wrote the following note to Theodore: —

"In your present condition, you have need of every comfort that can be procured you; and surely there is no cordial more valuable in illness than the presence of a friend. Suffer me, therefore, to acquaint your family with your situation: it will be a satisfaction to me, and, I doubt not, a consolation to you."

In a short time after she had sent the note, she received a message from Theodore, entreating most respectfully, but earnestly, to see her for a few minutes. She immediately went to his chamber, and found her worst apprehensions confirmed, by the languor expressed in his countenance; while the shock she received, together with her struggle to disguise her emotions, almost overcame her. I thank you for this goodness, said he, extending his hand, which she received, and sitting down by the bed, burst into a flood of tears. When her agitation had somewhat subsided, and, removing her handkerchief from her eyes, she again looked on Theodore, a smile of the tenderest love expressed his sense of the interest she took in his welfare, and administered a temporary relief to her heart.

Forgive this weakness, said she; my spirits have of late been so variously agitated—Theodore interrupted her: These tears are more flattering to my heart. But for my sake endeavour to support yourself: I doubt not I shall soon be better; the surgeon—

I do not like him, said Adeline; but tell me how you find yourself? He assured her that he was now much easier than he had yet been; and mentioning her kind note, he led to the subject on account of which he had solicited to see her. My family, said he, reside at a great distance from hence, and I well know their affection is such, that, were they informed of my situation, no consideration, however reasonable, could prevent their coming to my assistance: but before they can arrive, their presence will probably be unnecessary (Adeline looked earnestly at him.) I should probably be well, pursued he, smiling, before a letter could reach them; it would, therefore, occasion them unnecessary pain, and moreover a fruitless journey. For your sake, Adeline, I could wish they were here; but a few days will more fully show the consequences of my wound: let us wait at least till then, and be directed by circumstances.

Adeline forbore to press the subject further, and turned to one more immediately interesting. I much wish, said she, that you had a more able surgeon; you know the geography of the province better than I do; are we in the neighbourhood of any town likely to afford you other advice?

I believe not, said he; and this is an affair of little consequence, for my wound is so inconsiderable that a very moderate share of skill may suffice to cure it. But why, my beloved Adeline, do you give way to this anxiety? why suffer yourself to be disturbed by this tendency to forebode the worst? I am willing, perhaps presumptuously so, to attribute it to your kindness; and suffer me to assure you, that while it excites my gratitude, it increases my tenderest esteem. O Adeline! since you wish my speedy recovery, let me see you composed: while I believe you to be unhappy I cannot be well.—She assured him she would endeavour to be at least tranquil; and fearing the conversation, if prolonged, would be prejudicial to him, she left him to repose.

As she turned out of the gallery she met the hostess, upon whom certain words of Adeline had operated as a talisman, transforming neglect and impertinence into officious civility.

She came to inquire whether the gentleman above stairs had every thing that he liked, for she was sure it was her endeavour that he should. I have got him a nurse, Ma'mselle, to attend him, and I dare say she will do very well; but I will look to that, for I shall not mind helping him myself sometimes. Poor gentleman! how patiently he bears it! One would not think now that he believes he is going to die; yet the doctor told him so himself, or at least as good. Adeline was extremely shocked at this imprudent conduct of the surgeon, and dismissed the landlady, after ordering a slight dinner.

Towards evening the surgeon again made his appearance; and having passed some time with his patient, returned to the parlour, according to the desire of Adeline, to inform her of his condition. He answered Adeline's inquiries with great solemnity. It is impossible to determine positively at present. Madam, but I have reason to adhere to the opinion I gave you this morning. I am not apt indeed, to form opinions upon uncertain grounds—I will give you a singular instance of this:

It is not above a fortnight since I was sent for to a patient at some leagues distance: I was from home when the messenger arrived, and the case being urgent, before I could reach the patient another physician was consulted, who had ordered such medicines as he thought proper, and the patient had been apparently relieved by them. His friends were congratulating themselves upon his improvement when I arrived, and had agreed in opinion with the physician that there was no danger in his case. Depend upon it, said I, you are mistaken; these medicines cannot have relieved him; the patient is in the utmost danger. The patient groaned; but my brother physician persisted in affirming that the remedies he had prescribed would not only be certain, but speedy, some good effect having been already produced by them. Upon this I lost all patience; and adhering to my opinion, that these effects were fallacious and the case desperate, I assured the patient himself that his life was in the utmost danger. I am not one of those, Madam, who deceive their patients to the last moment;—but you shall hear the conclusion.

My brother physician was, I suppose, enraged by the firmness of my opposition, for he assumed a most angry look, which did not in the least affect me, and turning to the patient, desired he would decide upon which of our opinions to rely, for he must decline acting with me. The patient did me the honour, pursued the surgeon with a smile of complacency and smoothing his ruffles, to think more highly of me than, perhaps, I deserved, for he immediately dismissed my opponent. I could not have believed, said he, as the physician left the room—I could not have believed that a man who has been so many years in the profession could be so wholly ignorant of it.

I could not have believed it either, said I.—I am astonished that he was not aware of my danger, resumed the patient. I am astonished likewise, replied I. I was resolved to do what I could for the patient, for he was a man of understanding, as you perceive, and I had a regard for him. I therefore altered the prescriptions, and myself administered the medicines; but all would not do,—my opinion was verified, and he died even before the next morning.—Adeline, who had been compelled to listen to this long story, sighed at the conclusion of it. I don't wonder that you are affected, Madam, said the surgeon; the instance I have related is certainly a very affecting one. It distressed me so much, that it was some time before I could think or even speak concerning it. But you must allow, Madam, continued he, lowering his voice and bowing with a look of self-congratulation, that this was a striking instance of the infallibility of my judgment.

Adeline shuddered at the infallibility of his judgment, and made no reply. It was a shocking thing for the poor man, resumed the surgeon.—It was indeed, very shocking, said Adeline.—It affected me a good deal when it happened, continued he.—Undoubtedly, Sir, said Adeline.

But time wears away the most painful impressions.

I think you mention it was about a fortnight since this happened?

Somewhere thereabouts, replied the surgeon without seeming to understand the observation.—And will you permit me, Sir, to ask the name of the physician who so ignorantly opposed you?

Certainly, Madame; it is Lafance.

He lives in the obscurity he deserves, no doubt, said Adeline.

Why no, Madam, he lives in a town of some note, at about the distance of four leagues from hence; and affords one instance, among many others, that the public opinion, is generally erroneous. You will hardly believe it, but I assure you it is a fact, that this man comes into a great deal of practice, while I am suffered to remain here neglected, and, indeed very little known.

During his narrative Adeline had been considering by what means she could discover the name of the physician; for the instance that had been produced to prove his ignorance, and the infallibility of his opponent, had completely settled her opinion concerning them both. She now more than ever wished to deliver Theodore from the hands of the surgeon, and was musing on the possibility, when he with so much self-security, developed the means.

She asked him a few more questions concerning the state of Theodore's wound; and was told it was much as it had been, but that some degree of fever had come on. But I have ordered a fire to be made in the room, continued the surgeon, and some additional blankets to be laid on the bed; these, I doubt not, will have a proper effect. In the mean time they must be careful to keep from him every kind of liquid, except some cordial draughts which I shall send. He will naturally ask for drink, but it must on no account be given to him.

You do not approve then of the method which I have somewhere heard of, said Adeline, of attending to nature in these cases?

Nature, Madam! pursued he, nature is the most improper guide in the world: I always adopt a method directly contrary to what she would suggest; for what can be the use of art, if she is only to follow nature? This was my first opinion on setting out in life, and I have ever since strictly adhered to it. From what I have said, indeed, Madam, you may perhaps perceive that my opinions may be depended on; what they once are they always are, for my mind is not of that frivolous kind to be affected by circumstances.

Adeline was fatigued by this discourse, and impatient to impart to Theodore her discovery of a physician: but the surgeon seemed by no means disposed to leave her, and was expatiating upon various topics, with new instances of his surprising sagacity, when the waiter brought a message that some person desired to see him. He was, however, engaged upon too agreeable a topic to be easily prevailed upon to quit it, and it was not till after a second message was brought that he made his bow to Adeline and left the room. The moment he was gone she sent a note to Theodore, entreating his permission to call in the assistance of the physician.

The conceited manners of the surgeon had by this time given Theodore a very unfavourable opinion of his talents, and the last prescription had so fully confirmed it, that he now readily consented to have other advice. Adeline immediately inquired for a messenger; but recollecting that the residence of the physician was still a secret, she applied to the hostess, who being really ignorant of it, or pretending to be so, gave her no information. What further inquiries she made were equally ineffectual, and she passed some hours in extreme distress, while the disorder of Theodore rather increased than abated.

When supper appeared, she asked the boy who waited if he knew a physician of the name of Lafance in the neighbourhood. Not in the neighbourhood, Madame; but I know doctor Lafance of Chancy, for I come from the town. — Adeline inquired further, and received very satisfactory answers. But the town was at some leagues distance, and the delay this circumstance must occasion again alarmed her; she, however, ordered a messenger to be immediately dispatched, and having sent again to inquire concerning Theodore, retired to her chamber for the night.

The continued fatigue she had suffered for the last fourteen hours overcame anxiety, and her harassed spirits sunk to repose. She slept till late in the morning, and was then awakened by the landlady, who came to inform her that Theodore was much worse, and to inquire what should be done. Adeline, finding that the physician was not arrived, immediately arose, and hastened to inquire further concerning Theodore. The hostess informed her that he had passed a very disturbed night; that he had complained of being very hot, and desired that the fire in his room might be extinguished; but that the nurse knew her duty too well to obey him, and had strictly followed the doctor's orders.

She added, that he had taken the cordial draughts regularly, but had, notwithstanding, continued to grow worse, and at last became light-headed. In the mean time the boy who had been sent for the physician was still absent: — And no wonder, continued the hostess; why, only consider, it's eight leagues off, and the lad had to find the road, bad as it is, in the dark. But indeed, Ma'mselle, you might as well have trusted our doctor, for we never want any body else, not we, in the town here; and if I might speak my mind, Jaques had better have been sent off for the young gentleman's friends than for this strange doctor that nobody knows.

After asking some further questions concerning Theodore, the answers to which rather increased than diminished her alarm, Adeline endeavoured to compose her spirits, and await in patience the arrival of the physician. She was now more sensible than ever of the forlornness of her own condition, and of the danger of Theodore's, and earnestly wished that his friends could be informed of his situation; a wish which could not be gratified, for Theodore, who alone could acquaint her with their place of residence, was deprived of recollection.

When the surgeon arrived and perceived the situation of his patient, he expressed no surprise; but having asked some questions and given a few general directions, he went down to Adeline. After paying her his usual compliments, he suddenly assumed an air of importance, — I am sorry Madam, said he, that it is my office to communicate disagreeable intelligence, but I wish you to be prepared for the event, which I fear, is approaching. Adeline comprehended his meaning; and though she had hitherto given little faith to his judgment, she could not hear him hint at the immediate danger of Theodore without yielding to the influence of fear.

She entreated him to acquaint her with all he apprehended: and he then proceeded to say that Theodore was, as he had foreseen, much worse this morning than he had been the preceding night; and the disorder having now affected his head, there was every reason to fear it would prove fatal in a few hours. The worst consequences may ensue, continued he; if the wound becomes inflamed, there will be very little chance of his recovery.

Adeline listened to this sentence with a dreadful calmness, and gave no utterance to grief, either by words or tears. The gentleman, I suppose, Madam, has friends, and the sooner you inform them of his condition the better. If they reside at any distance, it is indeed too late; but there are other necessary — You are ill, Madam!

Adeline made an effort to speak, but in vain, and the surgeon now called loudly for a glass of water; she drank it, and a deep sigh that she uttered, seemed somewhat to relieve her oppressed heart: tears succeeded. In the mean time the surgeon perceiving she was better, though not well enough to listen to his conversation, took leave, and promised to return in an hour. The physician was not yet arrived, and Adeline awaited his appearance with a mixture of fear and anxious hope.

About noon he came; and having been informed of the accident by which the fever was produced, and of the treatment which the surgeon had given it, he ascended to Theodore's chamber. In a quarter of an hour he returned to the room where Adeline expected him: The gentleman is still delirious, said he, but I have ordered him a composing draught. — — Is there any hope, Sir? inquired Adeline. Yes, Madam, certainly there is hope; the case at present is somewhat doubtful, but a few hours may enable me to judge with more certainty: in the mean time, I have directed that he shall be kept quiet, and be allowed to drink freely of some diluting liquids.

He had scarcely, at Adeline's request, recommended a surgeon, instead of the one at present employed, when the latter gentleman entered the room, and perceiving the physician, threw a glance of mingled surprise and anger at Adeline, who retired with him to another apartment, where she dismissed him with a politeness which he did not deign to return, and which he certainly did not deserve.

Early the following morning the surgeon arrived; but either the medicines or the crisis of the disorder had thrown Theodore into a deep sleep, in which he remained for several hours. The physician now gave Adeline reason to hope for a favourable issue, and every precaution was taken to prevent his being disturbed. He awoke perfectly sensible and free from fever; and his first words inquired for Adeline, who soon learned that he was out of danger.

In a few days he was sufficiently recovered to be removed from his chamber to a room adjoining, where Adeline met him with a joy which she found it impossible to repress; and the observance of this lighted up his countenance with pleasure: indeed Adeline, sensible to the attachment he had so nobly testified, and softened by the danger he had encountered, no longer attempted to disguise the tenderness of her esteem, and was at length brought to confess the interest his first appearance had impressed upon her heart.

After an hour of affecting conversation, in which the happiness of a young and mutual attachment totally occupied their minds, and excluded every idea not in unison with delight, they returned to a sense of their present embarrassments. Adeline recollected that Theodore was arrested for disobedience of orders, and deserting his post; and Theodore, that he must shortly be torn away from Adeline, who would be left exposed to all the evils from which he had so lately rescued her. This thought overwhelmed his heart with anguish; and after a long

174

pause he ventured to propose what his wishes had often suggested — a marriage with Adeline before he departed from the village: this was the only means of preventing, perhaps, an eternal separation; and though he saw the many dangerous inconveniences to which she would be exposed by a marriage with a man circumstanced like himself, yet these appeared so unequal to those she would otherwise be left to encounter alone, that his reason could no longer scruple to adopt what his affection had suggested.

Adeline was for some time too much agitated to reply: and though she had little to oppose to the arguments and pleadings of Theodore; though she had no friends to control, and no contrariety of interests to perplex her, she could not bring herself to consent thus hastily to a marriage with a man of whom she had little knowledge, and to whose family and connexions she had no sort of introduction. At length she entreated he would drop the subject; and the conversation for the remainder of the day was more general, yet still interesting.

That similarity of taste and opinion which had at first attracted them, every moment now more fully disclosed. Their discourse was enriched by elegant literature, and endeared by mutual regard. Adeline had enjoyed few opportunities of reading; but the books to which she had access, operating upon a mind eager for knowledge, and upon a taste peculiarly sensible of the beautiful and the elegant, had impressed all their excellences upon her understanding. Theodore had received from nature many of the qualities of genius, and from education, all that it could bestow; to these were added a noble independency of spirit, a feeling heart, and manners which partook of a happy mixture of dignity and sweetness.

In the evening, one of the officers who, upon the representation of the sergeant, was sent by the person employed to prosecute military criminals, arrived at the village; and entering the apartment of Theodore, from which Adeline immediately withdrew, informed him with an air of infinite importance that he should set out on the following day for head-quarters. Theodore answered that he was not able to bear the journey, and referred him to his physician: but the officer replied that he should take no such trouble, it being certain that the physician might be instructed what to say, and that he should begin his journey on the morrow. Here has been delay enough, said he, already; and you will have sufficient business on your hands when you reach head-quarters; for the sergeant whom you have severely wounded intends to appear against you; and this, with the offence you have committed by deserting your post— —

Theodore's eyes flashed fire: Deserting! said he, rising from his seat and darting a look of menace at his accuser—who dares to brand me with the name of deserter? But instantly recollecting how much his conduct had appeared to justify the accusation, he endeavoured to stifle his emotions; and with a firm voice and composed manner said, that when he reached head-quarters he should be ready to answer whatever might be brought against him, but that till then he should be silent. The boldness of the officer was repressed by the spirit and dignity with which Theodore spoke these words, and muttering a reply that was scarcely audible, he left the room.

Theodore sat musing on the danger of his situation: he knew that he had much to apprehend from the peculiar circumstances attending his abrupt departure from his regiment, it having been stationed in a garrison town upon the Spanish frontiers, where the discipline was very severe, and from the power of his colonel, the Marquis de Montalt, whom pride and disappointment would now rouse to vengeance, and probably render indefatigable in the accomplishment of his destruction. But his thoughts soon fled from his own danger to that of Adeline; and in the consideration of this, all his fortitude forsook him: he could not support the idea of leaving her exposed to the evils he foreboded, nor, indeed, of a separation so sudden as that which now threatened him: and when she again entered the room, he renewed his solicitations for a speedy marriage, with all the arguments that tenderness and ingenuity could suggest.

Adeline, when she learned that he was to depart on the morrow, felt as if bereaved of her last comfort: all the horrors of his situation arose to her mind, and she turned from him in unutterable anguish. Considering her silence as a favourable presage, he repeated his entreaties that she would consent to be his, and thus give him a surety that their separation should not be eternal. Adeline sighed deeply to these words: And who can know that our separation will not be eternal, said she, even if I could consent to the marriage you propose? But while you hear my determination, forbear to accuse me of indifference; for indifference towards you would indeed be a crime, after the services you have rendered me.

And is a cold sentiment of gratitude all that I must expect from you? said Theodore. I know that you are going to distress me with a proof of your indifference, which you mistake for the suggestions of prudence; and that I shall be compelled to look

176

without reluctance upon the evils that may shortly await me. Ah, Adeline! if you mean to reject this, perhaps the last proposal which I can ever make to you, cease at least to deceive yourself with an idea that you love me — that delirium is fading even from my mind.

Can you then so soon forget our conversation of this morning? replied Adeline; and can you think so lightly of me as to believe I would profess a regard which I do not feel? If indeed you can believe this, I shall do well to forget that I ever made such an acknowledgement, and you that you heard it.

Forgive me, Adeline, forgive the doubts and inconsistencies I have betrayed: let the anxieties of love, and the emergency of my circumstances, plead for me. Adeline; smiling faintly through her tears, held out her hand, which he seized and pressed to his lips. Yet do not drive me to despair by a rejection of my suit, continued Theodore; think what I must suffer to leave you here destitute of friends and protection.

I am thinking how I may avoid a situation so deplorable, said Adeline. They say there is a convent which receives boarders, within a few miles, and thither I wish to go.

A convent! rejoined Theodore; would you go to a convent? Do you know the persecutions you would be liable to; and that if the Marquis should discover you, there is little probability the superior would resist his authority, or at least his bribes?

All this I have considered, said Adeline, and am prepared to encounter it, rather than enter into an engagement which at this time can be productive only of misery to us both.

Ah, Adeline! could you think thus, if you truly loved? I see myself about to be separated, and that perhaps for ever, from the object of my tenderest affections; and I cannot but express all the anguish I feel — I cannot forbear to repeat every argument that may afford even the slightest possibility of altering your determination. But you, Adeline, you look with complacency upon a circumstance which tortures me with despair.

Adeline, who had long strove to support her spirits in his presence, while she adhered to a resolution which reason suggested, but which the pleadings of her heart powerfully opposed, was unable longer to command her distress, and burst into tears. Theodore was in the same moment convinced of his error, and shocked at the grief he had occasioned. He drew his chair towards her, and taking her hand, again entreated her pardon, and endeavoured in the tenderest accents to soothe and comfort her. — What a wretch was I to cause you this distress, by questioning that regard with which I can no longer doubt you honour me! Forgive me, Adeline; say but you forgive me, and whatever may be the pain of this separation, I will no longer oppose it.

You have given me some pain, said Adeline, but you have not offended me. — She then mentioned some further particulars concerning the convent. Theodore endeavoured to conceal the distress which the approaching separation occasioned him, and to consult with her on these plans with composure. His judgment by degrees prevailed over his passions, and he now perceived that the plan she suggested, would afford her best chance of security. He considered, what in the first agitation of his mind had escaped him, that he might be condemned upon the charges brought against him, and that his death, should they have been married, would not only deprive her of her protector, but leave her more immediately exposed to the designs of the Marquis, who would doubtless attend his trial. Astonished that he had not noticed this before, and shocked at the unwariness by which he might have betrayed her into so dangerous a situation, he became at once reconciled to the idea of leaving her in a convent. He could have wished to place her in the asylum of his own family: but the circumstances under which she must be introduced were so awkward and painful, and above all, the distance at which they resided would render a journey so highly dangerous for her, that he forbore to propose it. He entreated only that she would allow him to write to her; but recollecting that his letters might be a means of betraying the place of her residence to the Marquis, he checked himself: I must deny myself even this melancholy pleasure, said he, lest my letters should discover your abode; yet hew shall I be able to endure the impatience and uncertainty to which prudence condemns me! If you are in danger, I shall be ignorant of it; though, indeed, did I know it, said he with a look of despair, I could not fly to save you. O exquisite misery! 'tis now only I perceive all the horrors of confinement — 'tis now only that I understand all the value of liberty.

His utterance was interrupted by the violent agitation of his mind; he arose from his chair, and walked with quick paces about the room. Adeline sat, overcome by the description which Theodore had given of his approaching situation, and by the consideration that she might remain in the most terrible suspense concerning his fate. She saw him in a prison — pale — emaciated, and in chains: — she saw all the vengeance of the Marquis descending upon him; and this for his noble exertions in her cause. Theodore, alarmed by the placid despair expressed in her countenance, threw himself into a chair by hers, and taking her hand, attempted to speak comfort to her; but the words faltered on his lips, and he could only bathe her hand with tears.

This mournful silence was interrupted by the arrival of the carriage at the inn, and Theodore, arising, went to the window that opened into the yard. The darkness of the night prevented his distinguishing the objects without, but a light now brought from the house showed him a carriage and four, attended by several servants. Presently he saw a gentleman, wrapped up in a roquelaure, alight and enter the inn, and in the next moment he heard the voice of the Marquis.

He had flown to support Adeline, who was sinking with terror, when the door opened, and the Marquis followed by the officers and several servants entered. Fury flashed from his eyes as they glanced upon Theodore, who hung over Adeline with a look of fearful solicitude—Seize that traitor, said he, turning to the officers; why have you suffered him to remain here so long?

I am no traitor, said Theodore with a firm voice and the dignity of conscious worth, but a defender of innocence, of one whom the treacherous Marquis de Montalt would destroy.

Obey your orders, said the Marquis to the officers. Adeline shrieked, held faster by Theodore's arm, and entreated the men not to part them. Force only can effect it, said Theodore, as he looked round for some instrument of defence; but he could see none, and in the same moment they surrounded and seized him. Dread every thing from my vengeance, said the Marquis to Theodore, as he caught the hand of Adeline, who had lost all power of resistance and was scarcely sensible of what passed; dread every thing from my vengeance; you know you have deserved it.

I defy your vengeance, cried Theodore, and dread only the pangs of conscience, which your power cannot inflict upon me, though your vices condemn you to its tortures.

Take him instantly from the room, and see that he is strongly fettered, said the Marquis; he shall soon know what a criminal who adds insolence to guilt may suffer.—Theodore exclaiming, Oh, Adeline! farewell! was now forced out of the room; while Adeline, whose torpid senses were roused by his voice and his last looks, fell at the feet of the Marquis, and with tears of agony implored compassion for Theodore: but her pleadings for his rival served only to irritate the pride and exasperate the hatred of the Marquis. He denounced vengeance on his head, and imprecations too dreadful for the spirits of Adeline, whom he compelled to rise; and then endeavouring to stifle the emotions of rage, which the presence of Theodore had excited, he began to address her with his usual expressions of admiration.

The wretched Adeline, who, regardless of what he said, still endeavoured to plead for her unhappy lover, was at length alarmed by the returning rage which the countenance of the Marquis expressed; and exerting all her remaining strength, she sprung from his grasp towards the door of the room: but he seized her hand before she could reach it, and regardless of her shrieks, bringing her back to her chair, was going to speak, when voices were heard in the passage, and immediately the landlord and his wife, whom Adeline's cries had alarmed, entered the apartment. The Marquis, turning furiously at them, demanded what they wanted; but not waiting for an answer, he bade them attend him, and quitting the room, she heard the door locked upon her.

Adeline now ran to the windows, which were unfastened and opened into the inn-yard. All was dark and silent. She called aloud for help, but no person appeared; and the windows were so high that it was impossible to escape unassisted. She walked about the room in an agony of terror and distress, now stooping to listen, and fancying she heard voices disputing below and now quickening her steps, as suspense increased the agitation of her mind.

She had continued in this state for near half an hour, when she suddenly heard a violent noise in the lower part of the house, which increased till all was uproar and confusion. People passed quickly through the passages, and doors were frequently opened and shut. She called, but received no answer. It immediately occurred to her that Theodore, having heard her screams, had attempted to come to her assistance, and that the bustle had been occasioned by the opposition of the officers. Knowing their fierceness and cruelty, she was seized with dreadful apprehensions for the life of Theodore.

A confused uproar of voices now sounded from below, and the screams of women convinced her there was fighting; she even thought she heard the clashing of swords: the image of Theodore dying by the hands of the Marquis now rose to her imagination, and the terrors of suspense became almost insupportable. She made a desperate effort to force the door, and again called for help; but her trembling hands were powerless, and every person in the house seemed to be too much engaged even to hear her. A loud shriek now pierced her ears, and amidst the tumult that followed she clearly distinguished deep groans. This confirmation of her fears deprived her of all her remaining spirits, and growing faint, she sunk almost lifeless into a chair near the door. The uproar gradually subsided till all was still, but nobody returned to her. Soon after she heard voices in the yard, but she had no power to walk across the room, even to ask the questions she wished, yet feared, to have answered.

About a quarter of an hour elapsed, when the door was unlocked, and the hostess appeared with a countenance as pale as death. For God's sake, said Adeline, tell me what has happened? Is he wounded? Is he killed?

He is not dead, Ma'mselle, but—

He is dying then?—tell me where he is—let me go.

Stop, Ma'mselle, cried the hostess, you are to stay here, I only want the hartshorn out of that cupboard there. Adeline tried to escape by the door; but the hostess, pushing her aside, locked it, and went down stairs.

Adeline's distress now entirely overcame her, and she sat motionless and scarcely conscious that she existed, till roused by a sound of footsteps near the door, which was again opened, and three men, whom she knew to be the Marquis's servants entered. She had sufficient recollection to repeat the questions she had asked the landlady; but they answered only that she must come with them, and that a chaise was waiting for her at the door. Still she urged her questions. Tell me if he lives, cried she.—Yes, Ma'mselle, he is alive, but he is terribly wounded, and the surgeon is just come to him. As they spoke they hurried her along the passage: and without noticing her entreaties and supplications to know whither she was going, they had reached the foot of the stairs, when her cries brought several people to the door. To these the hostess related that the lady was the wife of a gentleman just arrived, who had overtaken her in her flight with a gallant; an account which the Marquis's servants corroborated. 'Tis the gentleman who has just fought the duel, added the hostess, and it was on her account.

Adeline, partly disdaining to take any notice of this artful story, and partly from her desire to know the particulars of what had happened, contented herself with repeating her inquiries; to which one of the spectators at last replied, that the gentleman was desperately wounded. The Marquis's people would now have hurried her into the chaise, but she sunk lifeless in their arms; and her condition so interested the humanity of the spectators, that, notwithstanding their belief of what had been said, they opposed the effort made to carry her, senseless as she was, into the carriage.

She was at length taken into a room, and by proper applications restored to her senses. There she so earnestly besought an explanation of what had happened, that the hostess acquainted her with some particulars of the late rencounter. When the gentleman that was ill heard your screams, Madam, said she, he became quite outrageous, as they tell me, and nothing could pacify him. The Marquis, for they say he is a Marquis, but you know best, was then in the room with my husband and I, and when he heard the uproar, he went down to see what was the matter; and when he came into the room where the Captain was, he found him struggling with the sergeant. Then the Captain was more outrageous than ever; and notwithstanding he had one leg chained, and no sword, he contrived to get the sergeant's cutlass out of the scabbard, and immediately flew at the Marquis, and wounded him desperately; upon which he was secured. — It is the Marquis then who is wounded, said Adeline; the other gentleman is not hurt?

No, not he, replied the hostess; but he will smart for it by and by, for the Marquis swears he will do for him. Adeline for a moment forgot all her misfortunes and all her danger in thankfulness for the immediate escape of Theodore; and she was proceeding to make some further inquiries concerning him, when the Marquis's servants entered the room, and declared they could wait no longer. Adeline, now awakened to a sense of the evils with which she was threatened, endeavoured to win the pity of the hostess, who however was, or affected to be, convinced of the truth of the Marquis's story, and therefore insensible to all she could urge. Again she addressed his servants, but in vain; they would neither suffer her to remain longer at the inn, nor inform her whither she was going; but in the presence of several persons, already prejudiced by the injurious assertions of the hostess, Adeline was hurried into the chaise, and her conductors mounting their horses, the whole party was very soon beyond the village.

Thus ended Adeline's share of an adventure, begun with a prospect not only of security, but of happiness — an adventure which had attached her more closely to Theodore, and shown him to be more worthy of her love; but which, at the same time, had distressed her by new disappointment, produced the imprisonment of her generous and now adored lover, and delivered both himself and her into the power of a rival irritated by delay, contempt, and opposition.

CHAPTER XIII

Nor sea, nor shade, nor shield, nor rock, nor cave,

Nor silent deserts, nor the sullen grave,

Where flame-eyed fury means to frown — can save.

The surgeon of the place, having examined the Marquis's wound, gave him an immediate opinion upon it, and ordered that he should be put to bed: but the Marquis, ill as he was, had scarcely any other apprehension than that of losing Adeline, and declared he should be able to begin his journey in a few hours. With this intention he had begun to give orders for keeping horses in readiness, when the surgeon persisting most seriously, and even passionately to exclaim that his life would be the sacrifice of his rashness, he was carried to a bedchamber, where his valet alone was permitted to attend him.

This man, the convenient confident of all his intrigues, had been the chief instrument in assisting his designs concerning Adeline, and was indeed the very person who had brought her to the Marquis's villa on the borders of the forest. To him the Marquis gave his further directions concerning her: and, foreseeing the inconvenience as well as the danger of detaining her at the inn, he had ordered him, with several other servants, to carry her away immediately in a hired carriage. The valet having gone to execute his orders, the Marquis was left to his own reflections, and to the violence of contending passions.

The reproaches and continued opposition of Theodore, the favoured lover of Adeline, exasperated his pride and roused all his malice. He could not for a moment consider this opposition, which was in some respects successful, without feeling an excess of indignation and inveteracy, such as the prospect of a speedy revenge could alone enable him to support.

When he had discovered Adeline's escape from the villa, his surprise at first equalled his disappointment; and, after exhausting the paroxysms of his rage upon his domestics, he dispatched them all different ways in pursuit of her, going himself to the abbey, in the faint hope that, destitute as she was of other succour, she might have fled thither. La Motte, however, being as much surprised as himself, and as ignorant of the route which Adeline had taken, he returned to the villa impatient of intelligence, and found some of his servants arrived, without any news of Adeline, and those who came afterwards were as successless as the first.

A few days after, a letter from the lieutenant-colonel of the regiment informed him, that Theodore had quitted his company, and had been for some time absent, nobody knew where. This information, confirming a suspicion which had frequently occurred to him, that Theodore had been by some means or other instrumental in the escape of Adeline, all his other passions became for a time subservient to his revenge, and he gave orders for the immediate pursuit and apprehension of Theodore: but Theodore, in the mean time, had been overtaken and secured.

It was in consequence of having formerly observed the growing partiality between him and Adeline, and of intelligence received from La Motte, who had noticed their interview in the forest, that the Marquis had resolved to remove a rival so dangerous to his love, and so likely to be informed of his designs. He had therefore told Theodore, in a manner as plausible as he could, that it would be necessary for him to join the regiment; a notice which affected him only as it related to Adeline, and which seemed the less extraordinary, as he had already been at the villa a much longer time than was usual with the officers invited by the Marquis. Theodore, indeed, very well knew the character of the Marquis, and had accepted his invitation rather from an unwillingness to show any disrespect to his colonel by a refusal, than from a sanguine expectation of pleasure.

From the men who had apprehended Theodore, the Marquis received the information, which had enabled him to pursue and recover Adeline; but though he had now effected this, he was internally a prey to the corrosive effects of disappointed passion and exasperated pride. The anguish of his wound was almost forgotten in that of his mind, and every pang he felt seemed to increase his thirst of revenge, and to recoil with new torture upon his heart. While he was in this state, he heard the voice of the innocent Adeline imploring protection; but her cries excited in him neither pity nor remorse: and when, soon after, the carriage drove away, and he was certain both that she was secured and Theodore was wretched, he seemed to feel some cessation of mental pain.

Theodore, indeed, did suffer all that a virtuous mind, labouring under oppression so severe, could feel; but he was at least free from those inveterate and malignant passions which tore the bosom of the Marquis, and which inflict upon the professor a punishment more severe than any they can prompt him to imagine for another. What indignation he might feel towards the Marquis, was at this time secondary to his anxiety for Adeline. His captivity was painful, as it prevented his seeking a just and honourable revenge; but it was dreadful, as it withheld him from attempting the rescue of her whom he loved more than life.

When he heard the wheels of the carriage that contained her drive off, he felt an agony of despair which almost overcame his reason. Even the stern hearts of the soldiers who attended him were not wholly insensible to his wretchedness, and by venturing to blame the conduct of the Marquis they endeavoured to console their prisoner. The physician, who was just arrived, entered the room during this paroxysm of his distress, and both feeling and expressing much concern at his condition, inquired with strong surprise why he had been thus precipitately removed to a room so very unfit for his reception?

Theodore explained to him the reason of this, of the distress he suffered, and of the chains by which he was disgraced; and perceiving the physician listened to him with attention and compassion, he became desirous of acquainting him with some further particulars, for which purpose he desired the soldiers to leave the room. The men, complying with his request, stationed themselves on the outside of the door.

He then related all the particulars of the late transaction, and of his connection with the Marquis. The physician attended to his narrative with deep concern, and his countenance frequently expressed strong agitation. When Theodore concluded, he remained for some time silent and lost in thought; at length, awaking from his reverie, he said, I fear your situation is desperate: the character of the Marquis is too well known to suffer him either to be loved or respected; from such a man you have nothing to hope, for he has scarcely any thing to fear: I wish it was in my power to serve you, but I see no possibility of it.

Alas! said Theodore, my situation is indeed desperate, and— for that suffering angel—deep sobs interrupted his voice, and the violence of his agitation would not allow him to proceed. The physician could only express the sympathy he felt for his distress, and entreat him to be more calm, when a servant entered the room from the Marquis, who desired to see the physician immediately. After some time, he said he would attend the Marquis; and having endeavoured to attain a degree of composure which he found it difficult to assume, he wrung the hand of Theodore and quitted the room, promising to return before he left the house.

He found the Marquis much agitated both in body and mind, and rather more apprehensive for the consequences of the wound than he had expected. His anxiety for Theodore now suggested a plan, by the execution of which he hoped he might be able to serve him. Having felt his patient's pulse, and asked some questions, he assumed a very serious look; when the Marquis, who watched every turn of his countenance, desired he would, without hesitation, speak his opinion.

I am sorry to alarm you, my Lord, but here is some reason for apprehension: how long is it since you received the wound.

Good God! there is danger then! cried the Marquis, adding some bitter execrations against Theodore. — There certainly is danger, replied the physician; a few hours may enable me to determine its degree.

A few hours, Sir! interrupted the Marquis; a few hours! The physician entreated him to be more calm. Confusion! cried the Marquis: a man in health may, with great composure, entreat a dying man to be calm. Theodore will be broke upon the wheel for it, however.

You mistake me, Sir, said the physician; if I believed you a dying man, or, indeed, very near death, I should not have spoken as I did. But it is of consequence I should know how long the wound has been inflicted. — The Marquis's terror now began to subside, and he gave a circumstantial account of the affray with Theodore, representing that he had been basely used in an affair where his own conduct had been perfectly just and humane. The physician heard this relation with great coolness, and when it concluded without making any comment upon it, told the Marquis he would prescribe a medicine which he wished him to take immediately.

The Marquis again alarmed by the gravity of his manner, entreated he would declare most seriously, whether he thought him in immediate danger. The physician hesitated, and the anxiety of the Marquis increased: It is of consequence, said he, that I should know my exact situation. The physician then said, that if he had any worldly affairs to settle, it would be as well to attend to them, for that it was impossible to say what might be the event.

He then turned the discourse, and said he had just been with the young officer under arrest, who, he hoped, would not be removed at present, as such a procedure must endanger his life. The Marquis uttered a dreadful oath, and, cursing Theodore for having brought him to his present condition, said he should depart with the guard that very night. Against the cruelty of this sentence the physician ventured to expostulate; and endeavouring to awaken the Marquis to a sense of humanity, pleaded earnestly for Theodore. But these entreaties and arguments seemed, by displaying to the Marquis a part of his own character, to rouse his resentment and rekindle all the violence of his passions.

The physician at length withdrew in despondency, after promising, at the Marquis's request, not to leave the inn. He had hoped, by aggravating his danger, to obtain some advantages both for Adeline and Theodore; but the plan had quite a contrary effect: for the apprehension of death, so dreadful to the guilty mind of the Marquis, instead of awakening penitence, increased his desire of vengeance against the man who had brought him to such a situation. He determined to have Adeline conveyed where Theodore, should he by any accident escape, could never obtain her; and thus to secure to himself at least some means of revenge. He knew, however, that when Theodore was once safely conveyed to his regiment, his destruction was certain; for should he even be acquitted of the intention of deserting, he would be condemned for having assaulted his superior officer.

The physician returned to the room where Theodore was confined. The violence of his distress was now subsided into a stern despair more dreadful than the vehemence which had lately possessed him. The guard, in compliance with his request, having left the room, the physician repeated to him some part of his conversation with the Marquis. Theodore, after expressing his thanks, said he had nothing more to hope. For himself he felt little; it was for his family and Adeline he suffered. He inquired what route she had taken; and though he had no prospect of deriving advantage from the information, desired the physician to assist him in obtaining it: but the landlord and his wife either were, or affected to be, ignorant of the matter, and it was in vain to apply to any other person.

The sergeant now entered with orders from the Marquis for the immediate departure of Theodore, who heard the message with composure, though the physician could not help expressing his indignation at this precipitate removal, and his dread of the consequences that might attend it. Theodore had scarcely time to declare his gratitude for the kindness of this valuable friend, before the soldiers entered the room to conduct him to the carriage in waiting. As he bade him farewell, Theodore slipped his purse into his hand, and turning abruptly away, told the soldiers to lead on: but the physician stopped him, and refused the present with such serious warmth that he was compelled to resume it. He wrung the hand of his new friend, and being unable to speak, hurried away. The whole party immediately set off; and the unhappy Theodore was left to the remembrance of his past hopes and sufferings, to his anxiety for the fate of Adeline, the contemplation of his present wretchedness, and the apprehension of what might be reserved for him in future. For himself, indeed, he saw nothing but destruction, and was only relieved from total despair by a feeble hope that she whom he loved better than himself might one time enjoy that happiness of which he did not venture to look for a participation.

CHAPTER XIV

Have you the heart? When your head did but ache,

I knit my handkerchief about your brows,

And with my hand at midnight held your head;

And, like the watchful minutes to the hour.

Still and anon cheer'd up the heavy time.

KING JOHN.

If the midnight bell

Did, with his iron tongue and brazen mouth,

Sound one unto the drowsy race of night;

If this same were a church-yard where we stand,

And thou possessed with a thousand wrongs;

Or if that surly spirit Melancholy

Had baked thy blood and made it heavy, thick;

Then, in despite of broad-eyed watchful day,

I would into thy bosom pour my thoughts.

KING JOHN.

Meanwhile the persecuted Adeline continued to travel, with little interruption, all night. Her mind suffered such a tumult of grief, regret, despair, and terror, that she could not be said to think. The Marquis's valet, who had placed himself in the chaise with her, at first seemed inclined to talk; but her inattention soon silenced him, and left her to the indulgence of her own misery.

They seemed to travel through obscure lanes and by-ways, along which the carriage drove as furiously as the darkness would permit. When the dawn appeared, she perceived herself on the borders of a forest, and renewed her entreaties to know whither she was going. The man replied he had no orders to tell, but she would soon see. Adeline, who had hitherto supposed they were carrying her to the villa, now began to doubt it; and as every place appeared less terrible to her imagination than that, her despair began to abate, and she thought only of the devoted Theodore, whom she knew to be the victim of malice and revenge.

They now entered upon the forest, and it occurred to her that she was going to the abbey; for though she had no remembrance of the scenery through which she passed, it was not the less probable that this was the forest of Fontanville, whose boundaries were by much too extensive to have come within the circle of her former walks. This conjecture revived a terror little inferior to that occasioned by the idea of going to the villa; for at the abbey she would be equally in the power of the Marquis, and also in that of her cruel enemy La Motte. Her mind revolted at the picture her fancy drew; and as the carriage moved under the shades, she threw from the window a look of eager inquiry for some object which might confirm or destroy her present surmise: she did not long look, before an opening in the forest showed her the distant towers of the abbey — I am, indeed, lost then, said she, bursting into tears.

They were soon at the foot of the lawn, and Peter was seen running to open the gate, at which the carriage stopped. When he saw Adeline, he looked surprised and made an effort to speak; but the chaise now drove up to the abbey, where, at the door of the hall, La Motte himself appeared. As he advanced to take her from the carriage, an universal trembling seized her; it was with the utmost difficulty she supported herself, and for some moments she neither observed his countenance nor heard his voice. He offered his arm to assist her into the abbey, which she at first refused, but having tottered a few paces was obliged to accept; they then entered the vaulted room, where, sinking into a chair, a flood of tears came to her relief. La Motte did not interrupt the silence, which continued for some time, but paced the room in seeming agitation. When Adeline was sufficiently recovered to notice external objects, she observed his countenance, and there read the tumult of his soul, while he was struggling to assume a firmness which his better feelings opposed.

La Motte now took her hand, and would have led her from the room; but she stopped, and with a kind of desperate courage made an effort to engage him to pity and to save her. He interrupted her; It is not in my power, said he in a voice of emotion; I am not master of myself or my conduct; inquire no further — it is sufficient for you to know that I pity you; more I cannot do. He gave her no time to reply, but taking her hand led her to the stairs of the tower, and from thence to the chamber she had formerly occupied.

Here you must remain for the present, said he, in a confinement which is, perhaps, almost as involuntary on my part as it can be on yours. I am willing to render it as easy as possible, and have therefore ordered some books to be brought you.

Adeline made an effort to speak; but he hurried from the room, seemingly ashamed of the part he had undertaken, and unwilling to trust himself with her tears. She heard the door of the chamber locked; and then looking towards the windows, perceived they were secured: the door that led to the other apartments was also fastened. Such preparation for security shocked her; and hopeless as she had long believed herself, she now perceived her mind sink deeper in despair. When the tears she shed had somewhat relieved her, and her thoughts could turn from the subjects of her immediate concern, she was thankful for the total seclusion allotted her, since it would spare her the pain she must feel in the presence of Monsieur and Madame La Motte, and allow the unrestrained indulgence of her own sorrow and reflection; reflection which, however distressing, was preferable to the agony inflicted on the mind when, agitated by care and fear, it is obliged to assume an appearance of tranquillity.

In about a quarter of an hour her chamber door was unlocked, and Annette appeared with refreshments and books: she expressed satisfaction at seeing Adeline again, but seemed fearful of speaking, knowing, probably, that it was contrary to the orders of La Motte, who, she said, was waiting at the bottom of the stairs. When Annette was gone, Adeline took some refreshment, which was indeed necessary, for she had tasted nothing since she left the inn. She was pleased, but not surprised, that Madame La Motte did not appear, who, it was evident, shunned her from a consciousness of her own ungenerous conduct, — a consciousness which offered some presumption that she was still not wholly unfriendly to her. She reflected upon the words of La Motte, — I am not master of myself or my conduct, — and though they afforded her no hope, she derived some comfort, poor as it was, from the belief that he pitied her. After some time spent in miserable reflection and various conjectures, her long-agitated spirits seemed to demand repose, and she lay down to sleep.

Adeline slept quietly for several hours, and awoke with a mind refreshed and tranquillized. To prolong this temporary peace, and to prevent therefore the intrusion of her own thoughts, she examined the books La Motte had sent her: among these she found some that in happier times had elevated her mind and interested her heart: their effect was now weakened; they were still, however, able to soften for a time the sense of her misfortunes.

But this Lethean medicine to a wounded mind was but a temporary blessing; the entrance of La Motte dissolved the illusions of the page, and awakened her to a sense of her own situation. He came with food, and having placed it on the table left the room without speaking. Again she endeavoured to read, but his appearance had broken the enchantment; bitter reflection returned to her mind, and brought with it the image of Theodore—of Theodore lost to her for ever!

La Motte meanwhile experienced all the terrors that could be inflicted by a conscience not wholly hardened to guilt. He had been led on by passion to dissipation, and from dissipation to vice; but having once touched the borders of infamy, the progressive steps followed each other fast, and he now saw himself the pander of a villain, and the betrayer of an innocent girl whom every plea of justice and humanity called upon him to protect. He contemplated his picture—he shrunk from it, but he could change its deformity only by an effort too nobly daring for a mind already effeminated by vice. He viewed the dangerous labyrinth into which he was led, and perceived, as if for the first time, the progression of his guilt: from this labyrinth he weakly imagined further guilt could alone extricate him. Instead of employing his mind upon the means of saving Adeline from destruction, and himself from being instrumental to it, he endeavoured only to lull the pangs of conscience, and to persuade himself into a belief that he must proceed in the course he had begun. He knew himself to be in the power of the Marquis, and he dreaded that power more than the sure though distant punishment that awaits upon guilt. The honour of Adeline, and the quiet of his own conscience, he consented to barter for a few years of existence.

He was ignorant of the present illness of the Marquis, or he would have perceived that there was a chance of escaping the threatened punishment at a price less enormous than infamy, and he would perhaps have endeavoured to save Adeline and himself by flight. But the Marquis, foreseeing the possibility of this, had ordered his servants carefully to conceal the circumstance which detained him, and to acquaint La Motte that he should be at the abbey in a few days, at the same time directing his valet to await him there. Adeline, as he expected, had neither inclination nor opportunity to mention it; and thus La Motte remained ignorant of the circumstance which might have preserved him from further guilt and Adeline from misery.

Most unwillingly had La Motte made his wife acquainted with the action which had made him absolutely dependent upon the will of the Marquis; but the perturbation of his mind partly betrayed him: frequently in his sleep he muttered incoherent sentences, and frequently would start from his slumber, and call in passionate exclamation upon Adeline. These instances of a disturbed mind had alarmed and terrified Madame La Motte, who watched while he slept, and soon gathered from his words a confused idea of the Marquis's designs.

She hinted her suspicions to La Motte, who reproved her for having entertained them; but his manner, instead of repressing, increased her fears for Adeline; fears, which the conduct of the Marquis soon confirmed. On the night that he slept at the abbey, it had occurred to her that whatever scheme was in agitation it would now most probably be discussed; and anxiety for Adeline made her stoop to a meanness which, in other circumstances, would have been despicable. She quitted her room, and concealing herself in an apartment adjoining that in which she had left the Marquis and her husband, listened to their discourse. It turned upon the subject she had expected, and disclosed to her the full extent of their designs. Terrified for Adeline, and shocked at the guilty weakness of La Motte, she was for some time incapable of thinking, or determining how to proceed. She knew her husband to be under great obligation to the Marquis, whose territory thus afforded him a shelter from the world, and that it was in the power of the former to betray him into the hands of his enemies. She believed also that the Marquis would do this, if provoked: yet she thought, upon such an occasion, La Motte might find some way of appeasing the Marquis without subjecting himself to dishonour. After some further reflection, her mind became more composed, and she returned to her chamber, where La Motte soon followed. Her spirits, however, were not now in a state to encounter either his displeasure or his opposition, which she had too much reason to expect whenever she should mention the subject of her concern, and she therefore resolved not to notice it till the morrow.

On the morrow she told La Motte all he had uttered in his dreams; and mentioned other circumstances, which convinced him it was in vain any longer to deny the truth of her apprehensions. His wife then represented to him how possible it was to avoid the infamy into which he was about to plunge, by quitting the territories of the Marquis; and pleaded so warmly for Adeline, that La Motte in sullen silence appeared to meditate upon the plan. His thoughts were however very differently engaged. He was conscious of having deserved from the Marquis a dreadful punishment, and knew that if he exasperated him by refusing to acquiesce with his wishes, he had little to expect from flight, for the eye of justice and revenge would pursue him with indefatigable research.

La Motte meditated how to break this to his wife, for he perceived that there was no other method of counteracting her virtuous compassion for Adeline, and the dangerous consequences to be expected from it, than by opposing it with terror for his safety; and this could be done only by showing her the full extent of the evils that must attend the resentment of the Marquis. Vice had not yet so entirely darkened his conscience, but that the blush of shame stained his cheek, and his tongue faltered when he would have told his guilt. At length, finding it impossible to mention particulars, he told her that on account of an affair which no entreaties should ever induce him to explain, his life was in the power of the Marquis. You see the alternative, said he, take your choice of evils; and, if you can, tell Adeline of her danger, and sacrifice my life to save her from a situation which many would be ambitious to obtain. — Madame La Motte, condemned to the horrible alternative of permitting the seduction of innocence, or of dooming her husband to destruction, suffered a distraction of thought which defied all control. Perceiving, however, that an opposition to the designs of the Marquis would ruin La Motte and avail Adeline little, she determined to yield and endure in silence.

At the time when Adeline was planning her escape from the abbey, the significant looks of Peter had led La Motte to suspect the truth and to observe them more closely. He had seen them separate in the hall with apparent confusion, and had afterwards observed them conversing together in the cloisters. Circumstances so unusual left him not a doubt that Adeline had discovered her danger, and was concerting with Peter some means of escape. Affecting, therefore, to be informed of the whole affair, he charged Peter with treachery towards himself, and threatened him with the vengeance of the Marquis if he did not disclose all he knew. The menace intimidated Peter, and supposing that all chance of assisting Adeline was gone, he made a circumstantial confession, and promised to forbear acquainting Adeline with the discovery of the scheme. In this promise he was seconded by inclination, for he feared to meet the displeasure which Adeline, believing he had betrayed her, might express.

On the evening of the day on which Adeline's intended escape was discovered, the Marquis designed to come to the abbey, and it had been agreed that he should then take Adeline to his villa. La Motte had immediately perceived the advantage of permitting Adeline to repair, in the belief of being undiscovered, to the tomb. It would prevent much disturbance and opposition, and spare himself the pain he must feel in her presence, when she should know that he had betrayed her. A servant of the Marquis might go at the appointed hour to the tomb, and wrapt in the disguise of night might take her quietly thence in the character of Peter. Thus, without resistance she would be carried to the villa, nor discover her mistake till it was too late to prevent its consequence.

When the Marquis did arrive, La Motte, who was not so much intoxicated by the wine he had drunk as to forget his prudence, informed him of what had happened and what he had planned; and the Marquis approving it, his servant was made acquainted with the signal, which afterwards betrayed Adeline to his power.

A deep consciousness of the unworthy neutrality she had observed in Adeline's concerns, made Madame La Motte anxiously avoid seeing her now that she was again in the abbey. Adeline understood this conduct; and she rejoiced that she was spared the anguish of meeting her as an enemy, whom she had once considered as a friend. Several days now passed in solitude, in miserable retrospection, and dreadful expectation. The perilous situation of Theodore was almost the constant subject of her thoughts. Often did she breathe an agonizing wish for his safety, and often look round the sphere of possibility in search of hope: but hope had almost left the horizon of her prospect, and when it did appear, it sprung only from the death of the Marquis, whose vengeance threatened most certain destruction.

The Marquis, meanwhile, lay at the inn at Caux, in a state of very doubtful recovery. The physician and surgeon, neither of whom he would dismiss nor suffer to leave the village, proceeded upon contrary principles; and the good effect of what the one prescribed, was frequently counteracted by the injudicious treatment of the other. Humanity alone prevailed on the physician to continue his attendance. The malady of the Marquis was also heightened by the impatience of his temper, the terrors of death, and the irritation of his passions. One moment he believed himself dying, another he could scarcely be prevented from attempting to follow Adeline to the abbey. So various were the fluctuations of his mind, and so rapid the schemes that succeeded each other, that his passions were in a continual state of conflict. The physician attempted to persuade him that his recovery greatly depended upon tranquillity, and to prevail upon him to attempt at least some command of his feelings; but he was soon silenced in hopeless disgust by the impatient answers of the Marquis.

At length the servant who had carried off Adeline returned; and the Marquis having ordered him into his chamber, asked so many questions in a breath, that the man knew not which to answer. At length he pulled a folded paper from his pocket, which he said had been dropped in the chaise by Mademoiselle Adeline, and as he thought his Lordship would like to see it, he had taken care of it. The Marquis stretched forth his hand with eagerness, and received a note addressed to Theodore. On perceiving the superscription, the agitation of jealous rage for a moment overcame him, and he held it in his hand unable to open it.

He, however, broke the seal, and found it to be a note of inquiry, written by Adeline to Theodore during his illness, and which from some accident she had been prevented from sending him. The tender solicitude it expressed for his recovery stung the soul of the Marquis, and drew from him a comparison of her feelings on the illness of his rival and that of himself. She could be solicitous for his recovery, said he, but for mine she only dreads it. As if willing to prolong the pain this little billet had excited, he then read it again. Again he cursed his fate and execrated his rival. Giving himself up, as usual, to the transports of his passion, he was going to throw it from him, when his eyes caught the seal, and he looked earnestly at it: his anger seemed now to have subsided, he deposited the note carefully in his pocket-book, and was for some time lost in thought.

After many days of hopes and fears, the strength of his constitution overcame his illness, and he was well enough to write several letters, one of which he immediately sent off to prepare La Motte for his reception. The same policy which had prompted him to conceal his illness from La Motte, now urged him to say what he knew would not happen, that he should reach the abbey on the day after his servant. He repeated this injunction, that Adeline should be strictly guarded, and renewed his promises of reward for the future services of La Motte.

La Motte, to whom each succeeding day had brought new surprise and perplexity concerning the absence of the Marquis, received this notice with uneasiness; for he had begun to hope that the Marquis had altered his intentions concerning Adeline, being either engaged in some new adventure, or obliged to visit his estates in some distant province: he would have been willing thus to have got rid of an affair, which was to reflect so much dishonour on himself.

This hope was now vanished, and he directed Madame to prepare for the reception of the Marquis. Adeline passed these days in a state of suspense which was now cheered by hope and now darkened by despair. The delay, so much exceeding her expectation, seemed to prove that the illness of the Marquis was dangerous; and when she looked forward to the consequences of his recovery, she could not be sorry that it was so. So odious was the idea of him to her mind, that she would not suffer her lips to pronounce his name, nor make the inquiry of Annette, which was of such consequence to her peace.

It was about a week after the receipt of the Marquis's letter that Adeline one day saw from her window a party of horsemen enter the avenue, and knew them to be the Marquis and his attendants. She retired from the window, in a state of mind not to be described, and sinking into a chair, was for some time scarcely conscious of the objects around her. When she had recovered from the first terror which his appearance excited, she again tottered to the window; the party was not in sight, but she heard the trampling of horses, and knew that the Marquis had wound round to the great gate of the abbey. She addressed herself to Heaven for support and protection; and her mind being now somewhat composed, sat down to wait the event.

La Motte received the Marquis with expressions of surprise at his long absence; and the latter, merely saying he had been detained by illness, proceeded to inquire for Adeline. He was told she was in her chamber, from whence she might be summoned if he wished to see her. The Marquis hesitated, and at length excused himself, but desired she might be strictly watched. Perhaps, my Lord, said La Motte smiling, Adeline's obstinacy has been too powerful for your passion? you seem less interested concerning her than formerly.

O! by no means, replied the Marquis; she interests me if possible, more than ever; so much, indeed, that I cannot have her too closely guarded; and I therefore beg, La Motte, that you will suffer nobody to attend her but when you can observe them yourself. Is the room where she is confined sufficiently secure? La Motte assured him it was; but at the same time expressed his wish that she was removed to the villa. If by any means, said he, she should contrive to escape, I know what I must expect from your displeasure; and this reflection keeps my mind in continual anxiety.

This removal cannot be at present, said the Marquis; she is safer here, and you do wrong to disturb yourself with any apprehension of her escape, if her chamber is so secure as you represent it.

I can have no motive for deceiving you, my Lord, in this point.

I do not suspect you of any, said the Marquis; guard her carefully, and trust me she will not escape. I can rely upon my valet, and if you wish it he shall remain here. La Motte thought there could be no occasion for him, and it was agreed that the man should go home.

The Marquis, after remaining about half an hour in conversation with La Motte, left the abbey; and Adeline saw him depart with a mixture of surprise and thankfulness that almost overcame her. She had waited in momentary expectation of being summoned to appear, and had been endeavouring to arm herself with resolution to support his presence. She had listened to every voice that sounded from below; and at every step that crossed the passage her heart had palpitated with dread, lest it should be La Motte coming to lead her to the Marquis. This state of suffering had been prolonged almost beyond her power of enduring it, when she heard voices under her window, and rising, saw the Marquis ride away. After giving way to the joy and thankfulness that swelled her heart, she endeavoured to account for this circumstance, which, considering what had passed, was certainly very strange. It appeared, indeed, wholly inexplicable; and after much fruitless inquiry, she quitted the subject, endeavouring to persuade herself that it could only portend good.

The time of La Motte's usual visitation now drew near, and Adeline expected it in the trembling hope of hearing that the Marquis had ceased his persecution; but he was, as usual, sullen and silent, and it was not till he was about to quit the room that Adeline had the courage to inquire when the Marquis was expected again. La Motte, opening the door to depart, replied, on the following day; and Adeline, whom fear and delicacy embarrassed, saw she could obtain no intelligence of Theodore but by a direct question; she looked earnestly, as if she would have spoke, and he stopped; but she blushed and was still silent, till upon his again attempting to leave the room she faintly called him back.

I would ask, said she, after that unfortunate chevalier who has incurred the resentment of the Marquis, by endeavouring to serve me: Has the Marquis mentioned him?

He has, replied La Motte; and your indifference towards the Marquis is now fully explained.

Since I must feel resentment towards those who injure me, said Adeline, I may surely be allowed to be grateful towards those who serve me. Had the Marquis deserved my esteem, he would probably have possessed it.

Well, well, said La Motte, this young hero, who it seems has been brave enough to lift his arm against his Colonel, is taken care of, and I doubt not will soon be sensible of the value of his quixotism. — Indignation, grief, and fear, struggled in the bosom of Adeline; she disdained to give La Motte an opportunity of again pronouncing the name of Theodore; yet the uncertainty under which she laboured, urged her to inquire whether the Marquis had heard of him since he left Caux. Yes, said La Motte, he has been safely carried to his regiment, where he is confined till the Marquis can attend to appear against him.

Adeline had neither power nor inclination to inquire further; and La Motte quitting the chamber, she was left to the misery he had renewed. Though this information contained no new circumstance of misfortune, (for she now heard confirmed what she had always expected,) a weight of new sorrow seemed to fall upon her heart, and she perceived that she had unconsciously cherished a latent hope of Theodore's escape before he reached the place of his destination. All hope was now, however, gone; he was suffering the miseries of a prison, and the tortures of apprehension both for his own life and her safety. She pictured to herself the dark damp dungeon where he lay, loaded with chains and pale with sickness and grief; she heard him, in a voice that thrilled her heart, call upon her name, and raise his eyes to heaven in silent supplication: she saw the anguish of his countenance, the tears that fell slowly on his cheek; and remembering at the same time, the generous conduct that had brought him to this abyss of misery, and that it was for her sake he suffered, grief resolved itself into despair, her tears ceased to flow, and she sunk silently into a state of dreadful torpor.

On the morrow the Marquis arrived, and departed as before. Several days then elapsed, and he did not appear; till one evening, as La Motte and his wife were in their usual sitting-room, he entered, and conversed for some time upon general subjects, from which, however, he by degrees fell into a reverie, and after a pause of silence he rose and drew La Motte to the window. I would speak to you alone, said he, if you are at leisure; if not, another time will do. La Motte assuring him he was perfectly so, would have conducted him to another room, but the Marquis proposed a walk in the forest. They went out together; and when they had reached a solitary glade, where the spreading branches of the beech and oak deepened the shades of twilight and threw a solemn obscurity around, the Marquis turned to La Motte and addressed him:

Your condition, La Motte, is unhappy; this abbey is a melancholy residence for a man like you fond of society, and like you also qualified to adorn it. La Motte bowed. I wish it was in my power to restore you to the world, continued the Marquis; perhaps, if I knew the particulars of the affair which has driven you from it, I might perceive that my interest could effectually serve you:—I think I have heard you hint it was an affair of honour? La Motte was silent. I mean not to distress you, however; nor is it common curiosity that prompts this inquiry, but a sincere desire to befriend you. You have already informed me of some particulars of your misfortunes; I think the liberality of your temper led you into expenses which you afterwards endeavoured to retrieve by gaming?

Yes, my Lord, said La Motte, 'tis true that I dissipated the greater part of an affluent fortune in luxurious indulgencies, and that I afterwards took unworthy means to recover it: but I wish to be spared upon this subject. I would, if possible, lose the remembrance of a transaction which must for ever stain my character, and the rigorous effect of which, I fear, it is not in your power, my Lord, to soften.

You may be mistaken on this point, replied the Marquis; my interest at court is by no means inconsiderable. Fear not from me any severity of censure; I am not at all inclined to judge harshly of the faults of others: I well know how to allow for the emergency of circumstances; and I think La Motte, you have hitherto found me your friend.

I have, my Lord.

And when you recollect, that I have forgiven a certain transaction of late date— —

It is true, my Lord; and allow me to say, I have a just sense of your generosity. The transaction you allude to is by far the worst of my life; and what I have to relate cannot therefore lower me in your opinion. When I had dissipated the greatest part of my property in habits of voluptuous pleasure, I had recourse to gaming to supply the means of continuing them. A run of good luck for some time enabled me to do this; and encouraging my most sanguine expectations, I continued in the same career of success.

Soon after this, a sudden turn of fortune destroyed my hopes, and reduced me to the most desperate extremity. In one night my money was lowered to the sum of two hundred louis. These I resolved to stake also, and with them my life; for it was my resolution not to survive their loss. Never shall I forget the horrors of that moment on which hung my fate, nor the deadly anguish that seized my heart when my last stake was gone. I stood for some time in a state of stupefaction, till, roused to a sense of my misfortune, my passion made me pour forth execrations on my more fortunate rivals, and act all the phrensy of despair. During this paroxysm of madness, a gentleman, who had been a silent observer of all that passed, approached me. — You are unfortunate, Sir, said he. — I need not be informed of that. Sir, I replied.

You have perhaps been ill used? resumed he. — Yes, Sir, I am ruined, and therefore it may be said I am ill used.

Do you know the people you have played with?

No; but I have met them in the first circles.

Then I am probably mistaken, said he, and walked away. His last words roused me, and raised a hope that my money had not been fairly lost. Wishing for further information, I went in search of the gentleman, but he had left the rooms. I however stifled my transports, returned to the table where I had lost my money, placed myself behind the chair of one of the persons who had won it, and closely watched the game. For some time I saw nothing that could confirm my suspicions, but was at length convinced they were just.

When the game was ended I called one of my adversaries out of the room, and telling him what I had observed, threatened instantly to expose him if he did not restore my property. The man was for some time as positive as myself; and assuming the bully, threatened me with chastisement for my scandalous assertions. I was not, however, in a state of mind to be frightened; and his manner served only to exasperate my temper, already sufficiently inflamed by misfortune. After retorting his threats, I was about to return to the apartment we had left, and expose what had passed, when, with an insidious smile and a softened voice, he begged I would favour him with a few moments' attention, and allow him to speak with the gentleman his partner. To the latter part of his request I hesitated, but in the mean time the gentleman himself entered the room. His partner related to him, in few words, what had passed between us, and the terror that appeared in his countenance sufficiently declared his consciousness of guilt.

They then drew aside, and remained a few minutes in conversation together, after which they approached me with an offer, as they phrased it, of a compromise. I declared, however, against any thing of this kind, and swore nothing less than the whole sum I had lost should content me. — Is it not possible, Monsieur, that you may be offered something as advantageous as the whole? — I did not understand their meaning; but after they had continued for some time to give distant hints of the same sort, they proceeded to explain.

Perceiving their characters wholly in my power, they wished to secure my interest to their party, and therefore informing me that they belonged to an association of persons who lived upon the folly and inexperience of others, they offered me a share in their concern. My fortunes were desperate; and the proposal now made me would not only produce an immediate supply, but enable me to return to those scenes of dissipated pleasure to which passion had at first, and long habit afterwards, attached me. I closed with the offer, and thus sunk from dissipation into infamy.

La Motte paused, as if the recollection of these times filled him with remorse. The Marquis understood his feelings. You judge too rigorously of yourself, said he; there are few persons, let their appearance of honesty be what it may, who in such circumstances would have acted better than you have done. Had I been in your situation, I know not how I might have acted. That rigid virtue which shall condemn you, may dignify itself with the appellation of wisdom, but I wish not to possess it; let it still reside where it generally is to be found, in the cold bosoms of those who, wanting feeling to be men, dignify themselves with the title of philosophers. But pray proceed.

Our success was for some time unlimited, for we held the wheel of fortune, and trusted not to her caprice. Thoughtless and voluptuous by nature, my expenses fully kept pace with my income. An unlucky discovery of the practices of our party was at length made by a young nobleman, which obliged us to act for some time with the utmost circumspection. It would be tedious to relate the particulars, which made us at length so suspected, that the distant civility and cold reserve of our acquaintance rendered the frequenting public assemblies both painful and unprofitable. We turned our thoughts to other modes of obtaining money; and a swindling transaction, in which I engaged to a very large amount, soon compelled me to leave Paris. You know the rest my Lord.

La Motte was now silent, and the Marquis continued for some time musing. You perceive, my Lord, at length resumed La Motte, you perceive that my case is hopeless.

It is bad indeed, but not entirely hopeless. From my soul I pity you: yet, if you should return to the world, and incur the danger of prosecution, I think my interest with the minister might save you from any severe punishment. You seem, however, to have lost your relish for society, and perhaps do not wish to return to it.

Oh! my Lord can you doubt this? — But I am overcome with the excess of your goodness; would to heaven it were in my power to prove the gratitude it inspires!

Talk not of goodness, said the Marquis; I will not pretend that my desire of serving you is unalloyed by any degree of self-interest: I will not affect to be more than man, and trust me those who do are less. It is in your power to testify your gratitude, and bind me to your interest for ever. He paused. Name but the means, cried La Motte, — name but the means, and if they are within the compass of possibility they shall be executed. The Marquis was still silent. Do you doubt my sincerity, my Lord, that you are yet silent? Do you fear to repose a confidence in the man whom you have already loaded with obligation? who lives by your mercy, and almost by your means! The Marquis looked earnestly at him, but did not speak. I have not deserved this of you, my Lord; speak, I entreat you.

There are certain prejudices attached to the human mind, said the Marquis in a slow and solemn voice, which it requires all our wisdom to keep from interfering with our happiness; certain set notions, acquired in infancy, and cherished involuntarily by age, which grow up and assume a gloss so plausible, that few minds, in what is called a civilized country, can afterwards overcome them. Truth is often perverted by education. While the refined Europeans boast a standard of honour and a sublimity of virtue which often leads them from pleasure to misery, and from nature to error, the simple uninformed American follows the impulse of his heart, and obeys the inspiration of wisdom. The Marquis paused, and La Motte continued to listen in eager expectation.

Nature, uncontaminated by false refinement, resumed the Marquis, every where acts alike in the great occurrences of life. The Indian discovers his friend to be perfidious, and he kills him; the wild Asiatic does the same: the Turk, when ambition fires or revenge provokes, gratifies his passion at the expense of life, and does not call it murder. Even the polished Italian, distracted by jealousy, or tempted by a strong circumstance of advantage, draws his stiletto, and accomplishes his purpose. It is the first proof of a superior mind to liberate itself from prejudices of country or of education. You are silent, La Motte: are you not of my opinion?

I am attending, my Lord, to your reasoning.

There are, I repeat it, said the Marquis, people of minds so weak, as to shrink from acts they have been accustomed to hold wrong, however advantageous; they never suffer themselves to be guided by circumstances, but fix for life upon a certain standard, from which they will on no account depart. Self-preservation is the great law of nature; when a reptile hurts us, or an animal of prey threatens us, we think no further, but endeavour to annihilate it. When my life, or what may be essential to my life, requires the sacrifice of another, — or even if some passion, wholly unconquerable, requires it, — I should be a madman to hesitate. La Motte, I think I may confide in you — there are ways of doing certain things — you understand me? There are times, and circumstances, and opportunities — you comprehend my meaning?

Explain yourself, my Lord.

Kind services that — in short, there are services which excite all our gratitude, and which we can never think repaid. It is in your power to place me in such a situation.

Indeed! my Lord, name the means.

I have already named them. This abbey well suits the purpose; it is shut up from the eye of observation; any transaction may be concealed within its walls; the hour of midnight may witness the deed, and the morn shall not dawn to disclose it; these woods tell no tales. Ah! La Motte am I right in trusting this business with you? may I believe you are desirous of serving me, and of preserving yourself? The Marquis paused, and looked steadfastly at La Motte, whose countenance was almost concealed by the gloom of evening.

My Lord, you may trust me in any thing; explain yourself more fully.

What security will you give me of your faithfulness?

My life, my Lord; is it not already in your power? The Marquis hesitated, and then said, To-morrow about this time I shall return to the abbey, and will then explain my meaning, if indeed you shall not already have understood it. You in the mean time will consider your own powers of resolution, and be prepared either to adopt the purpose I shall suggest, or to declare you will not. La Motte made some confused reply. Farewell till to-morrow, said the Marquis; remember that freedom and affluence are now before you. He moved towards the abbey, and, mounting his horse, rode off with his attendants. La Motte walked slowly home, musing on the late conversation.

CHAPTER XV

Danger, whose limbs of giant mould

What mortal eye can fixed behold?

Who stalks his round, an hideous form!

Howling amidst the midnight storm! — —

And with him thousand phantoms join'd,

Who prompt to deeds accurst the mind!

On whom that rav'ning brood of Fate

Who lap the blood of Sorrow wait;

Who, Fear! this ghastly train can see,

And look not madly wild like thee!

COLLINS.

The Marquis was punctual to the hour. La Motte received him at the gate; but he declined entering, and said he preferred a walk in the forest. Thither, therefore, La Motte attended him. After some general conversation, Well, said the Marquis, have you considered what I said, and are you prepared to decide?

I have, my Lord, and will quickly decide, when you shall further explain yourself: till then I can form no resolution. The Marquis appeared dissatisfied, and was a moment silent. Is it then possible, he at length resumed, that you do not understand? This ignorance is surely affected. La Motte, I expect sincerity. Tell me, therefore, is it necessary I should say more?

It is, my Lord, said La Motte immediately. If you fear to confide in me freely, how can I fully accomplish your purpose?

Before I proceed further, said the Marquis, let me administer some oath which shall bind you to secrecy. But this is scarcely necessary; for, could I even doubt your word of honour, the remembrance of a certain transaction would point out to you the necessity of being as silent yourself as you must wish me to be. There was now a pause of silence, during which both the Marquis and La Motte betrayed some confusion. I think, La Motte, said he, I have given you sufficient proof that I can be grateful: the services you have already rendered me with respect to Adeline have not been unrewarded.

True, my Lord; I am ever willing to acknowledge this; and am sorry it has not been in my power to serve you more effectually. Your further views respecting her I am ready to assist.

I thank you. — Adeline — — the Marquis hesitated — Adeline, rejoined La Motte, eager to anticipate his wishes, has beauty worthy of your pursuit: she has inspired a passion of which she ought to be proud, and at any rate she shall soon be yours. Her charms are worthy of — —

Yes, yes, interrupted the Marquis; but — he paused. But they have given you too much trouble in the pursuit, said La Motte; and to be sure, my Lord, it must be confessed they have; but this trouble is all over — you may now consider her as your own.

I would do so, said the Marquis, fixing an eye of earnest regard upon La Motte — I would do so.

Name your hour, my Lord; you shall not be interrupted. Beauty such as Adeline's —

Watch her closely, interrupted the Marquis, and on no account suffer her to leave her apartment. Where is she now?

Confined in her chamber.

Very well. But I am impatient.

Name your time, my Lord — to-morrow night.

To-morrow night, said the Marquis, to-morrow night. Do you understand me now?

Yes, my Lord, this night if you wish it so. But had you not better dismiss your servants, and remain yourself in the forest? You know the door that opens upon the woods from the west tower. Come thither about twelve — I will be there to conduct you to her chamber. Remember then, my Lord, that to-night —

Adeline dies! interrupted the Marquis in a low voice scarcely human. Do you understand me now?

— — La Motte shrunk aghast — My Lord!

La Motte! said the Marquis. — There was a silence of several minutes, in which La Motte endeavoured to recover himself. Let me ask, my Lord, the meaning of this? said he, when he had breath to speak. Why should you wish the death of Adeline — of Adeline, whom so lately you loved?

Make no inquiries for my motive, said the Marquis; but it is as certain as that I live that she you name must die. This is sufficient. The surprise of La Motte equalled his horror. The means are various, resumed the Marquis. I could have wished that no blood might be spilt; and there are drugs sure and speedy in their effect, but they cannot be soon or safely procured. I also wish it over — it must be done quickly — this night.

This night, my Lord!

Aye, this night, La Motte; if it is to be, why not soon? Have you no convenient drug at hand?

None, my Lord.

I feared to trust a third person, or I should have been provided, said the Marquis. As it is, take this poniard! use it as occasion offers, but be resolute. La Motte received the poniard with a trembling hand, and continued to gaze upon it for some time, scarcely knowing what he did. Put it up, said the Marquis, and endeavour to recollect yourself. La Motte obeyed, but continued to muse in silence.

He saw himself entangled in the web which his own crimes had woven. Being in the power of the Marquis, he knew he must either consent to the commission of a deed, from the enormity of which, depraved as he was, he shrunk in horror, or sacrifice fortune, freedom, probably life itself, to the refusal. He had been led on by slow gradations from folly to vice, till he now saw before him an abyss of guilt which startled even the conscience that so long had slumbered. The means of retreating were desperate — to proceed was equally so.

When he considered the innocence and the helplessness of Adeline, her orphan state, her former affectionate conduct, and her confidence in his protection, his heart melted with compassion for the distress he had already occasioned her, and shrunk in terror from the deed he was urged to commit. But when, on the other hand, he contemplated the destruction that threatened him from the vengeance of the Marquis, and then considered the advantages that were offered him of favour, freedom, and probably fortune, — terror and temptation contributed to overcome the pleadings of humanity, and silence the voice of conscience. In this state of tumultuous uncertainty

209

he continued for some time silent, until the voice of the Marquis roused him to a conviction of the necessity of at least appearing to acquiesce in his designs.

Do you hesitate? said the Marquis. — No, my Lord, my resolution is fixed — I will obey you. But methinks it would be better to avoid bloodshed. Strange secrets have been revealed by — —

Aye, but how avoid it? interrupted the Marquis. — Poison I will not venture to procure. I have given you one sure instrument of death. You also may find it dangerous to inquire for a drug. La Motte perceived that he could not purchase poison without incurring a discovery much greater than that he wished to avoid. You are right, my Lord, and I will follow your orders implicitly. The Marquis now proceeded, in broken sentences, to give further directions concerning this dreadful scheme.

In her sleep, said he, at midnight; the family will then be at rest. Afterwards they planned a story which was to account for her disappearance, and by which it was to seem that she had sought an escape in consequence of her aversion to the addresses of the Marquis. The doors of her chamber and of the west tower were to be left open to corroborate this account, and many other circumstances were to be contrived to confirm the suspicion. They further consulted how the Marquis was to be informed of the event; and it was agreed that he should come as usual to the abbey on the following day. — To-night then, said the Marquis, I may rely upon your resolution?

You may, my Lord.

Farewell, then. When we meet again — —

When we meet again said La Motte, it will be done. He followed the Marquis to the abbey; and having seen him mount his horse and wished him a good night, he retired to his chamber, where he shut himself up.

Adeline, meanwhile, in the solitude of her prison gave way to the despair which her condition inspired. She tried to arrange her thoughts, and to argue herself into some degree of resignation; but reflection, by representing the past, and reason, by anticipating the future, brought before her mind the full picture, of her misfortunes, and she sunk in despondency. Of Theodore, who, by a conduct so noble, had testified his attachment and involved himself in ruin, she thought with a degree of anguish infinitely superior to any she had felt upon any other occasion.

That the very exertions which had deserved all her gratitude, and awakened all her tenderness, should be the cause of his destruction, was a circumstance so much beyond the ordinary bounds of misery, that her fortitude sunk at once before it. The idea of Theodore suffering — Theodore dying — was for ever present to her imagination; and frequently excluding the sense of her own danger, made her conscious only of his. Sometimes the hope he had given her of being able to vindicate his conduct, or at least to obtain a pardon, would return; but it was like the faint beam of an April morn, transient and cheerless. She knew that the Marquis, stung with jealousy and exasperated to revenge, would pursue him with unrelenting malice.

Against such an enemy what could Theodore oppose? Conscious rectitude would not avail him to ward off the blow which disappointed passion and powerful pride directed. Her distress was considerably heightened by reflecting that no intelligence of him could reach her at the abbey, and that she must remain she knew not how long in the most dreadful suspense concerning his fate. From the abbey she saw no possibility of escaping. She was a prisoner in a chamber inclosed at every avenue; she had no opportunity of conversing with any person who could afford her even a chance of relief; and she saw herself condemned to await in passive silence the impending destiny, infinitely more dreadful to her imagination than death itself.

Thus circumstanced, she yielded to the pressure of her misfortunes, and would sit for hours motionless and given up to thought. Theodore! she would frequently exclaim, you cannot hear my voice, you cannot fly to help me; yourself a prisoner and in chains. The picture was too horrid: the swelling anguish of her heart would subdue her utterance — tears bathed her cheeks — and she became insensible to every thing but the misery of Theodore.

On this evening her mind had been remarkably tranquil; and as she watched from her window, with a still and melancholy pleasure, the setting sun, the fading splendour of the western horizon, and the gradual approach of twilight, her thoughts bore her back to the time when in happier circumstances she had watched the same appearances. She recollected also the evening of her temporary escape from the abbey, when from this same window she had viewed the declining sun — how anxiously she had awaited the fall of twilight—how much she had endeavoured to anticipate the events of her future life—with what trembling fear she had descended from the tower and ventured into the forest. These reflections produced others that filled her heart with anguish and her eyes with tears.

While she was lost in her melancholy reverie she saw the Marquis mount his horse and depart from the gate. The sight of him revived in all its force a sense of the misery he inflicted on her beloved Theodore, and a consciousness of the evils which more immediately threatened herself. She withdrew from the window in an agony of tears, which continuing for a considerable time, her frame was at length quite exhausted, and she retired early to rest.

La Motte remained in his chamber till supper obliged him to descend. At table his wild and haggard countenance, which, in spite of all his endeavours, betrayed the disorder of his mind, and his long and frequent fits of abstraction, surprised as well as alarmed Madame La Motte. When Peter left the room she tenderly inquired what had disturbed him, and he with a distorted smile tried to be gay; but the effort was beyond his art, and he quickly relapsed into silence; or when Madame La Motte spoke, and he strove to conceal the absence of his thoughts, he answered so entirely from the purpose that his abstraction became still more apparent. Observing this, Madame La Motte appeared to take no notice of his present temper; and they continued to sit in uninterrupted silence till the hour of rest, when they retired to their chamber.

La Motte lay in a state of disturbed watchfulness for some time, and his frequent starts awoke Madame, who however, being pacified by some trifling excuse, soon went to sleep again. This agitation continued till near midnight, when recollecting that the time was now passing in idle reflection which ought to be devoted to action, he stole silently from his bed, wrapped himself in his night-gown, and taking the lamp which burned nightly in his chamber, passed up the spiral staircase. As he went he frequently looked back, and often started and listened to the hollow sighings of the blast.

His hand shook so violently when he attempted to unlock the door of Adeline's chamber, that he was obliged to set the lamp on the ground, and apply both his hands. The noise he made with the key induced him to suppose he must have awakened her; but when he opened the door, and perceived the stillness that reigned within, he was convinced she was asleep. When he approached the bed he heard her gently breathe, and soon after sigh—and he stopped: but silence returning he again advanced, and then heard her sing in her deep. As he listened he distinguished some notes of a melancholy little air, which in her happier days she had often sung to him. The low and mournful accent in which she now uttered them expressed too well the tone of her mind.

La Motte now stepped hastily towards the bed, when breathing a deep sigh she was again silent. He undrew the curtain and saw her lying in a profound sleep, her cheek, yet wet with tears, resting upon her arm. He stood a moment looking at her; and as he viewed her innocent and lovely countenance, pale in grief, the light of the lamp, which shone strong upon her eyes, awoke her, and perceiving a man, she uttered a scream. Her recollection returning, she knew him to be La Motte; and it instantly occurring to her that the Marquis was at hand, she raised herself in bed, and implored pity and protection. La Motte stood looking eagerly at her, but without replying.

The wildness of his looks and the gloomy silence he preserved increased her alarm, and with tears of terror she renewed her supplication. You once saved me from destruction, cried she; O save me now! have pity upon me—I have no protector but you.

What is it you fear? said La Motte in a tone scarcely articulate.—O save me—save me from the Marquis!

Rise then, said he, and dress yourself quickly: I shall be back again in a few minutes. He lighted a candle that stood on the table, and left the chamber; Adeline immediately arose and endeavoured to dress; but her thoughts were so bewildered that she scarcely knew what she did, and her whole frame so violently agitated, that it was with the utmost difficulty she preserved herself from fainting. She threw her clothes hastily on, and then sat down to await the return of La Motte. A considerable time elapsed, yet he did not appear; and having in vain endeavoured to compose her spirits, the pain of suspense became at length so insupportable, that she opened the door of her chamber, and went to the top of the staircase to listen. She thought she heard voices below; but considering that if the Marquis was there, her appearance could only increase her danger, she checked the step she had almost involuntarily taken to descend. Still she listened, and still thought she distinguished voices. Soon after, she heard a door shut, and then footsteps, and she hastened back to her chamber.

Near a quarter of an hour had elapsed and La Motte did not appear; when again she thought she heard a murmur of voices below and also passing steps: and at length, her anxiety not suffering her to remain in her room, she moved through the passage that communicated with the spiral staircase; but all was now still. In a few moments, however, a light flashed across the hall, and La Motte appeared at the door of the vaulted room. He looked up, and seeing Adeline in the gallery, beckoned her to descend.

She hesitated, and looked towards her chamber; but La Motte now approached the stairs, and with faltering steps she went to meet him. I fear the Marquis may see me, said she, whispering; where is he? La Motte took her hand and led her on, assuring her she had nothing to fear from the Marquis. The wildness of his looks, however, and the trembling of his hand, seemed to contradict this assurance, and she inquired whether he was leading her. To the forest, said La Motte, that you may escape from the abbey — a horse waits for you without: I can save you by no other means. New terror seized her. She could scarcely believe that La Motte, who had hitherto conspired with the Marquis, and had so closely confined her, should now himself undertake her escape; and she at this moment felt a dreadful presentiment which it was impossible to account for, that he was leading her out to murder her in the forest. Again shrinking back, she supplicated his mercy. He assured her he meant only to protect her, and desired she would not waste time.

There was something in his manner that spoke sincerity, and she suffered him to conduct her to a side door that opened into the forest, where she could just distinguish through the gloom a man on horseback. This brought to her remembrance the night in which she had quitted the tomb, when, trusting to the person who appeared, she had been carried to the Marquis's villa. La Motte called, and was answered by Peter, whose voice somewhat reassured Adeline.

He then told her that the Marquis would return to the abbey on the following morning and that this could be her only opportunity of escaping his designs; that she might rely upon his (La Motte's) word, that Peter had orders to carry her wherever she choose; but as he knew the Marquis would be indefatigable in search of her, he advised her by all means to leave the kingdom, which she might do with Peter, who was a native of Savoy, and would convey her to the house of his sister. There she might remain till La Motte himself, who did not now think it would be safe to continue much longer in France, should join her. He entreated her, whatever might happen, never to mention the events which had passed at the abbey. To save you, Adeline, I have risked my life; do not increase my danger and your own by any unnecessary discoveries. We may never meet again, but I hope you will be happy; and remember, when you think of me, that I am not quite so bad as I have been tempted to be.

Having said this, he gave her some money, which he told her would be necessary to defray the expenses of her journey. Adeline could no longer doubt his sincerity, and her transports of joy and gratitude would scarcely permit her to thank him. She wished to have bid Madame La Motte farewell, and indeed earnestly requested it; but he again told her she had no time to lose; and having wrapped her in a large cloak, he lifted her upon the horse. She bade him adieu with tears of gratitude, and Peter set off as fast as the darkness would permit.

When they were got some way,—I am glad with all my heart, Mam'selle, said he, to see you again. Who would have thought, after all, that my master himself would have bid me take you away! Well, to be sure, strange things come to pass; but I hope we shall have better luck this time. Adeline, not choosing to reproach him with the treachery of which she feared he had been formerly guilty, thanked him for his good wishes, and said she hoped they should be more fortunate: but Peter, in his usual strain of eloquence, proceeded to undeceive her in this point, and to acquaint her with every circumstance which his memory, and it was naturally a strong one could furnish.

Peter expressed such an artless interest in her welfare, and such a concern for her disappointment, that she could no longer doubt his faithfulness; and this conviction not only strengthened her confidence in the present undertaking, but made her listen to his conversation with kindness and pleasure. I should never have staid at the abbey till this time, said he, if I could have got away; but my master frighted me so much about the Marquis, and I had not money enough to carry me into my own country, so that I was forced to stay. It's well we have got some solid louis d'ors now; for I question, Ma'mselle, whether the people on the road would have taken those trinkets you formerly talked of for money.

Possibly not, said Adeline: I am thankful to Monsieur La Motte that we have more certain means of procuring conveniences. What route shall you take when we leave the forest, Peter?—Peter mentioned very correctly a great part of the road to Lyons; And then, said he, we can easily get to Savoy, and that will be nothing. My sister, God bless her! I hope, is living; I have not seen her many a year: but if she is not all the people will be glad to see me, and you will easily get a lodging, Ma'mselle, and every thing you want.

Adeline resolved to go with him to Savoy. La Motte, who knew the character and designs of the Marquis, had advised her to leave the kingdom, and had told her, what her fears would have suggested, that the Marquis would be indefatigable in search of her. His motive for this advice must be a desire of serving her; why else, when she was already in his power, should he remove her to another place, and even furnish her with money for the expenses of a journey?

At Leloncourt, where Peter said he was well known, she would be most likely to meet with protection and comfort, even should his sister be dead; and its distance and solitary situation pleased her. These reflections would have pointed out to her the prudence of proceeding to Savoy, had she been less destitute of resources in France; in her present situation they proved it to be necessary.

She inquired further concerning the route they were to take, and whether Peter was sufficiently acquainted with the road. When once I get to Thiers, I know it well enough, said Peter; for I have gone it many a time in my younger days, and any body will tell us the way there. They travelled for several hours in darkness and silence; and it was not till they emerged from the forest that Adeline saw the morning light streak the eastern clouds. The sight cheered and revived her; and as she travelled silently along, her mind revolved the events of the past night, and meditated plans for the future. The present kindness of La Motte appeared so very different from his former conduct, that it astonished and perplexed her; and she could only account for it by attributing it to one of those sudden impulses of humanity which sometimes operate even upon the most depraved hearts.

But when she recollected his former words — that he was not master of himself — she could scarcely believe that mere pity could induce him to break the bonds which had hitherto so strongly held him; and then, considering the altered conduct of the Marquis, she was inclined to think that she owed her liberty to some change in his sentiments towards her: yet the advice La Motte had given her to quit the kingdom, and the money with which he had supplied her for that purpose, seemed to contradict this opinion, and involved her again in doubt.

Peter now got directions to Thiers, which place they reached without any accident, and there stopped to refresh themselves. As soon as Peter thought the horse sufficiently rested, they again set forward, and from the rich plains of the Lyonnois, Adeline for the first time caught a view of the distant Alps, whose majestic heads, seeming to prop the vault of heaven, filled her mind with sublime emotions.

In a few hours they reached the vale in which stands the city of Lyons, whose beautiful environs, studded with villas and rich with cultivation, withdrew Adeline from the melancholy contemplation of her own circumstances, and her more painful anxiety for Theodore.

When they reached that busy city, her first care was to inquire concerning the passage of the Rhone; but she forbore to make these inquiries of the people of the inn, considering that if the Marquis should trace her thither, they might enable him to pursue her route. She, therefore, sent Peter to the quays to hire a boat, while she herself took a slight repast, it being her intention to embark immediately. Peter presently returned, having engaged a boat and men to take them up the Rhone to the nearest part of Savoy, from whence they were to proceed by land to the village of Leloncourt.

Having taken some refreshment, she ordered him to conduct her to the vessel. A new and striking scene presented itself to Adeline, who looked with surprise upon the river, gay with vessels, and the quay crowded with busy faces, and felt the contrast which the cheerful objects around bore to herself—to her, an orphan, desolate, helpless, and flying from persecution and her country. She spoke with the master of the boat; and having sent Peter back to the inn for the horse, (La Motte's gift to Peter in lieu of some arrears of wages,) they embarked.

As they slowly passed up the Rhone, whose steep banks, crowned with mountains, exhibited the most various, wild, and romantic scenery, Adeline sat in pensive reverie. The novelty of the scene through which she floated, now frowning with savage grandeur, and now smiling in fertility and gay with towns and villages, soothed her mind, and her sorrow gradually softened into a gentle and not unpleasing melancholy. She had seated herself at the head of the boat, where she watched its sides cleave the swift stream, and listened to the dashing of the waters.

The boat, slowly opposing the current, passed along for some hours, and at length the veil of evening was stretched over the landscape. The weather was fine, and Adeline, regardless of the dews that now fell, remained in the open air, observing the objects darken round her, the gay tints of the horizon fade away, and the stars gradually appear trembling upon the lucid mirror of the waters. The scene was now sunk in deep shadow, and the silence of the hour was broken only by the measured dashing of the oars, and now and then by the voice of Peter speaking to the boatmen. Adeline sat lost in thought—the forlornness of her circumstances came heightened to her imagination.

She saw herself surrounded by the darkness and stillness of night, in a strange place, far distant from any friends, going she scarcely knew whither, under the guidance of strangers, and pursued, perhaps, by an inveterate enemy. She pictured to herself the rage of the Marquis now that he had discovered her flight; and though she knew it very unlikely he should follow her by water, for which reason she had chosen that manner of travelling, she trembled at the portrait her fancy drew. Her thoughts then wandered to the plan she should adopt after reaching Savoy; and much as her experience had prejudiced her against the manners of a convent, she saw no place more likely to afford her a proper asylum. At length she retired to the little cabin for a few hours repose.

She awoke with the dawn: and her mind being too much disturbed to sleep again, she rose and watched the gradual approach of day. As she mused, she expressed the feelings of the moment in the following:

SONNET

Morn's beaming eyes at length unclose,

And wake the blushes of the rose,

That all night long oppress'd with dews,

And veil'd in chilly shade its hues,

Reclined, forlorn, the languid head,

And sadly sought its parent bed;

Warmth from her ray the trembling flower derives,

And, sweetly blushing, through its tears revives.

Morn's beaming eyes at length unclose,

And melt the tears that bend the rose;

But can their charms suppress the sigh,

Or chase the tear from Sorrow's eye?

Can all their lustrous light impart

One ray of peace to Sorrow's heart?

Ah! no; their fires her fainting soul oppress — —

Eve's pensive shades more soothe her meek distress!

When Adeline left the abbey, La Motte had remained for some time at the gate, listening to the steps of the horse that carried her, till the sound was lost in distance: he then turned into the hall with a lightness of heart to which he had long been a stranger. The satisfaction of having thus preserved her, as he hoped, from the designs of the Marquis, overcame for a while all sense of the danger in which this step must involve him. But when he returned entirely to his own situation, the terrors of the Marquis's resentment struck their full force upon his mind, and he considered how he might best escape it.

It was now past midnight — the Marquis was expected early on the following day; and in this interval it at first appeared probable to him that he might quit the forest. There was only one horse; but he considered whether it would be best to set off immediately for Auboine, where a carriage might be procured to convey his family and his moveables from the abbey, or quietly await the arrival of the Marquis, and endeavour to impose upon him by a forged story of Adeline's escape.

The time which must elapse before a carriage could reach the abbey would leave him scarcely sufficient to escape from the forest; what money he had remaining from the Marquis's bounty would not carry him far; and when it was expended he must probably be at a loss for subsistence, should he not before then be detected. By remaining at the abbey it would appear that he was unconscious of deserving the Marquis's resentment; and though he could not expect to impress a belief upon him that his orders had been executed, he might make it appear that Peter only had been accessary to the escape of Adeline; an account which would seem the more probable, from Peter's having been formerly detected in a similar scheme. He believed, also, that if the Marquis should threaten to deliver him into the hands of justice he might save himself by a menace of disclosing the crime he had commissioned him to perpetrate.

Thus arguing, La Motte resolved to remain at the abbey, and

await the event of the Marquis's disappointment.

When the Marquis did arrive, and was informed of Adeline's flight, the strong workings of his soul, which appeared in his countenance, for a while alarmed and terrified La Motte. He cursed himself and her in terms of such coarseness and vehemence, as La Motte was astonished to hear from a man whose manners were generally amiable, whatever might be the violence and criminality of his passions. To invent and express these terms seemed to give him not only relief, but delight; yet he appeared more shocked at the circumstance of her escape than exasperated at the carelessness of La Motte; and recollecting at length that he wasted time, he left the abbey, and dispatched several of his servants in pursuit of her.

When he was gone, La Motte, believing that his story had succeeded, returned to the pleasure of considering that he had done his duty, and to the hope that Adeline was now beyond the reach of pursuit. This calm was of short continuance. In a few hours the Marquis returned, accompanied by the officers of justice. The affrighted La Motte, perceiving him approach, endeavoured to conceal himself, but was seized and carried to the Marquis, who drew him aside.

I am not to be imposed upon, said he, by such a superficial story as you have invented; you know your life is in my hands; tell me instantly where you have secreted Adeline, or I will charge you with the crime you have committed against me; but upon your disclosing the place of her concealment I will dismiss the officers and, if you wish it, assist you to leave the kingdom. You have no time to hesitate, and may know that I will not be trifled with. La Motte attempted to appease the Marquis, and affirmed that Adeline was really fled he knew not whither. You will remember, my Lord, that your character is also in my power; and that, if you proceed to extremities, you will compel me to reveal in the face of day that you would have made me a murderer.

And who will believe you? said the Marquis. The crimes that banished you from society will be no testimony of your veracity, and that with which I now charge you will bring with it a sufficient presumption that your accusation is malicious. Officers, do your duty.

They then entered the room and seized La Motte, whom terror now deprived of all power of resistance, could resistance have availed him; and in the perturbation of his mind he informed the Marquis that Adeline had taken the road to Lyons.

This discovery, however, was made too late to serve himself; the Marquis seized the advantage it offered: but the charge had been given; and with the anguish of knowing that he had exposed Adeline to danger without benefiting himself, La Motte submitted in silence to his fate. Scarcely allowing him time to collect what little effects might easily be carried with him, the officers conveyed him from the abbey: but the Marquis, in consideration of the extreme distress of Madame La Motte, directed one of his servants to procure a carriage from Auboine, that she might follow her husband.

The Marquis in the mean time, now acquainted with the route Adeline had taken, sent forward his faithful valet to trace her to her place of concealment, and return immediately with intelligence to the villa.

Abandoned to despair, La Motte and his wife quitted the forest of Fontanville, which had for so many months afforded them an asylum, and embarked once more upon the tumultuous world, where justice would meet La Motte in the form of destruction. They had entered the forest as a refuge, rendered necessary by the former crimes of La Motte, and for sometime found in it the security they sought: but other offences, for even in that sequestered spot there happened to be temptation, soon succeeded; and his life, already sufficiently marked by the punishment of vice, now afforded him another instance of this great truth, "That where guilt is, there peace cannot enter."

CHAPTER XVI

Hail awful scenes, that calm the troubled breast,

And woo the weary to profound repose!

BEATTIE.

Adeline meanwhile, and Peter, proceeded on their voyage without any accident, and landed in Savoy, where Peter placed her upon the horse, and himself walked beside her. When he came within sight of his native mountains, his extravagant joy burst forth into frequent exclamations, and he would often ask Adeline if she had ever seen such hills in France. No, no, said he, the hills there are very well for French hills, but they are not to be named on the same day with ours. Adeline, lost in admiration of the astonishing and tremendous scenery around her, assented very warmly to the truth of Peter's assertion, which encouraged him to expatiate more largely upon the advantages of his country; its disadvantages he totally forgot; and though he gave away his last sous to the children of the peasantry that ran barefooted by the side of the horse, he spoke of nothing but the happiness and content of the inhabitants.

His native village, indeed, was an exception to the general character of the country, and to the usual effects of an arbitrary government; it was flourishing, healthy, and happy; and these advantages it chiefly owed to the activity and attention of the benevolent clergyman whose cure it was.

Adeline, who now began to feel the effects of long anxiety and fatigue, much wished to arrive at the end of her journey, and inquired impatiently of Peter concerning it. Her spirits thus weakened, the gloomy grandeur of the scenes which had so lately awakened emotions of delightful sublimity, now awed her into terror; she trembled at the sound of the torrents rolling among the cliffs and thundering in the vale below, and shrunk from the view of the precipices, which sometimes overhung the road and at others appeared beneath it. Fatigued as she was, she frequently dismounted to climb on foot the steep flinty road, which she feared to travel on horseback.

The day was closing when they drew near a small village at the foot of the Savoy Alps; and the sun, in all his evening splendour, now sinking behind their summits, threw a farewell gleam athwart the landscape so soft and glowing as drew from

Adeline, languid as she was, an exclamation of rapture.

The romantic situation of the village next attracted her notice. It stood at the foot of several stupendous mountains, which formed a chain round a lake at some little distance, and the woods that swept from their summits almost embosomed the village. The lake, unruffled by the lightest air, reflected the vermeil tints of the horizon with the sublime on its borders, darkening every instant with the falling twilight.

When Peter perceived the village, he burst into a shout of joy. Thank God, said he, we are near home; there is my dear native place: it looks just as it did twenty years ago: and there are the same old trees growing round our cottage yonder, and the huge rock that rises above it. My poor father died there, Ma'mselle. Pray Heaven my sister be alive! it is a long while since I saw her. Adeline listened with a melancholy pleasure to these artless expressions of Peter, who in retracing the scenes of his former days seemed to live them over again. As they approached the village, he continued to point out various objects of his remembrance. And there too is the good pastor's chateau; look, Ma'mselle, that white house with the smoke curling, that stands on the edge of the lake yonder. I wonder whether he is alive yet: he was not old when I left the place, and as much beloved as ever man was; but death spares nobody!

They had by this time reached the village, which was extremely neat, though it did not promise much accommodation. Peter had hardly advanced ten steps before he was accosted by some of his old acquaintance, who shook hands, and seemed not to know how to part with him. He inquired for his sister, and was told she was alive and well. As they passed on, so many of his old friends flocked round him, that Adeline became quite weary of the delay. Many whom he had left in the vigour of life were now tottering under the infirmities of age, while their sons and daughters, whom he had known only in the playfulness of infancy, were grown from his remembrance, and in the pride of youth. At length they approached the cottage, and were met by his sister, who having heard of his arrival, came and welcomed him with unfeigned joy.

On seeing Adeline, she seemed surprised, but assisted her to alight; and conducting her into a small but neat cottage, received her with a warmth of ready kindness which would have graced a better situation. Adeline desired to speak with her alone, for the room was now crowded with Peter's friends; and then acquainting her with such particulars of her circumstances as it was necessary to communicate, desired to know if she could be accommodated with lodging in the cottage. Yes, Ma'mselle, said the good woman, such as it is, you are heartily welcome: I am only sorry it is not better. But you seem ill Ma'mselle; what shall I get you?

Adeline, who had been long struggling with fatigue and indisposition, now yielded to their pressure. She said she was indeed ill; but hoped that rest would restore her, and desired a bed might be immediately prepared. The good woman went out to obey her, and soon returning showed her to a little cabin, where she retired to a bed whose cleanliness was its only recommendation.

But notwithstanding her fatigue, she could not sleep; and her mind, in spite of all her efforts, returned to the scenes that were passed, or presented gloomy and imperfect visions of the future.

The difference between her own condition and that of other persons, educated as she had been, struck her forcibly, and she wept. They, said she, have friends and relations, all striving to save them not only from what may hurt, but what may displease them; watching not only for their present safety, but for their future advantage, and preventing them even from injuring themselves. But during my whole life I have never known a friend; have been in general surrounded by enemies, and very seldom exempt from some circumstance either of danger or calamity. Yet surely I am not born to be for ever wretched; the time will come when— —She began to think she might one time be happy; but recollecting the desperate situation of Theodore,—No, said she, I can never hope even for peace!

Early the following morning the good woman of the house came to inquire how she had rested; and found she had slept little, and was much worse than on the preceding night. The uneasiness of her mind contributed to heighten the feverish symptoms that attended her, and in the course of the day her disorder began to assume a serious aspect. She observed its progress with composure, resigning herself to the will of God, and feeling little to regret in life. Her kind hostess did every thing in her power to relieve her, and there was neither physician nor apothecary in the village, so that nature was deprived of none of her advantages. Notwithstanding this, the disorder rapidly increased, and on the third day from its first attack she became delirious, after which she sunk into a state of stupefaction.

How long she remained in this deplorable condition she knew not; but on recovering her senses she found herself in an apartment very different from any she remembered. It was spacious and almost beautiful, the bed and every thing around being in one style of elegant simplicity. For some minutes she lay in a trance of surprise, endeavouring to recollect her scattered ideas of the past, and almost fearing to move lest the pleasing vision should vanish from her eyes.

At length she ventured to raise herself, when she presently heard a soft voice speaking near her, and the bed curtain on one side was gently undrawn by a beautiful girl. As she leaned forward over the bed, and with a smile of mingled tenderness and joy inquired of her patient how she did. Adeline gazed in silent admiration upon the most interesting female countenance she had ever seen, in which the expression of sweetness, united with lively sense and refinement, was chastened by simplicity.

Adeline at length recollected herself sufficiently to thank her kind inquirer, and begged to know to whom she was obliged, and where she was? The lovely girl pressed her hand, 'Tis we who are obliged, said she. Oh! how I rejoice to find that you have recovered your recollection! She said no more, but flew to the door of the apartment, and disappeared. In a few minutes she returned with an elderly lady, who approaching the bed with an air of tender interest, asked concerning the state of Adeline; to which the latter replied as well as the agitation of her spirits would permit, and repeated her desire of knowing to whom she was so greatly obliged. You shall know that hereafter, said the lady; at present be assured that you are with those who will think their care much overpaid by your recovery; submit, therefore, to every thing that may conduce to it, and consent to be kept as quiet as possible.

Adeline gratefully smiled and bowed her head in silent assent. The lady now quitted the room for a medicine; having given which to Adeline, the curtain was closed and she was left to repose. But her thoughts were too busy to suffer her to profit by the opportunity:—she contemplated the past and viewed the present; and when she compared them, the contrast struck her with astonishment: the whole appeared like one of those sudden transitions so frequent in dreams, in which we pass from grief and despair, we know not how, to comfort and delight.

Yet she looked forward to the future with a trembling anxiety that threatened to retard her recovery, and which when she remembered the words of her generous benefactress, she endeavoured to suppress. Had she better known the disposition of the persons in whose house she now was, her anxiety, as far as it regarded herself, must in a great measure have been done away; for La Luc, its owner, was one of those rare characters to whom misfortune seldom looks in vain, and whose native goodness, confirmed by principle, is uniform and unassuming in its acts. The following little picture of his domestic life, his family, and his manners, will more fully illustrate his character. It was drawn from the life, and its exactness will, it is hoped, compensate for its length.

THE FAMILY OF LA LUC.

But half mankind, like Handel's fool, destroy,

Through rage and ignorance, the strain of joy;

Irregularly wild, the passions roll

Through Nature's finest instrument, the soul: —

While men of sense, with Handel's happier skill,

Correct the taste and harmonize the will;

Teach their affections like his notes to flow,

Nor raised too high, nor ever sunk too low;

Till every virtue, measured and refined,

As fits the concert of the master mind,

Melts in its kindred sounds, and pours along

Th' according music of the moral song.

CAWTHORNE.

In the village of Leloncourt, celebrated for its picturesque situation at the foot of the Savoy Alps, lived Arnaud La Luc, a clergyman descended from an ancient family of France, whose decayed fortunes occasioned them to seek a retreat in Switzerland, in an age when the violence of civil commotion seldom spared the conquered. He was minister of the village, and equally loved for the piety and benevolence of the Christian, as respected for the dignity and elevation of the philosopher. His was the philosophy of nature, directed by common sense. He despised the jargon of the modern schools, and the brilliant absurdities of systems which dazzled without enlightening, and guided without convincing their disciples.

His mind was penetrating; his views extensive; and his systems, like his religion, were simple, rational, and sublime. The people of his parish looked up to him as to a father; for while his precepts directed their minds, his example touched their hearts.

In early youth La Luc lost a wife whom he tenderly loved. This event threw a tincture of soft and interesting melancholy over his character, which remained when time had mellowed the remembrance that occasioned it. Philosophy had strengthened, not hardened, his heart; it enabled him to resist the pressure of affliction, rather than to overcome it.

Calamity taught him to feel with peculiar sympathy the distresses of others. His income from the parish was small, and what remained from the divided and reduced estates of his ancestors did not much increase it; but though he could not always relieve the necessities of the indigent, his tender pity and holy conversation seldom failed in administering consolation to the mental sufferer. On these occasions the sweet and exquisite emotions of his heart have often induced him to say, that could the voluptuary be once sensible of these feelings, he would never after forego the luxury of doing good. Ignorance of true pleasure, he would say, more frequently than temptation to that which is false, leads to vice.

La Luc had one son and a daughter, who were too young when their mother died to lament their loss. He loved them with peculiar tenderness, as the children of her whom he never ceased to deplore; and it was for some time his sole amusement to observe the gradual unfolding of their infant minds, and to bend them to virtue. His was the deep and silent sorrow of the heart: his complaints he never obtruded upon others, and very seldom did he even mention his wife. His grief was too sacred for the eye of the vulgar. Often he retired to the deep solitude of the mountains, and amid their solemn and tremendous scenery would brood over the remembrance of times past, and resign himself to the luxury of grief. On his return from these little excursions he was always more placid and contented. A sweet tranquillity, which arose almost to happiness, was diffused over his mind, and his manners were more than usually benevolent. As he gazed on his children, and fondly kissed them, a tear would sometimes steal into his eye: but it was a tear of tender regret, unmingled with the darker qualities of sorrow, and was most precious to his heart.

On the death of his wife he received into his house a maiden sister, a sensible, worthy woman, who was deeply interested in the happiness of her brother. Her affectionate attention and judicious conduct anticipated the effect of time in softening the poignancy of his distress; and her unremitted care of his children, while it proved the goodness of her own heart, attracted her more closely to his.

It was with inexpressible pleasure that he traced in the infant features of Clara the resemblance of her mother. The same gentleness of manner and the same sweetness of disposition soon displayed themselves; and as she grew up, her actions frequently reminded him so strongly of his lost wife as to fix him in reveries, which absorbed all his soul.

Engaged in the duties of his parish, the education of his children, and in philosophic research, his years passed in tranquillity. The tender melancholy with which affliction had tinctured his mind, was by long indulgence become dear to him, and he would not have relinquished it for the brightest dream of airy happiness. When any passing incident disturbed him, he retired for consolation to the idea of her he so faithfully loved, and yielding to a gentle, and what the world would call a romantic, sadness, gradually reassumed his composure. This was the secret luxury to which he withdrew from temporary disappointment—the solitary enjoyment which dissipated the cloud of care, and blunted the sting of vexation—which elevated his mind above this world, and opened to his view the sublimity of another.

The spot he now inhabited, the surrounding scenery, the romantic beauties of the neighbouring walks, were dear to La Luc, for they had once been loved by Clara; they had been the scenes of her tenderness, and of his happiness.

His chateau stood on the borders of a small lake that was almost environed by mountains of stupendous height, which, shooting into a variety of grotesque forms, composed a scenery singularly solemn and sublime. Dark woods intermingled with bold projections of rock, sometimes barren and sometimes covered with the purple bloom of wild flowers, impended over the lake, and were seen in the clear mirror of its waters. The wild and alpine heights which rose above, were either crowned with perpetual snows, or exhibited tremendous crags and masses of solid rock, whose appearance was continually changing as the rays of light were variously reflected on their surface, and whose summits were often wrapt in impenetrable mists. Some cottages and hamlets, scattered on the margin of the lake or seated in picturesque points of view on the rocks above, were the only objects that reminded the beholder of humanity.

On the side of the lake, nearly opposite to the chateau, the mountains receded, and a long chain of Alps was seen stretching in perspective. Their innumerable tints and shades, some veiled in blue mists, some tinged with rich purple, and others glittering in partial light, gave luxurious and magical colouring to the scene.

The chateau was not large, but it was convenient, and was characterized by an air of elegant simplicity and good order. The entrance was a small hall, which opening by a glass door into the garden, afforded a view of the lake, with the magnificent scenery exhibited on its borders. On the left of the hall was La Luc's study, where he usually passed his mornings; and adjoining was a small room fitted up with chemical apparatus, astronomical instruments, and other implements of science. On the right hand was the family parlour, and behind it a room which belonged exclusively to Madame La Luc. Here were deposited various medicines and botanical distillations, together with the apparatus for preparing them. From this room the whole village was liberally supplied with medicinal comfort; for it was the pride of Madame to believe herself skilful in relieving the disorders of her neighbours.

Behind the chateau rose a tuft of pines, and in front a gentle declivity, covered with verdure and flowers, extended to the lake, whose waters flowed even with the grass, and gave freshness to the acacias that waved over its surface. Flowering shrubs, intermingled with mountain-ash, cypress, and ever-green oak, marked the boundary of the garden.

At the return of spring it was Clara's care to direct the young shoots of the plants, to nurse the budding flowers, and to shelter them with the luxuriant branches of the shrubs from the cold blasts that descended from the mountains. In summer she usually rose with the sun, and visited her favourite flowers while the dew yet hung glittering on their leaves. The freshness of early day, with the glowing colouring which then touched the scenery, gave a pure and exquisite delight to her innocent heart. Born amid scenes of grandeur and sublimity, she had quickly imbibed a taste for their charms, which taste was heightened by the influence of a warm imagination. To view the sun rising above the Alps, tinging their snowy heads with light, and suddenly darting his rays over the whole face of nature — to see the fiery splendour of the clouds reflected in the lake below, and the roseate tints first steal upon the rocks above — were among the earliest pleasures of which Clara was susceptible.

229

From being delighted with the observance of nature, she grew pleased with seeing her finely imitated, and soon displayed a taste for poetry and painting. When she was about sixteen she often selected from her father's library those of the Italian poets most celebrated for picturesque beauty, and would spend the first hours of morning in reading them under the shade of the acacias that bordered the lake. Here too she would often attempt rude sketches of the surrounding scenery; and at length by repeated efforts, assisted by some instruction from her brother she succeeded so well as to produce twelve drawings in crayon, which were judged worthy of decorating the parlour of the chateau.

Young La Luc played the flute, and she listened to him with exquisite delight, particularly when he stood on the margin of the lake, under her beloved acacias. Her voice was sweet and flexible, though not strong, and she soon learned to modulate it to the instrument. She knew nothing of the intricacies of execution; her airs were simple, and her style equally so; but she soon gave them a touching expression, inspired by the sensibility of her heart, which seldom left those of her hearers unaffected.

It was the happiness of La Luc to see his children happy; and in one of his excursions to Geneva, whither he went to visit some relations of his late wife, he bought Clara a lute. She received it with more gratitude than she could express; and having learned one air, she hastened to her favourite acacias, and played it again and again till she forgot every thing besides. Her little domestic duties, her books, her drawing, even the hour which her father dedicated to her improvement, when she met her brother in the library, and with him partook of knowledge, even this hour passed unheeded by. La Luc suffered it to pass. Madame was displeased that her niece neglected her domestic duties, and wished to reprove her, but La Luc begged she would be silent. Let experience teach her her error, said he, precept seldom brings conviction to young minds.

Madame objected that experience was a slow teacher. It is a sure one, replied La Luc, and is not unfrequently the quickest of all teachers: when it cannot lead us into serious evil, it is well to trust to it.

The second day passed with Clara as the first, and the third as the second. She could now play several tunes; she came to her father and repeated what she had learnt.

At supper the cream was not dressed, and there was no fruit on the table. La Luc inquired the reason; Clara recollected it, and blushed. She observed that her brother was absent, but nothing was said. Toward the conclusion of the repast he appeared; his countenance expressed unusual satisfaction, but he seated himself in silence. Clara inquired what had detained him from supper, and learnt that he had been to a sick family in the neighbourhood with the weekly allowance which her father gave them. La Luc had intrusted the care of this family to his daughter, and it was her duty to have carried them their little allowance on the preceding day, but she had forgotten every thing but music.

How did you find the woman? said La Luc to his son. Worse, Sir, he replied; for her medicines had not been regularly given and the children had had little or no food to-day.

Clara was shocked. No food to-day! said she to herself; and I have been playing all day on my lute, under the acacias by the lake! Her father did not seem to observe her emotion, but turned to his son. I left her better, said the latter; the medicines I carried eased her pain, and I had the pleasure to see her children make a joyful supper.

Clara, perhaps, for the first time in her life, envied him his pleasure; her heart was full, and she sat silent. No food to-day! thought she.

She retired pensively to her chamber. The sweet serenity with which she usually went to rest was vanished, for she could no longer reflect on the past day with satisfaction.

What a pity, said she, that what is so pleasing should be the cause of so much pain! This lute is my delight, and my torment! This reflection occasioned her much internal debate; but before she could come to any resolution upon the point in question, she fell asleep.

She awoke very early the next morning, and impatiently watched the progress of the dawn. The sun at length appearing, she arose, and determined to make all the atonement in her power for her former neglect, hastened to the cottage.

Here she remained a considerable time, and when she returned to the chateau, her countenance had recovered all its usual serenity. She resolved, however, not to touch her lute that day.

Till the hour of breakfast she busied herself in binding up the flowers and pruning the shoots that were too luxuriant, and she at length found herself, she scarcely knew how, beneath her beloved acacias by the side of the lake. Ah! said she with a sigh, how sweetly would the song I learned yesterday sound now over the waters! But she remembered her determination, and checked the step she was involuntarily taking towards the chateau.

She attended her father in the library at the usual hour, and learned from his discourse with her brother on what had been read the two preceding days, that she had lost much entertaining knowledge. She requested her father would inform her to what this conversation alluded; but he calmly replied, that she had preferred another amusement at the time when the subject was discussed, and must therefore content herself with ignorance. You would reap the rewards of study from the amusements of idleness, said he; learn to be reasonable—do not expect to unite inconsistencies.

Clara felt the justness of this rebuke, and remembered her lute. What mischief has it occasioned! sighed she. Yes, I am determined not to touch it at all this day. I will prove that I am able to control my inclinations when I see it is necessary so to do. Thus resolving, she applied herself to study with more than usual assiduity.

She adhered to her resolution, and towards the close of the day went into the garden to amuse herself. The evening was still and uncommonly beautiful. Nothing was heard but the faint shivering of the leaves, which returned but at intervals, making silence more solemn, and the distant murmurs of the torrents that rolled among the cliffs. As she stood by the lake, and watched the sun slowly sinking below the Alps, whose summits were tinged with gold and purple; as she saw the last rays of light gleam upon the waters, whose surface was not curled by the slightest air, she sighed, oh! how enchanting would be the sound of my lute at this moment, on this spot, and when every thing is so still around me!

The temptation was too powerful for the resolution of Clara: she ran to the chateau, returned with the instrument to her dear acacias, and beneath their shade continued to play till the surrounding objects faded in darkness from her sight. But the moon rose, and shedding a trembling lustre on the lake, made the scene more captivating than ever.

It was impossible to quit so delightful a spot; Clara repeated her favourite airs again and again. The beauty of the hour awakened all her genius; she never played with such expression before, and she listened with increasing rapture to the tones as they languished over the waters and died away on the distant air. She was perfectly enchanted—no! nothing was ever so delightful as to play on the lute beneath her acacias, on the margin of the lake, by moonlight!

When she returned to the chateau, supper was over. La Luc had observed Clara, and would not suffer her to be interrupted.

When the enthusiasm of the hour was passed, she recollected that she had broken her resolution, and the reflection gave her pain. I prided myself on controlling my inclinations, said she, and I have weakly yielded to their direction. But what evil have I incurred by indulging them this evening? I have neglected no duty, for I had none to perform. Of what then have I to accuse myself? It would have been absurd to have kept my resolution, and denied myself a pleasure when there appeared no reason for this self-denial.

She paused, not quite satisfied with this reasoning. Suddenly resuming her inquiry, But how, said she, am I certain that I should have resisted my inclinations if there had been a reason for opposing them? If the poor family whom I neglected yesterday had been unsupplied to-day, I fear I should again have forgotten them while I played on my lute on the banks of the lake.

She then recollected all that her father had at different times said on the subject of self-command, and she felt some pain.

No, said she, if I do not consider that to preserve a resolution, which I have once solemnly formed, is a sufficient reason to control my inclinations, I fear no other motive would long restrain me. I seriously determined not to touch my lute this whole day, and I have broken my resolution. To-morrow perhaps I may be tempted to neglect some duty, for I have discovered that I cannot rely on my own prudence. Since I cannot conquer temptation, I will fly from it.

On the following morning she brought her lute to La Luc, and begged he would receive it again, and at least keep it till she had taught her inclinations to submit to control.

The heart of La Luc swelled as she spoke. No, Clara, said he, it is unnecessary that I should receive your lute; the sacrifice you would make proves you worthy of my confidence. Take back the instrument; since you have sufficient resolution to resign it when it leads you from duty, I doubt not that you will be able to control its influence now that it is restored to you.

Clara felt a degree of pleasure and pride at these words, such as she had never before experienced; but she thought, that to deserve the commendation they bestowed, it was necessary to complete the sacrifice she had begun. In the virtuous enthusiasm of the moment the delights of music were forgotten in those of aspiring to well-earned praise; and when she refused the lute thus offered, she was conscious only of exquisite sensations. Dear Sir, said she, tears of pleasure, swelling in her eyes, allow me to deserve the praises you bestow, and then I shall indeed be happy.

La Luc thought she had never resembled her mother so much as at this instant, and tenderly kissing her, he for some moments wept in silence. When he was able to speak, You do already deserve my praises, said he, and I restore your lute as a reward for the conduct which excites them. This scene called back recollections too tender for the heart of La Luc, and giving Clara the instrument, he abruptly quitted the room.

La Luc's son, a youth of much promise, was designed by his father for the church, and had received from him an excellent education, which, however, it was thought necessary he should finish at an university. That of Geneva was fixed upon by La Luc. His scheme had been to make his son not a scholar only; he was ambitious that he should also be enviable as a man. From early infancy he had accustomed him to hardihood and endurance, and as he advanced in youth, he encouraged him in manly exercises, and acquainted him with the useful arts as well as with abstract science.

He was high-spirited and ardent in his temper, but his heart was generous and affectionate. He looked forward to Geneva, and to the new world it would disclose, with the sanguine expectations of youth; and in the delight of these expectations was absorbed the regret he would otherways have felt at a separation from his family.

A brother of the late Madame La Luc, who was by birth an Englishman, resided at Geneva with his family. To have been related to his wife was a sufficient claim upon the heart of La Luc, and he had therefore always kept up an intercourse with Mr. Audley, though the difference in their characters and manner of thinking would never permit this association to advance into friendship. La Luc now wrote to him, signifying an intention of sending his son to Geneva, and recommending him to his care. To this letter Mr. Audley returned a friendly answer; and a short time after, an acquaintance of La Luc's being called to Geneva, he determined that his son should accompany him. The separation was painful to La Luc, and almost insupportable to Clara. Madame was grieved, and took care that he should have a sufficient quantity of medicines put up in his travelling trunk; she was also at some pains to point out their virtues, and the different complaints for which they were requisite; but she was careful to deliver her lecture during the absence of her brother.

La Luc, with his daughter, accompanied his son on horseback to the next town, which was about eight miles from Leloncourt; and there again enforcing all the advice he had formerly given him respecting his conduct and pursuits, and again yielding to the tender weakness of the father, he bade him farewell. Clara wept, and felt more sorrow at this parting than the occasion could justify; but this was almost the first time she had known grief, and she artlessly yielded to its influence.

La Luc and Clara travelled pensively back, and the day was closing when they came within view of the lake, and soon after of the chateau. Never had it appeared gloomy till now; but now Clara wandered forlornly through every deserted apartment where she had been accustomed to see her brother, and recollected a thousand little circumstances which, had he been present, she would have thought immaterial, but on which imagination now stamped a value. The garden, the scenes around, all wore a melancholy aspect, and it was long ere they resumed their natural character and Clara recovered her vivacity.

Near four years had elapsed since this separation, when one evening, as Madame La Luc and her niece were sitting at work together in the parlour, a good woman in the neighbourhood desired to be admitted. She came to ask for some medicines, and the advice of Madame La Luc. Here is a sad accident happened at our house, Madame, said she; I am sure my heart aches for the poor young creature. — Madame La Luc desired she would explain herself, and the woman proceeded to say that her brother Peter, whom she had not seen for so many years, was arrived, and had brought a young lady to her cottage, who she verily believed was dying. She described her disorder, and acquainted Madame with what particulars of her mournful story Peter had related, failing not to exaggerate such as her compassion for the unhappy stranger and her love of the marvellous prompted.

The account appeared a very extraordinary one to Madame; but pity for the forlorn condition of the young sufferer induced her to inquire further into the affair. Do let me go to her, Madame, said Clara, who had been listening with ready compassion to the poor woman's narrative: Do suffer me to go—she must want comforts, and I wish much to see how she is. Madame asked some further questions concerning her disorder, and then, taking off her spectacles, she rose from her chair, and said she would go herself. Clara desired to accompany her. They put on their hats and followed the good woman to the cottage, where, in a very small close room, on a miserable bed, lay Adeline, pale, emaciated, and unconscious of all around her. Madame turned to the woman, and asked how long she had been in this way, while Clara went up to the bed, and taking the almost lifeless hand that lay on the quilt, looked anxiously in her face. She observes nothing, said she, poor creature! I wish she was at the chateau, she would be better accommodated, and I could nurse her there. The woman told Madame La Luc that the young lady had lain in that state for several hours. Madame examined her pulse, and shook her head. This room is very close, said she.—Very close indeed, cried Clara eagerly; surely she would be better at the chateau, if she could be moved.

We will see about that, said her aunt. In the mean time let me speak to Peter; it is some years since I saw him. She went to the outer room, and the woman ran out of the cottage to look for him. When she was gone, This is a miserable habitation for the poor stranger, said Clara; she will never be well here: do, Madame, let her be carried to our house; I am sure my father would wish it. Besides, there is something in her features, even inanimate as they now are, that prejudices me in her favour.

Shall I never persuade you to give up that romantic notion of judging people by their faces? said her aunt. What sort of a face she has is of very little consequence—her condition is lamentable, and I am desirous of altering it; but I wish first to ask Peter a few questions concerning her.

Thank you, my dear aunt, said Clara; she will be removed then. Madame La Luc was going to reply; but Peter now entered, and expressing great joy at seeing her again, inquired how Monsieur La Luc and Clara did. Clara immediately welcomed honest Peter to his native place, and he returned her salutation with many expressions of surprise at finding her so much grown. Though I have so often dandled you in my arms,

Ma'mselle, I should never have known you again: Young twigs shoot fast, as they say.

Madame La Luc now inquired into the particulars of Adeline's story; and heard as much as Peter knew of it, being only that his late master found her in a very distressed situation, and that he had himself brought her from the abbey to save her from a French Marquis. The simplicity of Peter's manner would not suffer her to question his veracity, though some of the circumstances he related excited all her surprise and awakened all her pity. Tears frequently stood in Clara's eyes during the course of his narrative; and when he concluded, she said, Dear Madame, I am sure when my father learns the history of this unhappy young woman he will not refuse to be a parent to her, and I will be her sister.

She deserves it all, said Peter, for she is very good indeed. He then proceeded in a strain of praise which was very unusual with him. — I will go home and consult with my brother about her, said Madame La Luc, rising: she certainly ought to be removed to a more airy room. The chateau is so near, that I think she may be carried thither without much risk.

Heaven bless you! Madam, cried Peter, rubbing his hands, for your goodness to my poor young lady.

La Luc had just returned from his evening walk when they reached the chateau. Madame told him where she had been, and related the history of Adeline and her present condition. — By all means have her removed hither, said La Luc, whose eyes bore testimony to the tenderness of his heart: she can be better attended to here than in Susan's cottage.

I knew you would say so, my dear father, said Clara: I will go and order the green bed to be prepared for her.

Be patient, niece, said Madame La Luc; there is no occasion for such haste: some things are to be considered first; but you are young and romantic. — La Luc smiled. — The evening is now closed, resumed Madame; it will therefore be dangerous to remove her before morning. Early to-morrow a room shall be got ready, and she shall be brought here; in the mean time I will go and make up a medicine which I hope may be of service to her. — Clara reluctantly assented to this delay, and Madame La Luc retired to her closet.

On the following morning Adeline, wrapped in blankets and sheltered as much as possible from the air, was brought to the chateau, where the good La Luc desired she might have every attention paid her, and where Clara watched over her with unceasing anxiety and tenderness. She remained in a state of torpor during the greater part of the day, but towards evening she breathed more freely; and Clara, who still watched by her bed, had at length the pleasure of perceiving that her senses were restored. It was at this moment that she found herself in the situation from which we have digressed to give this account of the venerable La Luc and his family. The reader will find that his virtues and his friendship to Adeline deserved this notice.

CHAPTER XVII

Still Fancy, to herself unkind,

Awakes to grief the soften'd mind.

And points the bleeding friend.

COLLINS.

Adeline, assisted by a fine constitution, and the kind attentions of her new friends, was in a little more than a week so much recovered as to leave her chamber. She was introduced to La Luc, whom she met with tears of gratitude, and thanked for his goodness in a manner so warm, yet so artless, as interested him still more in her favour. During the progress of her recovery, the sweetness of her behaviour had entirely won the heart of Clara, and greatly interested that of her aunt, whose reports of Adeline, together with the praises bestowed by Clara, had excited both esteem and curiosity in the breast of La Luc; and he now met her with an expression of benignity which spoke peace and comfort to her heart. She had acquainted Madame La Luc with such particulars of her story as Peter, either through ignorance or inattention, had not communicated, suppressing only, through a false delicacy perhaps, an acknowledgment of her attachment to Theodore. These circumstances were repeated to La Luc, who, ever sensible to the sufferings of others, was particularly interested by the singular misfortunes of Adeline.

Near a fortnight had elapsed since her removal to the chateau, when one morning La Luc desired to speak with her alone. She followed him into his study, and then in a manner the most delicate he told her, that as he found she was so unfortunate in her father, he desired she would henceforth consider him as her parent, and his house as her home. You and Clara shall be equally my daughters, continued he; I am rich in having such children. The strong emotions of surprise and gratitude for some time kept Adeline silent. Do not thank me, said La Luc; I know all you would say, and I know also that I am but doing my duty: I thank God that my duty and my pleasures are generally in unison. Adeline wiped away the tears which his goodness had excited, and was going to speak; but La Luc pressed her hand, and turning away to conceal his emotion, walked out of the room.

Adeline was now considered as a part of the family; and in the parental kindness of La Luc, the sisterly affection of Clara, and the steady and uniform regard of Madame, she would have been happy as she was thankful, had not unceasing anxiety for the fate of Theodore, of whom in this solitude she was less likely than ever to hear, corroded her heart, and embittered every moment of reflection. Even when sleep obliterated for awhile the memory of the past, his image frequently arose to her fancy, accompanied by all the exaggerations of terror. She saw him in chains, and struggling in the grasp of ruffians, or saw him led, amidst the dreadful preparations for execution, into the field: she saw the agony of his look, and heard him repeat her name in frantic accents, till the horrors of the scene overcame her and she awoke.

A similarity of taste and character attached her to Clara; yet the misery that preyed upon her heart was of a nature too delicate to be spoken of, and she never mentioned Theodore even to her friend. Her illness had yet left her weak and languid, and the perpetual anxiety of her mind contributed to prolong this state. She endeavoured by strong and almost continual efforts to abstract her thoughts from their mournful subject, and was often successful. La Luc had an excellent library, and the instruction it offered at once gratified her love of knowledge, and withdrew her mind from painful recollections. His conversation too afforded her another refuge from misery.

But her chief amusement was to wander among the sublime scenery of the adjacent country, sometimes with Clara, though often with no other companion than a book. There were indeed times when the conversation of her friend imposed a painful restraint, and, when, given up to reflection, she would ramble alone through scenes whose solitary grandeur assisted and soothed the melancholy of her heart. Here she would retrace all the conduct of her beloved Theodore, and endeavour to recollect his exact countenance, his air and manner. Now she would weep at the remembrance, and then, suddenly considering that he had perhaps already suffered an ignominious death for her sake, even in consequence of the very action which had proved his love, a dreadful despair would seize her, and, arresting her tears, would threaten to bear down every barrier that fortitude and reason could oppose.

Fearing longer to trust her own thoughts, she would hurry home, and by a desperate effort would try to lose, in the conversation of La Luc, the remembrance of the past. Her melancholy, when he observed it, La Luc attributed to a sense of

240

the cruel treatment she had received from her father; a circumstance which, by exciting his compassion, endeared her more strongly to his heart; while that love of rational conversation, which in her calmer hours so frequently appeared, opened to him a new source of amusement in the cultivation of a mind eager for knowledge, and susceptible of all the energies of genius. She found a melancholy pleasure in listening to the soft tones of Clara's lute, and would often soothe her mind by attempting to repeat the airs she heard.

The gentleness of her manners, partaking so much of that pensive character which marked La Luc's, was soothing to his heart, and tinctured his behaviour with a degree of tenderness that imparted comfort to her, and gradually won her entire confidence and affection. She saw with extreme concern the declining state of his health, and united her efforts with those of the family to amuse and revive him.

The pleasing society of which she partook, and the quietness of the country, at length restored her mind to a state of tolerable composure. She was now acquainted with all the wild walks of the neighbouring mountains; and never tired of viewing their astonishing scenery, she often indulged herself in traversing alone their unfrequented paths, where now and then a peasant from a neighbouring village was all that interrupted the profound solitude. She generally took with her a book, that if she perceived her thought inclined to fix on the one object of her grief, she might force them to a subject less dangerous to her peace. She had become a tolerable proficient in English while at the convent where she received her education, and the instruction of La Luc, who was well acquainted with the language, now served to perfect her. He was partial to the English; he admired their character, and the constitution of their laws, and his library contained a collection of their best authors, particularly of their philosophers and poets. Adeline found that no species of writing had power so effectually to withdraw her mind from the contemplation of its own misery as the higher kinds of poetry, and in these her taste soon taught her to distinguish the superiority of the English from that of the French. The genius of the language, more perhaps than the genius of the people, if indeed the distinction may be allowed, occasioned this.

She frequently took a volume of Shakespeare or of Milton, and, having gained some wild eminence, would seat herself beneath the pines, whose low murmurs soothed her heart, and conspired with the visions of the poet to lull her to forgetfulness of grief.

One evening, when Clara was engaged at home, Adeline wandered alone to a favourite spot among the rocks that bordered the lake. It was an eminence which commanded an entire view of the lake, and of the stupendous mountains that environed it. A few ragged thorns grew from the precipice beneath, which descended perpendicularly to the water's edge; and above rose a thick wood of larch, pine, and fir, intermingled with some chesnut and mountain ash. The evening was fine, and the air so still that it scarcely waved the light leaves of the trees around, or rippled the broad expanse of the waters below. Adeline gazed on the scene with a kind of still rapture, and watched the sun sinking amid a crimson glow, which tinted the bosom of the lake and the snowy heads of the distant Alps. The delight which the scenery inspired:

Soothing each gust of passion into peace,

All but the swellings of the soften'd heart,

That waken, not disturb, the tranquil mind; was now heightened by the tones of a French horn, and, looking on the lake, she perceived at some distance a pleasure-boat. As it was a spectacle rather uncommon in this solitude, she concluded the boat contained a party of foreigners come to view the wonderful scenery of the country, or perhaps of Genevois, who choose to amuse themselves on a lake as grand, though much less extensive, than their own; and the latter conjecture was probably just.

As she listened to the mellow and enchanting tones of the horn, which gradually sunk away in distance, the scene appeared more lovely than before; and finding it impossible to forbear attempting to paint in language what was so beautiful in reality, she composed the following:

STANZAS

How smooth that lake expands its ample breast!

Where smiles in soften'd glow the summer sky:

How vast the rocks that o'er its surface rest!

How wild the scenes its winding shores supply!

Now down the western steep slow sinks the sun,

And paints with yellow gleam the tufted woods;

While here the mountain-shadows, broad and dun,

Sweep o'er the crystal mirror of the floods.

Mark how his splendour tips with partial light

Those shatter'd battlements! that on the brow

Of yon bold promontory burst to sight

From o'er the woods that darkly spread below.

In the soft blush of light's reflected power,

The ridgy rock, the woods that crown its steep,

Th' illumin'd battlement, and darker tower,

On the smooth wave in trembling beauty sleep.

But, lo! the sun recalls his fervid ray,

And cold and dim the watery visions fail;

While o'er yon cliff, whose pointed crags decay,

Mild evening draws her thin empurpled veil!

How sweet that strain of melancholy horn!

That floats along the slowly-ebbing wave,

And up the far-receding mountains borne,

Returns a dying close from Echo's cave!

Hail! shadowy forms of still, expressive Eve!

Your pensive graces stealing on my heart,

Bid all the fine-attun'd emotions live,

And Fancy all her loveliest dreams impart.

La Luc observing how much Adeline was charmed with the features of the country, and desirous of amusing her melancholy, which, notwithstanding her efforts, was often too apparent, wished to show her other scenes than those to which her walks were circumscribed. He proposed a party on horseback to take a nearer view of the Glaciers; to attempt their ascent was a difficulty and fatigue to which neither La Luc, in his present state of health, nor Adeline were equal. She had not been accustomed to ride single, and the mountainous road they were to pass made the experiment rather dangerous; but she concealed her fears, and they were not sufficient to make her wish to forego an enjoyment such as was now offered her.

The following day was fixed for this excursion. La Luc and his party arose at an early hour, and having taken a slight breakfast, they set out towards the Glacier of Montanvert, which lay at a few leagues distance. Peter carried a small basket of provisions; and it was their plan to dine on some pleasant spot in the open air.

It is unnecessary to describe the high enthusiasm of Adeline, the more complacent pleasure of La Luc, and the transports of Clara, as the scenes of this romantic country shifted to their eyes. Now frowning in dark and gloomy grandeur, it exhibited only tremendous rocks and cataracts rolling from the heights into some deep and narrow valley, along which their united waters roared and foamed, and burst away to regions inaccessible to mortal foot: and now the scene arose less fiercely wild:

The pomp of groves and garniture of fields were intermingled with the ruder features of nature; and while the snow froze on the summit of the mountain, the vine blushed at its foot.

Engaged in interesting conversation, and by the admiration which the country excited, they travelled on till noon, when they looked round for a pleasant spot where they might rest and take refreshment. At some little distance they perceived the ruins of a fabric which had once been a castle; it stood almost on a point of rock that overhung a deep valley; and its broken turrets rising from among the woods that embosomed it, heightened the picturesque beauty of the object.

The edifice invited curiosity, and the shades repose—La Luc and his party advanced.

Deep struck with awe they mark'd the dome o'erthrown,

Where once the beauty bloom'd, the warrior shone:

They saw the castle's mouldering towers decay'd,

The loose stone tottering o'er the trembling shade.

They seated themselves on the grass under the shade of some high trees near the ruins. An opening in the woods afforded a view of the distant Alps—the deep silence of solitude reigned. For some time they were lost in meditation. Adeline felt a sweet complacency, such as she had long been a stranger to. Looking at La Luc, she perceived a tear stealing down his cheek, while the elevation of his mind was strongly expressed

244

on his countenance. He turned on Clara his eyes, which were now filled with tenderness, and made an effort to recover himself.

The stillness and total seclusion of this scene, said Adeline, those stupendous mountains, the gloomy grandeur of these woods, together with that monument of faded glory on which the hand of time is so emphatically impressed, diffuse a sacred enthusiasm over the mind, and awaken sensations truly sublime.

La Luc was going to speak; but Peter coming forward, desired to know whether he had not better open the wallet, as he fancied his honour and the young ladies must be main hungry, jogging on so far up hill and down before dinner. They acknowledged the truth of honest Peter's suspicion, and accepted his hint.

Refreshments were spread on the grass; and having seated themselves under the canopy of waving woods, surrounded by the sweets of wild flowers, they inhaled the pure breeze of the Alps, which might be called spirit of air, and partook of a repast which these circumstances rendered delicious.

When they arose to depart, — I am unwilling, said Clara, to quit this charming spot. How delightful would it be to pass one's life beneath these shades with the friends who are dear to one! — La Luc smiled at the romantic simplicity of the idea: but Adeline sighed deeply to the image of felicity and of Theodore which it recalled, and turned away to conceal her tears.

They now mounted their horses, and soon after arrived at the foot of Montanvert. The emotions of Adeline, as she contemplated in various points of view the astonishing objects around her, surpassed all expression; and the feelings of the whole party were too strong to admit of conversation. The profound stillness which reigned in these regions of solitude inspired awe, and heightened the sublimity of the scenery to an exquisite degree.

It seems, said Adeline, as if we were walking over the ruins of the world, and were the only persons who had survived the wreck. I can scarcely persuade myself that we are not left alone on the globe.

The view of these objects, said La Luc, lift the soul to their Great Author, and we contemplate with a feeling almost too vast for humanity — the sublimity of his nature in the grandeur of his works. — La Luc raised his eyes, filled with tears, to heaven, and was for some moments lost in silent adoration.

They quitted these scenes with extreme reluctance; but the hour of the day, and the appearance of the clouds, which seemed gathering for a storm, made them hasten their departure. Could she have been sheltered from its fury, Adeline almost wished to have witnessed the tremendous effect of a thunder storm in these regions.

They returned to Leloncourt by a different route, and the shade of the overhanging precipices was deepened by the gloom of the atmosphere. It was evening when they came within view of the lake, which the travelers rejoiced to see, for the storm so long threatened was now fast approaching; the thunder murmured among the Alps; and the dark vapours that rolled heavily along their sides heightened their dreadful sublimity. La Luc would have quickened his pace, but the road winding down the steep side of a mountain made caution necessary. The darkening air and the lightnings that now flashed along the horizon terrified Clara, but she withheld the expression of her fear in consideration of her father. A peal of thunder, which seemed to shake the earth to its foundations, and was reverberated in tremendous echoes from the cliffs, burst over their heads. Clara's horse took fright at the sound, and setting off, hurried her with amazing velocity down the mountain towards the lake, which washed its foot. The agony of La Luc, who viewed her progress in the horrible expectation of seeing her dashed down the precipice that bordered the road, is not to be described.

Clara kept her seat, but terror had almost deprived her of sense. Her efforts to preserve herself were mechanical, for she scarcely knew what she did. The horse, however, carried her safely almost to the foot of the mountain, but was making towards the lake, when a gentleman who travelled along the road caught the bridle as the animal endeavoured to pass. The sudden stopping of the horse threw Clara to the ground, and, impatient of restraint, the animal burst from the hand of the stranger, and plunged into the lake. The violence of the fall deprived her of recollection; but while the stranger endeavoured to support her, his servant ran to fetch water.

She soon recovered, and unclosing her eyes found herself in the arms of a chevalier, who appeared to support her with difficulty. The compassion expressed in his countenance while he inquired how she did, revived her spirits; and she was endeavouring to thank him for his kindness, when La Luc and

Adeline came up. The terror impressed on her father's features was perceived by Clara; languid as she was, she tried to raise herself, and said with a faint smile, which betrayed instead of disguising her sufferings, Dear Sir, I am not hurt. Her pale countenance and the blood that trickled down her cheek contradicted her words. But La Luc, to whom terror had suggested the utmost possible evil, now rejoiced to hear her speak; he recalled some presence of mind, and while Adeline applied her salts, he chafed her temples.

When she revived, she told him how much she was obliged to the stranger. La Luc endeavoured to express his gratitude; but the former interrupting him, begged he might be spared the pain of receiving thanks for having followed only an impulse of common humanity.

They were now not far from Leloncourt; but the evening was almost shut in, and the thunder murmured deeply among the hills. La Luc was distressed how to convey Clara home.

In endeavouring to raise her from the ground, the stranger betrayed such evident symptoms of pain, that La Luc inquired concerning it. The sudden jerk which the horse had given the arm of the chevalier, in escaping from his hold, had violently sprained his shoulder, and rendered his arm almost useless. The pain was exquisite; and La Luc, whose fears for his daughter were now subsiding, was shocked at the circumstance, and pressed the stranger to accompany him to the village, where relief might be obtained. He accepted the invitation; and Clara, being at length placed on a horse led by her father, was conducted to the chateau.

When Madame, who had been looking out for La Luc some time, perceived the cavalcade approaching, she was alarmed, and her apprehensions were confirmed when she saw the situation of her niece. Clara was carried into the house, and La Luc would have sent for a surgeon, but there was none within several leagues of the village, neither were there any of the physical profession within the same distance. Clara was assisted to her chamber by Adeline, and Madame La Luc undertook to examine the wounds. The result restored peace to the family, for though she was much bruised, she had escaped material injury; a slight contusion on the forehead had occasioned the bloodshed which at first alarmed La Luc. Madame undertook to restore her niece in a few days with the assistance of a balsam composed by herself, on the virtues of which she descanted with great eloquence, till La Luc interrupted her by reminding her of the condition of her patient.

247

Madame having bathed Clara's bruises, and given her a cordial of incomparable efficacy, left her; and Adeline watched in the chamber of her friend till she retired to her own for the night.

La Luc, whose spirits had suffered much perturbation, was now tranquillized by the report his sister made of Clara. He introduced the stranger; and having mentioned the accident he had met with, desired that he might have immediate assistance. Madame hastened to her closet; and it is perhaps difficult to determine whether she felt most concern for the sufferings of her guest, or pleasure at the opportunity thus offered of displaying her medical skill. However this might be, she quitted the room with great alacrity, and very quickly returned with a phial containing her inestimable balsam; and having given the necessary directions for the application of it, she left the stranger to the care of his servant.

La Luc insisted that the chevalier, M. Verneuil, should not leave the chateau that night, and he very readily submitted to be detained. His manners during the evening were as frank and engaging as the hospitality and gratitude of La Luc were sincere, and they soon entered into interesting conversation. M. Verneuil conversed like a man who had seen much, and thought more; and if he discovered any prejudice in his opinions, it was evidently the prejudice of a mind which, seeing objects through the medium of his own goodness, tinges them with the hue of its predominant quality. La Luc was much pleased, for in his retired situation he had not often an opportunity of receiving the pleasure which results from a communion of intelligent minds. He found that M. Verneuil had travelled. La Luc having asked some questions relative to England, they fell into discourse concerning the national characters of the French and English.

If it is the privilege of wisdom, said M. Verneuil, to look beyond happiness, I own I had rather be without it. When we observe the English, their laws, writings, and conversations, and at the same time mark their countenances, manners, and the frequency of suicide among them, we are apt to believe that wisdom and happiness are incompatible. If, on the other hand, we turn to their neighbours, the French, and see their wretched policy, their sparkling but sophistical discourse, frivolous occupations, and, withal, their gay animated air, we shall be compelled to acknowledge that happiness and folly too often dwell together.

It is the end of wisdom, said La Luc, to attain happiness, and I can hardly dignify that conduct or course of thinking which tends to misery with the name of wisdom. By this rule, perhaps, the folly, as we term it, of the French deserves, since its effect is happiness, to be called wisdom. That airy thoughtlessness, which alike to contemn reflection and anticipation, produces all the effect of it without reducing its subjects to the mortification of philosophy. But in truth wisdom is an exertion of mind to subdue folly; and as the happiness of the French is less the consequence of mind than of constitution, it deserves not the honours of wisdom.

Discoursing on the variety of opinions that are daily formed on the same conduct, La Luc observed how much that which is commonly called opinion is the result of passion and temper.

True, said M. Vernueil, there is a tone of thought, as there is a key note in music, that leads all its weaker affections. Thus, where the powers of judging may be equal, the disposition to judge is different; and the actions of men are but too often arraigned by whim and caprice, by partial vanity, and the humour of the moment.

Here La Luc took occasion to reprobate the conduct of those writers, who, by showing the dark side only of human nature, and by dwelling on the evils only which are incident to humanity, have sought to degrade man in his own eyes, and to make him discontented with life. What should we say of a painter, continued La Luc, who collected in his piece objects of a black hue only, who presents you with a black man, a black horse, a black dog, &c. &c., and tells you that his is a picture of nature, and that nature is black? — 'Tis true, you would reply, the objects you exhibit do exist in nature, but they form a very small part of her works. You say that nature is black, and, to prove it, you have collected on your canvass all the animals of this hue that exist. But you have forgot to paint the green earth, the blue sky, the white man, and objects of all those various hues with which creation abounds, and of which black is a very inconsiderable part.

The countenance of M. Verneuil lightened with peculiar animation during the discourse of La Luc. — To think well of his nature, said he, is necessary to the dignity and the happiness of man. There is a decent pride which becomes every mind, and is congenial to virtue. That consciousness of innate dignity, which shows him the glory of his nature, will be his best protection from the meanness of vice. Where this consciousness is wanting, continued M. Verneuil, there can be no sense of moral honour, and consequently none of the higher principles of action. What can be expected of him who says it is his nature to be mean and selfish? Or who can doubt that he who thinks thus, thinks from the experience of his own heart, from the tendency of his own inclinations? Let it always be remembered, that he who would persuade men to be good, ought to show them that they are great.

You speak, said La Luc, with the honest enthusiasm of a virtuous mind; and in obeying the impulse of your heart, you utter the truths of philosophy: and, trust me, a bad heart and a truly philosophic head have never yet been united in the same individual. Vicious inclinations not only corrupt the heart, but the understanding, and thus lead to false reasoning. Virtue only is on the side of truth.

La Luc and his guest, mutually pleased with each other, entered upon the discussion of subjects so interesting to them both, that it was late before they parted for the night.

It must be remembered that this was said in the seventeenth century.

CHAPTER XVIII

'Twas such a scene as gave a kind relief

To memory, in sweetly pensive grief.

VIRGIL'S TOMB.

Mine be the breezy hill, that skirts the down,

Where a green grassy turf is all I crave,

With here and there a violet bestrown,

And many an evening sun shine sweetly on my grave.

THE MINSTREL.

Repose had so much restored Clara, that when Adeline, anxious to know how she did, went early in the morning to her chamber, she found her already risen, and ready to attend the family at breakfast. Monsieur Verneuil appeared also; but his looks betrayed a want of rest, and indeed he had suffered during the night a degree of anguish from his arm which it was an effort of some resolution to endure in silence. It was now swelled and somewhat inflamed, and this might in some degree be attributed to the effect of Madame La Luc's balsam, the restorative qualities of which for once had failed. The whole family sympathized with his sufferings, and Madame at the request of M. Verneuil, abandoned her balsam, and substituted an emollient fomentation.

From an application of this, he in a short time found an abatement of the pain, and returned to the breakfast table with greater composure. The happiness which La Luc felt at seeing his daughter in safety was very apparent; but the warmth of his gratitude towards her preserver he found it difficult to express. Clara spoke the genuine emotions of her heart with artless but modest energy, and testified sincere concern for the sufferings which she had occasioned M. Verneuil.

The pleasure received from the company of his guest, and the consideration of the essential services he had rendered him, co-operated with the natural hospitality of La Luc, and he pressed M. Verneuil to remain some time at the chateau. — I can never repay the services you have done me, said La Luc; yet I seek to increase my obligations to you by requesting you will prolong your visit, and thus allow me an opportunity of cultivating your acquaintance.

M. Verneuil, who at the time he met La Luc was travelling from Geneva to a distant part of Savoy, merely for the purpose of viewing the country, being now delighted with his host and with every thing around him, willingly accepted the invitation. In this circumstance prudence concurred with inclination, for to have pursued his journey on horseback, in his present situation, would have been dangerous, if not impracticable.

The morning was spent in conversation, in which M. Verneuil displayed a mind enriched with taste, enlightened by science, and enlarged by observation. The situation of the chateau and the features of the surrounding scenery charmed him, and in the evening he found himself able to walk with La Luc and explore the beauties of this romantic region. As they passed through the village, the salutations of the peasants, in whom love and respect were equally blended, and their eager inquiries after Clara, bore testimony to the character of La Luc; while his countenance expressed a serene satisfaction, arising from the consciousness of deserving and possessing their love. —I live surrounded by my children, said he, turning to M. Verneuil, who had noticed their eagerness; for such I consider my parishioners. In discharging the duties of my office, I am repaid not only by my own conscience, but by their gratitude. There is a luxury in observing their simple and honest love, which I would not exchange for any thing the world calls blessings.

Yet the world, Sir, would call the pleasures of which you speak romantic, said M. Verneuil; for to be sensible of this pure and exquisite delight requires a heart untainted with the vicious pleasures of society — pleasures that deaden its finest feelings and poison the source of its truest enjoyments. — They pursued their way along the borders of the lake, sometimes under the shade of hanging woods, and sometimes over hillocks of turf, where the scene opened in all its wild magnificence. M. Verneuil often stopped in raptures to observe and point out the singular beauties it exhibited, while La Luc, pleased with the delight his friend expressed, surveyed with more than usual satisfaction the objects which had so often charmed him before. But there was a tender melancholy in the tone of his voice and his countenance, which arose from the recollection of having often traced those scenes, and partaken of the pleasure they inspired, with her who had long since bade them an eternal farewell.

They presently quitted the lake, and, winding up a steep ascent between the woods, came after a hour's walk to a green summit, which appeared, among the savage rocks that environed it, like the blossom on the thorn. It was a spot formed for solitary delight, inspiring that soothing tenderness so dear to the feeling mind, and which calls back to memory the images of past regret, softened by distance and endeared by frequent recollection. Wild shrubs grew from the crevices of the rocks beneath, and the high trees of pine and cedar that waved above, afforded a melancholy and romantic shade. The silence of the scene was interrupted only by the breeze as it rolled over the woods, and by the solitary notes of the birds that inhabited the cliffs.

From this point the eye commanded an entire view of those majestic and sublime Alps whose aspect fills the soul with emotions of indescribable awe, and seems to lift it to a nobler nature. The village and the chateau of La Luc appeared in the bosom of the mountains, a peaceful retreat from the storms that gathered on their tops. All the faculties of M. Verneuil were absorbed in admiration, and he was for some time quite silent; at length, bursting into a rhapsody, he turned, and would have addressed La Luc, when he perceived him at a distance leaning against a rustic urn, over which drooped in beautiful luxuriance the weeping willow.

As he approached, La Luc quitted his position, and advanced to meet him, while M. Verneuil inquired upon what occasion the urn had been erected. La Luc, unable to answer, pointed to it, and walked silently away, and M. Verneuil approaching the urn, read the following inscription:

TO

THE MEMORY OF CLARA LA LUC,

THIS URN

IS ERECTED ON THE SPOT WHICH SHE

LOVED, IN TESTIMONY OF

THE AFFECTION OF

A HUSBAND.

M. Verneuil now comprehended the whole, and, feeling for his friend, was hurt that he had noticed this monument of his grief. He rejoined La Luc, who was standing on the point of the eminence contemplating the landscape below with an air more placid, and touched with the sweetness of piety and resignation. He perceived that M. Verneuil was somewhat disconcerted, and he sought to remove his uneasiness. You will consider it, said he, as a mark of my esteem that I have brought you to this spot: it is never profaned by the presence of the unfeeling; they would deride the faithfulness of an attachment which has so long survived its object, and which, in their own breasts, would quickly have been lost amidst the dissipation of general society. I have cherished in my heart the remembrance of a woman whose virtues claimed all my love: I have cherished it as a treasure to which I could withdraw from temporary cares and vexations, in the certainty of finding a soothing, though melancholy comfort.

La Luc paused. M. Verneuil expressed the sympathy he felt, but he knew the sacredness of sorrow, and soon relapsed into silence. One of the brightest hopes of a future state, resumed La Luc, is, that we shall meet again those whom we have loved upon earth. And perhaps our happiness may be permitted to consist very much in the society of our friends, purified from the frailties of mortality, with the finer affections more sweetly attuned, and with the faculties of mind infinitely more elevated and enlarged. We shall then be enabled to comprehend subjects which are too vast for human conception; to comprehend, perhaps, the sublimity of that Deity who first called us into being. These views of futurity, my friend, elevate us above the evils of this world, and seem to communicate to us a portion of the nature we contemplate.

Call them not the illusions of a visionary brain, proceeded La Luc: I trust in their reality. Of this I am certain, that whether they are illusions or not, a faith in them ought to be cherished for the comfort it brings to the heart, and reverenced for the dignity it imparts to the mind. Such feelings make a happy and an important part of our belief in a future existence: they give energy to virtue, and stability to principle.

This, said M. Verneuil, is what I have often felt, and what every ingenuous mind must acknowledge.

La Luc and M. Verneuil continued in conversation till the sun had left the scene. The mountains, darkened by twilight, assumed a sublimer aspect, while the tops of some of the highest Alps were yet illuminated by the sun's rays, and formed a striking contrast to the shadowy obscurity of the world below. As they descended through the woods, and traversed the margin of the lake, the stillness and solemnity of the hour diffused a pensive sweetness over their minds, and sunk them into silence.

They found supper spread, as was usual, in the hall, of which the windows opened upon a garden, where the flowers might be said to yield their fragrance in gratitude to the refreshing dews. The windows were embowered with eglantine and other sweet shrubs, which hung in wild luxuriance around, and formed a beautiful and simple decoration. Clara and Adeline loved to pass their evenings in this hall, where they had acquired the first rudiments of astronomy, and from which they had a wide view of the heavens. La Luc pointed out to them the planets and the fixed stars, explained their laws, and from thence taking occasion to mingle moral with scientific instruction, would often ascend towards that great First Cause, whose nature soars beyond the grasp of human comprehension.

No study, he would sometimes say, so much enlarges the mind, or impresses it with so sublime an idea of the Deity, as that of astronomy. When the imagination launches into the regions of space, and contemplates the innumerable worlds which are scattered through it, we are lost in astonishment and awe. This globe appears as a mass of atoms in the immensity of the universe, and man a mere insect. Yet how wonderful! that man, whose frame is so diminutive in the scale of being, should have powers which spurn the narrow boundaries of time and place, soar beyond the sphere of his existence, penetrate the secret laws of nature, and calculate their progressive effects.

O! how expressively does this prove the spirituality of our being! Let the materialist consider it, and blush that he has ever doubted.

In this hall the whole family now met at supper; and during the remainder of the evening the conversation turned upon general subjects, in which Clara joined in modest and judicious remark. La Luc had taught her to familiarize her mind to reasoning, and had accustomed her to deliver her sentiments freely: she spoke them with a simplicity extremely engaging, and which convinced her hearers that the love of knowledge, not the vanity of talking, induced her to converse. M. Verneuil evidently endeavoured to draw forth her sentiments; and Clara, interested by the subjects he introduced, a stranger to affectation, and pleased with the opinions he expressed, answered them with frankness and animation. They retired mutually pleased with each other.

M. Verneuil was about six-and-thirty; his figure manly, his countenance frank and engaging. A quick penetrating eye, whose fire was softened by benevolence, disclosed the chief traits of his character; he was quick to discern, but generous to excuse, the follies of mankind; and while no one more sensibly felt an injury, none more readily accepted the concession of an enemy.

He was by birth a Frenchman. A fortune lately devolved to him, had enabled him to execute the plan which his active and inquisitive mind had suggested, of viewing the most remarkable parts of the continent. He was peculiarly susceptible of the beautiful and sublime in nature. To such a taste, Switzerland and the adjacent country was, of all others, the most interesting; and he found the scenery it exhibited infinitely surpassing all that his glowing imagination had painted; he saw with the eye of a painter, and felt with the rapture of a poet.

In the habitation of La Luc he met with the hospitality, the frankness, and the simplicity so characteristic of the country; in his venerable host he saw the strength of philosophy united with the finest tenderness of humanity—a philosophy which taught him to correct his feelings, not to annihilate them; in Clara, the bloom of beauty with the most perfect simplicity of heart; and in Adeline, all the charms of elegance and grace, with a genius deserving of the highest culture. In this family picture the goodness of Madame La Luc was not unperceived or forgotten. The cheerfulness and harmony that reigned within the chateau was delightful; but the philanthropy which, flowing from the heart of the pastor, was diffused through the whole village, and united the inhabitants in the sweet and firm bonds of social compact, was divine. The beauty of its situation conspired with these circumstances to make Leloncourt seem almost a paradise. M. Verneuil sighed that he must soon quit it. I ought to seek no further, said he, for here wisdom and happiness dwell together.

The admiration was reciprocal: La Luc and his family found themselves much interested in M. Verneuil, and looked forward to the time of his departure with regret. So warmly they pressed him to prolong his visit, and so powerfully his own inclinations seconded theirs, that he accepted the invitation. La Luc admitted no circumstance which might contribute to the amusement of his guest, who having in a few days recovered the use of his arm, they made several excursions among the mountains. Adeline and Clara, whom the care of Madame had restored to her usual health, were generally of the party.

After spending a week at the chateau, M. Verneuil bade adieu to La Luc and his family. They parted with mutual regret; and the former promised that when he returned to Geneva, he would take Leloncourt in his way. As he said this, Adeline, who had for some time observed with much alarm La Luc's declining health, looked mournfully on his languid countenance, and uttered a secret prayer that he might live to receive the visit of M. Verneuil.

Madame was the only person who did not lament his departure; she saw that the efforts of her brother to entertain his guest were more than his present state of health would admit of, and she rejoiced in the quiet that would now return to him.

But this quiet brought La Luc no respite from illness; the fatigue he had suffered in his late excursions seemed to have increased his disorder, which in a short time assumed the aspect of a consumption. Yielding to the solicitations of his family, he went to Geneva for advice, and was there recommended to try the air of Nice.

The journey thither, however, was of considerable length; and believing his life to be very precarious, he hesitated whether to go. He was also unwilling to leave the duty of his parish unperformed for so long a period as his health might require; but this was an objection which would not have withheld him from Nice, had his faith in the climate been equal to that of his physicians.

His parishioners felt the life of their pastor to be of the utmost consequence to them: it was a general cause, and they testified at once his worth, and their sense of it, by going in a body to solicit him to leave them. He was much affected by this instance of their attachment. Such a proof of regard, joined with the entreaties of his own family, and a consideration that for their sakes it was a duty to endeavour to prolong his life, was too powerful to be withstood, and he determined to set out for Italy.

It was settled that Clara and Adeline, whose health La Luc thought required change of air and scene, should accompany him, attended by the faithful Peter.

On the morning of his departure, a large body of his parishioners assembled round the door to bid him farewell. It was an affecting scene; — they might meet no more. At length, wiping the tears from his eyes, La Luc said, Let us trust in God, my friends; he has power to heal all disorders both of body and mind. We shall meet again, if not in this world, I hope in a better; — let our conduct be such as to ensure that better.

The sobs of his people prevented any reply. There was scarcely a dry eye in the village; for there was scarcely an inhabitant of it that was not now assembled in the presence of La Luc. He shook hands with them all; Farewell, my friends, said he, we shall meet again. — God grant we may! said they, with one voice of fervent petition.

Having mounted his horse, and Clara and Adeline being ready, they took a last leave of Madame La Luc, and quitted the chateau. The people unwilling to leave La Luc, the greater part of them accompanied him to some distance from the village. As he moved slowly on, he cast a last lingering look at his little home, where he had spent so many peaceful years, and which he now gazed on perhaps for the last time, and tears rose to his eyes; but he checked them. Every scene of the adjacent country called up, as he passed, some tender remembrance. He looked towards the spot consecrated to the memory of his deceased wife; the dewy vapours of the morning veiled it. La Luc felt the disappointment more deeply, perhaps, than reason could justify; but those who know from experience how much the imagination loves to dwell on any object, however remotely connected with that of our tenderness, will feel with him. This was an object round which the affections of La Luc had settled themselves; it was a memorial to the eye, and the view of it awakened more forcibly in the memory every tender idea that could associate with the primary subject of his regard. In such cases fancy gives to the illusions of strong affection the stamp of reality, and they are cherished by the heart with romantic fondness.

His people accompanied him for near a mile from the village, and could scarcely then be prevailed on to leave him: at length he once more bade them farewell, and went on his way, followed by their prayers and blessings.

La Luc and his little party travelled slowly on, sunk in pensive silence — a silence too pleasingly sad to be soon relinquished, and which they indulged without fear of interruption. The solitary grandeur of the scenes through which they passed, and the soothing murmur of the pines that waved above, aided this soft luxury of meditation.

They proceeded by easy stages; and after travelling for some days among the romantic mountains and green valleys of Piedmont, they entered the rich country of Nice. The gay and luxuriant views which now opened upon the travellers as they wound among the hills, appeared like scenes of fairy enchantment, or those produced by the lonely visions of the poets. While the spiral summits of the mountains exhibited the snowy severity of winter, the pine, the cypress, the olive, and the myrtle shaded their sides with the green tints of spring, and groves of orange, lemon, and citron, spread over their feet the full glow of autumn. As they advanced, the scenery became still more diversified; and at length, between the receding heights, Adeline caught a glimpse of the distant waters of the Mediterranean fading into the blue and cloudless horizon. She had never till now seen the ocean; and this transient view of it roused her imagination, and made her watch impatiently for a nearer prospect.

It was towards the close of day when the travellers, winding round an abrupt projection of that range of Alps which crowns the amphitheatre that environs Nice, looked down upon the green hills that stretch to the shores, on the city, and its ancient castle, and on the wide waters of the Mediterranean; with the mountains of Corsica in the furthest distance. Such a sweep of sea and land, so varied with the gay, the magnificent, and the awful, would have fixed any eye in admiration. For Adeline and Clara novelty and enthusiasm added their charms to the prospect. The soft and salubrious air seemed to welcome La Luc to this smiling region, and the serene atmosphere to promise invariable summer. They at length descended upon the little plain where stands the city of Nice, and which was the most extensive piece of level ground they had passed since they entered the country. Here, in the bosom of the mountains, sheltered from the north and the east, where the western gales alone seemed to breathe, all the blooms of spring and the riches of autumn were united. Trees of myrtle bordered the road, which wound among groves of orange, lemon, and bergamot, whose delicious fragrance came to the sense mingled with the breath of roses and carnations that blossomed in their shade. The gently swelling hills that rose from the plain were covered with vines, and crowned with cypresses, olives, and date trees; beyond, there appeared the sweep of lofty mountains whence the travellers had descended, and whence rose the little river Paglion, swollen by the snows that melt on their summits, and which, after meandering through the plain, washes the walls of Nice, where it falls into the Mediterranean. In this blooming region Adeline observed that the countenances of the peasants, meagre and discontented, formed a melancholy contrast to the face of the country; and she lamented again the effects of an arbitrary government, where the bounties of nature, which were designed for all, are monopolized by a few, and the many are suffered to starve, tantalized by surrounding plenty.

The city lost much of its enchantment on a nearer approach; its narrow streets and shabby houses but ill answered the expectation which a distant view of its ramparts and its harbour, gay with vessels, seemed to authorize. The appearance of the inn at which La Luc now alighted did not contribute to soften his disappointment: but if he was surprised to find such indifferent accommodation at the inn of a town celebrated as the resort of valetudinarians, he was still more so when he learned the difficulty of procuring furnished lodgings.

After much search, he procured apartments in a small but pleasant house situated a little way out of the town; it had a garden, and a terrace which overlooked the sea, and was distinguished by an air of neatness very unusual in the houses of Nice. He agreed to board with the family, whose table likewise accommodated a gentleman and lady, their lodgers; and thus he became a temporary inhabitant of this charming climate.

On the following morning Adeline rose at an early hour, eager to indulge the new and sublime emotion with which a view of the ocean inspired her, and walked with Clara toward the hills that afforded a more extensive prospect. They pursued their way for some time between high embowering banks, till they arrived at an eminence, whence:

Heaven, earth, ocean, smiled!

They sat down on a point of rock overshadowed by lofty palm-trees, to contemplate at leisure the magnificent scene. The sun was just emerged from the sea, over which his rays shed a flood of light, and darted a thousand brilliant tints on the vapours that ascend the horizon, and floated there in light clouds, leaving the bosom of the waters below clear as crystal, except where the white surges were seen to beat upon the rocks; and discovering the distant sails of the fishing-boats, and the far distant highlands of Corsica tinted with ethereal blue. Clara, after some time, drew forth her pencil, but threw it aside in despair. Adeline, as they returned home through a romantic glen, when her senses were no longer absorbed in the contemplation of this grand scenery, and when its images floated on her memory only in softened colours, repeated the following lines:

SUNRISE: A SONNET

Oft let me wander, at the break of day,

Through the cool vale o'erhung with waving woods,

Drink the rich fragrance of the budding May,

And catch the murmur of the distant floods;

Or rest on the fresh bank of limpid rill,

Where sleeps the violet in the dewy shade,

Where opening lilies balmy sweets distil,

And the wild musk-rose weeps along the glade:

Or climb the eastern cliff, whose airy head

Hangs rudely o'er the blue and misty main;

Watch the fine hues of morn through ether spread,

And paint with roseate glow the crystal plain.

Oh! who can speak the rapture of the soul

When o'er the waves the sun first steals to sight,

And all the world of waters, as they roll,

And Heaven's vast vault unveils in living light!

So life's young hour to man enchanting smiles,

With sparkling health, and joy, and fancy's fairy wiles!

La Luc in his walks met with some sensible and agreeable companions, who like himself came to Nice in search of health. Of these he soon formed a small but pleasant society, among whom was a Frenchman, whose mild manners, marked with a deep and interesting melancholy, had particularly attracted La Luc. He very seldom mentioned himself, or any circumstance that might lead to a knowledge of his family, but on other subjects conversed with frankness and much intelligence. La Luc had frequently invited him to his lodgings, but he had always declined the invitation; and this in a manner so gentle as to disarm displeasure, and convince La Luc that his refusal was the consequence of a certain dejection of mind which made him reluctant to meet other strangers.

The description which La Luc had given of this foreigner had excited the curiosity of Clara; and the sympathy which the unfortunate feel for each other called forth the commiseration of Adeline; for that he was unfortunate she could not doubt. On their return from an evening walk La Luc pointed out the chevalier, and quickened his pace to overtake him. Adeline was for a moment impelled to follow; but delicacy checked her steps, she knew how painful the presence of a stranger often is to a wounded mind, and forbore to intrude herself on his notice for the sake of only satisfying an idle curiosity. She turned therefore into another path: but the delicacy which now prevented the meeting, accident in a few days defeated, and La Luc introduced the stranger. Adeline received him with a soft smile, but endeavoured to restrain the expression of pity which her features had involuntarily assumed; she wished him not to know that she observed he was unhappy.

After this interview he no longer rejected the invitations of La Luc, but made him frequent visits, and often accompanied Adeline and Clara in their rambles. The mild and sensible conversation of the former seemed to soothe his mind, and in her presence he frequently conversed with a degree of animation which La Luc till then had not observed in him. Adeline too derived from the similarity of their taste, and his intelligent conversation, a degree of satisfaction which contributed, with the compassion his dejection inspired, to win her confidence, and she conversed with an easy frankness rather unusual to her.

His visits soon became more frequent. He walked with La Luc and his family; he attended them on their little excursions to view those magnificent remains of Roman antiquity which enrich the neighbourhood of Nice. When the ladies sat at home and worked, he enlivened the hours by reading to them, and they had the pleasure to observe his spirits somewhat relieved from the heavy melancholy that had oppressed him.

M. Amand was passionately fond of music. Clara had not forgot to bring her beloved lute: he would sometimes strike the chords in the most sweet and mournful symphonies, but never could be prevailed on to play. When Adeline or Clara played, he would sit in deep reverie, and lost to every object around him, except when he fixed his eyes in mournful gaze on Adeline, and a sigh would sometimes escape him.

One evening, Adeline having excused herself from accompanying La Luc and Clara in a visit to a neighbouring family, she retired to the terrace of the garden which overlooked the sea; and as she viewed the tranquil splendour of the setting sun, and his glories reflected on the polished surface of the waves, she touched the strings of the lute in softest harmony, her voice accompanying it with words which she had one day written after having read that rich effusion of Shakespeare's genius, "A Midsummer Night's Dream."

TITANIA TO HER LOVE.

O! fly with me through distant air

To isles that gem the western deep!

For laughing Summer revels there,

And hangs her wreath on every steep.

As through the green transparent sea

Light floating on the waves we go,

The nymphs shall gaily welcome me,

Far in their coral caves below.

For oft upon their margin sands,

When twilight leads the freshening hours,

I come with all my jocund bands

To charm them from their sea-green bowers.

And well they love our sports to view,

And on the ocean's breast to lave;

And oft as we the dance renew,

They call up music from the wave.

Swift hie we to that splendid clime,

Where gay Jamaica spreads her scene,

Lifts the blue mountain—wild—sublime!

And smooths her vales of vivid green.

Where throned high, in pomp of shade,

The power of vegetation reigns,

Expanding wide, o'er hill and glade,

Shrubs of all growth—fruit of all stains:

She steals the sun-beam's fervid glow,

To paint her flowers of mingling hue;
And o'er the grape the purple throw,
Breaking from verdant leaves to view.
There myrtle bowers, and citron grove,
O'er canopy our airy dance;
And there the sea-breeze loves to rove,
When trembles day's departing glance.
And when the false moon steals away,
Or ere the chasing morn doth rise,
Oft, fearless, we our gambols play
By the fire-worm's radiant eyes.
And suck the honey'd reeds that swell
In tufted plumes of silver white;
Or pierce the cocoa's milky cell,
To sip the nectar of delight!
And when the shaking thunders roll,
And lightnings strike athwart the gloom,
We shelter in the cedar's bole,
And revel 'mid the rich perfume!
But chief we love beneath the palm,
Or verdant plantain's spreading leaf,
To hear, upon the midnight calm,
Sweet Philomela pour her grief.
To mortal sprite such dulcet sound,
Such blissful hours, were never known!
O fly with me my airy round,
And I will make them all thine own!

Adeline ceased to sing—when she immediately heard repeated in a low voice:

To mortal sprite such dulcet sound,

Such blissful hours, were never known!

and turning her eyes whence it came, she saw M. Amand.
She blushed and laid down the lute, which he instantly took up,
and with a tremulous hand drew forth tones

That might create a soul,

Under the ribs of death:

In a melodious voice, that trembled with sensibility, he sang
the following

SONNET

How sweet is Love's first gentle sway,

When crown'd with flowers he softly smiles!

His blue eyes fraught with tearful wiles,

Where beams of tender transport play:

Hope leads him on his airy way,

And faith and fancy still beguiles — —

Faith quickly tangled in her toils — —

Fancy, whose magic forms so say

The fair deceiver's self deceive — —

How sweet is love's first gentle sway!

Ne'er would that heart he bids to grieve

From sorrow's soft enchantments stray — —

Ne'er — till the God exulting in his art,

Relentless frowns and wings th' envenom'd dart.

Monsieur Amand paused: he seemed much oppressed, and
at length, bursting into tears, laid down the instrument and
walked abruptly away to the further end of the terrace. Adeline,
without seeming to observe his agitation, arose and leaned
upon the wall, below which a group of fishermen were busily
employed in drawing a net. In a few moments he returned with
a composed and softened countenance. Forgive this abrupt

conduct, said he; I know not how to apologize for it but by
owning its cause. When I tell you, Madame, that my tears flow
to the memory of a lady who strongly resembled you, and who
is lost to me for ever, you will know how to pity me. — His voice
faltered, and he paused. Adeline was silent. The lute he
resumed, was her favourite instrument, and when you touched
it with such a melancholy expression, I saw her very image
before me. But, alas! why do I distress you with a knowledge of
my sorrows! she is gone, and never to return! And you, Adeline,
—you— — He checked his speech; and Adeline turning on him a
look of mournful regard, observed a wildness in his eyes which
alarmed her. These recollections are too painful, said she in a
gentle voice: let us return to the house; M. La Luc is probably
come home. O no! replied M. Amand; — No — this breeze
refreshes me. How often at this hour have I talked with her, as I
now talk with you! — such were the soft tones of her voice — such
the ineffable expression of her countenance. — Adeline
interrupted him. Let me beg of you to consider your health —
this dewy air cannot be good for invalids. He stood with his
hands clasped, and seemed not to hear her. She took up the lute
to go, and passed her fingers lightly over the chords. The
sounds recalled his scattered senses: he raised his eyes, and
fixed them in long unsettled gaze upon hers. Must I leave you
here? said she smiling, and standing in an attitude to depart — I
entreat you to play again the air I heard just now, said M.
Amand in a hurried voice. — Certainly; and she immediately
began to play. He leaned against a palm tree in an attitude of
deep attention, and as the sounds languished on the air, his
features gradually lost their wild expression, and he melted into
tears. He continued to weep silently till the song concluded, and
it was some time before he recovered voice enough to say,
Adeline, I cannot thank you for this goodness: my mind has
recovered its bias; you have soothed a broken heart. Increase the
kindness you have shown me, by promising never to mention
what you have witnessed this evening, and I will endeavour
never again to wound your sensibility by a similar offence. —
Adeline gave the required promise; and M. Amand, pressing
her hand, with a melancholy smile hurried from the garden,
and she saw him no more that night.

La Luc had been near a fortnight at Nice, and his health,
instead of amending seemed rather to decline, yet he wished to
make a longer experiment of the climate. The air which failed to
restore her venerable friend revived Adeline, and the variety
and novelty of the surrounding scenes amused her mind,
though, since they could not obliterate the memory of past, or
suppress the pang of present affection, they were ineffectual to
dissipate the sick languor of melancholy. Company, by

compelling her to withdraw her attention from the subject of her sorrow, afforded her a transient relief, but the violence of the exertion generally left her more depressed. It was in the stillness of solitude, in the tranquil observance of beautiful nature, that her mind recovered its tone, and, indulging the pensive inclination now become habitual to it, was soothed and fortified. Of all the grand objects which nature had exhibited, the ocean inspired her with the most sublime admiration. She loved to wander alone on its shores; and when she could escape so long from the duties or forms of society, she would sit for hours on the beach watching the rolling waves, and listening to their dying murmur, till her softened fancy recalled long-lost scenes, and restored the image of Theodore; when tears of despondency too often followed those of pity and regret. But these visions of memory, painful as they were, no longer excited that phrensy of grief they formerly awakened in Savoy; the sharpness of misery was passed, though its heavy influence was not perhaps less powerful. To these solitary indulgences generally succeeded calmness, and what Adeline endeavoured to believe was resignation.

She usually rose early, and walked down to the shore to enjoy, in the cool and silent hours of the morning, the cheering beauty of nature, and inhale the pure sea-breeze. Every object then smiled in fresh and lively colours. The blue sea, the brilliant sky, the distant fishing-boats with their white sails, and the voices of the fishermen borne at intervals on the air, were circumstances which reanimated her spirits; and in one of her rambles, yielding to that taste for poetry which had seldom forsaken her, she repeated the following lines: —

MORNING, ON THE SEA SHORE

What print of fairy feet is here

On Neptune's smooth and yellow sands?

What midnight revel's airy dance,

Beneath the moonbeam's trembling glance

Has blest these shores? — What sprightly bands

Have chased the waves uncheck'd by fear?

Whoe'er they were they fled from morn,

For now, all silent and forlorn,

These tide-forsaken sands appear —

Return, sweet sprites! the scene to cheer!

In vain the call! — Till moonlight's hour

Again diffuse its softer power,

Titania, nor her fairy loves,

Emerge from India's spicy groves.

Then, when the shadowy hour returns,

When silence reigns o'er air and earth,

And every star in ether burns,

They come to celebrate their mirth;

In frolic ringlet trip the ground,

Bid music's voice on silence win,

Till magic echoes answer round —

Thus do their festive rites begin.

O fairy forms so coy to mortal ken,

Your mystic steps to poets only shown;

O! lead me to the brook, or hollow'd glen,

Retiring far, with winding woods o'ergrown

Where'er ye best delight to rule;

If in some forest's lone retreat,

Thither conduct my willing feet

To the light brink of fountain cool,

Where, sleeping in the midnight dew,

Lie spring's young buds of every hue,

Yielding their sweet breath to the air;

To fold their silken leaves from harm,

And their chill heads in moonshine warm,

Is bright Titania's tender care.

There, to the night-birds's plaintive chaunt

Your carols sweet ye love to raise,

With oaten reed and pastoral lays;

And guard with forceful spell her haunt,

Who, when your antic sports are done,

Oft lulls ye in the lily's cell,

Sweet flower! that suits your slumbers well,

And shields ye from the rising sun.

When not to India's steeps ye fly

After twilight and the moon,

In honey buds ye love to lie,

While reigns supreme light's fervid noon;

Nor quit the cell where peace pervades.

Till night leads on the dews and shades.

E'en now your scenes enchanted meet my sight!

I see the earth unclose, the palace rise,

The high dome swell, and long arcades of light

Glitter among the deep embowering woods,

And glance reflecting from the trembling floods!

While to soft lutes the portals wide unfold,

And fairy forms, of fine ethereal dyes,

Advance with frolic step and laughing eyes,

Their hair with pearl, their garments deck'd with gold;

Pearls that in Neptune's briny waves they sought,

And gold from India's deepest caverns brought.

Thus your light visions to my eyes unveil,

Ye sportive pleasures, sweet illusion, hail!

But ah! at morn's first blush again ye fade!

So from youth's ardent gaze life's landscape gay,

And forms in fancy's summer hues array'd,

Dissolve at once in air at truth's resplendent day!

During several days succeeding that on which M. Amand had disclosed the cause of his melancholy, he did not visit La Luc. At length Adeline met him in one of her solitary rambles on the shore. He was pale, and dejected, and seemed much agitated when he observed her; she therefore endeavoured to avoid him, but he advanced with quickened steps and accosted her. He said it was his intention to leave Nice in a few days. I have found no benefit from the climate, added M. Amand; alas! what climate can relieve the sickness of the heart! I go to lose in the varieties of new scenes the remembrance of past happiness; yet the effort is vain; I am every where equally restless and unhappy. Adeline tried to encourage him to hope much from time and change of place. Time will blunt the sharpest edge of sorrow, said she; I know it from experience. Yet while she spoke, the tears in her eyes contradicted the assertions of her lips. — You have been unhappy, Adeline! — Yes — I knew it from the first. The smile of pity which you gave me, assured me that you knew what it was to suffer. The desponding air with which he spoke renewed her apprehension of a scene similar to the one she had lately witnessed, and she changed the subject; but he soon returned to it. You bid me hope much from time! — My wife! — My dear wife! — — his tongue faltered — It is now many months since I lost her — yet the moment of her death seems but as yesterday. Adeline faintly smiled. You can scarcely judge of the effect of time, yet you have much to hope for. He shook his head. But I am again intruding my misfortunes on your notice; forgive this perpetual egotism. There is a comfort in the pity of the good, such as nothing else can impart; this must plead my excuse; may you, Adeline, never want it! Ah! those tears — — Adeline hastily dried them. M. Amand forbore to press the subject, and immediately began to converse on indifferent topics. They returned towards the chateau; but La Luc being from home, M. Amand took leave at the door. Adeline retired to her chamber, oppressed by her own sorrows, and those of her amiable friend.

Near three weeks had now elapsed at Nice, during which the disorder of La Luc seemed rather to increase than abate, when his physician very honestly confessed the little hope he entertained from the climate, and advised him to try the effect of a sea voyage, adding that if the experiment failed, even the air of Montpellier appeared to him more likely to afford relief than that of Nice. La Luc received this disinterested advice with a mixture of gratitude and disappointment. The circumstances which had made him reluctant to quit Savoy, rendered him yet more so to protract his absence and increase his expenses; but the ties of affection that bound him to his family, and the love of life, which so seldom leaves us, again prevailed over inferior considerations; and he determined to coast the Mediterranean as far as Languedoc, where if the voyage did not answer his expectation he would land and proceed to Montpellier.

When M. Amand learned that La Luc designed to quit Nice in a few days, he determined not to leave it before him. During this interval he had not sufficient resolution to deny himself the frequent conversation of Adeline, though her presence, by reminding him of his lost wife, gave him more pain than comfort. He was the second son of a French gentleman of family, and had been married about a year to a lady to whom he had long been attached, when she died in her lying-in. The infant soon followed its mother, and left the disconsolate father abandoned to grief, which had preyed so heavily on his health, that his physician thought it necessary to send him to Nice. From the air of Nice, however, he had derived no benefit; and he now determined to travel further into Italy, though he no longer felt any interest in those charming scenes which in happier days and with her whom he never ceased to lament, would have afforded him the highest degree of mental luxury — now he sought only to escape from himself, or rather from the image of her who had once constituted his truest happiness.

La Luc having laid his plan, hired a small vessel, and in a few days embarked, with a sick hope, bidding adieu to the shores of Italy and the towering Alps, and seeking on a new element the health which had hitherto mocked his pursuit.

M. Amand took a melancholy leave of his new friends, whom he attended to the sea-side. When he assisted Adeline on board, his heart was too full to suffer him to say farewell; but he stood long on the beach pursuing with his eyes her course over the waters, and waving his hand, till tears dimmed his sight. The breeze wafted the vessel gently from the coast, and Adeline saw herself surrounded by the undulating waves of the ocean. The shore appeared to recede, its mountains to lessen, the gay colours of its landscape to melt into each other, and in a short time the figure of M. Amand was seen no more: the town of Nice, with its castle and harbour next faded away in distance, and the purple tint of the mountains was at length all that remained on the verge of the horizon. She sighed as she gazed, and her eyes filled with tears. So vanished my prospect of happiness, said she; and my future view is like the waste of waters that surround me. Her heart was full, and she retired from observation to a remote part of the deck, where she indulged her tears as she watched the vessel cut its way through the liquid glass. The water was so transparent that she saw the sun-beams playing at a considerable depth, and fish of various colours glance athwart the current. Innumerable marine plants spread their vigorous leaves on the rocks below, and the richness of their verdure formed a beautiful contrast to the glowing scarlet of the coral that branched beside them.

The distant coast at length entirely disappeared. Adeline gazed with an emotion the most sublime, on the boundless expanse of waters that spread on all sides: she seemed as if launched into a new world: the grandeur and immensity of the view astonished and overpowered her: for a moment she doubted the truth of the compass, and believed it to be almost impossible for the vessel to find its way over the pathless waters to any shore. And when she considered that a plank alone separated her from death, a sensation of unmixed terror superseded that of sublimity, and she hastily turned her eyes from the prospect, and her thoughts from the subject.

CHAPTER XIX

Is there a heart that music cannot melt?

Alas! how is that rugged heart forlorn!

Is there who ne'er the mystic transports felt

Of solitude and melancholy born?

He need not woo the Muse — he is her scorn.

BEATTIE.

Towards evening the captain, to avoid the danger of encountering a Barbary corsair steered for the French coast, and Adeline distinguished in the gleam of the setting sun the shores of Provence, feathered with wood and green with pasturage. La Luc, languid and ill, had retired to the cabin, whither Clara attended him. The pilot at the helm guiding the tall vessel through the sounding waters, and one solitary sailor leaning with crossed arms against the mast, and now and then singing parts of a mournful ditty, were all of the crew, except Adeline, that remained upon deck — and Adeline silently watched the declining sun, which threw a saffron glow upon the waves and on the sails gently swelling in the breeze that was now dying away. The sun at length sunk below the ocean, and twilight stole over the scene, leaving the shadowy shores yet visible, and touching with a solemn tint the waters that stretched wide around. She sketched the picture, but it was with a faint pencil.

NIGHT

O'er the dim breast of Ocean's wave

Night spreads afar her gloomy wings,

And pensive thought, and silence brings,

Save when the distant waters lave;

Or when the mariner's lone voice

Swells faintly in the passing gale,

Or when the screaming sea-gulls poise

O'er the tall mast and swelling sail.

Bounding the grey gleam of the deep,

Where fancied forms arouse the mind,

Dark sweep the shores, on whose rude steep

Sighs the sad spirit of the wind.

Sweet is its voice upon the air,

At Evening's melancholy close,

When the smooth wave in silence flows!

Sweet, sweet the peace its stealing accents bear!

Blest be thy shades, O Night! and blest the song

Thy low winds breathe the distant shores along!

As the shadows thickened, the scene sunk into deeper repose. Even the sailor's song had ceased; no sound was heard but that of the waters dashing beneath the vessel, and their fainter murmur on the pebbly coast. Adeline's mind was in unison with the tranquillity of the hour; lulled by the waves, she resigned herself to a still melancholy and sat lost in reverie. The present moment brought to her recollection her voyage up the Rhone, when seeking refuge from the terrors of the Marquis de Montalt, she so anxiously endeavoured to anticipate her future destiny. She then, as now, had watched the fall of evening and the fading prospect, and she remembered what a desolate feeling had accompanied the impression which those objects made. She had then no friends—no asylum—no certainty of escaping the pursuit of her enemy. Now she had found affectionate friends—a secure retreat—and was delivered from the terrors she then suffered—but still she was unhappy. The remembrance of Theodore—of Theodore who had loved her so truly, who had encountered and suffered so much for her sake, and of whose fate she was now as ignorant as when she traversed the Rhone, was an incessant pang to her heart. She seemed to be more remote than ever from the possibility of hearing of him. Sometimes a faint hope crossed her that he had escaped the malice of his persecutor; but when she considered the inveteracy and power of the latter, and the heinous light in which the law regards an assault upon a superior officer, even this poor hope vanished, and left her to tears and anguish, such as this reverie, which began with a sensation of only gentle melancholy, now led to. She continued to muse till the moon arose from the bosom of the ocean, and shed her trembling lustre upon the waves, diffusing peace, and making silence more solemn; beaming a soft light on the white sails, and throwing upon the waters the tall shadow of the vessel which now seemed to glide along unopposed by any current. Her tears had somewhat relieved the anguish of her mind, and she again reposed in placid melancholy, when a strain of such tender and entrancing sweetness stole on the silence of the hour, that it seemed more like celestial than mortal music—so soft, so soothing, it sunk upon her ear, that it recalled her from misery to hope and love. She wept again—but these were tears which she would not have exchanged for mirth and joy. She looked round, but perceived neither ship nor boat; and as the undulating sounds swelled on the distant air, she thought they came from the shore. Sometimes the breeze wafted them away, and again returned them in tones of the most languishing softness. The links of the air thus broken, it was music rather than melody that she caught, till, the pilot gradually steering nearer the coast, she distinguished the notes of a song familiar to her ear. She endeavoured to recollect where she had heard it, but in vain; yet her heart beat almost unconsciously with a something resembling hope. Still she listened, till the breeze again stole the sounds. With regret she now perceived that the vessel was moving from them, and at length they trembled faintly on the waves, sunk away at distance, and were heard no more. She remained upon deck a considerable time, unwilling to relinquish the expectation of hearing them again, and their sweetness still vibrating on her fancy, and at length retired to the cabin oppressed by a degree of disappointment which the occasion did not appear to justify.

La Luc grew better during the voyage, his spirits revived, and when the vessel entered that part of the Mediterranean called the Gulf of Lyons, he was sufficiently animated to enjoy from the deck the noble prospect which the sweeping shores of Provence, terminating in the far distant ones of Languedoc, exhibited. Adeline and Clara, who anxiously watched his looks, rejoiced in their amendment; and the fond wishes of the latter already anticipated his perfect recovery. The expectations of Adeline had been too often checked by disappointment permit her now to indulge an equal degree of hope with that of her friend, yet she confided much in the effect of this voyage.

La Luc amused himself at intervals with discoursing, and pointing out the situations of considerable ports on the coast, and the mouths of the rivers that, after wandering through Provence, disembogue themselves into the Mediterranean. The Rhone, however, was the only one of much consequence which he passed. On this object, though it was so distant that fancy perhaps, rather than the sense, beheld it, Clara gazed with peculiar pleasure, for it came from the banks of Savoy; and the wave which she thought she perceived, had washed the feet of her dear native mountains. The time passed with mingled pleasure and improvement as La Luc described to his attentive pupils the manners and commerce of the different inhabitants of the coast, and the natural history of the country: or as he traced in imagination the remote wanderings of rivers to their source, and delineated the characteristic beauties of their scenery.

After a pleasant voyage of a few days, the shores of Provence receded, and that of Languedoc, which had long bounded the distance, became the grand object of the scene, and the sailors drew near their port. They landed in the afternoon at a small town, situated at the foot of a woody eminence, on the right overlooking the sea, and on the left the rich plains of Languedoc gay with the purple vine. La Luc determined to defer his journey till the following day, and was directed to a small inn at the extremity of the town, where the accommodation, such as it was, he endeavoured to be contented with.

In the evening, the beauty of the hour and the desire of exploring new scenes, invited Adeline to walk. La Lac was fatigued, and did not go out, and Clara remained with him. Adeline took her way to the woods that rose from the margin of the sea, and climbed the wild eminence on which they hung. Often as she went she turned her eyes to catch between the dark foliage the blue waters of the bay, the white sail that flitted by, and the trembling gleam of the setting sun. When she reached the summit, and looked down over the dark tops of the woods on the wide and various prospect, she was seized with a kind of still rapture impossible to be expressed, and stood unconscious of the flight of time, till the sun had left the scene, and twilight threw its solemn shade upon the mountains. The sea alone reflected the fading splendour of the west; its tranquil surface was partially disturbed by the low wind that crept in tremulous lines along the waters, whence rising to the woods, it shivered their light leaves, and died away. Adeline, resigning herself to the luxury of sweet and tender emotions, repeated the following lines: —

SUNSET

Soft o'er the mountain's purple brow

Meek Twilight draws her shadows gray;

From tufted woods and valleys low,

Light's magic colours steal away.

Yet still, amid the spreading gloom,

Resplendent glow the western waves,

That roll o'er Neptune's coral caves,

A zone of light on Evening's dome.

On this lone summit let me rest,

And view the forms to Fancy dear,

Till on the Ocean's darken'd breast

The stars of Evening tremble clear;

Or the moon's pale orb appear,

Throwing her line of radiance wide,

Far o'er the lightly-curling tide,

That seems the yellow sands to chide.

No sounds o'er silence now prevail,

Save of the dying wave below,

Or sailor's song borne on the gale,

Or oar at distance striking slow.

So sweet! so tranquil! may my evening ray

Set to this world — and rise in future day!

Adeline quitted the heights, and followed a narrow path that wound to the beach below: her mind was now particularly sensible to fine impressions, and the sweet notes of the nightingale amid the stillness of the woods again awakened her enthusiasm.

TO THE NIGHTINGALE

Child of the melancholy song!

O yet that tender strain prolong!

Her lengthen'd shade when Evening flings,

From mountain-cliffs, and forests green,

And sailing slow on silent wings,

Along the glimmering West is seen;

I love o'er pathless hills to stray,
Or trace the winding vale remote,
And pause, sweet Bird! to hear thy lay
While moonbeams on the thin clouds float,
Till o'er the Mountain's dewy head
Pale Midnight steals to wake the dead.
Far through the heaven's ethereal blue,
Wafted on Spring's light airs you come,
With blooms, and flowers, and genial dew,
From climes where Summer joys to roam;
O! welcome to your long-lost home!
"Child of the melancholy song!"
Who lov'st the lonely woodland glade
To mourn, unseen, the boughs among,
When Twilight spreads her pensive shade,
Again thy dulcet voice I hail!
O pour again the liquid note
That dies upon the evening gale!
For Fancy loves the kindred tone;
Her griefs the plaintive accents own.
She loves to hear thy music float
At solemn Midnight's stillest hour,
And think on friends for ever lost,
On joys by disappointment crost,
And weep anew Love's charmful power!
Then Memory wakes the magic smile,
Th' impassion'd voice, the melting eye,
That wont the trusting heart beguile,
And wakes again the hopeless sigh.

Her skill the glowing tints revive

Of scenes that Time had bade decay;

She bids the soften'd Passions live —

The Passions urge again their sway.

Yet o'er the long-regretted scene

Thy song the grace of sorrow throws;

A melancholy charm serene,

More rare than all that mirth bestows,

Then hail, sweet Bird, and hail thy pensive tear!

To Taste, to Fancy, and to Virtue dear!

The spreading dusk at length reminded Adeline of her distance from the inn, and that she had her way to find through a wild and lonely wood: she bade adieu to the syren that had so long detained her, and pursued the path with quick steps. Having followed it for some time, she became bewildered among the thickets, and the increasing darkness did not allow her to judge of the direction she was in. Her apprehensions heightened her difficulties: she thought she distinguished the voices of men at some little distance, and she increased her speed till she found herself on the sea-sands over which the woods impended. Her breath was now exhausted — she paused a moment to recover herself, and fearfully listened: but instead of the voices of men, she heard faintly swelling in the breeze the notes of mournful music. — Her heart, ever sensible to the impressions of melody, melted with the tones, and her fears were for a moment lulled in sweet enchantment. Surprise was soon mingled with delight when, as the sound advanced, she distinguished the tone of that instrument, and the melody of that well-known air, she had heard a few preceding evenings from the shores of Provence. But she had no time for conjecture — footsteps approached, and she renewed her speed. She was now emerged from the darkness of the woods, and the moon, which shone bright, exhibited along the level sands the town and port in the distance. The steps that had followed now came up with her, and she perceived two men; but they passed in conversation without noticing her, and as they passed she was certain she recollected the voice of him who was then speaking. Its tones were so familiar to her ear, that she was surprised at the imperfect memory which did not suffer her to be assured by whom they were uttered. Another step now followed, and a rude voice called to her to stop. As she hastily turned her eyes she saw imperfectly by the moonlight a man in sailor's habit pursuing, while he renewed the call. Impelled by terror, she fled along the sands; but her steps were short and trembling—those of her pursuer strong and quick.

She had just strength sufficient to reach the men who had before passed her, and to implore their protection, when her pursuer came up with them, but suddenly turned into the woods on the left, and disappeared.

She had no breath to answer the inquiries of the strangers who supported her, till a sudden exclamation, and the sound of her own name, drew her eyes attentively upon the person who uttered them, and in the rays which shone strong from his features she distinguished M. Verneuil! Mutual satisfaction and explanation ensued; and when he learned that La Luc and his daughter were at the inn, he felt an increased pleasure in conducting her thither. He said that he had accidentally met with an old friend in Savoy, whom he now introduced by the name of Mauron, and who had prevailed on him to change his route and accompany him to the shores of the Mediterranean. They had embarked from the coast of Provence only a few preceding days, and had that evening landed in Languedoc on the estate of M. Mauron. Adeline had now no doubt that it was the flute of M. Verneuil, and which had so often delighted her at Leloncourt, that she had heard on the sea.

When they reached the inn, they found La Luc under great anxiety for Adeline, in search of whom he had sent several people. Anxiety yielded to surprise and pleasure, when he perceived her with M. Verneuil, whose eyes beamed with unusual animation on seeing Clara. After mutual congratulations, M. Verneuil observed, and lamented, the very indifferent accommodation which the inn afforded his friends, and M. Mauron immediately invited them to his chateau with a warmth of hospitality that overcame every scruple which delicacy or pride could oppose. The woods that Adeline had traversed formed a part of his domain, which extended almost to the inn; but he insisted that his carriage should take his guests to the chateau, and departed to give orders for their reception. The presence of M. Verneuil, and the kindness of his friend, gave to La Luc an unusual flow of spirits; he conversed with a degree of vigour and liveliness to which he had long been unaccustomed, and the smile of satisfaction that Clara gave to Adeline expressed how much she thought he was already benefited by the voyage. Adeline answered her look with a smile of less confidence, for she attributed his present animation to a more temporary cause.

About half an hour after the departure of M. Mauron, a boy who served as waiter brought a message from a chevalier then at the inn, requesting permission to speak with Adeline. The man who had pursued her along the sands instantly occurred to her, and she scarcely doubted that the stranger was some person belonging to the Marquis de Montalt, perhaps the Marquis himself, though that he should have discovered her accidentally, in so obscure a place, and so immediately upon her arrival, seemed very improbable. With trembling lips and a countenance pale as death she inquired the name of the chevalier. The boy was not acquainted with it. La Luc asked what sort of a person he was; but the boy, who understood little of the art of describing, gave such a confused account of him, that Adeline could only learn he was not large, but of a middle stature. This circumstance, however, convincing her it was not the Marquis de Montalt who desired to see her, she asked whether it would be agreeable to La Luc to have the stranger admitted. La Luc said, By all means; and the waiter withdrew. Adeline sat in trembling expectation till the door opened, and Louis de la Motte entered the room. He advanced with an embarrassed and melancholy air, though his countenance had been enlightened with a momentary pleasure when he first beheld Adeline — Adeline, who was still the idol of his heart. After the first salutations were over, all apprehensions of the Marquis being now dissipated, she inquired when Louis had seen Monsieur and Madame La Motte.

I ought rather to ask you that question, said Louis in some confusion, for I believe you have seen them since I have; and the pleasure of meeting you thus is equalled by my surprise. I have not heard from my father for some time, owing probably to my regiment being removed to new quarters.

He looked as if he wished to be informed with whom Adeline now was; but as this was a subject upon which it was impossible she could speak in the presence of La Luc, she led the conversation to general topics, after having said that Monsieur and Madame La Motte were well when she left them. Louis spoke little, and often looked anxiously at Adeline, while his mind seemed labouring under strong oppression. She observed this, and recollecting the declaration he had made her on the morning of his departure from the abbey, she attributed his present embarrassment to the effect of a passion yet unsubdued, and did not appear to notice it. After he had sat near a quarter of an hour, under a struggle of feelings which he could neither conquer nor conceal, he rose to leave the room; and as he passed Adeline, said, in a low voice, Do permit me to speak with you alone for five minutes. She hesitated in some confusion, and then, saying there were none but friends present, begged he would be seated. — Excuse me, said he, in the same low accent; what I would say nearly concerns you, and you only. Do favour me with a few moments' attention. He said this with a look that surprised her; and having ordered candles in another room, she went thither.

Louis sat for some moments silent, and seemingly in great perturbation of mind. At length he said, I know not whether to rejoice or to lament at this unexpected meeting, though, if you are in safe hands, I ought certainly to rejoice, however hard the task that now falls to my lot. I am not ignorant of the dangers and persecutions you have suffered, and cannot forbear expressing my anxiety to know how you are now circumstanced. Are you indeed with friends? — I am, said Adeline; M. La Motte has informed you — — No, replied Louis with a deep sigh, not my father. — He paused. — But I do indeed rejoice, resumed he, O! how sincerely rejoice! that you are in safety. Could you know, lovely Adeline, what I have suffered! — He checked himself. — I understood you had something of importance to say, Sir, said Adeline; you must excuse me if I remind you that I have not many moments to spare.

It is indeed of importance, replied Louis; yet I know not how to mention it — how to soften — — This task is too severe. Alas! my poor friend!

Whom is it you speak of, Sir? said Adeline with quickness. Louis rose from his chair and walked about the room. I would prepare you for what I have to say, he resumed, but upon my soul I am not equal to it.

I entreat you to keep me no longer in suspense, said Adeline, who had a wild idea that it was Theodore he would speak of. Louis still hesitated. Is it — O! is it? — I conjure you tell me the worst at once, said she in a voice of agony. I can bear it, — indeed I can.

My unhappy friend! exclaimed Louis. O! Theodore! — Theodore! faintly articulated Adeline; he lives then! — He does, said Louis, but — He stopped. — But what? cried Adeline, trembling violently; if he is living, you cannot tell me worse than my fears suggest; I entreat you therefore not to hesitate. — Louis resumed his seat and, endeavouring to assume a collected air, said, He is living, Madame, but he is a prisoner; and — for why should I deceive you? I fear he has little to hope in this world.

I have long feared so, Sir, said Adeline in a voice of forced composure; you have something more terrible than this to relate, and I again entreat you will explain yourself.

He has every thing to apprehend from the Marquis de Montalt, said Louis. Alas! why do I say to apprehend? His judgment is already fixed — he is condemned to die.

At this confirmation of her fears, a death-like paleness diffused itself over the countenance of Adeline; she sat motionless, and attempted to sigh, but seemed almost suffocated. Terrified at her situation, and expecting to see her faint, Louis would have supported her, but with her hand she waved him from her, and was unable to speak. He now called for assistance, and La Luc and Clara, with M. Verneuil, informed of Adeline's indisposition, were quickly by her side.

At the sound of their voices she looked up, and seemed to recollect herself, when uttering a heavy sigh she burst into tears. La Luc, rejoiced to see her weep, encouraged her tears, which after some time relieved her; and when she was able to speak, she desired to go back to La Luc's parlour. Louis attended her thither; when she was better he would have withdrawn, but La Luc begged he would stay.

You are perhaps a relation of this young lady, Sir, said he, and may have brought news of her father? — Not so, Sir, replied Louis, hesitating — This gentleman, said Adeline, who had now recollected her dissipated thoughts, is the son of the M. La Motte whom you may have heard me mention. — Louis seemed shocked to be declared the son of a man that had once acted so unworthily towards Adeline, who, instantly perceiving the pain her words occasioned, endeavoured to soften their effect by saying that La Motte had saved her from imminent danger, and had afforded her an asylum for many months. — Adeline sat in a state of dreadful solicitude to know the particulars of Theodore's situation, yet could not acquire courage to renew the subject in the presence of La Luc; she ventured, however, to ask Louis if his own regiment was quartered in the town.

He replied that his regiment lay at Vaceau, a French town on the frontiers of Spain; that he had just crossed a part of the Gulf of Lyons, and was on his way to Savoy, whither he should set out early in the morning.

We are lately come from thence, said Adeline; may I ask to what part of Savoy you are going? — -To Leloncourt, he replied. — To Leloncourt! said Adeline, in some surprise. — I am a stranger to the country, resumed Louis; but I go to serve my friend. You seem to know Leloncourt. — I do indeed, said Adeline. — You probably know then that M. La Luc lives there, and will guess the motive of my journey?

O Heavens! is it possible? exclaimed Adeline — is it possible that Theodore Peyrou is a relation of M. La Luc?

Theodore! what of my son? asked La Luc in surprise and apprehension — Your son! said Adeline, in a trembling voice — your son! — The astonishment and anguish depicted on her countenance increased the apprehensions of this unfortunate father, and he renewed his question. But Adeline was totally unable to answer him; and the distress of Louis, on thus unexpectedly discovering the father of his unhappy friend, and knowing that it was his task to disclose the fate of his son, deprived him for some time of all power of utterance; and La Luc and Clara, whose fears were every instant heightened by this dreadful silence, continued to repeat their questions.

At length a sense of the approaching sufferings of the good La Luc overcoming every other feeling, Adeline recovered strength of mind sufficient to try to soften the intelligence Louis had to communicate, and to conduct Clara to another room. Here she collected resolution to tell her, and with much tender consideration, the circumstances of her brother's situation, concealing only her knowledge of his sentence being already pronounced. This relation necessarily included the mention of their attachment, and in the friend of her heart Clara discovered the innocent cause of her brother's destruction. Adeline also learned the occasion of that circumstance which had contributed to keep her ignorant of Theodore's relationship to La Luc; she was told the former had taken the name of Peyrou, with an estate which had been left him about a year before by a relation of his mother's upon that condition. Theodore had been designed for the church, but his disposition inclined him to a more active life than the clerical habit would admit of; and on his accession to this estate he had entered into the service of the French king.

In the few and interrupted interviews which had been allowed them at Caux, Theodore had mentioned his family to Adeline only in general terms; and thus, when they were so suddenly separated, had, without designing it, left her in ignorance of his father's name and place of residence.

The sacredness and delicacy of Adeline's grief, which had never permitted her to mention the subject of it even to Clara, had since contributed to deceive her.

The distress of Clara, on learning the situation of her brother, could endure no restraint; Adeline, who had commanded her feelings so as to impart this intelligence with tolerable composure, only by a strong effort of mind, was now almost overwhelmed by her own and Clara's accumulated suffering. While they wept forth the anguish of their hearts; a scene if possible, more affecting passed between La Luc and Louis; who perceived it was necessary to inform him, though cautiously and by degrees, of the full extent of his calamity. He, therefore, told La Luc, that though Theodore had been first tried for the offence of having quitted his post, he was now condemned on a charge of assault made upon his general officer the Marquis de Montalt, who had brought witnesses to prove that his life had been endangered by the circumstance; and who, having pursued the prosecution with the most bitter rancour, had at length obtained the sentence which the law could not withhold, but which every other officer in the regiment deplored.

Louis added, that the sentence was to be executed in less than a fortnight, and that Theodore being very unhappy at receiving no answers to the letters he had sent his father, wishing to see him once more, and knowing that there was now no time to be lost, had requested him to go to Leloncourt and acquaint his father with his situation.

La Luc received the account of his son's condition with a distress that admitted neither of tears nor complaint. He asked where Theodore was; and desiring to be conducted to him, he thanked Louis for all his kindness, and ordered post horses immediately.

A carriage was soon ready; and this unhappy father, after taking a mournful leave of M. Verneuil, and sending a compliment to M. Mauron, attended by his family set out for the prison of his son. The journey was a silent one; each individual of the party endeavoured, in consideration of each other, to suppress the expression of grief, but was unable to do more. La Luc appeared calm and complacent; he seemed frequently to be engaged in prayer; but a struggle for resignation and composure was sometimes visible upon his countenance, notwithstanding the efforts of his mind.

CHAPTER XX

And venom'd with disgrace the dart of Death.

SEWARD.

We now return to the Marquis de Montalt, who having seen La Motte safely lodged in the prison of D— —y, and learning the trial would not come on immediately, had returned to his villa on the borders of the forest, where he expected to hear news of Adeline. It had been his intention to follow his servants to Lyons; but he now determined to wait a few days for letters, and he had little doubt that Adeline, since her flight had been so quickly pursued, would be overtaken, and probably before she could reach that city. In this expectation he had been miserably disappointed; for his servants informed him, that though they traced her thither, they had neither been able to follow her route beyond, nor to discover her at Lyons. This escape she probably owed to having embarked on the Rhone, for it does not appear that the Marquis's people thought of seeking her on the course of that river.

His presence was soon after required at Vaceau, where the court-martial was then sitting; thither therefore he went, with passions still more exasperated by his late disappointment, and procured the condemnation of Theodore. The sentence was universally lamented, for Theodore was much beloved in his regiment; and the occasion of the Marquis's personal resentment towards him being known, every heart was interested in his cause.

Louis de La Motte happening at this time to be stationed in the same town, heard an imperfect account of his story; and being convinced that the prisoner was the young chevalier whom he had formerly seen with the Marquis at the abbey, he was induced partly from compassion, and partly with a hope of hearing of his parents, to visit him. The compassionate sympathy which Louis expressed, and the zeal with which he tendered his services, affected Theodore, and excited in him a warm return of friendship; Louis made him frequent visits, did every thing that kindness could suggest to alleviate his sufferings, and a mutual esteem and confidence ensued.

Theodore at length communicated the chief subject of his concern to Louis; who discovered with inexpressible grief that it was Adeline whom the Marquis had thus cruelly persecuted,

286

and Adeline for whose sake the generous Theodore was about to suffer. He soon perceived also that Theodore was his favoured rival; but he generously suppressed the jealous pang this discovery occasioned, and determined that no prejudice of passion should withdraw him from the duties of humanity and friendship. He eagerly inquired where Adeline then resided. She is yet, I fear, in the power of the Marquis, said Theodore, sighing deeply. O God! — these chains! — and he threw an agonizing glance upon them. Louis sat silent and thoughtful; at length starting from his reverie, he said he would go to the Marquis, and immediately quitted the prison. The Marquis, was, however, already set off for Paris, where he had been summoned to appear at the approaching trial of La Motte; and Louis, yet ignorant of the late transactions at the abbey, returned to the prison; where he endeavoured to forget that Theodore was the favoured rival of his love, and to remember him only as the defender of Adeline. So earnestly he pressed his offers of service, that Theodore, whom the silence of his father equally surprised and afflicted, and who was very anxious to see him once again, accepted his proposal of going himself to Savoy. My letters I strongly suspect to have been intercepted by the Marquis, said Theodore; if so, my poor father will have the whole weight of this calamity to sustain at once, unless I avail myself of your kindness, and I shall neither see him nor hear from him before I die. Louis! there are moments when my fortitude shrinks from the conflict, and my senses threaten to desert me.

No time was to be lost; the warrant for his execution had already received the king's signature, and Louis immediately set forward for Savoy. The letters of Theodore had indeed been intercepted by order of the Marquis, who, in the hope of discovering the asylum of Adeline, had opened and afterwards destroyed them.

But to return to La Luc, who now drew near Vaceau, and whom his family observed to be greatly changed in his looks since he had heard the late calamitous intelligence; he uttered no complaint; but it was too obvious that his disorder had made a rapid progress. Louis, who during the journey proved the goodness of his disposition by the delicate attentions he paid this unhappy party, concealed his observation of the decline of La Luc, and to support Adeline's spirits, endeavoured to convince her that her apprehensions on this subject were groundless. Her spirits did indeed require support, for she was now within a few miles of the town that contained Theodore; and while her increasing perturbation almost overcame her, she yet tried to appear composed. When the carriage entered the town, she cast a timid and anxious glance from the window in search of the prison; but having passed through several streets without perceiving any building which corresponded with her idea of that she looked for, the coach stopped at the inn. The frequent changes in La Luc's countenance betrayed the violent agitation of his mind; and when he attempted to alight, feeble and exhausted, he was compelled to accept the support of Louis, to whom he faintly said as he passed to the parlour, I am indeed sick at heart, but I trust the pain will not be long. Louis pressed his hand without speaking, and hastened back for Adeline and Clara, who were already in the passage. La Luc wiped the tears from his eyes (they were the first he had shed) as they entered the room. I would go immediately to my poor boy, said he to Louis; yours, Sir, is a mournful office—be so good as to conduct me to him. He rose to go, but, feeble and overcome with grief, again sat down. Adeline and Clara united in entreating that he would compose himself, and take some refreshment; and Louis urging the necessity of preparing Theodore for the interview, prevailed with him to delay it till his son should be informed of his arrival, and immediately quitted the inn for the prison of his friend. When he was gone, La Luc, as a duty he owed those he loved, tried to take some support; but the convulsions of his throat would not suffer him to swallow the wine he held to his parched lips, and he was now so much disordered, that he desired to retire to his chamber, where alone, and in prayer, he passed the dreadful interval of Louis's absence.

Clara on the bosom of Adeline, who sat in calm but deep distress, yielded to the violence of her grief. I shall lose my dear father too, said she; I see it; I shall lose my father and my brother together. Adeline wept with her friend for some time in silence; and then attempted to persuade her that La Luc was not so ill as she apprehended.

Do not mislead me with hope, she replied that will not survive the shock of this calamity—I saw it from the first. Adeline knowing that La Luc's distress would be heightened by the observance of his daughter's, and that indulgence would only increase its poignancy, endeavoured to rouse her to an exertion of fortitude by urging the necessity of commanding her emotion in the presence of her father. This is possible, added she, however painful may be the effort. You must know, my dear, that my grief is not inferior to your own, yet I have hitherto been enabled to support my sufferings in silence; for M. La Luc I do, indeed, love and reverence as a parent.

Louis meanwhile reached the prison of Theodore, who received him with an air of mingled surprise and impatience. What brings you back so soon? said he, have you heard news of my father? Louis now gradually unfolded the circumstances of their meetings and La Luc's arrival at Vaceau. A various emotion agitated the countenance of Theodore on receiving this intelligence. My poor father! said he, he has then followed his son to this ignominious place! Little did I think when last we parted he would meet me in a prison under condemnation! This reflection roused an impetuosity of grief which deprived him for some time of speech? But where is he? said Theodore, recovering himself; now he is come I shrink from the interview I have so much wished for. The sight of his distress will be dreadful to me. Louis! when I am gone, comfort my poor father. His voice was again interrupted by sobs; and Louis, who had been fearful of acquainting him at the same time of the arrival of La Luc and the discovery of Adeline, now judged it proper to administer the cordial of this latter intelligence.

The glooms of a prison and of calamity vanished for a transient moment; those who had seen Theodore would have believed this to be the instant which gave him life and liberty. When his first emotions subsided, I will not repine, said he, since I know that Adeline is preserved, and that I shall once more see my father, I will endeavour to die with resignation. He inquired if La Luc was then in the prison, and was told he was at the inn with Clara and Adeline. Adeline! Is Adeline there too? — This is beyond my hopes. Yet why do I rejoice? I must never see her more: this is no place for Adeline. Again he relapsed into an agony of distress — and again repeated a thousand questions concerning Adeline, till he was reminded by Louis that his father was impatient to see him — when, shocked that he had so long detained his friend, he entreated him to conduct La Luc to the prison, and endeavoured to recollect fortitude for the approaching interview.

When Louis returned to the inn, La Luc was still in his chamber; and Clara quitting the room to call him, Adeline seized with trembling impatience the opportunity to inquire more particularly concerning Theodore, than she chose to do in the presence of his unhappy sister. Louis represented him to be much more tranquil than he really was. Adeline was somewhat soothed by the account; and her tears, hitherto restrained, flowed silently and fast till La Luc appeared. His countenance had recovered its serenity, but was impressed with a deep and steady sorrow, which excited in the beholder a mingled emotion of pity and reverence. How is my son, Sir? said he as he entered the room. We will go to him immediately.

289

Clara renewed the entreaties that had been already rejected, to accompany her father, who persisted in a refusal. To-morrow you shall see him, added he; but our first meeting must be alone. Stay with your friend, my dear; she has need of consolation. When La Luc was gone, Adeline, unable longer to struggle against the force of grief, retired to her chamber and her bed.

La Luc walked silently towards the prison, resting on the arm of Louis. It was now night: a dim lamp that hung above showed them the gates, and Louis rang a bell: La Luc, almost overcome with agitation, leaned against the postern till the porter appeared. He inquired for Theodore, and followed the man; but when he reached the second courtyard he seemed ready to faint, and again stopped. Louis desired the porter would fetch some water; but La Luc, recovering his voice, said he should soon be better, and would not suffer him to go. In a few minutes he was able to follow Louis, who led him through several dark passages, and up a flight of steps to a door which, being unbarred, disclosed to him the prison of his son. He was seated at a small table, on which stood a lamp that threw a feeble light across the place, sufficient only to show its desolation and wretchedness. When he perceived La Luc he sprung from his chair, and in the next moment was in his arms. My father! said he in a tremulous voice. My son! exclaimed La Luc; and they were for some time silent, and locked in each other's embrace. At length Theodore led him to the only chair the room afforded, and seating himself with Louis at the foot of the bed, had leisure to observe the ravages which illness and calamity had made on the features of his parent. La Luc made several efforts to speak; but, unable to articulate, laid his hand upon his breast and sighed deeply. Fearful of the consequence of so affecting a scene on his shattered frame, Louis endeavoured to call off his attention from the immediate object of his distress, and interrupted the silence; but La Luc shuddering, and complaining he was very cold, sunk back in his chair. His condition roused Theodore from the stupor of despair; and while he flew to support his father, Louis ran out for other assistance. — I shall soon be better, Theodore, said La Luc, unclosing his eyes, the faintness is already going off. I have not been well of late; and this sad meeting! — Unable any longer to command himself, Theodore wrung his hand, and the distress which had long struggled for utterance burst in convulsive throbs from his breast. La Lac gradually revived, and exerted himself to calm the transports of his son; but the fortitude of the latter had now entirely forsaken him, and he could only utter exclamation and complaint. Ah! little did I think we should ever meet under circumstances so dreadful as the present! But I have not deserved them, my father! the motives of my conduct have still been just.

That is my supreme consolation, said La Luc, and ought to support you in this hour of trial. The Almighty God, who is the judge of hearts, will reward you hereafter. Trust in him, my son; I look to him with no feeble hope, but with a firm reliance on his justice! La Luc's voice faltered; he raised his eyes to heaven with an expression of meek devotion, while the tears of humanity fell slowly on his cheek.

Still more affected by his last words, Theodore turned from him, and paced the room with quick steps: the entrance of Louis was a very seasonable relief to La Luc, who, taking a cordial he had brought, was soon sufficiently restored to discourse on the subject most interesting to him. Theodore tried to attain a command of his feelings, and succeeded. He conversed with tolerable composure for above an hour, during which La Luc endeavoured to elevate, by religious hope, the mind of his son, and to enable him to meet with fortitude the awful hour that approached. But the appearance of resignation which Theodore attained always vanished when he reflected that he was going to leave his father a prey to grief, and his beloved Adeline for ever. When La Luc was about to depart he again mentioned her. Afflicting as an interview must be in our present circumstances, said he, I cannot bear the thought of quitting the world without seeing her once more; yet I know not how to ask her to encounter, for my sake, the misery of a parting scene. Tell her that my thoughts never, for a moment, leave her; that— —La Luc interrupted, and assured him, that since he so much wished it, he should see her, though a meeting could serve only to heighten the mutual anguish of a final separation.

I know it—I know it too well, said Theodore; yet I cannot resolve to see her no more, and thus spare her the pain this interview must inflict. O my father! when I think of those whom I must soon leave for ever, my heart breaks. But I will, indeed, try to profit by your precept and example, and show that your paternal care has not been in vain. My good Louis, go with my father—he has need of support. How much I owe this generous friend, added Theodore, you well know, Sir.—I do, in truth, replied La Luc, and can never repay his kindness to you. He has contributed to support us all; but you require comfort more than myself—he shall remain with you—I will go alone.

This Theodore would not suffer; and La Luc no longer opposing him, they affectionately embraced, and separated for the night.

When they reached the inn, La Luc consulted with Louis on the possibility of addressing a petition to the sovereign time enough to save Theodore. His distance from Paris, and the short interval before the period fixed for this execution of the sentence, made this design difficult: but believing it was practicable, La Luc, incapable as he appeared of performing so long a journey, determined to attempt it. Louis, thinking that the undertaking would prove fatal to the father, without benefiting the son, endeavoured, though faintly, to dissuade him from it — but his resolution was fixed — If I sacrifice the small remains of my life in the service of my child, said he, I shall lose little: if I save him, I shall gain every thing. There is no time to be lost — I will set off immediately.

He would have ordered post-horses, but Louis and Clara, who were now come from the bed-side of her friend, urged the necessity of his taking a few hours' repose: he was at length compelled to acknowledge himself unequal to the immediate exertion which parental anxiety prompted, and consented to seek rest.

When he had retired to his chamber, Clara lamented the condition of her father. — He will not bear the journey, said she; he is greatly changed within these few days. — Louis was so entirely of her opinion, that he could not disguise it, even to flatter her with a hope. She added, what did not contribute to raise his spirits, that Adeline was so much indisposed by her grief for the situation of Theodore and the sufferings of La Luc that she dreaded the consequence.

It has been seen that the passion of young La Motte had suffered no abatement from time or absence; on the contrary, the persecution and the dangers which had pursued Adeline awakened all his tenderness, and drew her nearer to his heart. When he had discovered that Theodore loved her, and was beloved again, he experienced all the anguish of jealousy and disappointment; for, though she had forbidden him to hope, he found it too painful an effort to obey her, and had secretly cherished the flame which he ought to have stifled. His heart was, however, too noble to suffer his zeal for Theodore to abate because he was his favoured rival, and his mind too strong not to conceal the anguish this certainty occasioned. The attachment which Theodore had testified towards Adeline even endeared him to Louis, when he had recovered from the first shock of disappointment, and that conquest over jealousy which originated in principle, and was pursued with difficulty, became afterwards his pride and his glory. When, however, he again saw Adeline — saw her in the mild dignity of sorrow more interesting than ever — saw her, though sinking beneath its pressure, yet tender and solicitous to soften the afflictions of those around her — it was with the utmost difficulty he preserved his resolution, and forebore to express the sentiments she inspired. When he further considered that her acute sufferings arose from the strength of her affection, he more than ever wished himself the object of a heart capable of so tender a regard — and Thedore in prison and in chains was a momentary object of envy.

In the morning, when La Luc arose from short and disturbed slumbers, he found Louis, Clara, and Adeline, whom indisposition could not prevent from paying him this testimony of respect and affection, assembled in the parlour of the inn to see him depart. After a slight breakfast, during which his feelings permitted him to say little, he bade his friends a sad farewell, and stepped into the carriage, followed by their tears and prayers. — Adeline immediately retired to her chamber, which she was too ill to quit that day. In the evening Clara left her friend, and, conducted by Louis, went to visit her brother, whose emotions, on hearing of his father's departure, were various and strong.

CHAPTER XXI

'Tis only when with inbred horror smote

At some base act, or done, or to be done,

That the recoiling soul, with conscious dread.

Shrinks back into itself.

MASON.

We return now to Pierre de la Motte, who, after remaining some weeks in the prison of D— —y, was removed to take his trial in the courts of Paris, whether the Marquis de Montalt followed to prosecute the charge. Madame de la Motte accompanied her husband to the prison of the Chatelet. His mind sunk under the weight of his misfortunes; nor could all the efforts of his wife rouse him from the torpidity of despair which a consideration of his circumstances occasioned. Should he be even acquitted of the charge brought against him by the Marquis, (which was very unlikely,) he was now in the scene of his former crimes, and the moment that should liberate him from the walls of his prison would probably deliver him again into the hands of offended justice.

The prosecution of the Marquis was too well founded, and its object of a nature too serious, not to justify the terror of La Motte. Soon after the latter had settled at the abbey of St. Clair, the small stock of money which the emergency of his circumstances had left him being nearly exhausted, his mind became corroded with the most cruel anxiety concerning the means of his future subsistence. As he was one evening riding alone in a remote part of the forest, musing on his distressed circumstances, and meditating plans to relieve the exigencies which he saw approaching, he perceived among the trees at some distance a chevalier on horseback, who was riding deliberately along, and seemed wholly unattended. A thought darted across the mind of La Motte, that he might be spared the evils which threatened him by robbing this stranger. His former practices had passed the boundary of honesty—fraud was in some degree familiar to him—and the thought was not dismissed. He hesitated— —every moment of hesitation increased the power of temptation—the opportunity was such as might never occur again. He looked round, and as far as the trees opened saw no person but the chevalier, who seemed by his air to be a man of distinction. Summoning all his courage, La

294

Motte rode forward and attacked him. The Marquis de Montalt, for it was he, was unarmed; but knowing that his attendants were not far off, he refused to yield. While they were struggling for victory, La Motte saw several horsemen enter the extremity of the avenue, and rendered desperate by opposition and delay, he drew from his pocket a pistol, (which an apprehension of banditti made him usually carry when he rode to a distance from the abbey) and fired at the Marquis, who staggered and fell senseless to the ground. La Motte had time to tear from his coat a brilliant star, some diamond rings from his fingers, and to rifle his pockets before his attendants came up. Instead of pursuing the robber, they all, in their first confusion, flew to assist their Lord, and La Motte escaped.

He stopped before he reached the abbey at a little ruin, the tomb formerly mentioned, to examine his booty. It consisted of a purse containing seventy louis d'ors; of a diamond star, three rings of great value, and a miniature set with brilliants of the Marquis himself, which he had intended as a present for his favourite mistress. To La Motte, who but a few hours before had seen himself nearly destitute, the view of this treasure excited an almost ungovernable transport; but it was soon checked when he remembered the means he had employed to obtain it, and that he had paid for the wealth he contemplated, the price of blood. Naturally violent in his passions, this reflection sunk him from the summit of exultation to the abyss of despondency. He considered himself a murderer, and, startled as one awakened from a dream, would have given half the world, had it been his, to have been as poor, and comparatively as guiltless, as a few preceding hours had seen him. On examining the portrait he discovered the resemblance; and believing that his hand had deprived the original of life, he gazed upon the picture with unutterable anguish. To the horrors of remorse succeeded the perplexities of fear. Apprehensive of he knew not what, he lingered at the tomb, where he at length deposited his treasure, believing that if his offence should awaken justice, the abbey might be searched, and these jewels betray him. From Madame La Motte it was easy to conceal his increase of wealth; for as he had never made her acquainted with the exact state of his finances, she had not suspected the extreme poverty which menaced him; and as they continued to live as usual, she believed that their expenses were drawn from the usual supply. But it was not so easy to disguise the workings of remorse and horror: his manner became gloomy and reserved, and his frequent visits to the tomb, where he went partly to examine his treasure, but chiefly to indulge in the dreadful pleasure of contemplating the picture of the Marquis, excited curiosity. In the solitude of the forest, where no variety of objects occurred to renovate his ideas, the horrible one of having committed murder was ever present to him. — When the Marquis arrived at the abbey, the astonishment and terror of La Motte (for at first he scarce knew whether he held the shadow or the substance of a human form) were quickly succeeded by apprehension of the punishment due to the crime he had really committed. When his distress had prevailed on the Marquis to retire, he informed him that he was by birth a chevalier: he then touched upon such parts of his misfortunes as he thought would excite pity, expressed such abhorrence of his guilt, and voluntarily uttered such a solemn promise of returning the jewels he had yet in his possession, (for he had ventured to dispose only of a small part,) that the Marquis at length listened to him with some degree of compassion. This favourable sentiment, seconded by a selfish motive, induced the Marquis to compromise with La Motte. Of quick and inflammable passions, he had observed the beauty of Adeline with an eye of no common regard, and he resolved to spare the life of La Motte upon no other condition than the sacrifice of this unfortunate girl. La Motte had neither resolution nor virtue sufficient to reject the terms — the jewels were restored, and he consented to betray the innocent Adeline. But as he was too well acquainted with her heart to believe that she would easily be won to the practice of vice, and as he still felt a degree of pity and tenderness for her, he endeavoured to prevail on the Marquis to forbear precipitate measures, and to attempt gradually to undermine her principles by seducing her affections. He approved and adopted this plan: the failure of his first scheme induced him to employ the stratagems he afterwards pursued, and thus to multiply the misfortunes of Adeline.

Such were the circumstances which had brought La Motte to his present deplorable situation. The day of trial was now come, and he was led from prison into the court, where the Marquis appeared as his accuser. When the charge was delivered, La Motte, as is usual, pleaded Not guilty, and the Advocate Nemours, who had undertaken to plead for him, afterwards endeavoured to make it appear that the accusation, on the part of the Marquis de Montalt, was false and malicious. To this purpose he mentioned the circumstance of the latter having attempted to persuade his client to the murder of Adeline: he further urged that the Marquis had lived in habits of intimacy with La Motte for several months immediately preceding his arrest, and that it was not till he had disappointed the designs of his accuser, by conveying beyond his reach the unhappy object of his vengeance, that the Marquis had thought proper to charge La Motte with the crime for which he stood indicted. Nemours urged the improbability of one man's keeping up a friendly intercourse with another from whom he had suffered the double injury of assault and robbery; yet it was certain that the Marquis had observed a frequent intercourse with La Motte for some months following the time specified for the commission of the crime. If the Marquis intended to prosecute, why was it not immediately after his discovery of La Motte? and if not then, what had influenced him to prosecute at so distant a period?

To this nothing was replied on the part of the Marquis; for, as his conduct on this point had been subservient to his designs on Adeline, he could not justify it but by exposing schemes which would betray the darkness of his character, and invalidate his cause. He, therefore, contented himself with producing several of his servants as witnesses of the assault and robbery, who swore without scruple to the person of La Motte, though not one of them had seen him otherwise than through the gloom of evening and riding off at full speed. On a cross-examination most of them contradicted each other; their evidence was of course rejected: but as the Marquis had yet two other witnesses to produce, whose arrival at Paris had been hourly expected, the event of the trial was postponed, and the court adjourned.

La Motte was re-conducted to his prison under the same pressure of despondency with which he had quitted it. As he walked through one of the avenues he passed a man who stood by to let him proceed, and who regarded him with a fixed and earnest eye. La Motte thought he had seen him before; but the imperfect view he caught of his features through the darkness of the place made him uncertain as to this, and his mind was in too perturbed a state to suffer him to feel an interest on the subject. When he was gone, the stranger inquired of the keeper of the prison who La Motte was: on being told, and receiving answers to some further questions he put, he desired he might be admitted to speak with him. The request, as the man was only a debtor, was granted; but as the doors were now shut for the night, the interview was deferred till the morrow.

La Motte found Madame in his room, where she had been waiting for some hours to hear the event of the trial. They now wished more earnestly than ever to see their son; but they were, as he had suspected, ignorant of his change of quarters, owing to the letters which he had as usual, addressed to them under an assumed name, remaining at the post-house of Auboine. This circumstance occasioned Madame La Motte to address her letters to the place of her son's late residence, and he had thus continued ignorant of his father's misfortunes and removal. Madame La Motte, surprised at receiving no answers to her letters, sent off another, containing an account of the trial as far as it had proceeded, and a request that her son would obtain leave of absence, and set out for Paris instantly. As she was still ignorant, of the failure of her letters, and, had it been otherwise, would not have known whither to have sent them, she directed this as usual.

Meanwhile his approaching fate was never absent for a moment from the mind of La Motte, which, feeble by nature, and still more enervated by habits of indulgence, refused to support him at this dreadful period.

While these scenes were passing at Paris, La Luc arrived there without any accident, after performing a journey, during which he had been supported almost entirely by the spirit of his resolution. He hastened to throw himself at the feet of the sovereign; and such was the excess of his feeling on presenting the petition which was to decide the fate of his son, that he could only look silently up, and then fainted. The king received the paper, and giving orders for the unhappy father to be taken care of, passed on. He was carried back to his hotel, where he awaited the event of this his final effort.

Adeline, meanwhile, continued at Vaceau in a state of anxiety too powerful for her long-agitated frame, and the illness in consequence of this, confined her almost wholly to her chamber. Sometimes she ventured to flatter herself with a hope that the journey of La Luc would be successful: but these short and illusive intervals of comfort served only to heighten, by contrast, the despondency that succeeded; and in the alternate extremes of feeling she experienced a state more torturing than that produced either by the sharp sting of unexpected calamity, or the sullen pain of settled despair.

When she was well enough she came down to the parlour to converse with Louis, who brought her frequent accounts of Theodore, and who passed every moment he could snatch from the duty of his profession in endeavours to support and console his afflicted friends. Adeline and Theodore, both looked to him for the little comfort allotted them, for he brought them intelligence of each other, and whenever he appeared a transient melancholy kind of pleasure played round their hearts. He could not conceal from Theodore Adeline's indisposition, since it was necessary to account for her not indulging the earnest wish he repeatedly expressed to see her again. To Adeline he spoke chiefly of the fortitude and resignation of his friend, not however forgetting to mention the tender affection he constantly expressed for her. Accustomed to derive her sole consolation from the presence of Louis, and to observe his unwearied friendship towards him whom she so truly loved, she found her esteem for him ripen into gratitude, and her regard daily increase.

The fortitude with which he had said Theodore supported his calamities was somewhat exaggerated. He could not forget those ties which bound him to life sufficiently to meet his fate with firmness; but though the paroxysms of grief were acute and frequent, he sought, and often attained in the presence of his friends, a manly composure. From the event of his father's journey he hoped little, yet that little was sufficient to keep his mind in the torture of suspense till the issue should appear.

On the day preceding that fixed for the execution of the sentence, La Luc reached Vaceau. Adeline was at her chamber window when the carriage drew up to the inn; she saw him alight, and with feeble steps, supported by Peter, enter the house. From the languor of his air she drew no favourable omen, and, almost sinking under the violence of her emotion, she went to meet him. Clara was already with her father when Adeline entered the room. She approached him, but, dreading to receive from his lips a confirmation of the misfortune his countenance seemed to indicate, she looked expressively at him and sat down, unable to speak the question she would have asked. He held out his hand to her in silence, sunk back in his chair, and seemed to be fainting under oppression of heart. His manner confirmed all her fears; at this dreadful conviction her senses failed her, and she sat motionless and stupefied.

La Luc and Clara were too much occupied by their own distress to observe her situation; after some time she breathed a heavy sigh, and burst into tears. Relieved by weeping, her spirits gradually returned, and she at length said to La Luc, It is unnecessary, Sir, to ask the success of your journey; yet, when you can bear to mention the subject, I wish —

La Luc waved his hand — Alas! said he, I have nothing to tell but what you already guess too well. My poor Theodore! — His voice was convulsed with sorrow, and some moments of unutterable anguish followed.

Adeline was the first who recovered sufficient recollection to notice the extreme languor of La Luc, and attend to his support. She ordered him refreshments, and entreated he would retire to his bed and suffer her to send for a physician; adding, that the fatigue he had suffered made repose absolutely necessary. Would that I could find it, my dear child! said he; it is not in this world that I must look for it, but in a better, and that better, I trust, I shall soon attain. But where is our good friend, Louis La Motte? He must lead me to my son. — Grief again interrupted his utterance, and the entrance of Louis was a very seasonable relief to them all. Their tears explained the question he would have asked. La Luc immediately inquired for his son; and thanking Louis for all his kindness to him, desired to be conducted to the prison. Louis endeavoured to persuade him to defer his visit till the morning, and Adeline and Clara joined their entreaties with his, but La Luc determined to go that night. — His time is short, said he; a few hours and I shall see him no more, at least in this world; let me not neglect these precious moments. Adeline! I had promised my poor boy that he should see you once more; you are not now equal to the meeting; I will try to reconcile him to the disappointment: but if I fail, and you are better in the morning, I know you will exert yourself to sustain the interview. — Adeline looked impatient, and attempted to speak. La Luc rose to depart, but could only reach the door of the room, where, faint and feeble, he sat down in a chair. I must submit to necessity, said he; I find I am not able to go further to-night. Go to him, La Motte, and tell him I am somewhat disordered by my journey, but that I will be with him early in the morning. Do not flatter him with a hope; prepare him for the worst. — There was a pause of silence. La Luc at length recovering himself, desired Clara would order his bed to be got ready, and she willingly obeyed. When he withdrew, Adeline told Louis, what was indeed unnecessary, the event of La Luc's journey. I own, continued she, that I had sometimes suffered myself to hope, and I now feel this calamity with double force: I fear too that M. La Luc will sink under its pressure; he is much altered for the worse since he set out for Paris. Tell me your opinion sincerely.

The change was so obvious that Louis could not deny it; but he endeavoured to soothe her apprehension by ascribing this alteration, in a great measure, to the temporary fatigue of travelling. Adeline declared her resolution of accompanying La Luc to take leave of Theodore in the morning. I know not how I shall support the interview, said she; but to see him once more is a duty I owe both to him and myself. The remembrance of having neglected to give him this last proof of affection would pursue me with incessant remorse.

After some further conversation on this subject Louis withdrew to the prison, ruminating on the best means of imparting to his friend the fatal intelligence he had to communicate. Theodore received it with more composure than he had expected; but he asked with impatience why he did not see his father and Adeline; and on being informed that indisposition withheld them, his imagination seized on the worst possibility, and suggested that his father was dead. It was a considerable time before Louis could convince him of the contrary, and that Adeline was not dangerously ill: when, however, he was assured that he should see them in the morning, he became more tranquil. He desired his friend would not leave him that night. These are the last hours we can pass together, added he; I cannot sleep! Stay with me and lighten their heavy moments. I have need of comfort, Louis. Young as I am, and held by such strong attachments, I cannot quit the world with resignation. I know not how to credit those stories we hear of philosophic fortitude; wisdom cannot teach us cheerfully to resign a good, and life in my circumstances is surely such.

The night was passed in embarrassed conversation; sometimes interrupted by long fits of silence, and sometimes by the paroxysms of despair; and the morning of that day which was to lead Theodore to death, at length dawned through the grates of his prison.

La Luc meanwhile passed a sleepless and dreadful night. He prayed for fortitude and resignation both for himself and Theodore; but the pangs of nature were powerful in his heart, and not to be subdued. The idea of his lamented wife, and of what she would have suffered had she lived to witness the ignominious death which awaited her son, frequently occurred to him.

It seemed as if a destiny had hung over the life of Theodore; for it is probable that the king might have granted the petition of the unhappy father, had it not happened that the Marquis de Montalt was present at court when the paper was presented. The appearance and singular distress of the petitioner had interested the monarch, and, instead of putting by the paper, he opened it. As he threw his eyes over it, observing that the criminal was of the Marquis de Montalt's regiment, he turned to him and inquired the nature of the offence for which the culprit was about to suffer. The answer was such as might have been expected from the Marquis, and the king was convinced that Theodore was not a proper object of mercy.

But to return to La Luc, who was called, according to his order, at a very early hour. Having passed some time in prayer, he went down to the parlour, where Louis, punctual to the moment, already waited to conduct him to the prison. He appeared calm and collected, but his countenance was impressed with a fixed despair that sensibly affected his young friend. While they waited for Adeline he spoke little, and seemed struggling to attain the fortitude necessary to support him through the approaching scene. Adeline not appearing, he at length sent to hasten her, and was told she had been ill, but was recovering. She had indeed passed a night of such agitation, that her frame had sunk under it, and she was now endeavouring to recover strength and composure sufficient to sustain her in this dreadful hour. Every moment that brought her nearer to it had increased her emotion, and the apprehension of being prevented seeing Theodore had alone enabled her to struggle against the united pressure of illness and grief.

She now, with Clara, joined La Luc, who advanced as they entered the room, and took a hand of each in silence. After some moments he proposed to go, and they stepped into a carriage which conveyed them to the gates of the prison. The crowd had already begun to assemble there, and a confused murmur arose as the carriage moved forward; it was a grievous sight to the friends of Theodore. Louis supported Adeline when she alighted, she was scarcely able to walk, and with trembling steps she followed La Luc, whom the keeper led towards that part of the prison where his son was confined. It was now eight o'clock, the sentence was not to be executed till twelve, but a guard of soldiers was already placed in the court; and as this unhappy party passed along the narrow avenues, they were met by several officers who had been to take a last farewell of Theodore. As they ascended the stairs that led to his apartment. La Luc's ear caught the clink of chains, and heard him walking above with a quick irregular step. The unhappy father, overcome by the moment which now pressed upon him, stopped, and was obliged to support himself by the bannister. Louis fearing the consequence of his grief might be fatal, shattered as his frame already was, would have gone for assistance, but he made a sign to him to stay, I am better, said La Luc; O God! support me through this hour! — and in a few minutes he was able to proceed.

As the warder unlocked the door, the harsh grating of the key shocked Adeline, but in the next moment she was in the presence of Theodore, who sprung to meet her, and caught her in his arms before she sunk to the ground. As her head reclined on his shoulder, he again viewed that countenance so dear to him, which had so often lighted rapture in his heart, and which, though pale and inanimate as it now was, awakened him to momentary delight. When at length she unclosed her eyes, she fixed them in long and mournful gaze upon Theodore, who pressing her to his heart could answer her only with a smile of mingled tenderness and despair; the tears he endeavoured to restrain trembled in his eyes, and he forgot for a time every thing but Adeline. La Luc, who had seated himself at the foot of the bed, seemed unconscious of what passed around him, and entirely absorbed in his own grief; but Clara, as she clasped the hand of her brother and hung weeping on his arm, expressed aloud all the anguish of her heart, and at length recalled the attention of Adeline, who in a voice scarcely audible entreated she would spare her father. Her words roused Theodore, and supporting Adeline to a chair, he turned to La Luc. My dear child! said La Luc, grasping his hand and bursting into tears, my dear child! They wept together. After a long interval of silence, he said, I thought I could have supported this hour, but I am old and feeble. God knows my efforts for resignation, my faith in his goodness.

Theodore by a strong and sudden exertion assumed a composed and firm countenance, and endeavoured by every gentle argument to soothe and comfort his weeping friends. La Luc at length seemed to conquer his sufferings; drying his eyes, he said, My son, I ought to have set you a better example, and have practised the precepts of fortitude I have so often given you. But it is over; I know and will perform my duty. Adeline breathed a heavy sigh, and continued to weep. Be comforted, my love, we part but for a time, said Theodore as he kissed the tears from her cheek; and uniting her hand with that of his father's, he earnestly recommended her to his protection. Receive her, added he, as the most precious legacy I can bequeath; consider her as your child: she will console you when I am gone, she will more than supply the loss of your son.

La Luc assured him that he did now, and should continue to regard Adeline as his daughter. During those afflicting hours he endeavoured to dissipate the terrors of approaching death by inspiring his son with religious confidence. His conversation was pious, rational, and consolatory; he spoke not from the cold dictates of the head, but from the feelings of a heart which had long loved and practised the pure precepts of Christianity, and which now drew from them a comfort such as nothing earthly could bestow.

You are young, my son, said he, and are yet innocent of any great crime; you may therefore look on death without terror, for to the guilty only is his approach dreadful. I feel that I shall not long survive you, and I trust in a merciful God that we shall meet in a state where sorrow never comes; where the Sun of Righteousness shall arise with healing on his wings! As he spoke he looked up; the tears still trembled in his eyes, which beamed with meek yet fervent devotion, and his countenance glowed with the dignity of a superior being.

Let us not neglect the awful moments, said La Luc rising, let our united prayers ascend to Him who alone can comfort and support us! They all knelt down, and he prayed with that simple and sublime eloquence which true piety inspires. When he arose he embraced his children separately, and when he came to Theodore he paused, gazed upon him with an earnest, mournful expression, and was for some time unable to speak. Theodore could not bear this; he drew his hand before his eyes, and vainly endeavoured to stifle the deep sobs which convulsed his frame. At length recovering his voice, he entreated his father would leave him. This misery is too much for us all, said he, let us not prolong it. The time is now drawing on—leave me to compose myself; the sharpness of death consists in parting with those who are dear to us; when that is passed death is disarmed.

I will not leave you, my son, replied La Luc; my poor girls shall go, but for me, I will be with you in your last moments. Theodore felt that this would be too much for them both, and urged every argument which reason could suggest to prevail with his father to relinquish his design: but he remained firm in his determination. I will not suffer a selfish consideration of the pain I may endure, said La Luc, to tempt me to desert my child when he will most require my support. It is my duty to attend you, and nothing shall withhold me.

Theodore seized on the words of La Luc—As you would that I should be supported in my last hour, said he, I entreat that you will not be witness of it. Your presence, my dear father, would subdue all my fortitude—would destroy what little composure I may otherwise be able to attain. Add not to my sufferings the view of your distress, but leave me to forget, if possible, the dear parent I must quit for ever. His tears flowed anew. La Luc continued to gaze on him in silent agony. At length he said, Well, be it so. If indeed my presence would distress you, I will not go. His voice was broken and interrupted. After a pause of some moments he again embraced Theodore—We must part, said he, we must part, but it is only for a time—we shall soon be reunited in a higher world!—O God! thou seest my heart—thou seest all its feelings in this bitter hour!—Grief again overcame him. He pressed Theodore in his arms: and at length seeming to summon all his fortitude, he again said, Wemust part—Oh! my son, farewell for ever in this world!—The mercy of Almighty God support and bless you!

He turned away to leave the prison, but quite worn out with grief, sunk into a chair near the door he would have opened. Theodore gazed, with a distracted countenance, alternately on his father, on Clara, and on Adeline, whom he pressed to his throbbing heart, and their tears flowed together. And do I then, cried he, for the last time look upon that countenance!—Shall I never—never more behold it?—O! exquisite misery! Yet once again—once more, continued he, pressing her cheek; but it was insensible and cold as marble.

Louis, who had left the room soon after La Luc arrived, that his presence might not interrupt their farewell grief, now returned. Adeline raised her head, and perceiving who entered, it again sunk on the bosom of Theodore.

Louis appeared much agitated. La Luc arose. We must go, said he; Adeline, my love, exert yourself—Clara—my children, let us depart.—Yet one last—last embrace, and then!——Louis advanced and took his hand; My dear Sir, I have something to say; yet I fear to tell it.—What do you mean? said La Luc with quickness: no new misfortune can have power to afflict me at this moment; do not fear to speak.—I rejoice that I cannot put you to the proof, replied Louis; I have seen you sustain the most trying affliction with fortitude. Can you support the transports of hope?—La Luc gazed eagerly on Louis—Speak! said he, in a faint voice. Adeline raised her head, and, trembling between hope and fear, looked as if she would have searched his soul. He smiled cheerfully upon her. Is it—O! is it possible! she exclaimed, suddenly reanimated—He lives! He lives!—She said no more, but ran to La Luc, who sunk fainting in his chair, while Theodore and Clara with one voice called on Louis to relieve them from the tortures of suspense.

He proceeded to inform them that he had obtained from the commanding officer a respite for Theodore till the king's further pleasure could be known, and this in consequence of a letter received that morning from his mother, Madame de La Motte, in which she mentioned some very extraordinary circumstances that had appeared in the course of a trial lately conducted at Paris, and which so materially affected the character of the Marquis de Montalt as to render it possible a pardon might be obtained for Theodore.

These words darted with the rapidity of lightning upon the hearts of his hearers. La Luc revived, and that prison so lately the scene of despair now echoed only to the voices of gratitude and gladness. La Luc, raising his clasped hands to heaven, said, Great God! support me in this moment as thou hast already

305

supported me! — If my son lives, I die in peace.

He embraced Theodore, and remembering the anguish of his last embrace, tears of thankfulness and joy flowed to the contrast. So powerful indeed was the effect of this temporary reprieve, and of the hope it introduced, that if an absolute pardon had been obtained, it could scarcely for the moment have diffused a more lively joy. But when the first emotions were subsided, the uncertainty of Theodore's fate once more appeared. Adeline forbore to express this; but Clara without scruple lamented the possibility that her brother might yet be taken from them, and all their joy be turned to sorrow. A look from Adeline checked her. Joy was, however, so much the predominant feeling of the present moment, that the shade which reflection threw upon their hopes passed away like the cloud that is dispelled by the strength of the sunbeam; and Louis alone was pensive and abstracted.

When they were sufficiently composed, he informed them that the contents of Madame de La Motte's letter obliged him to set out for Paris immediately; and that the intelligence he had to communicate intimately concerned Adeline, who would undoubtedly judge it necessary to go thither also as soon as her health would permit. He then read to his impatient auditors such passages in the letter as were necessary to explain his meaning; but as Madame de La Motte had omitted to mention some circumstances of importance to be understood, the following is a relation of the occurrences that had lately happened at Paris.

It may be remembered that on the first day of his trial, La Motte, in passing from the courts to his prison, saw a person whose features, though imperfectly seen through the dusk, he thought he recollected; and that this same person, after inquiring the name of La Motte, desired to be admitted to him. On the following day the warder complied with his request, and the surprise of La Motte may be imagined when in the stronger light of his apartment, he distinguished the countenance of the man, from whose hands he had formerly received Adeline.

On observing Madame de La Motte in the room, he said he had something of consequence to impart, and desired to be left alone with the prisoner. When she was gone, he told De La Motte that he understood he was confined at the suit of the Marquis de Montalt. La Motte assented. — I know him for a villain, said the stranger boldly. Your case is desperate. Do you wish for life?

Need the question be asked?

Your trial, I understand proceeds to-morrow. I am now under confinement in this place for debt; but if you can obtain leave for me to go with you into the courts, and a condition from the judge that what I reveal shall not criminate myself, I will make discoveries that shall confound that same Marquis; I will prove him a villain; and it shall then be judged how far his word ought to be taken against you.

La Motte, whose interest was now strongly excited, desired he would explain himself; and the man proceeded to relate a long history of the misfortunes and consequent poverty which had tempted him to become subservient to the schemes of the Marquis, till he suddenly checked himself, and said. When I obtain from the court the promise I require, I will explain myself fully; till then, I cannot say more on the subject.

La Motte could not forbear expressing a doubt of his sincerity, and a curiosity concerning the motive that had induced him to become the Marquis's accuser. — As to my motive, it is a very natural one, replied the man: it is no easy matter to receive ill usage without resenting it, particularly from a villain whom you have served. — La Motte, for his own sake, endeavoured to check the vehemence with which this was uttered. I care not who hears me continued the stranger, but at the same time he lowered his voice; I repeat it — the Marquis has used me ill — I have kept his secret long enough: he does not think it worth while to secure my silence, or he would relieve my necessities. I am in prison for debt, and have applied to him for relief; since he does not choose to give it, let him take the consequence. I warrant he shall soon repent that he has provoked me, and 'tis fit he should.

The doubts of La Motte were now dissipated; the prospect of life again opened upon him, and he assured Du Bosse (which was the stranger's name) with much warmth, that he would commission his advocate to do all in his power to obtain leave for his appearance on the trial, and to procure the necessary condition. After some further conversation they parted.

CHAPTER XXII

Drag forth the legal monster into light,

Wrench from his hand oppression's iron rod,

And bid the cruel feel the pains they give.

Leave was at length granted for the appearance of Du Bosse, with a promise that his words should not criminate him, and he accompanied La Motte into court.

The confusion of the Marquis de Montalt on perceiving this man was observed by many persons present, and particularly by La Motte, who drew from this circumstance a favourable presage for himself.

When Du Bosse was called upon, he informed the court, that on the night of the twenty-first of April, in the preceding year, one Jean D'Aunoy, a man he had known many years, came to his lodging. After they had discoursed for some time on their circumstances, D'Aunoy said he knew a way by which Du Bosse might change all his poverty to riches, but that he would not say more till he was certain he would be willing to follow it. The distressed state in which Du Bosse then was, made him anxious to learn the means which would bring him relief; he eagerly inquired what his friend meant, and after some time D'Aunoy explained himself. He said he was employed by a nobleman (who he afterwards told Du Bosse was the Marquis de Montalt) to carry off a young girl from a convent, and that she was to be taken to a house a few leagues distant from Paris. I knew the house he described well, said Du Bosse, for I had been there many times with D'Aunoy, who lived there to avoid his creditors, though he often passed his nights at Paris. He would not tell me more of the scheme, but said he should want assistants, and if I and my brother, who is since dead, would join him, his employer would grudge no money, and we should be well rewarded. I desired him again to tell me more of the plan, but he was obstinate; and after I had told him I would consider of what he said, and speak to my brother, he went away.

When he called the next night for his answer, my brother and I agreed to engage, and accordingly we went home with him. He then told us that the young lady he was to bring thither was a natural daughter of the Marquis de Montalt and of a nun belonging to a convent of Ursulines; that his wife had received the child immediately on its birth, and had been allowed a handsome annuity to bring it up as her own, which she had done till her death. The child was then placed in a convent and designed for the veil; but when she was of an age to receive the vows, she had steadily persisted in refusing them. This circumstance had so much exasperated the Marquis, that in his rage he ordered that if she persisted in her obstinacy she should be removed from the convent, and got rid of any way; since if she lived in the world her birth might be discovered, and in consequence of this, her mother, for whom he had yet a regard, would be condemned to expiate her crime by a terrible death.

Du Bosse was interrupted in his narrative by the counsel of the Marquis, who contended that the circumstances alleged tending to criminate his client, the proceeding was both irrelevant and illegal. He was answered that it was not irrelevant, and therefore not illegal; for that the circumstances which threw light upon the character of the Marquis, affected his evidence against La Motte. Du Bosse was suffered to proceed.

D'Aunoy then said that the Marquis had ordered him to dispatch her, but that, as he had been used to see her from her infancy, he could not find in his heart to do it, and wrote to tell him so. The Marquis then commanded him to find those who would, and this was the business for which he wanted us. My brother and I were not so wicked as this came to, and so we told D'Aunoy; and I could not help asking why the Marquis resolved to murder his own child rather than expose her mother to the risque of suffering death. He said the Marquis had never seen his child and that, therefore, it could not be supposed he felt much kindness towards it, and still less that he could love it better than he loved its mother.

Du Bosse proceeded to relate how much he and his brother had endeavoured to soften the heart of D'Aunoy towards the Marquis's daughter, and that they prevailed with him to write again and plead for her. D'Aunoy went to Paris to await the answer, leaving them and the young girl at the house on the heath, where the former had consented to remain, seemingly for the purpose of executing the orders they might receive, but really with a design to save the unhappy victim from the sacrifice.

It is probable that Du Bosse, in this instance, gave a false account of his motive; since, if he was really guilty of an intention so atrocious as that of murder, he would naturally endeavour to conceal it. However this might be, he affirmed, that on the night of the twenty-sixth of April, he received an order from D'Aunoy for the destruction of the girl, whom he had afterwards delivered into the hands of La Motte.

La Motte listened to this relation in astonishment; when he knew that Adeline was the daughter of the Marquis, and remembered the crime to which he had once devoted her, his frame thrilled with horror. He now took up the story, and added an account of what had passed at the abbey between the Marquis and himself, concerning a design of the former upon the life of Adeline, and urged, as a proof of the present prosecution originating in malice, that it had commenced immediately after he had effected her escape from the Marquis. He concluded, however, with saying, that as the Marquis had immediately sent his people in pursuit of her, it was possible she might yet have fallen a victim to his vengeance.

Here the Marquis's counsel again interfered, and their objections were again overruled by the court. The uncommon degree of emotion which his countenance betrayed during the narrations of Du Bosse and De La Motte was generally observed. The court suspended the sentence of the latter, ordered that the Marquis should be put under immediate arrest, and that Adeline (the name given by her fostermother) and Jean D'Aunoy should be sought for.

The Marquis was accordingly seized at the suit of the crown, and put under confinement till Adeline should appear, or proof could be obtained that she died by his order; and till D'Aunoy should confirm or destroy the evidence of De La Motte.

Madame, who at length obtained intelligence of her son's residence from the town where he was formerly stationed, had acquainted him with his father's situation, and the proceedings of the trial; and as she believed that Adeline, if she had been so fortunate as to escape the Marquis's pursuit, was still in Savoy, she desired Louis would obtain leave of absence, and bring her to Paris, where her immediate presence was requisite to substantiate the evidence, and probably to save the life of La Motte.

On the receipt of her letter, which happened on the morning appointed for the execution of Theodore, Louis went immediately to the commanding officer to petition for a respite till the king's further pleasure should be known. He founded his plea on the arrest of the Marquis, and showed the letter he had just received. The commanding officer readily granted a reprieve; and Louis, who, on the arrival of this letter had forborne to communicate its contents to Theodore, lest it should torture him with false hope, now hastened to him with this comfortable news.

CHAPTER XXIII

Low on his funeral couch he lies!

No pitying heart, no eye, afford

A tear lo grace his obsequies.

GRAY.

On learning the purport of Madame de La Motte's letter, Adeline saw the necessity of her immediate departure for Paris. The life of La Motte, who had more than saved hers, the life perhaps of her beloved Theodore, depended on the testimony she should give. And she who had so lately been sinking under the influence of illness and despair, who could scarcely raise her languid head, or speak but in the faintest accents, now reanimated with hope, and invigorated by a sense of the importance of the business before her, prepared to perform a rapid journey of some hundred miles.

Theodore tenderly entreated that she would so far consider her health as to delay this journey for a few days: but with a smile of enchanting tenderness she assured him, that she was now too happy to be ill, and that the same cause which would confirm her happiness would confirm her health. So strong was the effect of hope upon her mind, now that it succeeded to the misery of despair, that it overcame the shock she suffered on believing herself a daughter of the Marquis, and every other painful reflection. She did not even foresee the obstacle that circumstance might produce to her union with Theodore, should he at last be permitted to live.

It was settled that she should set off for Paris in a few hours with Louis, and attended by Peter. These hours were passed by La Luc and his family in the prison.

When the time of her departure arrived, the spirits of Adeline again forsook her, and the illusions of joy disappeared. She no longer beheld Theodore as one respited from death, but took leave of him with a mournful presentiment that she should see him no more. So strongly was this presage impressed upon her mind, that it was long before she could summon resolution to bid him farewell; and when she had done so, and even left the apartment, she returned to take of him a last look. As she was once more quitting the room, her melancholy imagination represented Theodore at the place of execution, pale, and convulsed in death; she again turned her lingering eyes upon him; but fancy affected her sense, for she thought as she now gazed that his countenance changed, and assumed a ghastly hue. All her resolution vanished; and such was the anguish of her heart, that she resolved to defer her journey till the morrow, though she must by this means lose the protection of Louis, whose impatience to meet his father would not suffer the delay. The triumph of passion, however, was transient; soothed by the indulgence she promised herself, her grief subsided; reason resumed its influence; she again saw the necessity of her immediate departure, and recollected sufficient resolution to submit. La Luc would have accompanied her for the purpose of again soliciting the king in behalf of his son, had not the extreme weakness and lassitude to which he was reduced made travelling impracticable.

At length, Adeline with a heavy heart quitted Theodore, notwithstanding his entreaties that she would not undertake the journey in her present weak state, and was accompanied by Clara and La Luc to the inn. The former parted from her friend with many tears, and much anxiety for her welfare, but under a hope of soon meeting again. Should a pardon be granted to Theodore, La Luc designed to fetch Adeline from Paris; but should this be refused, she was to return with Peter. He bade her adieu with a father's kindness, which she repaid with a filial affection, and in her last words conjured him to attend to the recovery of his health: the languid smile he assumed seemed to express that her solicitude was vain, and that he thought his health past recovery.

Thus Adeline quitted the friends so justly dear to her, and so lately found, for Paris, where she was a stranger, almost without protection, and compelled to meet a father, who had pursued her with the utmost cruelty, in a public court of justice. The carriage in leaving Vaceau passed by the prison; she threw an eager look towards it as she passed; its heavy black walls, and narrow-grated windows, seemed to frown upon her hopes—but Theodore was there, and leaning from the window: she continued to gaze upon it till an abrupt turning in the street concealed it from her view. She then sunk back in the carriage, and yielding to the melancholy of her heart, wept in silence. Louis was not disposed to interrupt it; his thoughts were anxiously employed on his father's situation, and the travellers proceeded many miles without exchanging a word.

At Paris, whither we shall now return, the search after Jean D'Aunoy was prosecuted without success. The house on the heath, described by Du Bosse, was found uninhabited, and to the places of his usual resort in the city, where the officers of the police awaited him, he no longer came. It even appeared doubtful whether he was living, for he had absented himself from the houses of his customary rendezvous sometime before the trial of La Motte; it was therefore certain that his absence was not occasioned by any thing which had passed in the courts.

In the solitude of his confinement the Marquis de Montalt had leisure to reflect on the past, and to repent of his crimes; but reflection and repentance formed as yet no part of his disposition. He turned with impatience from recollections which produced only pain, and looked forward to the future with an endeavour to avert the disgrace and punishment which he saw impending. The elegance of his manners had so effectually veiled the depravity of his heart, that he was a favourite with his sovereign; and on this circumstance he rested his hope of security. He, however, severely repented that he had indulged the hasty spirit of revenge which had urged him to the prosecution of La Motte, and had thus unexpectedly involved him in a situation dangerous — if not fatal — since if Adeline could not be found he would be concluded guilty of her death. But the appearance of D'Aunoy was the circumstance he most dreaded; and to oppose the possibility of this, he employed secret emissaries to discover his retreat, and to bribe him to his interest. These were, however as unsuccessful in their research as the officers of police, and the Marquis at length began to hope that the man was really dead.

La Motte meanwhile awaited with trembling impatience the arrival of his son, when he should be relieved in some degree from his uncertainty concerning Adeline. On this appearance he rested his only hope of life, since the evidence against him would lose much of its validity from the confirmation she would give of the bad character of his prosecutor; and if the Parliament even condemned La Motte, the clemency of the king might yet operate in his favour.

Adeline arrived at Paris after a journey of several days, during which she was chiefly supported by the delicate attentions of Louis, whom she pitied and esteemed, though she could not love. She was immediately visited at the hotel by Madame La Motte: the meeting was affecting on both sides. A sense of her past conduct excited in the latter an embarrassment which the delicacy and goodness of Adeline would willingly have spared her; but the pardon solicited was given with so much sincerity, that Madame gradually became composed and reassured. This forgiveness, however, could not have been thus

easily granted, had Adeline believed her former conduct was
voluntary; a conviction of the restraint and terror under which
Madame had acted, alone induced her to excuse the past. In this
first meeting they forbore dwelling on particular subjects;
Madame La Motte proposed that Adeline should remove from
the hotel to her lodgings near the Chatelet; and Adeline, for
whom a residence at a public hotel was very improper, gladly
accepted the offer.

Madame there gave her a circumstantial account of La
Motte's situation, and concluded with saying, that as the
sentence of her husband had been suspended till some certainty
could be obtained concerning the late criminal designs of the
Marquis, and as Adeline could confirm the chief part of La
Motte's testimony, it was probable that now she was arrived the
court would proceed immediately. She now learnt the full
extent of her obligation to La Motte; for she was till now
ignorant that when he sent her from the forest he saved her
from death. Her horror of the Marquis, whom she could not
bear to consider as her father, and her gratitude to her deliverer,
redoubled, and she became impatient to give the testimony so
necessary to the hopes of her preserver. Madame then said, she
believed it was not too late to gain admittance that night to the
Chatelet; and as she knew how anxiously her husband wished
to see Adeline, she entreated her consent to go thither. Adeline,
though much harassed and fatigued, complied. When Louis
returned from M. Nemours, his father's advocate, whom he had
hastened to inform of her arrival, they all set out for the
Chatelet. The view of the prison into which they were now
admitted, so forcibly recalled to Adeline's mind the situation of
Theodore, that she with difficulty supported herself to the
apartment of La Motte. When he saw her, a gleam of joy passed
over his countenance; but again relapsing into despondency, he
looked mournfully at her, and then at Louis, and groaned
deeply. Adeline, in whom all remembrance of his former cruelty
was lost in his subsequent kindness, expressed her thankfulness
for the life he had preserved, and her anxiety to serve him, in
warm and repeated terms. But her gratitude evidently
distressed him; instead of reconciling him to himself, it seemed
to awaken a remembrance of the guilty designs he had once
assisted, and to strike the pangs of conscience deeper in his
heart. Endeavouring to conceal his emotions, he entered on the
subject of his present danger, and informed Adeline what
testimony would be required of her on the trial. After above an
hour's conversation with La Motte, she returned to the lodgings
of Madame, where, languid and ill, she withdrew to her
chamber, and tried to obliviate her anxieties in sleep.

The Parliament which conducted the trial re-assembled in a few days after the arrival of Adeline, and the two remaining witnesses of the Marquis, on whom he now rested his cause against La Motte, appeared. She was led trembling into the court, where almost the first object that met her eyes was the Marquis de Montalt, whom she now beheld with an emotion entirely new to her, and which was strongly tinctured with horror. When Du Bosse saw her he immediately swore to her identity; his testimony was confirmed by her manner; for, on perceiving him she grew pale, and an universal tremor seized her. Jean D'Aunoy could no where be found, and La Motte was thus deprived of an evidence which essentially affected his interest. Adeline, when called upon, gave her little narrative with clearness and precision; and Peter, who had conveyed her from the abbey, supported the testimony she offered. The evidence produced was sufficient to criminate the Marquis of the intention of murder, in the minds of most people present; but it was not sufficient to affect the testimony of his two last witnesses, who positively swore to the commission of the robbery, and to the person of La Motte, on whom sentence of death was accordingly pronounced. On receiving the sentence the unhappy criminal fainted, and the compassion of the assembly, whose feelings had been unusually interested in the decision, was expressed in a general groan.

Their attention was quickly called to a new object—it was Jean D'Aunoy, who now entered the court. But his evidence, if it could ever, indeed, have been the means of saving La Motte, came too late. He was reconducted to prison; but Adeline, who, extremely shocked by his sentence, was much indisposed, received orders to remain in the court during the examination of D'Aunoy. This man had been at length found in the prison of a provincial town, where some of his creditors had thrown him, and from which even the money which the Marquis had remitted to him for the purpose of satisfying the craving importunities of Du Bosse, had been insufficient to release him. Meanwhile the revenge of the latter had been roused against the Marquis by an imaginary neglect, and the money which was designed to relieve his necessities, was spent by D'Aunoy in riotous luxury.

He was confronted with Adeline and with Du Bosse, and ordered to confess all he knew concerning this mysterious affair, or to undergo the torture. D'Aunoy, who was ignorant how far the suspicions concerning the Marquis extended, and who was conscious that his own words might condemn him, remained for some time obstinately silent; but when the question was administered, his resolution gave way, and he confessed a crime of which he had not even been suspected.

It appeared, that, in the year 1642, D'Aunoy, together with one Jaques Martigny, and Francis Balliere, had way-laid and seized Henri, Marquis de Montalt, half-brother to Philippe; and after having robbed him, and bound his servant to a tree, according to the orders they had received, they conveyed him to the abbey of St. Clair, in the distant forest of Fontanville. Here he was confined for some time, till further directions were received from Philippe de Montalt, the present Marquis, who was then on his estates in a northern province of France. These orders were for death, and the unfortunate Henri was assassinated in his chamber in the third week of his confinement at the abbey.

On hearing this, Adeline grew faint: she remembered the MS. she had found, together with the extraordinary circumstances that had attended the discovery; every nerve thrilled with horror, and, raising her eyes, she saw the countenance of the Marquis overspread with the livid paleness of guilt. She endeavoured, however, to arrest her fleeting spirits while the man proceeded in his confession.

When the murder was perpetrated, D'Aunoy had returned to his employer, who gave him the reward agreed upon, and in a few months after delivered into his hands the infant daughter of the late Marquis, whom he conveyed to a distant part of the kingdom, where, assuming the name of St. Pierre, he brought her up as his own child, receiving from the present Marquis a considerable annuity for his secrecy.

Adeline, no longer able to struggle with the tumult of emotions that now rushed upon her heart, uttered a deep sigh and fainted away. She was carried from the court; and when the confusion occasioned by this circumstance subsided, Jean D'Aunoy went on. He related, that on the death of his wife, Adeline was placed in a convent, from whence she was afterwards removed to another, where the Marquis had destined her to receive the vows. That her determined rejection of them had occasioned him to resolve upon her death, and that she had accordingly been removed to the house on the heath. D'Aunoy added, that by the Marquis's order he had misled Du Bosse with a false story of her birth. Having, after some time, discovered that his comrades had deceived him concerning her death, D'Aunoy separated from them in enmity; but they unanimously determined to conceal her escape from the Marquis, that they might enjoy the recompense of their supposed crime. Some months subsequent to this period,

317

however, D'Aunoy received a letter from the Marquis, charging him with the truth, and promising him a large reward if he would confess where he had placed Adeline. In consequence of this letter, he acknowledged that she had been given into the hands of a stranger; but, who he was, or where he lived, was not known.

Upon these depositions Philippe de Montalt was committed to take his trial for the murder of Henri, his brother; D'Aunoy was thrown into a dungeon of the Chatelet, and Du Bosse was bound to appear as evidence.

The feelings of the Marquis, who, in a prosecution stimulated by revenge, had thus unexpectedly exposed his crimes to the public eye, and betrayed himself to justice, can only be imagined. The passions which had tempted him to the commission of a crime so horrid as that of murder, — and what, if possible, heightened its atrocity, the murder of one connected with him by the ties of blood, and by habits of even infantine association — the passions which had stimulated him to so monstrous a deed, were ambition and the love of pleasure. The first was more immediately gratified by the title of his brother; the latter, by the riches which would enable him to indulge his voluptuous inclinations.

The late Marquis de Montalt, the father of Adeline, received from his ancestors a patrimony very inadequate to support the splendour of his rank; but he had married the heiress of an illustrious family, whose fortune amply supplied the deficiency of his own. He had the misfortune to lose her, for she was amiable and beautiful, soon after the birth of a daughter, and it was then that the present Marquis formed the diabolical design of destroying his brother. The contrast of their characters prevented that cordial regard between them which their near relationship seemed to demand. Henri was benevolent, mild, and contemplative. In his heart reigned the love of virtue; in his manners the strictness of justice was tempered, not weakened, by mercy; his mind was enlarged by science, and adorned by elegant literature. The character of Philippe has been already delineated in his actions; its nicer shades were blended with some shining tints; but these served only to render more striking by contrast the general darkness of the portrait.

He had married a lady, who, by the death of her brother, inherited considerable estates, of which the abbey of St. Clair, and the villa on the borders of the forest of Fontanville, were the chief. His passion for magnificence and dissipation, however, soon involved him in difficulties, and pointed out to him the conveniency of possessing his brother's wealth. His brother and his infant daughter only stood between him and his wishes; how he removed the father has been already related; why he did not employ the same means to secure the child, seems somewhat surprising, unless we admit that a destiny hung over him on this occasion, and that she was suffered to live as an instrument to punish the murderer of her parent. When a retrospect is taken of the vicissitudes and dangers to which she had been exposed from her earliest infancy, it appears as if her preservation was the effect of something more than human policy, and affords a striking instance, that justice, however long delayed, will overtake the guilty.

While the late unhappy Marquis was suffering at the abbey, his brother, who, to avoid suspicion, remained in the north of France, delayed the execution of his horrid purpose from a timidity natural to a mind not yet inured to enormous guilt. Before he dared to deliver his final orders, he waited to know whether the story he contrived to propagate of his brother's death would veil his crime from suspicion. It succeeded but too well; for the servant, whose life had been spared that he might relate the tale, naturally enough concluded that his lord had been murdered by banditti; and the peasant, who, a few hours after, found the servant wounded, bleeding, and bound to a tree, and knew also that this spot was infested by robbers, as naturally believed him, and spread the report accordingly.

From this period the Marquis, to whom the abbey of St. Clair belonged in right of his wife, visited it only twice, and that at distant times, till, after an interval of several years, he accidentally found La Motte its inhabitant. He resided at Paris and on his estate in the north, except that once a year he usually passed a month at his delightful villa on the borders of the forest. In the busy scenes of the court, and in the dissipations of pleasure, he tried to lose the remembrance of his guilt; but there were times when the voice of conscience would be heard, though it was soon again lost in the tumult of the world.

It is probable, that on the night of his abrupt departure from the abbey, the solitary silence and gloom of the hour, in a place which had been the scene of his former crime, called up the remembrance of his brother with a force too powerful for fancy, and awakened horrors which compelled him to quit the polluted spot. If it was so, it is however certain that the spectres of conscience vanished with the darkness; for on the following day he returned to the abbey, though, it may be observed, he never attempted to pass another night there. But though terror was roused for a transient moment, neither pity nor repentance succeeded; since, when the discovery of Adeline's birth excited apprehension for his own life, he did not hesitate to repeat the crime, and would again have stained his soul with human blood. This discovery was effected by means of a seal bearing the arms of her mother's family, which was impressed on the note his servant had found, and had delivered to him at Caux. It may be remembered, that having read this note, he was throwing it from him in the fury of jealousy; but, that after examining it again, it was carefully deposited in his pocket-book. The violent agitation which a suspicion of this terrible truth occasioned, deprived him for awhile of all power to act. When he was well enough to write, he dispatched a letter to D'Aunoy, the purport of which has been already mentioned. From D'Aunoy he received the confirmation of his fears. Knowing that his life must pay the forfeiture of his crime, should Adeline ever obtain a knowledge of her birth, and not daring again to confide in the secrecy of a man who had once deceived him, he resolved, after some deliberation, on her death. He immediately set out for the abbey, and gave those directions concerning her which terror for his own safety, still more than a desire of retaining her estates, suggested.

As the history of the seal which revealed the birth of Adeline is rather remarkable, it may not be amiss to mention, that it was stolen from the Marquis, together with a gold watch, by Jean D'Aunoy: the watch was soon disposed of, but the seal had been kept as a pretty trinket by his wife, and at her death went with Adeline among her clothes to the convent. Adeline had carefully preserved it, because it had once belonged to the woman whom she believed to have been her mother.

CHAPTER XXIV

While anxious doubt distracts the tortured heart.

We now return to the course of the narrative, and to Adeline, who was carried from the court to the lodging of Madame de La Motte. Madame was, however, at the Chatelet with her husband, suffering all the distress which the sentence pronounced against him might be supposed to inflict. The feeble frame of Adeline, so long harassed by grief and fatigue, almost sunk under the agitation which the discovery of her birth excited. Her feelings on this occasion were too complex to be analysed. From an orphan, subsisting on the bounty of others, without family, with few friends, and pursued by a cruel and powerful enemy, she saw herself suddenly transformed to the daughter of an illustrious house, and the heiress of immense wealth. But she learned also that her father had been murdered — murdered in the prime of his days — murdered by means of his brother, against whom she must now appear, and in punishing the destroyer of her parent, doom her uncle to death.

When she remembered the manuscript so singularly found, and considered that when she wept to the sufferings it described, her tears had flowed for those of her father, her emotion cannot easily be imagined. The circumstances attending the discovery of these papers no longer appeared to be a work of chance, but of a Power whose designs are great and just. O, my father! she would exclaim, your last wish is fulfilled — the pitying heart you wished might trace your sufferings shall avenge them.

On the return of Madame La Motte, Adeline endeavoured, as usual, to suppress her own emotions, that she might soothe the affliction of her friend. She related what had passed in the courts after the departure of La Motte, and thus excited, even in the sorrowful heart of Madame, a momentary gleam of satisfaction. Adeline determined to recover, if possible, the manuscript. On inquiry she learned that La Motte, in the confusion of his departure, had left it among other things at the abbey. This circumstance much distressed her, the more so because she believed its appearance might be of importance on the approaching trial; she determined, however, if she could recover her rights, to have the manuscript sought for.

In the evening Louis joined this mournful party: he came immediately from his father, whom he left more tranquil than he had been since the fatal sentence was pronounced. After a silent and melancholy supper they separated for the night; and Adeline, in the solitude of her chamber, had leisure to meditate on the discoveries of this eventful day. The sufferings of her dead father, such as she had read them recorded by his own hand, pressed most forcibly to her thoughts. The narrative had formerly so much affected her heart, and interested her imagination, that her memory now faithfully reflected each particular circumstance there disclosed. But when she considered that she had been in the very chamber where her parent had suffered, where even his life had been sacrificed, and that she had probably seen the very dagger, seen it stained with rust, the rust of blood! by which he had fallen, the anguish and horror of her mind defied all control.

On the following day Adeline received orders to prepare for the prosecution of the Marquis de Montalt, which was to commence as soon as the requisite witnesses could be collected. Among these were the abbess of the convent, who had received her from the hands of D'Aunoy; Madame La Motte, who was present when Du Bosse compelled her husband to receive Adeline; and Peter, who had not only been witness to this circumstance, but who had conveyed her from the abbey that she might escape the designs of the Marquis. La Motte and Theodore La Luc were incapacitated by the sentence of the law from appearing on the trial.

When La Motte was informed of the discovery of Adeline's birth, and that her father had been murdered at the abbey of St. Clair, he instantly remembered, and mentioned to his wife, the skeleton he found in the stone room leading to the subterranean cells. Neither of them doubted, from the situation in which it lay, hid in a chest in an obscure room strongly guarded, that La Motte had seen the remains of the late Marquis. Madame, however, determined not to shock Adeline with the mention of this circumstance till it should be necessary to declare it on the trial.

As the time of this trial drew near, the distress and agitation of Adeline increased. Though justice demanded the life of the murderer, and though the tenderness and pity which the idea of her father called forth, urged her to revenge his death, she could not without horror consider herself as the instrument of dispensing that justice which would deprive a fellow-being of existence; and there were times when she wished the secret of her birth had never been revealed. If this sensibility was, in her peculiar circumstances, a weakness, it was at least an amiable one, and as such deserves to be reverenced.

The accounts she received from Vaceau of the health of M. La Luc did not contribute to tranquillize her mind. The symptoms described by Clara seemed to say that he was in the last stage of a consumption, and the grief of Theodore and herself on this occasion was expressed in her letters with the lively eloquence so natural to her. Adeline loved and revered La Luc for his own worth, and for the parental tenderness he had shown her; but he was still dearer to her as the father of Theodore and her concern for his declining state was not inferior to that of his children. It was increased by the reflection that she had probably been the means of shortening his life; for she too well knew that the distress occasioned him by the situation in which it had been her misfortune to involve Theodore, had shattered his frame to its present infirmity. The same cause also withheld him from seeking in the climate of Montpellier the relief he had formerly been taught to expect there. When she looked around on the condition of her friends, her heart was almost overwhelmed with the prospect; it seemed as if she was destined to involve all those most dear to her in calamity. With respect to La Motte, whatever were his vices, and whatever the designs in which he had formerly engaged against her, she forgot them all in the service he had finally rendered her; and considered it to be as much her duty, as she felt it to be her inclination, to intercede in his behalf. This, however, in her present situation, she could not do with any hope of success; but if the suit, upon which depended the establishment of her rank, her fortune, and consequently her influence, should be decided in her favour, she determined to throw herself at the king's feet, and when she pleaded the cause of Theodore, ask the life of La Motte.

A few days preceding that of the trial, Adeline was informed a stranger desired to speak with her; and on going to the room where he was, she found M. Verneuil. Her countenance expressed both surprise and satisfaction at this unexpected meeting, and she inquired, though with little expectation of an affirmative, if he had heard of M. La Luc. I have seen him, said M. Verneuil; I am just come from Vaceau: but, I am sorry I cannot give you a better account of his health; he is greatly altered since I saw him before.

Adeline could scarcely refrain from tears at the recollection these words revived of the calamities which had occasioned this lamented change. M. Verneuil delivered her a packet from Clara. As he presented it, he said, besides this introduction to your notice, I have a claim of a different kind, which I am proud to assert, and which will perhaps justify the permission I ask of speaking upon your affairs. — Adeline bowed; and M. Verneuil, with a countenance expressive of the most tender solicitude, added, that he had heard of the late proceedings of the Parliament of Paris, and of the discoveries that so intimately concerned her. I know not, continued he, whether I ought to congratulate or condole with you on this trying occasion. That I sincerely sympathize in all that concerns you I hope you will believe, and I cannot deny myself the pleasure of telling you that I am related, though distantly, to the late Marchioness your mother — for that she was your mother I cannot doubt.

Adeline rose hastily and advanced towards M. Verneuil; surprise and satisfaction reanimated her features. Do I indeed see a relation? said she in a sweet and tremulous voice; and one whom I can welcome as a friend? Tears trembled in her eyes; and she received M. Verneuil's embrace in silence. It was some time before her emotion would permit her to speak.

To Adeline, who from her earliest infancy had been abandoned to strangers, a forlorn and helpless orphan; who had never till lately known a relation, and who then found one in the person of an inveterate enemy; to her this discovery was as delightful as unexpected. But, after struggling for some time with the various emotions that pressed upon her heart, she begged of M. Verneuil permission to withdraw till she could recover composure. He would have taken leave, but she entreated him not to go.

The interest which M. Verneuil took in the concerns of La Luc, which was strengthened by his increasing regard for Clara, had drawn him to Vaceau, where he was informed of the family and peculiar circumstances of Adeline. On receiving this intelligence he immediately set out for Paris, to offer his protection and assistance to his newly-discovered relation, and to aid, if possible, the cause of Theodore.

Adeline in a short time returned, and could then bear to converse on the subject of her family. M. Verneuil offered her his support and assistance, if they should be found necessary. But I trust, added he, to the justice of your cause, and hope it will not require any adventitious aid. To those who remember the late Marchioness, your features bring sufficient evidence of your birth. As a proof that my judgment in this instance is not biassed by prejudice, the resemblance struck me when I was in Savoy, though I knew the Marchioness only by her portrait; and I believe I mentioned to M. La Luc that you often reminded me of a deceased relation. You may form some judgment of this yourself, added M. Verneuil, taking a miniature from his pocket. This was your amiable mother.

Adeline's countenance changed; she received the picture eagerly, gazed on it for a long time in silence, and her eyes filled with tears. It was not the resemblance she studied; but the countenance—the mild and beautiful countenance of her parent, whose blue eyes, full of tender sweetness, seemed bent upon hers, while a soft smile played on her lips; Adeline pressed the picture to hers, and again gazed in silent reverie. At length, with a deep sigh, she said. This surely was my mother. Had she but lived—O, my poor father! you had been spared. This reflection quite overcame her, and she burst into tears. M. Verneuil did not interrupt her grief, but took her hand and sat by her without speaking, till she became more composed. Again kissing the picture, she held it out to him with a hesitating look. No, said he, it is already with its true owner. She thanked him with a smile of ineffable sweetness; and after some conversation on the subject of the approaching trial, on which occasion she requested M. Verneuil would support her by his presence, he withdrew, having begged leave to repeat his visit on the following day.

Adeline now opened her packet, and saw once more the well known characters of Theodore: for a moment She felt as if in his presence, and the conscious blush overspread her cheek. With a trembling hand she broke the seal, and read the tenderest assurances and solicitudes of his love. She often paused that she might prolong the sweet emotions which these assurances awakened; but while tears of tenderness stood trembling on her eyelids, the bitter recollection of his situation would return, and they fell in anguish on her bosom.

He congratulated her, and with peculiar delicacy, on the prospects of life which were opening to her; said, every thing that might tend to animate and support her, but avoided dwelling on his own circumstances, except by expressing his sense of the zeal and kindness of his commanding officer, and adding that he did not despair of finally obtaining a pardon.

This hope, though but faintly expressed, and written evidently for the purpose of consoling Adeline, did not entirely fail of the desired effect. She yielded to its enchanting influence, and forgot for awhile the many subjects of care and anxiety which surrounded her. Theodore said little of his father's health; what he did say was by no means so discouraging as the accounts of Clara, who, less anxious to conceal a truth that must give pain to Adeline, expressed without reserve all her apprehension and concern.

CHAPTER XXV

...... Heaven is just!

And, when the measure of his crimes is full,

Will bare its red right arm, and launch its lightnings.

MASON.

The day of the trial so anxiously awaited, and on which the fate of so many persons depended, at length arrived. Adeline, accompanied by M. Verneuil and Madame La Motte, appeared as the prosecutor of the Marquis de Montalt; and D'Aunoy, Du Bosse, Louis de La Motte, and several other persons, as witnesses in her cause. The judges were some of the most distinguished in France, and the advocates on both sides men of eminent abilities. On a trial of such importance the court, as may be imagined, was crowded with persons of distinction, and the spectacle it presented was strikingly solemn, yet magnificent.

When she appeared before the tribunal, Adeline's emotion surpassed all the arts of disguise; but, adding to the natural dignity of her air an expression of soft timidity, and to her downcast eyes a sweet confusion, it rendered her an object still more interesting; and she attracted the universal pity and admiration of the assembly. When she ventured to raise her eyes, she perceived that the Marquis was not yet in the court; and while she awaited his appearance in trembling expectation, a confused murmuring rose in a distant part of the hall. Her spirits now almost forsook her; the certainty of seeing immediately, and consciously, the murderer of her father, chilled her with horror, and she was with difficulty preserved from fainting. A low sound now ran through the court, and an air of confusion appeared, which was soon communicated to the tribunal itself. Several of the members arose, some left the hall, the whole place exhibited a scene of disorder, and a report at length reached Adeline that the Marquis de Montalt was dying. A considerable time elapsed in uncertainty: but the confusion continued; the Marquis did not appear, and at Adeline's request M. Verneuil went in quest of more positive information.

He followed a crowd which was hurrying towards the Chatelet, and with some difficulty gained admittance into the prison; but the porter at the gate, whom he had bribed for a passport, could give him no certain information on the subject of his inquiry, and not being at liberty to quit his post, furnished M. Verneuil with only a vague direction to the Marquis's apartment. The courts were silent and deserted; but as he advanced, a distant hum of voices led him on, till, perceiving several persons running towards a staircase which appeared beyond the archway of a long passage, he followed thither, and learned that the Marquis was certainly dying. The staircase was filled with people; he endeavoured to press through the crowd, and after much struggle and difficulty he reached the door of an ante-room which communicated with the apartment where the Marquis lay, and whence several persons now issued. Here he learned that the object of his inquiry was already dead. M. Verneuil, however, pressed through the ante-room to the chamber where lay the Marquis on a bed surrounded by officers of the law, and two notaries, who appeared to have been taking down depositions. His countenance was suffused with a black and deadly hue, and impressed with the horrors of death. M. Verneuil turned away, shocked by the spectacle; and on inquiry heard that the Marquis had died by poison.

It appeared that, convinced he had nothing to hope from his trial, he had taken this method of avoiding an ignominious death. In the last hours of life, while tortured with the remembrance of his crime, he resolved to make all the atonement that remained for him; and having swallowed the potion, he immediately sent for a confessor to take a full confession of his guilt, and two notaries, and thus establish Adeline beyond dispute in the rights of her birth: and also bequeathed her a considerable legacy.

In consequence of these depositions she was soon after formally acknowledged as the daughter and heiress of Henri, Marquis de Montalt, and the rich estates of her father were restored to her. She immediately threw herself at the feet of the king in behalf of Theodore and of La Motte. The character of the former, the cause in which he had risked his life, the occasion of the late Marquis's enmity towards him, were circumstances so notorious and so forcible, that it is more than probable the monarch would have granted his pardon to a pleader less irresistible than was Adeline de Montalt. Theodore La Luc not only received an ample pardon, but, in consideration of his gallant conduct towards Adeline, he was soon after raised to a post of considerable rank in the army.

For La Motte, who had been condemned for the robbery on full evidence, and who had been also charged with the crime which had formerly compelled him to quit Paris, a pardon could not be obtained; but, at the earnest supplication of Adeline, and in consideration of the service he had finally rendered her, his sentence was softened from death to banishment. This indulgence, however, would have availed him little, had not the noble generosity of Adeline silenced other prosecutions that were preparing against him, and bestowed on him a sum more than sufficient to support his family in a foreign country. This kindness operated so powerfully upon his heart, which had been betrayed through weakness rather than natural depravity, and awakened so keen a remorse for the injuries he had once meditated against a benefactress so noble, that his former habits became odious to him, and his character gradually recovered the hue which it would probably always have worn had he never been exposed to the tempting dissipations of Paris.

The passion which Louis had so long owned for Adeline was raised almost to adoration by her late conduct; but he now relinquished even the faint hope which he had hitherto almost unconsciously cherished; and since the life which was granted to Theodore rendered this sacrifice necessary, he could not repine. He resolved, however, to seek in absence the tranquillity he had lost, and to place his future happiness on that of two persons so deservedly dear to him.

On the eve of his departure, La Motte and his family took a very affecting leave of Adeline; he left Paris for England, where it was his design to settle; and Louis, who was eager to fly from her enchantments, set out on the same day for his regiment.

Adeline remained some time at Paris to settle her affairs, where she was introduced by M. Verneuil to the few and distant relations that remained of her family. Among these were the Count and Countess D— —, and the Monsieur Amand who had so much engaged her pity and esteem at Nice. The lady whose death he lamented was of the family of De Montalt; and the resemblance which he had traced between her features and those of Adeline, her cousin, was something more than the effect of fancy. The death of his elder brother had abruptly recalled him from Italy; but Adeline had the satisfaction to observe, that the heavy melancholy which formerly oppressed him, had yielded to a sort of placid resignation, and that his countenance was often enlivened by a transient gleam of cheerfulness.

The Count and Countess D— —, who were much interested by her goodness and beauty, invited her to make their hotel her residence while she remained at Paris.

Her first care was to have the remains of her parent removed from the abbey of St. Clair, and deposited in the vault of his ancestors. D'Aunoy was tried, condemned, and hanged, for the murder. At the place of execution he had described the spot where the remains of the Marquis were concealed, which was in the stone room already mentioned belonging to the abbey. M. Verneuil accompanied the officers appointed for the search, and attended the ashes of the Marquis to St. Maur, an estate in one of the northern provinces. There they were deposited with the solemn funeral pomp becoming his rank; Adeline attended as chief mourner; and this last duty paid to the memory of her parent, she became more tranquil and resigned. The MS. that recorded his sufferings had been found at the abbey, and delivered to her by M. Verneuil, and she preserved it with the pious enthusiasm so sacred a relique deserved.

On her return to Paris, Theodore La Luc, who was come from Montpellier, awaited her arrival. The happiness of this meeting was clouded by the account he brought of his father, whose extreme danger had alone withheld him from hastening the moment he obtained his liberty to thank Adeline for the life she had preserved. She now received him as the friend to whom she was indebted for her preservation, and as the lover who deserved and possessed her tenderest affection. The remembrance of the circumstances under which they had last met, and of their mutual anguish, rendered more exquisite the happiness of the present moments, when, no longer oppressed by the horrid prospect of ignominious death and final separation, they looked forward only to the smiling days that awaited them, when hand in hand they should tread the flowery scenes of life. The contrast which memory drew of the past with the present, frequently drew tears of tenderness and gratitude to their eyes; and the sweet smile which seemed struggling to dispel from the countenance of Adeline those gems of sorrow, penetrated the heart of Theodore, and brought to his recollection a little song which in other circumstances he had formerly sung to her. He took up a lute that lay on the table, and touching the dulcet chords, accompanied it with the following words: —

SONG

The rose that weeps with morning dew,

And glitters in the sunny ray,

In tears and smiles resembles you,

When Love breaks sorrow's cloud away.

The dews that bend the blushing flower

Enrich the scent — renew the glow;

So Love's sweet tears exalt his power,

So bliss more brightly shines by woe!

Her affection for Theodore had induced Adeline to reject several suitors whom her goodness, beauty, and wealth, had already attracted, and who, though infinitely his superiors in point of fortune, were many of them inferior to him in family, and all of them in merit.

The various and tumultuous emotions which the late events had called forth in the bosom of Adeline were now subsided; but the memory of her father still tinctured her mind with a melancholy that time only could subdue; and she refused to listen to the supplications of Theodore, till the period she had prescribed for her mourning should be expired. The necessity of rejoining his regiment obliged him to leave Paris within the fortnight after his arrival; but he carried with him assurance of receiving her hand soon after she should lay aside her sable habit, and departed therefore with tolerable composure.

M. La Luc's very precarious state was a source of incessant disquietude to Adeline, and she determined to accompany M. Verneuil, who was now the declared lover of Clara, to Montpellier, whither La Luc had immediately gone on the liberation of his son. For this journey she was preparing, when she received from her friend a flattering account of his amendment; and as some further settlement of her affairs required her presence at Paris, she deferred her design, and M. Verneuil departed alone.

When Theodore's affairs assumed a more favourable aspect, M. Verneuil had written to La Luc, and communicated to him the secret of his heart respecting Clara. La Luc, who admired and esteemed M. Verneuil, and who was not ignorant of his family connexions, was pleased with the proposed alliance. Clara thought she had never seen any person whom she was so much inclined to love; and M. Verneuil received an answer favourable to his wishes, and which encouraged him to undertake the present journey to Montpellier.

The restoration of his happiness and the climate of Montpellier did all for the health of La Luc that his most anxious friends could wish, and he was at length so far recovered as to visit Adeline at her estate of St. Maur. Clara and

M. Verneuil accompanied him, and a cessation of hostilities between France and Spain soon after permitted Theodore to join this happy party. When La Luc, thus restored to those most dear to him, looked back on the miseries he had escaped, and forward to the blessings that awaited him, his heart dilated with emotions of exquisite joy and gratitude; and his venerable countenance, softened by an expression of complacent delight, exhibited a perfect picture of happy age.

CHAPTER XXVI

Last came Joy's ecstatic trial: —

They would have thought who heard the strain,

They saw in Tempe's vale her native maids

Amidst the festal sounding shades,

To some unwearied minstrel dancing,

While as his flying fingers kiss'd the strings,

Love framed with mirth a gay fantastic round.

ODE TO THE PASSIONS.

Adeline, in the society of friends so beloved, lost the impression of that melancholy which the fate of her parent had occasioned: she recovered all her natural vivacity; and when she threw off the mourning habit which filial piety had required her to assume, she gave her hand to Theodore. The nuptials, which were celebrated at St. Maur, were graced by the presence of the Count and Countess D — —; and La Luc had the supreme felicity of confirming on the same day the flattering destinies of both his children. When the ceremony was over, he blessed and embraced them all with tears of fatherly affection. I thank thee, O God! that I have been permitted to see this hour, said he; whenever it shall please thee to call me hence, I shall depart in peace.

Long, very long, may you be spared to bless your children! replied Adeline. Clara kissed her father's hand and wept: Long, very long! she repeated in a voice scarcely audible. La Luc smiled cheerfully, and turned the conversation to a subject less affecting.

But the time now drew nigh when La Luc thought it necessary to return to the duties of his parish, from which he had so long been absent. Madame La Luc too, who had attended him during the period of his danger at Montpellier, and hence returned to Savoy, complained much of the solitude of her life; and this was with her brother an additional motive for his speedy departure. Theodore and Adeline, who could not support the thought of a separation, endeavoured to persuade him to give up his chateau, and to reside with them in France; but he was held by many ties to Leloncourt. For many years he had constituted the comfort and happiness of his parishioners; they revered and loved him as a father — he regarded them with an affection little short of parental. The attachment they discovered towards him on his departure was not forgotten either; it had made a deep impression on his mind, and he could not bear the thought of forsaking them now that Heaven had showered on him its abundance. It is sweet to live for them, said he, and I will also die amongst them. A sentiment also of a more tender nature, — (and let not the stoic profane it with the name of weakness, or the man of the world scorn it as unnatural) — a sentiment still more tender attached him to Leloncourt, — the remains of his wife reposed there.

Since La Luc would not reside in France, Theodore and Adeline, to whom the splendid gaieties that courted them at Paris, were very inferior temptations to the sweet domestic pleasures and refined society which Leloncourt would afford, determined to accompany La Luc and Monsieur and Madame Verneuil abroad. Adeline arranged her affairs so as to render her residence in France unnecessary; and having bid an affectionate adieu to the Count and Countess D— —, and to M. Amand, who had recovered a tolerable degree of cheerfulness, she departed with her friends for Savoy.

They travelled leisurely, and frequently turned out of their way to view whatever was worthy of observation. After a long and pleasant journey they came once more within view of the Swiss mountains, the sight of which revived a thousand interesting recollections in the mind of Adeline. She remembered the circumstances and the sensations under which she had first seen them — when an orphan, flying from persecution to seek shelter among strangers, and lost to the only person on earth whom she loved — she remembered this, and the contrast of the present moment struck with all its force upon her heart.

The countenance of Clara brightened into smiles of the most animated delight as she drew near the beloved scenes of her infant pleasures; and Theodore, often looking from the windows, caught with patriotic enthusiasm the magnificent and changing scenery which the receding mountains successively disclosed.

It was evening when they approached within a few miles of Leloncourt, and the road winding round the foot of a stupendous crag, presented them a full view of the lake, and of the peaceful dwelling of La Luc. An exclamation of joy from the whole party announced the discovery, and the glance of

334

pleasure was reflected from every eye. The sun's last light gleamed upon the waters that reposed in "crystal purity" below, mellowed every feature of the landscape, and touched with purple splendour the clouds that rolled along the mountain tops.

La Luc welcomed his family to his happy home, and sent up a silent thanksgiving that he was permitted thus to return to it. Adeline continued to gaze upon each well known object; and again reflecting on the vicissitudes of grief and joy, and the surprising change of fortune which she had experienced since last she saw them, her heart dilated with gratitude and complacent delight. She looked at Theodore, whom in these very scenes she had lamented as lost to her for ever; who, when found again, was about to be torn from her by an ignominious death; but, who now sat by her side her secure and happy husband, the pride of his family and herself; and while the sensibility of her heart flowed in tears from her eyes, a smile of ineffable tenderness told him all she felt. He gently pressed her hand, and answered her with a look of love.

Peter, who now rode up to the carriage with a face fall of joy and of importance, interrupted a course of sentiment which was become almost too interesting. Ah! my dear master! cried he, welcome home again. Here is the village, God bless it! It is worth a million such places as Paris. Thank St. Jaques, we are all come safe back again.

This effusion of honest Peter's joy was received and answered with the kindness it deserved. As they drew near the lake, music sounded over the water, and they presently saw a large party of the villagers assembled on a green spot that sloped to the very margin of the waves, and dancing in all their holiday finery. It was the evening of a festival. The elder peasants sat under the shade of the trees that crowned this little eminence, eating milk and fruits, and watching their sons and daughters frisk it away to the sprightly notes of the tabor and pipe, which was joined by the softer tones of a mandolin.

The scene was highly interesting; and what added to its picturesque beauty was a group of cattle that stood, some on the brink, some half in the water, and others reposing on the green bank, while several peasant girls, dressed in the neat simplicity of their country, were dispensing the milky feast. Peter now rode on first, and a crowd soon collected round him, who, learning that their beloved master was at hand, went forth to meet and welcome him. Their warm and honest expressions of joy diffused an exquisite satisfaction over the heart of the good

La Luc, who met them with the kindness of a father, and could scarcely forbear shedding tears to this testimony of their attachment. When the younger part of the peasants heard the news of his arrival, the general joy was such, that, led by the tabor and pipe, they danced before his carriage to the chateau, where they again welcomed him and his family with the enlivening strains of music. At the gate of the chateau they were received by Madame La Luc, — and a happier party never met.

As the evening was uncommonly mild and beautiful, supper was spread in the garden. When the repast was over, Clara, whose heart was all glee, proposed a dance by moonlight. It will be delicious, said she; the moonbeams are already dancing on the waters. See what a stream of radiance they throw across the lake, and how they sparkle round that little promontory on the left. The freshness of the hour too invites to dancing.

They all agreed to the proposal. — And let the good people who have so heartily welcomed us home be called in too, said La Luc: they shall all partake our happiness: there is devotion in making others happy, and gratitude ought to make us devout. Peter, bring more wine, and set some tables under the trees. Peter flew; and while chairs and tables were placing, Clara ran for her favourite lute, the lute which had formerly afforded her such delight, and which Adeline had often touched with a melancholy expression. Clara's light hand now ran over the chords, and drew forth tones of tender sweetness, her voice accompanying the following:

AIR

Now at Moonlight's fairy hoar,

When faintly gleams each dewy steep,

And vale and mountain, lake and bower,

In solitary grandeur sleep;

When slowly sinks the evening breeze,

That lulls the mind in pensive care,

And Fancy loftier visions sees,

Bid music wake the silent air:

Bid the merry merry tabor sound,

And with the Fays of lawn or glade

In tripping circlet beat the ground

Under the high trees' trembling shade.

"Now at Moonlight's fairy hour"

Shall Music breathe her dulcet voice,

And o'er the waves, with magic power,

Call on Echo to rejoice!

Peter, who could not move in a sober step, had already spread refreshments under the trees, and in a short time the lawn was encircled with peasantry. The rural pipe and tabor were placed, at Clara's request, under the shade of her beloved acacias on the margin of the lake; the merry notes of music sounded, Adeline led off the dance, and the mountains answered only to the strains of mirth and melody.

The venerable La Luc, as he sat among the elder peasants, surveyed the scene — his children and people thus assembled round him in one grand compact of harmony and joy — the frequent tear bedewed his cheek, and he seemed to taste the fulness of an exalted delight.

So much was every heart roused to gladness, that the morning dawn began to peep upon the scene of their festivity, when every cottager returned to his home, blessing the benevolence of La Luc.

After passing some weeks with La Luc, M. Verneuil bought a chateau in the village of Leloncourt; and as it was the only one not already occupied, Theodore looked out for a residence in the neighbourhood. At the distance of a few leagues, on the beautiful banks of the lake of Geneva, where the waters retire into a small bay, he purchased a villa. The chateau was characterized by an air of simplicity and taste rather than of magnificence, which, however, was the chief trait in the surrounding scene. The chateau was almost encircled with woods, which formed a grand amphitheatre, swept down to the water's edge, and abounded with wild and romantic walks. Here nature was suffered to sport in all her beautiful luxuriance, except where, here and there, the hand of art formed the foliage to admit a view of the blue waters of the lake, with the white sail that glided by, or of the distant mountains. In front of the chateau the woods opened to a lawn, and the eye was suffered to wander over the lake, whose bosom presented an ever-moving picture, while its varied margin sprinkled with villas, woods, and towns, and crowned beyond with the snowy and sublime Alps, rising point behind point in awful confusion, exhibited a scenery of almost unequalled magnificence.

Here, contemning the splendour of false happiness, and possessing the pure and rational delights of love refined into the most tender friendship, surrounded by the friends so dear to them, and visited by a select and enlightened society — here, in the very bosom of felicity, lived Theodore and Adeline La Luc.

The passion of Louis de La Motte yielded at length to the powers of absence and necessity. He still loved Adeline, but it was with the placid tenderness of friendship; and when, at the earnest invitation of Theodore, he visited the villa, he beheld their happiness with a satisfaction unalloyed by any emotions of envy. He afterwards married a lady of some fortune at Geneva; and resigning his commission in the French service, settled on the borders of the lake, and increased the social delights of Theodore and Adeline.

Their former lives afforded an example of trials well endured — and their present, of virtues greatly rewarded; and this reward they continued to deserve — for, not to themselves was their happiness contracted, but diffused to all who came within the sphere of their influence. The indigent and unhappy rejoiced in their benevolence, the virtuous and enlightened in their friendship, and their children in parents whose example impressed upon their hearts, the precepts offered to their understandings.

The Monk: A Romance

By M.G. Lewis, Esq.

Somnia, terrores magicos, miracula, sagas,
Nocturnos lemures, portentaque.

HORAT.

Dreams, magic terrors, spells of mighty power,
Witches, and ghosts who rove at midnight hour.

IMITATION OF HORACE

Ep. 20. — B. 1.

Methinks, Oh! vain ill-judging Book,
I see thee cast a wishful look,
Where reputations won and lost are
In famous row called Paternoster.
Incensed to find your precious olio
Buried in unexplored port-folio,
You scorn the prudent lock and key,
And pant well bound and gilt to see
Your Volume in the window set
Of Stockdale, Hookham, or Debrett.

Go then, and pass that dangerous bourn
Whence never Book can back return:

And when you find, condemned, despised,
Neglected, blamed, and criticised,
Abuse from All who read you fall,
(If haply you be read at all
Sorely will you your folly sigh at,
And wish for me, and home, and quiet.

Assuming now a conjuror's office, I
Thus on your future Fortune prophesy:—
Soon as your novelty is o'er,
And you are young and new no more,
In some dark dirty corner thrown,
Mouldy with damps, with cobwebs strown,
Your leaves shall be the Book-worm's prey;
Or sent to Chandler-Shop away,
And doomed to suffer public scandal,
Shall line the trunk, or wrap the candle!

But should you meet with approbation,
And some one find an inclination
To ask, by natural transition
Respecting me and my condition;
That I am one, the enquirer teach,
Nor very poor, nor very rich;
Of passions strong, of hasty nature,
Of graceless form and dwarfish stature;
By few approved, and few approving;
Extreme in hating and in loving;

The Monk: A Romance

Abhorring all whom I dislike,
Adoring who my fancy strike;
In forming judgements never long,
And for the most part judging wrong;
In friendship firm, but still believing
Others are treacherous and deceiving,
And thinking in the present aera
That Friendship is a pure chimaera:
More passionate no creature living,
Proud, obstinate, and unforgiving,
But yet for those who kindness show,
Ready through fire and smoke to go.

Again, should it be asked your page,
"Pray, what may be the author's age?"
Your faults, no doubt, will make it clear,
I scarce have seen my twentieth year,
Which passed, kind Reader, on my word,
While England's Throne held George the Third.

Now then your venturous course pursue:
Go, my delight! Dear Book, adieu!

M. G. L.

Hague,

Oct. 28, 1794.

ADVERTISEMENT

The first idea of this Romance was suggested by the story of the Santon Barsisa, related in The Guardian. — The Bleeding Nun is a tradition still credited in many parts of Germany; and I have been told that the ruins of the Castle of Lauenstein, which She is supposed to haunt, may yet be seen upon the borders of Thuringia. — The Water-King, from the third to the twelfth stanza, is the fragment of an original Danish Ballad — And Belerma and Durandarte is translated from some stanzas to be found in a collection of old Spanish poetry, which contains also the popular song of Gayferos and Melesindra, mentioned in Don Quixote. — I have now made a full avowal of all the plagiarisms of which I am aware myself; but I doubt not, many more may be found, of which I am at present totally unconscious.

CHAPTER I.

— —Lord Angelo is precise;

Stands at a guard with envy; Scarce confesses

That his blood flows, or that his appetite

Is more to bread than stone.

MEASURE FOR MEASURE.

Scarcely had the Abbey Bell tolled for five minutes, and already was the Church of the Capuchins thronged with Auditors. Do not encourage the idea that the Crowd was assembled either from motives of piety or thirst of information. But very few were influenced by those reasons; and in a city where superstition reigns with such despotic sway as in Madrid, to seek for true devotion would be a fruitless attempt. The Audience now assembled in the Capuchin Church was collected by various causes, but all of them were foreign to the ostensible motive. The Women came to show themselves, the Men to see the Women: Some were attracted by curiosity to hear an Orator so celebrated; Some came because they had no better means of employing their time till the play began; Some, from being assured that it would be impossible to find places in the Church; and one half of Madrid was brought thither by expecting to meet the other half. The only persons truly anxious to hear the Preacher were a few antiquated devotees, and half a dozen rival Orators, determined to find fault with and ridicule the discourse. As to the remainder of the Audience, the Sermon might have been omitted altogether, certainly without their being disappointed, and very probably without their perceiving the omission.

Whatever was the occasion, it is at least certain that the Capuchin Church had never witnessed a more numerous assembly. Every corner was filled, every seat was occupied. The very Statues which ornamented the long aisles were pressed into the service. Boys suspended themselves upon the wings of Cherubims; St. Francis and St. Mark bore each a spectator on his shoulders; and St. Agatha found herself under the necessity of carrying double. The consequence was, that in spite of all their hurry and expedition, our two newcomers, on entering the Church, looked round in vain for places.

However, the old Woman continued to move forwards. In vain were exclamations of displeasure vented against her from all sides: In vain was She addressed with—"I assure you, Segnora, there are no places here."—"I beg, Segnora, that you will not crowd me so intolerably!"—"Segnora, you cannot pass this way. Bless me! How can people be so troublesome!"—The old Woman was obstinate, and on She went. By dint of perseverance and two brawny arms She made a passage through the Crowd, and managed to bustle herself into the very body of the Church, at no great distance from the Pulpit. Her companion had followed her with timidity and in silence, profiting by the exertions of her conductress.

"Holy Virgin!" exclaimed the old Woman in a tone of disappointment, while She threw a glance of enquiry round her; "Holy Virgin! What heat! What a Crowd! I wonder what can be the meaning of all this. I believe we must return: There is no such thing as a seat to be had, and nobody seems kind enough to accommodate us with theirs."

This broad hint attracted the notice of two Cavaliers, who occupied stools on the right hand, and were leaning their backs against the seventh column from the Pulpit. Both were young, and richly habited. Hearing this appeal to their politeness pronounced in a female voice, they interrupted their conversation to look at the speaker. She had thrown up her veil in order to take a clearer look round the Cathedral. Her hair was red, and She squinted. The Cavaliers turned round, and renewed their conversation.

"By all means," replied the old Woman's companion; "By all means, Leonella, let us return home immediately; The heat is excessive, and I am terrified at such a crowd."

These words were pronounced in a tone of unexampled sweetness. The Cavaliers again broke off their discourse, but for this time they were not contented with looking up: Both started involuntarily from their seats, and turned themselves towards the Speaker.

The voice came from a female, the delicacy and elegance of whose figure inspired the Youths with the most lively curiosity to view the face to which it belonged. This satisfaction was denied them. Her features were hidden by a thick veil; But struggling through the crowd had deranged it sufficiently to discover a neck which for symmetry and beauty might have vied with the Medicean Venus. It was of the most dazzling whiteness, and received additional charms from being shaded by the tresses of her long fair hair, which descended in ringlets to her waist. Her figure was rather below than above the middle size: It was light and airy as that of an Hamadryad. Her bosom was carefully veiled. Her dress was white; it was fastened by a blue sash, and just permitted to peep out from under it a little foot of the most delicate proportions. A chaplet of large grains hung upon her arm, and her face was covered with a veil of thick black gauze. Such was the female, to whom the youngest of the Cavaliers now offered his seat, while the other thought it necessary to pay the same attention to her companion.

The old Lady with many expressions of gratitude, but without much difficulty, accepted the offer, and seated herself: The young one followed her example, but made no other compliment than a simple and graceful reverence. Don Lorenzo (such was the Cavalier's name, whose seat She had accepted) placed himself near her; But first He whispered a few words in his Friend's ear, who immediately took the hint, and endeavoured to draw off the old Woman's attention from her lovely charge.

"You are doubtless lately arrived at Madrid," said Lorenzo to his fair Neighbour; "It is impossible that such charms should have long remained unobserved; and had not this been your first public appearance, the envy of the Women and adoration of the Men would have rendered you already sufficiently remarkable."

He paused, in expectation of an answer. As his speech did not absolutely require one, the Lady did not open her lips: After a few moments He resumed his discourse:

"Am I wrong in supposing you to be a Stranger to Madrid?"

The Lady hesitated; and at last, in so low a voice as to be scarcely intelligible, She made shift to answer, — "No, Segnor."

"Do you intend making a stay of any length?"

"Yes, Segnor."

"I should esteem myself fortunate, were it in my power to contribute to making your abode agreeable. I am well known at Madrid, and my Family has some interest at Court. If I can be of any service, you cannot honour or oblige me more than by permitting me to be of use to you." — "Surely," said He to himself, "She cannot answer that by a monosyllable; now She must say something to me."

Lorenzo was deceived, for the Lady answered only by a bow.

By this time He had discovered that his Neighbour was not very conversible; But whether her silence proceeded from pride, discretion, timidity, or idiotism, He was still unable to decide.

After a pause of some minutes — "It is certainly from your being a Stranger," said He, "and as yet unacquainted with our customs, that you continue to wear your veil. Permit me to remove it."

At the same time He advanced his hand towards the Gauze: The Lady raised hers to prevent him.

"I never unveil in public, Segnor."

"And where is the harm, I pray you?" interrupted her Companion somewhat sharply; "Do not you see that the other Ladies have all laid their veils aside, to do honour no doubt to the holy place in which we are? I have taken off mine already; and surely if I expose my features to general observation, you have no cause to put yourself in such a wonderful alarm! Blessed Maria! Here is a fuss and a bustle about a chit's face! Come, come, Child! Uncover it; I warrant you that nobody will run away with it from you —"

"Dear aunt, it is not the custom in Murcia."

"Murcia, indeed! Holy St. Barbara, what does that signify? You are always putting me in mind of that villainous Province. If it is the custom in Madrid, that is all that we ought to mind, and therefore I desire you to take off your veil immediately. Obey me this moment Antonia, for you know that I cannot bear contradiction—"

Her niece was silent, but made no further opposition to Don Lorenzo's efforts, who, armed with the Aunt's sanction hastened to remove the Gauze. What a Seraph's head presented itself to his admiration! Yet it was rather bewitching than beautiful; It was not so lovely from regularity of features as from sweetness and sensibility of Countenance. The several parts of her face considered separately, many of them were far from handsome; but when examined together, the whole was adorable. Her skin though fair was not entirely without freckles; Her eyes were not very large, nor their lashes particularly long. But then her lips were of the most rosy freshness; Her fair and undulating hair, confined by a simple ribband, poured itself below her waist in a profusion of ringlets; Her throat was full and beautiful in the extreme; Her hand and arm were formed with the most perfect symmetry; Her mild blue eyes seemed an heaven of sweetness, and the crystal in which they moved sparkled with all the brilliance of Diamonds: She appeared to be scarcely fifteen; An arch smile, playing round her mouth, declared her to be possessed of liveliness, which excess of timidity at present represt; She looked round her with a bashful glance; and whenever her eyes accidentally met Lorenzo's, She dropt them hastily upon her Rosary; Her cheek was immediately suffused with blushes, and She began to tell her beads; though her manner evidently showed that She knew not what She was about.

Lorenzo gazed upon her with mingled surprise and admiration; but the Aunt thought it necessary to apologize for Antonia's mauvaise honte.

"'Tis a young Creature," said She, "who is totally ignorant of the world. She has been brought up in an old Castle in Murcia; with no other Society than her Mother's, who, God help her! has no more sense, good Soul, than is necessary to carry her Soup to her mouth. Yet She is my own Sister, both by Father and Mother."

"And has so little sense?" said Don Christoval with feigned astonishment; "How very Extraordinary!"

"Very true, Segnor; Is it not strange? However, such is the fact; and yet only to see the luck of some people! A young Nobleman, of the very first quality, took it into his head that Elvira had some pretensions to Beauty — As to pretensions, in truth, She had always enough of THEM; But as to Beauty....! If I had only taken half the pains to set myself off which She did....! But this is neither here nor there. As I was saying, Segnor, a young Nobleman fell in love with her, and married her unknown to his Father. Their union remained a secret near three years, But at last it came to the ears of the old Marquis, who, as you may well suppose, was not much pleased with the intelligence. Away He posted in all haste to Cordova, determined to seize Elvira, and send her away to some place or other, where She would never be heard of more. Holy St. Paul! How He stormed on finding that She had escaped him, had joined her Husband, and that they had embarked together for the Indies. He swore at us all, as if the Evil Spirit had possessed him; He threw my Father into prison, as honest a painstaking Shoe-maker as any in Cordova; and when He went away, He had the cruelty to take from us my Sister's little Boy, then scarcely two years old, and whom in the abruptness of her flight, She had been obliged to leave behind her. I suppose, that the poor little Wretch met with bitter bad treatment from him, for in a few months after, we received intelligence of his death."

"Why, this was a most terrible old Fellow, Segnora!"

"Oh! shocking! and a Man so totally devoid of taste! Why, would you believe it, Segnor? When I attempted to pacify him, He cursed me for a Witch, and wished that to punish the Count, my Sister might become as ugly as myself! Ugly indeed! I like him for that."

"Ridiculous", cried Don Christoval; "Doubtless the Count would have thought himself fortunate, had he been permitted to exchange the one Sister for the other."

"Oh! Christ! Segnor, you are really too polite. However, I am heartily glad that the Condé was of a different way of thinking. A mighty pretty piece of business, to be sure, Elvira has made of it! After broiling and stewing in the Indies for thirteen long years, her Husband dies, and She returns to Spain, without an House to hide her head, or money to procure her one! This Antonia was then but an Infant, and her only remaining Child. She found that her Father-in-Law had married again, that he was irreconcileable to the Condé, and that his second Wife had produced him a Son, who is reported to be a very fine young Man. The old Marquis refused to see my Sister or her Child; But sent her word that on condition of never hearing any more of her, He would assign her a small pension, and She might live in an old Castle which He possessed in Murcia; This had been the favourite habitation of his eldest Son; But since his flight from Spain, the old Marquis could not bear the place, but let it fall to ruin and confusion—My Sister accepted the proposal; She retired to Murcia, and has remained there till within the last Month."

"And what brings her now to Madrid?" enquired Don Lorenzo, whom admiration of the young Antonia compelled to take a lively interest in the talkative old Woman's narration.

"Alas! Segnor, her Father-in-Law being lately dead, the Steward of his Murcian Estates has refused to pay her pension any longer.

With the design of supplicating his Son to renew it, She is now come to Madrid; But I doubt, that She might have saved herself the trouble! You young Noblemen have always enough to do with your money, and are not very often disposed to throw it away upon old Women. I advised my Sister to send Antonia with her petition; But She would not hear of such a thing. She is so obstinate! Well! She will find herself the worse for not following my counsels: the Girl has a good pretty face, and possibly might have done much."

"Ah! Segnora," interrupted Don Christoval, counterfeiting a passionate air; "If a pretty face will do the business, why has not your Sister recourse to you?"

"Oh! Jesus! my Lord, I swear you quite overpower me with your gallantry! But I promise you that I am too well aware of the danger of such Expeditions to trust myself in a young Nobleman's power! No, no; I have as yet preserved my reputation without blemish or reproach, and I always knew how to keep the Men at a proper distance."

"Of that, Segnora, I have not the least doubt. But permit me to ask you; Have you then any aversion to Matrimony?"

"That is an home question. I cannot but confess, that if an amiable Cavalier was to present himself...."

Here She intended to throw a tender and significant look upon Don Christoval; But, as She unluckily happened to squint most abominably, the glance fell directly upon his Companion: Lorenzo took the compliment to himself, and answered it by a profound bow.

"May I enquire," said He, "the name of the Marquis?"

"The Marquis de las Cisternas."

"I know him intimately well. He is not at present in Madrid, but is expected here daily. He is one of the best of Men; and if the lovely Antonia will permit me to be her Advocate with him, I doubt not my being able to make a favourable report of her cause."

Antonia raised her blue eyes, and silently thanked him for the offer by a smile of inexpressible sweetness. Leonella's satisfaction was much more loud and audible: Indeed, as her Niece was generally silent in her company, She thought it incumbent upon her to talk enough for both: This She managed without difficulty, for She very seldom found herself deficient in words.

"Oh! Segnor!" She cried; "You will lay our whole family under the most signal obligations! I accept your offer with all possible gratitude, and return you a thousand thanks for the generosity of your proposal. Antonia, why do not you speak, Child? While the Cavalier says all sorts of civil things to you, you sit like a Statue, and never utter a syllable of thanks, either bad, good, or indifferent!"

"My dear Aunt, I am very sensible that...."

"Fye, Niece! How often have I told you, that you never should interrupt a Person who is speaking!? When did you ever know me do such a thing? Are these your Murcian manners? Mercy on me! I shall never be able to make this Girl any thing like a Person of good breeding. But pray, Segnor," She continued, addressing herself to Don Christoval, "inform me, why such a Crowd is assembled today in this Cathedral?"

"Can you possibly be ignorant, that Ambrosio, Abbot of this Monastery, pronounces a Sermon in this Church every Thursday? All Madrid rings with his praises. As yet He has preached but thrice; But all who have heard him are so delighted with his eloquence, that it is as difficult to obtain a place at Church, as at the first representation of a new Comedy. His fame certainly must have reached your ears—"

"Alas! Segnor, till yesterday I never had the good fortune to see Madrid; and at Cordova we are so little informed of what is passing in the rest of the world, that the name of Ambrosio has never been mentioned in its precincts."

"You will find it in every one's mouth at Madrid. He seems to have fascinated the Inhabitants; and not having attended his Sermons myself, I am astonished at the Enthusiasm which He has excited. The adoration paid him both by Young and Old, by Man and Woman is unexampled. The Grandees load him with presents; Their Wives refuse to have any other Confessor, and he is known through all the city by the name of the 'Man of Holiness'."

"Undoubtedly, Segnor, He is of noble origin—"

"That point still remains undecided. The late Superior of the Capuchins found him while yet an Infant at the Abbey door. All attempts to discover who had left him there were vain, and the Child himself could give no account of his Parents. He was educated in the Monastery, where He has remained ever since. He early showed a strong inclination for study and retirement, and as soon as He was of a proper age, He pronounced his vows. No one has ever appeared to claim him, or clear up the mystery which conceals his birth; and the Monks, who find their account in the favour which is shewn to their establishment from respect to him, have not hesitated to publish that He is a present to them from the Virgin. In truth the singular austerity of his life gives some countenance to the report. He is now thirty years old, every hour of which period has been passed in study, total seclusion from the world, and mortification of the flesh. Till these last three weeks, when He was chosen superior of the Society to which He belongs, He had never been on the outside of the Abbey walls: Even now He never quits them except on Thursdays, when He delivers a discourse in this Cathedral which all Madrid assembles to hear. His knowledge is said to be the most profound, his eloquence the most persuasive. In the whole course of his life He has never been known to transgress a single rule of his order; The smallest stain is not to be discovered upon his character; and He is reported to be so strict an observer of Chastity, that He knows not in what consists the difference of Man and Woman. The common People therefore esteem him to be a Saint."

"Does that make a Saint?" enquired Antonia; "Bless me! Then am I one?"

"Holy St. Barbara!" exclaimed Leonella; "What a question! Fye, Child, Fye! These are not fit subjects for young Women to handle. You should not seem to remember that there is such a thing as a Man in the world, and you ought to imagine every body to be of the same sex with yourself. I should like to see you give people to understand, that you know that a Man has no breasts, and no hips, and no ...".

Luckily for Antonia's ignorance which her Aunt's lecture would soon have dispelled, an universal murmur through the Church announced the Preacher's arrival. Donna Leonella rose from her seat to take a better view of him, and Antonia followed her example.

He was a Man of noble port and commanding presence. His stature was lofty, and his features uncommonly handsome. His Nose was aquiline, his eyes large black and sparkling, and his dark brows almost joined together. His complexion was of a deep but clear Brown; Study and watching had entirely deprived his cheek of colour. Tranquillity reigned upon his smooth unwrinkled forehead; and Content, expressed upon every feature, seemed to announce the Man equally unacquainted with cares and crimes. He bowed himself with humility to the audience: Still there was a certain severity in his look and manner that inspired universal awe, and few could sustain the glance of his eye at once fiery and penetrating. Such was Ambrosio, Abbot of the Capuchins, and surnamed, "The Man of Holiness".

Antonia, while She gazed upon him eagerly, felt a pleasure fluttering in her bosom which till then had been unknown to her, and for which She in vain endeavoured to account. She waited with impatience till the Sermon should begin; and when at length the Friar spoke, the sound of his voice seemed to penetrate into her very soul. Though no other of the Spectators felt such violent sensations as did the young Antonia, yet every one listened with interest and emotion. They who were insensible to Religion's merits, were still enchanted with Ambrosio's oratory. All found their attention irresistibly attracted while He spoke, and the most profound silence reigned through the crowded Aisles.

Even Lorenzo could not resist the charm: He forgot that Antonia was seated near him, and listened to the Preacher with undivided attention.

In language nervous, clear, and simple, the Monk expatiated on the beauties of Religion. He explained some abstruse parts of the sacred writings in a style that carried with it universal conviction. His voice at once distinct and deep was fraught with all the terrors of the Tempest, while He inveighed against the vices of humanity, and described the punishments reserved for them in a future state. Every Hearer looked back upon his past offences, and trembled: The Thunder seemed to roll, whose bolt was destined to crush him, and the abyss of eternal destruction to open before his feet. But when Ambrosio, changing his theme, spoke of the excellence of an unsullied conscience, of the glorious prospect which Eternity presented to the Soul untainted with reproach, and of the recompense which awaited it in the regions of everlasting glory, His Auditors felt their scattered spirits insensibly return. They threw themselves with confidence upon the mercy of their Judge; They hung with delight upon the consoling words of the Preacher; and while his full voice swelled into melody, They were transported to those happy regions which He painted to their imaginations in colours so brilliant and glowing.

The discourse was of considerable length; Yet when it concluded, the Audience grieved that it had not lasted longer. Though the Monk had ceased to speak, enthusiastic silence still prevailed through the Church: At length the charm gradually dissolving, the general admiration was expressed in audible terms. As Ambrosio descended from the Pulpit, His Auditors crowded round him, loaded him with blessings, threw themselves at his feet, and kissed the hem of his Garment. He passed on slowly with his hands crossed devoutly upon his bosom, to the door opening into the Abbey Chapel, at which his Monks waited to receive him. He ascended the Steps, and then turning towards his Followers, addressed to them a few words of gratitude, and exhortation. While He spoke, his Rosary, composed of large grains of amber, fell from his hand, and dropped among the surrounding multitude. It was seized eagerly, and immediately divided amidst the Spectators. Whoever became possessor of a Bead, preserved it as a sacred relique; and had it been the Chaplet of thrice-blessed St. Francis himself, it could not have been disputed with greater vivacity. The Abbot, smiling at their eagerness, pronounced his benediction, and quitted the Church, while humility dwelt upon every feature. Dwelt She also in his heart?

Antonia's eyes followed him with anxiety. As the Door closed after him, it seemed to her as had she lost some one essential to her happiness. A tear stole in silence down her cheek.

"He is separated from the world!" said She to herself; "Perhaps, I shall never see him more!"

As she wiped away the tear, Lorenzo observed her action.

"Are you satisfied with our Orator?" said He; "Or do you think that Madrid overrates his talents?"

Antonia's heart was so filled with admiration for the Monk, that She eagerly seized the opportunity of speaking of him: Besides, as She now no longer considered Lorenzo as an absolute Stranger, She was less embarrassed by her excessive timidity.

"Oh! He far exceeds all my expectations," answered She; "Till this moment I had no idea of the powers of eloquence. But when He spoke, his voice inspired me with such interest, such esteem, I might almost say such affection for him, that I am myself astonished at the acuteness of my feelings."

Lorenzo smiled at the strength of her expressions.

"You are young and just entering into life," said He; "Your heart, new to the world and full of warmth and sensibility, receives its first impressions with eagerness. Artless yourself, you suspect not others of deceit; and viewing the world through the medium of your own truth and innocence, you fancy all who surround you to deserve your confidence and esteem. What pity, that these gay visions must soon be dissipated! What pity, that you must soon discover the baseness of mankind, and guard against your fellow-creatures as against your Foes!"

"Alas! Segnor," replied Antonia; "The misfortunes of my Parents have already placed before me but too many sad examples of the perfidy of the world! Yet surely in the present instance the warmth of sympathy cannot have deceived me."

"In the present instance, I allow that it has not. Ambrosio's character is perfectly without reproach; and a Man who has passed the whole of his life within the walls of a Convent cannot have found the opportunity to be guilty, even were He possessed of the inclination. But now, when, obliged by the duties of his situation, He must enter occasionally into the world, and be thrown into the way of temptation, it is now that it behoves him to show the brilliance of his virtue. The trial is dangerous; He is just at that period of life when the passions are most vigorous, unbridled, and despotic; His established reputation will mark him out to Seduction as an illustrious Victim; Novelty will give additional charms to the allurements of pleasure; and even the Talents with which Nature has endowed him will contribute to his ruin, by facilitating the means of obtaining his object. Very few would return victorious from a contest so severe."

"Ah! surely Ambrosio will be one of those few."

"Of that I have myself no doubt: By all accounts He is an exception to mankind in general, and Envy would seek in vain for a blot upon his character."

"Segnor, you delight me by this assurance! It encourages me to indulge my prepossession in his favour; and you know not with what pain I should have repressed the sentiment! Ah! dearest Aunt, entreat my Mother to choose him for our Confessor."

"I entreat her?" replied Leonella; "I promise you that I shall do no such thing. I do not like this same Ambrosio in the least; He has a look of severity about him that made me tremble from head to foot: Were He my Confessor, I should never have the courage to avow one half of my peccadilloes, and then I should be in a rare condition! I never saw such a stern-looking Mortal, and hope that I never shall see such another. His description of the Devil, God bless us! almost terrified me out of my wits, and when He spoke about Sinners He seemed as if He was ready to eat them."

"You are right, Segnora," answered Don Christoval; "Too great severity is said to be Ambrosio's only fault. Exempted himself from human failings, He is not sufficiently indulgent to those of others; and though strictly just and disinterested in his decisions, his government of the Monks has already shown some proofs of his inflexibility. But the crowd is nearly dissipated: Will you permit us to attend you home?"

"Oh! Christ! Segnor," exclaimed Leonella affecting to blush; "I would not suffer such a thing for the Universe! If I came home attended by so gallant a Cavalier, My Sister is so scrupulous that She would read me an hour's lecture, and I should never hear the last of it. Besides, I rather wish you not to make your proposals just at present."

"My proposals? I assure you, Segnora...."

"Oh! Segnor, I believe that your assurances of impatience are all very true; But really I must desire a little respite. It would not be quite so delicate in me to accept your hand at first sight."

"Accept my hand? As I hope to live and breathe...."

"Oh! dear Segnor, press me no further, if you love me! I shall consider your obedience as a proof of your affection; You shall hear from me tomorrow, and so farewell. But pray, Cavaliers, may I not enquire your names?"

"My Friend's," replied Lorenzo, "is the Condé d'Ossorio, and mine Lorenzo de Medina."

"'Tis sufficient. Well, Don Lorenzo, I shall acquaint my Sister with your obliging offer, and let you know the result with all expedition. Where may I send to you?"

"I am always to be found at the Medina Palace."

"You may depend upon hearing from me. Farewell, Cavaliers. Segnor Condé, let me entreat you to moderate the excessive ardour of your passion: However, to prove to you that I am not displeased with you, and prevent your abandoning yourself to despair, receive this mark of my affection, and sometimes bestow a thought upon the absent Leonella."

As She said this, She extended a lean and wrinkled hand; which her supposed Admirer kissed with such sorry grace and constraint so evident, that Lorenzo with difficulty repressed his inclination to laugh. Leonella then hastened to quit the Church; The lovely Antonia followed her in silence; but when She reached the Porch, She turned involuntarily, and cast back her eyes towards Lorenzo. He bowed to her, as bidding her farewell; She returned the compliment, and hastily withdrew.

"So, Lorenzo!" said Don Christoval as soon as they were alone, "You have procured me an agreeable Intrigue! To favour your designs upon Antonia, I obligingly make a few civil speeches which mean nothing to the Aunt, and at the end of an hour I find myself upon the brink of Matrimony! How will you reward me for having suffered so grievously for your sake? What can repay me for having kissed the leathern paw of that confounded old Witch? Diavolo! She has left such a scent upon my lips that I shall smell of garlick for this month to come! As I pass along the Prado, I shall be taken for a walking Omelet, or some large Onion running to seed!"

"I confess, my poor Count," replied Lorenzo, "that your service has been attended with danger; Yet am I so far from supposing it be past all endurance that I shall probably solicit you to carry on your amours still further."

"From that petition I conclude that the little Antonia has made some impression upon you."

"I cannot express to you how much I am charmed with her. Since my Father's death, My Uncle the Duke de Medina, has signified to me his wishes to see me married; I have till now eluded his hints, and refused to understand them; But what I have seen this Evening...."

"Well? What have you seen this Evening? Why surely, Don Lorenzo, You cannot be mad enough to think of making a Wife out of this Grand-daughter of 'as honest a painstaking Shoe-maker as any in Cordova'?"

"You forget, that She is also the Grand-daughter of the late Marquis de las Cisternas; But without disputing about birth and titles, I must assure you, that I never beheld a Woman so interesting as Antonia."

"Very possibly; But you cannot mean to marry her?"

"Why not, my dear Condé? I shall have wealth enough for both of us, and you know that my Uncle thinks liberally upon the subject.

From what I have seen of Raymond de las Cisternas, I am certain that he will readily acknowledge Antonia for his Niece. Her birth therefore will be no objection to my offering her my hand. I should be a Villain could I think of her on any other terms than marriage; and in truth She seems possessed of every quality requisite to make me happy in a Wife. Young, lovely, gentle, sensible...."

"Sensible? Why, She said nothing but 'Yes,' and 'No'."

"She did not say much more, I must confess — But then She always said 'Yes,' or 'No,' in the right place."

"Did She so? Oh! your most obedient! That is using a right Lover's argument, and I dare dispute no longer with so profound a Casuist. Suppose we adjourn to the Comedy?"

"It is out of my power. I only arrived last night at Madrid, and have not yet had an opportunity of seeing my Sister; You know that her Convent is in this Street, and I was going thither when the Crowd which I saw thronging into this Church excited my curiosity to know what was the matter. I shall now pursue my first intention, and probably pass the Evening with my Sister at the Parlour grate."

"Your Sister in a Convent, say you? Oh! very true, I had forgotten. And how does Donna Agnes? I am amazed, Don Lorenzo, how you could possibly think of immuring so charming a Girl within the walls of a Cloister!"

"I think of it, Don Christoval? How can you suspect me of such barbarity? You are conscious that She took the veil by her own desire, and that particular circumstances made her wish for a seclusion from the World. I used every means in my power to induce her to change her resolution; The endeavour was fruitless, and I lost a Sister!"

"The luckier fellow you; I think, Lorenzo, you were a considerable gainer by that loss: If I remember right, Donna Agnes had a portion of ten thousand pistoles, half of which reverted to your Lordship. By St. Jago! I wish that I had fifty Sisters in the same predicament. I should consent to losing them every soul without much heart-burning—"

"How, Condé?" said Lorenzo in an angry voice; "Do you suppose me base enough to have influenced my Sister's retirement? Do you suppose that the despicable wish to make myself Master of her fortune could...."

"Admirable! Courage, Don Lorenzo! Now the Man is all in a blaze. God grant that Antonia may soften that fiery temper, or we shall certainly cut each other's throat before the Month is over! However, to prevent such a tragical Catastrophe for the present, I shall make a retreat, and leave you Master of the field. Farewell, my Knight of Mount Aetna! Moderate that inflammable disposition, and remember that whenever it is necessary to make love to yonder Harridan, you may reckon upon my services."

He said, and darted out of the Cathedral.

"How wild-brained!" said Lorenzo; "With so excellent an heart, what pity that He possesses so little solidity of judgment!"

The night was now fast advancing. The Lamps were not yet lighted. The faint beams of the rising Moon scarcely could pierce through the gothic obscurity of the Church. Lorenzo found himself unable to quit the Spot. The void left in his bosom by Antonia's absence, and his Sister's sacrifice which Don Christoval had just recalled to his imagination, created that melancholy of mind which accorded but too well with the religious gloom surrounding him. He was still leaning against the seventh column from the Pulpit. A soft and cooling air breathed along the solitary Aisles: The Moonbeams darting into the Church through painted windows tinged the fretted roofs and massy pillars with a thousand various tints of light and colours:

Universal silence prevailed around, only interrupted by the occasional closing of Doors in the adjoining Abbey.

The calm of the hour and solitude of the place contributed to nourish Lorenzo's disposition to melancholy. He threw himself upon a seat which stood near him, and abandoned himself to the delusions of his fancy. He thought of his union with Antonia; He thought of the obstacles which might oppose his wishes; and a thousand changing visions floated before his fancy, sad 'tis true, but not unpleasing. Sleep insensibly stole over him, and the tranquil solemnity of his mind when awake for a while continued to influence his slumbers.

He still fancied himself to be in the Church of the Capuchins; but it was no longer dark and solitary. Multitudes of silver Lamps shed splendour from the vaulted Roof; Accompanied by the captivating chaunt of distant choristers, the Organ's melody swelled through the Church; The Altar seemed decorated as for some distinguished feast; It was surrounded by a brilliant Company; and near it stood Antonia arrayed in bridal white, and blushing with all the charms of Virgin Modesty.

Half hoping, half fearing, Lorenzo gazed upon the scene before him. Suddenly the door leading to the Abbey unclosed, and He saw, attended by a long train of Monks, the Preacher advance to whom He had just listened with so much admiration. He drew near Antonia.

"And where is the Bridegroom?" said the imaginary Friar.

Antonia seemed to look round the Church with anxiety. Involuntarily the Youth advanced a few steps from his concealment. She saw him; The blush of pleasure glowed upon her cheek; With a graceful motion of her hand She beckoned to him to advance. He disobeyed not the command; He flew towards her, and threw himself at her feet.

She retreated for a moment; Then gazing upon him with unutterable delight;—"Yes!" She exclaimed, "My Bridegroom! My destined Bridegroom!" She said, and hastened to throw herself into his arms; But before He had time to receive her, an Unknown rushed between them. His form was gigantic; His complexion was swarthy, His eyes fierce and terrible; his Mouth breathed out volumes of fire; and on his forehead was written in legible characters—"Pride! Lust! Inhumanity!"

Antonia shrieked. The Monster clasped her in his arms, and springing with her upon the Altar, tortured her with his odious caresses. She endeavoured in vain to escape from his embrace. Lorenzo flew to her succour, but ere He had time to reach her, a loud burst of thunder was heard. Instantly the Cathedral seemed crumbling into pieces; The Monks betook themselves to flight, shrieking fearfully; The Lamps were extinguished, the Altar sank down, and in its place appeared an abyss vomiting forth clouds of flame. Uttering a loud and terrible cry the Monster plunged into the Gulph, and in his fall attempted to drag Antonia with him. He strove in vain. Animated by supernatural powers She disengaged herself from his embrace; But her white Robe was left in his possession. Instantly a wing of brilliant splendour spread itself from either of Antonia's arms. She darted upwards, and while ascending cried to Lorenzo,

"Friend! we shall meet above!"

At the same moment the Roof of the Cathedral opened; Harmonious voices pealed along the Vaults; and the glory into which Antonia was received was composed of rays of such dazzling brightness, that Lorenzo was unable to sustain the gaze. His sight failed, and He sank upon the ground.

When He woke, He found himself extended upon the pavement of the Church: It was Illuminated, and the chaunt of Hymns sounded from a distance. For a while Lorenzo could not persuade himself that what He had just witnessed had been a dream, so strong an impression had it made upon his fancy. A little recollection convinced him of its fallacy: The Lamps had been lighted during his sleep, and the music which he heard was occasioned by the Monks, who were celebrating their Vespers in the Abbey Chapel.

Lorenzo rose, and prepared to bend his steps towards his Sister's Convent. His mind fully occupied by the singularity of his dream, He already drew near the Porch, when his attention was attracted by perceiving a Shadow moving upon the opposite wall. He looked curiously round, and soon descried a Man wrapped up in his Cloak, who seemed carefully examining whether his actions were observed. Very few people are exempt from the influence of curiosity. The Unknown seemed anxious to conceal his business in the Cathedral, and it was this very circumstance, which made Lorenzo wish to discover what He was about.

Our Hero was conscious that He had no right to pry into the secrets of this unknown Cavalier.

"I will go," said Lorenzo. And Lorenzo stayed, where He was.

The shadow thrown by the Column, effectually concealed him from the Stranger, who continued to advance with caution. At length He drew a letter from beneath his cloak, and hastily placed it beneath a Colossal Statue of St. Francis. Then retiring with precipitation, He concealed himself in a part of the Church at a considerable distance from that in which the Image stood.

"So!" said Lorenzo to himself; "This is only some foolish love affair. I believe, I may as well be gone, for I can do no good in it."

In truth till that moment it never came into his head that He could do any good in it; But He thought it necessary to make some little excuse to himself for having indulged his curiosity. He now made a second attempt to retire from the Church: For this time He gained the Porch without meeting with any impediment; But it was destined that He should pay it another visit that night. As He descended the steps leading into the Street, a Cavalier rushed against him with such violence, that Both were nearly overturned by the concussion. Lorenzo put his hand to his sword.

"How now, Segnor?" said He; "What mean you by this rudeness?"

"Ha! Is it you, Medina?" replied the Newcomer, whom Lorenzo by his voice now recognized for Don Christoval; "You are the luckiest Fellow in the Universe, not to have left the Church before my return. In, in! my dear Lad! They will be here immediately!"

"Who will be here?"

"The old Hen and all her pretty little Chickens! In, I say, and then you shall know the whole History."

Lorenzo followed him into the Cathedral, and they concealed themselves behind the Statue of St. Francis.

"And now," said our Hero, "may I take the liberty of asking, what is the meaning of all this haste and rapture?"

"Oh! Lorenzo, we shall see such a glorious sight! The Prioress of St. Clare and her whole train of Nuns are coming hither. You are to know, that the pious Father Ambrosio (The Lord reward him for it!) will upon no account move out of his own precincts: It being absolutely necessary for every fashionable Convent to have him for its Confessor, the Nuns are in consequence obliged to visit him at the Abbey; since when the Mountain will not come to Mahomet, Mahomet must needs go to the Mountain. Now the Prioress of St. Clare, the better to escape the gaze of such impure eyes as belong to yourself and your humble Servant, thinks proper to bring her holy flock to confession in the Dusk: She is to be admitted into the Abbey Chapel by yon private door. The Porteress of St. Clare, who is a worthy old Soul and a particular Friend of mine, has just assured me of their being here in a few moments. There is news for you, you Rogue! We shall see some of the prettiest faces in Madrid!"

"In truth, Christoval, we shall do no such thing. The Nuns are always veiled."

"No! No! I know better. On entering a place of worship, they ever take off their veils from respect to the Saint to whom 'tis dedicated. But Hark! They are coming! Silence, silence! Observe, and be convinced."

"Good!" said Lorenzo to himself; "I may possibly discover to whom the vows are addressed of this mysterious Stranger."

Scarcely had Don Christoval ceased to speak, when the Domina of St. Clare appeared, followed by a long procession of Nuns. Each upon entering the Church took off her veil. The Prioress crossed her hands upon her bosom, and made a profound reverence as She passed the Statue of St. Francis, the Patron of this Cathedral. The Nuns followed her example, and several moved onwards without having satisfied Lorenzo's curiosity. He almost began to despair of seeing the mystery cleared up, when in paying her respects to St. Francis, one of the Nuns happened to drop her Rosary. As She stooped to pick it up, the light flashed full upon her face. At the same moment She dexterously removed the letter from beneath the Image, placed it in her bosom, and hastened to resume her rank in the procession.

"Ha!" said Christoval in a low voice; "Here we have some

little Intrigue, no doubt."

"Agnes, by heaven!" cried Lorenzo.

"What, your Sister? Diavolo! Then somebody, I suppose, will have to pay for our peeping."

"And shall pay for it without delay," replied the incensed Brother.

The pious procession had now entered the Abbey; The Door was already closed upon it. The Unknown immediately quitted his concealment and hastened to leave the Church: Ere He could effect his intention, He descried Medina stationed in his passage. The Stranger hastily retreated, and drew his Hat over his eyes.

"Attempt not to fly me!" exclaimed Lorenzo; "I will know who you are, and what were the contents of that Letter."

"Of that Letter?" repeated the Unknown. "And by what title do you ask the question?"

"By a title of which I am now ashamed; But it becomes not you to question me. Either reply circumstantially to my demands, or answer me with your Sword."

"The latter method will be the shortest," rejoined the Other, drawing his Rapier; "Come on, Segnor Bravo! I am ready!"

Burning with rage, Lorenzo hastened to the attack: The Antagonists had already exchanged several passes before Christoval, who at that moment had more sense than either of them, could throw himself between their weapons.

"Hold! Hold! Medina!" He exclaimed; "Remember the consequences of shedding blood on consecrated ground!"

The Stranger immediately dropped his Sword.

"Medina?" He cried; "Great God, is it possible! Lorenzo, have you quite forgotten Raymond de las Cisternas?"

Lorenzo's astonishment increased with every succeeding moment. Raymond advanced towards him, but with a look of suspicion He drew back his hand, which the Other was preparing to take.

"You here, Marquis? What is the meaning of all this? You engaged in a clandestine correspondence with my Sister, whose affections...."

"Have ever been, and still are mine. But this is no fit place for an explanation. Accompany me to my Hotel, and you shall know every thing. Who is that with you?"

"One whom I believe you to have seen before," replied Don Christoval, "though probably not at Church."

"The Condé d'Ossorio?"

"Exactly so, Marquis."

"I have no objection to entrusting you with my secret, for I am sure that I may depend upon your silence."

"Then your opinion of me is better than my own, and therefore I must beg leave to decline your confidence. Do you go your own way, and I shall go mine. Marquis, where are you to be found?"

"As usual, at the Hotel de las Cisternas; But remember, that I am incognito, and that if you wish to see me, you must ask for Alphonso d'Alvarada."

"Good! Good! Farewell, Cavaliers!" said Don Christoval, and instantly departed.

"You, Marquis," said Lorenzo in the accent of surprise; "You, Alphonso d'Alvarada?"

"Even so, Lorenzo: But unless you have already heard my story from your Sister, I have much to relate that will astonish you. Follow me, therefore, to my Hotel without delay."

At this moment the Porter of the Capuchins entered the Cathedral to lock up the doors for the night. The two Noblemen instantly withdrew, and hastened with all speed to the Palace de las Cisternas.

"Well, Antonia!" said the Aunt, as soon as She had quitted the Church; "What think you of our Gallants? Don Lorenzo really seems a very obliging good sort of young Man: He paid you some attention, and nobody knows what may come of it. But as to Don Christoval, I protest to you, He is the very Phoenix of politeness. So gallant! so well-bred! So sensible, and so pathetic! Well! If ever Man can prevail upon me to break my vow never to marry, it will be that Don Christoval. You see, Niece, that every thing turns out exactly as I told you: The very moment that I produced myself in Madrid, I knew that I should be surrounded by Admirers. When I took off my veil, did you see, Antonia, what an effect the action had upon the Condé? And when I presented him my hand, did you observe the air of passion with which He kissed it? If ever I witnessed real love, I then saw it impressed upon Don Christoval's countenance!"

Now Antonia had observed the air, with which Don Christoval had kissed this same hand; But as She drew conclusions from it somewhat different from her Aunt's, She was wise enough to hold her tongue. As this is the only instance known of a Woman's ever having done so, it was judged worthy to be recorded here.

The old Lady continued her discourse to Antonia in the same strain, till they gained the Street in which was their Lodging. Here a Crowd collected before their door permitted them not to approach it; and placing themselves on the opposite side of the Street, they endeavoured to make out what had drawn all these people together. After some minutes the Crowd formed itself into a Circle; And now Antonia perceived in the midst of it a Woman of extraordinary height, who whirled herself repeatedly round and round, using all sorts of extravagant gestures. Her dress was composed of shreds of various-coloured silks and Linens fantastically arranged, yet not entirely without taste. Her head was covered with a kind of Turban, ornamented with vine leaves and wild flowers. She seemed much sun-burnt, and her complexion was of a deep olive: Her eyes looked fiery and strange; and in her hand She bore a long black Rod, with which She at intervals traced a variety of singular figures upon the ground, round about which She danced in all the eccentric attitudes of folly and delirium. Suddenly She broke off her dance, whirled herself round thrice with rapidity, and after a moment's pause She sang the following Ballad.

THE GYPSY'S SONG

Come, cross my hand! My art surpasses

    All that did ever Mortal know;

Come, Maidens, come! My magic glasses

    Your future Husband's form can show:

For 'tis to me the power is given
    Unclosed the book of Fate to see;
To read the fixed resolves of heaven,
    And dive into futurity.

I guide the pale Moon's silver waggon;
    The winds in magic bonds I hold;
I charm to sleep the crimson Dragon,
    Who loves to watch o'er buried gold:

Fenced round with spells, unhurt I venture
    Their sabbath strange where Witches keep;
Fearless the Sorcerer's circle enter,
    And woundless tread on snakes asleep.

Lo! Here are charms of mighty power!
    This makes secure an Husband's truth
And this composed at midnight hour
    Will force to love the coldest Youth:

If any Maid too much has granted,
    Her loss this Philtre will repair;
This blooms a cheek where red is wanted,
    And this will make a brown girl fair!

Then silent hear, while I discover
    What I in Fortune's mirror view;
And each, when many a year is over,

Shall own the Gypsy's sayings true.

"Dear Aunt!" said Antonia when the Stranger had finished, "Is She not mad?"

"Mad? Not She, Child; She is only wicked. She is a Gypsy, a sort of Vagabond, whose sole occupation is to run about the country telling lyes, and pilfering from those who come by their money honestly. Out upon such Vermin! If I were King of Spain, every one of them should be burnt alive who was found in my dominions after the next three weeks."

These words were pronounced so audibly that they reached the Gypsy's ears. She immediately pierced through the Crowd and made towards the Ladies. She saluted them thrice in the Eastern fashion, and then addressed herself to Antonia.

THE GYPSY

"Lady! gentle Lady! Know,

I your future fate can show;

Give your hand, and do not fear;

Lady! gentle Lady! hear!"

"Dearest Aunt!" said Antonia, "Indulge me this once! Let me have my fortune told me!"

"Nonsense, Child! She will tell you nothing but falsehoods."

"No matter; Let me at least hear what She has to say. Do, my dear Aunt! Oblige me, I beseech you!"

"Well, well! Antonia, since you are so bent upon the thing, ... Here, good Woman, you shall see the hands of both of us. There is money for you, and now let me hear my fortune."

As She said this, She drew off her glove, and presented her hand; The Gypsy looked at it for a moment, and then made this reply.

THE GYPSY

"Your fortune? You are now so old,

Good Dame, that 'tis already told:

Yet for your money, in a trice

I will repay you in advice.

Astonished at your childish vanity,

Your Friends all tax you with insanity,

And grieve to see you use your art

To catch some youthful Lover's heart.

Believe me, Dame, when all is done,

Your age will still be fifty one;

And Men will rarely take an hint

Of love, from two grey eyes that squint.

Take then my counsels; Lay aside

Your paint and patches, lust and pride,

And on the Poor those sums bestow,

Which now are spent on useless show.

Think on your Maker, not a Suitor;

Think on your past faults, not on future;

And think Time's Scythe will quickly mow

The few red hairs, which deck your brow.

The audience rang with laughter during the Gypsy's address; and — "fifty one," — "squinting eyes," "red hair," — "paint and patches," &c. were bandied from mouth to mouth. Leonella was almost choaked with passion, and loaded her malicious Adviser with the bitterest reproaches. The swarthy Prophetess for some time listened to her with a contemptuous smile: at length She made her a short answer, and then turned to Antonia.

THE GYPSY

"Peace, Lady! What I said was true;

And now, my lovely Maid, to you;

Give me your hand, and let me see

Your future doom, and heaven's decree."

In imitation of Leonella, Antonia drew off her glove, and

presented her white hand to the Gypsy, who having gazed upon it for some time with a mingled expression of pity and astonishment, pronounced her Oracle in the following words.

THE GYPSY

"Jesus! what a palm is there!

Chaste, and gentle, young and fair,

Perfect mind and form possessing,

You would be some good Man's blessing:

But Alas! This line discovers,

That destruction o'er you hovers;

Lustful Man and crafty Devil

Will combine to work your evil;

And from earth by sorrows driven,

Soon your Soul must speed to heaven.

Yet your sufferings to delay,

Well remember what I say.

When you One more virtuous see

Than belongs to Man to be,

One, whose self no crimes assailing,

Pities not his Neighbour's Failing,

Call the Gypsy's words to mind:

Though He seem so good and kind,

Fair Exteriors oft will hide

Hearts, that swell with lust and pride!

Lovely Maid, with tears I leave you!

Let not my prediction grieve you;

Rather with submission bending

Calmly wait distress impending,

And expect eternal bliss

In a better world than this.

Having said this, the Gypsy again whirled herself round thrice, and then hastened out of the Street with frantic gesture. The Crowd followed her; and Elvira's door being now unembarrassed Leonella entered the House out of humour with the Gypsy, with her Niece, and with the People; In short with every body, but herself and her charming Cavalier. The Gypsy's predictions had also considerably affected Antonia; But the impression soon wore off, and in a few hours She had forgotten the adventure as totally as had it never taken place.

CHAPTER II.

Fòrse sé tu gustassi una sòl volta

La millésima parte délle giòje,

Ché gusta un còr amato riamando,

Diresti ripentita sospirando,

Perduto è tutto il tempo

Ché in amar non si spènde.

TASSO.

Hadst Thou but tasted once the thousandth part

Of joys, which bless the loved and loving heart,

Your words repentant and your sighs would prove,

Lost is the time which is not past in love.

The monks having attended their Abbot to the door of his Cell, He dismissed them with an air of conscious superiority in which Humility's semblance combated with the reality of pride.

He was no sooner alone, than He gave free loose to the indulgence of his vanity. When He remembered the Enthusiasm which his discourse had excited, his heart swelled with rapture, and his imagination presented him with splendid visions of aggrandizement. He looked round him with exultation, and Pride told him loudly that He was superior to the rest of his fellow-Creatures.

"Who," thought He; "Who but myself has passed the ordeal of Youth, yet sees no single stain upon his conscience? Who else has subdued the violence of strong passions and an impetuous temperament, and submitted even from the dawn of life to voluntary retirement? I seek for such a Man in vain. I see no one but myself possessed of such resolution. Religion cannot boast Ambrosio's equal! How powerful an effect did my discourse produce upon its Auditors! How they crowded round me! How they loaded me with benedictions, and pronounced me the sole uncorrupted Pillar of the Church! What then now is left for me to do? Nothing, but to watch as carefully over the conduct of my Brothers as I have hitherto watched over my own. Yet hold! May I not be tempted from those paths which till now I have pursued without one moment's wandering? Am I not a Man, whose nature is frail, and prone to error? I must now abandon the solitude of my retreat; The fairest and noblest Dames of Madrid continually present themselves at the Abbey, and will use no other Confessor.

I must accustom my eyes to Objects of temptation, and expose myself to the seduction of luxury and desire. Should I meet in that world which I am constrained to enter some lovely Female, lovely ... as yon Madona....!"

As He said this, He fixed his eyes upon a picture of the Virgin, which was suspended opposite to him: This for two years had been the Object of his increasing wonder and adoration. He paused, and gazed upon it with delight.

"What Beauty in that countenance!" He continued after a silence of some minutes; "How graceful is the turn of that head! What sweetness, yet what majesty in her divine eyes! How softly her cheek reclines upon her hand! Can the Rose vie with the blush of that cheek? Can the Lily rival the whiteness of that hand? Oh! if such a Creature existed, and existed but for me! Were I permitted to twine round my fingers those golden ringlets, and press with my lips the treasures of that snowy bosom! Gracious God, should I then resist the temptation? Should I not barter for a single embrace the reward of my sufferings for thirty years? Should I not abandon.... Fool that I am! Whither do I suffer my admiration of this picture to hurry me? Away, impure ideas! Let me remember that Woman is for ever lost to me. Never was Mortal formed so perfect as this picture. But even did such exist, the trial might be too mighty for a common virtue, but Ambrosio's is proof against temptation. Temptation, did I say? To me it would be none. What charms me, when ideal and considered as a superior Being, would disgust me, become Woman and tainted with all the failings of Mortality. It is not the Woman's beauty that fills me with such enthusiasm; It is the Painter's skill that I admire, it is the Divinity that I adore! Are not the passions dead in my bosom? Have I not freed myself from the frailty of Mankind? Fear not, Ambrosio! Take confidence in the strength of your virtue. Enter boldly into a world to whose failings you are superior; Reflect that you are now exempted from Humanity's defects, and defy all the arts of the Spirits of Darkness. They shall know you for what you are!"

Here his Reverie was interrupted by three soft knocks at the door of his Cell. With difficulty did the Abbot awake from his delirium. The knocking was repeated.

"Who is there?" said Ambrosio at length.

"It is only Rosario," replied a gentle voice.

"Enter! Enter, my Son!"

The Door was immediately opened, and Rosario appeared with a small basket in his hand.

Rosario was a young Novice belonging to the Monastery, who in three Months intended to make his profession. A sort of mystery enveloped this Youth which rendered him at once an object of interest and curiosity. His hatred of society, his profound melancholy, his rigid observation of the duties of his order, and his voluntary seclusion from the world at his age so unusual, attracted the notice of the whole fraternity. He seemed fearful of being recognised, and no one had ever seen his face. His head was continually muffled up in his Cowl; Yet such of his features as accident discovered, appeared the most beautiful and noble. Rosario was the only name by which He was known in the Monastery.

No one knew from whence He came, and when questioned in the subject He preserved a profound silence. A Stranger, whose rich habit and magnificent equipage declared him to be of distinguished rank, had engaged the Monks to receive a Novice, and had deposited the necessary sums. The next day He returned with Rosario, and from that time no more had been heard of him.

The Youth had carefully avoided the company of the Monks: He answered their civilities with sweetness, but reserve, and evidently showed that his inclination led him to solitude. To this general rule the Superior was the only exception. To him He looked up with a respect approaching idolatry: He sought his company with the most attentive assiduity, and eagerly seized every means to ingratiate himself in his favour. In the Abbot's society his Heart seemed to be at ease, and an air of gaiety pervaded his whole manners and discourse. Ambrosio on his side did not feel less attracted towards the Youth; With him alone did He lay aside his habitual severity. When He spoke to him, He insensibly assumed a tone milder than was usual to him; and no voice sounded so sweet to him as did Rosario's. He repaid the Youth's attentions by instructing him in various sciences; The Novice received his lessons with docility; Ambrosio was every day more charmed with the vivacity of his Genius, the simplicity of his manners, and the rectitude of his heart: In short He loved him with all the affection of a Father. He could not help sometimes indulging a desire secretly to see the face of his Pupil; But his rule of self-denial extended even to curiosity, and prevented him from communicating his wishes to the Youth.

"Pardon my intrusion, Father," said Rosario, while He placed his basket upon the Table; "I come to you a Suppliant. Hearing that a dear Friend is dangerously ill, I entreat your prayers for his recovery. If supplications can prevail upon heaven to spare him, surely yours must be efficacious."

"Whatever depends upon me, my Son, you know that you may command.

What is your Friend's name?"

"Vincentio della Ronda."

"'Tis sufficient. I will not forget him in my prayers, and may our thrice-blessed St. Francis deign to listen to my intercession! — What have you in your basket, Rosario?"

"A few of those flowers, reverend Father, which I have observed to be most acceptable to you. Will you permit my arranging them in your chamber?"

"Your attentions charm me, my Son."

While Rosario dispersed the contents of his Basket in small Vases placed for that purpose in various parts of the room, the Abbot thus continued the conversation.

"I saw you not in the Church this evening, Rosario."

"Yet I was present, Father. I am too grateful for your protection to lose an opportunity of witnessing your Triumph."

"Alas! Rosario, I have but little cause to triumph: The Saint spoke by my mouth; To him belongs all the merit. It seems then you were contented with my discourse?"

"Contented, say you? Oh! you surpassed yourself! Never did I hear such eloquence ... save once!"

Here the Novice heaved an involuntary sigh.

"When was that once?" demanded the Abbot.

"When you preached upon the sudden indisposition of our late Superior."

"I remember it: That is more than two years ago. And were you present? I knew you not at that time, Rosario."

"'Tis true, Father; and would to God! I had expired, ere I beheld that day! What sufferings, what sorrows should I have escaped!"

"Sufferings at your age, Rosario?"

"Aye, Father; Sufferings, which if known to you, would equally raise your anger and compassion! Sufferings, which form at once the torment and pleasure of my existence! Yet in this retreat my bosom would feel tranquil, were it not for the tortures of apprehension. Oh God! Oh God! how cruel is a life of fear!—Father! I have given up all; I have abandoned the world and its delights for ever: Nothing now remains, Nothing now has charms for me, but your friendship, but your affection. If I lose that, Father! Oh! if I lose that, tremble at the effects of my despair!"

"You apprehend the loss of my friendship? How has my conduct justified this fear? Know me better, Rosario, and think me worthy of your confidence. What are your sufferings? Reveal them to me, and believe that if 'tis in my power to relieve them...."

"Ah! 'tis in no one's power but yours. Yet I must not let you know them. You would hate me for my avowal! You would drive me from your presence with scorn and ignominy!"

"My Son, I conjure you! I entreat you!"

"For pity's sake, enquire no further! I must not ... I dare not... Hark! The Bell rings for Vespers! Father, your benediction, and I leave you!"

As He said this, He threw himself upon his knees and received the blessing which He demanded. Then pressing the Abbot's hand to his lips, He started from the ground and hastily quitted the apartment. Soon after Ambrosio descended to Vespers (which were celebrated in a small chapel belonging to the Abbey), filled with surprise at the singularity of the Youth's behaviour.

Vespers being over, the Monks retired to their respective Cells. The Abbot alone remained in the Chapel to receive the Nuns of St. Clare. He had not been long seated in the confessional chair before the Prioress made her appearance. Each of the Nuns was heard in her turn, while the Others waited with the Domina in the adjoining Vestry. Ambrosio listened to the confessions with attention, made many exhortations, enjoined penance proportioned to each offence, and for some time every thing went on as usual: till at last one of the Nuns, conspicuous from the nobleness of her air and elegance of her figure, carelessly permitted a letter to fall from her bosom. She was retiring, unconscious of her loss. Ambrosio supposed it to have been written by some one of her Relations, and picked it up intending to restore it to her.

"Stay, Daughter," said He; "You have let fall...."

At this moment, the paper being already open, his eye involuntarily read the first words. He started back with surprise! The Nun had turned round on hearing his voice: She perceived her letter in his hand, and uttering a shriek of terror, flew hastily to regain it.

"Hold!" said the Friar in a tone of severity; "Daughter, I must read this letter."

"Then I am lost!" She exclaimed clasping her hands together wildly.

All colour instantly faded from her face; she trembled with agitation, and was obliged to fold her arms round a Pillar of the Chapel to save herself from sinking upon the floor. In the meanwhile the Abbot read the following lines:

"All is ready for your escape, my dearest Agnes. At twelve tomorrow night I shall expect to find you at the Garden door: I have obtained the Key, and a few hours will suffice to place you in a secure asylum. Let no mistaken scruples induce you to reject the certain means of preserving yourself and the innocent Creature whom you nourish in your bosom. Remember that you had promised to be mine, long ere you engaged yourself to the church; that your situation will soon be evident to the prying eyes of your Companions; and that flight is the only means of avoiding the effects of their malevolent resentment. Farewell, my Agnes! my dear and destined Wife! Fail not to be at the Garden door at twelve!"

As soon as He had finished, Ambrosio bent an eye stern and angry upon the imprudent Nun.

"This letter must to the Prioress!" said He, and passed her.

His words sounded like thunder to her ears: She awoke from her torpidity only to be sensible of the dangers of her situation. She followed him hastily, and detained him by his garment.

"Stay! Oh! stay!" She cried in the accents of despair, while She threw herself at the Friar's feet, and bathed them with her tears. "Father, compassionate my youth! Look with indulgence on a Woman's weakness, and deign to conceal my frailty! The remainder of my life shall be employed in expiating this single fault, and your lenity will bring back a soul to heaven!"

"Amazing confidence! What! Shall St. Clare's Convent become the retreat of Prostitutes? Shall I suffer the Church of Christ to cherish in its bosom debauchery and shame? Unworthy Wretch! such lenity would make me your accomplice. Mercy would here be criminal. You have abandoned yourself to a Seducer's lust; You have defiled the sacred habit by your impurity; and still dare you think yourself deserving my compassion? Hence, nor detain me longer! Where is the Lady Prioress?" He added, raising his voice.

"Hold! Father, Hold! Hear me but for one moment! Tax me not with impurity, nor think that I have erred from the warmth of temperament. Long before I took the veil, Raymond was Master of my heart: He inspired me with the purest, the most irreproachable passion, and was on the point of becoming my lawful husband. An horrible adventure, and the treachery of a Relation, separated us from each other: I believed him for ever lost to me, and threw myself into a Convent from motives of despair. Accident again united us; I could not refuse myself the melancholy pleasure of mingling my tears with his: We met nightly in the Gardens of St. Clare, and in an unguarded moment I violated my vows of Chastity. I shall soon become a Mother: Reverend Ambrosio, take compassion on me; take compassion on the innocent Being whose existence is attached to mine. If you discover my imprudence to the Domina, both of us are lost: The punishment which the laws of St. Clare assign to Unfortunates like myself is most severe and cruel. Worthy, worthy Father! Let not your own untainted conscience render you unfeeling towards those less able to withstand temptation! Let not mercy be the only virtue of which your heart is unsusceptible! Pity me, most reverend! Restore my letter, nor doom me to inevitable destruction!"

"Your boldness confounds me! Shall I conceal your crime, I whom you have deceived by your feigned confession? No, Daughter, no! I will render you a more essential service. I will rescue you from perdition in spite of yourself; Penance and mortification shall expiate your offence, and Severity force you back to the paths of holiness. What; Ho! Mother St. Agatha!"

"Father! By all that is sacred, by all that is most dear to you, I supplicate, I entreat...."

"Release me! I will not hear you. Where is the Domina? Mother St. Agatha, where are you?"

The door of the Vestry opened, and the Prioress entered the Chapel, followed by her Nuns.

"Cruel! Cruel!" exclaimed Agnes, relinquishing her hold.

Wild and desperate, She threw herself upon the ground, beating her bosom and rending her veil in all the delirium of despair. The Nuns gazed with astonishment upon the scene before them. The Friar now presented the fatal paper to the Prioress, informed her of the manner in which he had found it, and added, that it was her business to decide, what penance the delinquent merited.

While She perused the letter, the Domina's countenance grew inflamed with passion. What! Such a crime committed in her Convent, and made known to Ambrosio, to the Idol of Madrid, to the Man whom She was most anxious to impress with the opinion of the strictness and regularity of her House! Words were inadequate to express her fury. She was silent, and darted upon the prostrate Nun looks of menace and malignity.

"Away with her to the Convent!" said She at length to some of her Attendants.

Two of the oldest Nuns now approaching Agnes, raised her forcibly from the ground, and prepared to conduct her from the Chapel.

"What!" She exclaimed suddenly shaking off their hold with distracted gestures; "Is all hope then lost? Already do you drag me to punishment? Where are you, Raymond? Oh! save me! save me!"

Then casting upon the Abbot a frantic look, "Hear me!" She continued; "Man of an hard heart! Hear me, Proud, Stern, and

Cruel! You could have saved me; you could have restored me to happiness and virtue, but would not! You are the destroyer of my Soul; You are my Murderer, and on you fall the curse of my death and my unborn Infant's! Insolent in your yet-unshaken virtue, you disdained the prayers of a Penitent; But God will show mercy, though you show none. And where is the merit of your boasted virtue? What temptations have you vanquished? Coward! you have fled from it, not opposed seduction. But the day of Trial will arrive! Oh! then when you yield to impetuous passions! when you feel that Man is weak, and born to err; When shuddering you look back upon your crimes, and solicit with terror the mercy of your God, Oh! in that fearful moment think upon me! Think upon your Cruelty! Think upon Agnes, and despair of pardon!"

As She uttered these last words, her strength was exhausted, and She sank inanimate upon the bosom of a Nun who stood near her. She was immediately conveyed from the Chapel, and her Companions followed her.

Ambrosio had not listened to her reproaches without emotion. A secret pang at his heart made him feel, that He had treated this Unfortunate with too great severity. He therefore detained the Prioress and ventured to pronounce some words in favour of the Delinquent.

"The violence of her despair," said He, "proves, that at least Vice is not become familiar to her. Perhaps by treating her with somewhat less rigour than is generally practised, and mitigating in some degree the accustomed penance...."

"Mitigate it, Father?" interrupted the Lady Prioress; "Not I, believe me. The laws of our order are strict and severe; they have fallen into disuse of late, But the crime of Agnes shows me the necessity of their revival. I go to signify my intention to the Convent, and Agnes shall be the first to feel the rigour of those laws, which shall be obeyed to the very letter. Father, Farewell."

Thus saying, She hastened out of the Chapel.

"I have done my duty," said Ambrosio to himself.

Still did He not feel perfectly satisfied by this reflection. To dissipate the unpleasant ideas which this scene had excited in him, upon quitting the Chapel He descended into the Abbey Garden.

In all Madrid there was no spot more beautiful or better

regulated. It was laid out with the most exquisite taste. The choicest flowers adorned it in the height of luxuriance, and though artfully arranged, seemed only planted by the hand of Nature: Fountains, springing from basons of white Marble, cooled the air with perpetual showers; and the Walls were entirely covered by Jessamine, vines, and Honeysuckles. The hour now added to the beauty of the scene. The full Moon, ranging through a blue and cloudless sky, shed upon the trees a trembling lustre, and the waters of the fountains sparkled in the silver beam: A gentle breeze breathed the fragrance of Orange-blossoms along the Alleys; and the Nightingale poured forth her melodious murmur from the shelter of an artificial wilderness. Thither the Abbot bent his steps.

In the bosom of this little Grove stood a rustic Grotto, formed in imitation of an Hermitage. The walls were constructed of roots of trees, and the interstices filled up with Moss and Ivy. Seats of Turf were placed on either side, and a natural Cascade fell from the Rock above. Buried in himself the Monk approached the spot. The universal calm had communicated itself to his bosom, and a voluptuous tranquillity spread languor through his soul.

He reached the Hermitage, and was entering to repose himself, when He stopped on perceiving it to be already occupied. Extended upon one of the Banks lay a man in a melancholy posture.

His head was supported upon his arm, and He seemed lost in mediation. The Monk drew nearer, and recognised Rosario: He watched him in silence, and entered not the Hermitage. After some minutes the Youth raised his eyes, and fixed them mournfully upon the opposite Wall.

"Yes!" said He with a deep and plaintive sigh; "I feel all the happiness of thy situation, all the misery of my own! Happy were I, could I think like Thee! Could I look like Thee with disgust upon Mankind, could bury myself for ever in some impenetrable solitude, and forget that the world holds Beings deserving to be loved! Oh God! What a blessing would Misanthropy be to me!"

"That is a singular thought, Rosario," said the Abbot, entering the Grotto.

"You here, reverend Father?" cried the Novice.

At the same time starting from his place in confusion, He

drew his Cowl hastily over his face. Ambrosio seated himself upon the Bank, and obliged the Youth to place himself by him.

"You must not indulge this disposition to melancholy," said He; "What can possibly have made you view in so desirable a light, Misanthropy, of all sentiments the most hateful?"

"The perusal of these Verses, Father, which till now had escaped my observation. The Brightness of the Moonbeams permitted my reading them; and Oh! how I envy the feelings of the Writer!"

As He said this, He pointed to a marble Tablet fixed against the opposite Wall: On it were engraved the following lines.

INSCRIPTION IN AN HERMITAGE

Whoe'er Thou art these lines now reading,

Think not, though from the world receding

I joy my lonely days to lead in

    This Desart drear,

That with remorse a conscience bleeding

    Hath led me here.

No thought of guilt my bosom sowrs:

Free-willed I fled from courtly bowers;

For well I saw in Halls and Towers

    That Lust and Pride,

The Arch-Fiend's dearest darkest Powers,

    In state preside.

I saw Mankind with vice incrusted;

I saw that Honour's sword was rusted;

That few for aught but folly lusted;

That He was still deceiv'd, who trusted

    In Love or Friend;

And hither came with Men disgusted
        My life to end.

In this lone Cave, in garments lowly,
Alike a Foe to noisy folly,
And brow-bent gloomy melancholy
        I wear away
My life, and in my office holy
        Consume the day.

Content and comfort bless me more in
This Grot, than e'er I felt before in
A Palace, and with thoughts still soaring
        To God on high,
Each night and morn with voice imploring
        This wish I sigh.

"Let me, Oh! Lord! from life retire,
Unknown each guilty worldly fire,
Remorseful throb, or loose desire;
        And when I die,
Let me in this belief expire,
        'To God I fly'!"

Stranger, if full of youth and riot
As yet no grief has marred thy quiet,
Thou haply throw'st a scornful eye at
        The Hermit's prayer:
But if Thou hast a cause to sigh at

Thy fault, or care;

If Thou hast known false Love's vexation,

Or hast been exil'd from thy Nation,

Or guilt affrights thy contemplation,

And makes thee pine,

Oh! how must Thou lament thy station,

And envy mine!

"Were it possible" said the Friar, "for Man to be so totally wrapped up in himself as to live in absolute seclusion from human nature, and could yet feel the contented tranquillity which these lines express, I allow that the situation would be more desirable, than to live in a world so pregnant with every vice and every folly. But this never can be the case. This inscription was merely placed here for the ornament of the Grotto, and the sentiments and the Hermit are equally imaginary. Man was born for society. However little He may be attached to the World, He never can wholly forget it, or bear to be wholly forgotten by it. Disgusted at the guilt or absurdity of Mankind, the Misanthrope flies from it: He resolves to become an Hermit, and buries himself in the Cavern of some gloomy Rock. While Hate inflames his bosom, possibly He may feel contented with his situation: But when his passions begin to cool; when Time has mellowed his sorrows, and healed those wounds which He bore with him to his solitude, think you that Content becomes his Companion? Ah! no, Rosario. No longer sustained by the violence of his passions, He feels all the monotony of his way of living, and his heart becomes the prey of Ennui and weariness. He looks round, and finds himself alone in the Universe: The love of society revives in his bosom, and He pants to return to that world which He has abandoned. Nature loses all her charms in his eyes: No one is near him to point out her beauties, or share in his admiration of her excellence and variety. Propped upon the fragment of some Rock, He gazes upon the tumbling waterfall with a vacant eye, He views without emotion the glory of the setting Sun. Slowly He returns to his Cell at Evening, for no one there is anxious for his arrival; He has no comfort in his solitary unsavoury meal: He throws himself upon his couch of Moss despondent and dissatisfied, and wakes only to pass a day as joyless, as monotonous as the former."

"You amaze me, Father! Suppose that circumstances condemned you to solitude; Would not the duties of Religion and the consciousness of a life well spent communicate to your heart that calm which...."

"I should deceive myself, did I fancy that they could. I am convinced of the contrary, and that all my fortitude would not prevent me from yielding to melancholy and disgust. After consuming the day in study, if you knew my pleasure at meeting my Brethren in the Evening! After passing many a long hour in solitude, if I could express to you the joy which I feel at once more beholding a fellow-Creature! 'Tis in this particular that I place the principal merit of a Monastic Institution. It secludes Man from the temptations of Vice; It procures that leisure necessary for the proper service of the Supreme; It spares him the mortification of witnessing the crimes of the worldly, and yet permits him to enjoy the blessings of society. And do you, Rosario, do you envy an Hermit's life? Can you be thus blind to the happiness of your situation? Reflect upon it for a moment. This Abbey is become your Asylum: Your regularity, your gentleness, your talents have rendered you the object of universal esteem: You are secluded from the world which you profess to hate; yet you remain in possession of the benefits of society, and that a society composed of the most estimable of Mankind."

"Father! Father! 'tis that which causes my Torment! Happy had it been for me, had my life been passed among the vicious and abandoned! Had I never heard pronounced the name of Virtue! 'Tis my unbounded adoration of religion; 'Tis my soul's exquisite sensibility of the beauty of fair and good, that loads me with shame! that hurries me to perdition! Oh! that I had never seen these Abbey walls!"

"How, Rosario? When we last conversed, you spoke in a different tone. Is my friendship then become of such little consequence? Had you never seen these Abbey walls, you never had seen me: Can that really be your wish?"

"Had never seen you?" repeated the Novice, starting from the Bank, and grasping the Friar's hand with a frantic air; "You? You? Would to God, that lightning had blasted them, before you ever met my eyes! Would to God! that I were never to see you more, and could forget that I had ever seen you!"

With these words He flew hastily from the Grotto. Ambrosio remained in his former attitude, reflecting on the Youth's unaccountable behaviour. He was inclined to suspect the derangement of his senses: yet the general tenor of his conduct, the connexion of his ideas, and calmness of his demeanour till the moment of his quitting the Grotto, seemed to discountenance this conjecture. After a few minutes Rosario returned. He again seated himself upon the Bank: He reclined his cheek upon one hand, and with the other wiped away the tears which trickled from his eyes at intervals.

The Monk looked upon him with compassion, and forbore to interrupt his meditations. Both observed for some time a profound silence. The Nightingale had now taken her station upon an Orange Tree fronting the Hermitage, and poured forth a strain the most melancholy and melodious. Rosario raised his head, and listened to her with attention.

"It was thus," said He, with a deep-drawn sigh; "It was thus, that during the last month of her unhappy life, my Sister used to sit listening to the Nightingale. Poor Matilda! She sleeps in the Grave, and her broken heart throbs no more with passion."

"You had a Sister?"

"You say right, that I HAD; Alas! I have one no longer. She sunk beneath the weight of her sorrows in the very spring of life."

"What were those sorrows?"

"They will not excite your pity: you know not the power of those irresistible, those fatal sentiments, to which her Heart was a prey. Father, She loved unfortunately. A passion for One endowed with every virtue, for a Man, Oh! rather let me say, for a divinity, proved the bane of her existence. His noble form, his spotless character, his various talents, his wisdom solid, wonderful, and glorious, might have warmed the bosom of the most insensible. My Sister saw him, and dared to love though She never dared to hope."

"If her love was so well bestowed, what forbad her to hope the obtaining of its object?"

"Father, before He knew her, Julian had already plighted his vows to a Bride most fair, most heavenly! Yet still my Sister loved, and for the Husband's sake She doted upon the Wife. One morning She found means to escape from our Father's House: Arrayed in humble weeds She offered herself as a Domestic to the Consort of her Beloved, and was accepted. She was now continually in his presence: She strove to ingratiate herself into his favour: She succeeded. Her attentions attracted Julian's notice; The virtuous are ever grateful, and He distinguished Matilda above the rest of her Companions."

"And did not your Parents seek for her? Did they submit tamely to their loss, nor attempt to recover their wandering Daughter?"

"Ere they could find her, She discovered herself. Her love grew too violent for concealment; Yet She wished not for Julian's person, She ambitioned but a share of his heart. In an unguarded moment She confessed her affection. What was the return? Doating upon his Wife, and believing that a look of pity bestowed upon another was a theft from what He owed to her, He drove Matilda from his presence. He forbad her ever again appearing before him. His severity broke her heart: She returned to her Father's, and in a few Months after was carried to her Grave."

"Unhappy Girl! Surely her fate was too severe, and Julian was too cruel."

"Do you think so, Father?" cried the Novice with vivacity; "Do you think that He was cruel?"

"Doubtless I do, and pity her most sincerely."

"You pity her? You pity her? Oh! Father! Father! Then pity me!"

The Friar started; when after a moment's pause Rosario added with a faltering voice, — "for my sufferings are still greater. My Sister had a Friend, a real Friend, who pitied the acuteness of her feelings, nor reproached her with her inability to repress them. I ...! I have no Friend! The whole wide world cannot furnish an heart that is willing to participate in the sorrows of mine!"

As He uttered these words, He sobbed audibly. The Friar was affected. He took Rosario's hand, and pressed it with tenderness.

"You have no Friend, say you? What then am I? Why will you not confide in me, and what can you fear? My severity? Have I ever used it with you? The dignity of my habit? Rosario, I lay aside the Monk, and bid you consider me as no other than your Friend, your Father. Well may I assume that title, for never did Parent watch over a Child more fondly than I have watched over you. From the moment in which I first beheld you, I perceived sensations in my bosom till then unknown to me; I found a delight in your society which no one's else could afford; and when I witnessed the extent of your genius and information, I rejoiced as does a Father in the perfections of his Son. Then lay aside your fears; Speak to me with openness: Speak to me, Rosario, and say that you will confide in me. If my aid or my pity can alleviate your distress...."

"Yours can! Yours only can! Ah! Father, how willingly would I unveil to you my heart! How willingly would I declare the secret which bows me down with its weight! But Oh! I fear! I fear!"

"What, my Son?"

"That you should abhor me for my weakness; That the reward of my confidence should be the loss of your esteem."

"How shall I reassure you? Reflect upon the whole of my past conduct, upon the paternal tenderness which I have ever shown you. Abhor you, Rosario? It is no longer in my power. To give up your society would be to deprive myself of the greatest pleasure of my life. Then reveal to me what afflicts you, and believe me while I solemnly swear...."

"Hold!" interrupted the Novice; "Swear, that whatever be my secret, you will not oblige me to quit the Monastery till my Noviciate shall expire."

"I promise it faithfully, and as I keep my vows to you, may Christ keep his to Mankind. Now then explain this mystery, and rely upon my indulgence."

"I obey you. Know then.... Oh! how I tremble to name the word! Listen to me with pity, revered Ambrosio! Call up every latent spark of human weakness that may teach you compassion for mine! Father!" continued He throwing himself at the Friar's feet, and pressing his hand to his lips with eagerness, while agitation for a moment choked his voice; "Father!" continued He in faltering accents, "I am a Woman!"

The Abbot started at this unexpected avowal. Prostrate on the ground lay the feigned Rosario, as if waiting in silence the decision of his Judge. Astonishment on the one part, apprehension on the other, for some minutes chained them in the same attitudes, as had they been touched by the Rod of some Magician. At length recovering from his confusion, the

386

Monk quitted the Grotto, and sped with precipitation towards the Abbey. His action did not escape the Suppliant. She sprang from the ground; She hastened to follow him, overtook him, threw herself in his passage, and embraced his knees. Ambrosio strove in vain to disengage himself from her grasp.

"Do not fly me!" She cried; "Leave me not abandoned to the impulse of despair! Listen, while I excuse my imprudence; while I acknowledge my Sister's story to be my own! I am Matilda; You are her Beloved."

If Ambrosio's surprise was great at her first avowal, upon hearing her second it exceeded all bounds. Amazed, embarrassed, and irresolute He found himself incapable of pronouncing a syllable, and remained in silence gazing upon Matilda: This gave her opportunity to continue her explanation as follows.

"Think not, Ambrosio, that I come to rob your Bride of your affections. No, believe me: Religion alone deserves you; and far is it from Matilda's wish to draw you from the paths of virtue. What I feel for you is love, not licentiousness; I sigh to be possessor of your heart, not lust for the enjoyment of your person. Deign to listen to my vindication: A few moments will convince you that this holy retreat is not polluted by my presence, and that you may grant me your compassion without trespassing against your vows." —She seated herself: Ambrosio, scarcely conscious of what He did, followed her example, and She proceeded in her discourse.

"I spring from a distinguished family: My Father was Chief of the noble House of Villanegas. He died while I was still an Infant, and left me sole Heiress of his immense possessions. Young and wealthy, I was sought in marriage by the noblest Youths of Madrid; But no one succeeded in gaining my affections. I had been brought up under the care of an Uncle possessed of the most solid judgment and extensive erudition. He took pleasure in communicating to me some portion of his knowledge. Under his instructions my understanding acquired more strength and justness than generally falls to the lot of my sex: The ability of my Preceptor being aided by natural curiosity, I not only made a considerable progress in sciences universally studied, but in others, revealed but to few, and lying under censure from the blindness of superstition. But while my Guardian laboured to enlarge the sphere of my knowledge, He carefully inculcated every moral precept: He relieved me from the shackles of vulgar prejudice; He pointed out the beauty of Religion; He taught me to look with adoration upon the pure and virtuous, and, woe is me! I have obeyed him but too well!

"With such dispositions, Judge whether I could observe with any other sentiment than disgust the vice, dissipation, and ignorance, which disgrace our Spanish Youth. I rejected every offer with disdain. My heart remained without a Master till chance conducted me to the Cathedral of the Capuchins. Oh! surely on that day my Guardian Angel slumbered neglectful of his charge! Then was it that I first beheld you: You supplied the Superior's place, absent from illness. You cannot but remember the lively enthusiasm which your discourse created. Oh! how I drank your words! How your eloquence seemed to steal me from myself! I scarcely dared to breathe, fearing to lose a syllable; and while you spoke, Methought a radiant glory beamed round your head, and your countenance shone with the majesty of a God. I retired from the Church, glowing with admiration. From that moment you became the idol of my heart, the never-changing object of my Meditations. I enquired respecting you. The reports which were made me of your mode of life, of your knowledge, piety, and self-denial riveted the chains imposed on me by your eloquence. I was conscious that there was no longer a void in my heart; That I had found the Man whom I had sought till then in vain. In expectation of hearing you again, every day I visited your Cathedral: You remained secluded within the Abbey walls, and I always withdrew, wretched and disappointed. The Night was more propitious to me, for then you stood before me in my dreams; You vowed to me eternal friendship; You led me through the paths of virtue, and assisted me to support the vexations of life. The Morning dispelled these pleasing visions; I woke, and found myself separated from you by Barriers which appeared insurmountable. Time seemed only to increase the strength of my passion: I grew melancholy and despondent; I fled from society, and my health declined daily. At length no longer able to exist in this state of torture, I resolved to assume the disguise in which you see me. My artifice was fortunate: I was received into the Monastery, and succeeded in gaining your esteem.

"Now then I should have felt compleatly happy, had not my quiet been disturbed by the fear of detection. The pleasure which I received from your society, was embittered by the idea that perhaps I should soon be deprived of it: and my heart throbbed so rapturously at obtaining the marks of your friendship, as to convince me that I never should survive its loss. I resolved, therefore, not to leave the discovery of my sex to chance, to confess the whole to you, and throw myself entirely on your mercy and indulgence. Ah! Ambrosio, can I have been deceived? Can you be less generous than I thought you? I will not suspect it. You will not drive a Wretch to despair; I shall still be permitted to see you, to converse with you, to adore you! Your virtues shall be my example through life; and when we expire, our bodies shall rest in the same Grave."

She ceased. While She spoke, a thousand opposing sentiments combated in Ambrosio's bosom. Surprise at the singularity of this adventure, Confusion at her abrupt declaration, Resentment at her boldness in entering the Monastery, and Consciousness of the austerity with which it behoved him to reply, such were the sentiments of which He was aware; But there were others also which did not obtain his notice. He perceived not, that his vanity was flattered by the praises bestowed upon his eloquence and virtue; that He felt a secret pleasure in reflecting that a young and seemingly lovely Woman had for his sake abandoned the world, and sacrificed every other passion to that which He had inspired: Still less did He perceive that his heart throbbed with desire, while his hand was pressed gently by Matilda's ivory fingers.

By degrees He recovered from his confusion. His ideas became less bewildered: He was immediately sensible of the extreme impropriety, should Matilda be permitted to remain in the Abbey after this avowal of her sex. He assumed an air of severity, and drew away his hand.

"How, Lady!" said He; "Can you really hope for my permission to remain amongst us? Even were I to grant your request, what good could you derive from it? Think you that I ever can reply to an affection, which..."

"No, Father, No! I expect not to inspire you with a love like mine. I only wish for the liberty to be near you, to pass some hours of the day in your society; to obtain your compassion, your friendship and esteem. Surely my request is not unreasonable."

"But reflect, Lady! Reflect only for a moment on the impropriety of my harbouring a Woman in the Abbey; and that too a Woman, who confesses that She loves me. It must not be. The risque of your being discovered is too great, and I will not expose myself to so dangerous a temptation."

"Temptation, say you? Forget that I am a Woman, and it no longer exists: Consider me only as a Friend, as an Unfortunate, whose happiness, whose life depends upon your protection. Fear not lest I should ever call to your remembrance that love the most impetuous, the most unbounded, has induced me to disguise my sex; or that instigated by desires, offensive to your vows and my own honour, I should endeavour to seduce you from the path of rectitude. No, Ambrosio, learn to know me better. I love you for your virtues: Lose them, and with them you lose my affections. I look upon you as a Saint; Prove to me that you are no more than Man, and I quit you with disgust. Is it then from me that you fear temptation? From me, in whom the world's dazzling pleasures created no other sentiment than contempt? From me, whose attachment is grounded on your exemption from human frailty? Oh! dismiss such injurious apprehensions! Think nobler of me, think nobler of yourself. I am incapable of seducing you to error; and surely your Virtue is established on a basis too firm to be shaken by unwarranted desires. Ambrosio, dearest Ambrosio! drive me not from your presence; Remember your promise, and authorize my stay!"

"Impossible, Matilda; your interest commands me to refuse your prayer, since I tremble for you, not for myself. After vanquishing the impetuous ebullitions of Youth; After passing thirty years in mortification and penance, I might safely permit your stay, nor fear your inspiring me with warmer sentiments than pity. But to yourself, remaining in the Abbey can produce none but fatal consequences. You will misconstrue my every word and action; You will seize every circumstance with avidity, which encourages you to hope the return of your affection; Insensibly your passions will gain a superiority over your reason; and far from these being repressed by my presence, every moment which we pass together, will only serve to irritate and excite them. Believe me, unhappy Woman! you possess my sincere compassion. I am convinced that you have hitherto acted upon the purest motives; But though you are blind to the imprudence of your conduct, in me it would be culpable not to open your eyes. I feel that Duty obliges my treating you with harshness: I must reject your prayer, and remove every shadow of hope which may aid to nourish sentiments so pernicious to your repose. Matilda, you must from hence tomorrow."

"Tomorrow, Ambrosio? Tomorrow? Oh! surely you cannot mean it!

You cannot resolve on driving me to despair! You cannot have the cruelty...."

"You have heard my decision, and it must be obeyed. The Laws of our Order forbid your stay: It would be perjury to conceal that a Woman is within these Walls, and my vows will oblige me to declare your story to the Community. You must from hence! — I pity you, but can do no more!"

He pronounced these words in a faint and trembling voice: Then rising from his seat, He would have hastened towards the Monastery. Uttering a loud shriek, Matilda followed, and detained him.

"Stay yet one moment, Ambrosio! Hear me yet speak one word!"

"I dare not listen! Release me! You know my resolution!"

"But one word! But one last word, and I have done!"

"Leave me! Your entreaties are in vain! You must from hence tomorrow!"

"Go then, Barbarian! But this resource is still left me."

As She said this, She suddenly drew a poignard: She rent open her garment, and placed the weapon's point against her bosom.

"Father, I will never quit these Walls alive!"

"Hold! Hold, Matilda! What would you do?"

"You are determined, so am I: The Moment that you leave me, I plunge this Steel in my heart."

"Holy St. Francis! Matilda, have you your senses? Do you know the consequences of your action? That Suicide is the greatest of crimes? That you destroy your Soul? That you lose your claim to salvation? That you prepare for yourself everlasting torments?"

"I care not! I care not!" She replied passionately; "Either your hand guides me to Paradise, or my own dooms me to perdition! Speak to me, Ambrosio! Tell me that you will conceal my story, that I shall remain your Friend and your Companion, or this poignard drinks my blood!"

As She uttered these last words, She lifted her arm, and made a motion as if to stab herself. The Friar's eyes followed with dread the course of the dagger. She had torn open her habit, and her bosom was half exposed. The weapon's point rested upon her left breast: And Oh! that was such a breast! The

Moonbeams darting full upon it enabled the Monk to observe its dazzling whiteness. His eye dwelt with insatiable avidity upon the beauteous Orb. A sensation till then unknown filled his heart with a mixture of anxiety and delight: A raging fire shot through every limb; The blood boiled in his veins, and a thousand wild wishes bewildered his imagination.

"Hold!" He cried in an hurried faultering voice; "I can resist no longer! Stay, then, Enchantress; Stay for my destruction!"

He said, and rushing from the place, hastened towards the Monastery: He regained his Cell and threw himself upon his Couch, distracted irresolute and confused.

He found it impossible for some time to arrange his ideas. The scene in which He had been engaged had excited such a variety of sentiments in his bosom, that He was incapable of deciding which was predominant. He was irresolute what conduct He ought to hold with the disturber of his repose. He was conscious that prudence, religion, and propriety necessitated his obliging her to quit the Abbey: But on the other hand such powerful reasons authorized her stay that He was but too much inclined to consent to her remaining. He could not avoid being flattered by Matilda's declaration, and at reflecting that He had unconsciously vanquished an heart which had resisted the attacks of Spain's noblest Cavaliers: The manner in which He had gained her affections was also the most satisfactory to his vanity: He remembered the many happy hours which He had passed in Rosario's society, and dreaded that void in his heart which parting with him would occasion. Besides all this, He considered, that as Matilda was wealthy, her favour might be of essential benefit to the Abbey.

"And what do I risque," said He to himself, "by authorizing her stay? May I not safely credit her assertions? Will it not be easy for me to forget her sex, and still consider her as my Friend and my disciple? Surely her love is as pure as She describes. Had it been the offspring of mere licentiousness, would She so long have concealed it in her own bosom? Would She not have employed some means to procure its gratification? She has done quite the contrary: She strove to keep me in ignorance of her sex; and nothing but the fear of detection, and my instances, would have compelled her to reveal the secret. She has observed the duties of religion not less strictly than myself. She has made no attempts to rouze my slumbering passions, nor has She ever conversed with me till this night on the subject of Love. Had She been desirous to gain my affections, not my esteem, She would not have concealed from me her charms so carefully: At this very moment I have never seen her face: Yet certainly that face must be lovely, and her person beautiful, to judge by her ... by what I have seen."

As this last idea passed through his imagination, a blush spread itself over his cheek. Alarmed at the sentiments which He was indulging, He betook himself to prayer; He started from his Couch, knelt before the beautiful Madona, and entreated her assistance in stifling such culpable emotions. He then returned to his Bed, and resigned himself to slumber.

He awoke, heated and unrefreshed. During his sleep his inflamed imagination had presented him with none but the most voluptuous objects. Matilda stood before him in his dreams, and his eyes again dwelt upon her naked breast. She repeated her protestations of eternal love, threw her arms round his neck, and loaded him with kisses: He returned them; He clasped her passionately to his bosom, and ... the vision was dissolved. Sometimes his dreams presented the image of his favourite Madona, and He fancied that He was kneeling before her: As He offered up his vows to her, the eyes of the Figure seemed to beam on him with inexpressible sweetness. He pressed his lips to hers, and found them warm: The animated form started from the Canvas, embraced him affectionately, and his senses were unable to support delight so exquisite. Such were the scenes, on which his thoughts were employed while sleeping: His unsatisfied Desires placed before him the most lustful and provoking Images, and he rioted in joys till then unknown to him.

He started from his Couch, filled with confusion at the remembrance of his dreams. Scarcely was He less ashamed, when He reflected on his reasons of the former night which induced him to authorize Matilda's stay. The cloud was now dissipated which had obscured his judgment: He shuddered when He beheld his arguments blazoned in their proper colours, and found that He had been a slave to flattery, to avarice, and self-love. If in one hour's conversation Matilda had produced a change so remarkable in his sentiments, what had He not to dread from her remaining in the Abbey? Become sensible of his danger, awakened from his dream of confidence, He resolved to insist on her departing without delay. He began to feel that He was not proof against temptation; and that however Matilda might restrain herself within the bounds of modesty, He was unable to contend with those passions, from which He falsely thought himself exempted.

"Agnes! Agnes!" He exclaimed, while reflecting on his

embarrassments, "I already feel thy curse!"

He quitted his Cell, determined upon dismissing the feigned Rosario. He appeared at Matins; But his thoughts were absent, and He paid them but little attention. His heart and brain were both of them filled with worldly objects, and He prayed without devotion. The service over, He descended into the Garden. He bent his steps towards the same spot where, on the preceding night, He had made this embarrassing discovery. He doubted not but that Matilda would seek him there: He was not deceived. She soon entered the Hermitage, and approached the Monk with a timid air. After a few minutes during which both were silent, She appeared as if on the point of speaking; But the Abbot, who during this time had been summoning up all his resolution, hastily interrupted her. Though still unconscious how extensive was its influence, He dreaded the melodious seduction of her voice.

"Seat yourself by my side, Matilda," said He, assuming a look of firmness, though carefully avoiding the least mixture of severity; "Listen to me patiently, and believe, that in what I shall say, I am not more influenced by my own interest than by yours: Believe, that I feel for you the warmest friendship, the truest compassion, and that you cannot feel more grieved than I do, when I declare to you that we must never meet again."

"Ambrosio!" She cried, in a voice at once expressive of surprise and sorrow.

"Be calm, my Friend! My Rosario! Still let me call you by that name so dear to me! Our separation is unavoidable; I blush to own, how sensibly it affects me. — But yet it must be so. I feel myself incapable of treating you with indifference, and that very conviction obliges me to insist upon your departure. Matilda, you must stay here no longer."

"Oh! where shall I now seek for probity? Disgusted with a perfidious world, in what happy region does Truth conceal herself? Father, I hoped that She resided here; I thought that your bosom had been her favourite shrine. And you too prove false? Oh God! And you too can betray me?"

"Matilda!"

"Yes, Father, Yes! 'Tis with justice that I reproach you. Oh! where are your promises? My Noviciate is not expired, and yet will you compel me to quit the Monastery? Can you have the heart to drive me from you? And have I not received your solemn oath to the contrary?"

"I will not compell you to quit the Monastery: You have received my solemn oath to the contrary. But yet when I throw myself upon your generosity, when I declare to you the embarrassments in which your presence involves me, will you not release me from that oath? Reflect upon the danger of a discovery, upon the opprobrium in which such an event would plunge me: Reflect that my honour and reputation are at stake, and that my peace of mind depends on your compliance. As yet my heart is free; I shall separate from you with regret, but not with despair. Stay here, and a few weeks will sacrifice my happiness on the altar of your charms. You are but too interesting, too amiable! I should love you, I should doat on you! My bosom would become the prey of desires which Honour and my profession forbid me to gratify. If I resisted them, the impetuosity of my wishes unsatisfied would drive me to madness: If I yielded to the temptation, I should sacrifice to one moment of guilty pleasure my reputation in this world, my salvation in the next. To you then I fly for defence against myself. Preserve me from losing the reward of thirty years of sufferings! Preserve me from becoming the Victim of Remorse! your heart has already felt the anguish of hopeless love; Oh! then if you really value me, spare mine that anguish! Give me back my promise; Fly from these walls. Go, and you bear with you my warmest prayers for your happiness, my friendship, my esteem and admiration: Stay, and you become to me the source of danger, of sufferings, of despair! Answer me, Matilda; What is your resolve?" —She was silent—"Will you not speak, Matilda? Will you not name your choice?"

"Cruel! Cruel!" She exclaimed, wringing her hands in agony; "You know too well that you offer me no choice! You know too well that I can have no will but yours!"

"I was not then deceived! Matilda's generosity equals my expectations."

"Yes; I will prove the truth of my affection by submitting to a decree which cuts me to the very heart. Take back your promise. I will quit the Monastery this very day. I have a Relation, Abbess of a Covent in Estramadura: To her will I bend my steps, and shut myself from the world for ever. Yet tell me, Father, shall I bear your good wishes with me to my solitude? Will you sometimes abstract your attention from heavenly objects to bestow a thought upon me?"

"Ah! Matilda, I fear that I shall think on you but too often for my repose!"

"Then I have nothing more to wish for, save that we may meet in heaven. Farewell, my Friend! my Ambrosio! — And yet methinks, I would fain bear with me some token of your regard!"

"What shall I give you?"

"Something. — Any thing. — One of those flowers will be sufficient." (Here She pointed to a bush of Roses, planted at the door of the Grotto.) "I will hide it in my bosom, and when I am dead, the Nuns shall find it withered upon my heart."

The Friar was unable to reply: With slow steps, and a soul heavy with affliction, He quitted the Hermitage. He approached the Bush, and stooped to pluck one of the Roses. Suddenly He uttered a piercing cry, started back hastily, and let the flower, which He already held, fall from his hand. Matilda heard the shriek, and flew anxiously towards him.

"What is the matter?" She cried; "Answer me, for God's sake! What has happened?"

"I have received my death!" He replied in a faint voice; "Concealed among the Roses ... A Serpent...."

Here the pain of his wound became so exquisite, that Nature was unable to bear it: His senses abandoned him, and He sank inanimate into Matilda's arms.

Her distress was beyond the power of description. She rent her hair, beat her bosom, and not daring to quit Ambrosio, endeavoured by loud cries to summon the Monks to her assistance. She at length succeeded. Alarmed by her shrieks, Several of the Brothers hastened to the spot, and the Superior was conveyed back to the Abbey. He was immediately put to bed, and the Monk who officiated as Surgeon to the Fraternity prepared to examine the wound. By this time Ambrosio's hand had swelled to an extraordinary size; The remedies which had been administered to him, 'tis true, restored him to life, but not to his senses; He raved in all the horrors of delirium, foamed at the mouth, and four of the strongest Monks were scarcely able to hold him in his bed.

Father Pablos, such was the Surgeon's name, hastened to examine the wounded hand. The Monks surrounded the Bed, anxiously waiting for the decision: Among these the feigned

Rosario appeared not the most insensible to the Friar's calamity. He gazed upon the Sufferer with inexpressible anguish; and the groans which every moment escaped from his bosom sufficiently betrayed the violence of his affliction.

Father Pablos probed the wound. As He drew out his Lancet, its point was tinged with a greenish hue. He shook his head mournfully, and quitted the bedside.

"'Tis as I feared!" said He; "There is no hope."

"No hope?" exclaimed the Monks with one voice; "Say you, no hope?"

"From the sudden effects, I suspected that the Abbot was stung by a cientipedoro: The venom which you see upon my Lancet confirms my idea: He cannot live three days."

The cientipedoro is supposed to be a native of Cuba, and to have been brought into Spain from that island in the vessel of Columbus.

"And can no possible remedy be found?" enquired Rosario.

"Without extracting the poison, He cannot recover; and how to extract it is to me still a secret. All that I can do is to apply such herbs to the wound as will relieve the anguish: The Patient will be restored to his senses; But the venom will corrupt the whole mass of his blood, and in three days He will exist no longer."

Excessive was the universal grief at hearing this decision. Pablos, as He had promised, dressed the wound, and then retired, followed by his Companions: Rosario alone remained in the Cell, the Abbot at his urgent entreaty having been committed to his care. Ambrosio's strength worn out by the violence of his exertions, He had by this time fallen into a profound sleep. So totally was He overcome by weariness, that He scarcely gave any signs of life; He was still in this situation, when the Monks returned to enquire whether any change had taken place. Pablos loosened the bandage which concealed the wound, more from a principle of curiosity than from indulging the hope of discovering any favourable symptoms. What was his astonishment at finding, that the inflammation had totally subsided! He probed the hand; His Lancet came out pure and unsullied; No traces of the venom were perceptible; and had not the orifice still been visible, Pablos might have doubted that there had ever been a wound.

He communicated this intelligence to his Brethren; their delight was only equalled by their surprize. From the latter sentiment, however, they were soon released by explaining the circumstance according to their own ideas: They were perfectly convinced that their Superior was a Saint, and thought, that nothing could be more natural than for St. Francis to have operated a miracle in his favour. This opinion was adopted unanimously: They declared it so loudly, and vociferated, — "A miracle! a miracle!" — with such fervour, that they soon interrupted Ambrosio's slumbers.

The Monks immediately crowded round his Bed, and expressed their satisfaction at his wonderful recovery. He was perfectly in his senses, and free from every complaint except feeling weak and languid. Pablos gave him a strengthening medicine, and advised his keeping his bed for the two succeeding days: He then retired, having desired his Patient not to exhaust himself by conversation, but rather to endeavour at taking some repose. The other Monks followed his example, and the Abbot and Rosario were left without Observers.

For some minutes Ambrosio regarded his Attendant with a look of mingled pleasure and apprehension. She was seated upon the side of the Bed, her head bending down, and as usual enveloped in the Cowl of her Habit.

"And you are still here, Matilda?" said the Friar at length. "Are you not satisfied with having so nearly effected my destruction, that nothing but a miracle could have saved me from the Grave? Ah! surely Heaven sent that Serpent to punish..."

Matilda interrupted him by putting her hand before his lips with an air of gaiety.

"Hush! Father, Hush! You must not talk!"

"He who imposed that order, knew not how interesting are the subjects on which I wish to speak."

"But I know it, and yet issue the same positive command. I am appointed your Nurse, and you must not disobey my orders."

"You are in spirits, Matilda!"

"Well may I be so: I have just received a pleasure unexampled through my whole life."

"What was that pleasure?"

"What I must conceal from all, but most from you."

"But most from me? Nay then, I entreat you, Matilda...."

"Hush, Father! Hush! You must not talk. But as you do not seem inclined to sleep, shall I endeavour to amuse you with my Harp?"

"How? I knew not that you understood Music."

"Oh! I am a sorry Performer! Yet as silence is prescribed you for eight and forty hours, I may possibly entertain you, when wearied of your own reflections. I go to fetch my Harp."

She soon returned with it.

"Now, Father; What shall I sing? Will you hear the Ballad which treats of the gallant Durandarte, who died in the famous battle of Roncevalles?"

"What you please, Matilda."

"Oh! call me not Matilda! Call me Rosario, call me your Friend! Those are the names, which I love to hear from your lips. Now listen!"

She then tuned her harp, and afterwards preluded for some moments with such exquisite taste as to prove her a perfect Mistress of the Instrument. The air which She played was soft and plaintive:

Ambrosio, while He listened, felt his uneasiness subside, and a pleasing melancholy spread itself into his bosom. Suddenly Matilda changed the strain: With an hand bold and rapid She struck a few loud martial chords, and then chaunted the following Ballad to an air at once simple and melodious.

DURANDARTE AND BELERMA

Sad and fearful is the story

Of the Roncevalles fight;

On those fatal plains of glory

Perished many a gallant Knight.

There fell Durandarte; Never
Verse a nobler Chieftain named:
He, before his lips for ever
Closed in silence thus exclaimed.

"Oh! Belerma! Oh! my dear-one!
For my pain and pleasure born!
Seven long years I served thee, fair-one,
Seven long years my fee was scorn:

"And when now thy heart replying
To my wishes, burns like mine,
Cruel Fate my bliss denying
Bids me every hope resign.

"Ah! Though young I fall, believe me,
Death would never claim a sigh;
'Tis to lose thee, 'tis to leave thee,
Makes me think it hard to die!

"Oh! my Cousin Montesinos,
By that friendship firm and dear
Which from Youth has lived between us,
Now my last petition hear!

"When my Soul these limbs forsaking
Eager seeks a purer air,

From my breast the cold heart taking,
Give it to Belerma's care.

Say, I of my lands Possessor
Named her with my dying breath:
Say, my lips I op'd to bless her,
Ere they closed for aye in death:

"Twice a week too how sincerely
I adored her, Cousin, say;
Twice a week for one who dearly
Loved her, Cousin, bid her pray.

"Montesinos, now the hour
Marked by fate is near at hand:
Lo! my arm has lost its power!
Lo! I drop my trusty brand!

"Eyes, which forth beheld me going,
Homewards ne'er shall see me hie!
Cousin, stop those tears o'er-flowing,
Let me on thy bosom die!

"Thy kind hand my eyelids closing,
Yet one favour I implore:
Pray Thou for my Soul's reposing,
When my heart shall throb no more;

"So shall Jesus, still attending

Gracious to a Christian's vow,
Pleased accept my Ghost ascending,
And a seat in heaven allow."

Thus spoke gallant Durandarte;
Soon his brave heart broke in twain.
Greatly joyed the Moorish party,
That the gallant Knight was slain.

Bitter weeping Montesinos
Took from him his helm and glaive;
Bitter weeping Montesinos
Dug his gallant Cousin's grave.

To perform his promise made, He
Cut the heart from out the breast,
That Belerma, wretched Lady!
Might receive the last bequest.

Sad was Montesinos' heart, He
Felt distress his bosom rend.
"Oh! my Cousin Durandarte,
Woe is me to view thy end!

"Sweet in manners, fair in favour,
Mild in temper, fierce in fight,
Warrior, nobler, gentler, braver,
Never shall behold the light!

"Cousin, Lo! my tears bedew thee!

How shall I thy loss survive!

Durandarte, He who slew thee,

Wherefore left He me alive!"

While She sung, Ambrosio listened with delight: Never had He heard a voice more harmonious; and He wondered how such heavenly sounds could be produced by any but Angels. But though He indulged the sense of hearing, a single look convinced him that He must not trust to that of sight. The Songstress sat at a little distance from his Bed. The attitude in which She bent over her harp, was easy and graceful: Her Cowl had fallen backwarder than usual: Two coral lips were visible, ripe, fresh, and melting, and a Chin in whose dimples seemed to lurk a thousand Cupids. Her Habit's long sleeve would have swept along the Chords of the Instrument: To prevent this inconvenience She had drawn it above her elbow, and by this means an arm was discovered formed in the most perfect symmetry, the delicacy of whose skin might have contended with snow in whiteness. Ambrosio dared to look on her but once: That glance sufficed to convince him, how dangerous was the presence of this seducing Object. He closed his eyes, but strove in vain to banish her from his thoughts. There She still moved before him, adorned with all those charms which his heated imagination could supply: Every beauty which He had seen, appeared embellished, and those still concealed Fancy represented to him in glowing colours. Still, however, his vows and the necessity of keeping to them were present to his memory. He struggled with desire, and shuddered when He beheld how deep was the precipice before him.

Matilda ceased to sing. Dreading the influence of her charms, Ambrosio remained with his eyes closed, and offered up his prayers to St. Francis to assist him in this dangerous trial! Matilda believed that He was sleeping. She rose from her seat, approached the Bed softly, and for some minutes gazed upon him attentively.

"He sleeps!" said She at length in a low voice, but whose accents the Abbot distinguished perfectly; "Now then I may gaze upon him without offence! I may mix my breath with his; I may doat upon his features, and He cannot suspect me of impurity and deceit! — He fears my seducing him to the violation of his vows! Oh! the Unjust! Were it my wish to excite desire, should I conceal my features from him so carefully? Those features, of which I daily hear him...."

403

She stopped, and was lost in her reflections.

"It was but yesterday!" She continued; "But a few short hours have past, since I was dear to him! He esteemed me, and my heart was satisfied! Now!... Oh! now how cruelly is my situation changed! He looks on me with suspicion! He bids me leave him, leave him for ever! Oh! You, my Saint! my Idol! You, holding the next place to God in my breast! Yet two days, and my heart will be unveiled to you. — Could you know my feelings, when I beheld your agony! Could you know, how much your sufferings have endeared you to me! But the time will come, when you will be convinced that my passion is pure and disinterested. Then you will pity me, and feel the whole weight of these sorrows!"

As She said this, her voice was choaked by weeping. While She bent over Ambrosio, a tear fell upon his cheek.

"Ah! I have disturbed him!" cried Matilda, and retreated hastily.

Her alarm was ungrounded. None sleep so profoundly, as those who are determined not to wake. The Friar was in this predicament: He still seemed buried in a repose, which every succeeding minute rendered him less capable of enjoying. The burning tear had communicated its warmth to his heart.

"What affection! What purity!" said He internally; "Ah! since my bosom is thus sensible of pity, what would it be if agitated by love?"

Matilda again quitted her seat, and retired to some distance from the Bed. Ambrosio ventured to open his eyes, and to cast them upon her fearfully. Her face was turned from him. She rested her head in a melancholy posture upon her Harp, and gazed on the picture which hung opposite to the Bed.

"Happy, happy Image!" Thus did She address the beautiful Madona; "'Tis to you that He offers his prayers! 'Tis on you that He gazes with admiration! I thought you would have lightened my sorrows; You have only served to increase their weight: You have made me feel that had I known him ere his vows were pronounced, Ambrosio and happiness might have been mine. With what pleasure He views this picture! With what fervour He addresses his prayers to the insensible Image! Ah! may not his sentiments be inspired by some kind and secret Genius, Friend to my affection? May it not be Man's natural instinct which informs him... Be silent, idle hopes! Let me not encourage an idea which takes from the brilliance of Ambrosio's virtue. 'Tis Religion, not Beauty which attracts his admiration; 'Tis not to the Woman, but the Divinity that He kneels. Would He but address to me the least tender expression which He pours forth to this Madona! Would He but say that were He not already affianced to the Church, He would not have despised Matilda! Oh! let me nourish that fond idea! Perhaps He may yet acknowledge that He feels for me more than pity, and that affection like mine might well have deserved a return; Perhaps, He may own thus much when I lye on my deathbed! He then need not fear to infringe his vows, and the confession of his regard will soften the pangs of dying. Would I were sure of this! Oh! how earnestly should I sigh for the moment of dissolution!"

Of this discourse the Abbot lost not a syllable; and the tone in which She pronounced these last words pierced to his heart. Involuntarily He raised himself from his pillow.

"Matilda!" He said in a troubled voice; "Oh! my Matilda!"

She started at the sound, and turned towards him hastily. The suddenness of her movement made her Cowl fall back from her head; Her features became visible to the Monk's enquiring eye. What was his amazement at beholding the exact resemblance of his admired Madona? The same exquisite proportion of features, the same profusion of golden hair, the same rosy lips, heavenly eyes, and majesty of countenance adorned Matilda! Uttering an exclamation of surprize, Ambrosio sank back upon his pillow, and doubted whether the Object before him was mortal or divine.

Matilda seemed penetrated with confusion. She remained motionless in her place, and supported herself upon her Instrument. Her eyes were bent upon the earth, and her fair cheeks overspread with blushes. On recovering herself, her first action was to conceal her features. She then in an unsteady and troubled voice ventured to address these words to the Friar.

"Accident has made you Master of a secret, which I never would have revealed but on the Bed of death. Yes, Ambrosio; In Matilda de Villanegas you see the original of your beloved Madona. Soon after I conceived my unfortunate passion, I formed the project of conveying to you my Picture: Crowds of Admirers had persuaded me that I possessed some beauty, and I was anxious to know what effect it would produce upon you. I caused my Portrait to be drawn by Martin Galuppi, a celebrated Venetian at that time resident in Madrid. The resemblance was striking: I sent it to the Capuchin Abbey as if for sale, and the

Jew from whom you bought it was one of my Emissaries. You purchased it. Judge of my rapture, when informed that you had gazed upon it with delight, or rather with adoration; that you had suspended it in your Cell, and that you addressed your supplications to no other Saint. Will this discovery make me still more regarded as an object of suspicion? Rather should it convince you how pure is my affection, and engage you to suffer me in your society and esteem. I heard you daily extol the praises of my Portrait: I was an eyewitness of the transports, which its beauty excited in you: Yet I forbore to use against your virtue those arms, with which yourself had furnished me. I concealed those features from your sight, which you loved unconsciously. I strove not to excite desire by displaying my charms, or to make myself Mistress of your heart through the medium of your senses. To attract your notice by studiously attending to religious duties, to endear myself to you by convincing you that my mind was virtuous and my attachment sincere, such was my only aim. I succeeded; I became your companion and your Friend. I concealed my sex from your knowledge; and had you not pressed me to reveal my secret, had I not been tormented by the fear of a discovery, never had you known me for any other than Rosario. And still are you resolved to drive me from you? The few hours of life which yet remain for me, may I not pass them in your presence? Oh! speak, Ambrosio, and tell me that I may stay!"

This speech gave the Abbot an opportunity of recollecting himself. He was conscious that in the present disposition of his mind, avoiding her society was his only refuge from the power of this enchanting Woman.

"You declaration has so much astonished me," said He, "that I am at present incapable of answering you. Do not insist upon a reply, Matilda; Leave me to myself; I have need to be alone."

"I obey you — But before I go, promise not to insist upon my quitting the Abbey immediately."

"Matilda, reflect upon your situation; Reflect upon the consequences of your stay. Our separation is indispensable, and we must part."

"But not to-day, Father! Oh! in pity not today!"

"You press me too hard, but I cannot resist that tone of supplication. Since you insist upon it, I yield to your prayer: I consent to your remaining here a sufficient time to prepare in some measure the Brethren for your departure. Stay yet two days; But on the third," ... (He sighed involuntarily) — "Remember, that on the third we must part for ever!"

She caught his hand eagerly, and pressed it to her lips.

"On the third?" She exclaimed with an air of wild solemnity; "You are right, Father! You are right! On the third we must part for ever!"

There was a dreadful expression in her eye as She uttered these words, which penetrated the Friar's soul with horror: Again She kissed his hand, and then fled with rapidity from the chamber.

Anxious to authorise the presence of his dangerous Guest, yet conscious that her stay was infringing the laws of his order, Ambrosio's bosom became the Theatre of a thousand contending passions. At length his attachment to the feigned Rosario, aided by the natural warmth of his temperament, seemed likely to obtain the victory: The success was assured, when that presumption which formed the groundwork of his character came to Matilda's assistance. The Monk reflected that to vanquish temptation was an infinitely greater merit than to avoid it: He thought that He ought rather to rejoice in the opportunity given him of proving the firmness of his virtue. St. Anthony had withstood all seductions to lust; Then why should not He? Besides, St. Anthony was tempted by the Devil, who put every art into practice to excite his passions: Whereas, Ambrosio's danger proceeded from a mere mortal Woman, fearful and modest, whose apprehensions of his yielding were not less violent than his own.

"Yes," said He; "The Unfortunate shall stay; I have nothing to fear from her presence. Even should my own prove too weak to resist the temptation, I am secured from danger by the innocence of Matilda."

Ambrosio was yet to learn, that to an heart unacquainted with her, Vice is ever most dangerous when lurking behind the Mask of Virtue.

He found himself so perfectly recovered, that when Father Pablos visited him again at night, He entreated permission to quit his chamber on the day following. His request was granted. Matilda appeared no more that evening, except in company with the Monks when they came in a body to enquire after the Abbot's health. She seemed fearful of conversing with him in private, and stayed but a few minutes in his room. The Friar slept well; But the dreams of the former night were repeated, and his sensations of voluptuousness were yet more keen and exquisite. The same lust-exciting visions floated before his eyes: Matilda, in all the pomp of beauty, warm, tender, and luxurious, clasped him to her bosom, and lavished upon him the most ardent caresses. He returned them as eagerly, and already was on the point of satisfying his desires, when the faithless form disappeared, and left him to all the horrors of shame and disappointment.

The Morning dawned. Fatigued, harassed, and exhausted by his provoking dreams, He was not disposed to quit his Bed. He excused himself from appearing at Matins: It was the first morning in his life that He had ever missed them. He rose late. During the whole of the day He had no opportunity of speaking to Matilda without witnesses. His Cell was thronged by the Monks, anxious to express their concern at his illness; And He was still occupied in receiving their compliments on his recovery, when the Bell summoned them to the Refectory.

After dinner the Monks separated, and dispersed themselves in various parts of the Garden, where the shade of trees or retirement of some Grotto presented the most agreeable means of enjoying the Siesta. The Abbot bent his steps towards the Hermitage: A glance of his eye invited Matilda to accompany him.

She obeyed, and followed him thither in silence. They entered the Grotto, and seated themselves. Both seemed unwilling to begin the conversation, and to labour under the influence of mutual embarrassment. At length the Abbot spoke: He conversed only on indifferent topics, and Matilda answered him in the same tone. She seemed anxious to make him forget that the Person who sat by him was any other than Rosario. Neither of them dared, or indeed wished to make an allusion, to the subject which was most at the hearts of both.

Matilda's efforts to appear gay were evidently forced: Her spirits were oppressed by the weight of anxiety, and when She spoke her voice was low and feeble. She seemed desirous of finishing a conversation which embarrassed her; and complaining that She was unwell, She requested Ambrosio's permission to return to the Abbey. He accompanied her to the door of her cell; and when arrived there, He stopped her to declare his consent to her continuing the Partner of his solitude so long as should be agreeable to herself.

She discovered no marks of pleasure at receiving this intelligence, though on the preceding day She had been so anxious to obtain the permission.

"Alas! Father," She said, waving her head mournfully; "Your kindness comes too late! My doom is fixed. We must separate for ever. Yet believe, that I am grateful for your generosity, for your compassion of an Unfortunate who is but too little deserving of it!"

She put her handkerchief to her eyes. Her Cowl was only half drawn over her face. Ambrosio observed that She was pale, and her eyes sunk and heavy.

"Good God!" He cried; "You are very ill, Matilda! I shall send Father Pablos to you instantly."

"No; Do not. I am ill, 'tis true; But He cannot cure my malady. Farewell, Father! Remember me in your prayers tomorrow, while I shall remember you in heaven!"

She entered her cell, and closed the door.

The Abbot dispatched to her the Physician without losing a moment, and waited his report impatiently. But Father Pablos soon returned, and declared that his errand had been fruitless. Rosario refused to admit him, and had positively rejected his offers of assistance. The uneasiness which this account gave Ambrosio was not trifling: Yet He determined that Matilda should have her own way for that night: But that if her situation did not mend by the morning, he would insist upon her taking the advice of Father Pablos.

He did not find himself inclined to sleep. He opened his casement, and gazed upon the moonbeams as they played upon the small stream whose waters bathed the walls of the Monastery. The coolness of the night breeze and tranquillity of the hour inspired the Friar's mind with sadness. He thought upon Matilda's beauty and affection; Upon the pleasures which He might have shared with her, had He not been restrained by monastic fetters. He reflected, that unsustained by hope her love for him could not long exist; That doubtless She would succeed in extinguishing her passion, and seek for happiness in the arms of One more fortunate. He shuddered at the void which her absence would leave in his bosom. He looked with disgust on the monotony of a Convent, and breathed a sigh towards that world from which He was for ever separated. Such were the reflections which a loud knocking at his door interrupted. The

Bell of the Church had already struck Two. The Abbot hastened to enquire the cause of this disturbance. He opened the door of his Cell, and a Lay-Brother entered, whose looks declared his hurry and confusion.

"Hasten, reverend Father!" said He; "Hasten to the young Rosario.

He earnestly requests to see you; He lies at the point of death."

"Gracious God! Where is Father Pablos? Why is He not with him? Oh! I fear! I fear!"

"Father Pablos has seen him, but his art can do nothing. He says that He suspects the Youth to be poisoned."

"Poisoned? Oh! The Unfortunate! It is then as I suspected! But let me not lose a moment; Perhaps it may yet be time to save her!"

He said, and flew towards the Cell of the Novice. Several Monks were already in the chamber. Father Pablos was one of them, and held a medicine in his hand which He was endeavouring to persuade Rosario to swallow. The Others were employed in admiring the Patient's divine countenance, which They now saw for the first time. She looked lovelier than ever. She was no longer pale or languid; A bright glow had spread itself over her cheeks; her eyes sparkled with a serene delight, and her countenance was expressive of confidence and resignation.

"Oh! torment me no more!" was She saying to Pablos, when the terrified Abbot rushed hastily into the Cell; "My disease is far beyond the reach of your skill, and I wish not to be cured of it" — Then perceiving Ambrosio, — "Ah! 'tis He!" She cried; "I see him once again, before we part for ever! Leave me, my Brethren; Much have I to tell this holy Man in private."

The Monks retired immediately, and Matilda and the Abbot remained together.

"What have you done, imprudent Woman!" exclaimed the Latter, as soon as they were left alone; "Tell me; Are my suspicions just? Am I indeed to lose you? Has your own hand been the instrument of your destruction?"

She smiled, and grasped his hand.

"In what have I been imprudent, Father? I have sacrificed a pebble, and saved a diamond: My death preserves a life valuable to the world, and more dear to me than my own. Yes, Father; I am poisoned; But know that the poison once circulated in your veins."

"Matilda!"

"What I tell you I resolved never to discover to you but on the bed of death: That moment is now arrived. You cannot have forgotten the day already, when your life was endangered by the bite of a Cientipedoro. The Physician gave you over, declaring himself ignorant how to extract the venom: I knew but of one means, and hesitated not a moment to employ it. I was left alone with you: You slept; I loosened the bandage from your hand; I kissed the wound, and drew out the poison with my lips. The effect has been more sudden than I expected. I feel death at my heart; Yet an hour, and I shall be in a better world."

"Almighty God!" exclaimed the Abbot, and sank almost lifeless upon the Bed.

After a few minutes He again raised himself up suddenly, and gazed upon Matilda with all the wildness of despair.

"And you have sacrificed yourself for me! You die, and die to preserve Ambrosio! And is there indeed no remedy, Matilda? And is there indeed no hope? Speak to me, Oh! speak to me! Tell me, that you have still the means of life!"

"Be comforted, my only Friend! Yes, I have still the means of life in my power: But 'tis a means which I dare not employ. It is dangerous! It is dreadful! Life would be purchased at too dear a rate, ... unless it were permitted me to live for you."

"Then live for me, Matilda, for me and gratitude!" — (He caught her hand, and pressed it rapturously to his lips.) — "Remember our late conversations; I now consent to every thing: Remember in what lively colours you described the union of souls; Be it ours to realize those ideas. Let us forget the distinctions of sex, despise the world's prejudices, and only consider each other as Brother and Friend. Live then, Matilda! Oh! live for me!"

"Ambrosio, it must not be. When I thought thus, I deceived both you and myself. Either I must die at present, or expire by the lingering torments of unsatisfied desire. Oh! since we last conversed together, a dreadful veil has been rent from before my eyes. I love you no longer with the devotion which is paid to a Saint: I prize you no more for the virtues of your soul; I lust for the enjoyment of your person. The Woman reigns in my bosom, and I am become a prey to the wildest of passions. Away with friendship! 'tis a cold unfeeling word. My bosom burns with love, with unutterable love, and love must be its return. Tremble then, Ambrosio, tremble to succeed in your prayers. If I live, your truth, your reputation, your reward of a life past in sufferings, all that you value is irretrievably lost. I shall no longer be able to combat my passions, shall seize every opportunity to excite your desires, and labour to effect your dishonour and my own. No, no, Ambrosio; I must not live! I am convinced with every moment, that I have but one alternative; I feel with every heart-throb, that I must enjoy you, or die."

"Amazement!—Matilda! Can it be you who speak to me?"

He made a movement as if to quit his seat. She uttered a loud shriek, and raising herself half out of the Bed, threw her arms round the Friar to detain him.

"Oh! do not leave me! Listen to my errors with compassion! In a few hours I shall be no more; Yet a little, and I am free from this disgraceful passion."

"Wretched Woman, what can I say to you! I cannot ... I must not ... But live, Matilda! Oh! live!"

"You do not reflect on what you ask. What? Live to plunge myself in infamy? To become the Agent of Hell? To work the destruction both of you and of Myself? Feel this heart, Father!"

She took his hand: Confused, embarrassed, and fascinated, He withdrew it not, and felt her heart throb under it.

"Feel this heart, Father! It is yet the seat of honour, truth, and chastity: If it beats tomorrow, it must fall a prey to the blackest crimes. Oh! let me then die today! Let me die, while I yet deserve the tears of the virtuous! Thus will expire!"—(She reclined her head upon his shoulder; Her golden Hair poured itself over his Chest.)—"Folded in your arms, I shall sink to sleep; Your hand shall close my eyes for ever, and your lips receive my dying breath. And will you not sometimes think of me? Will you not sometimes shed a tear upon my Tomb? Oh!

Yes! Yes! Yes! That kiss is my assurance!"

The hour was night. All was silence around. The faint beams of a solitary Lamp darted upon Matilda's figure, and shed through the chamber a dim mysterious light. No prying eye, or curious ear was near the Lovers: Nothing was heard but Matilda's melodious accents. Ambrosio was in the full vigour of Manhood. He saw before him a young and beautiful Woman, the preserver of his life, the Adorer of his person, and whom affection for him had reduced to the brink of the Grave. He sat upon her Bed; His hand rested upon her bosom; Her head reclined voluptuously upon his breast. Who then can wonder, if He yielded to the temptation? Drunk with desire, He pressed his lips to those which sought them: His kisses vied with Matilda's in warmth and passion. He clasped her rapturously in his arms; He forgot his vows, his sanctity, and his fame: He remembered nothing but the pleasure and opportunity.

"Ambrosio! Oh! my Ambrosio!" sighed Matilda.

"Thine, ever thine!" murmured the Friar, and sank upon her bosom.

CHAPTER III

— —These are the Villains

Whom all the Travellers do fear so much.

— — — —Some of them are Gentlemen

Such as the fury of ungoverned Youth

Thrust from the company of awful Men.

TWO GENTLEMEN OF VERONA.

The Marquis and Lorenzo proceeded to the Hotel in silence. The Former employed himself in calling every circumstance to his mind, which related might give Lorenzo's the most favourable idea of his connexion with Agnes. The Latter, justly alarmed for the honour of his family, felt embarrassed by the presence of the Marquis: The adventure which He had just witnessed forbad his treating him as a Friend; and Antonia's interests being entrusted to his mediation, He saw the impolicy of treating him as a Foe. He concluded from these reflections, that profound silence would be the wisest plan, and waited with impatience for Don Raymond's explanation.

They arrived at the Hotel de las Cisternas. The Marquis immediately conducted him to his apartment, and began to express his satisfaction at finding him at Madrid. Lorenzo interrupted him.

"Excuse me, my Lord," said He with a distant air, "if I reply somewhat coldly to your expressions of regard. A Sister's honour is involved in this affair: Till that is established, and the purport of your correspondence with Agnes cleared up, I cannot consider you as my Friend. I am anxious to hear the meaning of your conduct, and hope that you will not delay the promised explanation."

"First give me your word, that you will listen with patience and indulgence."

"I love my Sister too well to judge her harshly; and till this moment I possessed no Friend so dear to me as yourself. I will also confess, that your having it in your power to oblige me in a business which I have much at heart, makes me very anxious to find you still deserving my esteem."

"Lorenzo, you transport me! No greater pleasure can be given me, than an opportunity of serving the Brother of Agnes."

"Convince me that I can accept your favours without dishonour, and there is no Man in the world to whom I am more willing to be obliged."

"Probably, you have already heard your Sister mention the name of Alphonso d'Alvarada?"

"Never. Though I feel for Agnes an affection truly fraternal, circumstances have prevented us from being much together. While yet a Child She was consigned to the care of her Aunt, who had married a German Nobleman. At his Castle She remained till two years since, when She returned to Spain, determined upon secluding herself from the world."

"Good God! Lorenzo, you knew of her intention, and yet strove not to make her change it?"

"Marquis, you wrong me. The intelligence, which I received at Naples, shocked me extremely, and I hastened my return to Madrid for the express purpose of preventing the sacrifice. The moment that I arrived, I flew to the Convent of St. Clare, in which Agnes had chosen to perform her Noviciate. I requested to see my Sister. Conceive my surprise when She sent me a refusal; She declared positively, that apprehending my influence over her mind, She would not trust herself in my society till the day before that on which She was to receive the Veil. I supplicated the Nuns; I insisted upon seeing Agnes, and hesitated not to avow my suspicions that her being kept from me was against her own inclinations. To free herself from the imputation of violence, the Prioress brought me a few lines written in my Sister's well-known hand, repeating the message already delivered. All future attempts to obtain a moment's conversation with her were as fruitless as the first. She was inflexible, and I was not permitted to see her till the day preceding that on which She entered the Cloister never to quit it more. This interview took place in the presence of our principal Relations. It was for the first time since her childhood that I saw her, and the scene was most affecting. She threw herself upon my bosom, kissed me, and wept bitterly. By every possible argument, by tears, by prayers, by kneeling, I strove to make her abandon her intention. I represented to her all the hardships of a religious life; I painted to her imagination all the pleasures which She was going to quit, and besought her to disclose to me, what occasioned her disgust to the world. At this last question She turned pale, and her tears flowed yet faster. She entreated me not to press her on that subject; That it sufficed me to know that her resolution was taken, and that a Convent was the only place where She could now hope for tranquillity. She persevered in her design, and made her profession. I visited her frequently at the Grate, and every moment that I passed with her, made me feel more affliction at her loss. I was shortly after obliged to quit Madrid; I returned but yesterday evening, and since then have not had time to call at St. Clare's Convent."

"Then till I mentioned it, you never heard the name of Alphonso d'Alvarada?"

"Pardon me: my Aunt wrote me word that an Adventurer so called had found means to get introduced into the Castle of Lindenberg; That He had insinuated himself into my Sister's good graces, and that She had even consented to elope with him. However, before the plan could be executed, the Cavalier discovered that the estates which He believed Agnes to possess in Hispaniola, in reality belonged to me. This intelligence made him change his intention; He disappeared on the day that the elopement was to have taken place, and Agnes, in despair at his perfidy and meanness, had resolved upon seclusion in a Convent. She added, that as this adventurer had given himself out to be a Friend of mine, She wished to know whether I had any knowledge of him. I replied in the negative. I had then very little idea, that Alphonso d'Alvarada and the Marquis de las Cisternas were one and the same person: The description given me of the first by no means tallied with what I knew of the latter."

"In this I easily recognize Donna Rodolpha's perfidious character. Every word of this account is stamped with marks of her malice, of her falsehood, of her talents for misrepresenting those whom She wishes to injure. Forgive me, Medina, for speaking so freely of your Relation. The mischief which She has done me authorises my resentment, and when you have heard my story, you will be convinced that my expressions have not been too severe."

He then began his narrative in the following manner:—

HISTORY OF DON RAYMOND,

MARQUIS DE LAS CISTERNAS

Long experience, my dear Lorenzo, has convinced me how generous is your nature: I waited not for your declaration of ignorance respecting your Sister's adventures to suppose that they had been purposely concealed from you. Had they reached your knowledge, from what misfortunes should both Agnes and myself have escaped! Fate had ordained it otherwise! You were on your Travels when I first became acquainted with your Sister; and as our Enemies took care to conceal from her your direction, it was impossible for her to implore by letter your protection and advice.

On leaving Salamanca, at which University as I have since heard, you remained a year after I quitted it, I immediately set out upon my Travels. My Father supplied me liberally with money; But He insisted upon my concealing my rank, and presenting myself as no more than a private Gentleman. This command was issued by the counsels of his Friend, the Duke of Villa Hermosa, a Nobleman for whose abilities and knowledge of the world I have ever entertained the most profound veneration.

"Believe me," said He, "my dear Raymond, you will hereafter feel the benefits of this temporary degradation. 'Tis true, that as the Condé de las Cisternas you would have been received with open arms; and your youthful vanity might have felt gratified by the attentions showered upon you from all sides. At present, much will depend upon yourself: You have excellent recommendations, but it must be your own business to make them of use to you. You must lay yourself out to please; You must labour to gain the approbation of those, to whom you are presented: They who would have courted the friendship of the Condé de las Cisternas will have no interest in finding out the merits, or bearing patiently with the faults, of Alphonso d'Alvarada. Consequently, when you find yourself really liked, you may safely ascribe it to your good qualities, not your rank, and the distinction shown you will be infinitely more flattering. Besides, your exalted birth would not permit your mixing with the lower classes of society, which will now be in your power, and from which, in my opinion, you will derive considerable benefit. Do not confine yourself to the Illustrious of those Countries through which you pass. Examine the manners and customs of the multitude: Enter into the Cottages; and by observing how the Vassals of Foreigners are treated, learn to diminish the burthens and augment the comforts of your own. According to my ideas, of those advantages which a Youth destined to the possession of power and wealth may reap from travel, He should not consider as the least essential, the opportunity of mixing with the classes below him, and becoming an eyewitness of the sufferings of the People."

Forgive me, Lorenzo, if I seem tedious in my narration. The close connexion which now exists between us, makes me anxious that you should know every particular respecting me; and in my fear of omitting the least circumstance which may induce you to think favourably of your Sister and myself, I may possibly relate many which you may think uninteresting.

I followed the Duke's advice; I was soon convinced of its wisdom.

I quitted Spain, calling myself by the assumed title of Don Alphonso d'Alvarada, and attended by a single Domestic of approved fidelity. Paris was my first station. For some time I was enchanted with it, as indeed must be every Man who is young, rich, and fond of pleasure. Yet among all its gaieties, I felt that something was wanting to my heart. I grew sick of dissipation: I discovered, that the People among whom I lived, and whose exterior was so polished and seducing, were at bottom frivolous, unfeeling and insincere. I turned from the Inhabitants of Paris with disgust, and quitted that Theatre of Luxury without heaving one sigh of regret.

I now bent my course towards Germany, intending to visit most of the principal courts: Prior to this expedition, I meant to make some little stay at Strasbourg. On quitting my Chaise at Luneville to take some refreshment, I observed a splendid Equipage, attended by four Domestics in rich liveries, waiting at the door of the Silver Lion. Soon after as I looked out of the window, I saw a Lady of noble presence, followed by two female Attendants, step into the Carriage, which drove off immediately.

I enquired of the Host, who the Lady was, that had just departed.

"A German Baroness, Monsieur, of great rank and fortune. She has been upon a visit to the Duchess of Longueville, as her Servants informed me; She is going to Strasbourg, where She will find her Husband, and then both return to their Castle in Germany."

I resumed my journey, intending to reach Strasbourg that night. My hopes, however were frustrated by the breaking down of my Chaise. The accident happened in the middle of a thick Forest, and I was not a little embarrassed as to the means of proceeding.

It was the depth of winter: The night was already closing round us; and Strasbourg, which was the nearest Town, was still distant from us several leagues. It seemed to me that my only alternative to passing the night in the Forest, was to take my Servant's Horse and ride on to Strasbourg, an undertaking at that season very far from agreeable. However, seeing no other resource, I was obliged to make up my mind to it. Accordingly I communicated my design to the Postillion, telling him that I would send People to assist him as soon as I reached Strasbourg. I had not much confidence in his honesty; But Stephano being well-armed, and the Driver to all appearance considerably advanced in years, I believed I ran no danger of losing my Baggage.

Luckily, as I then thought, an opportunity presented itself of passing the night more agreeably than I expected. On mentioning my design of proceeding by myself to Strasbourg, the Postillion shook his head in disapprobation.

"It is a long way," said He; "You will find it a difficult matter to arrive there without a Guide. Besides, Monsieur seems unaccustomed to the season's severity, and 'tis possible that unable to sustain the excessive cold...."

"What use is there to present me with all these objections?" said I, impatiently interrupting him; "I have no other resource: I run still greater risque of perishing with cold by passing the night in the Forest."

"Passing the night in the Forest?" He replied; "Oh! by St. Denis! We are not in quite so bad a plight as that comes to yet. If I am not mistaken, we are scarcely five minutes walk from the Cottage of my old Friend, Baptiste. He is a Wood-cutter, and a very honest Fellow. I doubt not but He will shelter you for the night with pleasure. In the meantime I can take the saddle-Horse, ride to Strasbourg, and be back with proper people to mend your Carriage by break of day."

"And in the name of God," said I, "How could you leave me so long in suspense? Why did you not tell me of this Cottage sooner? What excessive stupidity!"

"I thought that perhaps Monsieur would not deign to accept. ..."

"Absurd! Come, come! Say no more, but conduct us without delay to the Wood-man's Cottage."

He obeyed, and we moved onwards: The Horses contrived with some difficulty to drag the shattered vehicle after us. My Servant was become almost speechless, and I began to feel the effects of the cold myself, before we reached the wished-for Cottage. It was a small but neat Building: As we drew near it, I rejoiced at observing through the window the blaze of a comfortable fire. Our Conductor knocked at the door: It was some time before any one answered; The People within seemed in doubt whether we should be admitted.

"Come! Come, Friend Baptiste!" cried the Driver with impatience; "What are you about? Are you asleep? Or will you refuse a night's lodging to a Gentleman, whose Chaise has just broken down in the Forest?"

"Ah! is it you, honest Claude?" replied a Man's voice from within; "Wait a moment, and the door shall be opened."

Soon after the bolts were drawn back. The door was unclosed, and a Man presented himself to us with a Lamp in his hand. He gave the Guide an hearty reception, and then addressed himself to me.

"Walk in, Monsieur; Walk in, and welcome! Excuse me for not admitting you at first: But there are so many Rogues about this place, that saving your presence, I suspected you to be one."

Thus saying, He ushered me into the room, where I had observed the fire: I was immediately placed in an Easy Chair, which stood close to the Hearth. A Female, whom I supposed to be the Wife of my Host, rose from her seat upon my entrance, and received me with a slight and distant reverence. She made no answer to my compliment, but immediately re-seating herself, continued the work on which She had been employed. Her Husband's manners were as friendly as hers were harsh and repulsive.

"I wish, I could lodge you more conveniently, Monsieur," said He; "But we cannot boast of much spare room in this hovel. However, a chamber for yourself, and another for your Servant, I think, we can make shift to supply. You must content yourself with sorry fare; But to what we have, believe me, you are heartily welcome." — — Then turning to his wife — "Why, how you sit there, Marguerite, with as much tranquillity as if you had nothing better to do! Stir about, Dame! Stir about! Get some supper; Look out some sheets; Here, here; throw some logs upon the fire, for the Gentleman seems perished with cold."

The wife threw her work hastily upon the Table, and proceeded to execute his commands with every mark of unwillingness. Her countenance had displeased me on the first moment of my examining it. Yet upon the whole her features were handsome unquestionably; But her skin was sallow, and her person thin and meagre; A louring gloom over-spread her countenance; and it bore such visible marks of rancour and ill-will, as could not escape being noticed by the most inattentive Observer. Her every look and action expressed discontent and impatience, and the answers which She gave Baptiste, when He reproached her good-humouredly for her dissatisfied air, were tart, short, and cutting. In fine, I conceived at first sight equal disgust for her, and prepossession in favour of her Husband, whose appearance was calculated to inspire esteem and confidence. His countenance was open, sincere, and friendly; his manners had all the Peasant's honesty unaccompanied by his rudeness; His cheeks were broad, full, and ruddy; and in the solidity of his person He seemed to offer an ample apology for the leanness of his Wife's. From the wrinkles on his brow I judged him to be turned of sixty; But He bore his years well, and seemed still hearty and strong: The Wife could not be more than thirty, but in spirits and vivacity She was infinitely older than the Husband.

However, in spite of her unwillingness, Marguerite began to prepare the supper, while the Wood-man conversed gaily on different subjects. The Postillion, who had been furnished with a bottle of spirits, was now ready to set out for Strasbourg, and enquired, whether I had any further commands.

"For Strasbourg?" interrupted Baptiste; "You are not going thither tonight?"

"I beg your pardon: If I do not fetch Workmen to mend the Chaise, How is Monsieur to proceed tomorrow?"

"That is true, as you say; I had forgotten the Chaise. Well, but Claude; You may at least eat your supper here? That can make you lose very little time, and Monsieur looks too kind-hearted to send you out with an empty stomach on such a bitter cold night as this is."

To this I readily assented, telling the Postillion that my reaching Strasbourg the next day an hour or two later would be perfectly immaterial. He thanked me, and then leaving the Cottage with Stephano, put up his Horses in the Wood-man's Stable. Baptiste followed them to the door, and looked out with anxiety.

421

"'Tis a sharp biting wind!" said He; "I wonder, what detains my Boys so long! Monsieur, I shall show you two of the finest Lads, that ever stept in shoe of leather. The eldest is three and twenty, the second a year younger: Their Equals for sense, courage, and activity, are not to be found within fifty miles of Strasbourg. Would They were back again! I begin to feel uneasy about them."

Marguerite was at this time employed in laying the cloth.

"And are you equally anxious for the return of your Sons?" said I to her.

"Not I!" She replied peevishly; "They are no children of mine."

"Come! Come, Marguerite!" said the Husband; "Do not be out of humour with the Gentleman for asking a simple question. Had you not looked so cross, He would never have thought you old enough to have a Son of three and twenty: But you see how many years ill-temper adds to you!—Excuse my Wife's rudeness, Monsieur. A little thing puts her out, and She is somewhat displeased at your not thinking her to be under thirty. That is the truth, is it not, Marguerite? You know, Monsieur, that Age is always a ticklish subject with a Woman. Come! come! Marguerite, clear up a little. If you have not Sons as old, you will some twenty years hence, and I hope, that we shall live to see them just such Lads as Jacques and Robert."

Marguerite clasped her hands together passionately.

"God forbid!" said She; "God forbid! If I thought it, I would strangle them with my own hands!"

She quitted the room hastily, and went up stairs.

I could not help expressing to the Wood-man how much I pitied him for being chained for life to a Partner of such ill-humour.

"Ah! Lord! Monsieur, Every one has his share of grievances, and Marguerite has fallen to mine. Besides, after all She is only cross, and not malicious. The worst is, that her affection for two children by a former Husband makes her play the Step-mother with my two Sons. She cannot bear the sight of them, and by her good-will they would never set a foot within my door. But on this point I always stand firm, and never will consent to abandon the poor Lads to the world's mercy, as She has often

422

solicited me to do. In every thing else I let her have her own way; and truly She manages a family rarely, that I must say for her."

We were conversing in this manner, when our discourse was interrupted by a loud halloo, which rang through the Forest.

"My Sons, I hope!" exclaimed the Wood-man, and ran to open the door.

The halloo was repeated: We now distinguished the trampling of Horses, and soon after a Carriage, attended by several Cavaliers stopped at the Cottage door. One of the Horsemen enquired how far they were still from Strasbourg. As He addressed himself to me, I answered in the number of miles which Claude had told me; Upon which a volley of curses was vented against the Drivers for having lost their way. The Persons in the Coach were now informed of the distance of Strasbourg, and also that the Horses were so fatigued as to be incapable of proceeding further. A Lady, who appeared to be the principal, expressed much chagrin at this intelligence; But as there was no remedy, one of the Attendants asked the Wood-man, whether He could furnish them with lodging for the night.

He seemed much embarrassed, and replied in the negative; Adding that a Spanish Gentleman and his Servant were already in possession of the only spare apartments in his House. On hearing this, the gallantry of my nation would not permit me to retain those accommodations, of which a Female was in want. I instantly signified to the Wood-man, that I transferred my right to the Lady; He made some objections; But I overruled them, and hastening to the Carriage, opened the door, and assisted the Lady to descend. I immediately recognized her for the same person whom I had seen at the Inn at Luneville. I took an opportunity of asking one of her Attendants, what was her name?

"The Baroness Lindenberg," was the answer.

I could not but remark how different a reception our Host had given these newcomers and myself. His reluctance to admit them was visibly expressed on his countenance, and He prevailed on himself with difficulty to tell the Lady that She was welcome. I conducted her into the House, and placed her in the armed-chair, which I had just quitted. She thanked me very graciously; and made a thousand apologies for putting me to an inconvenience. Suddenly the Wood-man's countenance cleared up.

"At last I have arranged it!" said He, interrupting her excuses; "I can lodge you and your suite, Madam, and you will not be under the necessity of making this Gentleman suffer for his politeness.

We have two spare chambers, one for the Lady, the other, Monsieur, for you: My Wife shall give up hers to the two Waiting-women; As for the Men-servants, they must content themselves with passing the night in a large Barn, which stands at a few yards distance from the House. There they shall have a blazing fire, and as good a supper as we can make shift to give them."

After several expressions of gratitude on the Lady's part, and opposition on mine to Marguerite's giving up her bed, this arrangement was agreed to. As the Room was small, the Baroness immediately dismissed her Male Domestics: Baptiste was on the point of conducting them to the Barn which He had mentioned when two young Men appeared at the door of the Cottage.

"Hell and Furies!" exclaimed the first starting back; "Robert, the House is filled with Strangers!"

"Ha! There are my Sons!" cried our Host. "Why, Jacques! Robert! whither are you running, Boys? There is room enough still for you."

Upon this assurance the Youths returned. The Father presented them to the Baroness and myself: After which He withdrew with our Domestics, while at the request of the two Waiting-women, Marguerite conducted them to the room designed for their Mistress.

The two new-comers were tall, stout, well-made young Men, hard-featured, and very much sun-burnt. They paid their compliments to us in few words, and acknowledged Claude, who now entered the room, as an old acquaintance. They then threw aside their cloaks in which they were wrapped up, took off a leathern belt to which a large Cutlass was suspended, and each drawing a brace of pistols from his girdle laid them upon a shelf.

"You travel well-armed," said I.

"True, Monsieur;" replied Robert. "We left Strasbourg late this Evening, and 'tis necessary to take precautions at passing through this Forest after dark. It does not bear a good repute, I promise you."

"How?" said the Baroness; "Are there Robbers hereabout?"

"So it is said, Madame; For my own part, I have travelled through the wood at all hours, and never met with one of them."

Here Marguerite returned. Her Stepsons drew her to the other end of the room, and whispered her for some minutes. By the looks which they cast towards us at intervals, I conjectured them to be enquiring our business in the Cottage.

In the meanwhile the Baroness expressed her apprehensions, that her Husband would be suffering much anxiety upon her account. She had intended to send on one of her Servants to inform the Baron of her delay; But the account which the young Men gave of the Forest rendered this plan impracticable. Claude relieved her from her embarrassment. He informed her that He was under the necessity of reaching Strasbourg that night, and that would She trust him with a letter, She might depend upon its being safely delivered.

"And how comes it," said I, "that you are under no apprehension of meeting these Robbers?"

"Alas! Monsieur, a poor Man with a large family must not lose certain profit because 'tis attended with a little danger, and perhaps my Lord the Baron may give me a trifle for my pains. Besides, I have nothing to lose except my life, and that will not be worth the Robbers taking."

I thought his arguments bad, and advised his waiting till the Morning; But as the Baroness did not second me, I was obliged to give up the point. The Baroness Lindenberg, as I found afterwards, had long been accustomed to sacrifice the interests of others to her own, and her wish to send Claude to Strasbourg blinded her to the danger of the undertaking. Accordingly, it was resolved that He should set out without delay. The Baroness wrote her letter to her Husband, and I sent a few lines to my Banker, apprising him that I should not be at Strasbourg till the next day. Claude took our letters, and left the Cottage.

The Lady declared herself much fatigued by her journey: Besides having come from some distance, the Drivers had contrived to lose their way in the Forest. She now addressed herself to Marguerite, desiring to be shown to her chamber, and permitted to take half an hour's repose. One of the Waiting-

women was immediately summoned; She appeared with a
light, and the Baroness followed her up stairs. The cloth was
spreading in the chamber where I was, and Marguerite soon
gave me to understand that I was in her way. Her hints were
too broad to be easily mistaken; I therefore desired one of the
young Men to conduct me to the chamber where I was to sleep,
and where I could remain till supper was ready.

"Which chamber is it, Mother?" said Robert.

"The One with green hangings," She replied; "I have just
been at the trouble of getting it ready, and have put fresh sheets
upon the Bed; If the Gentleman chooses to lollop and lounge
upon it, He may make it again himself for me."

"You are out of humour, Mother, but that is no novelty.
Have the goodness to follow me, Monsieur."

He opened the door, and advanced towards a narrow
staircase.

"You have got no light!" said Marguerite; "Is it your own
neck or the Gentleman's that you have a mind to break?"

She crossed by me, and put a candle into Robert's hand,
having received which, He began to ascend the staircase.
Jacques was employed in laying the cloth, and his back was
turned towards me.

Marguerite seized the moment, when we were unobserved.
She caught my hand, and pressed it strongly.

"Look at the Sheets!" said She as She passed me, and
immediately resumed her former occupation.

Startled by the abruptness of her action, I remained as if
petrified. Robert's voice, desiring me to follow him, recalled me
to myself. I ascended the staircase. My conductor ushered me
into a chamber, where an excellent wood-fire was blazing upon
the hearth. He placed the light upon the Table, enquired
whether I had any further commands, and on my replying in
the negative, He left me to myself. You may be certain that the
moment when I found myself alone was that on which I
complied with Marguerite's injunction. I took the candle, hastily
approached the Bed, and turned down the Coverture. What was
my astonishment, my horror, at finding the sheets crimsoned
with blood!

At that moment a thousand confused ideas passed before my imagination. The Robbers who infested the Wood, Marguerite's exclamation respecting her Children, the arms and appearance of the two young Men, and the various Anecdotes which I had heard related, respecting the secret correspondence which frequently exists between Banditti and Postillions, all these circumstances flashed upon my mind, and inspired me with doubt and apprehension. I ruminated on the most probable means of ascertaining the truth of my conjectures. Suddenly I was aware of Someone below pacing hastily backwards and forwards. Every thing now appeared to me an object of suspicion. With precaution I drew near the window, which, as the room had been long shut up, was left open in spite of the cold. I ventured to look out. The beams of the Moon permitted me to distinguish a Man, whom I had no difficulty to recognize for my Host. I watched his movements.

He walked swiftly, then stopped, and seemed to listen: He stamped upon the ground, and beat his stomach with his arms as if to guard himself from the inclemency of the season. At the least noise, if a voice was heard in the lower part of the House, if a Bat flitted past him, or the wind rattled amidst the leafless boughs, He started, and looked round with anxiety.

"Plague take him!" said He at length with impatience; "What can He be about!"

He spoke in a low voice; but as He was just below my window, I had no difficulty to distinguish his words.

I now heard the steps of one approaching. Baptiste went towards the sound; He joined a man, whom his low stature and the Horn suspended from his neck, declared to be no other than my faithful Claude, whom I had supposed to be already on his way to Strasbourg. Expecting their discourse to throw some light upon my situation, I hastened to put myself in a condition to hear it with safety. For this purpose I extinguished the candle, which stood upon a table near the Bed: The flame of the fire was not strong enough to betray me, and I immediately resumed my place at the window.

The objects of my curiosity had stationed themselves directly under it. I suppose that during my momentary absence the Wood-man had been blaming Claude for tardiness, since when I returned to the window, the latter was endeavouring to excuse his fault.

"However," added He, "my diligence at present shall make

427

up for my past delay."

"On that condition," answered Baptiste, "I shall readily forgive you. But in truth as you share equally with us in our prizes, your own interest will make you use all possible diligence. 'Twould be a shame to let such a noble booty escape us! You say, that this Spaniard is rich?"

"His Servant boasted at the Inn, that the effects in his Chaise were worth above two thousand Pistoles."

Oh! how I cursed Stephano's imprudent vanity!

"And I have been told," continued the Postillion, "that this Baroness carries about her a casket of jewels of immense value."

"May be so, but I had rather She had stayed away. The Spaniard was a secure prey. The Boys and myself could easily have mastered him and his Servant, and then the two thousand Pistoles would have been shared between us four. Now we must let in the Band for a share, and perhaps the whole Covey may escape us. Should our Friends have betaken themselves to their different posts before you reach the Cavern, all will be lost. The Lady's Attendants are too numerous for us to overpower them: Unless our Associates arrive in time, we must needs let these Travellers set out tomorrow without damage or hurt."

"'Tis plaguy unlucky that my Comrades who drove the Coach should be those unacquainted with our Confederacy! But never fear, Friend Baptiste. An hour will bring me to the Cavern; It is now but ten o'clock, and by twelve you may expect the arrival of the Band. By the bye, take care of your Wife: You know how strong is her repugnance to our mode of life, and She may find means to give information to the Lady's Servants of our design."

"Oh! I am secure of her silence; She is too much afraid of me, and fond of her children, to dare to betray my secret. Besides, Jacques and Robert keep a strict eye over her, and She is not permitted to set a foot out of the Cottage. The Servants are safely lodged in the Barn; I shall endeavour to keep all quiet till the arrival of our Friends. Were I assured of your finding them, the Strangers should be dispatched this instant; But as it is possible for you to miss the Banditti, I am fearful of being summoned to produce them by their Domestics in the Morning."

"And suppose either of the Travellers should discover your

design?"

"Then we must poignard those in our power, and take our chance about mastering the rest. However, to avoid running such a risque, hasten to the Cavern: The Banditti never leave it before eleven, and if you use diligence, you may reach it in time to stop them."

"Tell Robert that I have taken his Horse: My own has broken his bridle, and escaped into the Wood. What is the watch-word?"

"The reward of Courage."

"'Tis sufficient. I hasten to the Cavern."

"And I to rejoin my Guests, lest my absence should create suspicion. Farewell, and be diligent."

These worthy Associates now separated: The One bent his course towards the Stable, while the Other returned to the House.

You may judge, what must have been my feelings during this conversation, of which I lost not a single syllable. I dared not trust myself to my reflections, nor did any means present itself to escape the dangers which threatened me. Resistance, I knew to be vain; I was unarmed, and a single Man against Three: However, I resolved at least to sell my life as dearly as I could. Dreading lest Baptiste should perceive my absence, and suspect me to have overheard the message with which Claude was dispatched, I hastily relighted my candle and quitted the chamber. On descending, I found the Table spread for six Persons. The Baroness sat by the fireside: Marguerite was employed in dressing a sallad, and her Step-sons were whispering together at the further end of the room. Baptiste having the round of the Garden to make, ere He could reach the Cottage door, was not yet arrived. I seated myself quietly opposite to the Baroness.

A glance upon Marguerite told her that her hint had not been thrown away upon me. How different did She now appear to me! What before seemed gloom and sullenness, I now found to be disgust at her Associates, and compassion for my danger. I looked up to her as to my only resource; Yet knowing her to be watched by her Husband with a suspicious eye, I could place but little reliance on the exertions of her good-will.

In spite of all my endeavours to conceal it, my agitation was but too visibly expressed upon my countenance. I was pale, and both my words and actions were disordered and embarrassed. The young Men observed this, and enquired the cause. I attributed it to excess of fatigue, and the violent effect produced on me by the severity of the season. Whether they believed me or not, I will not pretend to say: They at least ceased to embarrass me with their questions. I strove to divert my attention from the perils which surrounded me, by conversing on different subjects with the Baroness. I talked of Germany, declaring my intention of visiting it immediately: God knows, that I little thought at that moment of ever seeing it! She replied to me with great ease and politeness, professed that the pleasure of making my acquaintance amply compensated for the delay in her journey, and gave me a pressing invitation to make some stay at the Castle of Lindenberg. As She spoke thus, the Youths exchanged a malicious smile, which declared that She would be fortunate if She ever reached that Castle herself. This action did not escape me; But I concealed the emotion which it excited in my breast. I continued to converse with the Lady; But my discourse was so frequently incoherent, that as She has since informed me, She began to doubt whether I was in my right senses. The fact was, that while my conversation turned upon one subject, my thoughts were entirely occupied by another. I meditated upon the means of quitting the Cottage, finding my way to the Barn, and giving the Domestics information of our Host's designs. I was soon convinced, how impracticable was the attempt. Jacques and Robert watched my every movement with an attentive eye, and I was obliged to abandon the idea. All my hopes now rested upon Claude's not finding the Banditti: In that case, according to what I had overheard, we should be permitted to depart unhurt.

I shuddered involuntarily as Baptiste entered the room. He made many apologies for his long absence, but "He had been detained by affairs impossible to be delayed." He then entreated permission for his family to sup at the same table with us, without which, respect would not authorize his taking such a liberty. Oh! how in my heart I cursed the Hypocrite! How I loathed his presence, who was on the point of depriving me of an existence, at that time infinitely dear! I had every reason to be satisfied with life; I had youth, wealth, rank, and education; and the fairest prospects presented themselves before me. I saw those prospects on the point of closing in the most horrible manner: Yet was I obliged to dissimulate, and to receive with a semblance of gratitude the false civilities of him who held the dagger to my bosom.

The permission which our Host demanded, was easily obtained. We seated ourselves at the Table. The Baroness and myself occupied one side: The Sons were opposite to us with their backs to the door. Baptiste took his seat by the Baroness at the upper end, and the place next to him was left for his Wife. She soon entered the room, and placed before us a plain but comfortable Peasant's repast. Our Host thought it necessary to apologize for the poorness of the supper: "He had not been apprized of our coming; He could only offer us such fare as had been intended for his own family:"

"But," added He, "should any accident detain my noble Guests longer than they at present intend, I hope to give them a better treatment."

The Villain! I well knew the accident to which He alluded; I shuddered at the treatment which He taught us to expect!

My Companion in danger seemed entirely to have got rid of her chagrin at being delayed. She laughed, and conversed with the family with infinite gaiety. I strove but in vain to follow her example. My spirits were evidently forced, and the constraint which I put upon myself escaped not Baptiste's observation.

"Come, come, Monsieur, cheer up!" said He; "You seem not quite recovered from your fatigue. To raise your spirits, what say you to a glass of excellent old wine which was left me by my Father? God rest his soul, He is in a better world! I seldom produce this wine; But as I am not honoured with such Guests every day, this is an occasion which deserves a Bottle."

He then gave his Wife a Key, and instructed her where to find the wine of which He spoke. She seemed by no means pleased with the commission; She took the Key with an embarrassed air, and hesitated to quit the Table.

"Did you hear me?" said Baptiste in an angry tone.

Marguerite darted upon him a look of mingled anger and fear, and left the chamber. His eyes followed her suspiciously, till She had closed the door.

She soon returned with a bottle sealed with yellow wax. She placed it upon the table, and gave the Key back to her Husband. I suspected that this liquor was not presented to us without design, and I watched Marguerite's movements with inquietude. She was employed in rinsing some small horn Goblets. As She placed them before Baptiste, She saw that my eye was fixed upon her; and at the moment when She thought herself unobserved by the Banditti, She motioned to me with her head not to taste the liquor, She then resumed her place.

In the mean while our Host had drawn the Cork, and filling two of the Goblets, offered them to the Lady and myself. She at first made some objections, but the instances of Baptiste were so urgent, that She was obliged to comply. Fearing to excite suspicion, I hesitated not to take the Goblet presented to me. By its smell and colour I guessed it to be Champagne; But some grains of powder floating upon the top convinced me that it was not unadulterated. However, I dared not to express my repugnance to drinking it; I lifted it to my lips, and seemed to be swallowing it: Suddenly starting from my chair, I made the best of my way towards a Vase of water at some distance, in which Marguerite had been rinsing the Goblets. I pretended to spit out the wine with disgust, and took an opportunity unperceived of emptying the liquor into the Vase.

The Banditti seemed alarmed at my action. Jacques half rose from his chair, put his hand into his bosom, and I discovered the haft of a dagger. I returned to my seat with tranquillity, and affected not to have observed their confusion.

"You have not suited my taste, honest Friend," said I, addressing myself to Baptiste. "I never can drink Champagne without its producing a violent illness. I swallowed a few mouthfuls ere I was aware of its quality, and fear that I shall suffer for my imprudence."

Baptiste and Jacques exchanged looks of distrust.

"Perhaps," said Robert, "the smell may be disagreeable to you."

He quitted his chair, and removed the Goblet. I observed, that He examined, whether it was nearly empty.

"He must have drank sufficient," said He to his Brother in a low voice, while He reseated himself.

Marguerite looked apprehensive, that I had tasted the liquor: A glance from my eye reassured her.

I waited with anxiety for the effects which the Beverage would produce upon the Lady. I doubted not but the grains which I had observed were poisonous, and lamented that it had been impossible for me to warn her of the danger. But a few minutes had elapsed before I perceived her eyes grow heavy; Her head sank upon her shoulder, and She fell into a deep sleep. I affected not to attend to this circumstance, and continued my conversation with Baptiste, with all the outward gaiety in my power to assume. But He no longer answered me without constraint. He eyed me with distrust and astonishment, and I saw that the Banditti were frequently whispering among themselves. My situation became every moment more painful; I sustained the character of confidence with a worse grace than ever. Equally afraid of the arrival of their Accomplices and of their suspecting my knowledge of their designs, I knew not how to dissipate the distrust which the Banditti evidently entertained for me. In this new dilemma the friendly Marguerite again assisted me. She passed behind the Chairs of her Stepsons, stopped for a moment opposite to me, closed her eyes, and reclined her head upon her shoulder. This hint immediately dispelled my incertitude. It told me, that I ought to imitate the Baroness, and pretend that the liquor had taken its full effect upon me. I did so, and in a few minutes seemed perfectly overcome with slumber.

"So!" cried Baptiste, as I fell back in my chair; "At last He sleeps! I began to think that He had scented our design, and that we should have been forced to dispatch him at all events."

"And why not dispatch him at all events?" enquired the ferocious Jacques. "Why leave him the possibility of betraying our secret? Marguerite, give me one of my Pistols: A single touch of the trigger will finish him at once."

"And supposing," rejoined the Father, "Supposing that our Friends should not arrive tonight, a pretty figure we should make when the Servants enquire for him in the Morning! No, no, Jacques; We must wait for our Associates. If they join us, we are strong enough to dispatch the Domestics as well as their Masters, and the booty is our own; If Claude does not find the Troop, we must take patience, and suffer the prey to slip through our fingers. Ah! Boys, Boys, had you arrived but five minutes sooner, the Spaniard would have been done for, and two thousand Pistoles our own. But you are always out of the way when you are most wanted.

You are the most unlucky Rogues!"

"Well, well, Father!" answered Jacques; "Had you been of my mind, all would have been over by this time. You, Robert, Claude, and myself, why the Strangers were but double the number, and I warrant you we might have mastered them.

However, Claude is gone; 'Tis too late to think of it now. We must wait patiently for the arrival of the Gang; and if the Travellers escape us tonight, we must take care to waylay them tomorrow."

"True! True!" said Baptiste; "Marguerite, have you given the sleeping-draught to the Waiting-women?"

She replied in the affirmative.

"All then is safe. Come, come, Boys; Whatever falls out, we have no reason to complain of this adventure. We run no danger, may gain much, and can lose nothing."

At this moment I heard a trampling of Horses. Oh! how dreadful was the sound to my ears. A cold sweat flowed down my forehead, and I felt all the terrors of impending death. I was by no means reassured by hearing the compassionate Marguerite exclaim in the accents of despair,

"Almighty God! They are lost!"

Luckily the Wood-man and his Sons were too much occupied by the arrival of their Associates to attend to me, or the violence of my agitation would have convinced them that my sleep was feigned.

"Open! Open!" exclaimed several voices on the outside of the Cottage.

"Yes! Yes!" cried Baptiste joyfully; "They are our Friends sure enough! Now then our booty is certain. Away! Lads, Away! Lead them to the Barn; You know what is to be done there."

Robert hastened to open the door of the Cottage.

"But first," said Jacques, taking up his arms; "first let me dispatch these Sleepers."

"No, no, no!" replied his Father; "Go you to the Barn, where your presence is wanted. Leave me to take care of these and the Women above."

Jacques obeyed, and followed his Brother. They seemed to converse with the New-Comers for a few minutes: After which I heard the Robbers dismount, and as I conjectured, bend their course towards the Barn.

"So! That is wisely done!" muttered Baptiste; "They have quitted their Horses, that They may fall upon the Strangers by surprise. Good! Good! and now to business."

I heard him approach a small Cupboard which was fixed up in a distant part of the room, and unlock it. At this moment I felt myself shaken gently.

"Now! Now!" whispered Marguerite.

I opened my eyes. Baptiste stood with his back towards me. No one else was in the room save Marguerite and the sleeping Lady. The Villain had taken a dagger from the Cupboard and seemed examining whether it was sufficiently sharp. I had neglected to furnish myself with arms; But I perceived this to be my only chance of escaping, and resolved not to lose the opportunity. I sprang from my seat, darted suddenly upon Baptiste, and clasping my hands round his throat, pressed it so forcibly as to prevent his uttering a single cry. You may remember that I was remarkable at Salamanca for the power of my arm: It now rendered me an essential service. Surprised, terrified, and breathless, the Villain was by no means an equal Antagonist. I threw him upon the ground; I grasped him still tighter; and while I fixed him without motion upon the floor, Marguerite, wresting the dagger from his hand, plunged it repeatedly in his heart till He expired.

No sooner was this horrible but necessary act perpetrated than Marguerite called on me to follow her.

"Flight is our only refuge!" said She; "Quick! Quick! Away!"

I hesitated not to obey her: but unwilling to leave the Baroness a victim to the vengeance of the Robbers, I raised her in my arms still sleeping, and hastened after Marguerite. The Horses of the Banditti were fastened near the door: My Conductress sprang upon one of them. I followed her example, placed the Baroness before me, and spurred on my Horse. Our only hope was to reach Strasbourg, which was much nearer than the perfidious Claude had assured me. Marguerite was well acquainted with the road, and galloped on before me. We were obliged to pass by the Barn, where the Robbers were slaughtering our Domestics. The door was open: We distinguished the shrieks of the dying and imprecations of the Murderers! What I felt at that moment language is unable to describe!

Jacques heard the trampling of our Horses as we rushed by the Barn. He flew to the Door with a burning Torch in his hand, and easily recognised the Fugitives.

"Betrayed! Betrayed!" He shouted to his Companions.

Instantly they left their bloody work, and hastened to regain their Horses. We heard no more. I buried my spurs in the sides of my Courser, and Marguerite goaded on hers with the poignard, which had already rendered us such good service. We flew like lightning, and gained the open plains. Already was Strasbourg's Steeple in sight, when we heard the Robbers pursuing us. Marguerite looked back, and distinguished our followers descending a small Hill at no great distance. It was in vain that we urged on our Horses; The noise approached nearer with every moment.

"We are lost!" She exclaimed; "The Villains gain upon us!"

"On! On!" replied I; "I hear the trampling of Horses coming from the Town."

We redoubled our exertions, and were soon aware of a numerous band of Cavaliers, who came towards us at full speed. They were on the point of passing us.

"Stay! Stay!" shrieked Marguerite; "Save us! For God's sake, save us!"

The Foremost, who seemed to act as Guide, immediately reined in his Steed.

"'Tis She! 'Tis She!" exclaimed He, springing upon the ground; "Stop, my Lord, stop! They are safe! 'Tis my Mother!"

At the same moment Marguerite threw herself from her Horse, clasped him in her arms, and covered him with Kisses. The other Cavaliers stopped at the exclamation.

"The Baroness Lindenberg?" cried another of the Strangers eagerly; "Where is She? Is She not with you?"

He stopped on beholding her lying senseless in my arms. Hastily He caught her from me. The profound sleep in which She was plunged made him at first tremble for her life; but the beating of her heart soon reassured him.

"God be thanked!" said He; "She has escaped unhurt."

I interrupted his joy by pointing out the Brigands, who continued to approach. No sooner had I mentioned them than the greatest part of the Company, which appeared to be chiefly composed of soldiers, hastened forward to meet them. The Villains stayed not to receive their attack: Perceiving their danger they turned the heads of their Horses, and fled into the wood, whither they were followed by our Preservers. In the mean while the Stranger, whom I guessed to be the Baron Lindenberg, after thanking me for my care of his Lady, proposed our returning with all speed to the Town. The Baroness, on whom the effects of the opiate had not ceased to operate, was placed before him; Marguerite and her Son remounted their Horses; the Baron's Domestics followed, and we soon arrived at the Inn, where He had taken his apartments.

This was at the Austrian Eagle, where my Banker, whom before my quitting Paris I had apprised of my intention to visit Strasbourg, had prepared Lodgings for me. I rejoiced at this circumstance. It gave me an opportunity of cultivating the Baron's acquaintance, which I foresaw would be of use to me in Germany. Immediately upon our arrival the Lady was conveyed to bed; A Physician was sent for, who prescribed a medicine likely to counteract the effects of the sleepy potion, and after it had been poured down her throat, She was committed to the care of the Hostess. The Baron then addressed himself to me, and entreated me to recount the particulars of this adventure. I complied with his request instantaneously; for in pain respecting Stephano's fate, whom I had been compelled to abandon to the cruelty of the Banditti, I found it impossible for me to repose, till I had some news of him. I received but too soon the intelligence, that my trusty Servant had perished. The Soldiers who had pursued the Brigands returned while I was employed in relating my adventure to the Baron. By their account I found that the Robbers had been overtaken: Guilt and true courage are incompatible; They had thrown themselves at the feet of their Pursuers, had surrendered themselves without striking a blow, had discovered their secret retreat, made known their signals by which the rest of the Gang might be seized, and in short had betrayed ever mark of cowardice and baseness. By this means the whole of the Band, consisting of near sixty persons, had been made Prisoners, bound, and conducted to Strasbourg. Some of the Soldiers hastened to the Cottage, One of the Banditti serving them as Guide. Their first visit was to the fatal Barn, where they were fortunate enough to find two of the Baron's Servants still alive, though desperately wounded. The rest had expired beneath the swords of the Robbers, and of these my unhappy Stephano was one.

Alarmed at our escape, the Robbers in their haste to overtake us, had neglected to visit the Cottage. In consequence, the Soldiers found the two Waiting-women unhurt, and buried in the same death-like slumber which had overpowered their Mistress. There was nobody else found in the Cottage, except a child not above four years old, which the Soldiers brought away with them. We were busying ourselves with conjectures respecting the birth of this little unfortunate, when Marguerite rushed into the room with the Baby in her arms. She fell at the feet of the Officer who was making us this report, and blessed him a thousand times for the preservation of her Child.

When the first burst of maternal tenderness was over, I besought her to declare, by what means She had been united to a Man whose principles seemed so totally discordant with her own. She bent her eyes downwards, and wiped a few tears from her cheek.

"Gentlemen," said She after a silence of some minutes, "I would request a favour of you: You have a right to know on whom you confer an obligation. I will not therefore stifle a confession which covers me with shame; But permit me to comprise it in as few words as possible.

"I was born in Strasbourg of respectable Parents; Their names I must at present conceal: My Father still lives, and deserves not to be involved in my infamy; If you grant my request, you shall be informed of my family name. A Villain made himself Master of my affections, and to follow him I quitted my Father's House. Yet though my passions overpowered my virtue, I sank not into that degeneracy of vice, but too commonly the lot of Women who make the first false step. I loved my Seducer; dearly loved him! I was true to his Bed; this Baby, and the Youth who warned you, my Lord Baron, of your Lady's danger, are the pledges of our affection. Even at this moment I lament his loss, though 'tis to him that I owe all the miseries of my existence.

"He was of noble birth, but He had squandered away his paternal inheritance. His Relations considered him as a disgrace to their name, and utterly discarded him. His excesses drew upon him the indignation of the Police. He was obliged to fly from Strasbourg, and saw no other resource from beggary than an union with the Banditti who infested the neighbouring Forest, and whose Troop was chiefly composed of Young Men of family in the same predicament with himself. I was determined not to forsake him. I followed him to the Cavern of the Brigands, and shared with him the misery inseparable from

438

a life of pillage. But though I was aware that our existence was supported by plunder, I knew not all the horrible circumstances attached to my Lover's profession. These He concealed from me with the utmost care; He was conscious that my sentiments were not sufficiently depraved to look without horror upon assassination: He supposed, and with justice, that I should fly with detestation from the embraces of a Murderer. Eight years of possession had not abated his love for me; and He cautiously removed from my knowledge every circumstance, which might lead me to suspect the crimes in which He but too often participated. He succeeded perfectly: It was not till after my Seducer's death, that I discovered his hands to have been stained with the blood of innocence.

"One fatal night He was brought back to the Cavern covered with wounds: He received them in attacking an English Traveller, whom his Companions immediately sacrificed to their resentment. He had only time to entreat my pardon for all the sorrows which He had caused me: He pressed my hand to his lips, and expired. My grief was inexpressible. As soon as its violence abated, I resolved to return to Strasbourg, to throw myself with my two Children at my Father's feet, and implore his forgiveness, though I little hoped to obtain it. What was my consternation when informed that no one entrusted with the secret of their retreat was ever permitted to quit the troop of the Banditti; That I must give up all hopes of ever rejoining society, and consent instantly to accepting one of their Band for my Husband! My prayers and remonstrances were vain. They cast lots to decide to whose possession I should fall; I became the property of the infamous Baptiste. A Robber, who had once been a Monk, pronounced over us a burlesque rather than a religious Ceremony: I and my Children were delivered into the hands of my new Husband, and He conveyed us immediately to his home.

"He assured me that He had long entertained for me the most ardent regard; But that Friendship for my deceased Lover had obliged him to stifle his desires. He endeavoured to reconcile me to my fate, and for some time treated me with respect and gentleness: At length finding that my aversion rather increased than diminished, He obtained those favours by violence, which I persisted to refuse him. No resource remained for me but to bear my sorrows with patience; I was conscious that I deserved them but too well. Flight was forbidden: My Children were in the power of Baptiste, and He had sworn that if I attempted to escape, their lives should pay for it. I had had too many opportunities of witnessing the barbarity of his nature to doubt his fulfilling his oath to the very letter. Sad experience had convinced me of the horrors of my situation: My first Lover had carefully concealed them from me; Baptiste rather rejoiced in opening my eyes to the cruelties of his profession, and strove to familiarise me with blood and slaughter.

"My nature was licentious and warm, but not cruel: My conduct had been imprudent, but my heart was not unprincipled. Judge then what I must have felt at being a continual witness of crimes the most horrible and revolting! Judge how I must have grieved at being united to a Man who received the unsuspecting Guest with an air of openness and hospitality, at the very moment that He meditated his destruction. Chagrin and discontent preyed upon my constitution: The few charms bestowed on me by nature withered away, and the dejection of my countenance denoted the sufferings of my heart. I was tempted a thousand times to put an end to my existence; But the remembrance of my Children held my hand. I trembled to leave my dear Boys in my Tyrant's power, and trembled yet more for their virtue than their lives. The Second was still too young to benefit by my instructions; But in the heart of my Eldest I laboured unceasingly to plant those principles, which might enable him to avoid the crimes of his Parents. He listened to me with docility, or rather with eagerness. Even at his early age, He showed that He was not calculated for the society of Villains; and the only comfort which I enjoyed among my sorrows, was to witness the dawning virtues of my Theodore.

"Such was my situation, when the perfidy of Don Alphonso's postillion conducted him to the Cottage. His youth, air, and manners interested me most forcibly in his behalf. The absence of my Husband's Sons gave me an opportunity which I had long wished to find, and I resolved to risque every thing to preserve the Stranger. The vigilance of Baptiste prevented me from warning Don Alphonso of his danger: I knew that my betraying the secret would be immediately punished with death; and however embittered was my life by calamities, I wanted courage to sacrifice it for the sake of preserving that of another Person. My only hope rested upon procuring succour from Strasbourg: At this I resolved to try; and should an opportunity offer of warning Don Alphonso of his danger unobserved, I was determined to seize it with avidity. By Baptiste's orders I went upstairs to make the Stranger's Bed: I spread upon it Sheets in which a Traveller had been murdered but a few nights before, and which still were stained with blood. I hoped that these marks would not escape the vigilance of our Guest, and that He would collect from them the designs of my perfidious Husband. Neither was this the only step which I took to preserve the Stranger. Theodore was confined to his bed by illness. I stole into his room unobserved by my Tyrant, communicated to him my project, and He entered into it with eagerness. He rose in spite of his malady, and dressed himself with all speed. I fastened one of the Sheets round his arms, and lowered him from the Window. He flew to the Stable, took Claude's Horse, and hastened to Strasbourg. Had He been accosted by the Banditti, He was to have declared himself sent upon a message by Baptiste, but fortunately He reached the Town without meeting any obstacle. Immediately upon his arrival at Strasbourg, He entreated assistance from the Magistrature: His Story passed from mouth to mouth, and at length came to the knowledge of my Lord the Baron. Anxious for the safety of his Lady, whom He knew would be upon the road that Evening, it struck him that She might have fallen into the power of the Robbers. He accompanied Theodore who guided the Soldiers towards the Cottage, and arrived just in time to save us from falling once more into the hands of our Enemies."

Here I interrupted Marguerite to enquire why the sleepy potion had been presented to me. She said that Baptiste supposed me to have arms about me, and wished to incapacitate me from making resistance: It was a precaution which He always took, since as the Travellers had no hopes of escaping, Despair would have incited them to sell their lives dearly.

The Baron then desired Marguerite to inform him, what were her present plans. I joined him in declaring my readiness to show my gratitude to her for the preservation of my life.

"Disgusted with a world," She replied, "in which I have met with nothing but misfortunes, my only wish is to retire into a Convent. But first I must provide for my Children. I find that my Mother is no more, probably driven to an untimely grave by my desertion! My Father is still living; He is not an hard Man; Perhaps, Gentlemen, in spite of my ingratitude and imprudence, your intercessions may induce him to forgive me, and to take charge of his unfortunate Grand-sons. If you obtain this boon for me, you will repay my services a thousand-fold!"

Both the Baron and myself assured Marguerite, that we would spare no pains to obtain her pardon: and that even should her Father be inflexible, She need be under no apprehensions respecting the fate of her Children. I engaged myself to provide for Theodore, and the Baron promised to take the youngest under his protection.

The grateful Mother thanked us with tears for what She called generosity, but which in fact was no more than a proper sense of our obligations to her. She then left the room to put her little Boy to bed, whom fatigue and sleep had compleatly overpowered.

The Baroness, on recovering and being informed from what dangers I had rescued her, set no bounds to the expressions of her gratitude. She was joined so warmly by her Husband in pressing me to accompany them to their Castle in Bavaria, that I found it impossible to resist their entreaties. During a week which we passed at Strasbourg, the interests of Marguerite were not forgotten: In our application to her Father we succeeded as amply as we could wish. The good old Man had lost his Wife: He had no Children but this unfortunate Daughter, of whom He had received no news for almost fourteen years. He was surrounded by distant Relations, who waited with impatience for his decease in order to get possession of his money. When therefore Marguerite appeared again so unexpectedly, He considered her as a gift from heaven: He received her and her Children with open arms, and insisted upon their establishing themselves in his House without delay. The disappointed Cousins were obliged to give place. The old Man would not hear of his Daughter's retiring into a Convent: He said that She was too necessary to his happiness, and She was easily persuaded to relinquish her design. But no persuasions could induce Theodore to give up the plan which I had at first marked out for him. He had attached himself to me most sincerely during my stay at Strasbourg; and when I was on the point of leaving it, He besought me with tears to take him into my service: He set forth all his little talents in the most favourable colours, and tried to convince me that I should find him of infinite use to me upon the road. I was unwilling to charge myself with a Lad but scarcely turned of thirteen, whom I knew could only be a burthen to me: However, I could not resist the entreaties of this affectionate Youth, who in fact possessed a thousand estimable qualities. With some difficulty He persuaded his relations to let him follow me, and that permission once obtained, He was dubbed with the title of my Page. Having passed a week at Strasbourg, Theodore and myself set out for Bavaria in company with the Baron and his Lady. These Latter as well as myself had forced Marguerite to accept several presents of value, both for herself, and her youngest Son: On leaving her, I promised his Mother faithfully that I would restore Theodore to her within the year.

I have related this adventure at length, Lorenzo, that you might understand the means by which "The Adventurer,

Alphonso d'Alvarada got introduced into the Castle of Lindenberg." Judge from this specimen how much faith should be given to your Aunt's assertions!

CHAPTER IV.

Avaunt! and quit my sight! Let the Earth hide thee!

Thy bones are marrowless, thy blood is cold!

Thou hast no speculation in those eyes

Which Thou dost glare with! Hence, horrible shadow!

Unreal mockery hence!

MACBETH.

Continuation of the History of Don Raymond.

My journey was uncommonly agreeable: I found the Baron a Man of some sense, but little knowledge of the world. He had past a great part of his life without stirring beyond the precincts of his own domains, and consequently his manners were far from being the most polished: But He was hearty, good-humoured, and friendly. His attention to me was all that I could wish, and I had every reason to be satisfied with his behaviour. His ruling passion was Hunting, which He had brought himself to consider as a serious occupation; and when talking over some remarkable chace, He treated the subject with as much gravity as it had been a Battle on which the fate of two kingdoms was depending. I happened to be a tolerable Sportsman: Soon after my arrival at Lindenberg I gave some proofs of my dexterity. The Baron immediately marked me down for a Man of Genius, and vowed to me an eternal friendship.

That friendship was become to me by no means indifferent. At the Castle of Lindenberg I beheld for the first time your Sister, the lovely Agnes. For me whose heart was unoccupied, and who grieved at the void, to see her and to love her were the same. I found in Agnes all that was requisite to secure my affection. She was then scarcely sixteen; Her person light and elegant was already formed; She possessed several talents in perfection, particularly those of Music and drawing: Her character was gay, open, and good-humoured; and the graceful simplicity of her dress and manners formed an advantageous contrast to the art and studied Coquetry of the Parisian Dames, whom I had just quitted. From the moment that I beheld her, I felt the most lively interest in her fate. I made many enquiries respecting her of the Baroness.

"She is my Niece," replied that Lady; "You are still ignorant, Don Alphonso, that I am your Countrywoman. I am Sister to the Duke of Medina Celi: Agnes is the Daughter of my second Brother, Don Gaston: She has been destined to the Convent from her cradle, and will soon make her profession at Madrid."

(Here Lorenzo interrupted the Marquis by an exclamation of surprise.

"Intended for the Convent from her cradle?" said He; "By heaven, this is the first word that I ever heard of such a design!"

"I believe it, my dear Lorenzo," answered Don Raymond; "But you must listen to me with patience. You will not be less surprised, when I relate some particulars of your family still unknown to you, and which I have learnt from the mouth of Agnes herself."

He then resumed his narrative as follows.)

You cannot but be aware that your Parents were unfortunately Slaves to the grossest superstition: When this foible was called into play, their every other sentiment, their every other passion yielded to its irresistible strength. While She was big with Agnes, your Mother was seized by a dangerous illness, and given over by her Physicians. In this situation, Donna Inesilla vowed, that if She recovered from her malady, the Child then living in her bosom if a Girl should be dedicated to St. Clare, if a Boy to St. Benedict. Her prayers were heard; She got rid of her complaint; Agnes entered the world alive, and was immediately destined to the service of St. Clare.

Don Gaston readily chimed in with his Lady's wishes: But knowing the sentiments of the Duke, his Brother, respecting a Monastic life, it was determined that your Sister's destination should be carefully concealed from him. The better to guard the secret, it was resolved that Agnes should accompany her Aunt, Donna Rodolpha into Germany, whither that Lady was on the point of following her new-married Husband, Baron Lindenberg. On her arrival at that Estate, the young Agnes was put into a Convent, situated but a few miles from the Castle. The Nuns to whom her education was confided performed their charge with exactitude: They made her a perfect Mistress of many talents, and strove to infuse into her mind a taste for the retirement and tranquil pleasures of a Convent. But a secret instinct made the young Recluse sensible that She was not born for solitude: In all the freedom of youth and gaiety, She scrupled not to treat as ridiculous many ceremonies which the Nuns regarded with awe; and She was never more happy than when her lively imagination inspired her with some scheme to

plague the stiff Lady Abbess, or the ugly ill-tempered old
Porteress. She looked with disgust upon the prospect before her:
However no alternative was offered to her, and She submitted
to the decree of her Parents, though not without secret repining.

That repugnance She had not art enough to conceal long:
Don Gaston was informed of it. Alarmed, Lorenzo, lest your
affection for her should oppose itself to his projects, and lest you
should positively object to your Sister's misery, He resolved to
keep the whole affair from your knowledge as well as the
Duke's, till the sacrifice should be consummated. The season of
her taking the veil was fixed for the time when you should be
upon your travels: In the meanwhile no hint was dropped of
Donna Inesilla's fatal vow. Your Sister was never permitted to
know your direction. All your letters were read before She
received them, and those parts effaced, which were likely to
nourish her inclination for the world: Her answers were
dictated either by her Aunt, or by Dame Cunegonda, her
Governess. These particulars I learnt partly from Agnes, partly
from the Baroness herself.

I immediately determined upon rescuing this lovely Girl
from a fate so contrary to her inclinations, and ill-suited to her
merit. I endeavoured to ingratiate myself into her favour: I
boasted of my friendship and intimacy with you. She listened to
me with avidity; She seemed to devour my words while I spoke
in your praise, and her eyes thanked me for my affection to her
Brother. My constant and unremitted attention at length gained
me her heart, and with difficulty I obliged her to confess that
She loved me. When however, I proposed her quitting the
Castle of Lindenberg, She rejected the idea in positive terms.

"Be generous, Alphonso," She said; "You possess my heart,
but use not the gift ignobly. Employ not your ascendancy over
me in persuading me to take a step, at which I should hereafter
have to blush. I am young and deserted: My Brother, my only
Friend, is separated from me, and my other Relations act with
me as my Enemies. Take pity on my unprotected situation.
Instead of seducing me to an action which would cover me with
shame, strive rather to gain the affections of those who govern
me. The Baron esteems you. My Aunt, to others ever harsh
proud and contemptuous, remembers that you rescued her
from the hands of Murderers, and wears with you alone the
appearance of kindness and benignity. Try then your influence
over my Guardians. If they consent to our union my hand is
yours: From your account of my Brother, I cannot doubt your
obtaining his approbation: And when they find the
impossibility of executing their design, I trust that my Parents

will excuse my disobedience, and expiate by some other sacrifice my Mother's fatal vow."

From the first moment that I beheld Agnes, I had endeavoured to conciliate the favour of her Relations. Authorised by the confession of her regard, I redoubled my exertions. My principal Battery was directed against the Baroness; It was easy to discover that her word was law in the Castle: Her Husband paid her the most absolute submission, and considered her as a superior Being. She was about forty: In her youth She had been a Beauty; But her charms had been upon that large scale which can but ill sustain the shock of years: However She still possessed some remains of them. Her understanding was strong and excellent when not obscured by prejudice, which unluckily was but seldom the case. Her passions were violent: She spared no pains to gratify them, and pursued with unremitting vengeance those who opposed themselves to her wishes. The warmest of Friends, the most inveterate of Enemies, such was the Baroness Lindenberg.

I laboured incessantly to please her: Unluckily I succeeded but too well. She seemed gratified by my attention, and treated me with a distinction accorded by her to no one else. One of my daily occupations was reading to her for several hours: Those hours I should much rather have past with Agnes; But as I was conscious that complaisance for her Aunt would advance our union, I submitted with a good grace to the penance imposed upon me. Donna Rodolpha's Library was principally composed of old Spanish Romances: These were her favourite studies, and once a day one of these unmerciful Volumes was put regularly into my hands. I read the wearisome adventures of "Perceforest," "Tirante the White," "Palmerin of England," and "the Knight of the Sun," till the Book was on the point of falling from my hands through Ennui. However, the increasing pleasure which the Baroness seemed to take in my society, encouraged me to persevere; and latterly She showed for me a partiality so marked, that Agnes advised me to seize the first opportunity of declaring our mutual passion to her Aunt.

One Evening, I was alone with Donna Rodolpha in her own apartment. As our readings generally treated of love, Agnes was never permitted to assist at them. I was just congratulating myself on having finished "The Loves of Tristan and the Queen Iseult——"

"Ah! The Unfortunates!" cried the Baroness; "How say you, Segnor? Do you think it possible for Man to feel an attachment so disinterested and sincere?"

447

"I cannot doubt it," replied I; "My own heart furnishes me with the certainty. Ah! Donna Rodolpha, might I but hope for your approbation of my love! Might I but confess the name of my Mistress without incurring your resentment!"

She interrupted me.

"Suppose, I were to spare you that confession? Suppose I were to acknowledge that the object of your desires is not unknown to me? Suppose I were to say that She returns your affection, and laments not less sincerely than yourself the unhappy vows which separate her from you?"

"Ah! Donna Rodolpha!" I exclaimed, throwing myself upon my knees before her, and pressing her hand to my lips, "You have discovered my secret! What is your decision? Must I despair, or may I reckon upon your favour?"

She withdrew not the hand which I held; But She turned from me, and covered her face with the other.

"How can I refuse it you?" She replied; "Ah! Don Alphonso, I have long perceived to whom your attentions were directed, but till now I perceived not the impression which they made upon my heart.

At length I can no longer hide my weakness either from myself or from you. I yield to the violence of my passion, and own that I adore you! For three long months I stifled my desires; But grown stronger by resistance, I submit to their impetuosity. Pride, fear, and honour, respect for myself, and my engagements to the Baron, all are vanquished. I sacrifice them to my love for you, and it still seems to me that I pay too mean a price for your possession."

She paused for an answer. — Judge, my Lorenzo, what must have been my confusion at this discovery. I at once saw all the magnitude of this obstacle, which I had raised myself to my happiness. The Baroness had placed those attentions to her own account, which I had merely paid her for the sake of Agnes: And the strength of her expressions, the looks which accompanied them, and my knowledge of her revengeful disposition made me tremble for myself and my Beloved. I was silent for some minutes. I knew not how to reply to her declaration: I could only resolve to clear up the mistake without delay, and for the present to conceal from her knowledge the name of my Mistress. No sooner had She avowed her passion than the transports which before were evident in my features

448

gave place to consternation and constraint. I dropped her hand, and rose from my knees. The change in my countenance did not escape her observation.

"What means this silence?" said She in a trembling voice; "Where is that joy which you led me to expect?"

"Forgive me, Segnora," I answered, "if what necessity forces from me should seem harsh and ungrateful: To encourage you in an error, which, however it may flatter myself, must prove to you the source of disappointment, would make me appear criminal in every eye. Honour obliges me to inform you that you have mistaken for the solicitude of Love what was only the attention of Friendship. The latter sentiment is that which I wished to excite in your bosom: To entertain a warmer, respect for you forbids me, and gratitude for the Baron's generous treatment. Perhaps these reasons would not be sufficient to shield me from your attractions, were it not that my affections are already bestowed upon another. You have charms, Segnora, which might captivate the most insensible; No heart unoccupied could resist them. Happy is it for me that mine is no longer in my possession; or I should have to reproach myself for ever with having violated the Laws of Hospitality. Recollect yourself, noble Lady; Recollect what is owed by you to honour, by me to the Baron, and replace by esteem and friendship those sentiments which I never can return."

The Baroness turned pale at this unexpected and positive declaration: She doubted whether She slept or woke. At length recovering from her surprise, consternation gave place to rage, and the blood rushed back into her cheeks with violence.

"Villain!" She cried; "Monster of deceit! Thus is the avowal of my love received? Is it thus that.... But no, no! It cannot, it shall not be! Alphonso, behold me at your feet! Be witness of my despair! Look with pity on a Woman who loves you with sincere affection! She who possesses your heart, how has She merited such a treasure? What sacrifice has She made to you?

What raises her above Rodolpha?"

I endeavoured to lift her from her Knees.

"For God's sake, Segnora, restrain these transports: They disgrace yourself and me. Your exclamations may be heard, and your secret divulged to your Attendants. I see that my presence only irritates you: permit me to retire."

449

I prepared to quit the apartment: The Baroness caught me suddenly by the arm.

"And who is this happy Rival?" said She in a menacing tone; "I will know her name, and when I know it.... ! She is someone in my power; You entreated my favour, my protection! Let me but find her, let me but know who dares to rob me of your heart, and She shall suffer every torment which jealousy and disappointment can inflict! Who is She? Answer me this moment. Hope not to conceal her from my vengeance! Spies shall be set over you; every step, every look shall be watched; Your eyes will discover my Rival; I shall know her, and when She is found, tremble, Alphonso for her and for yourself!"

As She uttered these last words her fury mounted to such a pitch as to stop her powers of respiration. She panted, groaned, and at length fainted away. As She was falling I caught her in my arms, and placed her upon a Sopha. Then hastening to the door, I summoned her Women to her assistance; I committed her to their care, and seized the opportunity of escaping.

Agitated and confused beyond expression I bent my steps towards the Garden. The benignity with which the Baroness had listened to me at first raised my hopes to the highest pitch: I imagined her to have perceived my attachment for her Niece, and to approve of it. Extreme was my disappointment at understanding the true purport of her discourse. I knew not what course to take: The superstition of the Parents of Agnes, aided by her Aunt's unfortunate passion, seemed to oppose such obstacles to our union as were almost insurmountable.

As I past by a low parlour, whose windows looked into the Garden, through the door which stood half open I observed Agnes seated at a Table. She was occupied in drawing, and several unfinished sketches were scattered round her. I entered, still undetermined whether I should acquaint her with the declaration of the Baroness.

"Oh! is it only you?" said She, raising her head; "You are no Stranger, and I shall continue my occupation without ceremony. Take a Chair, and seat yourself by me."

I obeyed, and placed myself near the Table. Unconscious what I was doing, and totally occupied by the scene which had just passed, I took up some of the drawings, and cast my eye over them. One of the subjects struck me from its singularity. It represented the great Hall of the Castle of Lindenberg. A door conducting to a narrow staircase stood half open. In the foreground appeared a Groupe of figures, placed in the most grotesque attitudes; Terror was expressed upon every countenance.

Here was One upon his knees with his eyes cast up to heaven, and praying most devoutly; There Another was creeping away upon all fours. Some hid their faces in their cloaks or the laps of their Companions; Some had concealed themselves beneath a Table, on which the remnants of a feast were visible; While Others with gaping mouths and eyes wide-stretched pointed to a Figure, supposed to have created this disturbance. It represented a Female of more than human stature, clothed in the habit of some religious order. Her face was veiled; On her arm hung a chaplet of beads; Her dress was in several places stained with the blood which trickled from a wound upon her bosom. In one hand She held a Lamp, in the other a large Knife, and She seemed advancing towards the iron gates of the Hall.

"What does this mean, Agnes?" said I; "Is this some invention of your own?"

She cast her eye upon the drawing.

"Oh! no," She replied; "'Tis the invention of much wiser heads than mine. But can you possibly have lived at Lindenberg for three whole Months without hearing of the Bleeding Nun?"

"You are the first, who ever mentioned the name to me. Pray, who may the Lady be?"

"That is more than I can pretend to tell you. All my knowledge of her History comes from an old tradition in this family, which has been handed down from Father to Son, and is firmly credited throughout the Baron's domains. Nay, the Baron believes it himself; and as for my Aunt who has a natural turn for the marvellous, She would sooner doubt the veracity of the Bible, than of the Bleeding Nun. Shall I tell you this History?"

I answered that She would oblige me much by relating it: She resumed her drawing, and then proceeded as follows in a tone of burlesqued gravity.

"It is surprising that in all the Chronicles of past times, this remarkable Personage is never once mentioned. Fain would I recount to you her life; But unluckily till after her death She was never known to have existed. Then first did She think it necessary to make some noise in the world, and with that intention She made bold to seize upon the Castle of Lindenberg. Having a good taste, She took up her abode in the best room of the House: and once established there, She began to amuse herself by knocking about the tables and chairs in the middle of the night. Perhaps She was a bad Sleeper, but this I have never been able to ascertain. According to the tradition, this entertainment commenced about a Century ago. It was accompanied with shrieking, howling, groaning, swearing, and many other agreeable noises of the same kind. But though one particular room was more especially honoured with her visits, She did not entirely confine herself to it. She occasionally ventured into the old Galleries, paced up and down the spacious Halls, or sometimes stopping at the doors of the Chambers, She wept and wailed there to the universal terror of the Inhabitants. In these nocturnal excursions She was seen by different People, who all describe her appearance as you behold it here, traced by the hand of her unworthy Historian."

The singularity of this account insensibly engaged my attention.

"Did She never speak to those who met her?" said I.

"Not She. The specimens indeed, which She gave nightly of her talents for conversation, were by no means inviting. Sometimes the Castle rung with oaths and execrations: A Moment after She repeated her Paternoster: Now She howled out the most horrible blasphemies, and then chaunted De Profundis, as orderly as if still in the Choir. In short She seemed a mighty capricious Being: But whether She prayed or cursed, whether She was impious or devout, She always contrived to terrify her Auditors out of their senses. The Castle became scarcely habitable; and its Lord was so frightened by these midnight Revels, that one fine morning He was found dead in his bed. This success seemed to please the Nun mightily, for now She made more noise than ever. But the next Baron proved too cunning for her. He made his appearance with a celebrated Exorciser in his hand, who feared not to shut himself up for a night in the haunted Chamber. There it seems that He had an hard battle with the Ghost, before She would promise to be quiet. She was obstinate, but He was more so, and at length She consented to let the Inhabitants of the Castle take a good night's rest. For some time after no news was heard of her. But at the end of five years the Exorciser died, and then the Nun ventured to peep abroad again. However, She was now grown much more tractable and well-behaved. She walked about in silence, and never made her appearance above once in five years. This custom, if you will believe the Baron, She still continues. He is

452

fully persuaded, that on the fifth of May of every fifth year, as soon as the Clock strikes One, the Door of the haunted Chamber opens. (Observe, that this room has been shut up for near a Century.) Then out walks the Ghostly Nun with her Lamp and dagger: She descends the staircase of the Eastern Tower; and crosses the great Hall! On that night the Porter always leaves the Gates of the Castle open, out of respect to the Apparition: Not that this is thought by any means necessary, since She could easily whip through the Keyhole if She chose it; But merely out of politeness, and to prevent her from making her exit in a way so derogatory to the dignity of her Ghost-ship."

"And whither does She go on quitting the Castle?"

"To Heaven, I hope; But if She does, the place certainly is not to her taste, for She always returns after an hour's absence. The Lady then retires to her chamber, and is quiet for another five years."

"And you believe this, Agnes?"

"How can you ask such a question? No, no, Alphonso! I have too much reason to lament superstition's influence to be its Victim myself. However I must not avow my incredulity to the Baroness: She entertains not a doubt of the truth of this History. As to Dame Cunegonda, my Governess, She protests that fifteen years ago She saw the Spectre with her own eyes. She related to me one evening how She and several other Domestics had been terrified while at Supper by the appearance of the Bleeding Nun, as the Ghost is called in the Castle: 'Tis from her account that I drew this sketch, and you may be certain that Cunegonda was not omitted. There She is! I shall never forget what a passion She was in, and how ugly She looked while She scolded me for having made her picture so like herself!"

Here She pointed to a burlesque figure of an old Woman in an attitude of terror.

In spite of the melancholy which oppressed me, I could not help smiling at the playful imagination of Agnes: She had perfectly preserved Dame Cunegonda's resemblance, but had so much exaggerated every fault, and rendered every feature so irresistibly laughable, that I could easily conceive the Duenna's anger.

"The figure is admirable, my dear Agnes! I knew not that you possessed such talents for the ridiculous."

"Stay a moment," She replied; "I will show you a figure still more ridiculous than Dame Cunegonda's. If it pleases you, you may dispose of it as seems best to yourself."

She rose, and went to a Cabinet at some little distance. Unlocking a drawer, She took out a small case, which She opened, and presented to me.

"Do you know the resemblance?" said She smiling.

It was her own.

Transported at the gift, I pressed the portrait to my lips with passion: I threw myself at her feet, and declared my gratitude in the warmest and most affectionate terms. She listened to me with complaisance, and assured me that She shared my sentiments: When suddenly She uttered a loud shriek, disengaged the hand which I held, and flew from the room by a door which opened to the Garden. Amazed at this abrupt departure, I rose hastily from my knees. I beheld with confusion the Baroness standing near me glowing with jealousy, and almost choaked with rage. On recovering from her swoon, She had tortured her imagination to discover her concealed Rival. No one appeared to deserve her suspicions more than Agnes. She immediately hastened to find her Niece, tax her with encouraging my addresses, and assure herself whether her conjectures were well-grounded. Unfortunately She had already seen enough to need no other confirmation. She arrived at the door of the room at the precise moment, when Agnes gave me her Portrait. She heard me profess an everlasting attachment to her Rival, and saw me kneeling at her feet. She advanced to separate us; We were too much occupied by each other to perceive her approach, and were not aware of it, till Agnes beheld her standing by my side.

Rage on the part of Donna Rodolpha, embarrassment on mine, for some time kept us both silent. The Lady recovered herself first.

"My suspicions then were just," said She; "The Coquetry of my Niece has triumphed, and 'tis to her that I am sacrificed. In one respect however I am fortunate: I shall not be the only one who laments a disappointed passion. You too shall know, what it is to love without hope! I daily expect orders for restoring Agnes to her Parents. Immediately upon her arrival in Spain, She will take the veil, and place an insuperable barrier to your union. You may spare your supplications." She continued, perceiving me on the point of speaking; "My resolution is fixed and immoveable. Your Mistress shall remain a close Prisoner in her chamber till She exchanges this Castle for the Cloister. Solitude will perhaps recall her to a sense of her duty: But to prevent your opposing that wished event, I must inform you, Don Alphonso, that your presence here is no longer agreeable either to the Baron or Myself. It was not to talk nonsense to my Niece that your Relations sent you to Germany: Your business was to travel, and I should be sorry to impede any longer so excellent a design. Farewell, Segnor; Remember, that tomorrow morning we meet for the last time."

Having said this, She darted upon me a look of pride, contempt, and malice, and quitted the apartment. I also retired to mine, and consumed the night in planning the means of rescuing Agnes from the power of her tyrannical Aunt.

After the positive declaration of its Mistress, it was impossible for me to make a longer stay at the Castle of Lindenberg. Accordingly I the next day announced my immediate departure. The Baron declared that it gave him sincere pain; and He expressed himself in my favour so warmly, that I endeavoured to win him over to my interest. Scarcely had I mentioned the name of Agnes when He stopped me short, and said, that it was totally out of his power to interfere in the business. I saw that it was in vain to argue; The Baroness governed her Husband with despotic sway, and I easily perceived that She had prejudiced him against the match. Agnes did not appear: I entreated permission to take leave of her, but my prayer was rejected. I was obliged to depart without seeing her.

At quitting him the Baron shook my hand affectionately, and assured me that as soon as his Niece was gone, I might consider his House as my own.

"Farewell, Don Alphonso!" said the Baroness, and stretched out her hand to me.

I took it, and offered to carry it to my lips. She prevented me.

Her Husband was at the other end of the room, and out of hearing.

"Take care of yourself," She continued; "My love is become hatred, and my wounded pride shall not be unatoned. Go where you will, my vengeance shall follow you!"

She accompanied these words with a look sufficient to make

me tremble. I answered not, but hastened to quit the Castle.

As my Chaise drove out of the Court, I looked up to the windows of your Sister's chamber. Nobody was to be seen there: I threw myself back despondent in my Carriage. I was attended by no other servants than a Frenchman whom I had hired at Strasbourg in Stephano's room, and my little Page whom I before mentioned to you. The fidelity, intelligence, and good temper of Theodore had already made him dear to me; But He now prepared to lay an obligation on me, which made me look upon him as a Guardian Genius. Scarcely had we proceeded half a mile from the Castle, when He rode up to the Chaise-door.

"Take courage, Segnor!" said He in Spanish, which He had already learnt to speak with fluency and correctness. "While you were with the Baron, I watched the moment when Dame Cunegonda was below stairs, and mounted into the chamber over that of Donna Agnes. I sang as loud as I could a little German air well-known to her, hoping that She would recollect my voice. I was not disappointed, for I soon heard her window open. I hastened to let down a string with which I had provided myself: Upon hearing the casement closed again, I drew up the string, and fastened to it I found this scrap of paper."

He then presented me with a small note addressed to me. I opened it with impatience: It contained the following words written in pencil:

"Conceal yourself for the next fortnight in some neighbouring Village. My Aunt will believe you to have quitted Lindenberg, and I shall be restored to liberty. I will be in the West Pavilion at twelve on the night of the thirtieth. Fail not to be there, and we shall have an opportunity of concerting our future plans. Adieu.

"AGNES."

At perusing these lines my transports exceeded all bounds; Neither did I set any to the expressions of gratitude which I heaped upon Theodore. In fact his address and attention merited my warmest praise. You will readily believe that I had not entrusted him with my passion for Agnes; But the arch Youth had too much discernment not to discover my secret, and too much discretion not to conceal his knowledge of it. He observed in silence what was going on, nor strove to make himself an Agent in the business till my interests required his interference. I equally admired his judgment, his penetration, his address, and his fidelity. This was not the first occasion in which I had found him of infinite use, and I was every day more convinced of his quickness and capacity. During my short stay at Strasbourg, He had applied himself diligently to learning the rudiments of Spanish: He continued to study it, and with so much success that He spoke it with the same facility as his native language. He past the greatest part of his time in reading; He had acquired much information for his Age; and united the advantages of a lively countenance and prepossessing figure to an excellent understanding and the very best of hearts. He is now fifteen; He is still in my service, and when you see him, I am sure that He will please you. But excuse this digression: I return to the subject which I quitted.

I obeyed the instructions of Agnes. I proceeded to Munich. There I left my Chaise under the care of Lucas, my French Servant, and then returned on Horseback to a small Village about four miles distant from the Castle of Lindenberg. Upon arriving there a story was related to the Host at whose Inn I descended, which prevented his wondering at my making so long a stay in his House. The old Man fortunately was credulous and incurious: He believed all I said, and sought to know no more than what I thought proper to tell him. Nobody was with me but Theodore; Both were disguised, and as we kept ourselves close, we were not suspected to be other than what we seemed. In this manner the fortnight passed away. During that time I had the pleasing conviction that Agnes was once more at liberty. She past through the Village with Dame Cunegonda: She seemed in health and spirits, and talked to her Companion without any appearance of constraint.

"Who are those Ladies?" said I to my Host, as the Carriage past.

"Baron Lindenberg's Niece with her Governess," He replied; "She goes regularly every Friday to the Convent of St. Catharine, in which She was brought up, and which is situated about a mile from hence."

You may be certain that I waited with impatience for the ensuing Friday. I again beheld my lovely Mistress. She cast her eyes upon me, as She passed the Inn-door. A blush which overspread her cheek told me that in spite of my disguise I had been recognised. I bowed profoundly. She returned the compliment by a slight inclination of the head as if made to one inferior, and looked another way till the Carriage was out of sight.

The long-expected, long-wished for night arrived. It was calm, and the Moon was at the full. As soon as the Clock struck eleven I hastened to my appointment, determined not to be too late. Theodore had provided a Ladder; I ascended the Garden wall without difficulty; The Page followed me, and drew the Ladder after us. I posted myself in the West Pavilion, and waited impatiently for the approach of Agnes. Every breeze that whispered, every leaf that fell, I believed to be her footstep, and hastened to meet her. Thus was I obliged to pass a full hour, every minute of which appeared to me an age. The Castle Bell at length tolled twelve, and scarcely could I believe the night to be no further advanced. Another quarter of an hour elapsed, and I heard the light foot of my Mistress approaching the Pavilion with precaution. I flew to receive her, and conducted her to a seat. I threw myself at her feet, and was expressing my joy at seeing her, when She thus interrupted me.

"We have no time to lose, Alphonso: The moments are precious, for though no more a Prisoner, Cunegonda watches my every step. An express is arrived from my Father; I must depart immediately for Madrid, and 'tis with difficulty that I have obtained a week's delay. The superstition of my Parents, supported by the representations of my cruel Aunt, leaves me no hope of softening them to compassion. In this dilemma I have resolved to commit myself to your honour: God grant that you may never give me cause to repent my resolution! Flight is my only resource from the horrors of a Convent, and my imprudence must be excused by the urgency of the danger. Now listen to the plan by which I hope to effect my escape.

"We are now at the thirtieth of April. On the fifth day from this the Visionary Nun is expected to appear. In my last visit to the Convent I provided myself with a dress proper for the character: A Friend, whom I have left there and to whom I made no scruple to confide my secret, readily consented to supply me with a religious habit. Provide a carriage, and be with it at a little distance from the great Gate of the Castle. As soon as the Clock strikes "one," I shall quit my chamber, drest in the same apparel as the Ghost is supposed to wear. Whoever meets me will be too much terrified to oppose my escape. I shall easily reach the door, and throw myself under your protection. Thus far success is certain: But Oh! Alphonso, should you deceive me! Should you despise my imprudence and reward it with ingratitude, the World will not hold a Being more wretched than myself! I feel all the dangers to which I shall be exposed. I feel that I am giving you a right to treat me with levity: But I rely upon your love, upon your honour! The step which I am on the point of taking, will incense my Relations against me:

Should you desert me, should you betray the trust reposed in you, I shall have no friend to punish your insult, or support my cause. On yourself alone rests all my hope, and if your own heart does not plead in my behalf, I am undone for ever!"

The tone in which She pronounced these words was so touching, that in spite of my joy at receiving her promise to follow me, I could not help being affected. I also repined in secret at not having taken the precaution to provide a Carriage at the Village, in which case I might have carried off Agnes that very night. Such an attempt was now impracticable: Neither Carriage or Horses were to be procured nearer than Munich, which was distant from Lindenberg two good days journey. I was therefore obliged to chime in with her plan, which in truth seemed well arranged: Her disguise would secure her from being stopped in quitting the Castle, and would enable her to step into the Carriage at the very Gate without difficulty or losing time.

Agnes reclined her head mournfully upon my shoulder, and by the light of the Moon I saw tears flowing down her cheek. I strove to dissipate her melancholy, and encouraged her to look forward to the prospect of happiness. I protested in the most solemn terms that her virtue and innocence would be safe in my keeping, and that till the church had made her my lawful Wife, her honour should be held by me as sacred as a Sister's. I told her that my first care should be to find you out, Lorenzo, and reconcile you to our union; and I was continuing to speak in the same strain, when a noise without alarmed me. Suddenly the door of the Pavilion was thrown open, and Cunegonda stood before us. She had heard Agnes steal out of her chamber, followed her into the Garden, and perceived her entering the Pavilion. Favoured by the Trees which shaded it, and unperceived by Theodore who waited at a little distance, She had approached in silence, and overheard our whole conversation.

"Admirable!" cried Cunegonda in a voice shrill with passion, while Agnes uttered a loud shriek; "By St. Barbara, young Lady, you have an excellent invention! You must personate the Bleeding Nun, truly? What impiety! What incredulity! Marry, I have a good mind to let you pursue your plan: When the real Ghost met you, I warrant, you would be in a pretty condition! Don Alphonso, you ought to be ashamed of yourself for seducing a young ignorant Creature to leave her family and Friends: However, for this time at least I shall mar your wicked designs. The noble Lady shall be informed of the whole affair, and Agnes must defer playing the Spectre till a better opportunity. Farewell, Segnor— Donna Agnes, let me have the honour of conducting your Ghost-ship back to your apartment."

She approached the Sopha on which her trembling Pupil was seated, took her by the hand, and prepared to lead her from the Pavilion.

I detained her, and strove by entreaties, soothing, promises, and flattery to win her to my party: But finding all that I could say of no avail, I abandoned the vain attempt.

"Your obstinacy must be its own punishment," said I; "But one resource remains to save Agnes and myself, and I shall not hesitate to employ it."

Terrified at this menace, She again endeavoured to quit the Pavilion; But I seized her by the wrist, and detained her forcibly. At the same moment Theodore, who had followed her into the room, closed the door, and prevented her escape. I took the veil of Agnes: I threw it round the Duenna's head, who uttered such piercing shrieks that in spite of our distance from the Castle, I dreaded their being heard. At length I succeeded in gagging her so compleatly that She could not produce a single sound. Theodore and myself with some difficulty next contrived to bind her hands and feet with our handkerchiefs; And I advised Agnes to regain her chamber with all diligence. I promised that no harm should happen to Cunegonda, bad her remember that on the fifth of May I should be in waiting at the Great Gate of the Castle, and took of her an affectionate farewell. Trembling and uneasy She had scarce power enough to signify her consent to my plans, and fled back to her apartment in disorder and confusion.

In the meanwhile Theodore assisted me in carrying off my antiquated Prize. She was hoisted over the wall, placed before me upon my Horse like a Portmanteau, and I galloped away with her from the Castle of Lindenberg. The unlucky Duenna never had made a more disagreeable journey in her life: She was jolted and shaken till She was become little more than an animated Mummy; not to mention her fright when we waded through a small River through which it was necessary to pass in order to regain the Village. Before we reached the Inn, I had already determined how to dispose of the troublesome Cunegonda. We entered the Street in which the Inn stood, and while the page knocked, I waited at a little distance. The Landlord opened the door with a Lamp in his hand.

"Give me the light!" said Theodore; "My Master is coming."

He snatched the Lamp hastily, and purposely let it fall upon the ground: The Landlord returned to the Kitchen to re-light the Lamp, leaving the door open. I profited by the obscurity, sprang from my Horse with Cunegonda in my arms, darted up stairs, reached my chamber unperceived, and unlocking the door of a spacious Closet, stowed her within it, and then turned the Key. The Landlord and Theodore soon after appeared with lights: The Former expressed himself a little surprised at my returning so late, but asked no impertinent questions. He soon quitted the room, and left me to exult in the success of my undertaking.

I immediately paid a visit to my Prisoner. I strove to persuade her submitting with patience to her temporary confinement. My attempt was unsuccessful. Unable to speak or move, She expressed her fury by her looks, and except at meals I never dared to unbind her, or release her from the Gag. At such times I stood over her with a drawn sword, and protested, that if She uttered a single cry, I would plunge it in her bosom. As soon as She had done eating, the Gag was replaced. I was conscious that this proceeding was cruel, and could only be justified by the urgency of circumstances: As to Theodore, He had no scruples upon the subject. Cunegonda's captivity entertained him beyond measure. During his abode in the Castle, a continual warfare had been carried on between him and the Duenna; and now that He found his Enemy so absolutely in his power, He triumphed without mercy. He seemed to think of nothing but how to find out new means of plaguing her: Sometimes He affected to pity her misfortune, then laughed at, abused, and mimicked her; He played her a thousand tricks, each more provoking than the other, and amused himself by telling her that her elopement must have occasioned much surprise at the Baron's. This was in fact the case. No one except Agnes could imagine what was become of Dame Cunegonda: Every hole and corner was searched for her; The Ponds were dragged, and the Woods underwent a thorough examination. Still no Dame Cunegonda made her appearance. Agnes kept the secret, and I kept the Duenna: The Baroness, therefore, remained in total ignorance respecting the old Woman's fate, but suspected her to have perished by suicide. Thus past away five days, during which I had prepared every thing necessary for my enterprise. On quitting Agnes, I had made it my first business to dispatch a Peasant with a letter to Lucas at Munich, ordering him to take care that a Coach and four should arrive about ten o'clock on the fifth of May at the Village of Rosenwald. He obeyed my instructions punctually: The Equipage arrived at the time appointed. As the period of her Lady's elopement drew nearer, Cunegonda's rage increased. I verily believe that spight and passion would have killed her, had I not luckily discovered her prepossession in favour of Cherry Brandy. With this favourite liquor She was plentifully supplied, and Theodore always remaining to guard her, the Gag was occasionally removed. The liquor seemed to have a wonderful effect in softening the acrimony of her nature; and her confinement not admitting of any other amusement, She got drunk regularly once a day just by way of passing the time.

The fifth of May arrived, a period by me never to be forgotten! Before the Clock struck twelve, I betook myself to the scene of action. Theodore followed me on horseback. I concealed the Carriage in a spacious Cavern of the Hill, on whose brow the Castle was situated: This Cavern was of considerable depth, and among the peasants was known by the name of Lindenberg Hole. The night was calm and beautiful: The Moonbeams fell upon the antient Towers of the Castle, and shed upon their summits a silver light. All was still around me: Nothing was to be heard except the night breeze sighing among the leaves, the distant barking of Village Dogs, or the Owl who had established herself in a nook of the deserted Eastern Turret. I heard her melancholy shriek, and looked upwards. She sat upon the ride of a window, which I recognized to be that of the haunted Room. This brought to my remembrance the story of the Bleeding Nun, and I sighed while I reflected on the influence of superstition and weakness of human reason. Suddenly I heard a faint chorus steal upon the silence of the night.

"What can occasion that noise, Theodore?"

"A Stranger of distinction," replied He, "passed through the Village today in his way to the Castle: He is reported to be the Father of Donna Agnes. Doubtless, the Baron has given an entertainment to celebrate his arrival."

The Castle Bell announced the hour of midnight: This was the usual signal for the family to retire to Bed. Soon after I perceived lights in the Castle moving backwards and forwards in different directions. I conjectured the company to be separating. I could hear the heavy doors grate as they opened with difficulty, and as they closed again the rotten Casements rattled in their frames. The chamber of Agnes was on the other side of the Castle. I trembled lest She should have failed in obtaining the Key of the haunted Room: Through this it was necessary for her to pass in order to reach the narrow Staircase by which the Ghost was supposed to descend into the great

Hall. Agitated by this apprehension, I kept my eyes constantly fixed upon the window, where I hoped to perceive the friendly glare of a Lamp borne by Agnes. I now heard the massy Gates unbarred. By the candle in his hand I distinguished old Conrad, the Porter. He set the Portal doors wide open, and retired. The lights in the Castle gradually disappeared, and at length the whole Building was wrapt in darkness.

While I sat upon a broken ridge of the hill, the stillness of the scene inspired me with melancholy ideas not altogether unpleasing. The Castle which stood full in my sight, formed an object equally awful and picturesque. Its ponderous Walls tinged by the moon with solemn brightness, its old and partly-ruined Towers lifting themselves into the clouds and seeming to frown on the plains around them, its lofty battlements overgrown with ivy, and folding Gates expanding in honour of the Visionary Inhabitant, made me sensible of a sad and reverential horror. Yet did not these sensations occupy me so fully, as to prevent me from witnessing with impatience the slow progress of time. I approached the Castle, and ventured to walk round it. A few rays of light still glimmered in the chamber of Agnes. I observed them with joy. I was still gazing upon them, when I perceived a figure draw near the window, and the Curtain was carefully closed to conceal the Lamp which burned there. Convinced by this observation that Agnes had not abandoned our plan, I returned with a light heart to my former station.

The half-hour struck! The three-quarters struck! My bosom beat high with hope and expectation. At length the wished-for sound was heard. The Bell tolled "One," and the Mansion echoed with the noise loud and solemn. I looked up to the Casement of the haunted Chamber. Scarcely had five minutes elapsed, when the expected light appeared. I was now close to the Tower. The window was not so far from the Ground but that I fancied I perceived a female figure with a Lamp in her hand moving slowly along the Apartment. The light soon faded away, and all was again dark and gloomy.

Occasional gleams of brightness darted from the Staircase windows as the lovely Ghost past by them. I traced the light through the Hall: It reached the Portal, and at length I beheld Agnes pass through the folding gates. She was habited exactly as She had described the Spectre. A chaplet of Beads hung upon her arm; her head was enveloped in a long white veil; Her Nun's dress was stained with blood, and She had taken care to provide herself with a Lamp and dagger. She advanced towards the spot where I stood. I flew to meet her, and clasped her in my arms.

"Agnes!" said I while I pressed her to my bosom,

Agnes! Agnes! Thou art mine!

Agnes! Agnes! I am thine!

In my veins while blood shall roll,

Thou art mine!

I am thine!

Thine my body! Thine my soul!

Terrified and breathless She was unable to speak: She dropt her Lamp and dagger, and sank upon my bosom in silence. I raised her in my arms, and conveyed her to the Carriage. Theodore remained behind in order to release Dame Cunegonda. I also charged him with a letter to the Baroness explaining the whole affair, and entreating her good offices in reconciling Don Gaston to my union with his Daughter. I discovered to her my real name: I proved to her that my birth and expectations justified my pretending to her Niece, and assured her, though it was out of my power to return her love, that I would strive unceasingly to obtain her esteem and friendship.

I stepped into the Carriage, where Agnes was already seated. Theodore closed the door, and the Postillions drove away. At first I was delighted with the rapidity of our progress; But as soon as we were in no danger of pursuit, I called to the Drivers, and bad them moderate their pace. They strove in vain to obey me. The Horses refused to answer the rein, and continued to rush on with astonishing swiftness. The Postillions redoubled their efforts to stop them, but by kicking and plunging the Beasts soon released themselves from this restraint. Uttering a loud shriek, the Drivers were hurled upon the ground. Immediately thick clouds obscured the sky: The winds howled around us, the lightning flashed, and the Thunder roared tremendously. Never did I behold so frightful a Tempest! Terrified by the jar of contending elements, the Horses seemed every moment to increase their speed. Nothing could interrupt their career; They dragged the Carriage through Hedges and Ditches, dashed down the most dangerous precipices, and seemed to vye in swiftness with the rapidity of the winds.

All this while my Companion lay motionless in my arms. Truly alarmed by the magnitude of the danger, I was in vain attempting to recall her to her senses; when a loud crash announced, that a stop was put to our progress in the most disagreeable manner. The Carriage was shattered to pieces. In falling I struck my temple against a flint. The pain of the wound, the violence of the shock, and apprehension for the safety of Agnes combined to overpower me so compleatly, that my senses forsook me, and I lay without animation on the ground.

I probably remained for some time in this situation, since when I opened my eyes, it was broad daylight. Several Peasants were standing round me, and seemed disputing whether my recovery was possible. I spoke German tolerably well. As soon as I could utter an articulate sound, I enquired after Agnes. What was my surprise and distress, when assured by the Peasants, that nobody had been seen answering the description which I gave of her! They told me that in going to their daily labour they had been alarmed by observing the fragments of my Carriage, and by hearing the groans of an Horse, the only one of the four which remained alive: The other Three lay dead by my side. Nobody was near me when they came up, and much time had been lost, before they succeeded in recovering me. Uneasy beyond expression respecting the fate of my Companion, I besought the Peasants to disperse themselves in search of her: I described her dress, and promised immense rewards to whoever brought me any intelligence. As for myself, it was impossible for me to join in the pursuit: I had broken two of my ribs in the fall: My arm being dislocated hung useless by my side; and my left leg was shattered so terribly, that I never expected to recover its use.

The Peasants complied with my request: All left me except Four, who made a litter of boughs and prepared to convey me to the neighbouring Town. I enquired its name. It proved to be Ratisbon, and I could scarcely persuade myself that I had travelled to such a distance in a single night. I told the Countrymen that at one o'clock that morning I had past through the Village of Rosenwald. They shook their heads wistfully, and made signs to each other that I must certainly be delirious. I was conveyed to a decent Inn and immediately put to bed. A Physician was sent for, who set my arm with success. He then examined my other hurts, and told me that I need be under no apprehension of the consequences of any of them; But ordered me to keep myself quiet, and be prepared for a tedious and painful cure. I answered him that if He hoped to keep me quiet, He must first endeavour to procure me some news of a Lady who had quitted Rosenwald in my company the night before, and had been with me at the moment when the Coach broke down. He smiled, and only replied by advising me to make myself easy, for that all proper care should be taken of me. As He quitted me, the Hostess met him at the door of the room.

"The Gentleman is not quite in his right senses;" I heard him say to her in a low voice; "'Tis the natural consequence of his fall, but that will soon be over."

One after another the Peasants returned to the Inn, and informed me that no traces had been discovered of my unfortunate Mistress.

Uneasiness now became despair. I entreated them to renew their search in the most urgent terms, doubling the promises which I had already made them. My wild and frantic manner confirmed the bye-standers in the idea of my being delirious. No signs of the Lady having appeared, they believed her to be a creature fabricated by my over-heated brain, and paid no attention to my entreaties. However, the Hostess assured me that a fresh enquiry should be made, but I found afterwards that her promise was only given to quiet me. No further steps were taken in the business.

Though my Baggage was left at Munich under the care of my French Servant, having prepared myself for a long journey, my purse was amply furnished: Besides my equipage proved me to be of distinction, and in consequence all possible attention was paid me at the Inn. The day passed away: Still no news arrived of Agnes. The anxiety of fear now gave place to despondency. I ceased to rave about her and was plunged in the depth of melancholy reflections. Perceiving me to be silent and tranquil, my Attendants believed my delirium to have abated, and that my malady had taken a favourable turn. According to the Physician's order I swallowed a composing medicine; and as soon as the night shut in, my attendants withdrew and left me to repose.

That repose I wooed in vain. The agitation of my bosom chased away sleep. Restless in my mind, in spite of the fatigue of my body, I continued to toss about from side to side, till the Clock in a neighbouring Steeple struck "One." As I listened to the mournful hollow sound, and heard it die away in the wind, I felt a sudden chillness spread itself over my body. I shuddered without knowing wherefore; Cold dews poured down my forehead, and my hair stood bristling with alarm. Suddenly I heard slow and heavy steps ascending the staircase. By an involuntary movement I started up in my bed, and drew back the curtain. A single rush-light which glimmered upon the hearth shed a faint gleam through the apartment, which was hung with tapestry. The door was thrown open with violence. A figure entered, and drew near my Bed with solemn measured steps. With trembling apprehension I examined this midnight Visitor. God Almighty! It was the Bleeding Nun! It was my lost Companion! Her face was still veiled, but She no longer held her Lamp and dagger. She lifted up her veil slowly. What a sight presented itself to my startled eyes! I beheld before me an animated Corse. Her countenance was long and haggard; Her cheeks and lips were bloodless; The paleness of death was spread over her features, and her eyeballs fixed stedfastly upon me were lustreless and hollow.

I gazed upon the Spectre with horror too great to be described. My blood was frozen in my veins. I would have called for aid, but the sound expired ere it could pass my lips. My nerves were bound up in impotence, and I remained in the same attitude inanimate as a Statue.

The visionary Nun looked upon me for some minutes in silence: There was something petrifying in her regard. At length in a low sepulchral voice She pronounced the following words:

'Raymond! Raymond! Thou art mine!

Raymond! Raymond! I am thine!

In thy veins while blood shall roll,

I am thine!

Thou art mine!

Mine thy body! Mine thy soul! — —'

Breathless with fear, I listened while She repeated my own expressions. The Apparition seated herself opposite to me at the foot of the Bed, and was silent. Her eyes were fixed earnestly upon mine: They seemed endowed with the property of the Rattlesnake's, for I strove in vain to look off her. My eyes were fascinated, and I had not the power of withdrawing them from the Spectre's.

In this attitude She remained for a whole long hour without speaking or moving; nor was I able to do either. At length the Clock struck two. The Apparition rose from her seat, and approached the side of the bed. She grasped with her icy fingers my hand which hung lifeless upon the Coverture, and pressing her cold lips to mine, again repeated,

'Raymond! Raymond! Thou art mine!

Raymond! Raymond! I am thine! &c. — '

She then dropped my hand, quitted the chamber with slow steps, and the Door closed after her. Till that moment the faculties of my body had been all suspended; Those of my mind had alone been waking. The charm now ceased to operate: The blood which had been frozen in my veins rushed back to my heart with violence: I uttered a deep groan, and sank lifeless upon my pillow.

The adjoining room was only separated from mine by a thin partition: It was occupied by the Host and his Wife: The Former was rouzed by my groan, and immediately hastened to my chamber: The Hostess soon followed him. With some difficulty they succeeded in restoring me to my senses, and immediately sent for the Physician, who arrived in all diligence. He declared my fever to be very much increased, and that if I continued to suffer such violent agitation, He would not take upon him to ensure my life. Some medicines which He gave me in some degree tranquillized my spirits. I fell into a sort of slumber towards daybreak; But fearful dreams prevented me from deriving any benefit from my repose. Agnes and the Bleeding Nun presented themselves by turns to my fancy, and combined to harass and torment me. I awoke fatigued and unrefreshed. My fever seemed rather augmented than diminished; The agitation of my mind impeded my fractured bones from knitting: I had frequent fainting fits, and during the whole day the Physician judged it expedient not to quit me for two hours together.

The singularity of my adventure made me determine to conceal it from every one, since I could not expect that a circumstance so strange should gain credit. I was very uneasy about Agnes. I knew not what She would think at not finding me at the rendezvous, and dreaded her entertaining suspicions of my fidelity. However, I depended upon Theodore's discretion, and trusted that my letter to the Baroness would convince her of the rectitude of my intentions. These considerations somewhat lightened my inquietude upon her account: But the impression left upon my mind by my nocturnal Visitor grew stronger with every succeeding moment. The night drew near; I dreaded its arrival. Yet I strove to persuade myself that the Ghost would appear no more, and at all events I desired that a Servant might sit up in my chamber.

The fatigue of my body from not having slept on the former night, co-operating with the strong opiates administered to me in profusion, at length procured me that repose of which I was so much in need. I sank into a profound and tranquil slumber, and had already slept for some hours, when the neighbouring Clock rouzed me by striking "One". Its sound brought with it to my memory all the horrors of the night before. The same cold shivering seized me. I started up in my bed, and perceived the Servant fast asleep in an armed-Chair near me. I called him by his name: He made no answer. I shook him forcibly by the arm, and strove in vain to wake him. He was perfectly insensible to my efforts. I now heard the heavy steps ascending the staircase; The Door was thrown open, and again the Bleeding Nun stood before me. Once more my limbs were chained in second infancy. Once more I heard those fatal words repeated,

'Raymond! Raymond! Thou art mine!

Raymond! Raymond! I am thine! — —'

The scene which had shocked me so sensibly on the former night, was again presented. The Spectre again pressed her lips to mine, again touched me with her rotting fingers, and as on her first appearance, quitted the chamber as soon as the Clock told "Two."

Even night was this repeated. Far from growing accustomed to the Ghost, every succeeding visit inspired me with greater horror. Her idea pursued me continually, and I became the prey of habitual melancholy. The constant agitation of my mind naturally retarded the re-establishment of my health. Several months elapsed before I was able to quit my bed; and when at length I was moved to a Sopha, I was so faint, spiritless, and emaciated, that I could not cross the room without assistance. The looks of my Attendants sufficiently denoted the little hope, which they entertained of my recovery. The profound sadness, which oppressed me without remission made the Physician consider me to be an Hypochondriac. The cause of my distress I carefully concealed in my own bosom, for I knew that no one could give me relief: The Ghost was not even visible to any eye but mine. I had frequently caused Attendants to sit up in my room: But the moment that the Clock struck "One," irresistible slumber seized them, nor left them till the departure of the Ghost.

You may be surprized that during this time I made no enquiries after your Sister. Theodore, who with difficulty had discovered my abode, had quieted my apprehensions for her safety: At the same time He convinced me that all attempts to release her from captivity must be fruitless till I should be in a condition to return to Spain. The particulars of her adventure which I shall now relate to you, were partly communicated to me by Theodore, and partly by Agnes herself.

On the fatal night when her elopement was to have taken place, accident had not permitted her to quit her chamber at the appointed time. At length She ventured into the haunted room, descended the staircase leading into the Hall, found the Gates open as She expected, and left the Castle unobserved. What was her surprize at not finding me ready to receive her! She examined the Cavern, ranged through every Alley of the neighbouring wood, and passed two full hours in this fruitless enquiry. She could discover no traces either of me or of the Carriage. Alarmed and disappointed, her only resource was to return to the Castle before the Baroness missed her: But here She found herself in a fresh embarrassment. The Bell had already tolled "Two:" The Ghostly hour was past, and the careful Porter had locked the folding gates. After much irresolution She ventured to knock softly. Luckily for her, Conrad was still awake: He heard the noise and rose, murmuring at being called up a second time. No sooner had He opened one of the Doors, and beheld the supposed Apparition waiting there for admittance, than He uttered a loud cry, and sank upon his knees. Agnes profited by his terror. She glided by him, flew to her own apartment, and having thrown off her Spectre's trappings, retired to bed endeavouring in vain to account for my disappearing.

In the mean while Theodore having seen my Carriage drive off with the false Agnes, returned joyfully to the Village. The next morning He released Cunegonda from her confinement, and accompanied her to the Castle. There He found the Baron, his Lady, and Don Gaston, disputing together upon the Porter's relation. All of them agreed in believing the existence of Spectres: But the Latter contended, that for a Ghost to knock for admittance was a proceeding till then unwitnessed, and totally incompatible with the immaterial nature of a Spirit. They were still discussing this subject when the Page appeared with Cunegonda and cleared up the mystery. On hearing his deposition, it was agreed unanimously that the Agnes whom Theodore had seen step into my Carriage must have been the Bleeding Nun, and that the Ghost who had terrified Conrad was no other than Don Gaston's Daughter.

The first surprize which this discovery occasioned being over, the Baroness resolved to make it of use in persuading her

Niece to take the veil. Fearing lest so advantageous an establishment for his Daughter should induce Don Gaston to renounce his resolution, She suppressed my letter, and continued to represent me as a needy unknown Adventurer. A childish vanity had led me to conceal my real name even from my Mistress; I wished to be loved for myself, not for being the Son and Heir of the Marquis de las Cisternas. The consequence was that my rank was known to no one in the Castle except the Baroness, and She took good care to confine the knowledge to her own breast. Don Gaston having approved his Sister's design, Agnes was summoned to appear before them. She was taxed with having meditated an elopement, obliged to make a full confession, and was amazed at the gentleness with which it was received: But what was her affliction, when informed that the failure of her project must be attributed to me! Cunegonda, tutored by the Baroness, told her that when I released her, I had desired her to inform her Lady that our connexion was at an end, that the whole affair was occasioned by a false report, and that it by no means suited my circumstances to marry a Woman without fortune or expectations.

To this account my sudden disappearing gave but too great an air of probability. Theodore, who could have contradicted the story, by Donna Rodolpha's order was kept out of her sight: What proved a still greater confirmation of my being an Impostor, was the arrival of a letter from yourself declaring that you had no sort of acquaintance with Alphonso d'Alvarada. These seeming proofs of my perfidy, aided by the artful insinuations of her Aunt, by Cunegonda's flattery, and her Father's threats and anger, entirely conquered your Sister's repugnance to a Convent. Incensed at my behaviour, and disgusted with the world in general, She consented to receive the veil. She past another Month at the Castle of Lindenberg, during which my non-appearance confirmed her in her resolution, and then accompanied Don Gaston into Spain. Theodore was now set at liberty. He hastened to Munich, where I had promised to let him hear from me; But finding from Lucas that I had never arrived there, He pursued his search with indefatigable perseverance, and at length succeeded in rejoining me at Ratisbon.

So much was I altered, that scarcely could He recollect my features: The distress visible upon his sufficiently testified how lively was the interest which He felt for me. The society of this amiable Boy, whom I had always considered rather as a Companion than a Servant, was now my only comfort. His conversation was gay yet sensible, and his observations shrewd and entertaining: He had picked up much more knowledge than is usual at his Age: But what rendered him most agreeable to me, was his having a delightful voice, and some skill in Music. He had also acquired some taste in poetry, and even ventured sometimes to write verses himself. He occasionally composed little Ballads in Spanish, his compositions were but indifferent, I must confess; yet they were pleasing to me from their novelty, and hearing him sing them to his guitar was the only amusement, which I was capable of receiving. Theodore perceived well enough that something preyed upon my mind; But as I concealed the cause of my grief even from him, Respect would not permit him to pry into my secrets.

One Evening I was lying upon my Sopha, plunged in reflections very far from agreeable: Theodore amused himself by observing from the window a Battle between two Postillions, who were quarrelling in the Inn-yard.

"Ha! Ha!" cried He suddenly; "Yonder is the Great Mogul."

"Who?" said I.

"Only a Man who made me a strange speech at Munich."

"What was the purport of it?"

"Now you put me in mind of it, Segnor, it was a kind of message to you; but truly it was not worth delivering. I believe the Fellow to be mad, for my part. When I came to Munich in search of you, I found him living at "The King of the Romans," and the Host gave me an odd account of him. By his accent He is supposed to be a Foreigner, but of what Country nobody can tell. He seemed to have no acquaintance in the Town, spoke very seldom, and never was seen to smile. He had neither Servants or Baggage; But his Purse seemed well-furnished, and He did much good in the Town. Some supposed him to be an Arabian Astrologer, Others to be a Travelling Mountebank, and many declared that He was Doctor Faustus, whom the Devil had sent back to Germany. The Landlord, however told me, that He had the best reasons to believe him to be the Great Mogul incognito."

"But the strange speech, Theodore."

"True, I had almost forgotten the speech: Indeed for that matter, it would not have been a great loss if I had forgotten it altogether. You are to know, Segnor, that while I was enquiring about you of the Landlord, this Stranger passed by. He stopped, and looked at me earnestly. "Youth!" said He in a solemn voice,

"He whom you seek, has found that which He would fain lose. My hand alone can dry up the blood: Bid your Master wish for me when the Clock strikes, "One.""

"How?" cried I, starting from my Sopha. (The words which Theodore had repeated, seemed to imply the Stranger's knowledge of my secret) "Fly to him, my Boy! Entreat him to grant me one moment's conversation!"

Theodore was surprised at the vivacity of my manner: However, He asked no questions, but hastened to obey me. I waited his return impatiently. But a short space of time had elapsed when He again appeared and ushered the expected Guest into my chamber. He was a Man of majestic presence: His countenance was strongly marked, and his eyes were large, black, and sparkling: Yet there was a something in his look which, the moment that I saw him, inspired me with a secret awe, not to say horror. He was drest plainly, his hair was unpowdered, and a band of black velvet which encircled his forehead spread over his features an additional gloom. His countenance wore the marks of profound melancholy; his step was slow, and his manner grave, stately, and solemn.

He saluted me with politeness; and having replied to the usual compliments of introduction, He motioned to Theodore to quit the chamber. The Page instantly withdrew.

"I know your business," said He, without giving me time to speak.

"I have the power of releasing you from your nightly Visitor; But this cannot be done before Sunday. On the hour when the Sabbath Morning breaks, Spirits of darkness have least influence over Mortals. After Saturday the Nun shall visit you no more."

"May I not enquire," said I, "by what means you are in possession of a secret which I have carefully concealed from the knowledge of everyone?"

"How can I be ignorant of your distress, when their cause at this moment stands beside you?"

I started. The Stranger continued.

"Though to you only visible for one hour in the twenty-four, neither day or night does She ever quit you; Nor will She ever quit you till you have granted her request."

473

"And what is that request?"

"That She must herself explain: It lies not in my knowledge. Wait with patience for the night of Saturday: All shall be then cleared up."

I dared not press him further. He soon after changed the conversation and talked of various matters. He named People who had ceased to exist for many Centuries, and yet with whom He appeared to have been personally acquainted. I could not mention a Country however distant which He had not visited, nor could I sufficiently admire the extent and variety of his information. I remarked to him that having travelled, seen, and known so much, must have given him infinite pleasure. He shook his head mournfully.

"No one," He replied, "is adequate to comprehending the misery of my lot! Fate obliges me to be constantly in movement: I am not permitted to pass more than a fortnight in the same place. I have no Friend in the world, and from the restlessness of my destiny I never can acquire one. Fain would I lay down my miserable life, for I envy those who enjoy the quiet of the Grave: But Death eludes me, and flies from my embrace. In vain do I throw myself in the way of danger. I plunge into the Ocean; The Waves throw me back with abhorrence upon the shore: I rush into fire; The flames recoil at my approach: I oppose myself to the fury of Banditti; Their swords become blunted, and break against my breast: The hungry Tiger shudders at my approach, and the Alligator flies from a Monster more horrible than itself. God has set his seal upon me, and all his Creatures respect this fatal mark!"

He put his hand to the velvet, which was bound round his forehead. There was in his eyes an expression of fury, despair, and malevolence, that struck horror to my very soul. An involuntary convulsion made me shudder. The Stranger perceived it.

"Such is the curse imposed on me," he continued: "I am doomed to inspire all who look on me with terror and detestation. You already feel the influence of the charm, and with every succeeding moment will feel it more. I will not add to your sufferings by my presence. Farewell till Saturday. As soon as the Clock strikes twelve, expect me at your chamber door."

Having said this He departed, leaving me in astonishment at the mysterious turn of his manner and conversation.

His assurances that I should soon be relieved from the Apparition's visits produced a good effect upon my constitution. Theodore, whom I rather treated as an adopted Child than a Domestic, was surprized at his return to observe the amendment in my looks. He congratulated me on this symptom of returning health, and declared himself delighted at my having received so much benefit from my conference with the Great Mogul. Upon enquiry I found that the Stranger had already past eight days in Ratisbon: According to his own account, therefore, He was only to remain there six days longer. Saturday was still at the distance of Three. Oh! with what impatience did I expect its arrival! In the interim, the Bleeding Nun continued her nocturnal visits; But hoping soon to be released from them altogether, the effects which they produced on me became less violent than before.

The wished-for night arrived. To avoid creating suspicion I retired to bed at my usual hour: But as soon as my Attendants had left me, I dressed myself again, and prepared for the Stranger's reception. He entered my room upon the turn of midnight. A small Chest was in his hand, which He placed near the Stove. He saluted me without speaking; I returned the compliment, observing an equal silence. He then opened his Chest. The first thing which He produced was a small wooden Crucifix: He sank upon his knees, gazed upon it mournfully, and cast his eyes towards heaven. He seemed to be praying devoutly. At length He bowed his head respectfully, kissed the Crucifix thrice, and quitted his kneeling posture. He next drew from the Chest a covered Goblet: With the liquor which it contained, and which appeared to be blood, He sprinkled the floor, and then dipping in it one end of the Crucifix, He described a circle in the middle of the room. Round about this He placed various reliques, sculls, thigh-bones &c; I observed, that He disposed them all in the forms of Crosses. Lastly He took out a large Bible, and beckoned me to follow him into the Circle. I obeyed.

"Be cautious not to utter a syllable!" whispered the Stranger; "Step not out of the circle, and as you love yourself, dare not to look upon my face!"

Holding the Crucifix in one hand, the Bible in the other, He seemed to read with profound attention. The Clock struck "One"! As usual I heard the Spectre's steps upon the Staircase: But I was not seized with the accustomed shivering. I waited her approach with confidence. She entered the room, drew near the Circle, and stopped. The Stranger muttered some words, to me unintelligible. Then raising his head from the Book, and

475

extending the Crucifix towards the Ghost, He pronounced in a voice distinct and solemn,

"Beatrice! Beatrice! Beatrice!"

"What wouldst Thou?" replied the Apparition in a hollow faltering tone.

"What disturbs thy sleep? Why dost thou afflict and torture this Youth? How can rest be restored to thy unquiet Spirit?"

"I dare not tell! — I must not tell! — Fain would I repose in my Grave, but stern commands force me to prolong my punishment!"

"Knowest Thou this blood? Knowest Thou in whose veins it flowed?

Beatrice! Beatrice! In his name I charge thee to answer me!"

"I dare not disobey my taskers."

"Darest Thou disobey Me?"

He spoke in a commanding tone, and drew the sable band from his forehead. In spite of his injunctions to the contrary, Curiosity would not suffer me to keep my eyes off his face: I raised them, and beheld a burning Cross impressed upon his brow. For the horror with which this object inspired me I cannot account, but I never felt its equal! My senses left me for some moments; A mysterious dread overcame my courage, and had not the Exorciser caught my hand, I should have fallen out of the Circle.

When I recovered myself, I perceived that the burning Cross had produced an effect no less violent upon the Spectre. Her countenance expressed reverence, and horror, and her visionary limbs were shaken by fear.

"Yes!" She said at length; "I tremble at that mark! — respect it! — I obey you! Know then, that my bones lie still unburied: They rot in the obscurity of Lindenberg Hole. None but this Youth has the right of consigning them to the Grave. His own lips have made over to me his body and his soul: Never will I give back his promise, never shall He know a night devoid of terror, unless He engages to collect my mouldering bones, and deposit them in the family vault of his Andalusian Castle. Then let thirty Masses be said for the repose of my Spirit, and I trouble this world no more. Now let me depart! Those flames are scorching!"

He let the hand drop slowly which held the Crucifix, and which till then He had pointed towards her. The apparition bowed her head, and her form melted into air. The Exorciser led me out of the Circle. He replaced the Bible &c. in the Chest, and then addressed himself to me, who stood near him speechless from astonishment.

"Don Raymond, you have heard the conditions on which repose is promised you. Be it your business to fulfil them to the letter. For me nothing more remains than to clear up the darkness still spread over the Spectre's History, and inform you that when living, Beatrice bore the name of las Cisternas. She was the great Aunt of your Grandfather: In quality of your relation, her ashes demand respect from you, though the enormity of her crimes must excite your abhorrence. The nature of those crimes no one is more capable of explaining to you than myself: I was personally acquainted with the holy Man who proscribed her nocturnal riots in the Castle of Lindenberg, and I hold this narrative from his own lips.

"Beatrice de las Cisternas took the veil at an early age, not by her own choice, but at the express command of her Parents. She was then too young to regret the pleasures of which her profession deprived her: But no sooner did her warm and voluptuous character begin to be developed than She abandoned herself freely to the impulse of her passions, and seized the first opportunity to procure their gratification. This opportunity was at length presented, after many obstacles which only added new force to her desires. She contrived to elope from the Convent, and fled to Germany with the Baron Lindenberg. She lived at his Castle several months as his avowed Concubine: All Bavaria was scandalized by her impudent and abandoned conduct. Her feasts vied in luxury with Cleopatra's, and Lindenberg became the Theatre of the most unbridled debauchery. Not satisfied with displaying the incontinence of a Prostitute, She professed herself an Atheist: She took every opportunity to scoff at her monastic vows, and loaded with ridicule the most sacred ceremonies of Religion.

"Possessed of a character so depraved, She did not long confine her affections to one object. Soon after her arrival at the Castle, the Baron's younger Brother attracted her notice by his strong-marked features, gigantic Stature, and Herculean limbs. She was not of an humour to keep her inclinations long unknown; But She found in Otto von Lindenberg her equal in depravity. He returned her passion just sufficiently to increase it; and when He had worked it up to the desired pitch, He fixed the price of his love at his Brother's murder. The Wretch consented to this horrible agreement. A night was pitched upon for perpetrating the deed. Otto, who resided on a small Estate a few miles distant from the Castle, promised that at One in the morning He would be waiting for her at Lindenberg Hole; that He would bring with him a party of chosen Friends, by whose aid He doubted not being able to make himself Master of the Castle; and that his next step should be the uniting her hand to his. It was this last promise, which overruled every scruple of Beatrice, since in spite of his affection for her, the Baron had declared positively that He never would make her his Wife.

"The fatal night arrived. The Baron slept in the arms of his perfidious Mistress, when the Castle-Bell struck "One." Immediately Beatrice drew a dagger from underneath the pillow, and plunged it in her Paramour's heart. The Baron uttered a single dreadful groan, and expired. The Murderess quitted her bed hastily, took a Lamp in one hand, in the other the bloody dagger, and bent her course towards the cavern. The Porter dared not to refuse opening the Gates to one more dreaded in the Castle than its Master. Beatrice reached Lindenberg Hole unopposed, where according to promise She found Otto waiting for her. He received and listened to her narrative with transport: But ere She had time to ask why He came unaccompanied, He convinced her that He wished for no witnesses to their interview. Anxious to conceal his share in the murder, and to free himself from a Woman, whose violent and atrocious character made him tremble with reason for his own safety, He had resolved on the destruction of his wretched Agent. Rushing upon her suddenly, He wrested the dagger from her hand: He plunged it still reeking with his Brother's blood in her bosom, and put an end to her existence by repeated blows.

"Otto now succeeded to the Barony of Lindenberg. The murder was attributed solely to the fugitive Nun, and no one suspected him to have persuaded her to the action. But though his crime was unpunished by Man, God's justice permitted him not to enjoy in peace his blood-stained honours. Her bones lying still unburied in the Cave, the restless soul of Beatrice continued to inhabit the Castle. Drest in her religious habit in memory of her vows broken to heaven, furnished with the dagger which had drank the blood of her Paramour, and holding the Lamp which had guided her flying steps, every night did She stand before the Bed of Otto. The most dreadful confusion reigned through the Castle; The vaulted chambers resounded with shrieks and groans; And the Spectre, as She ranged along the antique Galleries, uttered an incoherent mixture of prayers and blasphemies. Otto was unable to withstand the shock which He felt at this fearful Vision: Its horror increased with every succeeding appearance: His alarm at length became so insupportable that his heart burst, and one morning He was found in his bed totally deprived of warmth and animation. His death did not put an end to the nocturnal riots. The bones of Beatrice continued to lie unburied, and her Ghost continued to haunt the Castle.

"The domains of Lindenberg now fell to a distant Relation. But terrified by the accounts given him of the Bleeding Nun (So was the Spectre called by the multitude), the new Baron called to his assistance a celebrated Exorciser. This holy Man succeeded in obliging her to temporary repose; But though She discovered to him her history, He was not permitted to reveal it to others, or cause her skeleton to be removed to hallowed ground. That Office was reserved for you, and till your coming, her Ghost was doomed to wander about the Castle and lament the crime which She had there committed. However, the Exorciser obliged her to silence during his lifetime. So long as He existed, the haunted chamber was shut up, and the Spectre was invisible. At his death which happened in five years after, She again appeared, but only once on every fifth year, on the same day and at the same hour when She plunged her Knife in the heart of her sleeping Lover: She then visited the Cavern which held her mouldering skeleton, returned to the Castle as soon as the Clock struck "Two," and was seen no more till the next five years had elapsed.

"She was doomed to suffer during the space of a Century. That period is past. Nothing now remains but to consign to the Grave the ashes of Beatrice. I have been the means of releasing you from your visionary Tormentor; and amidst all the sorrows which oppress me, to think that I have been of use to you, is some consolation. Youth, farewell! May the Ghost of your Relation enjoy that rest in the Tomb, which the Almighty's vengeance has denied to me for ever!"

Here the Stranger prepared to quit the apartment.

"Stay yet one moment!" said I; "You have satisfied my curiosity with regard to the Spectre, but you leave me in prey to yet greater respecting yourself. Deign to inform me, to whom I am under such real obligations. You mention circumstances long past, and persons long dead: You were personally acquainted with the Exorciser, who by your own account has been deceased near a Century. How am I to account for this? What means that burning Cross upon your forehead, and why did the sight of it strike such horror to my soul?"

On these points He for some time refused to satisfy me. At length overcome by my entreaties, He consented to clear up the whole, on condition that I would defer his explanation till the next day. With this request I was obliged to comply, and He left me. In the Morning my first care was to enquire after the mysterious Stranger. Conceive my disappointment when informed that He had already quitted Ratisbon. I dispatched messengers in pursuit of him but in vain. No traces of the Fugitive were discovered. Since that moment I never have heard any more of him, and 'tis most probable that I never shall."

(Lorenzo here interrupted his Friend's narrative.

"How?" said He; "You have never discovered who He was, or even formed a guess?"

"Pardon me," replied the Marquis; "When I related this adventure to my Uncle, the Cardinal-Duke, He told me that He had no doubt of this singular Man's being the celebrated Character known universally by the name of "the wandering Jew." His not being permitted to pass more than fourteen days on the same spot, the burning Cross impressed upon his forehead, the effect which it produced upon the Beholders, and many other circumstances give this supposition the colour of truth. The Cardinal is fully persuaded of it; and for my own part I am inclined to adopt the only solution which offers itself to this riddle. I return to the narrative from which I have digressed.")

From this period I recovered my health so rapidly as to astonish my Physicians. The Bleeding Nun appeared no more, and I was soon able to set out for Lindenberg. The Baron received me with open arms. I confided to him the sequel of my adventure; and He was not a little pleased to find that his Mansion would be no longer troubled with the Phantom's quiennial visits. I was sorry to perceive that absence had not weakened Donna Rodolpha's imprudent passion. In a private conversation which I had with her during my short stay at the Castle, She renewed her attempts to persuade me to return her affection. Regarding her as the primary cause of all my sufferings, I entertained for her no other sentiment than disgust. The Skeleton of Beatrice was found in the place which She had mentioned. This being all that I sought at Lindenberg, I hastened to quit the Baron's domains, equally anxious to perform the obsequies of the murdered Nun, and escape the importunity of a Woman whom I detested. I departed, followed by Donna Rodolpha's menaces that my contempt should not be long unpunished.

I now bent my course towards Spain with all diligence. Lucas with my Baggage had joined me during my abode at Lindenberg. I arrived in my native Country without any accident, and immediately proceeded to my Father's Castle in Andalusia. The remains of Beatrice were deposited in the family vault, all due ceremonies performed, and the number of Masses said which She had required. Nothing now hindered me from employing all my endeavours to discover the retreat of Agnes. The Baroness had assured me that her Niece had already taken the veil: This intelligence I suspected to have been forged by jealousy, and hoped to find my Mistress still at liberty to accept my hand. I enquired after her family; I found that before her Daughter could reach Madrid, Donna Inesilla was no more: You, my dear Lorenzo, were said to be abroad, but where I could not discover: Your Father was in a distant Province on a visit to the Duke de Medina, and as to Agnes, no one could or would inform me what was become of her. Theodore, according to promise, had returned to Strasbourg, where He found his Grandfather dead, and Marguerite in possession of his fortune. All her persuasions to remain with her were fruitless: He quitted her a second time, and followed me to Madrid. He exerted himself to the utmost in forwarding my search: But our united endeavours were unattended by success. The retreat which concealed Agnes remained an impenetrable mystery, and I began to abandon all hopes of recovering her.

About eight months ago I was returning to my Hotel in a melancholy humour, having past the evening at the Play-House. The Night was dark, and I was unaccompanied. Plunged in reflections which were far from being agreeable, I perceived not that three Men had followed me from the Theatre; till, on turning into an unfrequented Street, they all attacked me at the same time with the utmost fury. I sprang back a few paces, drew my sword, and threw my cloak over my left arm. The obscurity of the night was in my favour. For the most part the blows of the Assassins, being aimed at random, failed to touch me. I at length was fortunate enough to lay one of my Adversaries at my feet; But before this I had already received so many wounds, and was so warmly pressed, that my destruction would have been inevitable, had not the clashing of swords called a Cavalier to my assistance. He ran towards me with his sword drawn: Several Domestics followed him with torches. His arrival made the combat equal: Yet would not the Bravoes abandon their design till the Servants were on the point of joining us. They then fled away, and we lost them in the obscurity.

The Stranger now addressed himself to me with politeness, and enquired whether I was wounded. Faint with the loss of blood, I could scarcely thank him for his seasonable aid, and entreat him to let some of his Servants convey me to the Hotel de las Cisternas. I no sooner mentioned the name than He profest himself an acquaintance of my Father's, and declared that He would not permit my being transported to such a distance before my wounds had been examined. He added that his House was hard by, and begged me to accompany him thither. His manner was so earnest, that I could not reject his offer, and leaning upon his arm, a few minutes brought me to the Porch of a magnificent Hotel.

On entering the House, an old grey-headed Domestic came to welcome my Conductor: He enquired when the Duke, his Master, meant to quit the Country, and was answered that He would remain there yet some months. My Deliverer then desired the family Surgeon to be summoned without delay. His orders were obeyed. I was seated upon a Sopha in a noble apartment; and my wounds being examined, they were declared to be very slight. The Surgeon, however, advised me not to expose myself to the night air; and the Stranger pressed me so earnestly to take a bed in his House, that I consented to remain where I was for the present.

Being now left alone with my Deliverer, I took the opportunity of thanking him in more express terms, than I had done hitherto: But He begged me to be silent upon the subject.

"I esteem myself happy," said He, "in having had it in my power to render you this little service; and I shall think myself eternally obliged to my Daughter for detaining me so late at the Convent of St. Clare. The high esteem in which I have ever held the Marquis de las Cisternas, though accident has not permitted our being so intimate as I could wish, makes me rejoice in the opportunity of making his Son's acquaintance. I am certain that my Brother in whose House you now are, will lament his not being at Madrid to receive you himself: But in the Duke's absence I am Master of the family, and may assure you in his name, that every thing in the Hotel de Medina is perfectly at your disposal."

Conceive my surprize, Lorenzo, at discovering in the person of my Preserver Don Gaston de Medina: It was only to be equalled by my secret satisfaction at the assurance that Agnes inhabited the Convent of St. Clare. This latter sensation was not a little weakened, when in answer to my seemingly indifferent questions He told me that his Daughter had really taken the veil. I suffered not my grief at this circumstance to take root in my mind: I flattered myself with the idea that my Uncle's credit at the Court of Rome would remove this obstacle, and that without difficulty I should obtain for my Mistress a dispensation from her vows. Buoyed up with this hope I calmed the uneasiness of my bosom; and I redoubled my endeavours to appear grateful for the attention and pleased with the society of Don Gaston.

A Domestic now entered the room, and informed me that the Bravo whom I had wounded discovered some signs of life. I desired that He might be carried to my Father's Hotel, and that as soon as He recovered his voice, I would examine him respecting his reasons for attempting my life. I was answered that He was already able to speak, though with difficulty: Don Gaston's curiosity made him press me to interrogate the Assassin in his presence, but this curiosity I was by no means inclined to gratify. One reason was, that doubting from whence the blow came, I was unwilling to place before Don Gaston's eyes the guilt of a Sister: Another was, that I feared to be recognized for Alphonso d'Alvarada, and precautions taken in consequence to keep me from the sight of Agnes. To avow my passion for his Daughter, and endeavour to make him enter into my schemes, what I knew of Don Gaston's character convinced me would be an imprudent step: and considering it to be essential that He should know me for no other than the Condé de las Cisternas, I was determined not to let him hear the Bravo's confession. I insinuated to him, that as I suspected a Lady to be concerned in the Business, whose name might accidentally escape from the Assassin, it was necessary for me to examine the Man in private. Don Gaston's delicacy would not permit his urging the point any longer, and in consequence the Bravo was conveyed to my Hotel.

The next Morning I took leave of my Host, who was to return to the Duke on the same day. My wounds had been so trifling that, except being obliged to wear my arm in a sling for a short time, I felt no inconvenience from the night's adventure. The Surgeon who examined the Bravo's wound declared it to be mortal: He had just time to confess that He had been instigated to murder me by the revengeful Donna Rodolpha, and expired in a few minutes after.

All my thoughts were now bent upon getting to the speech of my lovely Nun. Theodore set himself to work, and for this time with better success. He attacked the Gardener of St. Clare so forcibly with bribes and promises that the Old Man was entirely gained over to my interests; and it was settled that I should be introduced into the Convent in the character of his Assistant. The plan was put into execution without delay. Disguised in a common habit, and a black patch covering one of my eyes, I was presented to the Lady Prioress, who condescended to approve of the Gardener's choice. I immediately entered upon my employment. Botany having been a favourite study with me, I was by no means at a loss in my new station. For some days I continued to work in the Convent Garden without meeting the Object of my disguise: On the fourth Morning I was more successful. I heard the voice of Agnes, and was speeding towards the sound, when the sight of the Domina stopped me. I drew back with caution, and concealed myself behind a thick clump of Trees.

The Prioress advanced and seated herself with Agnes on a Bench at no great distance. I heard her in an angry tone blame her Companion's continual melancholy: She told her that to weep the loss of any Lover in her situation was a crime; But that to weep the loss of a faithless one was folly and absurdity in the extreme. Agnes replied in so low a voice that I could not distinguish her words, but I perceived that She used terms of gentleness and submission. The conversation was interrupted by the arrival of a young Pensioner who informed the Domina that She was waited for in the Parlour. The old Lady rose, kissed the cheek of Agnes, and retired. The newcomer remained. Agnes spoke much to her in praise of somebody whom I could not make out, but her Auditor seemed highly delighted, and interested by the conversation. The Nun showed her several letters; the Other perused them with evident pleasure, obtained permission to copy them, and withdrew for that purpose to my great satisfaction.

No sooner was She out of sight, than I quitted my concealment. Fearing to alarm my lovely Mistress, I drew near her gently, intending to discover myself by degrees. But who for a moment can deceive the eyes of love? She raised her head at my approach, and recognised me in spite of my disguise at a single glance. She rose hastily from her seat with an exclamation of surprize, and attempted to retire; But I followed her, detained her, and entreated to be heard. Persuaded of my falsehood She refused to listen to me, and ordered me positively to quit the Garden. It was now my turn to refuse. I protested that however dangerous might be the consequences, I would not leave her till

She had heard my justification. I assured her that She had been deceived by the artifices of her Relations; that I could convince her beyond the power of doubt that my passion had been pure and disinterested; and I asked her what should induce me to seek her in the Convent, were I influenced by the selfish motives which my Enemies had ascribed to me.

My prayers, my arguments, and vows not to quit her, till She had promised to listen to me, united to her fears lest the Nuns should see me with her, to her natural curiosity, and to the affection which She still felt for me in spite of my supposed desertion, at length prevailed. She told me that to grant my request at that moment was impossible; But She engaged to be in the same spot at eleven that night, and to converse with me for the last time. Having obtained this promise I released her hand, and She fled back with rapidity towards the Convent.

I communicated my success to my Ally, the old Gardener: He pointed out an hiding place where I might shelter myself till night without fear of a discovery. Thither I betook myself at the hour when I ought to have retired with my supposed Master, and waited impatiently for the appointed time. The chillness of the night was in my favour, since it kept the other Nuns confined to their Cells. Agnes alone was insensible of the inclemency of the Air, and before eleven joined me at the spot which had witnessed our former interview. Secure from interruption, I related to her the true cause of my disappearing on the fatal fifth of May. She was evidently much affected by my narrative: When it was concluded, She confessed the injustice of her suspicions, and blamed herself for having taken the veil through despair at my ingratitude.

"But now it is too late to repine!" She added; "The die is thrown: I have pronounced my vows, and dedicated myself to the service of heaven. I am sensible, how ill I am calculated for a Convent. My disgust at a monastic life increases daily: Ennui and discontent are my constant Companions; and I will not conceal from you that the passion which I formerly felt for one so near being my Husband is not yet extinguished in my bosom. But we must part! Insuperable Barriers divide us from each other, and on this side the Grave we must never meet again!"

I now exerted myself to prove that our union was not so impossible as She seemed to think it. I vaunted to her the Cardinal-Duke of Lerma's influence at the Court of Rome: I assured her that I should easily obtain a dispensation from her vows; and I doubted not but Don Gaston would coincide with my views, when informed of my real name and long attachment. Agnes replied that since I encouraged such an hope, I could know but little of her Father. Liberal and kind in every other respect, Superstition formed the only stain upon his character. Upon this head He was inflexible; He sacrificed his dearest interests to his scruples, and would consider it an insult to suppose him capable of authorising his daughter to break her vows to heaven.

"But suppose," said I interrupting her; "Suppose that He should disapprove of our union; Let him remain ignorant of my proceedings, till I have rescued you from the prison in which you are now confined. Once my Wife, you are free from his authority: I need from him no pecuniary assistance; and when He sees his resentment to be unavailing, He will doubtless restore you to his favour. But let the worst happen; Should Don Gaston be irreconcileable, my Relations will vie with each other in making you forget his loss: and you will find in my Father a substitute for the Parent of whom I shall deprive you."

"Don Raymond," replied Agnes in a firm and resolute voice, "I love my Father: He has treated me harshly in this one instance; but I have received from him in every other so many proofs of love that his affection is become necessary to my existence. Were I to quit the Convent, He never would forgive me; nor can I think that on his deathbed He would leave me his curse, without shuddering at the very idea. Besides, I am conscious myself, that my vows are binding: Wilfully did I contract my engagement with heaven; I cannot break it without a crime. Then banish from your mind the idea of our being ever united. I am devoted to religion; and however I may grieve at our separation, I would oppose obstacles myself, to what I feel would render me guilty."

I strove to overrule these ill-grounded scruples: We were still disputing upon the subject, when the Convent Bell summoned the Nuns to Matins. Agnes was obliged to attend them; But She left me not till I had compelled her to promise that on the following night She would be at the same place at the same hour. These meetings continued for several Weeks uninterrupted; and 'tis now, Lorenzo, that I must implore your indulgence. Reflect upon our situation, our youth, our long attachment: Weigh all the circumstances which attended our assignations, and you will confess the temptation to have been irresistible; you will even pardon me when I acknowledge, that in an unguarded moment, the honour of Agnes was sacrificed to my passion."

(Lorenzo's eyes sparkled with fury: A deep crimson spread itself over his face. He started from his seat, and attempted to draw his sword. The Marquis was aware of his movement, and caught his hand: He pressed it affectionately.

"My Friend! My Brother! Hear me to the conclusion! Till then restrain your passion, and be at least convinced, that if what I have related is criminal, the blame must fall upon me, and not upon your Sister."

Lorenzo suffered himself to be prevailed upon by Don Raymond's entreaties. He resumed his place, and listened to the rest of the narrative with a gloomy and impatient countenance. The Marquis thus continued.)

"Scarcely was the first burst of passion past when Agnes, recovering herself, started from my arms with horror. She called me infamous Seducer, loaded me with the bitterest reproaches, and beat her bosom in all the wildness of delirium. Ashamed of my imprudence, I with difficulty found words to excuse myself. I endeavoured to console her; I threw myself at her feet, and entreated her forgiveness. She forced her hand from me, which I had taken, and would have prest to my lips.

"Touch me not!" She cried with a violence which terrified me; "Monster of perfidy and ingratitude, how have I been deceived in you! I looked upon you as my Friend, my Protector: I trusted myself in your hands with confidence, and relying upon your honour, thought that mine ran no risque. And 'tis by you, whom I adored, that I am covered with infamy! 'Tis by you that I have been seduced into breaking my vows to God, that I am reduced to a level with the basest of my sex! Shame upon you, Villain, you shall never see me more!"

She started from the Bank on which She was seated. I endeavoured to detain her; But She disengaged herself from me with violence, and took refuge in the Convent.

I retired, filled with confusion and inquietude. The next morning I failed not as usual to appear in the Garden; but Agnes was no where to be seen. At night I waited for her at the place where we generally met; I found no better success. Several days and nights passed away in the same manner. At length I saw my offended Mistress cross the walk on whose borders I was working: She was accompanied by the same young Pensioner, on whose arm She seemed from weakness obliged to support herself. She looked upon me for a moment, but instantly turned her head away. I waited her return; But She passed on to the Convent without paying any attention to me, or the penitent looks with which I implored her forgiveness.

As soon as the Nuns were retired, the old Gardener joined me with a sorrowful air.

"Segnor," said He, "it grieves me to say, that I can be no longer of use to you. The Lady whom you used to meet has just assured me that if I admitted you again into the Garden, She would discover the whole business to the Lady Prioress. She bade me tell you also, that your presence was an insult, and that if you still possess the least respect for her, you will never attempt to see her more. Excuse me then for informing you that I can favour your disguise no longer. Should the Prioress be acquainted with my conduct, She might not be contented with dismissing me her service: Out of revenge She might accuse me of having profaned the Convent, and cause me to be thrown into the Prisons of the Inquisition."

Fruitless were my attempts to conquer his resolution. He denied me all future entrance into the Garden, and Agnes persevered in neither letting me see or hear from her. In about a fortnight after, a violent illness which had seized my Father obliged me to set out for Andalusia. I hastened thither, and as I imagined, found the Marquis at the point of death. Though on its first appearance his complaint was declared mortal, He lingered out several Months; during which my attendance upon him during his malady, and the occupation of settling his affairs after his decease, permitted not my quitting Andalusia. Within these four days I returned to Madrid, and on arriving at my Hotel, I there found this letter waiting for me.

(Here the Marquis unlocked the drawer of a Cabinet: He took out a folded paper, which He presented to his Auditor. Lorenzo opened it, and recognised his Sister's hand. The contents were as follows:

"Into what an abyss of misery have you plunged me! Raymond, you force me to become as criminal as yourself. I had resolved never to see you more; if possible, to forget you; If not, only to remember you with hate. A Being for whom I already feel a Mother's tenderness, solicits me to pardon my Seducer, and apply to his love for the means of preservation. Raymond, your child lives in my bosom. I tremble at the vengeance of the Prioress; I tremble much for myself, yet more for the innocent Creature whose existence depends upon mine. Both of us are lost, should my situation be discovered. Advise me then what steps to take, but seek not to see me. The Gardener, who undertakes to deliver this, is dismissed, and we have nothing to hope from that quarter: The Man engaged in his place is of incorruptible fidelity. The best means of conveying to me your answer, is by concealing it under the great Statue of St. Francis, which stands in the Capuchin Cathedral. Thither I go every Thursday to confession, and shall easily have an opportunity of securing your letter. I hear that you are now absent from Madrid; Need I entreat you to write the very moment of your return? I will not think it. Ah! Raymond! Mine is a cruel situation! Deceived by my nearest Relations, compelled to embrace a profession the duties of which I am ill-calculated to perform, conscious of the sanctity of those duties, and seduced into violating them by One whom I least suspected of perfidy, I am now obliged by circumstances to chuse between death and perjury. Woman's timidity, and maternal affection, permit me not to balance in the choice. I feel all the guilt into which I plunge myself, when I yield to the plan which you before proposed to me. My poor Father's death which has taken place since we met, has removed one obstacle. He sleeps in his grave, and I no longer dread his anger. But from the anger of God, Oh! Raymond! who shall shield me? Who can protect me against my conscience, against myself? I dare not dwell upon these thoughts; They will drive me mad. I have taken my resolution: Procure a dispensation from my vows; I am ready to fly with you. Write to me, my Husband! Tell me, that absence has not abated your love, tell me that you will rescue from death your unborn Child, and its unhappy Mother. I live in all the agonies of terror: Every eye which is fixed upon me seems to read my secret and my shame. And you are the cause of those agonies! Oh! When my heart first loved you, how little did it suspect you of making it feel such pangs!

"AGNES."

Having perused the letter, Lorenzo restored it in silence. The Marquis replaced it in the Cabinet, and then proceeded.)

"Excessive was my joy at reading this intelligence so earnestly-desired, so little expected. My plan was soon arranged. When Don Gaston discovered to me his Daughter's retreat, I entertained no doubt of her readiness to quit the Convent: I had, therefore, entrusted the Cardinal-Duke of Lerma with the whole affair, who immediately busied himself in obtaining the necessary Bull. Fortunately I had afterwards neglected to stop his proceedings. Not long since I received a letter from him, stating that He expected daily to receive the order from the Court of Rome. Upon this I would willingly have relyed: But the Cardinal wrote me word, that I must find some means of conveying Agnes out of the Convent, unknown to the Prioress. He doubted not but this Latter would be much incensed by losing a Person of such high rank from her society, and consider the renunciation of Agnes as an insult to her House. He represented her as a Woman of a violent and revengeful character, capable of proceeding to the greatest extremities. It was therefore to be feared, lest by confining Agnes in the Convent She should frustrate my hopes, and render the Pope's mandate unavailing. Influenced by this consideration, I resolved to carry off my Mistress, and conceal her till the arrival of the expected Bull in the Cardinal-Duke's Estate. He approved of my design, and profest himself ready to give a shelter to the Fugitive. I next caused the new Gardener of St. Clare to be seized privately, and confined in my Hotel. By this means I became Master of the Key to the Garden door, and I had now nothing more to do than prepare Agnes for the elopement. This was done by the letter, which you saw me deliver this Evening. I told her in it, that I should be ready to receive her at twelve tomorrow night, that I had secured the Key of the Garden, and that She might depend upon a speedy release.

You have now, Lorenzo, heard the whole of my long narrative. I have nothing to say in my excuse, save that my intentions towards your Sister have been ever the most honourable: That it has always been, and still is my design to make her my Wife: And that I trust, when you consider these circumstances, our youth, and our attachment, you will not only forgive our momentary lapse from virtue, but will aid me in repairing my faults to Agnes, and securing a lawful title to her person and her heart.

CHAPTER V.

O You! whom Vanity's light bark conveys

On Fame's mad voyage by the wind of praise,

With what a shifting gale your course you ply,

For ever sunk too low, or borne too high!

Who pants for glory finds but short repose,

A breath revives him, and a breath o'er-throws.

POPE.

Here the Marquis concluded his adventures. Lorenzo, before He could determine on his reply, past some moments in reflection. At length He broke silence.

"Raymond," said He taking his hand, "strict honour would oblige me to wash off in your blood the stain thrown upon my family; But the circumstances of your case forbid me to consider you as an Enemy. The temptation was too great to be resisted. 'Tis the superstition of my Relations which has occasioned these misfortunes, and they are more the Offenders than yourself and Agnes. What has past between you cannot be recalled, but may yet be repaired by uniting you to my Sister. You have ever been, you still continue to be, my dearest and indeed my only Friend. I feel for Agnes the truest affection, and there is no one on whom I would bestow her more willingly than on yourself. Pursue then your design. I will accompany you tomorrow night, and conduct her myself to the House of the Cardinal. My presence will be a sanction for her conduct, and prevent her incurring blame by her flight from the Convent."

The Marquis thanked him in terms by no means deficient in gratitude. Lorenzo then informed him that He had nothing more to apprehend from Donna Rodolpha's enmity. Five Months had already elapsed since, in an excess of passion, She broke a blood-vessel and expired in the course of a few hours. He then proceeded to mention the interests of Antonia. The Marquis was much surprized at hearing of this new Relation: His Father had carried his hatred of Elvira to the Grave, and had never given the least hint that He knew what was become of his eldest Son's Widow. Don Raymond assured his friend

491

that He was not mistaken in supposing him ready to acknowledge his Sister-in-law and her amiable Daughter. The preparations for the elopement would not permit his visiting them the next day; But in the meanwhile He desired Lorenzo to assure them of his friendship, and to supply Elvira upon his account with any sums which She might want. This the Youth promised to do, as soon as her abode should be known to him: He then took leave of his future Brother, and returned to the Palace de Medina.

The day was already on the point of breaking when the Marquis retired to his chamber. Conscious that his narrative would take up some hours, and wishing to secure himself from interruption on returning to the Hotel, He ordered his Attendants not to sit up for him. Consequently, He was somewhat surprised on entering his Antiroom, to find Theodore established there. The Page sat near a Table with a pen in his hand, and was so totally occupied by his employment that He perceived not his Lord's approach. The Marquis stopped to observe him. Theodore wrote a few lines, then paused, and scratched out a part of the writing: Then wrote again, smiled, and seemed highly pleased with what He had been about. At last He threw down his pen, sprang from his chair, and clapped his hands together joyfully.

"There it is!" cried He aloud: "Now they are charming!"

His transports were interrupted by a laugh from the Marquis, who suspected the nature of his employment.

"What is so charming, Theodore?"

The Youth started, and looked round. He blushed, ran to the Table, seized the paper on which He had been writing, and concealed it in confusion.

"Oh! my Lord, I knew not that you were so near me. Can I be of use to you? Lucas is already gone to bed."

"I shall follow his example when I have given my opinion of your verses."

"My verses, my Lord?"

"Nay, I am sure that you have been writing some, for nothing else could have kept you awake till this time of the morning. Where are they, Theodore? I shall like to see your composition."

Theodore's cheeks glowed with still deeper crimson: He longed to show his poetry, but first chose to be pressed for it.

"Indeed, my Lord, they are not worthy your attention."

"Not these verses, which you just now declared to be so charming?

Come, come, let me see whether our opinions are the same. I promise that you shall find in me an indulgent Critic."

The Boy produced his paper with seeming reluctance; but the satisfaction which sparkled in his dark expressive eyes betrayed the vanity of his little bosom. The Marquis smiled while He observed the emotions of an heart as yet but little skilled in veiling its sentiments. He seated himself upon a Sopha: Theodore, while Hope and fear contended on his anxious countenance, waited with inquietude for his Master's decision, while the Marquis read the following lines.

LOVE AND AGE

The night was dark; The wind blew cold;

Anacreon, grown morose and old,

Sat by his fire, and fed the chearful flame:

Suddenly the Cottage-door expands,

And lo! before him Cupid stands,

Casts round a friendly glance, and greets him by his name.

"What is it Thou?" the startled Sire

In sullen tone exclaimed, while ire

With crimson flushed his pale and wrinkled cheek:

"Wouldst Thou again with amorous rage

Inflame my bosom? Steeled by age,

Vain Boy, to pierce my breast thine arrows are too weak.

"What seek You in this desart drear?

No smiles or sports inhabit here;

Ne'er did these vallies witness dalliance sweet:

Eternal winter binds the plains;

Age in my house despotic reigns,

My Garden boasts no flower, my bosom boasts no heat.

"Begone, and seek the blooming bower,

Where some ripe Virgin courts thy power,

Or bid provoking dreams flit round her bed;

On Damon's amorous breast repose;

Wanton — on Chloe's lip of rose,

Or make her blushing cheek a pillow for thy head.

"Be such thy haunts; These regions cold

Avoid! Nor think grown wise and old

This hoary head again thy yoke shall bear:

Remembering that my fairest years

By Thee were marked with sighs and tears,

I think thy friendship false, and shun the guileful snare.

"I have not yet forgot the pains

I felt, while bound in Julia's chains;

The ardent flames with which my bosom burned;

The nights I passed deprived of rest;

The jealous pangs which racked my breast;

My disappointed hopes, and passion unreturned.

"Then fly, and curse mine eyes no more!

Fly from my peaceful Cottage-door!
No day, no hour, no moment shalt Thou stay.
   I know thy falsehood, scorn thy arts,
   Distrust thy smiles, and fear thy darts;
Traitor, begone, and seek some other to betray!"

"Does Age, old Man, your wits confound?"
Replied the offended God, and frowned;
(His frown was sweet as is the Virgin's smile!)
   "Do You to Me these words address?
   To Me, who do not love you less,
Though You my friendship scorn, and pleasures past revile!

"If one proud Fair you chanced to find,
   An hundred other Nymphs were kind,
Whose smiles might well for Julia's frowns atone:
   But such is Man! His partial hand
   Unnumbered favours writes on sand,
But stamps one little fault on solid lasting stone.

"Ingrate! Who led Thee to the wave,
   At noon where Lesbia loved to lave?
Who named the bower alone where Daphne lay?
   And who, when Caelia shrieked for aid,
   Bad you with kisses hush the Maid?
What other was't than Love, Oh! false Anacreon, say!

"Then You could call me—'Gentle Boy!
   'My only bliss! my source of joy!'—

495

Then You could prize me dearer than your soul!

    Could kiss, and dance me on your knees;

    And swear, not wine itself would please,

Had not the lip of Love first touched the flowing bowl!

    "Must those sweet days return no more?

    Must I for aye your loss deplore,

Banished your heart, and from your favour driven?

    Ah! no; My fears that smile denies;

    That heaving breast, those sparkling eyes

Declare me ever dear and all my faults forgiven.

    "Again beloved, esteemed, carest,

    Cupid shall in thine arms be prest,

Sport on thy knees, or on thy bosom sleep:

    My Torch thine age-struck heart shall warm;

    My Hand pale Winter's rage disarm,

And Youth and Spring shall here once more their revels
keep." —

    A feather now of golden hue

    He smiling from his pinion drew;

This to the Poet's hand the Boy commits;

    And straight before Anacreon's eyes

    The fairest dreams of fancy rise,

And round his favoured head wild inspiration flits.

    His bosom glows with amorous fire

    Eager He grasps the magic lyre;

Swift o'er the tuneful chords his fingers move:
> The Feather plucked from Cupid's wing
> Sweeps the too-long-neglected string,

While soft Anacreon sings the power and praise of Love.

> Soon as that name was heard, the Woods
> Shook off their snows; The melting floods

Broke their cold chains, and Winter fled away.
> Once more the earth was deckt with flowers;
> Mild Zephyrs breathed through blooming bowers;

High towered the glorious Sun, and poured the blaze of day.

> Attracted by the harmonious sound,
> Sylvans and Fauns the Cot surround,

And curious crowd the Minstrel to behold:
> The Wood-nymphs haste the spell to prove;
> Eager They run; They list, they love,

And while They hear the strain, forget the Man is old.

> Cupid, to nothing constant long,
> Perched on the Harp attends the song,

Or stifles with a kiss the dulcet notes:
> Now on the Poet's breast reposes,
> Now twines his hoary locks with roses,

Or borne on wings of gold in wanton circle floats.

> Then thus Anacreon—"I no more
> At other shrine my vows will pour,

Since Cupid deigns my numbers to inspire:

497

From Phœbus or the blue-eyed Maid

Now shall my verse request no aid,

For Love alone shall be the Patron of my Lyre.

"In lofty strain, of earlier days,

I spread the King's or Hero's praise,

And struck the martial Chords with epic fire:

But farewell, Hero! farewell, King!

Your deeds my lips no more shall sing,

For Love alone shall be the subject of my Lyre.

The Marquis returned the paper with a smile of encouragement.

"Your little poem pleases me much," said He; "However, you must not count my opinion for anything. I am no judge of verses, and for my own part, never composed more than six lines in my life: Those six produced so unlucky an effect that I am fully resolved never to compose another. But I wander from my subject. I was going to say that you cannot employ your time worse than in making verses. An Author, whether good or bad, or between both, is an Animal whom everybody is privileged to attack; For though All are not able to write books, all conceive themselves able to judge them. A bad composition carries with it its own punishment, contempt and ridicule. A good one excites envy, and entails upon its Author a thousand mortifications. He finds himself assailed by partial and ill-humoured Criticism: One Man finds fault with the plan, Another with the style, a Third with the precept, which it strives to inculcate; and they who cannot succeed in finding fault with the Book, employ themselves in stigmatizing its Author. They maliciously rake out from obscurity every little circumstance which may throw ridicule upon his private character or conduct, and aim at wounding the Man, since They cannot hurt the Writer. In short, to enter the lists of literature is wilfully to expose yourself to the arrows of neglect, ridicule, envy, and disappointment. Whether you write well or ill, be assured that you will not escape from blame; Indeed this circumstance contains a young Author's chief consolation: He remembers that Lope de Vega and Calderona had unjust and envious Critics, and He modestly conceives himself to be exactly in their predicament. But I am conscious that all these sage observations

498

are thrown away upon you. Authorship is a mania to conquer which no reasons are sufficiently strong; and you might as easily persuade me not to love, as I persuade you not to write. However, if you cannot help being occasionally seized with a poetical paroxysm, take at least the precaution of communicating your verses to none but those whose partiality for you secures their approbation."

"Then, my Lord, you do not think these lines tolerable?" said Theodore with an humble and dejected air.

"You mistake my meaning. As I said before, they have pleased me much; But my regard for you makes me partial, and Others might judge them less favourably. I must still remark that even my prejudice in your favour does not blind me so much as to prevent my observing several faults. For instance, you make a terrible confusion of metaphors; You are too apt to make the strength of your lines consist more in the words than sense; Some of the verses only seem introduced in order to rhyme with others; and most of the best ideas are borrowed from other Poets, though possibly you are unconscious of the theft yourself. These faults may occasionally be excused in a work of length; But a short Poem must be correct and perfect."

"All this is true, Segnor; But you should consider that I only write for pleasure."

"Your defects are the less excusable. Their incorrectness may be forgiven in those who work for money, who are obliged to compleat a given task in a given time, and are paid according to the bulk, not value of their productions. But in those whom no necessity forces to turn Author, who merely write for fame, and have full leisure to polish their compositions, faults are impardonable, and merit the sharpest arrows of criticism."

The Marquis rose from the Sopha; the Page looked discouraged and melancholy, and this did not escape his Master's observation.

"However" added He smiling, "I think that these lines do you no discredit. Your versification is tolerably easy, and your ear seems to be just. The perusal of your little poem upon the whole gave me much pleasure; and if it is not asking too great a favour, I shall be highly obliged to you for a Copy."

The Youth's countenance immediately cleared up. He perceived not the smile, half approving, half ironical, which accompanied the request, and He promised the Copy with great readiness. The Marquis withdrew to his chamber, much amused by the instantaneous effect produced upon Theodore's vanity by the conclusion of his Criticism. He threw himself upon his Couch; Sleep soon stole over him, and his dreams presented him with the most flattering pictures of happiness with Agnes.

On reaching the Hotel de Medina, Lorenzo's first care was to enquire for Letters. He found several waiting for him; but that which He sought was not amongst them. Leonella had found it impossible to write that evening. However, her impatience to secure Don Christoval's heart, on which She flattered herself with having made no slight impression, permitted her not to pass another day without informing him where She was to be found. On her return from the Capuchin Church, She had related to her Sister with exultation how attentive an handsome Cavalier had been to her; as also how his Companion had undertaken to plead Antonia's cause with the Marquis de las Cisternas. Elvira received this intelligence with sensations very different from those with which it was communicated. She blamed her Sister's imprudence in confiding her history to an absolute Stranger, and expressed her fears lest this inconsiderate step should prejudice the Marquis against her. The greatest of her apprehensions She concealed in her own breast. She had observed with inquietude that at the mention of Lorenzo, a deep blush spread itself over her Daughter's cheek. The timid Antonia dared not to pronounce his name: Without knowing wherefore, She felt embarrassed when He was made the subject of discourse, and endeavoured to change the conversation to Ambrosio. Elvira perceived the emotions of this young bosom: In consequence, She insisted upon Leonella's breaking her promise to the Cavaliers. A sigh, which on hearing this order escaped from Antonia, confirmed the wary Mother in her resolution.

Through this resolution Leonella was determined to break: She conceived it to be inspired by envy, and that her Sister dreaded her being elevated above her. Without imparting her design to anyone, She took an opportunity of dispatching the following note to Lorenzo; It was delivered to him as soon as he woke:

"Doubtless, Segnor Don Lorenzo, you have frequently accused me of ingratitude and forgetfulness: But on the word of a Virgin, it was out of my power to perform my promise yesterday. I know not in what words to inform you how strange a reception my Sister gave your kind wish to visit her. She is an odd Woman, with many good points about her; But her jealousy of me frequently makes her conceive notions quite unaccountable. On hearing that your Friend had paid some little attention to me, She immediately took the alarm: She blamed my conduct, and has absolutely forbidden me to let you know our abode. My strong sense of gratitude for your kind offers of service, and ... Shall I confess it? my desire to behold once more the too amiable Don Christoval, will not permit my obeying her injunctions. I have therefore stolen a moment to inform you, that we lodge in the Strada di San Iago, four doors from the Palace d'Albornos, and nearly opposite to the Barber's Miguel Coello. Enquire for Donna Elvira Dalfa, since in compliance with her Father-in-law's order, my Sister continues to be called by her maiden name. At eight this evening you will be sure of finding us: But let not a word drop which may raise a suspicion of my having written this letter. Should you see the Condé d'Ossorio, tell him ... I blush while I declare it ... Tell him that his presence will be but too acceptable to the sympathetic

LEONELLA.

The latter sentences were written in red ink, to express the blushes of her cheek, while She committed an outrage upon her virgin modesty.

Lorenzo had no sooner perused this note than He set out in search of Don Christoval. Not being able to find him in the course of the day, He proceeded to Donna Elvira's alone, to Leonella's infinite disappointment. The Domestic by whom He sent up his name, having already declared his Lady to be at home, She had no excuse for refusing his visit: Yet She consented to receive it with much reluctance. That reluctance was increased by the changes which his approach produced in Antonia's countenance; nor was it by any means abated when the Youth himself appeared. The symmetry of his person, animation of his features, and natural elegance of his manners and address, convinced Elvira that such a Guest must be dangerous for her Daughter. She resolved to treat him with distant politeness, to decline his services with gratitude for the tender of them, and to make him feel, without offence, that his future visits would be far from acceptable.

On his entrance He found Elvira, who was indisposed, reclining upon a Sopha: Antonia sat by her embroidery frame, and Leonella, in a pastoral dress, held "Montemayor's Diana." In spite of her being the Mother of Antonia, Lorenzo could not help expecting to find in Elvira Leonella's true Sister, and the Daughter of "as honest a painstaking Shoe-maker, as any in Cordova." A single glance was sufficient to undeceive him. He beheld a Woman whose features, though impaired by time and sorrow, still bore the marks of distinguished beauty: A serious dignity reigned upon her countenance, but was tempered by a grace and sweetness which rendered her truly enchanting. Lorenzo fancied that She must have resembled her Daughter in her youth, and readily excused the imprudence of the late Condé de las Cisternas. She desired him to be seated, and immediately resumed her place upon the Sopha.

Antonia received him with a simple reverence, and continued her work: Her cheeks were suffused with crimson, and She strove to conceal her emotion by leaning over her embroidery frame. Her Aunt also chose to play off her airs of modesty; She affected to blush and tremble, and waited with her eyes cast down to receive, as She expected, the compliments of Don Christoval. Finding after some time that no sign of his approach was given, She ventured to look round the room, and perceived with vexation that Medina was unaccompanied. Impatience would not permit her waiting for an explanation: Interrupting Lorenzo, who was delivering Raymond's message, She desired to know what was become of his Friend.

He, who thought it necessary to maintain himself in her good graces, strove to console her under her disappointment by committing a little violence upon truth.

"Ah! Segnora," He replied in a melancholy voice "How grieved will He be at losing this opportunity of paying you his respects! A Relation's illness has obliged him to quit Madrid in haste: But on his return, He will doubtless seize the first moment with transport to throw himself at your feet!"

As He said this, his eyes met those of Elvira: She punished his falsehood sufficiently by darting at him a look expressive of displeasure and reproach. Neither did the deceit answer his intention. Vexed and disappointed Leonella rose from her seat, and retired in dudgeon to her own apartment.

Lorenzo hastened to repair the fault, which had injured him in Elvira's opinion. He related his conversation with the Marquis respecting her: He assured her that Raymond was prepared to acknowledge her for his Brother's Widow; and that till it was in his power to pay his compliments to her in person, Lorenzo was commissioned to supply his place. This intelligence relieved Elvira from an heavy weight of uneasiness: She had now found a Protector for the fatherless Antonia, for whose future fortunes She had suffered the greatest apprehensions. She was not sparing of her thanks to him who had interfered so generously in her behalf; But still She gave

...o invitation to repeat his visit.

However, when upon rising to depart He requested permission to enquire after her health occasionally, the polite earnestness of his manner, gratitude for his services, and respect for his Friend the Marquis, would not admit of a refusal. She consented reluctantly to receive him: He promised not to abuse her goodness, and quitted the House.

Antonia was now left alone with her Mother: A temporary silence ensued. Both wished to speak upon the same subject, but Neither knew how to introduce it. The one felt a bashfulness which sealed up her lips, and for which She could not account: The other feared to find her apprehensions true, or to inspire her Daughter with notions to which She might be still a Stranger. At length Elvira began the conversation.

"That is a charming young Man, Antonia; I am much pleased with him. Was He long near you yesterday in the Cathedral?"

"He quitted me not for a moment while I staid in the Church: He gave me his seat, and was very obliging and attentive."

"Indeed? Why then have you never mentioned his name to me? Your Aunt lanched out in praise of his Friend, and you vaunted Ambrosio's eloquence: But Neither said a word of Don Lorenzo's person and accomplishments. Had not Leonella spoken of his readiness to undertake our cause, I should not have known him to be in existence."

She paused. Antonia coloured, but was silent.

"Perhaps you judge him less favourably than I do. In my opinion his figure is pleasing, his conversation sensible, and manners engaging. Still He may have struck you differently: You may think him disagreeable, and ...".

"Disagreeable? Oh! dear Mother, how should I possibly think him so? I should be very ungrateful were I not sensible of his kindness yesterday, and very blind if his merits had escaped me. His figure is so graceful, so noble! His manners so gentle, yet so manly! I never yet saw so many accomplishments united in one person, and I doubt whether Madrid can produce his equal."

"Why then were you so silent in praise of this Phoenix of Madrid?

Why was it concealed from me that his society had afforded you pleasure?"

"In truth, I know not: You ask me a question which I cannot resolve myself. I was on the point of mentioning him a thousand times: His name was constantly upon my lips, but when I would have pronounced it, I wanted courage to execute my design. However, if I did not speak of him, it was not that I thought of him the less."

"That I believe; But shall I tell you why you wanted courage? It was because, accustomed to confide to me your most secret thoughts, you knew not how to conceal, yet feared to acknowledge, that your heart nourished a sentiment which you were conscious I should disapprove. Come hither to me, my Child."

Antonia quitted her embroidery frame, threw herself upon her knees by the Sopha, and hid her face in her Mother's lap.

"Fear not, my sweet Girl! Consider me equally as your Friend and Parent, and apprehend no reproof from me. I have read the emotions of your bosom; you are yet ill-skilled in concealing them, and they could not escape my attentive eye. This Lorenzo is dangerous to your repose; He has already made an impression upon your heart. 'Tis true that I perceive easily that your affection is returned; But what can be the consequences of this attachment? You are poor and friendless, my Antonia; Lorenzo is the Heir of the Duke of Medina Celi. Even should Himself mean honourably, his Uncle never will consent to your union; Nor without that Uncle's consent, will I. By sad experience I know what sorrows She must endure, who marries into a family unwilling to receive her. Then struggle with your affection: Whatever pains it may cost you, strive to conquer it. Your heart is tender and susceptible: It has already received a strong impression; But when once convinced that you should not encourage such sentiments, I trust, that you have sufficient fortitude to drive them from your bosom."

Antonia kissed her hand, and promised implicit obedience. Elvira then continued.

"To prevent your passion from growing stronger, it will be needful to prohibit Lorenzo's visits. The service which He has rendered me permits not my forbidding them positively; But unless I judge too favourably of his character, He will discontinue them without taking offence, if I confess to him my reasons, and throw myself entirely on his generosity. The next time that I see him, I will honestly avow to him the embarrassment which his presence occasions. How say you, my Child? Is not this measure necessary?"

Antonia subscribed to every thing without hesitation, though not without regret. Her Mother kissed her affectionately, and retired to bed. Antonia followed her example, and vowed so frequently never more to think of Lorenzo, that till Sleep closed her eyes She thought of nothing else.

While this was passing at Elvira's, Lorenzo hastened to rejoin the Marquis. Every thing was ready for the second elopement of Agnes; and at twelve the two Friends with a Coach and four were at the Garden wall of the Convent. Don Raymond drew out his Key, and unlocked the door. They entered, and waited for some time in expectation of being joined by Agnes. At length the Marquis grew impatient: Beginning to fear that his second attempt would succeed no better than the first, He proposed to reconnoitre the Convent. The Friends advanced towards it. Every thing was still and dark. The Prioress was anxious to keep the story a secret, fearing lest the crime of one of its members should bring disgrace upon the whole community, or that the interposition of powerful Relations should deprive her vengeance of its intended victim. She took care therefore to give the Lover of Agnes no cause to suppose that his design was discovered, and his Mistress on the point of suffering the punishment of her fault. The same reason made her reject the idea of arresting the unknown Seducer in the Garden; Such a proceeding would have created much disturbance, and the disgrace of her Convent would have been noised about Madrid. She contented herself with confining Agnes closely; As to the Lover, She left him at liberty to pursue his designs. What She had expected was the result. The Marquis and Lorenzo waited in vain till the break of day: They then retired without noise, alarmed at the failure of their plan, and ignorant of the cause of its ill-success.

The next morning Lorenzo went to the Convent, and requested to see his Sister. The Prioress appeared at the Grate with a melancholy countenance: She informed him that for several days Agnes had appeared much agitated; That She had been prest by the Nuns in vain to reveal the cause, and apply to their tenderness for advice and consolation; That She had obstinately persisted in concealing the cause of her distress; But that on Thursday Evening it had produced so violent an effect upon her constitution, that She had fallen ill, and was actually confined to her bed. Lorenzo did not credit a syllable of this account: He insisted upon seeing his Sister; If She was unable to come to the Grate, He desired to be admitted to her Cell. The Prioress crossed herself! She was shocked at the very idea of a Man's profane eye pervading the interior of her holy Mansion, and professed herself astonished that Lorenzo could think of such a thing. She told him that his request could not be granted; But that if He returned the next day, She hoped that her beloved Daughter would then be sufficiently recovered to join him at the Parlour grate.

With this answer Lorenzo was obliged to retire, unsatisfied and trembling for his Sister's safety.

He returned the next morning at an early hour. "Agnes was worse; The Physician had pronounced her to be in imminent danger; She was ordered to remain quiet, and it was utterly impossible for her to receive her Brother's visit." Lorenzo stormed at this answer, but there was no resource. He raved, He entreated, He threatened: No means were left untried to obtain a sight of Agnes. His endeavours were as fruitless as those of the day before, and He returned in despair to the Marquis. On his side, the Latter had spared no pains to discover what had occasioned his plot to fail: Don Christoval, to whom the affair was now entrusted, endeavoured to worm out the secret from the Old Porteress of St. Clare, with whom He had formed an acquaintance; But She was too much upon her guard, and He gained from her no intelligence. The Marquis was almost distracted, and Lorenzo felt scarcely less inquietude. Both were convinced that the purposed elopement must have been discovered: They doubted not but the malady of Agnes was a pretence, But they knew not by what means to rescue her from the hands of the Prioress.

Regularly every day did Lorenzo visit the Convent: As regularly was He informed that his Sister rather grew worse than better. Certain that her indisposition was feigned, these accounts did not alarm him: But his ignorance of her fate, and of the motives which induced the Prioress to keep her from him, excited the most serious uneasiness. He was still uncertain what steps He ought to take, when the Marquis received a letter from the Cardinal-Duke of Lerma. It inclosed the Pope's expected Bull, ordering that Agnes should be released from her vows, and restored to her Relations. This essential paper decided at once the proceedings of her Friends: They resolved that Lorenzo should carry it to the Domina without delay, and demand that his Sister should be instantly given up to him. Against this mandate illness could not be pleaded: It gave her Brother the power of removing her instantly to the Palace de Medina, and He determined to use that power on the following day.

His mind relieved from inquietude respecting his Sister, and his Spirits raised by the hope of soon restoring her to freedom, He now had time to give a few moments to love and to Antonia. At the same hour as on his former visit He repaired to Donna Elvira's: She had given orders for his admission. As soon as He was announced, her Daughter retired with Leonella, and when He entered the chamber, He found the Lady of the House alone. She received him with less distance than before, and desired him to place himself near her upon the Sopha. She then without losing time opened her business, as had been agreed between herself and Antonia.

"You must not think me ungrateful, Don Lorenzo, or forgetful how essential are the services which you have rendered me with the Marquis. I feel the weight of my obligations; Nothing under the Sun should induce my taking the step to which I am now compelled but the interest of my Child, of my beloved Antonia. My health is declining; God only knows how soon I may be summoned before his Throne. My Daughter will be left without Parents, and should She lose the protection of the Cisternas family, without Friends.

She is young and artless, uninstructed in the world's perfidy, and with charms sufficient to render her an object of seduction. Judge then, how I must tremble at the prospect before her! Judge how anxious I must be to keep her from their society who may excite the yet dormant passions of her bosom. You are amiable, Don Lorenzo: Antonia has a susceptible, a loving heart, and is grateful for the favours conferred upon us by your interference with the Marquis. Your presence makes me tremble: I fear lest it should inspire her with sentiments which may embitter the remainder of her life, or encourage her to cherish hopes in her situation unjustifiable and futile. Pardon me when I avow my terrors, and let my frankness plead in my excuse. I cannot forbid you my House, for gratitude restrains me; I can only throw myself upon your generosity, and entreat you to spare the feelings of an anxious, of a doting Mother. Believe me when I assure you that I lament the necessity of rejecting your acquaintance; But there is no remedy, and Antonia's interest obliges me to beg you to forbear your visits. By complying with my request, you will increase the esteem which I already feel for you, and of which everything convinces me that you are truly deserving."

"Your frankness charms me," replied Lorenzo; "You shall find that in your favourable opinion of me you were not deceived. Yet I hope that the reasons, now in my power to allege, will persuade you to withdraw a request which I cannot obey without infinite reluctance. I love your Daughter, love her most sincerely: I wish for no greater happiness than to inspire her with the same sentiments, and receive her hand at the Altar as her Husband. 'Tis true, I am not rich myself; My Father's death has left me but little in my own possession; But my expectations justify my pretending to the Condé de las Cisternas' Daughter."

He was proceeding, but Elvira interrupted him.

"Ah! Don Lorenzo, you forget in that pompous title the meanness of my origin. You forget that I have now past fourteen years in Spain, disavowed by my Husband's family, and existing upon a stipend barely sufficient for the support and education of my Daughter. Nay, I have even been neglected by most of my own Relations, who out of envy affect to doubt the reality of my marriage. My allowance being discontinued at my Father-in-law's death, I was reduced to the very brink of want. In this situation I was found by my Sister, who amongst all her foibles possesses a warm, generous, and affectionate heart. She aided me with the little fortune which my Father left her, persuaded me to visit Madrid, and has supported my Child and myself since our quitting Murcia. Then consider not Antonia as descended from the Condé de la Cisternas: Consider her as a poor and unprotected Orphan, as the Grand-child of the Tradesman Torribio Dalfa, as the needy Pensioner of that Tradesman's Daughter. Reflect upon the difference between such a situation, and that of the Nephew and Heir of the potent Duke of Medina. I believe your intentions to be honourable; But as there are no hopes that your Uncle will approve of the union, I foresee that the consequences of your attachment must be fatal to my Child's repose."

"Pardon me, Segnora; You are misinformed if you suppose the Duke of Medina to resemble the generality of Men. His sentiments are liberal and disinterested: He loves me well; and I have no reason to dread his forbidding the marriage when He perceives that my happiness depends upon Antonia. But supposing him to refuse his sanction, what have I still to fear? My Parents are no more; My little fortune is in my own possession: It will be sufficient to support Antonia, and I shall exchange for her hand Medina's Dukedom without one sigh of regret."

"You are young and eager; It is natural for you to entertain such ideas. But Experience has taught me to my cost that curses accompany an unequal alliance. I married the Condé de las Cisternas in opposition to the will of his Relations; Many an heart-pang has punished me for the imprudent step. Whereever we bent our course, a Father's execration pursued Gonzalvo. Poverty overtook us, and no Friend was near to relieve our wants. Still our mutual affection existed, but alas! not without interruption.

Accustomed to wealth and ease, ill could my Husband support the transition to distress and indigence. He looked back with repining to the comforts which He once enjoyed. He regretted the situation which for my sake He had quitted; and in moments when Despair possessed his mind, has reproached me with having made him the Companion of want and wretchedness! He has called me his bane! The source of his sorrows, the cause of his destruction! Ah God! He little knew how much keener were my own heart's reproaches! He was ignorant that I suffered trebly, for myself, for my Children, and for him! 'Tis true that his anger seldom lasted long: His sincere affection for me soon revived in his heart; and then his repentance for the tears which He had made me shed tortured me even more than his reproaches. He would throw himself on the ground, implore my forgiveness in the most frantic terms, and load himself with curses for being the Murderer of my repose. Taught by experience that an union contracted against the inclinations of families on either side must be unfortunate, I will save my Daughter from those miseries which I have suffered. Without your Uncle's consent, while I live, She never shall be yours. Undoubtedly He will disapprove of the union; His power is immense, and Antonia shall not be exposed to his anger and persecution."

"His persecution? How easily may that be avoided! Let the worst happen, it is but quitting Spain. My wealth may easily be realised; The Indian Islands will offer us a secure retreat; I have an estate, though not of value, in Hispaniola: Thither will we fly, and I shall consider it to be my native Country, if it gives me Antonia's undisturbed possession."

"Ah! Youth, this is a fond romantic vision. Gonzalvo thought the same. He fancied that He could leave Spain without regret; But the moment of parting undeceived him. You know not yet what it is to quit your native land; to quit it, never to behold it more!

You know not, what it is to exchange the scenes where you have passed your infancy, for unknown realms and barbarous climates! To be forgotten, utterly eternally forgotten, by the Companions of your Youth! To see your dearest Friends, the fondest objects of your affection, perishing with diseases incidental to Indian atmospheres, and find yourself unable to procure for them necessary assistance! I have felt all this! My Husband and two sweet Babes found their Graves in Cuba: Nothing would have saved my young Antonia but my sudden return to Spain. Ah! Don Lorenzo, could you conceive what I suffered during my absence! Could you know how sorely I regretted all that I left behind, and how dear to me was the very name of Spain! I envied the winds which blew towards it: And when the Spanish Sailor chaunted some well-known air as He past my window, tears filled my eyes while I thought upon my native land. Gonzalvo too ... My Husband ...".

Elvira paused. Her voice faltered, and She concealed her face with her handkerchief. After a short silence She rose from the Sopha, and proceeded.

"Excuse my quitting you for a few moments: The remembrance of what I have suffered has much agitated me, and I need to be alone. Till I return peruse these lines. After my Husband's death I found them among his papers; Had I known sooner that He entertained such sentiments, Grief would have killed me. He wrote these verses on his voyage to Cuba, when his mind was clouded by sorrow, and He forgot that He had a Wife and Children.

What we are losing, ever seems to us the most precious: Gonzalvo was quitting Spain for ever, and therefore was Spain dearer to his eyes than all else which the World contained. Read them, Don Lorenzo; They will give you some idea of the feelings of a banished Man!"

Elvira put a paper into Lorenzo's hand, and retired from the chamber. The Youth examined the contents, and found them to be as follows.

THE EXILE

Farewell, Oh! native Spain! Farewell for ever!

  These banished eyes shall view thy coasts no more;

A mournful presage tells my heart, that never

  Gonzalvo's steps again shall press thy shore.

Hushed are the winds; While soft the Vessel sailing
  With gentle motion plows the unruffled Main,
I feel my bosom's boasted courage failing,
  And curse the waves which bear me far from Spain.

I see it yet! Beneath yon blue clear Heaven
  Still do the Spires, so well beloved, appear;
From yonder craggy point the gale of Even
  Still wafts my native accents to mine ear:

Propped on some moss-crowned Rock, and gaily singing,
  There in the Sun his nets the Fisher dries;
Oft have I heard the plaintive Ballad, bringing
  Scenes of past joys before my sorrowing eyes.

Ah! Happy Swain! He waits the accustomed hour,
  When twilight-gloom obscures the closing sky;
Then gladly seeks his loved paternal bower,
  And shares the feast his native fields supply:

Friendship and Love, his Cottage Guests, receive him
  With honest welcome and with smile sincere;
No threatening woes of present joys bereave him,
  No sigh his bosom owns, his cheek no tear.

Ah! Happy Swain! Such bliss to me denying,
  Fortune thy lot with envy bids me view;
Me, who from home and Spain an Exile flying,

Bid all I value, all I love, adieu.

No more mine ear shall list the well-known ditty
   Sung by some Mountain-Girl, who tends her Goats,
Some Village-Swain imploring amorous pity,
   Or Shepherd chaunting wild his rustic notes:

No more my arms a Parent's fond embraces,
   No more my heart domestic calm, must know;
Far from these joys, with sighs which Memory traces,
   To sultry skies, and distant climes I go.

Where Indian Suns engender new diseases,
   Where snakes and tigers breed, I bend my way
To brave the feverish thirst no art appeases,
   The yellow plague, and madding blaze of day:

But not to feel slow pangs consume my liver,
   To die by piece-meal in the bloom of age,
My boiling blood drank by insatiate fever,
   And brain delirious with the day-star's rage,

Can make me know such grief, as thus to sever
   With many a bitter sigh, Dear Land, from Thee;
To feel this heart must doat on thee for ever,
   And feel, that all thy joys are torn from me!

Ah me! How oft will Fancy's spells in slumber
   Recall my native Country to my mind!

The Monk: A Romance

How oft regret will bid me sadly number
    Each lost delight and dear Friend left behind!

Wild Murcia's Vales, and loved romantic bowers,
    The River on whose banks a Child I played,
My Castle's antient Halls, its frowning Towers,
    Each much-regretted wood, and well-known Glade,

Dreams of the land where all my wishes centre,
    Thy scenes, which I am doomed no more to know,
Full oft shall Memory trace, my soul's Tormentor,
    And turn each pleasure past to present woe.

But Lo! The Sun beneath the waves retires;
    Night speeds apace her empire to restore:
Clouds from my sight obscure the village-spires,
    Now seen but faintly, and now seen no more.

Oh! breathe not, Winds! Still be the Water's motion!
    Sleep, sleep, my Bark, in silence on the Main!
So when to-morrow's light shall gild the Ocean,
    Once more mine eyes shall see the coast of Spain.

Vain is the wish! My last petition scorning,
    Fresh blows the Gale, and high the Billows swell:
Far shall we be before the break of Morning;
    Oh! then for ever, native Spain, farewell!

Lorenzo had scarcely time to read these lines, when Elvira returned to him: The giving a free course to her tears had relieved her, and her spirits had regained their usual composure.

"I have nothing more to say, my Lord," said She; "You have heard my apprehensions, and my reasons for begging you not to repeat your visits. I have thrown myself in full confidence upon your honour: I am certain that you will not prove my opinion of you to have been too favourable."

"But one question more, Segnora, and I leave you. Should the Duke of Medina approve my love, would my addresses be unacceptable to yourself and the fair Antonia?"

"I will be open with you, Don Lorenzo: There being little probability of such an union taking place, I fear that it is desired but too ardently by my Daughter. You have made an impression upon her young heart, which gives me the most serious alarm: To prevent that impression from growing stronger, I am obliged to decline your acquaintance. For me, you may be sure that I should rejoice at establishing my Child so advantageously. Conscious that my constitution, impaired by grief and illness, forbids me to expect a long continuance in this world, I tremble at the thought of leaving her under the protection of a perfect Stranger. The Marquis de las Cisternas is totally unknown to me:

He will marry; His Lady may look upon Antonia with an eye of displeasure, and deprive her of her only Friend. Should the Duke, your Uncle, give his consent, you need not doubt obtaining mine, and my Daughter's: But without his, hope not for ours. At all events, what ever steps you may take, what ever may be the Duke's decision, till you know it let me beg your forbearing to strengthen by your presence Antonia's prepossession. If the sanction of your Relations authorises your addressing her as your Wife, my Doors fly open to you: If that sanction is refused, be satisfied to possess my esteem and gratitude, but remember, that we must meet no more."

Lorenzo promised reluctantly to conform to this decree: But He added that He hoped soon to obtain that consent which would give him a claim to the renewal of their acquaintance. He then explained to her why the Marquis had not called in person, and made no scruple of confiding to her his Sister's History. He concluded by saying that He hoped to set Agnes at liberty the next day; and that as soon as Don Raymond's fears were quieted upon this subject, He would lose no time in assuring

Donna Elvira of his friendship and protection.

The Lady shook her head.

"I tremble for your Sister," said She; "I have heard many traits of the Domina of St. Clare's character, from a Friend who was educated in the same Convent with her. She reported her to be haughty, inflexible, superstitious, and revengeful. I have since heard that She is infatuated with the idea of rendering her Convent the most regular in Madrid, and never forgave those whose imprudence threw upon it the slightest stain. Though naturally violent and severe, when her interests require it, She well knows how to assume an appearance of benignity. She leaves no means untried to persuade young Women of rank to become Members of her Community: She is implacable when once incensed, and has too much intrepidity to shrink at taking the most rigorous measures for punishing the Offender. Doubtless, She will consider your Sister's quitting the Convent as a disgrace thrown upon it: She will use every artifice to avoid obeying the mandate of his Holiness, and I shudder to think that Donna Agnes is in the hands of this dangerous Woman."

Lorenzo now rose to take leave. Elvira gave him her hand at parting, which He kissed respectfully; and telling her that He soon hoped for the permission to salute that of Antonia, He returned to his Hotel. The Lady was perfectly satisfied with the conversation which had past between them. She looked forward with satisfaction to the prospect of his becoming her Son-in-law; But Prudence bad her conceal from her Daughter's knowledge the flattering hopes which Herself now ventured to entertain.

Scarcely was it day, and already Lorenzo was at the Convent of St. Clare, furnished with the necessary mandate. The Nuns were at Matins. He waited impatiently for the conclusion of the service, and at length the Prioress appeared at the Parlour Grate. Agnes was demanded. The old Lady replied, with a melancholy air, that the dear Child's situation grew hourly more dangerous; That the Physicians despaired of her life; But that they had declared the only chance for her recovery to consist in keeping her quiet, and not to permit those to approach her whose presence was likely to agitate her. Not a word of all this was believed by Lorenzo, any more than He credited the expressions of grief and affection for Agnes, with which this account was interlarded. To end the business, He put the Pope's Bull into the hands of the Domina, and insisted that, ill or in health, his Sister should be delivered to him without delay.

The Prioress received the paper with an air of humility: But no sooner had her eye glanced over the contents, than her resentment baffled all the efforts of Hypocrisy. A deep crimson spread itself over her face, and She darted upon Lorenzo looks of rage and menace.

"This order is positive," said She in a voice of anger, which She in vain strove to disguise; "Willingly would I obey it; But unfortunately it is out of my power."

Lorenzo interrupted her by an exclamation of surprize.

"I repeat it, Segnor; to obey this order is totally out of my power. From tenderness to a Brother's feelings, I would have communicated the sad event to you by degrees, and have prepared you to hear it with fortitude. My measures are broken through: This order commands me to deliver up to you the Sister Agnes without delay; I am therefore obliged to inform you without circumlocution, that on Friday last, She expired."

Lorenzo started back with horror, and turned pale. A moment's recollection convinced him that this assertion must be false, and it restored him to himself.

"You deceive me!" said He passionately; "But five minutes past since you assured me that though ill She was still alive. Produce her this instant! See her I must and will, and every attempt to keep her from me will be unavailing."

"You forget yourself, Segnor; You owe respect to my age as well as my profession. Your Sister is no more. If I at first concealed her death, it was from dreading lest an event so unexpected should produce on you too violent an effect. In truth, I am but ill repaid for my attention. And what interest, I pray you, should I have in detaining her? To know her wish of quitting our society is a sufficient reason for me to wish her absence, and think her a disgrace to the Sisterhood of St. Clare: But She has forfeited my affection in a manner yet more culpable. Her crimes were great, and when you know the cause of her death, you will doubtless rejoice, Don Lorenzo, that such a Wretch is no longer in existence. She was taken ill on Thursday last on returning from confession in the Capuchin Chapel. Her malady seemed attended with strange circumstances; But She persisted in concealing its cause: Thanks to the Virgin, we were too ignorant to suspect it! Judge then what must have been our consternation, our horror, when She was delivered the next day of a stillborn Child, whom She immediately followed to the Grave. How, Segnor? Is it possible that your countenance expresses no surprize, no indignation? Is it possible that your Sister's infamy was known to you, and that still She possessed your affection? In that case, you have no need of my compassion. I can say nothing more, except repeat my inability of obeying the orders of his Holiness. Agnes is no more, and to convince you that what I say is true, I swear by our blessed Saviour, that three days have past since She was buried."

Here She kissed a small crucifix which hung at her girdle. She then rose from her chair, and quitted the Parlour. As She withdrew, She cast upon Lorenzo a scornful smile.

"Farewell, Segnor," said She; "I know no remedy for this accident: I fear that even a second Bull from the Pope will not procure your Sister's resurrection."

Lorenzo also retired, penetrated with affliction: But Don Raymond's at the news of this event amounted to Madness. He would not be convinced that Agnes was really dead, and continued to insist that the Walls of St. Clare still confined her. No arguments could make him abandon his hopes of regaining her: Every day some fresh scheme was invented for procuring intelligence of her, and all of them were attended with the same success.

On his part, Medina gave up the idea of ever seeing his Sister more: Yet He believed that She had been taken off by unfair means. Under this persuasion, He encouraged Don Raymond's researches, determined, should He discover the least warrant for his suspicions, to take a severe vengeance upon the unfeeling Prioress. The loss of his Sister affected him sincerely; Nor was it the least cause of his distress that propriety obliged him for some time to defer mentioning Antonia to the Duke. In the meanwhile his emissaries constantly surrounded Elvira's Door. He had intelligence of all the movements of his Mistress: As She never failed every Thursday to attend the Sermon in the Capuchin Cathedral, He was secure of seeing her once a week, though in compliance with his promise, He carefully shunned her observation. Thus two long Months passed away. Still no information was procured of Agnes: All but the Marquis credited her death; and now Lorenzo determined to disclose his sentiments to his Uncle. He had already dropt some hints of his intention to marry; They had been as favourably received as He could expect, and He harboured no doubt of the success of his application.

CHAPTER VI.

While in each other's arms entranced They lay,

They blessed the night, and curst the coming day.

LEE.

The burst of transport was past: Ambrosio's lust was satisfied; Pleasure fled, and Shame usurped her seat in his bosom. Confused and terrified at his weakness, He drew himself from Matilda's arms. His perjury presented itself before him: He reflected on the scene which had just been acted, and trembled at the consequences of a discovery. He looked forward with horror; His heart was despondent, and became the abode of satiety and disgust. He avoided the eyes of his Partner in frailty; A melancholy silence prevailed, during which Both seemed busied with disagreeable reflections.

Matilda was the first to break it. She took his hand gently, and pressed it to her burning lips.

"Ambrosio!" She murmured in a soft and trembling voice.

The Abbot started at the sound. He turned his eyes upon Matilda's: They were filled with tears; Her cheeks were covered with blushes, and her supplicating looks seemed to solicit his compassion.

"Dangerous Woman!" said He; "Into what an abyss of misery have you plunged me! Should your sex be discovered, my honour, nay my life, must pay for the pleasure of a few moments. Fool that I was, to trust myself to your seductions! What can now be done? How can my offence be expiated? What atonement can purchase the pardon of my crime? Wretched Matilda, you have destroyed my quiet for ever!"

"To me these reproaches, Ambrosio? To me, who have sacrificed for you the world's pleasures, the luxury of wealth, the delicacy of sex, my Friends, my fortune, and my fame? What have you lost, which I preserved? Have I not shared in your guilt? Have you not shared in my pleasure? Guilt, did I say? In what consists ours, unless in the opinion of an ill-judging World? Let that World be ignorant of them, and our joys become divine and blameless! Unnatural were your vows of Celibacy; Man was not created for such a state; And were Love

518

a crime, God never would have made it so sweet, so irresistible! Then banish those clouds from your brow, my Ambrosio! Indulge in those pleasures freely, without which life is a worthless gift: Cease to reproach me with having taught you what is bliss, and feel equal transports with the Woman who adores you!"

As She spoke, her eyes were filled with a delicious languor. Her bosom panted: She twined her arms voluptuously round him, drew him towards her, and glewed her lips to his. Ambrosio again raged with desire: The die was thrown: His vows were already broken; He had already committed the crime, and why should He refrain from enjoying its reward? He clasped her to his breast with redoubled ardour. No longer repressed by the sense of shame, He gave a loose to his intemperate appetites. While the fair Wanton put every invention of lust in practice, every refinement in the art of pleasure which might heighten the bliss of her possession, and render her Lover's transports still more exquisite, Ambrosio rioted in delights till then unknown to him: Swift fled the night, and the Morning blushed to behold him still clasped in the embraces of Matilda.

Intoxicated with pleasure, the Monk rose from the Syren's luxurious Couch. He no longer reflected with shame upon his incontinence, or dreaded the vengeance of offended heaven. His only fear was lest Death should rob him of enjoyments, for which his long Fast had only given a keener edge to his appetite. Matilda was still under the influence of poison, and the voluptuous Monk trembled less for his Preserver's life than his Concubine's. Deprived of her, He would not easily find another Mistress with whom He could indulge his passions so fully, and so safely. He therefore pressed her with earnestness to use the means of preservation which She had declared to be in her possession.

"Yes!" replied Matilda; "Since you have made me feel that Life is valuable, I will rescue mine at any rate. No dangers shall appall me: I will look upon the consequences of my action boldly, nor shudder at the horrors which they present. I will think my sacrifice scarcely worthy to purchase your possession, and remember that a moment past in your arms in this world o'er-pays an age of punishment in the next. But before I take this step, Ambrosio, give me your solemn oath never to enquire by what means I shall preserve myself."

He did so in a manner the most binding.

"I thank you, my Beloved. This precaution is necessary, for though you know it not, you are under the command of vulgar prejudices: The Business on which I must be employed this night, might startle you from its singularity, and lower me in your opinion. Tell me; Are you possessed of the Key of the low door on the western side of the Garden?"

"The Door which opens into the burying-ground common to us and the Sisterhood of St. Clare? I have not the Key, but can easily procure it."

"You have only this to do. Admit me into the burying-ground at midnight; Watch while I descend into the vaults of St. Clare, lest some prying eye should observe my actions; Leave me there alone for an hour, and that life is safe which I dedicate to your pleasures. To prevent creating suspicion, do not visit me during the day. Remember the Key, and that I expect you before twelve. Hark! I hear steps approaching! Leave me; I will pretend to sleep."

The Friar obeyed, and left the Cell. As He opened the door, Father Pablos made his appearance.

"I come," said the Latter, "to enquire after the health of my young Patient."

"Hush!" replied Ambrosio, laying his finger upon his lip; "Speak softly; I am just come from him. He has fallen into a profound slumber, which doubtless will be of service to him. Do not disturb him at present, for He wishes to repose."

Father Pablos obeyed, and hearing the Bell ring, accompanied the Abbot to Matins. Ambrosio felt embarrassed as He entered the Chapel. Guilt was new to him, and He fancied that every eye could read the transactions of the night upon his countenance. He strove to pray; His bosom no longer glowed with devotion; His thoughts insensibly wandered to Matilda's secret charms. But what He wanted in purity of heart, He supplied by exterior sanctity. The better to cloak his transgression, He redoubled his pretensions to the semblance of virtue, and never appeared more devoted to Heaven as since He had broken through his engagements. Thus did He unconsciously add Hypocrisy to perjury and incontinence; He had fallen into the latter errors from yielding to seduction almost irresistible; But he was now guilty of a voluntary fault by endeavouring to conceal those into which Another had betrayed him.

The Matins concluded, Ambrosio retired to his Cell. The pleasures which He had just tasted for the first time were still impressed upon his mind. His brain was bewildered, and presented a confused Chaos of remorse, voluptuousness, inquietude, and fear. He looked back with regret to that peace of soul, that security of virtue, which till then had been his portion. He had indulged in excesses whose very idea but four and twenty hours before He had recoiled at with horror. He shuddered at reflecting that a trifling indiscretion on his part, or on Matilda's, would overturn that fabric of reputation which it had cost him thirty years to erect, and render him the abhorrence of that People of whom He was then the Idol. Conscience painted to him in glaring colours his perjury and weakness; Apprehension magnified to him the horrors of punishment, and He already fancied himself in the prisons of the Inquisition. To these tormenting ideas succeeded Matilda's beauty, and those delicious lessons which, once learnt, can never be forgotten. A single glance thrown upon these reconciled him with himself. He considered the pleasures of the former night to have been purchased at an easy price by the sacrifice of innocence and honour. Their very remembrance filled his soul with ecstacy; He cursed his foolish vanity, which had induced him to waste in obscurity the bloom of life, ignorant of the blessings of Love and Woman. He determined at all events to continue his commerce with Matilda, and called every argument to his aid which might confirm his resolution. He asked himself, provided his irregularity was unknown, in what would his fault consist, and what consequences He had to apprehend? By adhering strictly to every rule of his order save Chastity, He doubted not to retain the esteem of Men, and even the protection of heaven. He trusted easily to be forgiven so slight and natural a deviation from his vows: But He forgot that having pronounced those vows, Incontinence, in Laymen the most venial of errors, became in his person the most heinous of crimes.

Once decided upon his future conduct, his mind became more easy. He threw himself upon his bed, and strove by sleeping to recruit his strength exhausted by his nocturnal excesses. He awoke refreshed, and eager for a repetition of his pleasures. Obedient to Matilda's order, He visited not her Cell during the day. Father Pablos mentioned in the Refectory that Rosario had at length been prevailed upon to follow his prescription; But that the medicine had not produced the slightest effect, and that He believed no mortal skill could rescue him from the Grave. With this opinion the Abbot agreed, and affected to lament the untimely fate of a Youth, whose talents had appeared so promising.

521

The night arrived. Ambrosio had taken care to procure from the Porter the Key of the low door opening into the Cemetery. Furnished with this, when all was silent in the Monastery, He quitted his Cell, and hastened to Matilda's. She had left her bed, and was drest before his arrival.

"I have been expecting you with impatience," said She; "My life depends upon these moments. Have you the Key?"

"I have."

"Away then to the garden. We have no time to lose. Follow me!"

She took a small covered Basket from the Table. Bearing this in one hand, and the Lamp, which was flaming upon the Hearth, in the other, She hastened from the Cell. Ambrosio followed her. Both maintained a profound silence. She moved on with quick but cautious steps, passed through the Cloisters, and reached the Western side of the Garden. Her eyes flashed with a fire and wildness which impressed the Monk at once with awe and horror. A determined desperate courage reigned upon her brow. She gave the Lamp to Ambrosio; Then taking from him the Key, She unlocked the low Door, and entered the Cemetery. It was a vast and spacious Square planted with yew trees: Half of it belonged to the Abbey; The other half was the property of the Sisterhood of St. Clare, and was protected by a roof of Stone. The Division was marked by an iron railing, the wicket of which was generally left unlocked.

Thither Matilda bent her course. She opened the wicket and sought for the door leading to the subterraneous Vaults, where reposed the mouldering Bodies of the Votaries of St. Clare. The night was perfectly dark; Neither Moon or Stars were visible. Luckily there was not a breath of Wind, and the Friar bore his Lamp in full security: By the assistance of its beams, the door of the Sepulchre was soon discovered. It was sunk within the hollow of a wall, and almost concealed by thick festoons of ivy hanging over it. Three steps of rough-hewn Stone conducted to it, and Matilda was on the point of descending them when She suddenly started back.

"There are People in the Vaults!" She whispered to the Monk; "Conceal yourself till they are past."

She took refuge behind a lofty and magnificent Tomb, erected in honour of the Convent's Foundress. Ambrosio followed her example, carefully hiding his Lamp lest its beams should betray them. But a few moments had elapsed when the Door was pushed open leading to the subterraneous Caverns. Rays of light proceeded up the Staircase: They enabled the concealed Spectators to observe two Females drest in religious habits, who seemed engaged in earnest conversation. The Abbot had no difficulty to recognize the Prioress of St. Clare in the first, and one of the elder Nuns in her Companion.

"Every thing is prepared," said the Prioress; "Her fate shall be decided tomorrow. All her tears and sighs will be unavailing. No! In five and twenty years that I have been Superior of this Convent, never did I witness a transaction more infamous!"

"You must expect much opposition to your will;" the Other replied in a milder voice; "Agnes has many Friends in the Convent, and in particular the Mother St. Ursula will espouse her cause most warmly. In truth, She merits to have Friends; and I wish I could prevail upon you to consider her youth, and her peculiar situation. She seems sensible of her fault; The excess of her grief proves her penitence, and I am convinced that her tears flow more from contrition than fear of punishment. Reverend Mother, would you be persuaded to mitigate the severity of your sentence, would you but deign to overlook this first transgression, I offer myself as the pledge of her future conduct."

"Overlook it, say you? Mother Camilla, you amaze me! What? After disgracing me in the presence of Madrid's Idol, of the very Man on whom I most wished to impress an idea of the strictness of my discipline? How despicable must I have appeared to the reverend Abbot! No, Mother, No! I never can forgive the insult. I cannot better convince Ambrosio that I abhor such crimes, than by punishing that of Agnes with all the rigour of which our severe laws admit. Cease then your supplications; They will all be unavailing. My resolution is taken: Tomorrow Agnes shall be made a terrible example of my justice and resentment."

The Mother Camilla seemed not to give up the point, but by this time the Nuns were out of hearing. The Prioress unlocked the door which communicated with St. Clare's Chapel, and having entered with her Companion, closed it again after them.

Matilda now asked, who was this Agnes with whom the Prioress was thus incensed, and what connexion She could have with Ambrosio. He related her adventure; and He added, that since that time his ideas having undergone a thorough revolution, He now felt much compassion for the unfortunate

Nun.

"I design," said He, "to request an audience of the Domina tomorrow, and use every means of obtaining a mitigation of her sentence."

"Beware of what you do!" interrupted Matilda; "Your sudden change of sentiment may naturally create surprize, and may give birth to suspicions which it is most our interest to avoid. Rather, redouble your outward austerity, and thunder out menaces against the errors of others, the better to conceal your own. Abandon the Nun to her fate. Your interfering might be dangerous, and her imprudence merits to be punished: She is unworthy to enjoy Love's pleasures, who has not wit enough to conceal them. But in discussing this trifling subject I waste moments which are precious. The night flies apace, and much must be done before morning. The Nuns are retired; All is safe. Give me the Lamp, Ambrosio. I must descend alone into these Caverns: Wait here, and if any one approaches, warn me by your voice; But as you value your existence, presume not to follow me. Your life would fall a victim to your imprudent curiosity."

Thus saying She advanced towards the Sepulchre, still holding her Lamp in one hand, and her little Basket in the other. She touched the door: It turned slowly upon its grating hinges, and a narrow winding staircase of black marble presented itself to her eyes. She descended it. Ambrosio remained above, watching the faint beams of the Lamp as they still proceeded up the stairs. They disappeared, and He found himself in total darkness.

Left to himself He could not reflect without surprize on the sudden change in Matilda's character and sentiments. But a few days had past since She appeared the mildest and softest of her sex, devoted to his will, and looking up to him as to a superior Being. Now She assumed a sort of courage and manliness in her manners and discourse but ill-calculated to please him. She spoke no longer to insinuate, but command: He found himself unable to cope with her in argument, and was unwillingly obliged to confess the superiority of her judgment. Every moment convinced him of the astonishing powers of her mind: But what She gained in the opinion of the Man, She lost with interest in the affection of the Lover. He regretted Rosario, the fond, the gentle, and submissive: He grieved that Matilda preferred the virtues of his sex to those of her own; and when He thought of her expressions respecting the devoted Nun, He could not help blaming them as cruel and unfeminine. Pity is a sentiment so natural, so appropriate to the female character, that it is scarcely a merit for a Woman to possess it, but to be without it is a grievous crime. Ambrosio could not easily forgive his Mistress for being deficient in this amiable quality. However, though he blamed her insensibility, He felt the truth of her observations; and though He pitied sincerely the unfortunate Agnes, He resolved to drop the idea of interposing in her behalf.

Near an hour had elapsed, since Matilda descended into the Caverns; Still She returned not. Ambrosio's curiosity was excited. He drew near the Staircase. He listened. All was silent, except that at intervals He caught the sound of Matilda's voice, as it wound along the subterraneous passages, and was re-echoed by the Sepulchre's vaulted roofs. She was at too great a distance for him to distinguish her words, and ere they reached him they were deadened into a low murmur. He longed to penetrate into this mystery. He resolved to disobey her injunctions and follow her into the Cavern. He advanced to the Staircase; He had already descended some steps when his courage failed him. He remembered Matilda's menaces if He infringed her orders, and his bosom was filled with a secret unaccountable awe. He returned up the stairs, resumed his former station, and waited impatiently for the conclusion of this adventure.

Suddenly He was sensible of a violent shock: An earthquake rocked the ground. The Columns which supported the roof under which He stood were so strongly shaken, that every moment menaced him with its fall, and at the same moment He heard a loud and tremendous burst of thunder. It ceased, and his eyes being fixed upon the Staircase, He saw a bright column of light flash along the Caverns beneath. It was seen but for an instant. No sooner did it disappear, than all was once more quiet and obscure. Profound Darkness again surrounded him, and the silence of night was only broken by the whirring Bat, as She flitted slowly by him.

With every instant Ambrosio's amazement increased. Another hour elapsed, after which the same light again appeared and was lost again as suddenly. It was accompanied by a strain of sweet but solemn Music, which as it stole through the Vaults below, inspired the Monk with mingled delight and terror. It had not long been hushed, when He heard Matilda's steps upon the Staircase. She ascended from the Cavern; The most lively joy animated her beautiful features.

"Did you see any thing?" She asked.

"Twice I saw a column of light flash up the Staircase."

"Nothing else?"

"Nothing."

"The Morning is on the point of breaking. Let us retire to the Abbey, lest daylight should betray us."

With a light step She hastened from the burying-ground. She regained her Cell, and the curious Abbot still accompanied her. She closed the door, and disembarrassed herself of her Lamp and Basket.

"I have succeeded!" She cried, throwing herself upon his bosom: "Succeeded beyond my fondest hopes! I shall live, Ambrosio, shall live for you! The step which I shuddered at taking proves to me a source of joys inexpressible! Oh! that I dared communicate those joys to you! Oh! that I were permitted to share with you my power, and raise you as high above the level of your sex, as one bold deed has exalted me above mine!"

"And what prevents you, Matilda?" interrupted the Friar; "Why is your business in the Cavern made a secret? Do you think me undeserving of your confidence? Matilda, I must doubt the truth of your affection, while you have joys in which I am forbidden to share."

"You reproach me with injustice. I grieve sincerely that I am obliged to conceal from you my happiness. But I am not to blame: The fault lies not in me, but in yourself, my Ambrosio! You are still too much the Monk. Your mind is enslaved by the prejudices of Education; And Superstition might make you shudder at the idea of that which experience has taught me to prize and value. At present you are unfit to be trusted with a secret of such importance: But the strength of your judgment; and the curiosity which I rejoice to see sparkling in your eyes, makes me hope that you will one day deserve my confidence. Till that period arrives, restrain your impatience. Remember that you have given me your solemn oath never to enquire into this night's adventures. I insist upon your keeping this oath: For though" She added smiling, while She sealed his lips with a wanton kiss; "Though I forgive your breaking your vows to heaven, I expect you to keep your vows to me."

The Friar returned the embrace which had set his blood on fire. The luxurious and unbounded excesses of the former night were renewed, and they separated not till the Bell rang for Matins.

The same pleasures were frequently repeated. The Monks rejoiced in the feigned Rosario's unexpected recovery, and none of them suspected his real sex. The Abbot possessed his Mistress in tranquillity, and perceiving his frailty unsuspected, abandoned himself to his passions in full security. Shame and remorse no longer tormented him. Frequent repetitions made him familiar with sin, and his bosom became proof against the stings of Conscience. In these sentiments He was encouraged by Matilda; But She soon was aware that She had satiated her Lover by the unbounded freedom of her caresses. Her charms becoming accustomed to him, they ceased to excite the same desires which at first they had inspired. The delirium of passion being past, He had leisure to observe every trifling defect: Where none were to be found, Satiety made him fancy them. The Monk was glutted with the fullness of pleasure: A Week had scarcely elapsed before He was wearied of his Paramour: His warm constitution still made him seek in her arms the gratification of his lust: But when the moment of passion was over, He quitted her with disgust, and his humour, naturally inconstant, made him sigh impatiently for variety.

Possession, which cloys Man, only increases the affection of Woman. Matilda with every succeeding day grew more attached to the Friar. Since He had obtained her favours, He was become dearer to her than ever, and She felt grateful to him for the pleasures in which they had equally been Sharers. Unfortunately as her passion grew ardent, Ambrosio's grew cold; The very marks of her fondness excited his disgust, and its excess served to extinguish the flame which already burned but feebly in his bosom. Matilda could not but remark that her society seemed to him daily less agreeable: He was inattentive while She spoke: her musical talents, which She possessed in perfection, had lost the power of amusing him; Or if He deigned to praise them, his compliments were evidently forced and cold. He no longer gazed upon her with affection, or applauded her sentiments with a Lover's partiality. This Matilda well perceived, and redoubled her efforts to revive those sentiments which He once had felt. She could not but fail, since He considered as importunities the pains which She took to please him, and was disgusted by the very means which She used to recall the Wanderer. Still, however, their illicit Commerce continued: But it was clear that He was led to her arms, not by love, but the cravings of brutal appetite. His constitution made a

Woman necessary to him, and Matilda was the only one with whom He could indulge his passions safely: In spite of her beauty, He gazed upon every other Female with more desire; But fearing that his Hypocrisy should be made public, He confined his inclinations to his own breast.

It was by no means his nature to be timid: But his education had impressed his mind with fear so strongly, that apprehension was now become part of his character. Had his Youth been passed in the world, He would have shown himself possessed of many brilliant and manly qualities. He was naturally enterprizing, firm, and fearless: He had a Warrior's heart, and He might have shone with splendour at the head of an Army. There was no want of generosity in his nature: The Wretched never failed to find in him a compassionate Auditor: His abilities were quick and shining, and his judgment, vast, solid, and decisive. With such qualifications He would have been an ornament to his Country: That He possessed them, He had given proofs in his earliest infancy, and his Parents had beheld his dawning virtues with the fondest delight and admiration. Unfortunately, while yet a Child He was deprived of those Parents. He fell into the power of a Relation whose only wish about him was never to hear of him more; For that purpose He gave him in charge to his Friend, the former Superior of the Capuchins. The Abbot, a very Monk, used all his endeavours to persuade the Boy that happiness existed not without the walls of a Convent. He succeeded fully. To deserve admittance into the order of St. Francis was Ambrosio's highest ambition. His Instructors carefully repressed those virtues whose grandeur and disinterestedness were ill-suited to the Cloister. Instead of universal benevolence, He adopted a selfish partiality for his own particular establishment: He was taught to consider compassion for the errors of Others as a crime of the blackest dye: The noble frankness of his temper was exchanged for servile humility; and in order to break his natural spirit, the Monks terrified his young mind by placing before him all the horrors with which Superstition could furnish them: They painted to him the torments of the Damned in colours the most dark, terrible, and fantastic, and threatened him at the slightest fault with eternal perdition. No wonder that his imagination constantly dwelling upon these fearful objects should have rendered his character timid and apprehensive. Add to this, that his long absence from the great world, and total unacquaintance with the common dangers of life, made him form of them an idea far more dismal than the reality. While the Monks were busied in rooting out his virtues and narrowing his sentiments, they allowed every vice which had fallen to his share to arrive at full perfection. He was suffered to be proud, vain, ambitious, and disdainful: He was jealous of his Equals, and despised all merit but his own: He was implacable when offended, and cruel in his revenge. Still in spite of the pains taken to pervert them, his natural good qualities would occasionally break through the gloom cast over them so carefully:

At such times the contest for superiority between his real and acquired character was striking and unaccountable to those unacquainted with his original disposition. He pronounced the most severe sentences upon Offenders, which, the moment after, Compassion induced him to mitigate: He undertook the most daring enterprizes, which the fear of their consequences soon obliged him to abandon: His inborn genius darted a brilliant light upon subjects the most obscure; and almost instantaneously his Superstition replunged them in darkness more profound than that from which they had just been rescued. His Brother Monks, regarding him as a Superior Being, remarked not this contradiction in their Idol's conduct. They were persuaded that what He did must be right, and supposed him to have good reasons for changing his resolutions. The fact was, that the different sentiments with which Education and Nature had inspired him were combating in his bosom: It remained for his passions, which as yet no opportunity had called into play, to decide the victory. Unfortunately his passions were the very worst Judges, to whom He could possibly have applied. His monastic seclusion had till now been in his favour, since it gave him no room for discovering his bad qualities. The superiority of his talents raised him too far above his Companions to permit his being jealous of them: His exemplary piety, persuasive eloquence, and pleasing manners had secured him universal Esteem, and consequently He had no injuries to revenge: His Ambition was justified by his acknowledged merit, and his pride considered as no more than proper confidence. He never saw, much less conversed with, the other sex: He was ignorant of the pleasures in Woman's power to bestow, and if He read in the course of his studies

"That men were fond, he smiled, and wondered how!"

For a time, spare diet, frequent watching, and severe penance cooled and represt the natural warmth of his constitution: But no sooner did opportunity present itself, no sooner did He catch a glimpse of joys to which He was still a Stranger, than Religion's barriers were too feeble to resist the overwhelming torrent of his desires. All impediments yielded before the force of his temperament, warm, sanguine, and voluptuous in the excess.

529

As yet his other passions lay dormant; But they only needed to be once awakened, to display themselves with violence as great and irresistible.

He continued to be the admiration of Madrid. The Enthusiasm created by his eloquence seemed rather to increase than diminish.

Every Thursday, which was the only day when He appeared in public, the Capuchin Cathedral was crowded with Auditors, and his discourse was always received with the same approbation. He was named Confessor to all the chief families in Madrid; and no one was counted fashionable who was injoined penance by any other than Ambrosio. In his resolution of never stirring out of his Convent, He still persisted. This circumstance created a still greater opinion of his sanctity and self-denial. Above all, the Women sang forth his praises loudly, less influenced by devotion than by his noble countenance, majestic air, and well-turned, graceful figure. The Abbey door was thronged with Carriages from morning to night; and the noblest and fairest Dames of Madrid confessed to the Abbot their secret peccadilloes.

The eyes of the luxurious Friar devoured their charms: Had his Penitents consulted those Interpreters, He would have needed no other means of expressing his desires. For his misfortune, they were so strongly persuaded of his continence, that the possibility of his harbouring indecent thoughts never once entered their imaginations. The climate's heat, 'tis well known, operates with no small influence upon the constitutions of the Spanish Ladies: But the most abandoned would have thought it an easier task to inspire with passion the marble Statue of St. Francis than the cold and rigid heart of the immaculate Ambrosio.

On his part, the Friar was little acquainted with the depravity of the world; He suspected not that but few of his Penitents would have rejected his addresses. Yet had He been better instructed on this head, the danger attending such an attempt would have sealed up his lips in silence. He knew that it would be difficult for a Woman to keep a secret so strange and so important as his frailty; and He even trembled lest Matilda should betray him. Anxious to preserve a reputation which was infinitely dear to him, He saw all the risque of committing it to the power of some vain giddy Female; and as the Beauties of Madrid affected only his senses without touching his heart, He forgot them as soon as they were out of his sight. The danger of discovery, the fear of being repulsed, the loss of reputation, all these considerations counselled him to stifle his desires: And though He now felt for it the most perfect indifference, He was necessitated to confine himself to Matilda's person.

One morning, the confluence of Penitents was greater than usual. He was detained in the Confessional Chair till a late hour. At length the crowd was dispatched, and He prepared to quit the Chapel, when two Females entered and drew near him with humility. They threw up their veils, and the youngest entreated him to listen to her for a few moments. The melody of her voice, of that voice to which no Man ever listened without interest, immediately caught Ambrosio's attention. He stopped. The Petitioner seemed bowed down with affliction: Her cheeks were pale, her eyes dimmed with tears, and her hair fell in disorder over her face and bosom. Still her countenance was so sweet, so innocent, so heavenly, as might have charmed an heart less susceptible, than that which panted in the Abbot's breast. With more than usual softness of manner He desired her to proceed, and heard her speak as follows with an emotion which increased every moment.

"Reverend Father, you see an Unfortunate, threatened with the loss of her dearest, of almost her only Friend! My Mother, my excellent Mother lies upon the bed of sickness. A sudden and dreadful malady seized her last night; and so rapid has been its progress, that the Physicians despair of her life. Human aid fails me; Nothing remains for me but to implore the mercy of Heaven. Father, all Madrid rings with the report of your piety and virtue. Deign to remember my Mother in your prayers: Perhaps they may prevail on the Almighty to spare her; and should that be the case, I engage myself every Thursday in the next three Months to illuminate the Shrine of St. Francis in his honour."

"So!" thought the Monk; "Here we have a second Vincentio della Ronda. Rosario's adventure began thus," and He wished secretly that this might have the same conclusion.

He acceded to the request. The Petitioner returned him thanks with every mark of gratitude, and then continued.

"I have yet another favour to ask. We are Strangers in Madrid; My Mother needs a Confessor, and knows not to whom She should apply. We understand that you never quit the Abbey, and Alas! my poor Mother is unable to come hither! If you would have the goodness, reverend Father, to name a proper person, whose wise and pious consolations may soften the agonies of my Parent's deathbed, you will confer an everlasting favour upon hearts not ungrateful."

With this petition also the Monk complied. Indeed, what petition would He have refused, if urged in such enchanting accents? The suppliant was so interesting! Her voice was so sweet, so harmonious! Her very tears became her, and her affliction seemed to add new lustre to her charms. He promised to send to her a Confessor that same Evening, and begged her to leave her address. The Companion presented him with a Card on which it was written, and then withdrew with the fair Petitioner, who pronounced before her departure a thousand benedictions on the Abbot's goodness. His eyes followed her out of the Chapel. It was not till She was out of sight that He examined the Card, on which He read the following words.

"Donna Elvira Dalfa, Strada di San Iago, four doors from the Palace d'Albornos."

The Suppliant was no other than Antonia, and Leonella was her Companion. The Latter had not consented without difficulty to accompany her Niece to the Abbey: Ambrosio had inspired her with such awe that She trembled at the very sight of him. Her fears had conquered even her natural loquacity, and while in his presence She uttered not a single syllable.

The Monk retired to his Cell, whither He was pursued by Antonia's image. He felt a thousand new emotions springing in his bosom, and He trembled to examine into the cause which gave them birth. They were totally different from those inspired by Matilda, when She first declared her sex and her affection. He felt not the provocation of lust; No voluptuous desires rioted in his bosom; Nor did a burning imagination picture to him the charms which Modesty had veiled from his eyes. On the contrary, what He now felt was a mingled sentiment of tenderness, admiration, and respect. A soft and delicious melancholy infused itself into his soul, and He would not have exchanged it for the most lively transports of joy. Society now disgusted him: He delighted in solitude, which permitted his indulging the visions of Fancy: His thoughts were all gentle, sad, and soothing, and the whole wide world presented him with no other object than Antonia.

"Happy Man!" He exclaimed in his romantic enthusiasm; "Happy Man, who is destined to possess the heart of that lovely Girl! What delicacy in her features! What elegance in her form! How enchanting was the timid innocence of her eyes, and how different from the wanton expression, the wild luxurious fire which sparkles in Matilda's! Oh! sweeter must one kiss be snatched from the rosy lips of the First, than all the full and lustful favours bestowed so freely by the Second. Matilda gluts me with enjoyment even to loathing, forces me to her arms, apes the Harlot, and glories in her prostitution. Disgusting! Did She know the inexpressible charm of Modesty, how irresistibly it enthralls the heart of Man, how firmly it chains him to the Throne of Beauty, She never would have thrown it off. What would be too dear a price for this lovely Girl's affections? What would I refuse to sacrifice, could I be released from my vows, and permitted to declare my love in the sight of earth and heaven? While I strove to inspire her with tenderness, with friendship and esteem, how tranquil and undisturbed would the hours roll away! Gracious God! To see her blue downcast eyes beam upon mine with timid fondness! To sit for days, for years listening to that gentle voice! To acquire the right of obliging her, and hear the artless expressions of her gratitude! To watch the emotions of her spotless heart! To encourage each dawning virtue! To share in her joy when happy, to kiss away her tears when distrest, and to see her fly to my arms for comfort and support! Yes; If there is perfect bliss on earth, 'tis his lot alone, who becomes that Angel's Husband."

While his fancy coined these ideas, He paced his Cell with a disordered air. His eyes were fixed upon vacancy: His head reclined upon his shoulder; A tear rolled down his cheek, while He reflected that the vision of happiness for him could never be realized.

"She is lost to me!" He continued; "By marriage She cannot be mine: And to seduce such innocence, to use the confidence reposed in me to work her ruin.... Oh! it would be a crime, blacker than yet the world ever witnessed! Fear not, lovely Girl! Your virtue runs no risque from me. Not for Indies would I make that gentle bosom know the tortures of remorse."

Again He paced his chamber hastily. Then stopping, his eye fell upon the picture of his once-admired Madona. He tore it with indignation from the wall: He threw it on the ground, and spurned it from him with his foot.

"The Prostitute!"

Unfortunate Matilda! Her Paramour forgot that for his sake alone She had forfeited her claim to virtue; and his only reason for despising her was that She had loved him much too well.

He threw himself into a Chair which stood near the Table. He saw the card with Elvira's address. He took it up, and it brought to his recollection his promise respecting a Confessor. He passed a few minutes in doubt: But Antonia's Empire over him was already too much decided to permit his making a long resistance to the idea which struck him. He resolved to be the Confessor himself. He could leave the Abbey unobserved without difficulty: By wrapping up his head in his Cowl He hoped to pass through the Streets without being recognised: By taking these precautions, and by recommending secrecy to Elvira's family, He doubted not to keep Madrid in ignorance that He had broken his vow never to see the outside of the Abbey walls. Matilda was the only person whose vigilance He dreaded: But by informing her at the Refectory that during the whole of that day, Business would confine him to his Cell, He thought himself secure from her wakeful jealousy. Accordingly, at the hours when the Spaniards are generally taking their Siesta, He ventured to quit the Abbey by a private door, the Key of which was in his possession. The Cowl of his habit was thrown over his face: From the heat of the weather the Streets were almost totally deserted: The Monk met with few people, found the Strada di San Iago, and arrived without accident at Donna Elvira's door. He rang, was admitted, and immediately ushered into an upper apartment.

It was here that He ran the greatest risque of a discovery. Had Leonella been at home, She would have recognized him directly: Her communicative disposition would never have permitted her to rest till all Madrid was informed that Ambrosio had ventured out of the Abbey, and visited her Sister. Fortune here stood the Monk's Friend. On Leonella's return home, She found a letter instructing her that a Cousin was just dead, who had left what little He possessed between Herself and Elvira. To secure this bequest She was obliged to set out for Cordova without losing a moment. Amidst all her foibles her heart was truly warm and affectionate, and She was unwilling to quit her Sister in so dangerous a state. But Elvira insisted upon her taking the journey, conscious that in her Daughter's forlorn situation no increase of fortune, however trifling, ought to be neglected. Accordingly, Leonella left Madrid, sincerely grieved at her Sister's illness, and giving some few sighs to the memory of the amiable but inconstant Don Christoval. She was fully persuaded that at first She had made a terrible breach in his heart: But hearing nothing more of him, She supposed that He had quitted the pursuit, disgusted by the lowness of her origin, and knowing upon other terms than marriage He had nothing to hope from such a Dragon of Virtue as She professed herself; Or else, that being naturally capricious and changeable,

the remembrance of her charms had been effaced from the
Condé's heart by those of some newer Beauty. Whatever was
the cause of her losing him, She lamented it sorely. She strove in
vain, as She assured every body who was kind enough to listen
to her, to tear his image from her too susceptible heart. She
affected the airs of a lovesick Virgin, and carried them all to the
most ridiculous excess. She heaved lamentable sighs, walked
with her arms folded, uttered long soliloquies, and her
discourse generally turned upon some forsaken Maid who
expired of a broken heart! Her fiery locks were always
ornamented with a garland of willow; Every evening She was
seen straying upon the Banks of a rivulet by Moonlight; and She
declared herself a violent Admirer of murmuring Streams and
Nightingales;

"Of lonely haunts, and twilight Groves,

"Places which pale Passion loves!"

Such was the state of Leonella's mind, when obliged to quit
Madrid. Elvira was out of patience at all these follies, and
endeavoured at persuading her to act like a reasonable Woman.
Her advice was thrown away: Leonella assured her at parting
that nothing could make her forget the perfidious Don
Christoval. In this point She was fortunately mistaken. An
honest Youth of Cordova, Journeyman to an Apothecary, found
that her fortune would be sufficient to set him up in a genteel
Shop of his own: In consequence of this reflection He avowed
himself her Admirer. Leonella was not inflexible. The ardour of
his sighs melted her heart, and She soon consented to make him
the happiest of Mankind. She wrote to inform her Sister of her
marriage; But, for reasons which will be explained hereafter,
Elvira never answered her letter.

Ambrosio was conducted into the Antichamber to that
where Elvira was reposing. The Female Domestic who had
admitted him left him alone while She announced his arrival to
her Mistress. Antonia, who had been by her Mother's Bedside,
immediately came to him.

"Pardon me, Father," said She, advancing towards him;
when recognizing his features, She stopped suddenly, and
uttered a cry of joy. "Is it possible!" She continued;

"Do not my eyes deceive me? Has the worthy Ambrosio
broken through his resolution, that He may soften the agonies
of the best of Women? What pleasure will this visit give my
Mother! Let me not delay for a moment the comfort which your

piety and wisdom will afford her."

Thus saying, She opened the chamber door, presented to her Mother her distinguished Visitor, and having placed an armed-chair by the side of the Bed, withdrew into another department.

Elvira was highly gratified by this visit: Her expectations had been raised high by general report, but She found them far exceeded. Ambrosio, endowed by nature with powers of pleasing, exerted them to the utmost while conversing with Antonia's Mother. With persuasive eloquence He calmed every fear, and dissipated every scruple: He bad her reflect on the infinite mercy of her Judge, despoiled Death of his darts and terrors, and taught her to view without shrinking the abyss of eternity, on whose brink She then stood. Elvira was absorbed in attention and delight: While She listened to his exhortations, confidence and comfort stole insensibly into her mind. She unbosomed to him without hesitation her cares and apprehensions. The latter respecting a future life He had already quieted: And He now removed the former, which She felt for the concerns of this. She trembled for Antonia. She had none to whose care She could recommend her, save to the Marquis de las Cisternas and her Sister Leonella. The protection of the One was very uncertain; and as to the Other, though fond of her Niece, Leonella was so thoughtless and vain as to make her an improper person to have the sole direction of a Girl so young and ignorant of the World. The Friar no sooner learnt the cause of her alarms than He begged her to make herself easy upon that head. He doubted not being able to secure for Antonia a safe refuge in the House of one of his Penitents, the Marchioness of Villa-Franca: This was a Lady of acknowledged virtue, remarkable for strict principles and extensive charity. Should accident deprive her of this resource, He engaged to procure Antonia a reception in some respectable Convent: That is to say, in quality of boarder; for Elvira had declared herself no Friend to a monastic life, and the Monk was either candid or complaisant enough to allow that her disapprobation was not unfounded.

These proofs of the interest which He felt for her completely won Elvira's heart. In thanking him She exhausted every expression which Gratitude could furnish, and protested that now She should resign herself with tranquillity to the Grave. Ambrosio rose to take leave: He promised to return the next day at the same hour, but requested that his visits might be kept secret.

"I am unwilling" said He, "that my breaking through a rule imposed by necessity should be generally known. Had I not resolved never to quit my Convent, except upon circumstances as urgent as that which has conducted me to your door, I should be frequently summoned upon insignificant occasions: That time would be engrossed by the Curious, the Unoccupied, and the fanciful, which I now pass at the Bedside of the Sick, in comforting the expiring Penitent, and clearing the passage to Eternity from Thorns."

Elvira commended equally his prudence and compassion, promising to conceal carefully the honour of his visits. The Monk then gave her his benediction, and retired from the chamber.

In the Antiroom He found Antonia: He could not refuse himself the pleasure of passing a few moments in her society. He bad her take comfort, for that her Mother seemed composed and tranquil, and He hoped that She might yet do well. He enquired who attended her, and engaged to send the Physician of his Convent to see her, one of the most skilful in Madrid. He then launched out in Elvira's commendation, praised her purity and fortitude of mind, and declared that She had inspired him with the highest esteem and reverence. Antonia's innocent heart swelled with gratitude: Joy danced in her eyes, where a tear still sparkled. The hopes which He gave her of her Mother's recovery, the lively interest which He seemed to feel for her, and the flattering way in which She was mentioned by him, added to the report of his judgment and virtue, and to the impression made upon her by his eloquence, confirmed the favourable opinion with which his first appearance had inspired Antonia. She replied with diffidence, but without restraint: She feared not to relate to him all her little sorrows, all her little fears and anxieties; and She thanked him for his goodness with all the genuine warmth which favours kindle in a young and innocent heart. Such alone know how to estimate benefits at their full value. They who are conscious of Mankind's perfidy and selfishness, ever receive an obligation with apprehension and distrust: They suspect that some secret motive must lurk behind it: They express their thanks with restraint and caution, and fear to praise a kind action to its full extent, aware that some future day a return may be required. Not so Antonia; She thought the world was composed only of those who resembled her, and that vice existed, was to her still a secret. The Monk had been of service to her; He said that He wished her well; She was grateful for his kindness, and thought that no terms were strong enough to be the vehicle of her thanks. With what delight did Ambrosio listen to the declaration of her artless gratitude!

The natural grace of her manners, the unequalled sweetness of her voice, her modest vivacity, her unstudied elegance, her expressive countenance, and intelligent eyes united to inspire him with pleasure and admiration, While the solidity and correctness of her remarks received additional beauty from the unaffected simplicity of the language in which they were conveyed.

Ambrosio was at length obliged to tear himself from this conversation which possessed for him but too many charms. He repeated to Antonia his wishes that his visits should not be made known, which desire She promised to observe. He then quitted the House, while his Enchantress hastened to her Mother, ignorant of the mischief which her Beauty had caused. She was eager to know Elvira's opinion of the Man whom She had praised in such enthusiastic terms, and was delighted to find it equally favourable, if not even more so, than her own.

"Even before He spoke," said Elvira, "I was prejudiced in his favour: The fervour of his exhortations, dignity of his manner, and closeness of his reasoning, were very far from inducing me to alter my opinion. His fine and full-toned voice struck me particularly; But surely, Antonia, I have heard it before. It seemed perfectly familiar to my ear. Either I must have known the Abbot in former times, or his voice bears a wonderful resemblance to that of some other, to whom I have often listened.

There were certain tones which touched my very heart, and made me feel sensations so singular, that I strive in vain to account for them."

"My dearest Mother, it produced the same effect upon me: Yet certainly neither of us ever heard his voice till we came to Madrid. I suspect that what we attribute to his voice, really proceeds from his pleasant manners, which forbid our considering him as a Stranger. I know not why, but I feel more at my ease while conversing with him than I usually do with people who are unknown to me. I feared not to repeat to him all my childish thoughts; and somehow I felt confident that He would hear my folly with indulgence. Oh! I was not deceived in him! He listened to me with such an air of kindness and attention! He answered me with such gentleness, such condescension! He did not call me an Infant, and treat me with contempt, as our cross old Confessor at the Castle used to do. I verily believe that if I had lived in Murcia a thousand years, I never should have liked that fat old Father Dominic!"

"I confess that Father Dominic had not the most pleasing manners in the world; But He was honest, friendly, and well-meaning."

"Ah! my dear Mother, those qualities are so common!"

"God grant, my Child, that Experience may not teach you to think them rare and precious: I have found them but too much so! But tell me, Antonia; Why is it impossible for me to have seen the Abbot before?"

"Because since the moment when He entered the Abbey, He has never been on the outside of its walls. He told me just now, that from his ignorance of the Streets, He had some difficulty to find the Strada di San Iago, though so near the Abbey."

"All this is possible, and still I may have seen him BEFORE He entered the Abbey: In order to come out, it was rather necessary that He should first go in."

"Holy Virgin! As you say, that is very true. — Oh! But might He not have been born in the Abbey?"

Elvira smiled.

"Why, not very easily."

"Stay, Stay! Now I recollect how it was. He was put into the Abbey quite a Child; The common People say that He fell from heaven, and was sent as a present to the Capuchins by the Virgin."

"That was very kind of her. And so He fell from heaven, Antonia?

He must have had a terrible tumble."

"Many do not credit this, and I fancy, my dear Mother, that I must number you among the Unbelievers. Indeed, as our Landlady told my Aunt, the general idea is that his Parents, being poor and unable to maintain him, left him just born at the Abbey door. The late Superior from pure charity had him educated in the Convent, and He proved to be a model of virtue, and piety, and learning, and I know not what else besides: In consequence, He was first received as a Brother of the order, and not long ago was chosen Abbot. However, whether this account or the other is the true one, at least all agree that when the Monks took him under their care, He could not speak: Therefore, you could not have heard his voice before He entered the Monastery, because at that time He had no voice at all."

"Upon my word, Antonia, you argue very closely! Your conclusions are infallible! I did not suspect you of being so able a Logician."

"Ah! You are mocking me! But so much the better. It delights me to see you in spirits: Besides you seem tranquil and easy, and I hope that you will have no more convulsions. Oh! I was sure the Abbot's visit would do you good!"

"It has indeed done me good, my Child. He has quieted my mind upon some points which agitated me, and I already feel the effects of his attention. My eyes grow heavy, and I think I can sleep a little. Draw the curtains, my Antonia: But if I should not wake before midnight, do not sit up with me, I charge you."

Antonia promised to obey her, and having received her blessing drew the curtains of the Bed. She then seated herself in silence at her embroidery frame, and beguiled the hours with building Castles in the air. Her spirits were enlivened by the evident change for the better in Elvira, and her fancy presented her with visions bright and pleasing. In these dreams Ambrosio made no despicable figure. She thought of him with joy and gratitude; But for every idea which fell to the Friar's share, at least two were unconsciously bestowed upon Lorenzo. Thus passed the time, till the Bell in the neighbouring Steeple of the Capuchin Cathedral announced the hour of midnight: Antonia remembered her Mother's injunctions, and obeyed them, though with reluctance. She undrew the curtains with caution. Elvira was enjoying a profound and quiet slumber; Her cheek glowed with health's returning colours: A smile declared that her dreams were pleasant, and as Antonia bent over her, She fancied that She heard her name pronounced. She kissed her Mother's forehead softly, and retired to her chamber. There She knelt before a Statue of St. Rosolia, her Patroness; She recommended herself to the protection of heaven, and as had been her custom from infancy, concluded her devotions by chaunting the following Stanzas.

The Monk: A Romance
MIDNIGHT HYMN

Now all is hushed; The solemn chime
No longer swells the nightly gale:
Thy awful presence, Hour sublime,
With spotless heart once more I hail.

'Tis now the moment still and dread,
When Sorcerers use their baleful power;
When Graves give up their buried dead
To profit by the sanctioned hour:

From guilt and guilty thoughts secure,
To duty and devotion true,
With bosom light and conscience pure,
Repose, thy gentle aid I woo.

Good Angels, take my thanks, that still
The snares of vice I view with scorn;
Thanks, that to-night as free from ill
I sleep, as when I woke at morn.

Yet may not my unconscious breast
Harbour some guilt to me unknown?
Some wish impure, which unreprest
You blush to see, and I to own?

If such there be, in gentle dream
Instruct my feet to shun the snare;

Bid truth upon my errors beam,
And deign to make me still your care.

Chase from my peaceful bed away
The witching Spell, a foe to rest,
The nightly Goblin, wanton Fay,
The Ghost in pain, and Fiend unblest:

Let not the Tempter in mine ear
Pour lessons of unhallowed joy;
Let not the Night-mare, wandering near
My Couch, the calm of sleep destroy;

Let not some horrid dream affright
With strange fantastic forms mine eyes;
But rather bid some vision bright
Display the bliss of yonder skies.

Show me the crystal Domes of Heaven,
The worlds of light where Angels lie;
Shew me the lot to Mortals given,
Who guiltless live, who guiltless die.

Then show me how a seat to gain
Amidst those blissful realms of
Air; Teach me to shun each guilty stain,
And guide me to the good and fair.

So every morn and night, my Voice

To heaven the grateful strain shall raise;

In You as Guardian Powers rejoice,

Good Angels, and exalt your praise:

So will I strive with zealous fire

Each vice to shun, each fault correct;

Will love the lessons you inspire,

And Prize the virtues you protect.

Then when at length by high command

My body seeks the Grave's repose,

When Death draws nigh with friendly hand

My failing Pilgrim eyes to close;

Pleased that my soul has 'scaped the wreck,

Sighless will I my life resign,

And yield to God my Spirit back,

As pure as when it first was mine.

aving finished her usual devotions, Antonia retired to bed. Sleep soon stole over her senses; and for several hours She enjoyed that calm repose which innocence alone can know, and for which many a Monarch with pleasure would exchange his Crown.

— — Ah! how dark

These long-extended realms and rueful wastes;

Where nought but silence reigns, and night, dark night,

Dark as was Chaos ere the Infant Sun

Was rolled together, or had tried its beams

Athwart the gloom profound!

The sickly Taper

By glimmering through thy low-browed misty vaults,

Furred round with mouldy damps, and ropy slime,

Lets fall a supernumerary horror,

And only serves to make

Thy night more irksome!

BLAIR.

Returned undiscovered to the Abbey, Ambrosio's mind was filled with the most pleasing images. He was wilfully blind to the danger of exposing himself to Antonia's charms: He only remembered the pleasure which her society had afforded him, and rejoiced in the prospect of that pleasure being repeated. He failed not to profit by Elvira's indisposition to obtain a sight of her Daughter every day. At first He bounded his wishes to inspire Antonia with friendship: But no sooner was He convinced that She felt that sentiment in its fullest extent, than his aim became more decided, and his attentions assumed a warmer colour. The innocent familiarity with which She treated him, encouraged his desires: Grown used to her modesty, it no longer commanded the same respect and awe: He still admired it, but it only made him more anxious to deprive her of that quality which formed her principal charm. Warmth of passion, and natural penetration, of which latter unfortunately both for himself and Antonia He possessed an ample share, supplied a knowledge of the arts of seduction. He easily distinguished the emotions which were favourable to his designs, and seized every means with avidity of infusing corruption into Antonia's bosom. This He found no easy matter. Extreme simplicity prevented her from perceiving the aim to which the Monk's insinuations tended; But the excellent morals which She owed to Elvira's care, the solidity and correctness of her understanding, and a strong sense of what was right implanted in her heart by Nature, made her feel that his precepts must be faulty. By a few simple words She frequently overthrew the whole bulk of his sophistical arguments, and made him conscious how weak they were when opposed to Virtue and Truth. On such occasion He took refuge in his eloquence; He overpowered her with a torrent of Philosophical paradoxes, to which, not understanding them, it was impossible for her to reply; And thus though He did not convince her that his reasoning was just, He at least prevented her from discovering it to be false. He perceived that her respect for his judgment augmented daily, and doubted not with time to bring her to the point desired.

He was not unconscious that his attempts were highly criminal: He saw clearly the baseness of seducing the innocent Girl: But his passion was too violent to permit his abandoning his design. He resolved to pursue it, let the consequences be what they might. He depended upon finding Antonia in some unguarded moment; And seeing no other Man admitted into her society, nor hearing any mentioned either by her or by Elvira, He imagined that her young heart was still unoccupied. While He waited for the opportunity of satisfying his unwarrantable lust, every day increased his coldness for Matilda. Not a little was this occasioned by the consciousness of his faults to her. To hide them from her He was not sufficiently master of himself: Yet He dreaded lest, in a transport of jealous rage, She should betray the secret on which his character and even his life depended. Matilda could not but remark his indifference: He was conscious that She remarked it, and fearing her reproaches, shunned her studiously. Yet when He could not avoid her, her mildness might have convinced him that He had nothing to dread from her resentment. She had resumed the character of the gentle interesting Rosario: She taxed him not with ingratitude; But her eyes filled with involuntary tears, and the soft melancholy of her countenance and voice uttered complaints far more touching than words could have conveyed. Ambrosio was not unmoved by her sorrow; But unable to remove its cause, He forbore to show that it affected him. As her conduct convinced him that He needed not fear her vengeance, He continued to neglect her, and avoided her company with care. Matilda saw that She in vain attempted to regain his affections: Yet She stifled the impulse of resentment, and continued to treat her inconstant Lover with her former fondness and attention.

545

By degrees Elvira's constitution recovered itself. She was no longer troubled with convulsions, and Antonia ceased to tremble for her Mother. Ambrosio beheld this reestablishment with displeasure. He saw that Elvira's knowledge of the world would not be the Dupe of his sanctified demeanour, and that She would easily perceive his views upon her Daughter. He resolved therefore, before She quitted her chamber, to try the extent of his influence over the innocent Antonia.

One evening, when He had found Elvira almost perfectly restored to health, He quitted her earlier than was his usual custom. Not finding Antonia in the Antichamber, He ventured to follow her to her own. It was only separated from her Mother's by a Closet, in which Flora, the Waiting-Woman, generally slept. Antonia sat upon a Sopha with her back towards the door, and read attentively. She heard not his approach, till He had seated himself by her. She started, and welcomed him with a look of pleasure: Then rising, She would have conducted him to the sitting-room; But Ambrosio taking her hand, obliged her by gentle violence to resume her place. She complied without difficulty: She knew not that there was more impropriety in conversing with him in one room than another. She thought herself equally secure of his principles and her own, and having replaced herself upon the Sopha, She began to prattle to him with her usual ease and vivacity.

He examined the Book which She had been reading, and had now placed upon the Table. It was the Bible.

"How!" said the Friar to himself; "Antonia reads the Bible, and is still so ignorant?"

But, upon a further inspection, He found that Elvira had made exactly the same remark. That prudent Mother, while She admired the beauties of the sacred writings, was convinced that, unrestricted, no reading more improper could be permitted a young Woman. Many of the narratives can only tend to excite ideas the worst calculated for a female breast: Every thing is called plainly and roundly by its name; and the annals of a Brothel would scarcely furnish a greater choice of indecent expressions. Yet this is the Book which young Women are recommended to study; which is put into the hands of Children, able to comprehend little more than those passages of which they had better remain ignorant; and which but too frequently inculcates the first rudiments of vice, and gives the first alarm to the still sleeping passions. Of this was Elvira so fully convinced, that She would have preferred putting into her Daughter's hands "Amadis de Gaul," or "The Valiant Champion, Tirante the White;" and would sooner have authorised her studying the lewd exploits of "Don Galaor," or the lascivious jokes of the "Damsel Plazer di mi vida." She had in consequence made two resolutions respecting the Bible. The first was that Antonia should not read it till She was of an age to feel its beauties, and profit by its morality: The second, that it should be copied out with her own hand, and all improper passages either altered or omitted. She had adhered to this determination, and such was the Bible which Antonia was reading: It had been lately delivered to her, and She perused it with an avidity, with a delight that was inexpressible. Ambrosio perceived his mistake, and replaced the Book upon the Table.

Antonia spoke of her Mother's health with all the enthusiastic joy of a youthful heart.

"I admire your filial affection," said the Abbot; "It proves the excellence and sensibility of your character; It promises a treasure to him whom Heaven has destined to possess your affections. The Breast, so capable of fondness for a Parent, what will it feel for a Lover? Nay, perhaps, what feels it for one even now? Tell me, my lovely Daughter; Have you known what it is to love? Answer me with sincerity: Forget my habit, and consider me only as a Friend."

"What it is to love?" said She, repeating his question; "Oh! yes, undoubtedly; I have loved many, many People."

"That is not what I mean. The love of which I speak can be felt only for one. Have you never seen the Man whom you wished to be your Husband?"

"Oh! No, indeed!"

This was an untruth, but She was unconscious of its falsehood: She knew not the nature of her sentiments for Lorenzo; and never having seen him since his first visit to Elvira, with every day his Image grew less feebly impressed upon her bosom. Besides, She thought of an Husband with all a Virgin's terror, and negatived the Friar's demand without a moment's hesitation.

"And do you not long to see that Man, Antonia? Do you feel no void in your heart which you fain would have filled up? Do you heave no sighs for the absence of some one dear to you, but who that some one is, you know not? Perceive you not that what formerly could please, has charms for you no longer? That a thousand new wishes, new ideas, new sensations, have sprang in your bosom, only to be felt, never to be described? Or while you fill every other heart with passion, is it possible that your own remains insensible and cold? It cannot be! That melting eye, that blushing cheek, that enchanting voluptuous melancholy which at times overspreads your features, all these marks belye your words. You love, Antonia, and in vain would hide it from me."

"Father, you amaze me! What is this love of which you speak? I neither know its nature, nor if I felt it, why I should conceal the sentiment."

"Have you seen no Man, Antonia, whom though never seen before, you seemed long to have sought? Whose form, though a Stranger's, was familiar to your eyes? The sound of whose voice soothed you, pleased you, penetrated to your very soul? In whose presence you rejoiced, for whose absence you lamented? With whom your heart seemed to expand, and in whose bosom with confidence unbounded you reposed the cares of your own? Have you not felt all this, Antonia?"

"Certainly I have: The first time that I saw you, I felt it."

Ambrosio started. Scarcely dared He credit his hearing.

"Me, Antonia?" He cried, his eyes sparkling with delight and impatience, while He seized her hand, and pressed it rapturously to his lips. "Me, Antonia? You felt these sentiments for me?"

"Even with more strength than you have described. The very moment that I beheld you, I felt so pleased, so interested! I waited so eagerly to catch the sound of your voice, and when I heard it, it seemed so sweet! It spoke to me a language till then so unknown! Methought, it told me a thousand things which I wished to hear! It seemed as if I had long known you; as if I had a right to your friendship, your advice, and your protection.

I wept when you departed, and longed for the time which should restore you to my sight."

"Antonia! my charming Antonia!" exclaimed the Monk, and caught her to his bosom; "Can I believe my senses? Repeat it to me, my sweet Girl! Tell me again that you love me, that you love me truly and tenderly!"

"Indeed, I do: Let my Mother be excepted, and the world holds no one more dear to me!"

At this frank avowal Ambrosio no longer possessed himself; Wild with desire, He clasped the blushing Trembler in his arms. He fastened his lips greedily upon hers, sucked in her pure delicious breath, violated with his bold hand the treasures of her bosom, and wound around him her soft and yielding limbs. Startled, alarmed, and confused at his action, surprize at first deprived her of the power of resistance. At length recovering herself, She strove to escape from his embrace.

"Father! .... Ambrosio!" She cried; "Release me, for God's sake!"

But the licentious Monk heeded not her prayers: He persisted in his design, and proceeded to take still greater liberties. Antonia prayed, wept, and struggled: Terrified to the extreme, though at what She knew not, She exerted all her strength to repulse the Friar, and was on the point of shrieking for assistance when the chamber door was suddenly thrown open. Ambrosio had just sufficient presence of mind to be sensible of his danger. Reluctantly He quitted his prey, and started hastily from the Couch. Antonia uttered an exclamation of joy, flew towards the door, and found herself clasped in the arms of her Mother.

Alarmed at some of the Abbot's speeches, which Antonia had innocently repeated, Elvira resolved to ascertain the truth of her suspicions. She had known enough of Mankind not to be imposed upon by the Monk's reputed virtue. She reflected on several circumstances, which though trifling, on being put together seemed to authorize her fears. His frequent visits, which as far as She could see, were confined to her family; His evident emotion, whenever She spoke of Antonia; His being in the full prime and heat of Manhood; and above all, his pernicious philosophy communicated to her by Antonia, and which accorded but ill with his conversation in her presence, all these circumstances inspired her with doubts respecting the purity of Ambrosio's friendship. In consequence, She resolved, when He should next be alone with Antonia, to endeavour at surprizing him. Her plan had succeeded. 'Tis true, that when She entered the room, He had already abandoned his prey; But the disorder of her Daughter's dress, and the shame and confusion stamped upon the Friar's countenance, sufficed to prove that her suspicions were but too well-founded. However, She was too prudent to make those suspicions known. She judged that to unmask the Imposter would be no easy matter, the public being so much prejudiced in his favour: and having but few Friends, She thought it dangerous to make herself so powerful an Enemy. She affected therefore not to remark his agitation, seated herself tranquilly upon the Sopha, assigned some trifling reason for having quitted her room unexpectedly, and conversed on various subjects with seeming confidence and ease.

Reassured by her behaviour, the Monk began to recover himself. He strove to answer Elvira without appearing embarrassed: But He was still too great a novice in dissimulation, and He felt that He must look confused and awkward. He soon broke off the conversation, and rose to depart. What was his vexation, when on taking leave, Elvira told him in polite terms, that being now perfectly reestablished, She thought it an injustice to deprive Others of his company, who might be more in need of it! She assured him of her eternal gratitude, for the benefit which during her illness She had derived from his society and exhortations: And She lamented that her domestic affairs, as well as the multitude of business which his situation must of necessity impose upon him, would in future deprive her of the pleasure of his visits. Though delivered in the mildest language this hint was too plain to be mistaken. Still, He was preparing to put in a remonstrance when an expressive look from Elvira stopped him short. He dared not press her to receive him, for her manner convinced him that He was discovered: He submitted without reply, took an hasty leave, and retired to the Abbey, his heart filled with rage and shame, with bitterness and disappointment.

Antonia's mind felt relieved by his departure; Yet She could not help lamenting that She was never to see him more. Elvira also felt a secret sorrow; She had received too much pleasure from thinking him her Friend, not to regret the necessity of changing her opinion: But her mind was too much accustomed to the fallacy of worldly friendships to permit her present disappointment to weigh upon it long. She now endeavoured to make her Daughter aware of the risque which She had ran: But She was obliged to treat the subject with caution, lest in removing the bandage of ignorance, the veil of innocence should be rent away. She therefore contented herself with warning Antonia to be upon her guard, and ordering her, should the Abbot persist in his visits, never to receive them but in company. With this injunction Antonia promised to comply.

Ambrosio hastened to his Cell. He closed the door after him, and threw himself upon the bed in despair. The impulse of desire, the stings of disappointment, the shame of detection, and the fear of being publicly unmasked, rendered his bosom a scene of the most horrible confusion. He knew not what course to pursue. Debarred the presence of Antonia, He had no hopes of satisfying that passion which was now become a part of his existence. He reflected that his secret was in a Woman's power: He trembled with apprehension when He beheld the precipice before him, and with rage, when He thought that had it not been for Elvira, He should now have possessed the object of his desires. With the direct imprecations He vowed vengeance against her; He swore that, cost what it would, He still would possess Antonia. Starting from the Bed, He paced the chamber with disordered steps, howled with impotent fury, dashed himself violently against the walls, and indulged all the transports of rage and madness.

He was still under the influence of this storm of passions when He heard a gentle knock at the door of his Cell. Conscious that his voice must have been heard, He dared not refuse admittance to the Importuner: He strove to compose himself, and to hide his agitation. Having in some degree succeeded, He drew back the bolt: The door opened, and Matilda appeared.

At this precise moment there was no one with whose presence He could better have dispensed. He had not sufficient command over himself to conceal his vexation. He started back, and frowned.

"I am busy," said He in a stern and hasty tone; "Leave me!"

Matilda heeded him not: She again fastened the door, and then advanced towards him with an air gentle and supplicating.

"Forgive me, Ambrosio," said She; "For your own sake I must not obey you. Fear no complaints from me; I come not to reproach you with your ingratitude. I pardon you from my heart, and since your love can no longer be mine, I request the next best gift, your confidence and friendship. We cannot force our inclinations; The little beauty which you once saw in me has perished with its novelty, and if it can no longer excite desire, mine is the fault, not yours. But why persist in shunning me? Why such anxiety to fly my presence? You have sorrows, but will not permit me to share them; You have disappointments, but will not accept my comfort; You have wishes, but forbid my aiding your pursuits. 'Tis of this which I complain, not of your indifference to my person. I have given up the claims of the Mistress, but nothing shall prevail on me to give up those of the Friend."

Her mildness had an instantaneous effect upon Ambrosio's feelings.

"Generous Matilda!" He replied, taking her hand, "How far do you rise superior to the foibles of your sex! Yes, I accept your offer. I have need of an adviser, and a Confident: In you I find every needful quality united. But to aid my pursuits .... Ah! Matilda, it lies not in your power!"

"It lies in no one's power but mine. Ambrosio, your secret is none to me; Your every step, your every action has been observed by my attentive eye. You love."

"Matilda!"

"Why conceal it from me? Fear not the little jealousy which taints the generality of Women: My soul disdains so despicable a passion. You love, Ambrosio; Antonia Dalfa is the object of your flame. I know every circumstance respecting your passion: Every conversation has been repeated to me. I have been informed of your attempt to enjoy Antonia's person, your disappointment, and dismission from Elvira's House. You now despair of possessing your Mistress; But I come to revive your hopes, and point out the road to success."

"To success? Oh! impossible!"

"To them who dare nothing is impossible. Rely upon me, and you may yet be happy. The time is come, Ambrosio, when regard for your comfort and tranquillity compels me to reveal a part of my History, with which you are still unacquainted. Listen, and do not interrupt me: Should my confession disgust you, remember that in making it my sole aim is to satisfy your wishes, and restore that peace to your heart which at present has abandoned it. I formerly mentioned that my Guardian was a Man of uncommon knowledge: He took pains to instil that knowledge into my infant mind. Among the various sciences which curiosity had induced him to explore, He neglected not that which by most is esteemed impious, and by many chimerical. I speak of those arts which relate to the world of Spirits. His deep researches into causes and effects, his unwearied application to the study of natural philosophy, his profound and unlimited knowledge of the properties and virtues of every gem which enriches the deep, of every herb which the earth produces, at length procured him the distinction which He had sought so long, so earnestly. His curiosity was fully slaked, his ambition amply gratified. He gave laws to the elements; He could reverse the order of nature; His eye read the mandates of futurity, and the infernal Spirits were submissive to his commands. Why shrink you from me? I understand that enquiring look. Your suspicions are right,

552

though your terrors are unfounded. My Guardian concealed not from me his most precious acquisition. Yet, had I never seen you, I should never have exerted my power. Like you I shuddered at the thoughts of Magic: Like you I had formed a terrible idea of the consequences of raising a daemon. To preserve that life which your love had taught me to prize, I had recourse to means which I trembled at employing. You remember that night which I past in St. Clare's Sepulchre? Then was it that, surrounded by mouldering bodies, I dared to perform those mystic rites which summoned to my aid a fallen Angel. Judge what must have been my joy at discovering that my terrors were imaginary: I saw the Dæmon obedient to my orders, I saw him trembling at my frown, and found that, instead of selling my soul to a Master, my courage had purchased for myself a slave."

"Rash Matilda! What have you done? You have doomed yourself to endless perdition; You have bartered for momentary power eternal happiness! If on witchcraft depends the fruition of my desires, I renounce your aid most absolutely. The consequences are too horrible: I doat upon Antonia, but am not so blinded by lust as to sacrifice for her enjoyment my existence both in this world and the next."

"Ridiculous prejudices! Oh! blush, Ambrosio, blush at being subjected to their dominion. Where is the risque of accepting my offers? What should induce my persuading you to this step, except the wish of restoring you to happiness and quiet. If there is danger, it must fall upon me: It is I who invoke the ministry of the Spirits; Mine therefore will be the crime, and yours the profit. But danger there is none: The Enemy of Mankind is my Slave, not my Sovereign. Is there no difference between giving and receiving laws, between serving and commanding? Awake from your idle dreams, Ambrosio! Throw from you these terrors so ill-suited to a soul like yours; Leave them for common Men, and dare to be happy! Accompany me this night to St. Clare's Sepulchre, witness my incantations, and Antonia is your own."

"To obtain her by such means I neither can, or will. Cease then to persuade me, for I dare not employ Hell's agency.

"You DARE not? How have you deceived me! That mind which I esteemed so great and valiant, proves to be feeble, puerile, and grovelling, a slave to vulgar errors, and weaker than a Woman's."

"What? Though conscious of the danger, wilfully shall I expose myself to the Seducer's arts? Shall I renounce for ever my title to salvation? Shall my eyes seek a sight which I know will blast them? No, no, Matilda; I will not ally myself with God's Enemy."

"Are you then God's Friend at present? Have you not broken your engagements with him, renounced his service, and abandoned yourself to the impulse of your passions? Are you not planning the destruction of innocence, the ruin of a Creature whom He formed in the mould of Angels? If not of Dæmons, whose aid would you invoke to forward this laudable design? Will the Seraphims protect it, conduct Antonia to your arms, and sanction with their ministry your illicit pleasures? Absurd! But I am not deceived, Ambrosio! It is not virtue which makes you reject my offer: You WOULD accept it, but you dare not. 'Tis not the crime which holds your hand, but the punishment; 'Tis not respect for God which restrains you, but the terror of his vengeance! Fain would you offend him in secret, but you tremble to profess yourself his Foe. Now shame on the coward soul, which wants the courage either to be a firm Friend or open Enemy!"

"To look upon guilt with horror, Matilda, is in itself a merit: In this respect I glory to confess myself a Coward. Though my passions have made me deviate from her laws, I still feel in my heart an innate love of virtue. But it ill becomes you to tax me with my perjury: You, who first seduced me to violate my vows; You, who first rouzed my sleeping vices, made me feel the weight of Religion's chains, and bad me be convinced that guilt had pleasures. Yet though my principles have yielded to the force of temperament, I still have sufficient grace to shudder at Sorcery, and avoid a crime so monstrous, so unpardonable!"

"Unpardonable, say you? Where then is your constant boast of the Almighty's infinite mercy? Has He of late set bounds to it? Receives He no longer a Sinner with joy? You injure him, Ambrosio; You will always have time to repent, and He have goodness to forgive. Afford him a glorious opportunity to exert that goodness: The greater your crime, the greater his merit in pardoning. Away then with these childish scruples: Be persuaded to your good, and follow me to the Sepulchre."

"Oh! cease, Matilda! That scoffing tone, that bold and impious language, is horrible in every mouth, but most so in a Woman's. Let us drop a conversation which excites no other sentiments than horror and disgust. I will not follow you to the Sepulchre, or accept the services of your infernal Agents.

Antonia shall be mine, but mine by human means."

"Then yours She will never be! You are banished her presence; Her Mother has opened her eyes to your designs, and She is now upon her guard against them. Nay more, She loves another. A Youth of distinguished merit possesses her heart, and unless you interfere, a few days will make her his Bride. This intelligence was brought me by my invisible Servants, to whom I had recourse on first perceiving your indifference. They watched your every action, related to me all that past at Elvira's, and inspired me with the idea of favouring your designs. Their reports have been my only comfort. Though you shunned my presence, all your proceedings were known to me: Nay, I was constantly with you in some degree, thanks to this precious gift!"

With these words She drew from beneath her habit a mirror of polished steel, the borders of which were marked with various strange and unknown characters.

"Amidst all my sorrows, amidst all my regrets for your coldness, I was sustained from despair by the virtues of this Talisman. On pronouncing certain words, the Person appears in it on whom the Observer's thoughts are bent: thus though I was exiled from your sight, you, Ambrosio, were ever present to mine."

The Friar's curiosity was excited strongly.

"What you relate is incredible! Matilda, are you not amusing yourself with my credulity?"

"Be your own eyes the Judge."

She put the Mirror into his hand. Curiosity induced him to take it, and Love, to wish that Antonia might appear. Matilda pronounced the magic words. Immediately, a thick smoke rose from the characters traced upon the borders, and spread itself over the surface. It dispersed again gradually; A confused mixture of colours and images presented themselves to the Friar's eyes, which at length arranging themselves in their proper places, He beheld in miniature Antonia's lovely form.

The scene was a small closet belonging to her apartment. She was undressing to bathe herself. The long tresses of her hair were already bound up. The amorous Monk had full opportunity to observe the voluptuous contours and admirable symmetry of her person. She threw off her last garment, and advancing to the Bath prepared for her, She put her foot into the water. It struck cold, and She drew it back again. Though unconscious of being observed, an inbred sense of modesty induced her to veil her charms; and She stood hesitating upon the brink, in the attitude of the Venus de Medicis. At this moment a tame Linnet flew towards her, nestled its head between her breasts, and nibbled them in wanton play. The smiling Antonia strove in vain to shake off the Bird, and at length raised her hands to drive it from its delightful harbour. Ambrosio could bear no more: His desires were worked up to phrenzy.

"I yield!" He cried, dashing the mirror upon the ground: "Matilda, I follow you! Do with me what you will!"

She waited not to hear his consent repeated. It was already midnight. She flew to her Cell, and soon returned with her little basket and the Key of the Cemetery, which had remained in her possession since her first visit to the Vaults. She gave the Monk no time for reflection.

"Come!" She said, and took his hand; "Follow me, and witness the effects of your resolve!"

This said, She drew him hastily along. They passed into the Burying-ground unobserved, opened the door of the Sepulchre, and found themselves at the head of the subterraneous Staircase. As yet the beams of the full Moon had guided their steps, but that resource now failed them. Matilda had neglected to provide herself with a Lamp. Still holding Ambrosio's hand She descended the marble steps; But the profound obscurity with which they were overspread obliged them to walk slow and cautiously.

"You tremble!" said Matilda to her Companion; "Fear not; The destined spot is near."

They reached the foot of the Staircase, and continued to proceed, feeling their way along the Walls. On turning a corner suddenly, they descried faint gleams of light which seemed burning at a distance. Thither they bent their steps: The rays proceeded from a small sepulchral Lamp which flamed unceasingly before the Statue of St. Clare. It tinged with dim and cheerless beams the massy Columns which supported the Roof, but was too feeble to dissipate the thick gloom in which the Vaults above were buried.

Matilda took the Lamp.

"Wait for me!" said She to the Friar; "In a few moments I am here again."

With these words She hastened into one of the passages which branched in various directions from this spot, and formed a sort of Labyrinth. Ambrosio was now left alone: Darkness the most profound surrounded him, and encouraged the doubts which began to revive in his bosom. He had been hurried away by the delirium of the moment: The shame of betraying his terrors, while in Matilda's presence, had induced him to repress them; But now that he was abandoned to himself, they resumed their former ascendancy. He trembled at the scene which He was soon to witness. He knew not how far the delusions of Magic might operate upon his mind, and possibly might force him to some deed whose commission would make the breach between himself and Heaven irreparable. In this fearful dilemma, He would have implored God's assistance, but was conscious that He had forfeited all claim to such protection. Gladly would He have returned to the Abbey; But as He had past through innumerable Caverns and winding passages, the attempt of regaining the Stairs was hopeless. His fate was determined: No possibility of escape presented itself: He therefore combated his apprehensions, and called every argument to his succour, which might enable him to support the trying scene with fortitude. He reflected that Antonia would be the reward of his daring: He inflamed his imagination by enumerating her charms. He persuaded himself that (as Matilda had observed), He always should have time sufficient for repentance, and that as He employed her assistance, not that of the Dæmons, the crime of Sorcery could not be laid to his charge. He had read much respecting witchcraft: He understood that unless a formal Act was signed renouncing his claim to salvation, Satan would have no power over him. He was fully determined not to execute any such act, whatever threats might be used, or advantages held out to him.

Such were his meditations while waiting for Matilda. They were interrupted by a low murmur which seemed at no great distance from him. He was startled. He listened. Some minutes past in silence, after which the murmur was repeated. It appeared to be the groaning of one in pain. In any other situation, this circumstance would only have excited his attention and curiosity:

In the present, his predominant sensation was that of terror. His imagination totally engrossed by the ideas of sorcery and Spirits, He fancied that some unquiet Ghost was wandering near him; or else that Matilda had fallen a Victim to her presumption, and was perishing under the cruel fangs of the Dæmons. The noise seemed not to approach, but continued to be heard at intervals. Sometimes it became more audible, doubtless as the sufferings of the person who uttered the groans became more acute and insupportable. Ambrosio now and then thought that He could distinguish accents; and once in particular He was almost convinced that He heard a faint voice exclaim,

"God! Oh! God! No hope! No succour!"

Yet deeper groans followed these words. They died away gradually, and universal silence again prevailed.

"What can this mean?" thought the bewildered Monk.

At that moment an idea which flashed into his mind, almost petrified him with horror. He started, and shuddered at himself.

"Should it be possible!" He groaned involuntarily; "Should it but be possible, Oh! what a Monster am I!"

He wished to resolve his doubts, and to repair his fault, if it were not too late already: But these generous and compassionate sentiments were soon put to flight by the return of Matilda. He forgot the groaning Sufferer, and remembered nothing but the danger and embarrassment of his own situation. The light of the returning Lamp gilded the walls, and in a few moments after Matilda stood beside him. She had quitted her religious habit: She was now cloathed in a long sable Robe, on which was traced in gold embroidery a variety of unknown characters: It was fastened by a girdle of precious stones, in which was fixed a poignard. Her neck and arms were uncovered. In her hand She bore a golden wand. Her hair was loose and flowed wildly upon her shoulders; Her eyes sparkled with terrific expression; and her whole Demeanour was calculated to inspire the beholder with awe and admiration.

"Follow me!" She said to the Monk in a low and solemn voice; "All is ready!"

His limbs trembled, while He obeyed her. She led him through various narrow passages; and on every side as they past along, the beams of the Lamp displayed none but the most revolting objects; Skulls, Bones, Graves, and Images whose eyes seemed to glare on them with horror and surprize. At length they reached a spacious Cavern, whose lofty roof the eye sought in vain to discover. A profound obscurity hovered through the void. Damp vapours struck cold to the Friar's heart; and He listened sadly to the blast while it howled along the lonely Vaults. Here Matilda stopped. She turned to Ambrosio. His cheeks and lips were pale with apprehension. By a glance of mingled scorn and anger She reproved his pusillanimity, but She spoke not. She placed the Lamp upon the ground, near the Basket. She motioned that Ambrosio should be silent, and began the mysterious rites. She drew a circle round him, another round herself, and then taking a small Phial from the Basket, poured a few drops upon the ground before her. She bent over the place, muttered some indistinct sentences, and immediately a pale sulphurous flame arose from the ground. It increased by degrees, and at length spread its waves over the whole surface, the circles alone excepted in which stood Matilda and the Monk. It then ascended the huge Columns of unhewn stone, glided along the roof, and formed the Cavern into an immense chamber totally covered with blue trembling fire. It emitted no heat: On the contrary, the extreme chillness of the place seemed to augment with every moment. Matilda continued her incantations: At intervals She took various articles from the Basket, the nature and name of most of which were unknown to the Friar: But among the few which He distinguished, He particularly observed three human fingers, and an Agnus Dei which She broke in pieces. She threw them all into the flames which burned before her, and they were instantly consumed.

The Monk beheld her with anxious curiosity. Suddenly She uttered a loud and piercing shriek. She appeared to be seized with an access of delirium; She tore her hair, beat her bosom, used the most frantic gestures, and drawing the poignard from her girdle plunged it into her left arm. The blood gushed out plentifully, and as She stood on the brink of the circle, She took care that it should fall on the outside. The flames retired from the spot on which the blood was pouring. A volume of dark clouds rose slowly from the ensanguined earth, and ascended gradually, till it reached the vault of the Cavern. At the same time a clap of thunder was heard: The echo pealed fearfully along the subterraneous passages, and the ground shook beneath the feet of the Enchantress.

It was now that Ambrosio repented of his rashness. The solemn singularity of the charm had prepared him for something strange and horrible. He waited with fear for the Spirit's appearance, whose coming was announced by thunder and earthquakes. He looked wildly round him, expecting that some dreadful Apparition would meet his eyes, the sight of which would drive him mad. A cold shivering seized his body, and He sank upon one knee, unable to support himself.

"He comes!" exclaimed Matilda in a joyful accent.

Ambrosio started, and expected the Dæmon with terror. What was his surprize, when the Thunder ceasing to roll, a full strain of melodious Music sounded in the air. At the same time the cloud dispersed, and He beheld a Figure more beautiful than Fancy's pencil ever drew. It was a Youth seemingly scarce eighteen, the perfection of whose form and face was unrivalled. He was perfectly naked: A bright Star sparkled upon his forehead; Two crimson wings extended themselves from his shoulders; and his silken locks were confined by a band of many-coloured fires, which played round his head, formed themselves into a variety of figures, and shone with a brilliance far surpassing that of precious Stones. Circlets of Diamonds were fastened round his arms and ankles, and in his right hand He bore a silver branch, imitating Myrtle. His form shone with dazzling glory: He was surrounded by clouds of rose-coloured light, and at the moment that He appeared, a refreshing air breathed perfumes through the Cavern. Enchanted at a vision so contrary to his expectations, Ambrosio gazed upon the Spirit with delight and wonder: Yet however beautiful the Figure, He could not but remark a wildness in the Dæmon's eyes, and a mysterious melancholy impressed upon his features, betraying the Fallen Angel, and inspiring the Spectators with secret awe.

The Music ceased. Matilda addressed herself to the Spirit: She spoke in a language unintelligible to the Monk, and was answered in the same. She seemed to insist upon something which the Dæmon was unwilling to grant. He frequently darted upon Ambrosio angry glances, and at such times the Friar's heart sank within him. Matilda appeared to grow incensed. She spoke in a loud and commanding tone, and her gestures declared that She was threatening him with her vengeance. Her menaces had the desired effect: The Spirit sank upon his knee, and with a submissive air presented to her the branch of Myrtle. No sooner had She received it, than the Music was again heard; A thick cloud spread itself over the Apparition; The blue flames disappeared, and total obscurity reigned through the Cave. The Abbot moved not from his place: His faculties were all bound up in pleasure, anxiety, and surprize. At length the darkness dispersing, He perceived Matilda standing near him in her religious habit, with the Myrtle in her hand. No traces of the incantation, and the Vaults were only illuminated by the faint rays of the sepulchral Lamp.

"I have succeeded," said Matilda, "though with more difficulty than I expected. Lucifer, whom I summoned to my assistance, was at first unwilling to obey my commands: To enforce his compliance I was constrained to have recourse to my strongest charms. They have produced the desired effect, but I have engaged never more to invoke his agency in your favour. Beware then, how you employ an opportunity which never will return. My magic arts will now be of no use to you: In future you can only hope for supernatural aid by invoking the Dæmons yourself, and accepting the conditions of their service. This you will never do: You want strength of mind to force them to obedience, and unless you pay their established price, they will not be your voluntary Servants. In this one instance they consent to obey you: I offer you the means of enjoying your Mistress, and be careful not to lose the opportunity. Receive this constellated Myrtle: While you bear this in your hand, every door will fly open to you. It will procure you access tomorrow night to Antonia's chamber: Then breathe upon it thrice, pronounce her name, and place it upon her pillow. A death-like slumber will immediately seize upon her, and deprive her of the power of resisting your attempts. Sleep will hold her till break of Morning. In this state you may satisfy your desires without danger of being discovered; since when daylight shall dispel the effects of the enchantment, Antonia will perceive her dishonour, but be ignorant of the Ravisher. Be happy then, my Ambrosio, and let this service convince you that my friendship is disinterested and pure. The night must be near expiring: Let us return to the Abbey, lest our absence should create surprize."

The Abbot received the talisman with silent gratitude. His ideas were too much bewildered by the adventures of the night to permit his expressing his thanks audibly, or indeed as yet to feel the whole value of her present. Matilda took up her Lamp and Basket, and guided her Companion from the mysterious Cavern. She restored the Lamp to its former place, and continued her route in darkness, till She reached the foot of the Staircase. The first beams of the rising Sun darting down it facilitated the ascent. Matilda and the Abbot hastened out of the Sepulchre, closed the door after them, and soon regained the Abbey's western Cloister. No one met them, and they retired unobserved to their respective Cells.

The confusion of Ambrosio's mind now began to appease. He rejoiced in the fortunate issue of his adventure, and reflecting upon the virtues of the Myrtle, looked upon Antonia as already in his power. Imagination retraced to him those secret charms betrayed to him by the Enchanted Mirror, and He waited with impatience for the approach of midnight.

CHAPTER VIII.

The crickets sing, and Man's o'er-laboured sense

Repairs itself by rest: Our Tarquin thus

Did softly press the rushes, ere He wakened

The chastity He wounded—Cytherea,

How bravely thou becom'st thy bed! Fresh Lily!

And whiter than the sheets!

CYMBELINE.

All the researches of the Marquis de las Cisternas proved vain: Agnes was lost to him for ever. Despair produced so violent an effect upon his constitution, that the consequence was a long and severe illness. This prevented him from visiting Elvira as He had intended; and She being ignorant of the cause of his neglect, it gave her no trifling uneasiness. His Sister's death had prevented Lorenzo from communicating to his Uncle his designs respecting Antonia: The injunctions of her Mother forbad his presenting himself to her without the Duke's consent; and as She heard no more of him or his proposals, Elvira conjectured that He had either met with a better match, or had been commanded to give up all thoughts of her Daughter. Every day made her more uneasy respecting Antonia's fate: While She retained the Abbot's protection, She bore with fortitude the disappointment of her hopes with regard to Lorenzo and the Marquis. That resource now failed her. She was convinced that Ambrosio had meditated her Daughter's ruin: And when She reflected that her death would leave Antonia friendless and unprotected in a world so base, so perfidious and depraved, her heart swelled with the bitterness of apprehension. At such times She would sit for hours gazing upon the lovely Girl; and seeming to listen to her innocent prattle, while in reality her thoughts dwelt upon the sorrows into which a moment would suffice to plunge her. Then She would clasp her in her arms suddenly, lean her head upon her Daughter's bosom, and bedew it with her tears.

An event was in preparation which, had She known it, would have relieved her from her inquietude. Lorenzo now waited only for a favourable opportunity to inform the Duke of his intended marriage: However, a circumstance which occurred at this period, obliged him to delay his explanation for a few days longer.

Don Raymond's malady seemed to gain ground. Lorenzo was constantly at his bedside, and treated him with a tenderness truly fraternal. Both the cause and effects of the disorder were highly afflicting to the Brother of Agnes: yet Theodore's grief was scarcely less sincere. That amiable Boy quitted not his Master for a moment, and put every means in practice to console and alleviate his sufferings. The Marquis had conceived so rooted an affection for his deceased Mistress, that it was evident to all that He never could survive her loss: Nothing could have prevented him from sinking under his grief but the persuasion of her being still alive, and in need of his assistance. Though convinced of its falsehood, his Attendants encouraged him in a belief which formed his only comfort. He was assured daily that fresh perquisitions were making respecting the fate of Agnes: Stories were invented recounting the various attempts made to get admittance into the Convent; and circumstances were related which, though they did not promise her absolute recovery, at least were sufficient to keep his hopes alive. The Marquis constantly fell into the most terrible excess of passion when informed of the failure of these supposed attempts. Still He would not credit that the succeeding ones would have the same fate, but flattered himself that the next would prove more fortunate.

Theodore was the only one who exerted himself to realize his Master's Chimoeras. He was eternally busied in planning schemes for entering the Convent, or at least of obtaining from the Nuns some intelligence of Agnes. To execute these schemes was the only inducement which could prevail on him to quit Don Raymond. He became a very Proteus, changing his shape every day; but all his metamorphoses were to very little purpose: He regularly returned to the Palace de las Cisternas without any intelligence to confirm his Master's hopes. One day He took it into his head to disguise himself as a Beggar. He put a patch over his left eye, took his Guitar in hand, and posted himself at the Gate of the Convent.

"If Agnes is really confined in the Convent," thought He, "and hears my voice, She will recollect it, and possibly may find means to let me know that She is here."

With this idea He mingled with a crowd of Beggars who assembled daily at the Gate of St. Clare to receive Soup, which the Nuns were accustomed to distribute at twelve o'clock. All were provided with jugs or bowls to carry it away; But as Theodore had no utensil of this kind, He begged leave to eat his portion at the Convent door. This was granted without difficulty: His sweet voice, and in spite of his patched eye, his engaging countenance, won the heart of the good old Porteress, who, aided by a Lay-Sister, was busied in serving to each his Mess. Theodore was bad to stay till the Others should depart, and promised that his request should then be granted. The Youth desired no better, since it was not to eat Soup that He presented himself at the Convent. He thanked the Porteress for her permission, retired from the Door, and seating himself upon a large stone, amused himself in tuning his Guitar while the Beggars were served.

As soon as the Crowd was gone, Theodore was beckoned to the Gate, and desired to come in. He obeyed with infinite readiness, but affected great respect at passing the hallowed Threshold, and to be much daunted by the presence of the Reverend Ladies. His feigned timidity flattered the vanity of the Nuns, who endeavoured to reassure him. The Porteress took him into her awn little Parlour: In the meanwhile, the Lay-Sister went to the Kitchen, and soon returned with a double portion of Soup, of better quality than what was given to the Beggars. His Hostess added some fruits and confections from her own private store, and Both encouraged the Youth to dine heartily. To all these attentions He replied with much seeming gratitude, and abundance of blessings upon his benefactresses. While He ate, the Nuns admired the delicacy of his features, the beauty of his hair, and the sweetness and grace which accompanied all his actions. They lamented to each other in whispers, that so charming a Youth should be exposed to the seductions of the World, and agreed, that He would be a worthy Pillar of the Catholic Church. They concluded their conference by resolving that Heaven would be rendered a real service if they entreated the Prioress to intercede with Ambrosio for the Beggar's admission into the order of Capuchins.

This being determined, the Porteress, who was a person of great influence in the Convent, posted away in all haste to the Domina's Cell. Here She made so flaming a narrative of Theodore's merits that the old Lady grew curious to see him. Accordingly, the Porteress was commissioned to convey him to the Parlour grate. In the interim, the supposed Beggar was sifting the Lay-Sister with respect to the fate of Agnes: Her evidence only corroborated the Domina's assertions. She said that Agnes had been taken ill on returning from confession, had never quitted her bed from that moment, and that She had herself been present at the Funeral. She even attested having seen her dead body, and assisted with her own hands in adjusting it upon the Bier. This account discouraged Theodore:

Yet as He had pushed the adventure so far, He resolved to witness its conclusion.

The Porteress now returned, and ordered him to follow her. He obeyed, and was conducted into the Parlour, where the Lady Prioress was already posted at the Grate. The Nuns surrounded her, who all flocked with eagerness to a scene which promised some diversion. Theodore saluted them with profound respect, and his presence had the power to smooth for a moment even the stern brow of the Superior. She asked several questions respecting his Parents, his religion, and what had reduced him to a state of Beggary. To these demands his answers were perfectly satisfactory and perfectly false. He was then asked his opinion of a monastic life: He replied in terms of high estimation and respect for it. Upon this, the Prioress told him that his obtaining an entrance into a religious order was not impossible; that her recommendation would not permit his poverty to be an obstacle, and that if She found him deserving it, He might depend in future upon her protection. Theodore assured her that to merit her favour would be his highest ambition; and having ordered him to return next day, when She would talk with him further, the Domina quitted the Parlour.

The Nuns, whom respect for the Superior had till then kept silent, now crowded all together to the Grate, and assailed the Youth with a multitude of questions. He had already examined each with attention: Alas! Agnes was not amongst them. The Nuns heaped question upon question so thickly that it was scarcely possible for him to reply. One asked where He was born, since his accent declared him to be a Foreigner: Another wanted to know, why He wore a patch upon his left eye: Sister Helena enquired whether He had not a Sister like him, because She should like such a Companion; and Sister Rachael was fully persuaded that the Brother would be the pleasanter Companion of the Two. Theodore amused himself with retailing to the credulous Nuns for truths all the strange stories which his imagination could invent. He related to them his supposed adventures, and penetrated every Auditor with astonishment, while He talked of Giants, Savages, Ship-wrecks, and Islands inhabited

"By anthropophagi, and men whose heads

Do grow beneath their shoulders," with many other circumstances to the full as remarkable. He said, that He was born in Terra Incognita, was educated at an Hottentot University, and had past two years among the Americans of Silesia.

"For what regards the loss of my eye" said He, "it was a just punishment upon me for disrespect to the Virgin, when I made my second pilgrimage to Loretto. I stood near the Altar in the miraculous Chapel: The Monks were proceeding to array the Statue in her best apparel. The Pilgrims were ordered to close their eyes during this ceremony: But though by nature extremely religious, curiosity was too powerful. At the moment ..... I shall penetrate you with horror, reverend Ladies, when I reveal my crime! .... At the moment that the Monks were changing her shift, I ventured to open my left eye, and gave a little peep towards the Statue. That look was my last! The Glory which surrounded the Virgin was too great to be supported. I hastily shut my sacrilegious eye, and never have been able to unclose it since!"

At the relation of this miracle the Nuns all crossed themselves, and promised to intercede with the blessed Virgin for the recovery of his sight. They expressed their wonder at the extent of his travels, and at the strange adventures which He had met with at so early an age. They now remarked his Guitar, and enquired whether he was an adept in Music. He replied with modesty that it was not for him to decide upon his talents, but requested permission to appeal to them as Judges. This was granted without difficulty.

"But at least," said the old Porteress, "take care not to sing any thing profane."

"You may depend upon my discretion," replied Theodore: "You shall hear how dangerous it is for young Women to abandon themselves to their passions, illustrated by the adventure of a Damsel who fell suddenly in love with an unknown Knight."

"But is the adventure true?" enquired the Porteress.

"Every word of it. It happened in Denmark, and the Heroine was thought so beautiful that She was known by no other name but that of 'the lovely Maid'."

"In Denmark, say you?" mumbled an old Nun; "Are not the People all Blacks in Denmark?"

"By no means, reverend Lady; They are of a delicate pea-green with flame-coloured hair and whiskers."

"Mother of God! Pea-green?" exclaimed Sister Helena; "Oh! 'tis impossible!"

"Impossible?" said the Porteress with a look of contempt and exultation: "Not at all: When I was a young Woman, I remember seeing several of them myself."

Theodore now put his instrument in proper order. He had read the story of a King of England whose prison was discovered by a Minstrel; and He hoped that the same scheme would enable him to discover Agnes, should She be in the Convent. He chose a Ballad which She had taught him herself in the Castle of Lindenberg: She might possibly catch the sound, and He hoped to hear her replying to some of the Stanzas. His Guitar was now in tune, and He prepared to strike it.

"But before I begin," said He "it is necessary to inform you, Ladies, that this same Denmark is terribly infested by Sorcerers, Witches, and Evil Spirits. Every element possesses its appropriate Dæmons. The Woods are haunted by a malignant power, called 'the Erl- or Oak-King:' He it is who blights the Trees, spoils the Harvest, and commands the Imps and Goblins: He appears in the form of an old Man of majestic figure, with a golden Crown and long white beard: His principal amusement is to entice young Children from their Parents, and as soon as He gets them into his Cave, He tears them into a thousand pieces — The Rivers are governed by another Fiend, called 'the Water-King:' His province is to agitate the deep, occasion ship-wrecks, and drag the drowning Sailors beneath the waves: He wears the appearance of a Warrior, and employs himself in luring young Virgins into his snare: What He does with them, when He catches them in the water, Reverend Ladies, I leave for you to imagine — 'The Fire-King' seems to be a Man all formed of flames: He raises the Meteors and wandering lights which beguile Travellers into ponds and marshes, and He directs the lightning where it may do most mischief — The last of these elementary Dæmons is called 'the Cloud-King:' His figure is that of a beautiful Youth, and He is distinguished by two large sable Wings: Though his outside is so enchanting, He is not a bit better disposed than the Others: He is continually employed in raising Storms, tearing up Forests by the roots, and blowing Castles and Convents about the ears of their Inhabitants. The First has a Daughter, who is Queen of the Elves and Fairies; The Second has a Mother, who is a powerful Enchantress: Neither of these Ladies are worth more than the Gentlemen: I do not remember to have heard any family assigned to the two other Dæmons, but at present I have no business with any of them except the Fiend of the Waters. He is the Hero of my Ballad; but I thought it necessary before I began, to give you some account of his proceedings —"

Theodore then played a short symphony; After which, stretching his voice to its utmost extent to facilitate its reaching the ear of Agnes, He sang the following Stanzas.

THE WATER-KING

A DANISH BALLAD

With gentle murmur flowed the tide,
While by the fragrant flowery side
The lovely Maid with carols gay
To Mary's church pursued her way.

The Water-Fiend's malignant eye
Along the Banks beheld her hie;
Straight to his Mother-witch he sped,
And thus in suppliant accents said:

"Oh! Mother! Mother! now advise,
How I may yonder Maid surprize:
Oh! Mother! Mother! Now explain,
How I may yonder Maid obtain."

The Witch She gave him armour white;
She formed him like a gallant Knight;
Of water clear next made her hand
A Steed, whose housings were of sand.

The Water-King then swift He went;
To Mary's Church his steps He bent:

He bound his Courser to the Door,
And paced the Church-yard three times four.

His Courser to the door bound He,
And paced the Church-yard four time three:
Then hastened up the Aisle, where all
The People flocked, both great and small.

The Priest said, as the Knight drew near,
"And wherefore comes the white Chief here?"
The lovely Maid She smiled aside;
"Oh! would I were the white Chief's Bride!"

He stept o'er Benches one and two;
"Oh! lovely Maid, I die for You!"
He stept o'er Benches two and three;
"Oh! lovely Maiden, go with me!"

Then sweet She smiled, the lovely Maid,
And while She gave her hand, She said,
"Betide me joy, betide me woe,
O'er Hill, o'er dale, with thee I go."

The Priest their hands together joins:
They dance, while clear the moon-beam shines;
And little thinks the Maiden bright,
Her Partner is the Water-spright.

Oh! had some spirit deigned to sing,

"Your Partner is the Water-King!"
The Maid had fear and hate confest,
And cursed the hand which then She prest.

But nothing giving cause to think,
How near She strayed to danger's brink,
Still on She went, and hand in hand
The Lovers reached the yellow sand.

"Ascend this Steed with me, my Dear;
We needs must cross the streamlet here;
Ride boldly in; It is not deep;
The winds are hushed, the billows sleep."

Thus spoke the Water-King. The Maid
Her Traitor-Bride-groom's wish obeyed:
And soon She saw the Courser lave
Delighted in his parent wave.

"Stop! Stop! my Love! The waters blue
E'en now my shrinking foot bedew!"
"Oh! lay aside your fears, sweet Heart!
We now have reached the deepest part."

"Stop! Stop! my Love! For now I see
The waters rise above my knee."
"Oh! lay aside your fears, sweet Heart!
We now have reached the deepest part."

"Stop! Stop! for God's sake, stop! For Oh!

The waters o'er my bosom flow!" —

Scarce was the word pronounced, when Knight

And Courser vanished from her sight.

She shrieks, but shrieks in vain; for high

The wild winds rising dull the cry;

The Fiend exults; The Billows dash,

And o'er their hapless Victim wash.

Three times while struggling with the stream,

The lovely Maid was heard to scream;

But when the Tempest's rage was o'er,

The lovely Maid was seen no more.

Warned by this Tale, ye Damsels fair,

To whom you give your love beware!

Believe not every handsome Knight,

And dance not with the Water-Spright!

The Youth ceased to sing. The Nuns were delighted with the sweetness of his voice and masterly manner of touching the Instrument: But however acceptable this applause would have been at any other time, at present it was insipid to Theodore. His artifice had not succeeded. He paused in vain between the Stanzas: No voice replied to his, and He abandoned the hope of equalling Blondel.

The Convent Bell now warned the Nuns that it was time to assemble in the Refectory. They were obliged to quit the Grate; They thanked the Youth for the entertainment which his Music had afforded them, and charged him to return the next day. This He promised: The Nuns, to give him the greater inclination to keep his word, told him that He might always depend upon the Convent for his meals, and each of them made him some little present. One gave him a box of sweetmeats; Another, an

Agnus Dei; Some brought reliques of Saints, waxen Images, and consecrated Crosses; and Others presented him with pieces of those works in which the Religious excel, such as embroidery, artificial flowers, lace, and needlework. All these He was advised to sell, in order to put himself into better case; and He was assured that it would be easy to dispose of them, since the Spaniards hold the performances of the Nuns in high estimation. Having received these gifts with seeming respect and gratitude, He remarked that, having no Basket, He knew not how to convey them away. Several of the Nuns were hastening in search of one, when they were stopped by the return of an elderly Woman, whom Theodore had not till then observed: Her mild countenance, and respectable air prejudiced him immediately in her favour.

"Hah!" said the Porteress; "Here comes the Mother St. Ursula with a Basket."

The Nun approached the Grate, and presented the Basket to Theodore: It was of willow, lined with blue satin, and upon the four sides were painted scenes from the legend of St. Genevieve.

"Here is my gift," said She, as She gave it into his hand; "Good Youth, despise it not; Though its value seems insignificant, it has many hidden virtues."

She accompanied these words with an expressive look. It was not lost upon Theodore; In receiving the present, He drew as near the Grate as possible.

"Agnes!" She whispered in a voice scarcely intelligible. Theodore, however, caught the sound: He concluded that some mystery was concealed in the Basket, and his heart beat with impatience and joy. At this moment the Domina returned. Her air was gloomy and frowning, and She looked if possible more stern than ever.

"Mother St. Ursula, I would speak with you in private."

The Nun changed colour, and was evidently disconcerted.

"With me?" She replied in a faltering voice.

The Domina motioned that She must follow her, and retired. The Mother St. Ursula obeyed her; Soon after, the Refectory Bell ringing a second time, the Nuns quitted the Grate, and Theodore was left at liberty to carry off his prize. Delighted that at length He had obtained some intelligence for the Marquis, He flew rather than ran, till He reached the Hotel de las Cisternas. In a few minutes He stood by his Master's Bed with the Basket in his hand. Lorenzo was in the chamber, endeavouring to reconcile his Friend to a misfortune which He felt himself but too severely. Theodore related his adventure, and the hopes which had been created by the Mother St. Ursula's gift. The Marquis started from his pillow: That fire which since the death of Agnes had been extinguished, now revived in his bosom, and his eyes sparkled with the eagerness of expectation. The emotions which Lorenzo's countenance betrayed, were scarcely weaker, and He waited with inexpressible impatience for the solution of this mystery. Raymond caught the basket from the hands of his Page: He emptied the contents upon the bed, and examined them with minute attention. He hoped that a letter would be found at the bottom; Nothing of the kind appeared. The search was resumed, and still with no better success. At length Don Raymond observed that one corner of the blue satin lining was unripped; He tore it open hastily, and drew forth a small scrap of paper neither folded or sealed. It was addressed to the Marquis de las Cisternas, and the contents were as follows:

"Having recognised your Page, I venture to send these few lines. Procure an order from the Cardinal-Duke for seizing my Person, and that of the Domina; But let it not be executed till Friday at midnight. It is the Festival of St. Clare: There will be a procession of Nuns by torch-light, and I shall be among them. Beware not to let your intention be known: Should a syllable be dropt to excite the Domina's suspicions, you will never hear of me more. Be cautious, if you prize the memory of Agnes, and wish to punish her Assassins. I have that to tell, will freeze your blood with horror.

"ST. URSULA."

No sooner had the Marquis read the note than He fell back upon his pillow deprived of sense or motion. The hope failed him which till now had supported his existence; and these lines convinced him but too positively that Agnes was indeed no more. Lorenzo felt this circumstance less forcibly, since it had always been his idea that his Sister had perished by unfair means. When He found by the Mother St. Ursula's letter how true were his suspicions, the confirmation excited no other sentiment in his bosom than a wish to punish the Murderers as they deserved. It was no easy task to recall the Marquis to himself. As soon as He recovered his speech, He broke out into execrations against the Assassins of his Beloved, and vowed to take upon them a signal vengeance. He continued to rave and torment himself with impotent passion till his constitution, enfeebled by grief and illness, could support itself no longer, and He relapsed into insensibility. His melancholy situation sincerely affected Lorenzo, who would willingly have remained in the apartment of his Friend; But other cares now demanded his presence. It was necessary to procure the order for seizing the Prioress of St. Clare. For this purpose, having committed Raymond to the care of the best Physicians in Madrid, He quitted the Hotel de las Cisternas, and bent his course towards the Palace of the Cardinal-Duke.

His disappointment was excessive, when He found that affairs of State had obliged the Cardinal to set out for a distant Province.

It wanted but five to Friday: Yet by travelling day and night, He hoped to return in time for the Pilgrimage of St. Clare. In this He succeeded. He found the Cardinal-Duke; and represented to him the supposed culpability of the Prioress, as also the violent effects which it had produced upon Don Raymond. He could have used no argument so forcible as this last. Of all his Nephews, the Marquis was the only one to whom the Cardinal-Duke was sincerely attached: He perfectly doated upon him, and the Prioress could have committed no greater crime in his eyes than to have endangered the life of the Marquis. Consequently, He granted the order of arrest without difficulty: He also gave Lorenzo a letter to a principal Officer of the Inquisition, desiring him to see his mandate executed. Furnished with these papers, Medina hastened back to Madrid, which He reached on the Friday a few hours before dark. He found the Marquis somewhat easier, but so weak and exhausted that without great exertion He could neither speak or more. Having past an hour by his Bedside, Lorenzo left him to communicate his design to his Uncle, as also to give Don Ramirez de Mello the Cardinal's letter. The First was petrified with horror when He learnt the fate of his unhappy Niece: He encouraged Lorenzo to punish her Assassins, and engaged to accompany him at night to St. Clare's Convent. Don Ramirez promised his firmest support, and selected a band of trusty Archers to prevent opposition on the part of the Populace.

But while Lorenzo was anxious to unmask one religious Hypocrite, He was unconscious of the sorrows prepared for him by Another. Aided by Matilda's infernal Agents, Ambrosio had resolved upon the innocent Antonia's ruin. The moment destined to be so fatal to her arrived. She had taken leave of her Mother for the night.

575

As She kissed her, She felt an unusual despondency infuse itself into her bosom. She left her, and returned to her instantly, threw herself into her maternal arms, and bathed her cheek with tears: She felt uneasy at quitting her, and a secret presentiment assured her that never must they meet again. Elvira observed, and tried to laugh her out of this childish prejudice: She chid her mildly for encouraging such ungrounded sadness, and warned her how dangerous it was to encourage such ideas.

To all her remonstrances She received no other answer than,

"Mother! Dear Mother! Oh! would to God, it were Morning!"

Elvira, whose inquietude respecting her Daughter was a great obstacle to her perfect reestablishment, was still labouring under the effects of her late severe illness. She was this Evening more than usually indisposed, and retired to bed before her accustomed hour. Antonia withdrew from her Mother's chamber with regret, and till the Door closed, kept her eyes fixed upon her with melancholy expression. She retired to her own apartment; Her heart was filled with bitterness: It seemed to her that all her prospects were blasted, and the world contained nothing for which it was worth existing. She sank into a Chair, reclined her head upon her arm, and gazed upon the floor with a vacant stare, while the most gloomy images floated before her fancy. She was still in this state of insensibility when She was disturbed by hearing a strain of soft Music breathed beneath her window. She rose, drew near the Casement, and opened it to hear it more distinctly. Having thrown her veil over her face, She ventured to look out. By the light of the Moon She perceived several Men below with Guitars and Lutes in their hands; and at a little distance from them stood Another wrapped in his cloak, whose stature and appearance bore a strong resemblance to Lorenzo's. She was not deceived in this conjecture. It was indeed Lorenzo himself, who bound by his word not to present himself to Antonia without his Uncle's consent, endeavoured by occasional Serenades, to convince his Mistress that his attachment still existed. His stratagem had not the desired effect. Antonia was far from supposing that this nightly music was intended as a compliment to her: She was too modest to think herself worthy such attentions; and concluding them to be addressed to some neighbouring Lady, She grieved to find that they were offered by Lorenzo.

The air which was played, was plaintive and melodious. It accorded with the state of Antonia's mind, and She listened with pleasure. After a symphony of some length, it was succeeded by the sound of voices, and Antonia distinguished the following words.

SERENADE

Chorus

Oh! Breathe in gentle strain, my Lyre!
'Tis here that Beauty loves to rest:
Describe the pangs of fond desire,
Which rend a faithful Lover's breast.

Song

In every heart to find a Slave,
In every Soul to fix his reign,
In bonds to lead the wise and brave,
And make the Captives kiss his chain,
Such is the power of Love, and Oh!
I grieve so well Love's power to know.

In sighs to pass the live-long day,
To taste a short and broken sleep,
For one dear Object far away,
All others scorned, to watch and weep,
Such are the pains of Love, and Oh!
I grieve so well Love's pains to know!

To read consent in virgin eyes,

To press the lip ne'er prest till then

To hear the sigh of transport rise,

And kiss, and kiss, and kiss again,

Such are thy pleasures, Love, But Oh!

When shall my heart thy pleasures know?

Chorus

Now hush, my Lyre! My voice be still!

Sleep, gentle Maid! May fond desire

With amorous thoughts thy visions fill,

Though still my voice, and hushed my Lyre.

The Music ceased: The Performers dispersed, and silence prevailed through the Street. Antonia quitted the window with regret: She as usual recommended herself to the protection of St. Rosolia, said her accustomed prayers, and retired to bed. Sleep was not long absent, and his presence relieved her from her terrors and inquietude.

It was almost two o'clock before the lustful Monk ventured to bend his steps towards Antonia's dwelling. It has been already mentioned that the Abbey was at no great distance from the Strada di San Iago. He reached the House unobserved. Here He stopped, and hesitated for a moment. He reflected on the enormity of the crime, the consequences of a discovery, and the probability, after what had passed, of Elvira's suspecting him to be her Daughter's Ravisher: On the other hand it was suggested that She could do no more than suspect; that no proofs of his guilt could be produced; that it would seem impossible for the rape to have been committed without Antonia's knowing when, where, or by whom; and finally, He believed that his fame was too firmly established to be shaken by the unsupported accusations of two unknown Women. This latter argument was perfectly false: He knew not how uncertain is the air of popular applause, and that a moment suffices to make him today the detestation of the world, who yesterday was its Idol. The result of the Monk's deliberations was that He should proceed in his enterprize. He ascended the steps leading to the House. No sooner did He touch the door with the silver Myrtle, than it flew open, and presented him with a free passage. He entered, and the door closed after him of its own accord.

Guided by the moonbeams, He proceeded up the Staircase with slow and cautious steps. He looked round him every moment with apprehension and anxiety. He saw a Spy in every shadow, and heard a voice in every murmur of the night breeze. Consciousness of the guilty business on which He was employed appalled his heart, and rendered it more timid than a Woman's. Yet still He proceeded. He reached the door of Antonia's chamber. He stopped, and listened. All was hushed within. The total silence persuaded him that his intended Victim was retired to rest, and He ventured to lift up the Latch. The door was fastened, and resisted his efforts: But no sooner was it touched by the Talisman, than the Bolt flew back. The Ravisher stept on, and found himself in the chamber, where slept the innocent Girl, unconscious how dangerous a Visitor was drawing near her Couch. The door closed after him, and the Bolt shot again into its fastening.

Ambrosio advanced with precaution. He took care that not a board should creak under his foot, and held in his breath as He approached the Bed. His first attention was to perform the magic ceremony, as Matilda had charged him: He breathed thrice upon the silver Myrtle, pronounced over it Antonia's name, and laid it upon her pillow. The effects which it had already produced permitted not his doubting its success in prolonging the slumbers of his devoted Mistress. No sooner was the enchantment performed than He considered her to be absolutely in his power, and his eyes flamed with lust and impatience. He now ventured to cast a glance upon the sleeping Beauty. A single Lamp, burning before the Statue of St. Rosolia, shed a faint light through the room, and permitted him to examine all the charms of the lovely Object before him. The heat of the weather had obliged her to throw off part of the Bed-cloathes: Those which still covered her, Ambrosio's insolent hand hastened to remove. She lay with her cheek reclining upon one ivory arm; The Other rested on the side of the Bed with graceful indolence. A few tresses of her hair had escaped from beneath the Muslin which confined the rest, and fell carelessly over her bosom, as it heaved with slow and regular suspiration. The warm air had spread her cheek with higher colour than usual. A smile inexpressibly sweet played round her ripe and coral lips, from which every now and then escaped a gentle sigh or an half-pronounced sentence. An air of enchanting innocence and candour pervaded her whole form; and there was a sort of modesty in her very nakedness which added fresh stings to the desires of the lustful Monk.

579

He remained for some moments devouring those charms with his eyes which soon were to be subjected to his ill-regulated passions. Her mouth half-opened seemed to solicit a kiss: He bent over her; he joined his lips to hers, and drew in the fragrance of her breath with rapture. This momentary pleasure increased his longing for still greater. His desires were raised to that frantic height by which Brutes are agitated. He resolved not to delay for one instant longer the accomplishment of his wishes, and hastily proceeded to tear off those garments which impeded the gratification of his lust.

"Gracious God!" exclaimed a voice behind him; "Am I not deceived? Is not this an illusion?"

Terror, confusion, and disappointment accompanied these words, as they struck Ambrosio's hearing. He started, and turned towards it. Elvira stood at the door of the chamber, and regarded the Monk with looks of surprize and detestation.

A frightful dream had represented to her Antonia on the verge of a precipice. She saw her trembling on the brink: Every moment seemed to threaten her fall, and She heard her exclaim with shrieks, "Save me, Mother! Save me! — Yet a moment, and it will be too late!" Elvira woke in terror. The vision had made too strong an impression upon her mind, to permit her resting till assured of her Daughter's safety. She hastily started from her Bed, threw on a loose night-gown, and passing through the Closet in which slept the Waiting-woman, She reached Antonia's chamber just in time to rescue her from the grasp of the Ravisher.

His shame and her amazement seemed to have petrified into Statues both Elvira and the Monk: They remained gazing upon each other in silence. The Lady was the first to recover herself.

"It is no dream!" She cried; "It is really Ambrosio, who stands before me! It is the Man whom Madrid esteems a Saint, that I find at this late hour near the Couch of my unhappy Child! Monster of Hypocrisy! I already suspected your designs, but forbore your accusation in pity to human frailty. Silence would now be criminal: The whole City shall be informed of your incontinence. I will unmask you, Villain, and convince the Church what a Viper She cherishes in her bosom."

Pale and confused the baffled Culprit stood trembling before her.

He would fain have extenuated his offence, but could find no apology for his conduct: He could produce nothing but broken sentences, and excuses which contradicted each other. Elvira was too justly incensed to grant the pardon which He requested. She protested that She would raise the neighbourhood, and make him an example to all future Hypocrites. Then hastening to the Bed, She called to Antonia to wake; and finding that her voice had no effect, She took her arm, and raised her forcibly from the pillow. The charm operated too powerfully. Antonia remained insensible, and on being released by her Mother, sank back upon the pillow.

"This slumber cannot be natural!" cried the amazed Elvira, whose indignation increased with every moment. "Some mystery is concealed in it; But tremble, Hypocrite; all your villainy shall soon be unravelled! Help! Help!" She exclaimed aloud; "Within there! Flora! Flora!"

"Hear me for one moment, Lady!" cried the Monk, restored to himself by the urgency of the danger; "By all that is sacred and holy, I swear that your Daughter's honour is still unviolated. Forgive my transgression! Spare me the shame of a discovery, and permit me to regain the Abbey undisturbed. Grant me this request in mercy! I promise not only that Antonia shall be secure from me in future, but that the rest of my life shall prove ....."

Elvira interrupted him abruptly.

"Antonia secure from you? I will secure her! You shall betray no longer the confidence of Parents! Your iniquity shall be unveiled to the public eye: All Madrid shall shudder at your perfidy, your hypocrisy and incontinence. What Ho! there! Flora! Flora, I say!"

While She spoke thus, the remembrance of Agnes struck upon his mind. Thus had She sued to him for mercy, and thus had He refused her prayer! It was now his turn to suffer, and He could not but acknowledge that his punishment was just. In the meanwhile Elvira continued to call Flora to her assistance; but her voice was so choked with passion that the Servant, who was buried in profound slumber, was insensible to all her cries: Elvira dared not go towards the Closet in which Flora slept, lest the Monk should take that opportunity to escape. Such indeed was his intention: He trusted that could He reach the Abbey unobserved by any other than Elvira, her single testimony would not suffice to ruin a reputation so well established as his was in Madrid. With this idea He gathered up such garments as He had already thrown off, and hastened towards the Door. Elvira was aware of his design; She followed him, and ere He could draw back the bolt, seized him by the arm, and detained him.

"Attempt not to fly!" said She; "You quit not this room without Witnesses of your guilt."

Ambrosio struggled in vain to disengage himself. Elvira quitted not her hold, but redoubled her cries for succour. The Friar's danger grew more urgent. He expected every moment to hear people assembling at her voice; And worked up to madness by the approach of ruin, He adopted a resolution equally desperate and savage. Turning round suddenly, with one hand He grasped Elvira's throat so as to prevent her continuing her clamour, and with the other, dashing her violently upon the ground, He dragged her towards the Bed. Confused by this unexpected attack, She scarcely had power to strive at forcing herself from his grasp: While the Monk, snatching the pillow from beneath her Daughter's head, covering with it Elvira's face, and pressing his knee upon her stomach with all his strength, endeavoured to put an end to her existence. He succeeded but too well. Her natural strength increased by the excess of anguish, long did the Sufferer struggle to disengage herself, but in vain. The Monk continued to kneel upon her breast, witnessed without mercy the convulsive trembling of her limbs beneath him, and sustained with inhuman firmness the spectacle of her agonies, when soul and body were on the point of separating. Those agonies at length were over. She ceased to struggle for life. The Monk took off the pillow, and gazed upon her. Her face was covered with a frightful blackness:

Her limbs moved no more; The blood was chilled in her veins; Her heart had forgotten to beat, and her hands were stiff and frozen.

Ambrosio beheld before him that once noble and majestic form, now become a Corse, cold, senseless and disgusting.

This horrible act was no sooner perpetrated, than the Friar beheld the enormity of his crime. A cold dew flowed over his limbs; his eyes closed; He staggered to a chair, and sank into it almost as lifeless as the Unfortunate who lay extended at his feet. From this state He was rouzed by the necessity of flight, and the danger of being found in Antonia's apartment. He had no desire to profit by the execution of his crime. Antonia now appeared to him an object of disgust. A deadly cold had usurped the place of that warmth which glowed in his bosom: No ideas offered themselves to his mind but those of death and guilt, of present shame and future punishment. Agitated by remorse and fear He prepared for flight: Yet his terrors did not so compleatly master his recollection, as to prevent his taking the precautions necessary for his safety. He replaced the pillow upon the bed, gathered up his garments, and with the fatal Talisman in his hand, bent his unsteady steps towards the door. Bewildered by fear, He fancied that his flight was opposed by Legions of Phantoms; Whereever He turned, the disfigured Corse seemed to lie in his passage, and it was long before He succeeded in reaching the door. The enchanted Myrtle produced its former effect. The door opened, and He hastened down the staircase. He entered the Abbey unobserved, and having shut himself into his Cell, He abandoned his soul to the tortures of unavailing remorse, and terrors of impending detection.

CHAPTER IX.

Tell us, ye Dead, will none of you in pity

To those you left behind disclose the secret?

O! That some courteous Ghost would blab it out,

What 'tis you are, and we must shortly be.

I've heard that Souls departed have sometimes

Fore-warned Men of their deaths:

'Twas kindly done

To knock, and give the alarum.

BLAIR.

Ambrosio shuddered at himself, when He reflected on his rapid advances in iniquity. The enormous crime which He had just committed filled him with real horror. The murdered Elvira was continually before his eyes, and his guilt was already punished by the agonies of his conscience. Time, however, considerably weakened these impressions: One day passed away, another followed it, and still not the least suspicion was thrown upon him. Impunity reconciled him to his guilt: He began to resume his spirits; and as his fears of detection died away, He paid less attention to the reproaches of remorse. Matilda exerted herself to quiet his alarms. At the first intelligence of Elvira's death, She seemed greatly affected, and joined the Monk in deploring the unhappy catastrophe of his adventure: But when She found his agitation to be somewhat calmed, and himself better disposed to listen to her arguments, She proceeded to mention his offence in milder terms, and convince him that He was not so highly culpable as He appeared to consider himself. She represented that He had only availed himself of the rights which Nature allows to every one, those of self-preservation: That either Elvira or himself must have perished, and that her inflexibility and resolution to ruin him had deservedly marked her out for the Victim. She next stated, that as He had before rendered himself suspected to Elvira, it was a fortunate event for him that her lips were closed by death; since without this last adventure, her suspicions if made public might have produced very disagreeable consequences. He had therefore freed himself from an Enemy, to whom the errors of his conduct were sufficiently known to

584

make her dangerous, and who was the greatest obstacle to his designs upon Antonia. Those designs She encouraged him not to abandon. She assured him that, no longer protected by her Mother's watchful eye, the Daughter would fall an easy conquest; and by praising and enumerating Antonia's charms, She strove to rekindle the desires of the Monk. In this endeavour She succeeded but too well.

As if the crimes into which his passion had seduced him had only increased its violence, He longed more eagerly than ever to enjoy Antonia. The same success in concealing his present guilt, He trusted would attend his future. He was deaf to the murmurs of conscience, and resolved to satisfy his desires at any price. He waited only for an opportunity of repeating his former enterprize; But to procure that opportunity by the same means was now impracticable. In the first transports of despair He had dashed the enchanted Myrtle into a thousand pieces: Matilda told him plainly that He must expect no further assistance from the infernal Powers unless He was willing to subscribe to their established conditions. This Ambrosio was determined not to do: He persuaded himself that however great might be his iniquity, so long as he preserved his claim to salvation, He need not despair of pardon. He therefore resolutely refused to enter into any bond or compact with the Fiends; and Matilda finding him obstinate upon this point, forbore to press him further. She exerted her invention to discover some means of putting Antonia into the Abbot's power: Nor was it long before that means presented itself.

While her ruin was thus meditating, the unhappy Girl herself suffered severely from the loss of her Mother. Every morning on waking, it was her first care to hasten to Elvira's chamber. On that which followed Ambrosio's fatal visit, She woke later than was her usual custom: Of this She was convinced by the Abbey Chimes. She started from her bed, threw on a few loose garments hastily, and was speeding to enquire how her Mother had passed the night, when her foot struck against something which lay in her passage. She looked down. What was her horror at recognizing Elvira's livid Corse! She uttered a loud shriek, and threw herself upon the floor. She clasped the inanimate form to her bosom, felt that it was dead-cold, and with a movement of disgust, of which She was not the Mistress, let it fall again from her arms. The cry had alarmed Flora, who hastened to her assistance. The sight which She beheld penetrated her with horror; but her alarm was more audible than Antonia's. She made the House ring with her lamentations, while her Mistress, almost suffocated with grief, could only mark her distress by sobs and groans. Flora's shrieks soon reached the ears of the Hostess, whose terror and surprize were excessive on learning the cause of this disturbance. A Physician was immediately sent for: But on the first moment of beholding the Corse, He declared that Elvira's recovery was beyond the power of art. He proceeded therefore to give his assistance to Antonia, who by this time was truly in need of it. She was conveyed to bed, while the Landlady busied herself in giving orders for Elvira's Burial. Dame Jacintha was a plain good kind of Woman, charitable, generous, and devout: But her intellects were weak, and She was a Miserable Slave to fear and superstition. She shuddered at the idea of passing the night in the same House with a dead Body: She was persuaded that Elvira's Ghost would appear to her, and no less certain that such a visit would kill her with fright. From this persuasion, She resolved to pass the night at a Neighbour's, and insisted that the Funeral should take place the next day. St. Clare's Cemetery being the nearest, it was determined that Elvira should be buried there. Dame Jacintha engaged to defray every expence attending the burial. She knew not in what circumstances Antonia was left, but from the sparing manner in which the Family had lived, She concluded them to be indifferent.

Consequently, She entertained very little hope of ever being recompensed; But this consideration prevented her not from taking care that the Interment was performed with decency, and from showing the unfortunate Antonia all possible respect.

Nobody dies of mere grief; Of this Antonia was an instance. Aided by her youth and healthy constitution, She shook off the malady which her Mother's death had occasioned; But it was not so easy to remove the disease of her mind. Her eyes were constantly filled with tears: Every trifle affected her, and She evidently nourished in her bosom a profound and rooted melancholy. The slightest mention of Elvira, the most trivial circumstance recalling that beloved Parent to her memory, was sufficient to throw her into serious agitation. How much would her grief have been increased, had She known the agonies which terminated her Mother's existence! But of this no one entertained the least suspicion. Elvira was subject to strong convulsions: It was supposed that, aware of their approach, She had dragged herself to her Daughter's chamber in hopes of assistance; that a sudden access of her fits had seized her, too violent to be resisted by her already enfeebled state of health; and that She had expired ere She had time to reach the medicine which generally relieved her, and which stood upon a shelf in Antonia's room. This idea was firmly credited by the few people, who interested themselves about Elvira: Her Death was esteemed a natural event, and soon forgotten by all save by her, who had but too much reason to deplore her loss.

In truth Antonia's situation was sufficiently embarrassing and unpleasant. She was alone in the midst of a dissipated and expensive City; She was ill provided with money, and worse with Friends. Her aunt Leonella was still at Cordova, and She knew not her direction. Of the Marquis de las Cisternas She heard no news: As to Lorenzo, She had long given up the idea of possessing any interest in his bosom. She knew not to whom She could address herself in her present dilemma. She wished to consult Ambrosio; But She remembered her Mother's injunctions to shun him as much as possible, and the last conversation which Elvira had held with her upon the subject had given her sufficient lights respecting his designs to put her upon her guard against him in future. Still all her Mother's warnings could not make her change her good opinion of the Friar. She continued to feel that his friendship and society were requisite to her happiness: She looked upon his failings with a partial eye, and could not persuade herself that He really had intended her ruin. However, Elvira had positively commanded her to drop his acquaintance, and She had too much respect for her orders to disobey them.

At length She resolved to address herself for advice and protection to the Marquis de las Cisternas, as being her nearest Relation. She wrote to him, briefly stating her desolate situation; She besought him to compassionate his Brother's Child, to continue to her Elvira's pension, and to authorise her retiring to his old Castle in Murcia, which till now had been her retreat. Having sealed her letter, She gave it to the trusty Flora, who immediately set out to execute her commission. But Antonia was born under an unlucky Star. Had She made her application to the Marquis but one day sooner, received as his Niece and placed at the head of his Family, She would have escaped all the misfortunes with which She was now threatened. Raymond had always intended to execute this plan: But first, his hopes of making the proposal to Elvira through the lips of Agnes, and afterwards, his disappointment at losing his intended Bride, as well as the severe illness which for some time had confined him to his Bed, made him defer from day to day the giving an Asylum in his House to his Brother's Widow. He had commissioned Lorenzo to supply her liberally with money: But Elvira, unwilling to receive obligations from that Nobleman, had assured him that She needed no immediate pecuniary assistance. Consequently, the Marquis did not imagine that a trifling delay on his part could create any embarrassment; and the distress and agitation of his mind might well excuse his negligence.

Had He been informed that Elvira's death had left her Daughter Friendless and unprotected, He would doubtless have taken such measures, as would have ensured her from every danger: But Antonia was not destined to be so fortunate. The day on which She sent her letter to the Palace de las Cisternas was that following Lorenzo's departure from Madrid. The Marquis was in the first paroxysms of despair at the conviction that Agnes was indeed no more: He was delirious, and his life being in danger, no one was suffered to approach him. Flora was informed that He was incapable of attending to Letters, and that probably a few hours would decide his fate. With this unsatisfactory answer She was obliged to return to her Mistress, who now found herself plunged into greater difficulties than ever.

Flora and Dame Jacintha exerted themselves to console her. The Latter begged her to make herself easy, for that as long as She chose to stay with her, She would treat her like her own Child. Antonia, finding that the good Woman had taken a real affection for her, was somewhat comforted by thinking that She had at least one Friend in the World. A Letter was now brought to her, directed to Elvira. She recognized Leonella's writing, and opening it with joy, found a detailed account of her Aunt's adventures at Cordova. She informed her Sister that She had recovered her Legacy, had lost her heart, and had received in exchange that of the most amiable of Apothecaries, past, present, and to come. She added that She should be at Madrid on the Tuesday night, and meant to have the pleasure of presenting her Caro Sposo in form. Though her nuptials were far from pleasing Antonia, Leonella's speedy return gave her Niece much delight. She rejoiced in thinking that She should once more be under a Relation's care. She could not but judge it to be highly improper, for a young Woman to be living among absolute Strangers, with no one to regulate her conduct, or protect her from the insults to which, in her defenceless situation, She was exposed. She therefore looked forward with impatience to the Tuesday night.

It arrived. Antonia listened anxiously to the Carriages, as they rolled along the Street. None of them stopped, and it grew late without Leonella's appearing. Still, Antonia resolved to sit up till her Aunt's arrival, and in spite of all her remonstrances, Dame Jacintha and Flora insisted upon doing the same. The hours passed on slow and tediously. Lorenzo's departure from Madrid had put a stop to the nightly Serenades: She hoped in vain to hear the usual sound of Guitars beneath her window. She took up her own, and struck a few chords: But Music that evening had lost its charms for her, and She soon replaced the

Instrument in its case. She seated herself at her embroidery frame, but nothing went right: The silks were missing, the thread snapped every moment, and the needles were so expert at falling that they seemed to be animated. At length a flake of wax fell from the Taper which stood near her upon a favourite wreath of Violets: This compleatly discomposed her; She threw down her needle, and quitted the frame. It was decreed that for that night nothing should have the power of amusing her. She was the prey of Ennui, and employed herself in making fruitless wishes for the arrival of her Aunt.

As She walked with a listless air up and down the chamber, the Door caught her eye conducting to that which had been her Mother's. She remembered that Elvira's little Library was arranged there, and thought that She might possibly find in it some Book to amuse her till Leonella should arrive. Accordingly She took her Taper from the table, passed through the little Closet, and entered the adjoining apartment. As She looked around her, the sight of this room brought to her recollection a thousand painful ideas. It was the first time of her entering it since her Mother's death. The total silence prevailing through the chamber, the Bed despoiled of its furniture, the cheerless hearth where stood an extinguished Lamp, and a few dying Plants in the window which, since Elvira's loss, had been neglected, inspired Antonia with a melancholy awe. The gloom of night gave strength to this sensation. She placed her light upon the Table, and sank into a large chair, in which She had seen her Mother seated a thousand and a thousand times. She was never to see her seated there again! Tears unbidden streamed down her cheek, and She abandoned herself to the sadness which grew deeper with every moment.

Ashamed of her weakness, She at length rose from her seat: She proceeded to seek for what had brought her to this melancholy scene. The small collection of Books was arranged upon several shelves in order. Antonia examined them without finding any thing likely to interest her, till She put her hand upon a volume of old Spanish Ballads. She read a few Stanzas of one of them: They excited her curiosity. She took down the Book, and seated herself to peruse it with more ease. She trimmed the Taper, which now drew towards its end, and then read the following Ballad.

ALONZO THE BRAVE, AND FAIR IMOGINE

A Warrior so bold, and a Virgin so bright
   Conversed, as They sat on the green:
They gazed on each other with tender delight;
Alonzo the Brave was the name of the Knight,
   The Maid's was the Fair Imogine.

"And Oh!" said the Youth, "since to-morrow I go
   To fight in a far distant land,
Your tears for my absence soon leaving to flow,
Some Other will court you, and you will bestow
   On a wealthier Suitor your hand."

"Oh! hush these suspicions," Fair Imogine said,
   "Offensive to Love and to me!
For if ye be living, or if ye be dead,
I swear by the Virgin, that none in your stead
   Shall Husband of Imogine be.

"If e'er I by lust or by wealth led aside
   Forget my Alonzo the Brave,
God grant, that to punish my falsehood and pride
Your Ghost at the Marriage may sit by my side,
May tax me with perjury, claim me as Bride,
   And bear me away to the Grave!"

To Palestine hastened the Hero so bold;
   His Love, She lamented him sore:

But scarce had a twelve-month elapsed, when behold,
A Baron all covered with jewels and gold
   Arrived at Fair Imogine's door.

His treasure, his presents, his spacious domain
   Soon made her untrue to her vows:
He dazzled her eyes; He bewildered her brain;
He caught her affections so light and so vain,
   And carried her home as his Spouse.

And now had the Marriage been blest by the Priest;
   The revelry now was begun:
The Tables, they groaned with the weight of the Feast;
Nor yet had the laughter and merriment ceased,
   When the Bell of the Castle told, — "One!"

Then first with amazement Fair Imogine found
terrific;That a Stranger was placed by her side: His air was
He uttered no sound; He spoke not, He moved not,
He looked not around,
   But earnestly gazed on the Bride.

His vizor was closed, and gigantic his height;
   His armour was sable to view:
All pleasure and laughter were hushed at his sight;
The Dogs as They eyed him drew back in affright,
   The Lights in the chamber burned blue!

His presence all bosoms appeared to dismay;
    The Guests sat in silence and fear.
At length spoke the Bride, while She trembled;
"I pray, Sir Knight, that your Helmet aside you would lay,
    And deign to partake of our chear."

The Lady is silent: The Stranger complies.
    His vizor lie slowly unclosed:
Oh! God! what a sight met Fair Imogine's eyes!
What words can express her dismay and surprize,
    When a Skeleton's head was exposed.

All present then uttered a terrified shout;
    All turned with disgust from the scene.
The worms, They crept in, and the worms, They crept out,
And sported his eyes and his temples about,
    While the Spectre addressed Imogine.

"Behold me, Thou false one! Behold me!" He cried;
    "Remember Alonzo the Brave!
God grants, that to punish thy falsehood and pride
My Ghost at thy marriage should sit by thy side,
Should tax thee with perjury, claim thee as Bride
    And bear thee away to the Grave!"

Thus saying, his arms round the Lady He wound,
    While loudly She shrieked in dismay;
Then sank with his prey through the wide-yawning ground:
Nor ever again was Fair Imogine found,

Or the Spectre who bore her away.

Not long lived the Baron; and none since that time
　　To inhabit the Castle presume:
For Chronicles tell, that by order sublime
There Imogine suffers the pain of her crime,
　　And mourns her deplorable doom.

At midnight four times in each year does her Spright
　　When Mortals in slumber are bound,
Arrayed in her bridal apparel of white,
Appear in the Hall with the Skeleton-Knight,
　　And shriek, as He whirls her around.

While They drink out of skulls newly torn from the grave,
　　Dancing round them the Spectres are seen:
Their liquor is blood, and this horrible Stave
They howl. — "To the health of Alonzo the Brave,
　　And his Consort, the False Imogine!"

　　The perusal of this story was ill-calculated to dispel Antonia's melancholy. She had naturally a strong inclination to the marvellous; and her Nurse, who believed firmly in Apparitions, had related to her when an Infant so many horrible adventures of this kind, that all Elvira's attempts had failed to eradicate their impressions from her Daughter's mind. Antonia still nourished a superstitious prejudice in her bosom: She was often susceptible of terrors which, when She discovered their natural and insignificant cause, made her blush at her own weakness. With such a turn of mind, the adventure which She had just been reading sufficed to give her apprehensions the alarm. The hour and the scene combined to authorize them. It was the dead of night: She was alone, and in the chamber once occupied by her deceased Mother. The weather was comfortless and stormy: The wind howled around the House, the doors rattled in their frames, and the heavy rain pattered against the windows. No other sound was heard. The Taper, now burnt down to the socket, sometimes flaring upwards shot a gleam of light through the room, then sinking again seemed upon the point of expiring. Antonia's heart throbbed with agitation: Her eyes wandered fearfully over the objects around her, as the trembling flame illuminated them at intervals. She attempted to rise from her seat; But her limbs trembled so violently that She was unable to proceed. She then called Flora, who was in a room at no great distance: But agitation choked her voice, and her cries died away in hollow murmurs.

She passed some minutes in this situation, after which her terrors began to diminish. She strove to recover herself, and acquire strength enough to quit the room: Suddenly She fancied, that She heard a low sigh drawn near her. This idea brought back her former weakness. She had already raised herself from her seat, and was on the point of taking the Lamp from the Table. The imaginary noise stopped her: She drew back her hand, and supported herself upon the back of a Chair. She listened anxiously, but nothing more was heard.

"Gracious God!" She said to herself; "What could be that sound? Was I deceived, or did I really hear it?"

Her reflections were interrupted by a noise at the door scarcely audible: It seemed as if somebody was whispering. Antonia's alarm increased: Yet the Bolt She knew to be fastened, and this idea in some degree reassured her. Presently the Latch was lifted up softly, and the Door moved with caution backwards and forwards. Excess of terror now supplied Antonia with that strength, of which She had till then been deprived. She started from her place and made towards the Closet door, whence She might soon have reached the chamber where She expected to find Flora and Dame Jacintha. Scarcely had She reached the middle of the room when the Latch was lifted up a second time. An involuntary movement obliged her to turn her head. Slowly and gradually the Door turned upon its hinges, and standing upon the Threshold She beheld a tall thin Figure, wrapped in a white shroud which covered it from head to foot.

This vision arrested her feet: She remained as if petrified in the middle of the apartment. The Stranger with measured and solemn steps drew near the Table. The dying Taper darted a blue and melancholy flame as the Figure advanced towards it. Over the Table was fixed a small Clock; The hand of it was upon the stroke of three. The Figure stopped opposite to the Clock: It raised its right arm, and pointed to the hour, at the same time looking earnestly upon Antonia, who waited for the conclusion of this scene, motionless and silent.

The figure remained in this posture for some moments. The clock struck. When the sound had ceased, the Stranger advanced yet a few steps nearer Antonia.

"Yet three days," said a voice faint, hollow, and sepulchral; "Yet three days, and we meet again!"

Antonia shuddered at the words.

"We meet again?" She pronounced at length with difficulty: "Where shall we meet? Whom shall I meet?"

The figure pointed to the ground with one hand, and with the other raised the Linen which covered its face.

"Almighty God! My Mother!"

Antonia shrieked, and fell lifeless upon the floor.

Dame Jacintha who was at work in a neighbouring chamber, was alarmed by the cry: Flora was just gone down stairs to fetch fresh oil for the Lamp, by which they had been sitting. Jacintha therefore hastened alone to Antonia's assistance, and great was her amazement to find her extended upon the floor. She raised her in her arms, conveyed her to her apartment, and placed her upon the Bed still senseless. She then proceeded to bathe her temples, chafe her hands, and use all possible means of bringing her to herself. With some difficulty She succeeded. Antonia opened her eyes, and looked round her wildly.

"Where is She?" She cried in a trembling voice; "Is She gone? Am I safe? Speak to me! Comfort me! Oh! speak to me for God's sake!"

"Safe from whom, my Child?" replied the astonished Jacintha; "What alarms you? Of whom are you afraid?"

"In three days! She told me that we should meet in three days! I heard her say it! I saw her, Jacintha, I saw her but this moment!"

She threw herself upon Jacintha's bosom.

"You saw her? Saw whom?"

"My Mother's Ghost!"

"Christ Jesus!" cried Jacintha, and starting from the Bed, let fall Antonia upon the pillow, and fled in consternation out of the room.

As She hastened down stairs, She met Flora ascending them.

"Go to your Mistress, Flora," said She; "Here are rare doings! Oh! I am the most unfortunate Woman alive! My House is filled with Ghosts and dead Bodies, and the Lord knows what besides; Yet I am sure, nobody likes such company less than I do. But go your way to Donna Antonia, Flora, and let me go mine."

Thus saying, She continued her course to the Street door, which She opened, and without allowing herself time to throw on her veil, She made the best of her way to the Capuchin Abbey. In the meanwhile, Flora hastened to her Lady's chamber, equally surprized and alarmed at Jacintha's consternation. She found Antonia lying upon the bed insensible. She used the same means for her recovery that Jacintha had already employed; But finding that her Mistress only recovered from one fit to fall into another, She sent in all haste for a Physician. While expecting his arrival, She undrest Antonia, and conveyed her to Bed.

Heedless of the storm, terrified almost out of her senses, Jacintha ran through the Streets, and stopped not till She reached the Gate of the Abbey. She rang loudly at the bell, and as soon as the Porter appeared, She desired permission to speak to the Superior. Ambrosio was then conferring with Matilda upon the means of procuring access to Antonia. The cause of Elvira's death remaining unknown, He was convinced that crimes were not so swiftly followed by punishment, as his Instructors the Monks had taught him, and as till then He had himself believed. This persuasion made him resolve upon Antonia's ruin, for the enjoyment of whose person dangers and difficulties only seemed to have increased his passion. The Monk had already made one attempt to gain admission to her presence; But Flora had refused him in such a manner as to convince him that all future endeavours must be vain. Elvira had confided her suspicions to that trusty Servant: She had desired her never to leave Ambrosio alone with her Daughter, and if possible to prevent their meeting altogether. Flora promised to obey her, and had executed her orders to the very letter. Ambrosio's visit had been rejected that morning, though Antonia was ignorant of it. He saw that to obtain a sight of his Mistress by open means was out of the question; and both Himself and Matilda had consumed the night, in endeavouring to invent some plan, whose event might be more successful. Such was their employment, when a Lay-Brother entered the Abbot's Cell, and informed him that a Woman calling herself Jacintha Zuniga requested audience for a few minutes.

Ambrosio was by no means disposed to grant the petition of his Visitor. He refused it positively, and bad the Lay-Brother tell the Stranger to return the next day. Matilda interrupted him.

"See this Woman," said She in a low voice; "I have my reasons."

The Abbot obeyed her, and signified that He would go to the Parlour immediately. With this answer the Lay-Brother withdrew. As soon as they were alone Ambrosio enquired why Matilda wished him to see this Jacintha.

"She is Antonia's Hostess," replied Matilda; "She may possibly be of use to you: but let us examine her, and learn what brings her hither."

They proceeded together to the Parlour, where Jacintha was already waiting for the Abbot. She had conceived a great opinion of his piety and virtue; and supposing him to have much influence over the Devil, thought that it must be an easy matter for him to lay Elvira's Ghost in the Red Sea. Filled with this persuasion She had hastened to the Abbey. As soon as She saw the Monk enter the Parlour, She dropped upon her knees, and began her story as follows.

"Oh! Reverend Father! Such an accident! Such an adventure! I know not what course to take, and unless you can help me, I shall certainly go distracted. Well, to be sure, never was Woman so unfortunate, as myself! All in my power to keep clear of such abomination have I done, and yet that all is too little. What signifies my telling my beads four times a day, and observing every fast prescribed by the Calendar? What signifies my having made three Pilgrimages to St. James of Compostella, and purchased as many pardons from the Pope as would buy off Cain's punishment? Nothing prospers with me! All goes wrong, and God only knows, whether any thing will ever go right again! Why now, be your Holiness the Judge. My Lodger dies in convulsions; Out of pure kindness I bury her at my own expence; (Not that she is any relation of mine, or that I shall be benefited a single pistole by her death: I got nothing by it, and therefore you know, reverend Father, that her living or dying was just the same to me. But that is nothing to the purpose; To return to what I was saying,) I took care of her funeral, had every thing performed decently and properly, and put myself to expence enough, God knows! And how do you think the Lady repays me for my kindness? Why truly by refusing to sleep quietly in her comfortable deal Coffin, as a peaceable well-disposed Spirit ought to do, and coming to plague me, who never wish to set eyes on her again. Forsooth, it well becomes her to go racketing about my House at midnight, popping into her Daughter's room through the Keyhole, and frightening the poor Child out of her wits! Though She be a Ghost, She might be more civil than to bolt into a Person's House, who likes her company so little. But as for me, reverend Father, the plain state of the case is this: If She walks into my House, I must walk out of it, for I cannot abide such Visitors, not I! Thus you see, your Sanctity, that without your assistance I am ruined and undone for ever. I shall be obliged to quit my House; Nobody will take it, when 'tis known that She haunts it, and then I shall find myself in a fine situation! Miserable Woman that I am! What shall I do! What will become of me!"

Here She wept bitterly, wrung her hands, and begged to know the Abbot's opinion of her case.

"In truth, good Woman," replied He, "It will be difficult for me to relieve you without knowing what is the matter with you. You have forgotten to tell me what has happened, and what it is you want."

"Let me die" cried Jacintha, "but your Sanctity is in the right! This then is the fact stated briefly. A lodger of mine is lately dead, a very good sort of Woman that I must needs say for her as far as my knowledge of her went, though that was not a great way:

She kept me too much at a distance; for indeed She was given to be upon the high ropes, and whenever I ventured to speak to her, She had a look with her which always made me feel a little queerish, God forgive me for saying so. However, though She was more stately than needful, and affected to look down upon me (Though if I am well informed, I come of as good Parents as She could do for her ears, for her Father was a Shoe-maker at Cordova, and Mine was an Hatter at Madrid, aye, and a very creditable Hatter too, let me tell you,) Yet for all her pride, She was a quiet well-behaved Body, and I never wish to have a better Lodger. This makes me wonder the more at her not sleeping quietly in her Grave: But there is no trusting to people in this world! For my part, I never saw her do amiss, except on the Friday before her death. To be sure, I was then much scandalized by seeing her eat the wing of a Chicken! 'How, Madona Flora!' quoth I; (Flora, may it please your Reverence, is the name of the waiting Maid) — 'How, Madona Flora!' quoth I; 'Does your Mistress eat flesh upon Fridays? Well! Well! See the event, and then remember that Dame Jacintha warned you of it!' These were my very words, but Alas! I might as well have held my tongue! Nobody minded me; and Flora, who is somewhat pert and snappish, (More is the pity, say I) told me that there was no more harm in eating a Chicken than the egg from which it came. Nay, She even declared that if her Lady added a slice of bacon, She would not be an inch nearer Damnation, God protect us! A poor ignorant sinful soul! I protest to your Holiness, I trembled to hear her utter such blasphemies, and expected every moment to see the ground open and swallow her up, Chicken and all! For you must know, worshipful Father, that while She talked thus, She held the plate in her hand, on which lay the identical roast Fowl. And a fine Bird it was, that I must say for it! Done to a turn, for I superintended the cooking of it myself: It was a little Gallician of my own raising, may it please your Holiness, and the flesh was as white as an egg-shell, as indeed Donna Elvira told me herself. 'Dame Jacintha,' said She, very good-humouredly, though to say the truth, She was always very polite to me ....."

Here Ambrosio's patience failed him. Eager to know Jacintha's business in which Antonia seemed to be concerned, He was almost distracted while listening to the rambling of this prosing old Woman. He interrupted her, and protested that if She did not immediately tell her story and have done with it, He should quit the Parlour, and leave her to get out of her difficulties by herself. This threat had the desired effect. Jacintha related her business in as few words as She could manage; But her account was still so prolix that Ambrosio had need of his patience to bear him to the conclusion.

"And so, your Reverence," said She, after relating Elvira's death and burial, with all their circumstances; "And so, your Reverence, upon hearing the shriek, I put away my work, and away posted I to Donna Antonia's chamber. Finding nobody there, I past on to the next; But I must own, I was a little timorous at going in, for this was the very room where Donna Elvira used to sleep. However, in I went, and sure enough, there lay the young Lady at full length upon the floor, as cold as a stone, and as white as a sheet. I was surprized at this, as your Holiness may well suppose; But Oh me! how I shook when I saw a great tall figure at my elbow whose head touched the ceiling! The face was Donna Elvira's, I must confess; But out of its mouth came clouds of fire, its arms were loaded with heavy chains which it rattled piteously, and every hair on its head was a Serpent as big as my arm! At this I was frightened enough, and began to say my Ave-Maria: But the Ghost interrupting me uttered three loud groans, and roared out in a terrible voice, 'Oh! That Chicken's wing! My poor soul suffers for it!' As soon as She had said this, the Ground opened, the Spectre sank down, I heard a clap of thunder, and the room was filled with a smell of brimstone. When I recovered from my fright, and had brought Donna Antonia to herself, who told me that She had cried out upon seeing her Mother's Ghost, (And well might She cry, poor Soul! Had I been in her place, I should have cried ten times louder) it directly came into my head, that if any one had power to quiet this Spectre, it must be your Reverence. So hither I came in all diligence, to beg that you will sprinkle my House with holy water, and lay the Apparition in the Red Sea."

Ambrosio stared at this strange story, which He could not credit.

"Did Donna Antonia also see the Ghost?" said He.

"As plain as I see you, Reverend Father!"

Ambrosio paused for a moment. Here was an opportunity offered him of gaining access to Antonia, but He hesitated to employ it. The reputation which He enjoyed in Madrid was still dear to him; and since He had lost the reality of virtue, it appeared as if its semblance was become more valuable. He was conscious that publicly to break through the rule never to quit the Abbey precincts, would derogate much from his supposed austerity. In visiting Elvira, He had always taken care to keep his features concealed from the Domestics. Except by the Lady, her Daughter, and the faithful Flora, He was known in the Family by no other name than that of Father Jerome. Should He comply with Jacintha's request, and accompany her to her House, He knew that the violation of his rule could not be kept a secret. However, his eagerness to see Antonia obtained the victory: He even hoped, that the singularity of this adventure would justify him in the eyes of Madrid: But whatever might be the consequences, He resolved to profit by the opportunity which chance had presented to him. An expressive look from Matilda confirmed him in this resolution.

"Good Woman," said He to Jacintha, "what you tell me is so extraordinary that I can scarcely credit your assertions. However, I will comply with your request. Tomorrow after Matins you may expect me at your House: I will then examine into what I can do for you, and if it is in my power, will free you from this unwelcome Visitor. Now then go home, and peace be with you!"

"Home?" exclaimed Jacintha; "I go home? Not I by my troth! except under your protection, I set no foot of mine within the threshold. God help me, the Ghost may meet me upon the Stairs, and whisk me away with her to the devil! Oh! That I had accepted young Melchior Basco's offer! Then I should have had somebody to protect me; But now I am a lone Woman, and meet with nothing but crosses and misfortunes! Thank Heaven, it is not yet too late to repent! There is Simon Gonzalez will have me any day of the week, and if I live till daybreak, I will marry him out of hand: An Husband I will have, that is determined, for now this Ghost is once in my House, I shall be frightened out of my wits to sleep alone. But for God's sake, reverend Father, come with me now. I shall have no rest till the House is purified, or the poor young Lady either. The dear Girl! She is in a piteous taking: I left her in strong convulsions, and I doubt, She will not easily recover her fright."

The Friar started, and interrupted her hastily.

"In convulsions, say you? Antonia in convulsions? Lead on, good Woman! I follow you this moment!"

Jacintha insisted upon his stopping to furnish himself with the vessel of holy water: With this request He complied. Thinking herself safe under his protection should a Legion of Ghosts attack her, the old Woman returned the Monk a profusion of thanks, and they departed together for the Strada di San Iago.

So strong an impression had the Spectre made upon Antonia, that for the first two or three hours the Physician declared her life to be in danger. The fits at length becoming less frequent induced him to alter his opinion. He said that to keep her quiet was all that was necessary; and He ordered a medicine to be prepared which would tranquillize her nerves, and procure her that repose which at present She much wanted. The sight of Ambrosio, who now appeared with Jacintha at her Bedside, contributed essentially to compose her ruffled spirits. Elvira had not sufficiently explained herself upon the nature of his designs, to make a Girl so ignorant of the world as her

Daughter aware how dangerous was his acquaintance. At this moment, when penetrated with horror at the scene which had just past, and dreading to contemplate the Ghost's prediction, her mind had need of all the succours of friendship and religion, Antonia regarded the Abbot with an eye doubly partial. That strong prepossession in his favour still existed which She had felt for him at first sight: She fancied, yet knew not wherefore, that his presence was a safeguard to her from every danger, insult, or misfortune.

She thanked him gratefully for his visit, and related to him the adventure, which had alarmed her so seriously.

The Abbot strove to reassure her, and convince her that the whole had been a deception of her overheated fancy. The solitude in which She had passed the Evening, the gloom of night, the Book which She had been reading, and the Room in which She sat, were all calculated to place before her such a vision. He treated the idea of Ghosts with ridicule, and produced strong arguments to prove the fallacy of such a system. His conversation tranquillized and comforted her, but did not convince her. She could not believe that the Spectre had been a mere creature of her imagination; Every circumstance was impressed upon her mind too forcibly, to permit her flattering herself with such an idea. She persisted in asserting that She had really seen her Mother's Ghost, had heard the period of her dissolution announced and declared that She never should quit her bed alive. Ambrosio advised her against encouraging these sentiments, and then quitted her chamber, having promised to repeat his visit on the morrow. Antonia received this assurance with every mark of joy: But the Monk easily perceived that He was not equally acceptable to her Attendant. Flora obeyed Elvira's injunctions with the most scrupulous observance. She examined every circumstance with an anxious eye likely in the least to prejudice her young Mistress, to whom She had been attached for many years. She was a Native of Cuba, had followed Elvira to Spain, and loved the young Antonia with a Mother's affection. Flora quitted not the room for a moment while the Abbot remained there: She watched his every word, his every look, his every action. He saw that her suspicious eye was always fixed upon him, and conscious that his designs would not bear inspection so minute, He felt frequently confused and disconcerted. He was aware that She doubted the purity of his intentions; that She would never leave him alone with Antonia, and his Mistress defended by the presence of this vigilant Observer, He despaired of finding the means to gratify his passion.

As He quitted the House, Jacintha met him, and begged that some Masses might be sung for the repose of Elvira's soul, which She doubted not was suffering in Purgatory. He promised not to forget her request; But He perfectly gained the old Woman's heart by engaging to watch during the whole of the approaching night in the haunted chamber. Jacintha could find no terms sufficiently strong to express her gratitude, and the Monk departed loaded with her benedictions.

It was broad day when He returned to the Abbey. His first care was to communicate what had past to his Confident. He felt too sincere a passion for Antonia to have heard unmoved the prediction of her speedy death, and He shuddered at the idea of losing an object so dear to him. Upon this head Matilda reassured him. She confirmed the arguments which Himself had already used: She declared Antonia to have been deceived by the wandering of her brain, by the Spleen which opprest her at the moment, and by the natural turn of her mind to superstition, and the marvellous. As to Jacintha's account, the absurdity refuted itself; The Abbot hesitated not to believe that She had fabricated the whole story, either confused by terror, or hoping to make him comply more readily with her request. Having overruled the Monk's apprehensions, Matilda continued thus.

"The prediction and the Ghost are equally false; But it must be your care, Ambrosio, to verify the first. Antonia within three days must indeed be dead to the world; But She must live for you.

Her present illness, and this fancy which She has taken into her head, will colour a plan which I have long meditated, but which was impracticable without your procuring access to Antonia. She shall be yours, not for a single night, but for ever. All the vigilance of her Duenna shall not avail her: You shall riot unrestrained in the charms of your Mistress. This very day must the scheme be put in execution, for you have no time to lose. The Nephew of the Duke of Medina Celi prepares to demand Antonia for his Bride: In a few days She will be removed to the Palace of her Relation, the Marquis de las Cisternas, and there She will be secure from your attempts. Thus during your absence have I been informed by my Spies, who are ever employed in bringing me intelligence for your service. Now then listen to me. There is a juice extracted from certain herbs, known but to few, which brings on the Person who drinks it the exact image of Death. Let this be administered to Antonia: You may easily find means to pour a few drops into her medicine. The effect will be throwing her into strong convulsions for an hour: After which her blood will gradually cease to flow, and heart to beat; A mortal paleness will spread itself over her features, and She will appear a Corse to every eye. She has no Friends about her: You may charge yourself unsuspected with the superintendence of her funeral, and cause her to be buried in the Vaults of St. Clare. Their solitude and easy access render these Caverns favourable to your designs. Give Antonia the soporific draught this Evening: Eight and forty hours after She has drank it, Life will revive to her bosom. She will then be absolutely in your power: She will find all resistance unavailing, and necessity will compel her to receive you in her arms."

"Antonia will be in my power!" exclaimed the Monk; "Matilda, you transport me! At length then, happiness will be mine, and that happiness will be Matilda's gift, will be the gift of friendship!

I shall clasp Antonia in my arms, far from every prying eye, from every tormenting Intruder! I shall sigh out my soul upon her bosom; Shall teach her young heart the first rudiments of pleasure, and revel uncontrouled in the endless variety of her charms! And shall this delight indeed by mine? Shall I give the reins to my desires, and gratify every wild tumultuous wish? Oh! Matilda, how can I express to you my gratitude?"

"By profiting by my counsels. Ambrosio, I live but to serve you:

Your interest and happiness are equally mine. Be your person Antonia's, but to your friendship and your heart I still assert my claim. Contributing to yours forms now my only pleasure. Should my exertions procure the gratification of your wishes, I shall consider my trouble to be amply repaid. But let us lose no time. The liquor of which I spoke is only to be found in St. Clare's Laboratory. Hasten then to the Prioress; Request of her admission to the Laboratory, and it will not be denied. There is a Closet at the lower end of the great Room, filled with liquids of different colours and qualities. The Bottle in question stands by itself upon the third shelf on the left. It contains a greenish liquor: Fill a small phial with it when you are unobserved, and Antonia is your own."

The Monk hesitated not to adopt this infamous plan. His desires, but too violent before, had acquired fresh vigour from the sight of Antonia. As He sat by her bedside, accident had discovered to him some of those charms which till then had been concealed from him: He found them even more perfect, than his ardent imagination had pictured them. Sometimes her white and polished arm was displayed in arranging the pillow: Sometimes a sudden movement discovered part of her swelling bosom: But whereever the new-found charm presented itself, there rested the Friar's gloting eyes. Scarcely could He master himself sufficiently to conceal his desires from Antonia and her vigilant Duenna. Inflamed by the remembrance of these beauties, He entered into Matilda's scheme without hesitation.

No sooner were Matins over than He bent his course towards the Convent of St. Clare: His arrival threw the whole Sisterhood into the utmost amazement. The Prioress was sensible of the honour done her Convent by his paying it his first visit, and strove to express her gratitude by every possible attention. He was paraded through the Garden, shown all the reliques of Saints and Martyrs, and treated with as much respect and distinction as had He been the Pope himself. On his part, Ambrosio received the Domina's civilities very graciously, and strove to remove her surprize at his having broken through his resolution. He stated, that among his penitents, illness prevented many from quitting their Houses. These were exactly the People who most needed his advice and the comforts of Religion: Many representations had been made to him upon this account, and though highly repugnant to his own wishes, He had found it absolutely necessary for the service of heaven to change his determination, and quit his beloved retirement. The Prioress applauded his zeal in his profession and his charity towards Mankind: She declared that Madrid was happy in possessing a Man so perfect and irreproachable. In such discourse, the Friar at length reached the Laboratory. He found the Closet: The Bottle stood in the place which Matilda had described, and the Monk seized an opportunity to fill his phial unobserved with the soporific liquor. Then having partaken of a Collation in the Refectory, He retired from the Convent pleased with the success of his visit, and leaving the Nuns delighted by the honour conferred upon them.

He waited till Evening before He took the road to Antonia's dwelling. Jacintha welcomed him with transport, and besought him not to forget his promise to pass the night in the haunted Chamber: That promise He now repeated. He found Antonia tolerably well, but still harping upon the Ghost's prediction. Flora moved not from her Lady's Bed, and by symptoms yet stronger than on the former night testified her dislike to the Abbot's presence. Still Ambrosio affected not to observe them. The Physician arrived, while He was conversing with Antonia. It was dark already; Lights were called for, and Flora was compelled to descend for them herself. However, as She left a third Person in the room, and expected to be absent but a few minutes, She believed that She risqued nothing in quitting her post. No sooner had She left the room, than Ambrosio moved towards the Table, on which stood Antonia's medicine: It was placed in a recess of the window. The Physician seated in an armed-chair, and employed in questioning his Patient, paid no attention to the proceedings of the Monk. Ambrosio seized the opportunity: He drew out the fatal Phial, and let a few drops fall into the medicine. He then hastily left the Table, and returned to the seat which He had quitted. When Flora made her appearance with lights, every thing seemed to be exactly as She had left it.

The Physician declared that Antonia might quit her chamber the next day with perfect safety. He recommended her following the same prescription which, on the night before, had procured her a refreshing sleep: Flora replied that the draught stood ready upon the Table: He advised the Patient to take it without delay, and then retired. Flora poured the medicine into a Cup and presented it to her Mistress. At that moment Ambrosio's courage failed him. Might not Matilda have deceived him? Might not Jealousy have persuaded her to destroy her Rival, and substitute poison in the room of an opiate? This idea appeared so reasonable that He was on the point of preventing her from swallowing the medicine. His resolution was adopted too late: The Cup was already emptied, and Antonia restored it into Flora's hands. No remedy was now to be found: Ambrosio could only expect the moment impatiently, destined to decide upon Antonia's life or death, upon his own happiness or despair.

Dreading to create suspicion by his stay, or betray himself by his mind's agitation, He took leave of his Victim, and withdrew from the room. Antonia parted from him with less cordiality than on the former night. Flora had represented to her Mistress that to admit his visits was to disobey her Mother's orders: She described to her his emotion on entering the room, and the fire which sparkled in his eyes while He gazed upon her. This had escaped Antonia's observation, but not her Attendant's; Who explaining the Monk's designs and their probable consequences in terms much clearer than Elvira's, though not quite so delicate, had succeeded in alarming her young Lady, and persuading her to treat him more distantly than She had done hitherto. The idea of obeying her Mother's will at once determined Antonia. Though She grieved at losing his society, She conquered herself sufficiently to receive the Monk with some degree of reserve and coldness. She thanked him with respect and gratitude for his former visits, but did not invite his repeating them in future. It now was not the Friar's interest to solicit admission to her presence, and He took leave of her as if not designing to return. Fully persuaded that the acquaintance which She dreaded was now at an end, Flora was so much worked upon by his easy compliance that She began to doubt the justice of her suspicions. As She lighted him down Stairs, She thanked him for having endeavoured to root out from Antonia's mind her superstitious terrors of the Spectre's prediction: She added, that as He seemed interested in Donna Antonia's welfare, should any change take place in her situation, She would be careful to let him know it. The Monk in replying took pains to raise his voice, hoping that Jacintha would hear it. In this He succeeded; As He reached the foot of the Stairs with his Conductress, the Landlady failed not to make her appearance.

"Why surely you are not going away, reverend Father?" cried She; "Did you not promise to pass the night in the haunted Chamber? Christ Jesus! I shall be left alone with the Ghost, and a fine pickle I shall be in by morning! Do all I could, say all I could, that obstinate old Brute, Simon Gonzalez, refused to marry me today; And before tomorrow comes, I suppose, I shall be torn to pieces, by the Ghosts, and Goblins, and Devils, and what not! For God's sake, your Holiness, do not leave me in such a woeful condition! On my bended knees I beseech you to keep your promise: Watch this night in the haunted chamber; Lay the Apparition in the Red Sea, and Jacintha remembers you in her prayers to the last day of her existence!"

This request Ambrosio expected and desired; Yet He affected to raise objections, and to seem unwilling to keep his word. He told Jacintha that the Ghost existed nowhere but in her own brain, and that her insisting upon his staying all night in the House was ridiculous and useless. Jacintha was obstinate: She was not to be convinced, and pressed him so urgently not to leave her a prey to the Devil, that at length He granted her request. All this show of resistance imposed not upon Flora, who was naturally of a suspicious temper. She suspected the Monk to be acting a part very contrary to his own inclinations, and that He wished for no better than to remain where He was. She even went so far as to believe that Jacintha was in his interest; and the poor old Woman was immediately set down, as no better than a Procuress. While She applauded herself for having penetrated into this plot against her Lady's honour, She resolved in secret to render it fruitless.

"So then," said She to the Abbot with a look half-satirical and half indignant; "So then you mean to stay here tonight? Do so, in God's name! Nobody will prevent you. Sit up to watch for the Ghost's arrival: I shall sit up too, and the Lord grant that I may see nothing worse than a Ghost! I quit not Donna Antonia's Bedside during this blessed night: Let me see any one dare to enter the room, and be He mortal or immortal, be He Ghost, Devil, or Man, I warrant his repenting that ever He crossed the threshold!"

This hint was sufficiently strong, and Ambrosio understood its meaning. But instead of showing that He perceived her suspicions; He replied mildly that He approved the Duenna's precautions, and advised her to persevere in her intention. This, She assured him faithfully that He might depend upon her doing. Jacintha then conducted him into the chamber where the Ghost had appeared, and Flora returned to her Lady's.

Jacintha opened the door of the haunted room with a trembling hand: She ventured to peep in; But the wealth of India would not have tempted her to cross the threshold. She gave the Taper to the Monk, wished him well through the adventure, and hastened to be gone. Ambrosio entered. He bolted the door, placed the light upon the Table, and seated himself in the Chair which on the former night had sustained Antonia. In spite of Matilda's assurances that the Spectre was a mere creation of fancy, his mind was impressed with a certain mysterious horror. He in vain endeavoured to shake it off. The silence of the night, the story of the Apparition, the chamber wainscotted with dark oak pannells, the recollection which it brought with it of the murdered Elvira, and his incertitude respecting the nature of the drops given by him to Antonia, made him feel uneasy at his present situation. But He thought much less of the Spectre, than of the poison. Should He have destroyed the only object which rendered life dear to him; Should the Ghost's prediction prove true; Should Antonia in three days be no more, and He the wretched cause of her death . ..... The supposition was too horrible to dwell upon. He drove away these dreadful images, and as often they presented themselves again before him. Matilda had assured him that the effects of the Opiate would be speedy. He listened with fear, yet with eagerness, expecting to hear some disturbance in the adjoining chamber. All was still silent. He concluded that the drops had not begun to operate. Great was the stake, for which He now played: A moment would suffice to decide upon his misery or happiness. Matilda had taught him the means of ascertaining that life was not extinct for ever: Upon this assay depended all his hopes. With every instant his impatience redoubled; His terrors grew more lively, his anxiety more awake. Unable to bear this state of incertitude, He endeavoured to divert it by substituting the thoughts of Others to his own.

The Books, as was before mentioned, were ranged upon shelves near the Table: This stood exactly opposite to the Bed, which was placed in an Alcove near the Closet door. Ambrosio took down a Volume, and seated himself by the Table: But his attention wandered from the Pages before him. Antonia's image and that of the murdered Elvira persisted to force themselves before his imagination. Still He continued to read, though his eyes ran over the characters without his mind being conscious of their import. Such was his occupation, when He fancied that He heard a footstep. He turned his head, but nobody was to be seen.

He resumed his Book; But in a few minutes after the same sound was repeated, and followed by a rustling noise close behind him. He now started from his seat, and looking round him, perceived the Closet door standing half-unclosed. On his first entering the room He had tried to open it, but found it bolted on the inside.

"How is this?" said He to himself; "How comes this door unfastened?"

He advanced towards it: He pushed it open, and looked into the closet: No one was there. While He stood irresolute, He thought that He distinguished a groaning in the adjacent chamber: It was Antonia's, and He supposed that the drops began to take effect: But upon listening more attentively, He found the noise to be caused by Jacintha, who had fallen asleep by the Lady's Bedside, and was snoring most lustily. Ambrosio drew back, and returned to the other room, musing upon the sudden opening of the Closet door, for which He strove in vain to account.

He paced the chamber up and down in silence. At length He stopped, and the Bed attracted his attention. The curtain of the Recess was but half-drawn. He sighed involuntarily.

"That Bed," said He in a low voice, "That Bed was Elvira's! There has She past many a quiet night, for She was good and innocent. How sound must have been her sleep! And yet now She sleeps sounder! Does She indeed sleep? Oh! God grant that She may! What if She rose from her Grave at this sad and silent hour? What if She broke the bonds of the Tomb, and glided angrily before my blasted eyes? Oh! I never could support the sight! Again to see her form distorted by dying agonies, her blood-swollen veins, her livid countenance, her eyes bursting from their sockets with pain! To hear her speak of future punishment, menace me with Heaven's vengeance, tax me with

the crimes I have committed, with those I am going to commit ...
.. Great God! What is that?"

As He uttered these words, his eyes which were fixed upon
the Bed, saw the curtain shaken gently backwards and
forwards. The Apparition was recalled to his mind, and He
almost fancied that He beheld Elvira's visionary form reclining
upon the Bed. A few moments consideration sufficed to
reassure him.

"It was only the wind," said He, recovering himself.

Again He paced the chamber; But an involuntary movement
of awe and inquietude constantly led his eye towards the
Alcove. He drew near it with irresolution. He paused before He
ascended the few steps which led to it. He put out his hand
thrice to remove the curtain, and as often drew it back.

"Absurd terrors!" He cried at length, ashamed of his own
weakness — —

Hastily he mounted the steps; When a Figure drest in white
started from the Alcove, and gliding by him, made with
precipitation towards the Closet. Madness and despair now
supplied the Monk with that courage, of which He had till then
been destitute. He flew down the steps, pursued the Apparition,
and attempted to grasp it.

"Ghost, or Devil, I hold you!" He exclaimed, and seized the
Spectre by the arm.

"Oh! Christ Jesus!" cried a shrill voice; "Holy Father, how
you gripe me! I protest that I meant no harm!"

This address, as well as the arm which He held, convinced
the Abbot that the supposed Ghost was substantial flesh and
blood. He drew the Intruder towards the Table, and holding up
the light, discovered the features of ...... Madona Flora!

Incensed at having been betrayed by this trifling cause into
fears so ridiculous, He asked her sternly, what business had
brought her to that chamber. Flora, ashamed at being found out,
and terrified at the severity of Ambrosio's looks, fell upon her
knees, and promised to make a full confession.

"I protest, reverend Father," said She, "that I am quite
grieved at having disturbed you: Nothing was further from my
intention. I meant to get out of the room as quietly as I got in;

and had you been ignorant that I watched you, you know, it would have been the same thing as if I had not watched you at all. To be sure, I did very wrong in being a Spy upon you, that I cannot deny; But Lord! your Reverence, how can a poor weak Woman resist curiosity? Mine was so strong to know what you were doing, that I could not but try to get a little peep, without any body knowing any thing about it. So with that I left old Dame Jacintha sitting by my Lady's Bed, and I ventured to steal into the Closet. Being unwilling to interrupt you, I contented myself at first with putting my eye to the Keyhole; But as I could see nothing by this means, I undrew the bolt, and while your back was turned to the Alcove, I whipt me in softly and silently. Here I lay snug behind the curtain, till your Reverence found me out, and seized me ere I had time to regain the Closet door. This is the whole truth, I assure you, Holy Father, and I beg your pardon a thousand times for my impertinence."

During this speech the Abbot had time to recollect himself: He was satisfied with reading the penitent Spy a lecture upon the dangers of curiosity, and the meanness of the action in which She had been just discovered. Flora declared herself fully persuaded that She had done wrong; She promised never to be guilty of the same fault again, and was retiring very humble and contrite to Antonia's chamber, when the Closet door was suddenly thrown open, and in rushed Jacintha pale and out of breath.

"Oh! Father! Father!" She cried in a voice almost choaked with terror; "What shall I do! What shall I do! Here is a fine piece of work! Nothing but misfortunes! Nothing but dead people, and dying people! Oh! I shall go distracted! I shall go distracted!"

"Speak! Speak!" cried Flora and the Monk at the same time; "What has happened? What is the matter?"

"Oh! I shall have another Corse in my House! Some Witch has certainly cast a spell upon it, upon me, and upon all about me! Poor Donna Antonia! There She lies in just such convulsions, as killed her Mother! The Ghost told her true! I am sure, the Ghost has told her true!"

Flora ran, or rather flew to her Lady's chamber: Ambrosio followed her, his bosom trembling with hope and apprehension. They found Antonia as Jacintha had described, torn by racking convulsions from which they in vain endeavoured to relieve her. The Monk dispatched Jacintha to the Abbey in all haste, and commissioned her to bring Father Pablos back with her, without losing a moment.

"I will go for him," replied Jacintha, "and tell him to come hither; But as to bringing him myself, I shall do no such thing. I am sure that the House is bewitched, and burn me if ever I set foot in it again."

With this resolution She set out for the Monastery, and delivered to Father Pablos the Abbot's orders. She then betook herself to the House of old Simon Gonzalez, whom She resolved never to quit, till She had made him her Husband, and his dwelling her own.

Father Pablos had no sooner beheld Antonia, than He pronounced her incurable. The convulsions continued for an hour: During that time her agonies were much milder than those which her groans created in the Abbot's heart. Her every pang seemed a dagger in his bosom, and He cursed himself a thousand times for having adopted so barbarous a project. The hour being expired, by degrees the Fits became less frequent, and Antonia less agitated. She felt that her dissolution was approaching, and that nothing could save her.

"Worthy Ambrosio," She said in a feeble voice, while She pressed his hand to her lips; "I am now at liberty to express, how grateful is my heart for your attention and kindness. I am upon the bed of death; Yet an hour, and I shall be no more. I may therefore acknowledge without restraint, that to relinquish your society was very painful to me: But such was the will of a Parent, and I dared not disobey. I die without repugnance: There are few, who will lament my leaving them; There are few, whom I lament to leave. Among those few, I lament for none more than for yourself; But we shall meet again, Ambrosio! We shall one day meet in heaven: There shall our friendship be renewed, and my Mother shall view it with pleasure!"

She paused. The Abbot shuddered when She mentioned Elvira: Antonia imputed his emotion to pity and concern for her.

"You are grieved for me, Father," She continued; "Ah! sigh not for my loss. I have no crimes to repent, at least none of which I am conscious, and I restore my soul without fear to him from whom I received it. I have but few requests to make: Yet let me hope that what few I have shall be granted. Let a solemn Mass be said for my soul's repose, and another for that of my beloved Mother. Not that I doubt her resting in her Grave: I am now convinced that my reason wandered, and the falsehood of the Ghost's prediction is sufficient to prove my error. But every one has some failing: My Mother may have had hers, though I knew them not: I therefore wish a Mass to be celebrated for her repose, and the expence may be defrayed by the little wealth of which I am possessed. Whatever may then remain, I bequeath to my Aunt Leonella. When I am dead, let the Marquis de las Cisternas know that his Brother's unhappy family can no longer importune him. But disappointment makes me unjust: They tell me that He is ill, and perhaps had it been in his power, He wished to have protected me. Tell him then, Father, only that I am dead, and that if He had any faults to me, I forgave him from my heart. This done, I have nothing more to ask for, than your prayers: Promise to remember my requests, and I shall resign my life without a pang or sorrow."

Ambrosio engaged to comply with her desires, and proceeded to give her absolution. Every moment announced the approach of Antonia's fate: Her sight failed; Her heart beat sluggishly; Her fingers stiffened, and grew cold, and at two in the morning She expired without a groan. As soon as the breath had forsaken her body, Father Pablos retired, sincerely affected at the melancholy scene. On her part, Flora gave way to the most unbridled sorrow.

Far different concerns employed Ambrosio: He sought for the pulse whose throbbing, so Matilda had assured him, would prove Antonia's death but temporal. He found it; He pressed it; It palpitated beneath his hand, and his heart was filled with ecstacy. However, He carefully concealed his satisfaction at the success of his plan. He assumed a melancholy air, and addressing himself to Flora, warned her against abandoning herself to fruitless sorrow. Her tears were too sincere to permit her listening to his counsels, and She continued to weep unceasingly.

The Friar withdrew, first promising to give orders himself about the Funeral, which, out of consideration for Jacintha as He pretended, should take place with all expedition. Plunged in grief for the loss of her beloved Mistress, Flora scarcely attended to what He said. Ambrosio hastened to command the Burial. He obtained permission from the Prioress, that the Corse should be deposited in St. Clare's Sepulchre: and on the Friday Morning, every proper and needful ceremony being performed, Antonia's body was committed to the Tomb.

On the same day Leonella arrived at Madrid, intending to present her young Husband to Elvira. Various circumstances had obliged her to defer her journey from Tuesday to Friday, and She had no opportunity of making this alteration in her plans known to her Sister. As her heart was truly affectionate, and as She had ever entertained a sincere regard for Elvira and her Daughter, her surprize at hearing of their sudden and melancholy fate was fully equalled by her sorrow and disappointment. Ambrosio sent to inform her of Antonia's bequest: At her solication, He promised, as soon as Elvira's trifling debts were discharged, to transmit to her the remainder. This being settled, no other business detained Leonella in Madrid, and She returned to Cordova with all diligence.

CHAPTER X.

Oh! could I worship aught beneath the skies

That earth hath seen or fancy could devise,

Thine altar, sacred Liberty, should stand,

Built by no mercenary vulgar hand,

With fragrant turf, and flowers as wild and fair,

As ever dressed a bank, or scented summer air.

COWPER.

His whole attention bent upon bringing to justice the Assassins of his Sister, Lorenzo little thought how severely his interest was suffering in another quarter. As was before mentioned, He returned not to Madrid till the evening of that day on which Antonia was buried. Signifying to the Grand Inquisitor the order of the Cardinal-Duke (a ceremony not to be neglected, when a Member of the Church was to be arrested publicly) communicating his design to his Uncle and Don Ramirez, and assembling a troop of Attendants sufficiently to prevent opposition, furnished him with full occupation during the few hours preceding midnight. Consequently, He had no opportunity to enquire about his Mistress, and was perfectly ignorant both of her death and her Mother's.

The Marquis was by no means out of danger: His delirium was gone, but had left him so much exhausted that the Physicians declined pronouncing upon the consequences likely to ensue. As for Raymond himself, He wished for nothing more earnestly than to join Agnes in the grave. Existence was hateful to him: He saw nothing in the world deserving his attention; and He hoped to hear that Agnes was revenged, and himself given over in the same moment.

Followed by Raymond's ardent prayers for success, Lorenzo was at the Gates of St. Clare a full hour before the time appointed by the Mother St. Ursula. He was accompanied by his Uncle, by Don Ramirez de Mello, and a party of chosen Archers. Though in considerable numbers their appearance created no surprise: A great Crowd was already assembled before the Convent doors, in order to witness the Procession. It was naturally supposed that Lorenzo and his Attendants were conducted thither by the same design. The Duke of Medina being recognised, the People drew back, and made way for his party to advance. Lorenzo placed himself opposite to the great Gate, through which the Pilgrims were to pass. Convinced that the Prioress could not escape him, He waited patiently for her appearance, which She was expected to make exactly at Midnight.

The Nuns were employed in religious duties established in honour of St. Clare, and to which no Prophane was ever admitted. The Chapel windows were illuminated. As they stood on the outside, the Auditors heard the full swell of the organ, accompanied by a chorus of female voices, rise upon the stillness of the night. This died away, and was succeeded by a single strain of harmony: It was the voice of her who was destined to sustain in the procession the character of St. Clare. For this office the most beautiful Virgin of Madrid was always selected, and She upon whom the choice fell esteemed it as the highest of honours. While listening to the Music, whose melody distance only seemed to render sweeter, the Audience was wrapped up in profound attention. Universal silence prevailed through the Crowd, and every heart was filled with reverence for religion. Every heart but Lorenzo's. Conscious that among those who chaunted the praises of their God so sweetly, there were some who cloaked with devotion the foulest sins, their hymns inspired him with detestation at their Hypocrisy. He had long observed with disapprobation and contempt the superstition which governed Madrid's Inhabitants. His good sense had pointed out to him the artifices of the Monks, and the gross absurdity of their miracles, wonders, and supposititious reliques. He blushed to see his Countrymen the Dupes of deceptions so ridiculous, and only wished for an opportunity to free them from their monkish fetters. That opportunity, so long desired in vain, was at length presented to him. He resolved not to let it slip, but to set before the People in glaring colours how enormous were the abuses but too frequently practised in Monasteries, and how unjustly public esteem was bestowed indiscriminately upon all who wore a religious habit. He longed for the moment destined to unmask the Hypocrites, and convince his Countrymen that a sanctified exterior does not always hide a virtuous heart.

The service lasted, till Midnight was announced by the Convent Bell. That sound being heard, the Music ceased: The voices died away softly, and soon after the lights disappeared from the Chapel windows. Lorenzo's heart beat high, when He found the execution of his plan to be at hand. From the natural superstition of the People He had prepared himself for some resistance. But He trusted that the Mother St. Ursula would bring good reasons to justify his proceeding. He had force with him to repel the first impulse of the Populace, till his arguments should be heard: His only fear was lest the Domina, suspecting his design, should have spirited away the Nun on whose deposition every thing depended. Unless the Mother St. Ursula should be present, He could only accuse the Prioress upon suspicion; and this reflection gave him some little apprehension for the success of his enterprize. The tranquillity which seemed to reign through the Convent in some degree re-assured him: Still He expected the moment eagerly, when the presence of his Ally should deprive him of the power of doubting.

The Abbey of Capuchins was only separated from the Convent by the Garden and Cemetery. The Monks had been invited to assist at the Pilgrimage. They now arrived, marching two by two with lighted Torches in their hands, and chaunting Hymns in honour of St. Clare. Father Pablos was at their head, the Abbot having excused himself from attending. The people made way for the holy Train, and the Friars placed themselves in ranks on either side of the great Gates. A few minutes sufficed to arrange the order of the Procession. This being settled, the Convent doors were thrown open, and again the female Chorus sounded in full melody. First appeared a Band of Choristers: As soon as they had passed, the Monks fell in two by two, and followed with steps slow and measured. Next came the Novices; They bore no Tapers, as did the Professed, but moved on with eyes bent downwards, and seemed to be occupied by telling their Beads. To them succeeded a young and lovely Girl, who represented St. Lucia: She held a golden bason in which were two eyes: Her own were covered by a velvet bandage, and She was conducted by another Nun habited as an Angel. She was followed by St. Catherine, a palm-branch in one hand, a flaming Sword in the other: She was robed in white, and her brow was ornamented with a sparkling Diadem. After her appeared St. Genevieve, surrounded by a number of Imps, who putting themselves into grotesque attitudes, drawing her by the robe, and sporting round her with antic gestures, endeavoured to distract her attention from the Book, on which her eyes were constantly fixed. These merry Devils greatly entertained the Spectators, who testified their pleasure by repeated bursts of Laughter. The Prioress had been careful to select a Nun whose disposition was naturally solemn and saturnine. She had every reason to be satisfied with her choice: The drolleries of the Imps were entirely thrown away, and St. Genevieve moved on without discomposing a muscle.

Each of these Saints was separated from the Other by a band of Choristers, exalting her praise in their Hymns, but declaring her to be very much inferior to St. Clare, the Convent's avowed Patroness. These having passed, a long train of Nuns appeared, bearing like the Choristers each a burning Taper. Next came the reliques of St. Clare, inclosed in vases equally precious for their materials and workmanship: But they attracted not Lorenzo's attention. The Nun who bore the heart occupied him entirely. According to Theodore's description, He doubted not her being the Mother St. Ursula. She seemed to look round with anxiety. As He stood foremost in the rank by which the procession past, her eye caught Lorenzo's. A flush of joy overspread her till then pallid cheek. She turned to her Companion eagerly.

"We are safe!" He heard her whisper; "'tis her Brother!"

His heart being now at ease, Lorenzo gazed with tranquillity upon the remainder of the show. Now appeared its most brilliant ornament. It was a Machine fashioned like a throne, rich with jewels and dazzling with light. It rolled onwards upon concealed wheels, and was guided by several lovely Children, dressed as Seraphs. The summit was covered with silver clouds, upon which reclined the most beautiful form that eyes ever witnessed. It was a Damsel representing St. Clare: Her dress was of inestimable price, and round her head a wreath of Diamonds formed an artificial glory: But all these ornaments yielded to the lustre of her charms. As She advanced, a murmur of delight ran through the Crowd. Even Lorenzo confessed secretly, that He never beheld more perfect beauty, and had not his heart been Antonia's, it must have fallen a sacrifice to this enchanting Girl. As it was, He considered her only as a fine Statue: She obtained from him no tribute save cold admiration, and when She had passed him, He thought of her no more.

"Who is She?" asked a By-stander in Lorenzo's hearing.

"One whose beauty you must often have heard celebrated. Her name is Virginia de Villa-Franca: She is a Pensioner of St. Clare's Convent, a Relation of the Prioress, and has been selected with justice as the ornament of the Procession."

The Throne moved onwards. It was followed by the Prioress herself: She marched at the head of the remaining Nuns with a devout and sanctified air, and closed the procession. She moved on slowly: Her eyes were raised to heaven: Her countenance calm and tranquil seemed abstracted from all sublunary things, and no feature betrayed her secret pride at displaying the pomp and opulence of her Convent. She passed along, accompanied by the prayers and benedictions of the Populace: But how great was the general confusion and surprize, when Don Ramirez starting forward, challenged her as his Prisoner.

For a moment amazement held the Domina silent and
immoveable: But no sooner did She recover herself, than She
exclaimed against sacrilege and impiety, and called the People
to rescue a Daughter of the Church. They were eagerly
preparing to obey her; when Don Ramirez, protected by the
Archers from their rage, commanded them to forbear, and
threatened them with the severest vengeance of the Inquisition.
At that dreaded word every arm fell, every sword shrunk back
into its scabbard. The Prioress herself turned pale, and
trembled. The general silence convinced her that She had
nothing to hope but from innocence, and She besought Don
Ramirez in a faultering voice, to inform her of what crime She
was accused.

"That you shall know in time," replied He; "But first I must
secure the Mother St. Ursula."

"The Mother St. Ursula?" repeated the Domina faintly.

At this moment casting her eyes round, She saw near her
Lorenzo and the Duke, who had followed Don Ramirez.

"Ah! great God!" She cried, clasping her hands together with
a frantic air; "I am betrayed!"

"Betrayed?" replied St. Ursula, who now arrived conducted
by some of the Archers, and followed by the Nun her
Companion in the procession: "Not betrayed, but discovered. In
me recognise your Accuser: You know not how well I am
instructed in your guilt!—Segnor!" She continued, turning to
Don Ramirez; "I commit myself to your custody. I charge the
Prioress of St. Clare with murder, and stake my life for the
justice of my accusation."

A general cry of surprize was uttered by the whole
Audience, and an explanation was demanded loudly. The
trembling Nuns, terrified at the noise and universal confusion,
had dispersed, and fled different ways. Some regained the
Convent; Others sought refuge in the dwellings of their
Relations; and Many, only sensible of their present danger, and
anxious to escape from the tumult, ran through the Streets, and
wandered, they knew not whither. The lovely Virginia was one
of the first to fly: And in order that She might be better seen and
heard, the People desired that St. Ursula should harangue them
from the vacant Throne. The Nun complied; She ascended the
glittering Machine, and then addressed the surrounding

multitude as follows.

"However strange and unseemly may appear my conduct, when considered to be adopted by a Female and a Nun, necessity will justify it most fully. A secret, an horrible secret weighs heavy upon my soul: No rest can be mine till I have revealed it to the world, and satisfied that innocent blood which calls from the Grave for vengeance. Much have I dared to gain this opportunity of lightening my conscience. Had I failed in my attempt to reveal the crime, had the Domina but suspected that the mystery was none to me, my ruin was inevitable. Angels who watch unceasingly over those who deserve their favour, have enabled me to escape detection: I am now at liberty to relate a Tale, whose circumstances will freeze every honest soul with horror. Mine is the task to rend the veil from Hypocrisy, and show misguided Parents to what dangers the Woman is exposed, who falls under the sway of a monastic Tyrant.

"Among the Votaries of St. Clare, none was more lovely, none more gentle, than Agnes de Medina. I knew her well; She entrusted to me every secret of her heart; I was her Friend and Confident, and I loved her with sincere affection. Nor was I singular in my attachment. Her piety unfeigned, her willingness to oblige, and her angelic disposition, rendered her the Darling of all that was estimable in the Convent. The Prioress herself, proud, scrupulous and forbidding, could not refuse Agnes that tribute of approbation which She bestowed upon no one else. Every one has some fault: Alas! Agnes had her weakness! She violated the laws of our order, and incurred the inveterate hate of the unforgiving Domina. St. Clare's rules are severe: But grown antiquated and neglected, many of late years have either been forgotten, or changed by universal consent into milder punishments. The penance, adjudged to the crime of Agnes, was most cruel, most inhuman! The law had been long exploded: Alas! It still existed, and the revengeful Prioress now determined to revive it.

This law decreed that the Offender should be plunged into a private dungeon, expressly constituted to hide from the world for ever the Victim of Cruelty and tyrannic superstition. In this dreadful abode She was to lead a perpetual solitude, deprived of all society, and believed to be dead by those whom affection might have prompted to attempt her rescue. Thus was She to languish out the remainder of her days, with no other food than bread and water, and no other comfort than the free indulgence of her tears."

The indignation created by this account was so violent, as for some moments to interrupt St. Ursula's narrative. When the disturbance ceased, and silence again prevailed through the Assembly, She continued her discourse, while at every word the Domina's countenance betrayed her increasing terrors.

"A council of the twelve elder nuns was called: I was of the number. The Prioress in exaggerated colours described the offence of Agnes, and scrupled not to propose the revival of this almost forgotten law. To the shame of our sex be it spoken, that either so absolute was the Domina's will in the Convent, or so much had disappointment, solitude, and self-denial hardened their hearts and soured their tempers that this barbarous proposal was assented to by nine voices out of the twelve. I was not one of the nine. Frequent opportunities had convinced me of the virtues of Agnes, and I loved and pitied her most sincerely. The Mothers Bertha and Cornelia joined my party: We made the strongest opposition possible, and the Superior found herself compelled to change her intention. In spite of the majority in her favour, She feared to break with us openly. She knew that supported by the Medina family, our forces would be too strong for her to cope with: And She also knew that after being once imprisoned and supposed dead, should Agnes be discovered, her ruin would be inevitable. She therefore gave up her design, though which much reluctance. She demanded some days to reflect upon a mode of punishment which might be agreeable to the whole Community; and She promised, that as soon as her resolution was fixed, the same Council should be again summoned. Two days passed away: On the Evening of the Third it was announced that on the next day Agnes should be examined; and that according to her behaviour on that occasion, her punishment should be either strengthened or mitigated.

"On the night preceding this examination, I stole to the Cell of Agnes at an hour when I supposed the other Nuns to be buried in sleep. I comforted her to the best of my power: I bad her take courage, told her to rely upon the support of her friends, and taught her certain signs, by which I might instruct her to answer the Domina's questions by an assent or negative. Conscious that her Enemy would strive to confuse, embarrass, and daunt her, I feared her being ensnared into some confession prejudicial to her interests. Being anxious to keep my visit secret, I stayed with Agnes but a short time. I bad her not let her spirits be cast down; I mingled my tears with those which streamed down her cheek, embraced her fondly, and was on the point of retiring, when I heard the sound of steps approaching the Cell. I started back. A Curtain which veiled a large Crucifix offered me a retreat, and I hastened to place myself behind it.

The door opened. The Prioress entered, followed by four other Nuns. They advanced towards the bed of Agnes. The Superior reproached her with her errors in the bitterest terms: She told her that She was a disgrace to the Convent, that She was resolved to deliver the world and herself from such a Monster, and commanded her to drink the contents of a Goblet now presented to her by one of the Nuns. Aware of the fatal properties of the liquor, and trembling to find herself upon the brink of Eternity, the unhappy Girl strove to excite the Domina's pity by the most affecting prayers.

She sued for life in terms which might have melted the heart of a Fiend: She promised to submit patiently to any punishment, to shame, imprisonment, and torture, might She but be permitted to live! Oh! might She but live another month, or week, or day! Her merciless Enemy listened to her complaints unmoved: She told her that at first She meant to have spared her life, and that if She had altered her intention, She had to thank the opposition of her Friends. She continued to insist upon her swallowing the poison: She bad her recommend herself to the Almighty's mercy, not to hers, and assured her that in an hour She would be numbered with the Dead. Perceiving that it was vain to implore this unfeeling Woman, She attempted to spring from her bed, and call for assistance: She hoped, if She could not escape the fate announced to her, at least to have witnesses of the violence committed. The Prioress guessed her design. She seized her forcibly by the arm, and pushed her back upon her pillow. At the same time drawing a dagger, and placing it at the breast of the unfortunate Agnes, She protested that if She uttered a single cry, or hesitated a single moment to drink the poison, She would pierce her heart that instant. Already half-dead with fear, She could make no further resistance. The Nun approached with the fatal Goblet. The Domina obliged her to take it, and swallow the contents. She drank, and the horrid deed was accomplished. The Nuns then seated themselves round the Bed. They answered her groans with reproaches; They interrupted with sarcasms the prayers in which She recommended her parting soul to mercy: They threatened her with heaven's vengeance and eternal perdition: They bad her despair of pardon, and strowed with yet sharper thorns Death's painful pillow. Such were the sufferings of this young Unfortunate, till released by fate from the malice of her Tormentors. She expired in horror of the past, in fears for the future; and her agonies were such as must have amply gratified the hate and vengeance of her Enemies. As soon as her Victim ceased to breathe, the Domina retired, and was followed by her Accomplices.

"It was now that I ventured from my concealment. I dared not to assist my unhappy Friend, aware that without preserving her, I should only have brought on myself the same destruction. Shocked and terrified beyond expression at this horrid scene, scarcely had I sufficient strength to regain my Cell. As I reached the door of that of Agnes, I ventured to look towards the bed, on which lay her lifeless body, once so lovely and so sweet! I breathed a prayer for her departed Spirit, and vowed to revenge her death by the shame and punishment of her Assassins. With danger and difficulty have I kept my oath. I unwarily dropped some words at the funeral of Agnes, while thrown off my guard by excessive grief, which alarmed the guilty conscience of the Prioress. My every action was observed; My every step was traced. I was constantly surrounded by the Superior's spies. It was long before I could find the means of conveying to the unhappy Girl's Relations an intimation of my secret. It was given out that Agnes had expired suddenly: This account was credited not only by her Friends in Madrid, but even by those within the Convent. The poison had left no marks upon her body: No one suspected the true cause of her death, and it remained unknown to all, save the Assassins and Myself.

"I have no more to say: for what I have already said, I will answer with my life. I repeat that the Prioress is a Murderess; that she has driven from the world, perhaps from heaven, an Unfortunate whose offence was light and venial; that She has abused the power intrusted to her hands, and has been a Tyrant, a Barbarian, and an Hypocrite. I also accuse the four Nuns, Violante, Camilla, Alix, and Mariana, as being her Accomplices, and equally criminal."

Here St. Ursula ended her narrative. It created horror and surprize throughout: But when She related the inhuman murder of Agnes, the indignation of the Mob was so audibly testified, that it was scarcely possible to hear the conclusion. This confusion increased with every moment: At length a multitude of voices exclaimed that the Prioress should be given up to their fury. To this Don Ramirez refused to consent positively. Even Lorenzo bad the People remember that She had undergone no trial, and advised them to leave her punishment to the Inquisition. All representations were fruitless: The disturbance grew still more violent, and the Populace more exasperated. In vain did Ramirez attempt to convey his Prisoner out of the Throng. Wherever He turned, a band of Rioters barred his passage, and demanded her being delivered over to them more loudly than before. Ramirez ordered his Attendants to cut their way through the multitude: Oppressed by numbers, it was impossible for them to draw their swords. He threatened the

Mob with the vengeance of the Inquisition: But in this moment of popular phrenzy even this dreadful name had lost its effect. Though regret for his Sister made him look upon the Prioress with abhorrence, Lorenzo could not help pitying a Woman in a situation so terrible: But in spite of all his exertions, and those of the Duke, of Don Ramirez, and the Archers, the People continued to press onwards. They forced a passage through the Guards who protected their destined Victim, dragged her from her shelter, and proceeded to take upon her a most summary and cruel vengeance. Wild with terror, and scarcely knowing what She said, the wretched Woman shrieked for a moment's mercy: She protested that She was innocent of the death of Agnes, and could clear herself from the suspicion beyond the power of doubt. The Rioters heeded nothing but the gratification of their barbarous vengeance. They refused to listen to her: They showed her every sort of insult, loaded her with mud and filth, and called her by the most opprobrious appellations. They tore her one from another, and each new Tormentor was more savage than the former. They stifled with howls and execrations her shrill cries for mercy; and dragged her through the Streets, spurning her, trampling her, and treating her with every species of cruelty which hate or vindictive fury could invent. At length a Flint, aimed by some well-directing hand, struck her full upon the temple. She sank upon the ground bathed in blood, and in a few minutes terminated her miserable existence. Yet though She no longer felt their insults, the Rioters still exercised their impotent rage upon her lifeless body. They beat it, trod upon it, and ill-used it, till it became no more than a mass of flesh, unsightly, shapeless, and disgusting.

Unable to prevent this shocking event, Lorenzo and his Friends had beheld it with the utmost horror: But they were rouzed from their compelled inactivity, on hearing that the Mob was attacking the Convent of St. Clare. The incensed Populace, confounding the innocent with the guilty, had resolved to sacrifice all the Nuns of that order to their rage, and not to leave one stone of the building upon another. Alarmed at this intelligence, they hastened to the Convent, resolved to defend it if possible, or at least to rescue the Inhabitants from the fury of the Rioters. Most of the Nuns had fled, but a few still remained in their habitation. Their situation was truly dangerous. However, as they had taken the precaution of fastening the inner Gates, with this assistance Lorenzo hoped to repel the Mob, till Don Ramirez should return to him with a more sufficient force.

Having been conducted by the former disturbance to the distance of some Streets from the Convent, He did not immediately reach it: When He arrived, the throng surrounding it was so excessive as to prevent his approaching the Gates. In the interim, the Populace besieged the Building with persevering rage: They battered the walls, threw lighted torches in at the windows, and swore that by break of day not a Nun of St. Clare's order should be left alive. Lorenzo had just succeeded in piercing his way through the Crowd, when one of the Gates was forced open. The Rioters poured into the interior part of the Building, where they exercised their vengeance upon every thing which found itself in their passage. They broke the furniture into pieces, tore down the pictures, destroyed the reliques, and in their hatred of her Servant forgot all respect to the Saint. Some employed themselves in searching out the Nuns, Others in pulling down parts of the Convent, and Others again in setting fire to the pictures and valuable furniture which it contained. These Latter produced the most decisive desolation: Indeed the consequences of their action were more sudden than themselves had expected or wished. The Flames rising from the burning piles caught part of the Building, which being old and dry, the conflagration spread with rapidity from room to room. The Walls were soon shaken by the devouring element: The Columns gave way: The Roofs came tumbling down upon the Rioters, and crushed many of them beneath their weight. Nothing was to be heard but shrieks and groans; The Convent was wrapped in flames, and the whole presented a scene of devastation and horror.

Lorenzo was shocked at having been the cause, however innocent, of this frightful disturbance: He endeavoured to repair his fault by protecting the helpless Inhabitants of the Convent. He entered it with the Mob, and exerted himself to repress the prevailing Fury, till the sudden and alarming progress of the flames compelled him to provide for his own safety. The People now hurried out, as eagerly as they had before thronged in; But their numbers clogging up the doorway, and the fire gaining upon them rapidly, many of them perished ere they had time to effect their escape. Lorenzo's good fortune directed him to a small door in a farther Aisle of the Chapel. The bolt was already undrawn: He opened the door, and found himself at the foot of St. Clare's Sepulchre.

Here he stopped to breathe. The Duke and some of his Attendants had followed him, and thus were in security for the present. They now consulted, what steps they should take to escape from this scene of disturbance: But their deliberations were considerably interrupted by the sight of volumes of fire rising from amidst the Convent's massy walls, by the noise of some heavy Arch tumbling down in ruins, or by the mingled shrieks of the Nuns and Rioters, either suffocating in the press, perishing in the flames, or crushed beneath the weight of the falling Mansion.

Lorenzo enquired, whither the Wicket led? He was answered, to the Garden of the Capuchins, and it was resolved to explore an outlet upon that side. Accordingly the Duke raised the Latch, and passed into the adjoining Cemetery. The Attendants followed without ceremony. Lorenzo, being the last, was also on the point of quitting the Colonnade, when He saw the door of the Sepulchre opened softly. Someone looked out, but on perceiving Strangers uttered a loud shriek, started back again, and flew down the marble Stairs.

"What can this mean?" cried Lorenzo; "Here is some mystery concealed. Follow me without delay!"

Thus saying, He hastened into the Sepulchre, and pursued the person who continued to fly before him. The Duke knew not the cause of his exclamation, but supposing that He had good reasons for it, he followed him without hesitation. The Others did the same, and the whole Party soon arrived at the foot of the Stairs.

The upper door having been left open, the neighbouring flames darted from above a sufficient light to enable Lorenzo's catching a glance of the Fugitive running through the long passages and distant Vaults: But when a sudden turn deprived him of this assistance, total darkness succeeded, and He could only trace the object of his enquiry by the faint echo of retiring feet. The Pursuers were now compelled to proceed with caution: As well as they could judge, the Fugitive also seemed to slacken pace, for they heard the steps follow each other at longer intervals. They at length were bewildered by the Labyrinth of passages, and dispersed in various directions. Carried away by his eagerness to clear up this mystery, and to penetrate into which He was impelled by a movement secret and unaccountable, Lorenzo heeded not this circumstance till He found himself in total solitude. The noise of footsteps had ceased. All was silent around, and no clue offered itself to guide him to the flying Person. He stopped to reflect on the means most likely to aid his pursuit. He was persuaded that no common cause would have induced the Fugitive to seek that dreary place at an hour so unusual: The cry which He had heard, seemed uttered in a voice of terror, and He was convinced that some mystery was attached to this event. After some minutes past in hesitation He continued to proceed, feeling his way along the walls of the passage. He had already past some time in this slow progress, when He descried a spark of light glimmering at a distance. Guided by this observation, and having drawn his sword, He bent his steps towards the place, whence the beam seemed to be emitted.

It proceeded from the Lamp which flamed before St. Clare's Statue. Before it stood several Females, their white Garments streaming in the blast, as it howled along the vaulted dungeons. Curious to know what had brought them together in this melancholy spot, Lorenzo drew near with precaution. The Strangers seemed earnestly engaged in conversation. They heard not Lorenzo's steps, and He approached unobserved, till He could hear their voices distinctly.

"I protest," continued She who was speaking when He arrived, and to whom the rest were listening with great attention; "I protest, that I saw them with my own eyes. I flew down the steps; They pursued me, and I escaped falling into their hands with difficulty. Had it not been for the Lamp, I should never have found you."

"And what could bring them hither?" said another in a trembling voice; "Do you think that they were looking for us?"

"God grant that my fears may be false," rejoined the First; "But I doubt they are Murderers! If they discover us, we are lost! As for me, my fate is certain: My affinity to the Prioress will be a sufficient crime to condemn me; and though till now these Vaults have afforded me a retreat......."

Here looking up, her eye fell upon Lorenzo, who had continued to approach softly.

"The Murderers!" She cried—

She started away from the Statue's Pedestal on which She had been seated, and attempted to escape by flight. Her Companions at the same moment uttered a terrified scream, while Lorenzo arrested the Fugitive by the arm. Frightened and desperate She sank upon her knees before him.

"Spare me!" She exclaimed; "For Christ's sake, spare me! I am innocent, indeed, I am!"

While She spoke, her voice was almost choked with fear. The beams of the Lamp darting full upon her face which was unveiled, Lorenzo recognized the beautiful Virginia de Villa-Franca. He hastened to raise her from the ground, and besought her to take courage. He promised to protect her from the Rioters, assured her that her retreat was still a secret, and that She might depend upon his readiness to defend her to the last drop of his blood. During this conversation, the Nuns had thrown themselves into various attitudes: One knelt, and addressed herself to heaven; Another hid her face in the lap of her Neighbour; Some listened motionless with fear to the discourse of the supposed Assassin; while Others embraced the Statue of St. Clare, and implored her protection with frantic cries. On perceiving their mistake, they crowded round Lorenzo and heaped benedictions on him by dozens. He found that, on hearing the threats of the Mob, and terrified by the cruelties which from the Convent Towers they had seen inflicted on the Superior, many of the Pensioners and Nuns had taken refuge in the Sepulchre. Among the former was to be reckoned the lovely Virginia. Nearly related to the Prioress, She had more reason than the rest to dread the Rioters, and now besought Lorenzo earnestly not to abandon her to their rage. Her Companions, most of whom were Women of noble family, made the same request, which He readily granted. He promised not to quit them, till He had seen each of them safe in the arms of her Relations: But He advised their deferring to quit the Sepulchre for some time longer, when the popular fury should be somewhat calmed, and the arrival of military force have dispersed the multitude.

"Would to God!" cried Virginia, "That I were already safe in my Mother's embraces! How say you, Segnor; Will it be long, ere we may leave this place? Every moment that I pass here, I pass in torture!"

"I hope, not long," said He; "But till you can proceed with security, this Sepulchre will prove an impenetrable asylum. Here you run no risque of a discovery, and I would advise your remaining quiet for the next two or three hours."

"Two or three hours?" exclaimed Sister Helena; "If I stay another hour in these vaults, I shall expire with fear! Not the wealth of worlds should bribe me to undergo again what I have suffered since my coming hither. Blessed Virgin! To be in this melancholy place in the middle of night, surrounded by the mouldering bodies of my deceased Companions, and expecting every moment to be torn in pieces by their Ghosts who wander about me, and complain, and groan, and wail in accents that make my blood run cold, ... Christ Jesus! It is enough to drive me to madness!"

"Excuse me," replied Lorenzo, "if I am surprized that while menaced by real woes you are capable of yielding to imaginary dangers. These terrors are puerile and groundless: Combat them, holy Sister; I have promised to guard you from the Rioters, but against the attacks of superstition you must depend for protection upon yourself. The idea of Ghosts is ridiculous in the extreme; And if you continue to be swayed by ideal terrors .."

"Ideal?" exclaimed the Nuns with one voice; "Why we heard it ourselves, Segnor! Every one of us heard it! It was frequently repeated, and it sounded every time more melancholy and deep. You will never persuade me that we could all have been deceived. Not we, indeed; No, no; Had the noise been merely created by fancy ...."

"Hark! Hark!" interrupted Virginia in a voice of terror; "God preserve us! There it is again!"

The Nuns clasped their hands together, and sank upon their knees.

Lorenzo looked round him eagerly, and was on the point of yielding to the fears which already had possessed the Women. Universal silence prevailed. He examined the Vault, but nothing was to be seen. He now prepared to address the Nuns, and ridicule their childish apprehensions, when his attention was arrested by a deep and long-drawn groan.

"What was that?" He cried, and started.

"There, Segnor!" said Helena; "Now you must be convinced! You have heard the noise yourself! Now judge, whether our terrors are imaginary. Since we have been here, that groaning has been repeated almost every five minutes. Doubtless, it proceeds from some Soul in pain, who wishes to be prayed out of purgatory: But none of us here dares ask it the question. As for me, were I to see an Apparition, the fright, I am very certain, would kill me out of hand."

As She said this, a second groan was heard yet more distinctly. The Nuns crossed themselves, and hastened to repeat their prayers against evil Spirits. Lorenzo listened attentively. He even thought that He could distinguish sounds, as of one speaking in complaint; But distance rendered them inarticulate. The noise seemed to come from the midst of the small Vault in which He and the Nuns then were, and which a multitude of passages branching out in various directions, formed into a sort of Star. Lorenzo's curiosity which was ever awake, made him anxious to solve this mystery. He desired that silence might be kept. The Nuns obeyed him. All was hushed, till the general stillness was again disturbed by the groaning, which was repeated several times successively. He perceived it to be most audible, when upon following the sound He was conducted close to the shrine of St. Clare:

"The noise comes from hence," said He; "Whose is this Statue?"

Helena, to whom He addressed the question, paused for a moment. Suddenly She clapped her hands together.

"Aye!" cried she, "it must be so. I have discovered the meaning of these groans."

The nuns crowded round her, and besought her eagerly to explain herself. She gravely replied that for time immemorial the Statue had been famous for performing miracles: From this She inferred that the Saint was concerned at the conflagration of a Convent which She protected, and expressed her grief by audible lamentations. Not having equal faith in the miraculous Saint, Lorenzo did not think this solution of the mystery quite so satisfactory, as the Nuns, who subscribed to it without hesitation. In one point, 'tis true, that He agreed with Helena.

He suspected that the groans proceeded from the Statue: The more He listened, the more was He confirmed in this idea. He drew nearer to the Image, designing to inspect it more closely: But perceiving his intention, the Nuns besought him for God's sake to desist, since if He touched the Statue, his death was inevitable.

"And in what consists the danger?" said He.

"Mother of God! In what?" replied Helena, ever eager to relate a miraculous adventure; "If you had only heard the hundredth part of those marvellous Stories about this Statue which the Domina used to recount! She assured us often and often, that if we only dared to lay a finger upon it, we might expect the most fatal consequences. Among other things She told us that a Robber having entered these Vaults by night, He observed yonder Ruby, whose value is inestimable. Do you see it, Segnor? It sparkles upon the third finger of the hand, in which She holds a crown of Thorns. This Jewel naturally excited the Villain's cupidity. He resolved to make himself Master of it. For this purpose He ascended the Pedestal: He supported himself by grasping the Saint's right arm, and extended his own towards the Ring. What was his surprize, when He saw the Statue's hand raised in a posture of menace, and heard her lips pronounce his eternal perdition! Penetrated with awe and consternation, He desisted from his attempt, and prepared to quit the Sepulchre. In this He also failed. Flight was denied him. He found it impossible to disengage the hand, which rested upon the right arm of the Statue. In vain did He struggle: He remained fixed to the Image, till the insupportable and fiery anguish which darted itself through his veins, compelled his shrieking for assistance.

The Sepulchre was now filled with Spectators. The Villain confessed his sacrilege, and was only released by the separation of his hand from his body. It has remained ever since fastened to the Image. The Robber turned Hermit, and led ever after an exemplary life: But yet the Saint's decree was performed, and Tradition says that He continues to haunt this Sepulchre, and implore St. Clare's pardon with groans and lamentations. Now I think of it, those which we have just heard, may very possibly have been uttered by the Ghost of this Sinner: But of this I will not be positive. All that I can say is, that since that time no one has ever dared to touch the Statue: Then do not be foolhardy, good Segnor! For the love of heaven, give up your design, nor expose yourself unnecessarily to certain destruction."

Not being convinced that his destruction would be so certain as Helena seemed to think it, Lorenzo persisted in his resolution. The Nuns besought him to desist in piteous terms, and even pointed out the Robber's hand, which in effect was still visible upon the arm of the Statue. This proof, as they imagined, must convince him. It was very far from doing so; and they were greatly scandalized when he declared his suspicion that the dried and shrivelled fingers had been placed there by order of the Prioress. In spite of their prayers and threats He approached the Statue. He sprang over the iron Rails which defended it, and the Saint underwent a thorough examination. The Image at first appeared to be of Stone, but proved on further inspection to be formed of no more solid materials than coloured Wood. He shook it, and attempted to move it; But it appeared to be of a piece with the Base which it stood upon. He examined it over and over: Still no clue guided him to the solution of this mystery, for which the Nuns were become equally solicitous, when they saw that He touched the Statue with impunity. He paused, and listened: The groans were repeated at intervals, and He was convinced of being in the spot nearest to them. He mused upon this singular event, and ran over the Statue with enquiring eyes. Suddenly they rested upon the shrivelled hand. It struck him, that so particular an injunction was not given without cause, not to touch the arm of the Image. He again ascended the Pedestal; He examined the object of his attention, and discovered a small knob of iron concealed between the Saint's shoulder and what was supposed to have been the hand of the Robber. This observation delighted him. He applied his fingers to the knob, and pressed it down forcibly. Immediately a rumbling noise was heard within the Statue, as if a chain tightly stretched was flying back. Startled at the sound the timid Nuns started away, prepared to hasten from the Vault at the first appearance of danger. All remaining quiet and still, they again gathered round Lorenzo, and beheld his proceedings with anxious curiosity.

Finding that nothing followed this discovery, He descended. As He took his hand from the Saint, She trembled beneath his touch. This created new terrors in the Spectators, who believed the Statue to be animated. Lorenzo's ideas upon the subject were widely different. He easily comprehended that the noise which He had heard, was occasioned by his having loosened a chain which attached the Image to its Pedestal. He once more attempted to move it, and succeeded without much exertion. He placed it upon the ground, and then perceived the Pedestal to be hollow, and covered at the opening with an heavy iron grate.

This excited such general curiosity that the Sisters forgot both their real and imaginary dangers. Lorenzo proceeded to raise the Grate, in which the Nuns assisted him to the utmost of their strength. The attempt was accomplished with little difficulty. A deep abyss now presented itself before them, whose thick obscurity the eye strove in vain to pierce. The rays of the Lamp were too feeble to be of much assistance. Nothing was discernible, save a flight of rough unshapen steps which sank into the yawning Gulph and were soon lost in darkness. The groans were heard no more; But All believed them to have ascended from this Cavern. As He bent over it, Lorenzo fancied that He distinguished something bright twinkling through the gloom. He gazed attentively upon the spot where it showed itself, and was convinced that He saw a small spark of light, now visible, now disappearing. He communicated this circumstance to the Nuns: They also perceived the spark; But when He declared his intention to descend into the Cave, they united to oppose his resolution. All their remonstrances could not prevail on him to alter it. None of them had courage enough to accompany him; neither could He think of depriving them of the Lamp. Alone therefore, and in darkness, He prepared to pursue his design, while the Nuns were contented to offer up prayers for his success and safety.

The steps were so narrow and uneven, that to descend them was like walking down the side of a precipice. The obscurity by which He was surrounded rendered his footing insecure. He was obliged to proceed with great caution, lest He should miss the steps and fall into the Gulph below him. This He was several times on the point of doing. However, He arrived sooner upon solid ground than He had expected: He now found that the thick darkness and impenetrable mists which reigned through the Cavern had deceived him into the belief of its being much more profound than it proved upon inspection. He reached the foot of the Stairs unhurt: He now stopped, and looked round for the spark which had before caught his attention. He sought it in vain: All was dark and gloomy. He listened for the groans; But his ear caught no sound, except the distant murmur of the Nuns above, as in low voices they repeated their Ave-Marias. He stood irresolute to which side He should address his steps. At all events He determined to proceed: He did so, but slowly, fearing lest instead of approaching, He should be retiring from the object of his search. The groans seemed to announce one in pain, or at least in sorrow, and He hoped to have the power of relieving the Mourner's calamities. A plaintive tone, sounding at no great distance, at length reached his hearing; He bent his course joyfully towards it. It became more audible as He advanced; and He soon beheld again the spark of light, which a low projecting Wall had hitherto concealed from him.

It proceeded from a small lamp which was placed upon an heap of stones, and whose faint and melancholy rays served rather to point out, than dispell the horrors of a narrow gloomy dungeon formed in one side of the Cavern; It also showed several other recesses of similar construction, but whose depth was buried in obscurity. Coldly played the light upon the damp walls, whose dew-stained surface gave back a feeble reflection. A thick and pestilential fog clouded the height of the vaulted dungeon. As Lorenzo advanced, He felt a piercing chillness spread itself through his veins. The frequent groans still engaged him to move forwards. He turned towards them, and by the Lamp's glimmering beams beheld in a corner of this loathsome abode, a Creature stretched upon a bed of straw, so wretched, so emaciated, so pale, that He doubted to think her Woman. She was half-naked: Her long dishevelled hair fell in disorder over her face, and almost entirely concealed it. One wasted Arm hung listlessly upon a tattered rug which covered her convulsed and shivering limbs: The Other was wrapped round a small bundle, and held it closely to her bosom. A large Rosary lay near her: Opposite to her was a Crucifix, on which She bent her sunk eyes fixedly, and by her side stood a Basket and a small Earthen Pitcher.

Lorenzo stopped: He was petrified with horror. He gazed upon the miserable Object with disgust and pity. He trembled at the spectacle; He grew sick at heart: His strength failed him, and his limbs were unable to support his weight. He was obliged to lean against the low Wall which was near him, unable to go forward, or to address the Sufferer. She cast her eyes towards the Staircase: The Wall concealed Lorenzo, and She observed him not.

"No one comes!" She at length murmured.

As She spoke, her voice was hollow, and rattled in her throat: She sighed bitterly.

"No one comes!" She repeated; "No! They have forgotten me! They will come no more!"

She paused for a moment: Then continued mournfully.

"Two days! Two long, long days, and yet no food! And yet no hope, no comfort! Foolish Woman! How can I wish to lengthen a life so wretched! Yet such a death! O! God! To perish by such a death! To linger out such ages in torture! Till now, I knew not what it was to hunger! Hark! No. No one comes! They will come no more!"

She was silent. She shivered, and drew the rug over her naked shoulders.

"I am very cold! I am still unused to the damps of this dungeon!

'Tis strange: But no matter. Colder shall I soon be, and yet not feel it—I shall be cold, cold as Thou art!"

She looked at the bundle which lay upon her breast. She bent over it, and kissed it: Then drew back hastily, and shuddered with disgust.

"It was once so sweet! It would have been so lovely, so like him! I have lost it for ever! How a few days have changed it! I should not know it again myself! Yet it is dear to me! God! how dear! I will forget what it is: I will only remember what it was, and love it as well, as when it was so sweet! so lovely! so like him! I thought that I had wept away all my tears, but here is one still lingering."

She wiped her eyes with a tress of her hair. She put out her hand for the Pitcher, and reached it with difficulty. She cast into it a look of hopeless enquiry. She sighed, and replaced it upon the ground.

"Quite a void! Not a drop! Not one drop left to cool my scorched-up burning palate! Now would I give treasures for a draught of water! And they are God's Servants, who make me suffer thus! They think themselves holy, while they torture me like Fiends! They are cruel and unfeeling; And 'tis they who bid me repent; And 'tis they, who threaten me with eternal perdition! Saviour, Saviour! You think not so!"

She again fixed her eyes upon the Crucifix, took her Rosary, and while She told her beads, the quick motion of her lips declared her to be praying with fervency.

While He listened to her melancholy accents, Lorenzo's sensibility became yet more violently affected. The first sight of such misery had given a sensible shock to his feelings: But that being past, He now advanced towards the Captive. She heard his steps, and uttering a cry of joy, dropped the Rosary.

"Hark! Hark! Hark!" She cried: "Some one comes!"

She strove to raise herself, but her strength was unequal to the attempt: She fell back, and as She sank again upon the bed of straw, Lorenzo heard the rattling of heavy chains. He still approached, while the Prisoner thus continued.

"Is it you, Camilla? You are come then at last? Oh! it was time! I thought that you had forsaken me; that I was doomed to perish of hunger. Give me to drink, Camilla, for pity's sake! I am faint with long fasting, and grown so weak that I cannot raise myself from the ground. Good Camilla, give me to drink, lest I expire before you!"

Fearing that surprize in her enfeebled state might be fatal, Lorenzo was at a loss how to address her.

"It is not Camilla," said He at length, speaking in a slow and gentle voice.

"Who is it then?" replied the Sufferer: "Alix, perhaps, or Violante. My eyes are grown so dim and feeble that I cannot distinguish your features. But whichever it is, if your breast is sensible of the least compassion, if you are not more cruel than Wolves and Tigers, take pity on my sufferings. You know that I

635

am dying for want of sustenance. This is the third day, since these lips have received nourishment. Do you bring me food? Or come you only to announce my death, and learn how long I have yet to exist in agony?"

"You mistake my business," replied Lorenzo; "I am no Emissary of the cruel Prioress. I pity your sorrows, and come hither to relieve them."

"To relieve them?" repeated the Captive; "Said you, to relieve them?"

At the same time starting from the ground, and supporting herself upon her hands, She gazed upon the Stranger earnestly.

"Great God! It is no illusion! A Man! Speak! Who are you? What brings you hither? Come you to save me, to restore me to liberty, to life and light? Oh! speak, speak quickly, lest I encourage an hope whose disappointment will destroy me."

"Be calm!" replied Lorenzo in a voice soothing and compassionate; "The Domina of whose cruelty you complain, has already paid the forfeit of her offences: You have nothing more to fear from her.

A few minutes will restore you to liberty, and the embraces of your Friends from whom you have been secluded. You may rely upon my protection. Give me your hand, and be not fearful. Let me conduct you where you may receive those attentions which your feeble state requires."

"Oh! Yes! Yes! Yes!" cried the Prisoner with an exulting shriek; "There is a God then, and a just one! Joy! Joy! I shall once more breath the fresh air, and view the light of the glorious sunbeams! I will go with you! Stranger, I will go with you! Oh! Heaven will bless you for pitying an Unfortunate! But this too must go with me," She added pointing to the small bundle which She still clasped to her bosom; "I cannot part with this. I will bear it away: It shall convince the world how dreadful are the abodes so falsely termed religious. Good Stranger, lend me your hand to rise: I am faint with want, and sorrow, and sickness, and my forces have quite forsaken me! So, that is well!"

As Lorenzo stooped to raise her, the beams of the Lamp struck full upon his face.

"Almighty God!" She exclaimed; "Is it possible! That look! Those features! Oh! Yes, it is, it is ....."

She extended her arms to throw them round him; But her enfeebled frame was unable to sustain the emotions which agitated her bosom. She fainted, and again sank upon the bed of straw.

Lorenzo was surprized at her last exclamation. He thought that He had before heard such accents as her hollow voice had just formed, but where He could not remember. He saw that in her dangerous situation immediate physical aid was absolutely necessary, and He hastened to convey her from the dungeon. He was at first prevented from doing so by a strong chain fastened round the prisoner's body, and fixing her to the neighbouring Wall. However, his natural strength being aided by anxiety to relieve the Unfortunate, He soon forced out the Staple to which one end of the Chain was attached. Then taking the Captive in his arms, He bent his course towards the Staircase. The rays of the Lamp above, as well as the murmur of female voices, guided his steps. He gained the Stairs, and in a few minutes after arrived at the iron-grate.

The nuns during his absence had been terribly tormented by curiosity and apprehension: They were equally surprized and delighted on seeing him suddenly emerge from the Cave. Every heart was filled with compassion for the miserable Creature whom He bore in his arms. While the Nuns, and Virginia in particular, employed themselves in striving to recall her to her senses, Lorenzo related in few words the manner of his finding her. He then observed to them that by this time the tumult must have been quelled, and that He could now conduct them to their Friends without danger. All were eager to quit the Sepulchre: Still to prevent all possibility of ill-usage, they besought Lorenzo to venture out first alone, and examine whether the Coast was clear. With this request He complied. Helena offered to conduct him to the Staircase, and they were on the point of departing, when a strong light flashed from several passages upon the adjacent walls. At the same time Steps were heard of people approaching hastily, and whose number seemed to be considerable. The Nuns were greatly alarmed at this circumstance: They supposed their retreat to be discovered, and the Rioters to be advancing in pursuit of them. Hastily quitting the Prisoner who remained insensible, they crowded round Lorenzo, and claimed his promise to protect them. Virginia alone forgot her own danger by striving to relieve the sorrows of Another. She supported the Sufferer's head upon her knees, bathing her temples with rose-water, chafing her cold hands, and sprinkling her face with tears which were drawn from her by compassion. The Strangers approaching nearer, Lorenzo was enabled to dispel the fears of the Suppliants. His name, pronounced by a number of voices among which He distinguished the Duke's, pealed along the Vaults, and convinced him that He was the object of their search. He communicated this intelligence to the Nuns, who received it with rapture. A few moments after confirmed his idea. Don Ramirez, as well as the Duke, appeared, followed by Attendants with Torches. They had been seeking him through the Vaults, in order to let him know that the Mob was dispersed, and the riot entirely over. Lorenzo recounted briefly his adventure in the Cavern, and explained how much the Unknown was in want of medical assistance. He besought the Duke to take charge of her, as well as of the Nuns and Pensioners.

"As for me," said He, "Other cares demand my attention. While you with one half of the Archers convey these Ladies to their respective homes, I wish the other half to be left with me. I will examine the Cavern below, and pervade the most secret recesses of the Sepulchre. I cannot rest till convinced that yonder wretched Victim was the only one confined by Superstition in these vaults."

The Duke applauded his intention. Don Ramirez offered to assist him in his enquiry, and his proposal was accepted with gratitude.

The Nuns having made their acknowledgments to Lorenzo, committed themselves to the care of his Uncle, and were conducted from the Sepulchre. Virginia requested that the Unknown might be given to her in charge, and promised to let Lorenzo know whenever She was sufficiently recovered to accept his visits. In truth, She made this promise more from consideration for herself than for either Lorenzo or the Captive. She had witnessed his politeness, gentleness, and intrepidity with sensible emotion. She wished earnestly to preserve his acquaintance; and in addition to the sentiments of pity which the Prisoner excited, She hoped that her attention to this Unfortunate would raise her a degree in the esteem of Lorenzo. She had no occasion to trouble herself upon this head. The kindness already displayed by her and the tender concern which She had shown for the Sufferer had gained her an exalted place in his good graces. While occupied in alleviating the Captive's sorrows, the nature of her employment adorned her with new charms, and rendered her beauty a thousand times more interesting. Lorenzo viewed her with admiration and delight: He considered her as a ministering Angel descended to the aid of afflicted innocence; nor could his heart have resisted her attractions, had it not been steeled by the remembrance of Antonia.

The duke now conveyed the nuns in safety to the dwellings of their respective friends. The rescued Prisoner was still insensible and gave no signs of life, except by occasional groans. She was borne upon a sort of litter; Virginia, who was constantly by the side of it, was apprehensive that exhausted by long abstinence, and shaken by the sudden change from bonds and darkness to liberty and light, her frame would never get the better of the shock. Lorenzo and Don Ramirez still remained in the Sepulchre. After deliberating upon their proceedings, it was resolved that to prevent losing time, the Archers should be divided into two Bodies: That with one Don Ramirez should examine the cavern, while Lorenzo with the other might penetrate into the further Vaults. This being arranged, and his Followers being provided with Torches, Don Ramirez advanced to the Cavern. He had already descended some steps when He heard People approaching hastily from the interior part of the Sepulchre. This surprized him, and He quitted the Cave precipitately.

"Do you hear footsteps?" said Lorenzo; "Let us bend our course towards them. 'Tis from this side that they seem to proceed."

At that moment a loud and piercing shriek induced him to quicken his steps.

"Help! Help, for God's sake! cried a voice, whose melodious tone penetrated Lorenzo's heart with terror.

He flew towards the cry with the rapidity of lightning, and was followed by Don Ramirez with equal swiftness.

CHAPTER XI.

Great Heaven! How frail thy creature Man is made!

How by himself insensibly betrayed!

In our own strength unhappily secure,

Too little cautious of the adverse power,

On pleasure's flowery brink we idly stray,

Masters as yet of our returning way:

Till the strong gusts of raging passion rise,

Till the dire Tempest mingles earth and skies,

And swift into the boundless Ocean borne,

Our foolish confidence too late we mourn:

Round our devoted heads the billows beat,

And from our troubled view the lessening lands retreat.

PRIOR.

All this while, Ambrosio was unconscious of the dreadful scenes which were passing so near. The execution of his designs upon Antonia employed his every thought. Hitherto, He was satisfied with the success of his plans. Antonia had drank the opiate, was buried in the vaults of St. Clare, and absolutely in his disposal. Matilda, who was well acquainted with the nature and effects of the soporific medicine, had computed that it would not cease to operate till one in the Morning. For that hour He waited with impatience. The Festival of St. Clare presented him with a favourable opportunity of consummating his crime. He was certain that the Friars and Nuns would be engaged in the Procession, and that He had no cause to dread an interruption: From appearing himself at the head of his Monks, He had desired to be excused. He doubted not, that being beyond the reach of help, cut off from all the world, and totally in his power, Antonia would comply with his desires. The affection which She had ever exprest for him, warranted this persuasion: But He resolved that should She prove obstinate, no consideration whatever should prevent him from enjoying her. Secure from a discovery, He shuddered not at the idea of employing force: If He felt any repugnance, it arose not from a principle of shame or compassion, but from his feeling for

Antonia the most sincere and ardent affection, and wishing to owe her favours to no one but herself.

The Monks quitted the Abbey at midnight. Matilda was among the Choristers, and led the chaunt. Ambrosio was left by himself, and at liberty to pursue his own inclinations. Convinced that no one remained behind to watch his motions, or disturb his pleasures, He now hastened to the Western Aisles. His heart beating with hope not unmingled with anxiety, He crossed the Garden, unlocked the door which admitted him into the Cemetery, and in a few minutes He stood before the Vaults. Here He paused.

He looked round him with suspicion, conscious that his business was unfit for any other eye. As He stood in hesitation, He heard the melancholy shriek of the screech-Owl: The wind rattled loudly against the windows of the adjacent Convent, and as the current swept by him, bore with it the faint notes of the chaunt of Choristers. He opened the door cautiously, as if fearing to be overheard: He entered; and closed it again after him. Guided by his Lamp, He threaded the long passages, in whose windings Matilda had instructed him, and reached the private Vault which contained his sleeping Mistress.

Its entrance was by no means easy to discover: But this was no obstacle to Ambrosio, who at the time of Antonia's Funeral had observed it too carefully to be deceived. He found the door, which was unfastened, pushed it open, and descended into the dungeon. He approached the humble Tomb in which Antonia reposed. He had provided himself with an iron crow and a pick-axe; But this precaution was unnecessary. The Grate was slightly fastened on the outside: He raised it, and placing the Lamp upon its ridge, bent silently over the Tomb. By the side of three putrid half-corrupted Bodies lay the sleeping Beauty. A lively red, the forerunner of returning animation, had already spread itself over her cheek; and as wrapped in her shroud She reclined upon her funeral Bier, She seemed to smile at the Images of Death around her. While He gazed upon their rotting bones and disgusting figures, who perhaps were once as sweet and lovely, Ambrosio thought upon Elvira, by him reduced to the same state. As the memory of that horrid act glanced upon his mind, it was clouded with a gloomy horror. Yet it served but to strengthen his resolution to destroy Antonia's honour.

"For your sake, Fatal Beauty!" murmured the Monk, while gazing on his devoted prey; "For your sake, have I committed this murder, and sold myself to eternal tortures. Now you are in my power: The produce of my guilt will at least be mine. Hope not that your prayers breathed in tones of unequalled melody, your bright eyes filled with tears, and your hands lifted in supplication, as when seeking in penitence the Virgin's pardon; Hope not that your moving innocence, your beauteous grief, or all your suppliant arts shall ransom you from my embraces. Before the break of day, mine you must, and mine you shall be!"

He lifted her still motionless from the Tomb: He seated himself upon a bank of Stone, and supporting her in his arms, watched impatiently for the symptoms of returning animation. Scarcely could He command his passions sufficiently, to restrain himself from enjoying her while yet insensible. His natural lust was increased in ardour by the difficulties which had opposed his satisfying it: As also by his long abstinence from Woman, since from the moment of resigning her claim to his love, Matilda had exiled him from her arms for ever.

"I am no Prostitute, Ambrosio;" Had She told him, when in the fullness of his lust He demanded her favours with more than usual earnestness; "I am now no more than your Friend, and will not be your Mistress. Cease then to solicit my complying with desires, which insult me. While your heart was mine, I gloried in your embraces: Those happy times are past: My person is become indifferent to you, and 'tis necessity, not love, which makes you seek my enjoyment. I cannot yield to a request so humiliating to my pride."

Suddenly deprived of pleasures, the use of which had made them an absolute want, the Monk felt this restraint severely. Naturally addicted to the gratification of the senses, in the full vigour of manhood, and heat of blood, He had suffered his temperament to acquire such ascendency that his lust was become madness. Of his fondness for Antonia, none but the grosser particles remained: He longed for the possession of her person; and even the gloom of the vault, the surrounding silence, and the resistance which He expected from her, seemed to give a fresh edge to his fierce and unbridled desires.

Gradually He felt the bosom which rested against his, glow with returning warmth. Her heart throbbed again; Her blood flowed swifter, and her lips moved. At length She opened her eyes, but still opprest and bewildered by the effects of the strong opiate, She closed them again immediately. Ambrosio watched her narrowly, nor permitted a movement to escape him. Perceiving that She was fully restored to existence, He caught her in rapture to his bosom, and closely pressed his lips to hers. The suddenness of his action sufficed to dissipate the fumes which obscured Antonia's reason. She hastily raised herself, and cast a wild look round her. The strange Images which presented themselves on every side contributed to confuse her. She put her hand to her head, as if to settle her disordered imagination. At length She took it away, and threw her eyes through the dungeon a second time. They fixed upon the Abbot's face.

"Where am I?" She said abruptly. "How came I here? Where is my Mother? Methought, I saw her! Oh! a dream, a dreadful dreadful dream told me ...... But where am I? Let me go! I cannot stay here!"

She attempted to rise, but the Monk prevented her.

"Be calm, lovely Antonia!" He replied; "No danger is near you: Confide in my protection. Why do you gaze on me so earnestly? Do you not know me? Not know your Friend? Ambrosio?"

"Ambrosio? My Friend? Oh! yes, yes; I remember ...... But why am I here? Who has brought me? Why are you with me? Oh! Flora bad me beware .....! Here are nothing but Graves, and Tombs, and Skeletons! This place frightens me! Good Ambrosio take me away from it, for it recalls my fearful dream! Methought I was dead, and laid in my grave! Good Ambrosio, take me from hence. Will you not? Oh! will you not? Do not look on me thus!

Your flaming eyes terrify me! Spare me, Father! Oh! spare me for God's sake!"

"Why these terrors, Antonia?" rejoined the Abbot, folding her in his arms, and covering her bosom with kisses which She in vain struggled to avoid: "What fear you from me, from one who adores you? What matters it where you are? This Sepulchre seems to me Love's bower; This gloom is the friendly night of mystery which He spreads over our delights! Such do I think it, and such must my Antonia. Yes, my sweet Girl! Yes! Your veins shall glow with fire which circles in mine, and my transports shall be doubled by your sharing them!"

While He spoke thus, He repeated his embraces, and permitted himself the most indecent liberties. Even Antonia's ignorance was not proof against the freedom of his behaviour. She was sensible of her danger, forced herself from his arms, and her shroud being her only garment, She wrapped it closely round her.

"Unhand me, Father!" She cried, her honest indignation tempered by alarm at her unprotected position; "Why have you brought me to this place? Its appearance freezes me with horror! Convey me from hence, if you have the least sense of pity and humanity! Let me return to the House which I have quitted I know not how; But stay here one moment longer, I neither will, or ought."

Though the Monk was somewhat startled by the resolute tone in which this speech was delivered, it produced upon him no other effect than surprize. He caught her hand, forced her upon his knee, and gazing upon her with gloting eyes, He thus replied to her.

"Compose yourself, Antonia. Resistance is unavailing, and I need disavow my passion for you no longer. You are imagined dead: Society is for ever lost to you. I possess you here alone; You are absolutely in my power, and I burn with desires which I must either gratify or die: But I would owe my happiness to yourself. My lovely Girl! My adorable Antonia! Let me instruct you in joys to which you are still a Stranger, and teach you to feel those pleasures in my arms which I must soon enjoy in yours. Nay, this struggling is childish," He continued, seeing her repell his caresses, and endeavour to escape from his grasp; "No aid is near: Neither heaven or earth shall save you from my embraces. Yet why reject pleasures so sweet, so rapturous? No one observes us: Our loves will be a secret to all the world: Love and opportunity invite your giving loose to your passions. Yield to them, my Antonia! Yield to them, my lovely Girl! Throw your arms thus fondly round me; Join your lips thus closely to mine! Amidst all her gifts, has Nature denied her most precious, the sensibility of Pleasure? Oh! impossible! Every feature, look, and motion declares you formed to bless, and to be blessed yourself! Turn not on me those supplicating eyes: Consult your own charms; They will tell you that I am proof against entreaty. Can I relinquish these limbs so white, so soft, so delicate; These swelling breasts, round, full, and elastic! These lips fraught with such inexhaustible sweetness? Can I relinquish these treasures, and leave them to another's enjoyment? No, Antonia; never, never! I swear it by this kiss, and this! and this!"

With every moment the Friar's passion became more ardent, and Antonia's terror more intense. She struggled to disengage herself from his arms: Her exertions were unsuccessful; and finding that Ambrosio's conduct became still freer, She shrieked for assistance with all her strength. The aspect of the Vault, the pale glimmering of the Lamp, the surrounding obscurity, the sight of the Tomb, and the objects of mortality which met her eyes on either side, were ill-calculated to inspire her with those emotions by which the Friar was agitated. Even his caresses terrified her from their fury, and created no other sentiment than fear. On the contrary, her alarm, her evident disgust, and incessant opposition, seemed only to inflame the Monk's desires, and supply his brutality with additional strength. Antonia's shrieks were unheard: Yet She continued them, nor abandoned her endeavours to escape, till exhausted and out of breath She sank from his arms upon her knees, and once more had recourse to prayers and supplications. This attempt had no better success than the former. On the contrary, taking advantage of her situation, the Ravisher threw himself by her side: He clasped her to his bosom almost lifeless with terror, and faint with struggling. He stifled her cries with kisses, treated her with the rudeness of an unprincipled Barbarian, proceeded from freedom to freedom, and in the violence of his lustful delirium, wounded and bruised her tender limbs. Heedless of her tears, cries and entreaties, He gradually made himself Master of her person, and desisted not from his prey, till He had accomplished his crime and the dishonour of Antonia.

Scarcely had He succeeded in his design than He shuddered at himself and the means by which it was effected. The very excess of his former eagerness to possess Antonia now contributed to inspire him with disgust; and a secret impulse made him feel how base and unmanly was the crime which He had just committed. He started hastily from her arms. She, who so lately had been the object of his adoration, now raised no other sentiment in his heart than aversion and rage. He turned away from her; or if his eyes rested upon her figure involuntarily, it was only to dart upon her looks of hate. The Unfortunate had fainted ere the completion of her disgrace: She only recovered life to be sensible of her misfortune. She remained stretched upon the earth in silent despair: The tears chased each other slowly down her cheeks, and her bosom heaved with frequent sobs. Oppressed with grief, She continued for some time in this state of torpidity. At length She rose with difficulty, and dragging her feeble steps towards the door, prepared to quit the dungeon.

The sound of her footsteps rouzed the Monk from his sullen apathy. Starting from the Tomb against which He reclined, while his eyes wandered over the images of corruption contained in it, He pursued the Victim of his brutality, and soon overtook her. He seized her by the arm, and violently forced her back into the dungeon.

645

"Whither go you?" He cried in a stern voice; "Return this instant!"

Antonia trembled at the fury of his countenance.

"What, would you more?" She said with timidity: "Is not my ruin compleated? Am I not undone, undone for ever? Is not your cruelty contented, or have I yet more to suffer? Let me depart. Let me return to my home, and weep unrestrained my shame and my affliction!"

"Return to your home?" repeated the Monk, with bitter and contemptuous mockery; Then suddenly his eyes flaming with passion, "What? That you may denounce me to the world? That you may proclaim me an Hypocrite, a Ravisher, a Betrayer, a Monster of cruelty, lust, and ingratitude? No, no, no! I know well the whole weight of my offences; Well that your complaints would be too just, and my crimes too notorious! You shall not from hence to tell Madrid that I am a Villain; that my conscience is loaded with sins which make me despair of Heaven's pardon. Wretched Girl, you must stay here with me! Here amidst these lonely Tombs, these images of Death, these rotting loathsome corrupted bodies! Here shall you stay, and witness my sufferings; witness what it is to die in the horrors of despondency, and breathe the last groan in blasphemy and curses! And who am I to thank for this? What seduced me into crimes, whose bare remembrance makes me shudder? Fatal Witch! was it not thy beauty? Have you not plunged my soul into infamy? Have you not made me a perjured Hypocrite, a Ravisher, an Assassin! Nay, at this moment, does not that angel look bid me despair of God's forgiveness? Oh! when I stand before his judgment-throne, that look will suffice to damn me! You will tell my Judge that you were happy, till I saw you; that you were innocent, till I polluted you! You will come with those tearful eyes, those cheeks pale and ghastly, those hands lifted in supplication, as when you sought from me that mercy which I gave not! Then will my perdition be certain! Then will come your Mother's Ghost, and hurl me down into the dwellings of Fiends, and flames, and Furies, and everlasting torments! And 'tis you, who will accuse me! 'Tis you, who will cause my eternal anguish! You, wretched Girl! You! You!"

As He thundered out these words, He violently grasped Antonia's arm, and spurned the earth with delirious fury.

Supposing his brain to be turned, Antonia sank in terror upon her knees: She lifted up her hands, and her voice almost died away, ere She could give it utterance.

"Spare me! Spare me!" She murmured with difficulty.

"Silence!" cried the Friar madly, and dashed her upon the ground — —

He quitted her, and paced the dungeon with a wild and disordered air. His eyes rolled fearfully: Antonia trembled whenever She met their gaze. He seemed to meditate on something horrible, and She gave up all hopes of escaping from the Sepulchre with life. Yet in harbouring this idea, She did him injustice. Amidst the horror and disgust to which his soul was a prey, pity for his Victim still held a place in it. The storm of passion once over, He would have given worlds had He possest them, to have restored to her that innocence of which his unbridled lust had deprived her. Of the desires which had urged him to the crime, no trace was left in his bosom: The wealth of India would not have tempted him to a second enjoyment of her person. His nature seemed to revolt at the very idea, and fain would He have wiped from his memory the scene which had just past. As his gloomy rage abated, in proportion did his compassion augment for Antonia. He stopped, and would have spoken to her words of comfort; But He knew not from whence to draw them, and remained gazing upon her with mournful wildness. Her situation seemed so hopeless, so woebegone, as to baffle mortal power to relieve her. What could He do for her? Her peace of mind was lost, her honour irreparably ruined. She was cut off for ever from society, nor dared He give her back to it. He was conscious that were She to appear in the world again, his guilt would be revealed, and his punishment inevitable. To one so laden with crimes, Death came armed with double terrors. Yet should He restore Antonia to light, and stand the chance of her betraying him, how miserable a prospect would present itself before her. She could never hope to be creditably established; She would be marked with infamy, and condemned to sorrow and solitude for the remainder of her existence. What was the alternative? A resolution far more terrible for Antonia, but which at least would insure the Abbot's safety. He determined to leave the world persuaded of her death, and to retain her a captive in this gloomy prison: There He proposed to visit her every night, to bring her food, to profess his penitence, and mingle his tears with hers. The Monk felt that this resolution was unjust and cruel; but it was his only means to prevent Antonia from publishing his guilt and her own infamy. Should He release her, He could not depend upon her silence: His offence was too flagrant to permit his hoping for her forgiveness. Besides, her reappearing would excite universal curiosity, and the violence of her affliction would prevent her from concealing its cause. He determined therefore, that Antonia should remain a Prisoner in the dungeon.

He approached her with confusion painted on his countenance. He raised her from the ground. Her hand trembled, as He took it, and He dropped it again as if He had touched a Serpent. Nature seemed to recoil at the touch. He felt himself at once repulsed from and attracted towards her, yet could account for neither sentiment. There was something in her look which penetrated him with horror; and though his understanding was still ignorant of it, Conscience pointed out to him the whole extent of his crime. In hurried accents yet the gentlest He could find, while his eye was averted, and his voice scarcely audible, He strove to console her under a misfortune which now could not be avoided. He declared himself sincerely penitent, and that He would gladly shed a drop of his blood, for every tear which his barbarity had forced from her. Wretched and hopeless, Antonia listened to him in silent grief: But when He announced her confinement in the Sepulchre, that dreadful doom to which even death seemed preferable roused her from her insensibility at once. To linger out a life of misery in a narrow loathsome Cell, known to exist by no human Being save her Ravisher, surrounded by mouldering Corses, breathing the pestilential air of corruption, never more to behold the light, or drink the pure gale of heaven, the idea was more terrible than She could support. It conquered even her abhorrence of the Friar. Again She sank upon her knees: She besought his compassion in terms the most pathetic and urgent. She promised, would He but restore her to liberty, to conceal her injuries from the world; to assign any reason for her reappearance which He might judge proper; and in order to prevent the least suspicion from falling upon him, She offered to quit Madrid immediately. Her entreaties were so urgent as to make a considerable impression upon the Monk. He reflected that as her person no longer excited his desires, He had no interest in keeping her concealed as He had at first intended; that He was adding a fresh injury to those which She had already suffered; and that if She adhered to her promises, whether She was confined or at liberty, his life and reputation were equally secure. On the other hand, He trembled lest in her affliction Antonia should unintentionally break her engagement; or that her excessive simplicity and ignorance of deceit should permit some one more artful to surprize her secret. However well-founded were these apprehensions, compassion, and a sincere wish to repair his fault as much as possible solicited his complying with the prayers of his Suppliant. The difficulty of colouring Antonia's unexpected return to life, after her supposed death and public interment, was the only point which kept him irresolute. He was still pondering on the means of removing this obstacle, when He heard the sound of feet approaching with precipitation. The door of the Vault was thrown open, and Matilda rushed in, evidently much confused and terrified.

On seeing a Stranger enter, Antonia uttered a cry of joy: But her hopes of receiving succour from him were soon dissipated. The supposed Novice, without expressing the least surprize at finding a Woman alone with the Monk, in so strange a place, and at so late an hour, addressed him thus without losing a moment.

"What is to be done, Ambrosio? We are lost, unless some speedy means is found of dispelling the Rioters. Ambrosio, the Convent of St. Clare is on fire; The Prioress has fallen a victim to the fury of the Mob. Already is the Abbey menaced with a similar fate. Alarmed at the threats of the People, the Monks seek for you everywhere. They imagine that your authority alone will suffice to calm this disturbance. No one knows what is become of you, and your absence creates universal astonishment and despair. I profited by the confusion, and fled hither to warn you of the danger."

"This will soon be remedied," answered the Abbot; "I will hasten back to my Cell: a trivial reason will account for my having been missed."

"Impossible!" rejoined Matilda: "The Sepulchre is filled with Archers. Lorenzo de Medina, with several Officers of the Inquisition, searches through the Vaults, and pervades every passage. You will be intercepted in your flight; Your reasons for being at this late hour in the Sepulchre will be examined; Antonia will be found, and then you are undone for ever!"

"Lorenzo de Medina? Officers of the Inquisition? What brings them here? Seek they for me? Am I then suspected? Oh! speak, Matilda! Answer me, in pity!"

"As yet they do not think of you, but I fear that they will ere long. Your only chance of escaping their notice rests upon the difficulty of exploring this Vault. The door is artfully hidden:

Haply it may not be observed, and we may remain concealed till the search is over."

"But Antonia ..... Should the Inquisitors draw near, and her cries be heard ...."

649

"Thus I remove that danger!" interrupted Matilda.

At the same time drawing a poignard, She rushed upon her devoted prey.

"Hold! Hold!" cried Ambrosio, seizing her hand, and wresting from it the already lifted weapon. "What would you do, cruel Woman? The Unfortunate has already suffered but too much, thanks to your pernicious consels! Would to God that I had never followed them! Would to God that I had never seen your face!"

Matilda darted upon him a look of scorn.

"Absurd!" She exclaimed with an air of passion and majesty which impressed the Monk with awe. "After robbing her of all that made it dear, can you fear to deprive her of a life so miserable? But 'tis well! Let her live to convince you of your folly. I abandon you to your evil destiny! I disclaim your alliance! Who trembles to commit so insignificant a crime, deserves not my protection. Hark! Hark! Ambrosio; Hear you not the Archers? They come, and your destruction is inevitable!"

At this moment the Abbot heard the sound of distant voices. He flew to close the door on whose concealment his safety depended, and which Matilda had neglected to fasten. Ere He could reach it, He saw Antonia glide suddenly by him, rush through the door, and fly towards the noise with the swiftness of an arrow. She had listened attentively to Matilda: She heard Lorenzo's name mentioned, and resolved to risque every thing to throw herself under his protection. The door was open. The sounds convinced her that the Archers could be at no great distance. She mustered up her little remaining strength, rushed by the Monk ere He perceived her design, and bent her course rapidly towards the voices. As soon as He recovered from his first surprize, the Abbot failed not to pursue her. In vain did Antonia redouble her speed, and stretch every nerve to the utmost. Her Enemy gained upon her every moment: She heard his steps close after her, and felt the heat of his breath glow upon her neck. He overtook her; He twisted his hand in the ringlets of her streaming hair, and attempted to drag her back with him to the dungeon. Antonia resisted with all her strength: She folded her arms round a Pillar which supported the roof, and shrieked loudly for assistance. In vain did the Monk strive to threaten her to silence.

"Help!" She continued to exclaim; "Help! Help! for God's sake!"

Quickened by her cries, the sound of footsteps was heard approaching. The Abbot expected every moment to see the Inquisitors arrive. Antonia still resisted, and He now enforced her silence by means the most horrible and inhuman. He still grasped Matilda's dagger: Without allowing himself a moment's reflection, He raised it, and plunged it twice in the bosom of Antonia! She shrieked, and sank upon the ground. The Monk endeavoured to bear her away with him, but She still embraced the Pillar firmly. At that instant the light of approaching Torches flashed upon the Walls. Dreading a discovery, Ambrosio was compelled to abandon his Victim, and hastily fled back to the Vault, where He had left Matilda.

He fled not unobserved. Don Ramirez happening to arrive the first, perceived a Female bleeding upon the ground, and a Man flying from the spot, whose confusion betrayed him for the Murderer. He instantly pursued the Fugitive with some part of the Archers, while the Others remained with Lorenzo to protect the wounded Stranger. They raised her, and supported her in their arms. She had fainted from excess of pain, but soon gave signs of returning life. She opened her eyes, and on lifting up her head, the quantity of fair hair fell back which till then had obscured her features.

"God Almighty! It is Antonia!"

Such was Lorenzo's exclamation, while He snatched her from the Attendant's arms, and clasped her in his own.

Though aimed by an uncertain hand, the poignard had answered but too well the purpose of its Employer. The wounds were mortal, and Antonia was conscious that She never could recover. Yet the few moments which remained for her were moments of happiness. The concern exprest upon Lorenzo's countenance, the frantic fondness of his complaints, and his earnest enquiries respecting her wounds, convinced her beyond a doubt that his affections were her own. She would not be removed from the Vaults, fearing lest motion should only hasten her death; and She was unwilling to lose those moments which She past in receiving proofs of Lorenzo's love, and assuring him of her own. She told him that had She still been undefiled She might have lamented the loss of life; But that deprived of honour and branded with shame, Death was to her a blessing: She could not have been his Wife, and that hope being denied her, She resigned herself to the Grave without one sigh of regret. She bad him take courage, conjured him not to abandon himself to fruitless sorrow, and declared that She mourned to leave nothing in the whole world but him. While every sweet accent increased rather than lightened Lorenzo's grief, She continued to converse with him till the moment of dissolution. Her voice grew faint and scarcely audible; A thick cloud spread itself over her eyes; Her heart beat slow and irregular, and every instant seemed to announce that her fate was near at hand.

She lay, her head reclining upon Lorenzo's bosom, and her lips still murmuring to him words of comfort. She was interrupted by the Convent Bell, as tolling at a distance, it struck the hour. Suddenly Antonia's eyes sparkled with celestial brightness: Her frame seemed to have received new strength and animation. She started from her Lover's arms.

"Three o'clock!" She cried; "Mother, I come!"

She clasped her hands, and sank lifeless upon the ground. Lorenzo in agony threw himself beside her: He tore his hair, beat his breast, and refused to be separated from the Corse. At length his force being exhausted, He suffered himself to be led from the Vault, and was conveyed to the Palace de Medina scarcely more alive than the unfortunate Antonia.

In the meanwhile, though closely pursued, Ambrosio succeeded in regaining the Vault. The Door was already fastened when Don Ramirez arrived, and much time elapsed, ere the Fugitive's retreat was discovered. But nothing can resist perseverance. Though so artfully concealed, the Door could not escape the vigilance of the Archers. They forced it open, and entered the Vault to the infinite dismay of Ambrosio and his Companion. The Monk's confusion, his attempt to hide himself, his rapid flight, and the blood sprinkled upon his cloaths, left no room to doubt his being Antonia's Murderer. But when He was recognized for the immaculate Ambrosio, "The Man of Holiness," the Idol of Madrid, the faculties of the Spectators were chained up in surprize, and scarcely could they persuade themselves that what they saw was no vision. The Abbot strove not to vindicate himself, but preserved a sullen silence. He was secured and bound. The same precaution was taken with Matilda: Her Cowl being removed, the delicacy of her features and profusion of her golden hair betrayed her sex, and this incident created fresh amazement. The dagger was also found in the Tomb, where the Monk had thrown it; and the dungeon having undergone a thorough search, the two Culprits were conveyed to the prisons of the Inquisition.

Don Ramirez took care that the populace should remain ignorant both of the crimes and profession of the Captives. He feared a repetition of the riots which had followed the apprehending the Prioress of St. Clare. He contented himself with stating to the Capuchins the guilt of their Superior. To avoid the shame of a public accusation, and dreading the popular fury from which they had already saved their Abbey with much difficulty, the Monks readily permitted the Inquisitors to search their Mansion without noise. No fresh discoveries were made. The effects found in the Abbot's and Matilda's Cells were seized, and carried to the Inquisition to be produced in evidence. Every thing else remained in its former position, and order and tranquillity once more prevailed through Madrid.

St. Clare's Convent was completely ruined by the united ravages of the Mob and conflagration. Nothing remained of it but the principal Walls, whose thickness and solidity had preserved them from the flames. The Nuns who had belonged to it were obliged in consequence to disperse themselves into other Societies: But the prejudice against them ran high, and the Superiors were very unwilling to admit them. However, most of them being related to Families the most distinguished for their riches, birth and power, the several Convents were compelled to receive them, though they did it with a very ill grace. This prejudice was extremely false and unjustifiable: After a close investigation, it was proved that All in the Convent were persuaded of the death of Agnes, except the four Nuns whom St. Ursula had pointed out. These had fallen Victims to the popular fury; as had also several who were perfectly innocent and unconscious of the whole affair. Blinded by resentment, the Mob had sacrificed every Nun who fell into their hands: They who escaped were entirely indebted to the Duke de Medina's prudence and moderation. Of this they were conscious, and felt for that Nobleman a proper sense of gratitude.

Virginia was not the most sparing of her thanks: She wished equally to make a proper return for his attentions, and to obtain the good graces of Lorenzo's Uncle. In this She easily succeeded.

The Duke beheld her beauty with wonder and admiration; and while his eyes were enchanted with her Form, the sweetness of her manners and her tender concern for the suffering Nun prepossessed his heart in her favour. This Virginia had discernment enough to perceive, and She redoubled her attention to the Invalid. When He parted from her at the door of her Father's Palace, the Duke entreated permission to enquire occasionally after her health. His request was readily granted: Virginia assured him that the Marquis de Villa-Franca would be proud of an opportunity to thank him in person for the protection afforded to her. They now separated, He enchanted with her beauty and gentleness, and She much pleased with him and more with his Nephew.

On entering the Palace, Virginia's first care was to summon the family Physician, and take care of her unknown charge. Her Mother hastened to share with her the charitable office. Alarmed by the riots, and trembling for his Daughter's safety, who was his only child, the Marquis had flown to St. Clare's Convent, and was still employed in seeking her. Messengers were now dispatched on all sides to inform him that He would find her safe at his Hotel, and desire him to hasten thither immediately. His absence gave Virginia liberty to bestow her whole attention upon her Patient; and though much disordered herself by the adventures of the night, no persuasion could induce her to quit the bedside of the Sufferer. Her constitution being much enfeebled by want and sorrow, it was some time before the Stranger was restored to her senses. She found great difficulty in swallowing the medicines prescribed to her: But this obstacle being removed, She easily conquered her disease which proceeded from nothing but weakness. The attention which was paid her, the wholesome food to which She had been long a Stranger, and her joy at being restored to liberty, to society, and, as She dared to hope, to Love, all this combined to her speedy re-establishment.

From the first moment of knowing her, her melancholy situation, her sufferings almost unparalleled had engaged the affections of her amiable Hostess: Virginia felt for her the most lively interest; But how was She delighted, when her Guest being sufficiently recovered to relate her History, She recognized in the captive Nun the Sister of Lorenzo!

This victim of monastic cruelty was indeed no other than the unfortunate Agnes. During her abode in the Convent, She had been well known to Virginia: But her emaciated form, her features altered by affliction, her death universally credited, and her overgrown and matted hair which hung over her face and bosom in disorder at first had prevented her being recollected. The Prioress had put every artifice in practice to induce Virginia to take the veil; for the Heiress of Villa-Franca would have been no despicable acquisition. Her seeming kindness and unremitted attention so far succeeded that her young Relation began to think seriously upon compliance. Better instructed in the disgust and ennui of a monastic life, Agnes had penetrated the designs of the Domina: She trembled for the innocent Girl,

and endeavoured to make her sensible of her error. She painted
in their true colours the numerous inconveniencies attached to a
Convent, the continued restraint, the low jealousies, the petty
intrigues, the servile court and gross flattery expected by the
Superior. She then bad Virginia reflect on the brilliant prospect
which presented itself before her: The Idol of her Parents, the
admiration of Madrid, endowed by nature and education with
every perfection of person and mind, She might look forward to
an establishment the most fortunate. Her riches furnished her
with the means of exercising in their fullest extent, charity and
benevolence, those virtues so dear to her; and her stay in the
world would enable her discovering Objects worthy her
protection, which could not be done in the seclusion of a
Convent.

Her persuasions induced Virginia to lay aside all thoughts of
the Veil: But another argument, not used by Agnes, had more
weight with her than all the others put together. She had seen
Lorenzo, when He visited his Sister at the Grate. His Person
pleased her, and her conversations with Agnes generally used
to terminate in some question about her Brother. She, who
doted upon Lorenzo, wished for no better than an opportunity
to trumpet out his praise. She spoke of him in terms of rapture;
and to convince her Auditor how just were his sentiments, how
cultivated his mind, and elegant his expressions, She showed
her at different times the letters which She received from him.
She soon perceived that from these communications the heart of
her young Friend had imbibed impressions, which She was far
from intending to give, but was truly happy to discover. She
could not have wished her Brother a more desirable union:
Heiress of Villa-Franca, virtuous, affectionate, beautiful, and
accomplished, Virginia seemed calculated to make him happy.
She sounded her Brother upon the subject, though without
mentioning names or circumstances. He assured her in his
answers that his heart and hand were totally disengaged, and
She thought that upon these grounds She might proceed
without danger. She in consequence endeavoured to strengthen
the dawning passion of her Friend. Lorenzo was made the
constant topic of her discourse; and the avidity with which her
Auditor listened, the sighs which frequently escaped from her
bosom, and the eagerness with which upon any digression She
brought back the conversation to the subject whence it had
wandered, sufficed to convince Agnes that her Brother's
addresses would be far from disagreeable. She at length
ventured to mention her wishes to the Duke: Though a Stranger
to the Lady herself, He knew enough of her situation to think
her worthy his Nephew's hand. It was agreed between him and
his Niece, that She should insinuate the idea to Lorenzo, and

She only waited his return to Madrid to propose her Friend to him as his Bride. The unfortunate events which took place in the interim, prevented her from executing her design. Virginia wept her loss sincerely, both as a Companion, and as the only Person to whom She could speak of Lorenzo. Her passion continued to prey upon her heart in secret, and She had almost determined to confess her sentiments to her Mother, when accident once more threw their object in her way. The sight of him so near her, his politeness, his compassion, his intrepidity, had combined to give new ardour to her affection. When She now found her Friend and Advocate restored to her, She looked upon her as a Gift from Heaven; She ventured to cherish the hope of being united to Lorenzo, and resolved to use with him his Sister's influence.

Supposing that before her death Agnes might possibly have made the proposal, the Duke had placed all his Nephew's hints of marriage to Virginia's account: Consequently, He gave them the most favourable reception. On returning to his Hotel, the relation given him of Antonia's death, and Lorenzo's behaviour on the occasion, made evident his mistake. He lamented the circumstances; But the unhappy Girl being effectually out of the way, He trusted that his designs would yet be executed. 'Tis true that Lorenzo's situation just then ill-suited him for a Bridegroom. His hopes disappointed at the moment when He expected to realize them, and the dreadful and sudden death of his Mistress had affected him very severely. The Duke found him upon the Bed of sickness. His Attendants expressed serious apprehensions for his life; But the Uncle entertained not the same fears. He was of opinion, and not unwisely, that "Men have died, and worms have eat them; but not for Love!" He therefore flattered himself that however deep might be the impression made upon his Nephew's heart, Time and Virginia would be able to efface it. He now hastened to the afflicted Youth, and endeavoured to console him: He sympathised in his distress, but encouraged him to resist the encroachments of despair. He allowed that He could not but feel shocked at an event so terrible, nor could He blame his sensibility; But He besought him not to torment himself with vain regrets, and rather to struggle with affliction, and preserve his life, if not for his own sake, at least for the sake of those who were fondly attached to him. While He laboured thus to make Lorenzo forget Antonia's loss, the Duke paid his court assiduously to Virginia, and seized every opportunity to advance his Nephew's interest in her heart.

It may easily be expected that Agnes was not long without enquiring after Don Raymond. She was shocked to hear the wretched situation to which grief had reduced him; Yet She could not help exulting secretly, when She reflected, that his illness proved the sincerity of his love. The Duke undertook the office himself, of announcing to the Invalid the happiness which awaited him. Though He omitted no precaution to prepare him for such an event, at this sudden change from despair to happiness Raymond's transports were so violent, as nearly to have proved fatal to him. These once passed, the tranquillity of his mind, the assurance of felicity, and above all the presence of Agnes, (Who was no sooner reestablished by the care of Virginia and the Marchioness, than She hastened to attend her Lover) soon enabled him to overcome the effects of his late dreadful malady. The calm of his soul communicated itself to his body, and He recovered with such rapidity as to create universal surprize.

No so Lorenzo. Antonia's death accompanied with such terrible circumstances weighed upon his mind heavily. He was worn down to a shadow. Nothing could give him pleasure. He was persuaded with difficulty to swallow nourishment sufficient for the support of life, and a consumption was apprehended. The society of Agnes formed his only comfort. Though accident had never permitted their being much together, He entertained for her a sincere friendship and attachment. Perceiving how necessary She was to him, She seldom quitted his chamber. She listened to his complaints with unwearied attention, and soothed him by the gentleness of her manners, and by sympathising with his distress. She still inhabited the Palace de Villa-Franca, the Possessors of which treated her with marked affection. The Duke had intimated to the Marquis his wishes respecting Virginia. The match was unexceptionable: Lorenzo was Heir to his Uncle's immense property, and was distinguished in Madrid for his agreeable person, extensive knowledge, and propriety of conduct: Add to this, that the Marchioness had discovered how strong was her Daughter's prepossession in his favour.

In consequence the Duke's proposal was accepted without hesitation: Every precaution was taken to induce Lorenzo's seeing the Lady with those sentiments which She so well merited to excite. In her visits to her Brother Agnes was frequently accompanied by the Marchioness; and as soon as He was able to move into his Antichamber, Virginia under her mother's protection was sometimes permitted to express her wishes for his recovery. This She did with such delicacy, the manner in which She mentioned Antonia was so tender and soothing, and when She lamented her Rival's melancholy fate, her bright eyes shone so beautiful through her tears, that Lorenzo could not behold, or listen to her without emotion. His Relations, as well as the Lady, perceived that with every day her society seemed to give him fresh pleasure, and that He spoke of her in terms of stronger admiration. However, they prudently kept their observations to themselves. No word was dropped which might lead him to suspect their designs. They continued their former conduct and attention, and left Time to ripen into a warmer sentiment the friendship which He already felt for Virginia.

In the mean while, her visits became more frequent; and latterly there was scarce a day, of which She did not pass some part by the side of Lorenzo's Couch. He gradually regained his strength, but the progress of his recovery was slow and doubtful. One evening He seemed to be in better spirits than usual: Agnes and her Lover, the Duke, Virginia, and her Parents were sitting round him. He now for the first time entreated his Sister to inform him how She had escaped the effects of the poison which St. Ursula had seen her swallow. Fearful of recalling those scenes to his mind in which Antonia had perished, She had hitherto concealed from him the history of her sufferings. As He now started the subject himself, and thinking that perhaps the narrative of her sorrows might draw him from the contemplation of those on which He dwelt too constantly, She immediately complied with his request. The rest of the company had already heard her story; But the interest which all present felt for its Heroine made them anxious to hear it repeated. The whole society seconding Lorenzo's entreaties, Agnes obeyed. She first recounted the discovery which had taken place in the Abbey Chapel, the Domina's resentment, and the midnight scene of which St. Ursula had been a concealed witness. Though the Nun had already described this latter event, Agnes now related it more circumstantially and at large: After which She proceeded in her narrative as follows.

Conclusion of the History of Agnes de Medina

My supposed death was attended with the greatest agonies. Those moments which I believed my last, were embittered by the Domina's assurances that I could not escape perdition; and as my eyes closed, I heard her rage exhale itself in curses on my offence. The horror of this situation, of a death-bed from which hope was banished, of a sleep from which I was only to wake to find myself the prey of flames and Furies, was more dreadful than I can describe. When animation revived in me, my soul was still impressed with these terrible ideas: I looked round with fear, expecting to behold the Ministers of divine vengeance. For the first hour, my senses were so bewildered, and my brain so dizzy, that I strove in vain to arrange the strange images which floated in wild confusion before me. If I endeavoured to raise myself from the ground, the wandering of my head deceived me. Every thing around me seemed to rock, and I sank once more upon the earth. My weak and dazzled eyes were unable to bear a nearer approach to a gleam of light which I saw trembling above me. I was compelled to close them again, and remain motionless in the same posture.

A full hour elapsed, before I was sufficiently myself to examine the surrounding Objects. When I did examine them, what terror filled my bosom I found myself extended upon a sort of wicker Couch: It had six handles to it, which doubtless had served the Nuns to convey me to my grave. I was covered with a linen cloth:

Several faded flowers were strown over me: On one side lay a small wooden Crucifix; On the other, a Rosary of large Beads. Four low narrow walls confined me. The top was also covered, and in it was practised a small grated Door: Through this was admitted the little air which circulated in this miserable place. A faint glimmering of light which streamed through the Bars, permitted me to distinguish the surrounding horrors. I was opprest by a noisome suffocating smell; and perceiving that the grated door was unfastened, I thought that I might possibly effect my escape. As I raised myself with this design, my hand rested upon something soft: I grasped it, and advanced it towards the light. Almighty God! What was my disgust, my consternation! In spite of its putridity, and the worms which preyed upon it, I perceived a corrupted human head, and recognised the features of a Nun who had died some months before!

I threw it from me, and sank almost lifeless upon my Bier.

When my strength returned, this circumstance, and the consciousness of being surrounded by the loathsome and mouldering Bodies of my Companions, increased my desire to escape from my fearful prison. I again moved towards the light. The grated door was within my reach: I lifted it without difficulty; Probably it had been left unclosed to facilitate my quitting the dungeon. Aiding myself by the irregularity of the Walls some of whose stones projected beyond the rest, I contrived to ascend them, and drag myself out of my prison. I now found Myself in a Vault tolerably spacious. Several Tombs, similar in appearance to that whence I had just escaped, were ranged along the sides in order, and seemed to be considerably sunk within the earth. A sepulchral Lamp was suspended from the roof by an iron chain, and shed a gloomy light through the dungeon. Emblems of Death were seen on every side: Skulls, shoulder-blades, thigh-bones, and other leavings of Mortality were scattered upon the dewy ground. Each Tomb was ornamented with a large Crucifix, and in one corner stood a wooden Statue of St. Clare. To these objects I at first paid no attention: A Door, the only outlet from the Vault, had attracted my eyes. I hastened towards it, having wrapped my winding-sheet closely round me. I pushed against the door, and to my inexpressible terror found that it was fastened on the outside.

I guessed immediately that the Prioress, mistaking the nature of the liquor which She had compelled me to drink, instead of poison had administered a strong Opiate. From this I concluded that being to all appearance dead I had received the rites of burial; and that deprived of the power of making my existence known, it would be my fate to expire of hunger. This idea penetrated me with horror, not merely for my own sake, but that of the innocent Creature, who still lived within my bosom. I again endeavoured to open the door, but it resisted all my efforts. I stretched my voice to the extent of its compass, and shrieked for aid: I was remote from the hearing of every one: No friendly voice replied to mine. A profound and melancholy silence prevailed through the Vault, and I despaired of liberty. My long abstinence from food now began to torment me. The tortures which hunger inflicted on me, were the most painful and insupportable: Yet they seemed to increase with every hour which past over my head. Sometimes I threw myself upon the ground, and rolled upon it wild and desperate: Sometimes starting up, I returned to the door, again strove to force it open, and repeated my fruitless cries for succour. Often was I on the point of striking my temple against the sharp corner of some Monument, dashing out my brains, and thus terminating my woes at once; But still the remembrance of my Baby vanquished my resolution: I trembled at a deed which equally endangered my Child's existence and my own. Then would I vent my anguish in loud exclamations and passionate complaints; and then again my strength failing me, silent and hopeless I would sit me down upon the base of St. Clare's Statue, fold my arms, and abandon myself to sullen despair. Thus passed several wretched hours. Death advanced towards me with rapid strides, and I expected that every succeeding moment would be that of my dissolution. Suddenly a neighbouring Tomb caught my eye: A Basket stood upon it, which till then I had not observed. I started from my seat: I made towards it as swiftly as my exhausted frame would permit. How eagerly did I seize the

Basket, on finding it to contain a loaf of coarse bread and a small bottle of water.

I threw myself with avidity upon these humble aliments. They had to all appearance been placed in the Vault for several days; The bread was hard, and the water tainted; Yet never did I taste food to me so delicious. When the cravings of appetite were satisfied, I busied myself with conjectures upon this new circumstance: I debated whether the Basket had been placed there with a view to my necessity. Hope answered my doubts in the affirmative. Yet who could guess me to be in need of such assistance? If my existence was known, why was I detained in this gloomy Vault? If I was kept a Prisoner, what meant the ceremony of committing me to the Tomb? Or if I was doomed to perish with hunger, to whose pity was I indebted for provisions placed within my reach? A Friend would not have kept my dreadful punishment a secret; Neither did it seem probable that an Enemy would have taken pains to supply me with the means of existence. Upon the whole I was inclined to think that the Domina's designs upon my life had been discovered by some one of my Partizans in the Convent, who had found means to substitute an opiate for poison: That She had furnished me with food to support me, till She could effect my delivery: And that She was then employed in giving intelligence to my Relations of my danger, and pointing out a way to release me from captivity. Yet why then was the quality of my provisions so coarse? How could my Friend have entered the Vault without the Domina's knowledge? And if She had entered, why was the Door fastened so carefully? These reflections staggered me: Yet still this idea was the most favourable to my hopes, and I dwelt upon it in preference.

My meditations were interrupted by the sound of distant footsteps. They approached, but slowly. Rays of light now darted through the crevices of the Door. Uncertain whether the Persons who advanced came to relieve me, or were conducted by some other motive to the Vault, I failed not to attract their notice by loud cries for help. Still the sounds drew near: The light grew stronger: At length with inexpressible pleasure I heard the Key turning in the Lock. Persuaded that my deliverance was at hand, I flew towards the Door with a shriek of joy. It opened: But all my hopes of escape died away, when the Prioress appeared followed by the same four Nuns, who had been witnesses of my supposed death. They bore torches in their hands, and gazed upon me in fearful silence.

I started back in terror. The Domina descended into the Vault, as did also her Companions. She bent upon me a stern resentful eye, but expressed no surprize at finding me still living. She took the seat which I had just quitted: The door was again closed, and the Nuns ranged themselves behind their Superior, while the glare of their torches, dimmed by the vapours and dampness of the Vault, gilded with cold beams the surrounding Monuments. For some moments all preserved a dead and solemn silence. I stood at some distance from the Prioress. At length She beckoned me to advance. Trembling at the severity of her aspect my strength scarce sufficed me to obey her. I drew near, but my limbs were unable to support their burthen. I sank upon my knees; I clasped my hands, and lifted them up to her for mercy, but had no power to articulate a syllable.

She gazed upon me with angry eyes.

"Do I see a Penitent, or a Criminal?" She said at length; "Are those hands raised in contrition for your crimes, or in fear of meeting their punishment? Do those tears acknowledge the justice of your doom, or only solicit mitigation of your sufferings? I fear me, 'tis the latter!"

She paused, but kept her eye still fixt upon mine.

"Take courage;" She continued: "I wish not for your death, but your repentance. The draught which I administered, was no poison, but an opiate. My intention in deceiving you was to make you feel the agonies of a guilty conscience, had Death overtaken you suddenly while your crimes were still unrepented. You have suffered those agonies: I have brought you to be familiar with the sharpness of death, and I trust that your momentary anguish will prove to you an eternal benefit. It is not my design to destroy your immortal soul; or bid you seek the grave, burthened with the weight of sins unexpiated. No, Daughter, far from it: I will purify you with wholesome chastisement, and furnish you with full leisure for contrition and remorse. Hear then my sentence; The ill-judged zeal of your Friends delayed its execution, but cannot now prevent it. All Madrid believes you to be no more; Your Relations are thoroughly persuaded of your death, and the Nuns your Partizans have assisted at your funeral. Your existence can never be suspected; I have taken such precautions, as must render it an impenetrable mystery. Then abandon all thoughts of a World from which you are eternally separated, and employ the few hours which are allowed you, in preparing for the next."

This exordium led me to expect something terrible. I trembled, and would have spoken to deprecate her wrath: but a motion of the Domina commanded me to be silent. She proceeded.

"Though of late years unjustly neglected, and now opposed by many of our misguided Sisters, (whom Heaven convert!) it is my intention to revive the laws of our order in their full force. That against incontinence is severe, but no more than so monstrous an offence demands: Submit to it, Daughter, without resistance; You will find the benefit of patience and resignation in a better life than this. Listen then to the sentence of St. Clare. Beneath these Vaults there exist Prisons, intended to receive such criminals as yourself: Artfully is their entrance concealed, and She who enters them, must resign all hopes of liberty. Thither must you now be conveyed. Food shall be supplied you, but not sufficient for the indulgence of appetite: You shall have just enough to keep together body and soul, and its quality shall be the simplest and coarsest. Weep, Daughter, weep, and moisten your bread with your tears: God knows that you have ample cause for sorrow! Chained down in one of these secret dungeons, shut out from the world and light for ever, with no comfort but religion, no society but repentance, thus must you groan away the remainder of your days. Such are St. Clare's orders; Submit to them without repining. Follow me!"

Thunderstruck at this barbarous decree, my little remaining strength abandoned me. I answered only by falling at her feet, and bathing them with tears. The Domina, unmoved by my affliction, rose from her seat with a stately air. She repeated her commands in an absolute tone: But my excessive faintness made me unable to obey her. Mariana and Alix raised me from the ground, and carried me forwards in their arms. The Prioress moved on, leaning upon Violante, and Camilla preceded her with a Torch. Thus passed our sad procession along the passages, in silence only broken by my sighs and groans. We stopped before the principal shrine of St. Clare. The Statue was removed from its Pedestal, though how I knew not. The Nuns afterwards raised an iron grate till then concealed by the Image, and let it fall on the other side with a loud crash. The awful sound, repeated by the vaults above, and Caverns below me, rouzed me from the despondent apathy in which I had been plunged. I looked before me: An abyss presented itself to my affrighted eyes, and a steep and narrow Staircase, whither my Conductors were leading me. I shrieked, and started back. I implored compassion, rent the air with my cries, and summoned both heaven and earth to my assistance. In vain! I was hurried down the Staircase, and forced into one of the Cells which lined the Cavern's sides.

My blood ran cold, as I gazed upon this melancholy abode. The cold vapours hovering in the air, the walls green with damp, the bed of Straw so forlorn and comfortless, the Chain destined to bind me for ever to my prison, and the Reptiles of every description which as the torches advanced towards them, I descried hurrying to their retreats, struck my heart with terrors almost too exquisite for nature to bear. Driven by despair to madness, I burst suddenly from the Nuns who held me: I threw myself upon my knees before the Prioress, and besought her mercy in the most passionate and frantic terms.

"If not on me," said I, "look at least with pity on that innocent Being, whose life is attached to mine! Great is my crime, but let not my Child suffer for it! My Baby has committed no fault: Oh! spare me for the sake of my unborn Offspring, whom ere it tastes life your severity dooms to destruction!"

The Prioress drew back haughtily: She forced her habit from my grasp, as if my touch had been contagious.

"What?" She exclaimed with an exasperated air; "What? Dare you plead for the produce of your shame? Shall a Creature be permitted to live, conceived in guilt so monstrous? Abandoned Woman, speak for him no more! Better that the Wretch should perish than live: Begotten in perjury, incontinence, and pollution, It cannot fail to prove a Prodigy of vice. Hear me, thou Guilty! Expect no mercy from me either for yourself, or Brat. Rather pray that Death may seize you before you produce it; Or if it must see the light, that its eyes may immediately be closed again for ever! No aid shall be given you in your labour; Bring your Offspring into the world yourself, Feed it yourself, Nurse it yourself, Bury it yourself: God grant that the latter may happen soon, lest you receive comfort from the fruit of your iniquity!"

This inhuman speech, the threats which it contained, the dreadful sufferings foretold to me by the Domina, and her prayers for my Infant's death, on whom though unborn I already doated, were more than my exhausted frame could support. Uttering a deep groan, I fell senseless at the feet of my unrelenting Enemy. I know not how long I remained in this situation; But I imagine that some time must have elapsed before my recovery, since it sufficed the Prioress and her Nuns to quit the Cavern. When my senses returned, I found myself in silence and solitude. I heard not even the retiring footsteps of my Persecutors. All was hushed, and all was dreadful! I had been thrown upon the bed of Straw: The heavy Chain which I had already eyed with terror, was wound around my waist, and fastened me to the Wall. A Lamp glimmering with dull, melancholy rays through my dungeon, permitted my distinguishing all its horrors: It was separated from the Cavern by a low and irregular Wall of Stone: A large Chasm was left open in it which formed the entrance, for door there was none. A leaden Crucifix was in front of my straw Couch. A tattered rug lay near me, as did also a Chaplet of Beads; and not far from me stood a pitcher of water, and a wicker Basket containing a small loaf, and a bottle of oil to supply my Lamp.

With a despondent eye did I examine this scene of suffering: When I reflected that I was doomed to pass in it the remainder of my days, my heart was rent with bitter anguish. I had once been taught to look forward to a lot so different! At one time my prospects had appeared so bright, so flattering! Now all was lost to me. Friends, comfort, society, happiness, in one moment I was deprived of all! Dead to the world, Dead to pleasure, I lived to nothing but the sense of misery. How fair did that world seem to me, from which I was for ever excluded! How many loved objects did it contain, whom I never should behold again! As I threw a look of terror round my prison, as I shrunk from the cutting wind which howled through my subterraneous dwelling, the change seemed so striking, so abrupt, that I doubted its reality.

That the Duke de Medina's Niece, that the destined Bride of the Marquis de las Cisternas, One bred up in affluence, related to the noblest families in Spain, and rich in a multitude of affectionate Friends, that She should in one moment become a Captive, separated from the world for ever, weighed down with chains, and reduced to support life with the coarsest aliments, appeared a change so sudden and incredible, that I believed myself the sport of some frightful vision. Its continuance convinced me of my mistake with but too much certainty. Every morning my hopes were disappointed. At length I abandoned all idea of escaping: I resigned myself to my fate, and only expected Liberty when She came the Companion of Death.

My mental anguish, and the dreadful scenes in which I had been an Actress, advanced the period of my labour. In solitude and misery, abandoned by all, unassisted by Art, uncomforted by Friendship, with pangs which if witnessed would have touched the hardest heart, was I delivered of my wretched burthen. It came alive into the world; But I knew not how to treat it, or by what means to preserve its existence. I could only bathe it with tears, warm it in my bosom, and offer up prayers for its safety. I was soon deprived of this mournful employment: The want of proper attendance, my ignorance how to nurse it, the bitter cold of the dungeon, and the unwholesome air which inflated its lungs, terminated my sweet Babe's short and painful existence. It expired in a few hours after its birth, and I witnessed its death with agonies which beggar all description.

But my grief was unavailing. My Infant was no more; nor could all my sighs impart to its little tender frame the breath of a moment. I rent my winding-sheet, and wrapped in it my lovely Child. I placed it on my bosom, its soft arm folded round my neck, and its pale cold cheek resting upon mine. Thus did its lifeless limbs repose, while I covered it with kisses, talked to it, wept, and moaned over it without remission, day or night. Camilla entered my prison regularly once every twenty-four hours, to bring me food. In spite of her flinty nature, She could not behold this spectacle unmoved. She feared that grief so excessive would at length turn my brain, and in truth I was not always in my proper senses. From a principle of compassion She urged me to permit the Corse to be buried: But to this I never would consent. I vowed not to part with it while I had life: Its presence was my only comfort, and no persuasion could induce me to give it up. It soon became a mass of putridity, and to every eye was a loathsome and disgusting Object; To every eye but a Mother's. In vain did human feelings bid me recoil from this emblem of mortality with repugnance: I withstood, and vanquished that repugnance. I persisted in holding my Infant to my bosom, in lamenting it, loving it, adoring it! Hour after hour have I passed upon my sorry Couch, contemplating what had once been my Child: I endeavoured to retrace its features through the livid corruption, with which they were overspread: During my confinement this sad occupation was my only delight; and at that time Worlds should not have bribed me to give it up. Even when released from my prison, I brought away my Child in my arms. The representations of my two kind Friends,' — (Here She took the hands of the Marchioness and Virginia, and pressed them alternately to her lips) — 'at length persuaded me to resign my unhappy Infant to the Grave. Yet I parted from it with reluctance: However, reason at length prevailed; I suffered it to be taken from me, and it now reposes in consecrated ground.

I before mentioned that regularly once a day Camilla brought me food. She sought not to embitter my sorrows with reproach: She bad me, 'tis true, resign all hopes of liberty and worldly happiness; But She encouraged me to bear with patience my temporary distress, and advised me to draw comfort from religion.

My situation evidently affected her more than She ventured to express: But She believed that to extenuate my fault would make me less anxious to repent it. Often while her lips painted the enormity of my guilt in glaring colours, her eyes betrayed, how sensible She was to my sufferings. In fact I am certain that none of my Tormentors, (for the three other Nuns entered my prison occasionally) were so much actuated by the spirit of oppressive cruelty as by the idea that to afflict my body was the only way to preserve my soul. Nay, even this persuasion might not have had such weight with them, and they might have thought my punishment too severe, had not their good dispositions been represt by blind obedience to their Superior. Her resentment existed in full force. My project of elopement having been discovered by the Abbot of the Capuchins, She supposed herself lowered in his opinion by my disgrace, and in consequence her hate was inveterate. She told the Nuns to whose custody I was committed that my fault was of the most heinous nature, that no sufferings could equal the offence, and that nothing could save me from eternal perdition but punishing my guilt with the utmost severity. The Superior's word is an oracle to but too many of a Convent's Inhabitants. The Nuns believed whatever the Prioress chose to assert: Though contradicted by reason and charity, they hesitated not to admit the truth of her arguments. They followed her injunctions to the very letter, and were fully persuaded that to treat me with lenity, or to show the least pity for my woes, would be a direct means to destroy my chance for salvation.

Camilla, being most employed about me, was particularly charged by the Prioress to treat me with harshness. In compliance with these orders, She frequently strove to convince me, how just was my punishment, and how enormous was my crime: She bad me think myself too happy in saving my soul by mortifying my body, and even threatened me sometimes with eternal perdition. Yet as I before observed, She always concluded by words of encouragement and comfort; and though uttered by Camilla's lips, I easily recognised the Domina's expressions. Once, and once only, the Prioress visited me in my dungeon. She then treated me with the most unrelenting cruelty: She loaded me with reproaches, taunted me with my frailty, and when I implored her mercy, told me to ask it of heaven, since I deserved none on earth. She even gazed upon my lifeless Infant without emotion; and when She left me, I heard her charge Camilla to increase the hardships of my Captivity. Unfeeling Woman! But let me check my resentment: She has expiated her errors by her sad and unexpected death.

Peace be with her; and may her crimes be forgiven in heaven, as I forgive her my sufferings on earth!

Thus did I drag on a miserable existence. Far from growing familiar with my prison, I beheld it every moment with new horror. The cold seemed more piercing and bitter, the air more thick and pestilential. My frame became weak, feverish, and emaciated. I was unable to rise from the bed of Straw, and exercise my limbs in the narrow limits, to which the length of my chain permitted me to move. Though exhausted, faint, and weary, I trembled to profit by the approach of Sleep: My slumbers were constantly interrupted by some obnoxious Insect crawling over me.

Sometimes I felt the bloated Toad, hideous and pampered with the poisonous vapours of the dungeon, dragging his loathsome length along my bosom: Sometimes the quick cold Lizard rouzed me leaving his slimy track upon my face, and entangling itself in the tresses of my wild and matted hair: Often have I at waking found my fingers ringed with the long worms which bred in the corrupted flesh of my Infant. At such times I shrieked with terror and disgust, and while I shook off the reptile, trembled with all a Woman's weakness.

Such was my situation, when Camilla was suddenly taken ill. A dangerous fever, supposed to be infectious, confined her to her bed. Every one except the Lay-Sister appointed to nurse her, avoided her with caution, and feared to catch the disease. She was perfectly delirious, and by no means capable of attending to me. The Domina and the Nuns admitted to the mystery, had latterly given me over entirely to Camilla's care: In consequence, they busied themselves no more about me; and occupied by preparing for the approaching Festival, it is more than probable that I never once entered into their thoughts. Of the reason of Camilla's negligence, I have been informed since my release by the Mother St. Ursula; At that time I was very far from suspecting its cause. On the contrary, I waited for my Gaoler's appearance at first with impatience, and afterwards with despair. One day passed away; Another followed it; The Third arrived. Still no Camilla! Still no food! I knew the lapse of time by the wasting of my Lamp, to supply which fortunately a week's supply of Oil had been left me. I supposed, either that the Nuns had forgotten me, or that the Domina had ordered them to let me perish. The latter idea seemed the most probable; Yet so natural is the love of life, that I trembled to find it true. Though embittered by every species of misery, my existence was still dear to me, and I dreaded to lose it. Every succeeding minute proved to me that I must abandon all hopes of relief. I was become an absolute skeleton: My eyes already failed me, and my limbs were beginning to stiffen. I could only express my anguish, and the pangs of that hunger which gnawed my heart-strings, by frequent groans, whose melancholy sound the vaulted roof of the dungeon re-echoed. I resigned myself to my fate: I already expected the moment of dissolution, when my Guardian Angel, when my beloved Brother arrived in time to save me. My sight grown dim and feeble at first refused to recognize him; and when I did distinguish his features, the sudden burst of rapture was too much for me to bear. I was overpowered by the swell of joy at once more beholding a Friend, and that a Friend so dear to me. Nature could not support my emotions, and took her refuge in insensibility.

You already know, what are my obligations to the Family of Villa-Franca: But what you cannot know is the extent of my gratitude, boundless as the excellence of my Benefactors. Lorenzo! Raymond! Names so dear to me! Teach me to bear with fortitude this sudden transition from misery to bliss. So lately a Captive, opprest with chains, perishing with hunger, suffering every inconvenience of cold and want, hidden from the light, excluded from society, hopeless, neglected, and as I feared, forgotten; Now restored to life and liberty, enjoying all the comforts of affluence and ease, surrounded by those who are most loved by me, and on the point of becoming his Bride who has long been wedded to my heart, my happiness is so exquisite, so perfect, that scarcely can my brain sustain the weight. One only wish remains ungratified: It is to see my Brother in his former health, and to know that Antonia's memory is buried in her grave.

Granted this prayer, I have nothing more to desire. I trust, that my past sufferings have purchased from heaven the pardon of my momentary weakness. That I have offended, offended greatly and grievously, I am fully conscious; But let not my Husband, because He once conquered my virtue, doubt the propriety of my future conduct. I have been frail and full of error: But I yielded not to the warmth of constitution; Raymond, affection for you betrayed me. I was too confident of my strength; But I depended no less on your honour than my own. I had vowed never to see you more: Had it not been for the consequences of that unguarded moment, my resolution had been kept. Fate willed it otherwise, and I cannot but rejoice at its decree. Still my conduct has been highly blameable, and while I attempt to justify myself, I blush at recollecting my imprudence. Let me then dismiss the ungrateful subject; First assuring you, Raymond, that you shall have no cause to repent our union, and that the more culpable have been the errors of your Mistress, the more exemplary shall be the conduct of your Wife.

Here Agnes ceased, and the Marquis replied to her address in terms equally sincere and affectionate. Lorenzo expressed his satisfaction at the prospect of being so closely connected with a Man for whom He had ever entertained the highest esteem. The Pope's Bull had fully and effectually released Agnes from her religious engagements: The marriage was therefore celebrated as soon as the needful preparations had been made, for the Marquis wished to have the ceremony performed with all possible splendour and publicity. This being over, and the Bride having received the compliments of Madrid, She departed with Don Raymond for his Castle in Andalusia: Lorenzo accompanied them, as did also the Marchioness de Villa-Franca and her lovely Daughter. It is needless to say that Theodore was of the party, and would be impossible to describe his joy at his Master's marriage. Previous to his departure, the Marquis, to atone in some measure for his past neglect, made some enquiries relative to Elvira. Finding that She as well as her Daughter had received many services from Leonella and Jacintha, He showed his respect to the memory of his Sister-in-law by making the two Women handsome presents. Lorenzo followed his example—Leonella was highly flattered by the attentions of Noblemen so distinguished, and Jacintha blessed the hour on which her House was bewitched.

On her side, Agnes failed not to reward her Convent Friends. The worthy Mother St. Ursula, to whom She owed her liberty, was named at her request Superintendent of "The Ladies of Charity:" This was one of the best and most opulent Societies throughout Spain. Bertha and Cornelia not choosing to quit their Friend, were appointed to principal charges in the same establishment. As to the Nuns who had aided the Domina in persecuting Agnes, Camilla being confined by illness to her bed, had perished in the flames which consumed St. Clare's Convent. Mariana, Alix, and Violante, as well as two more, had fallen victims to the popular rage. The three Others who in Council had supported the Domina's sentence, were severely reprimanded, and banished to religious Houses in obscure and distant Provinces: Here they languished away a few years, ashamed of their former weakness, and shunned by their Companions with aversion and contempt.

Nor was the fidelity of Flora permitted to go unrewarded. Her wishes being consulted, She declared herself impatient to revisit her native land. In consequence, a passage was procured for her to Cuba, where She arrived in safety, loaded with the presents of Raymond and Lorenzo.

The debts of gratitude discharged, Agnes was at liberty to pursue her favourite plan. Lodged in the same House, Lorenzo and Virginia were eternally together. The more He saw of her, the more was He convinced of her merit. On her part, She laid herself out to please, and not to succeed was for her impossible.

Lorenzo witnessed with admiration her beautiful person, elegant manners, innumerable talents, and sweet disposition: He was also much flattered by her prejudice in his favour, which She had not sufficient art to conceal. However, his sentiments partook not of that ardent character which had marked his affection for Antonia. The image of that lovely and unfortunate Girl still lived in his heart, and baffled all Virginia's efforts to displace it. Still when the Duke proposed to him the match, which He wished to earnestly to take place, his Nephew did not reject the offer. The urgent supplications of his Friends, and the Lady's merit conquered his repugnance to entering into new engagements. He proposed himself to the Marquis de Villa-Franca, and was accepted with joy and gratitude. Virginia became his Wife, nor did She ever give him cause to repent his choice. His esteem increased for her daily. Her unremitted endeavours to please him could not but succeed. His affection assumed stronger and warmer colours. Antonia's image was gradually effaced from his bosom; and Virginia became sole Mistress of that heart, which She well deserved to possess without a Partner.

The remaining years of Raymond and Agnes, of Lorenzo and Virginia, were happy as can be those allotted to Mortals, born to be the prey of grief, and sport of disappointment. The exquisite sorrows with which they had been afflicted, made them think lightly of every succeeding woe. They had felt the sharpest darts in misfortune's quiver; Those which remained appeared blunt in comparison. Having weathered Fate's heaviest Storms, they looked calmly upon its terrors: or if ever they felt Affliction's casual gales, they seemed to them gentle as Zephyrs which breathe over summer-seas.

CHAPTER XII.

— — He was a fell despightful Fiend:

Hell holds none worse in baleful bower below:

By pride, and wit, and rage, and rancor keened;

Of Man alike, if good or bad the Foe.

THOMSON.

On the day following Antonia's death, all Madrid was a scene of consternation and amazement. An Archer who had witnessed the adventure in the Sepulchre had indiscreetly related the circumstances of the murder: He had also named the Perpetrator. The confusion was without example which this intelligence raised among the Devotees. Most of them disbelieved it, and went themselves to the Abbey to ascertain the fact. Anxious to avoid the shame to which their Superior's ill-conduct exposed the whole Brotherhood, the Monks assured the Visitors that Ambrosio was prevented from receiving them as usual by nothing but illness. This attempt was unsuccessful: The same excuse being repeated day after day, the Archer's story gradually obtained confidence. His Partizans abandoned him: No one entertained a doubt of his guilt; and they who before had been the warmest in his praise were now the most vociferous in his condemnation.

While his innocence or guilt was debated in Madrid with the utmost acrimony, Ambrosio was a prey to the pangs of conscious villainy, and the terrors of punishment impending over him. When He looked back to the eminence on which He had lately stood, universally honoured and respected, at peace with the world and with himself, scarcely could He believe that He was indeed the culprit whose crimes and whose fate He trembled to envisage. But a few weeks had elapsed, since He was pure and virtuous, courted by the wisest and noblest in Madrid, and regarded by the People with a reverence that approached idolatry: He now saw himself stained with the most loathed and monstrous sins, the object of universal execration, a Prisoner of the Holy Office, and probably doomed to perish in tortures the most severe. He could not hope to deceive his Judges: The proofs of his guilt were too strong. His being in the Sepulchre at so late an hour, his confusion at the discovery, the dagger which in his first alarm He owned had been concealed by him, and the blood which had spirted upon his habit from

Antonia's wound, sufficiently marked him out for the Assassin. He waited with agony for the day of examination: He had no resource to comfort him in his distress. Religion could not inspire him with fortitude: If He read the Books of morality which were put into his hands, He saw in them nothing but the enormity of his offences; If he attempted to pray, He recollected that He deserved not heaven's protection, and believed his crimes so monstrous as to baffle even God's infinite goodness. For every other Sinner He thought there might be hope, but for him there could be none. Shuddering at the past, anguished by the present, and dreading the future, thus passed He the few days preceding that which was marked for his Trial.

That day arrived. At nine in the morning his prison door was unlocked, and his Gaoler entering, commanded him to follow him. He obeyed with trembling. He was conducted into a spacious Hall, hung with black cloth. At the Table sat three grave, stern-looking Men, also habited in black: One was the Grand Inquisitor, whom the importance of this cause had induced to examine into it himself. At a smaller table at a little distance sat the Secretary, provided with all necessary implements for writing. Ambrosio was beckoned to advance, and take his station at the lower end of the Table. As his eye glanced downwards, He perceived various iron instruments lying scattered upon the floor. Their forms were unknown to him, but apprehension immediately guessed them to be engines of torture. He turned pale, and with difficulty prevented himself from sinking upon the ground.

Profound silence prevailed, except when the Inquisitors whispered a few words among themselves mysteriously. Near an hour past away, and with every second of it Ambrosio's fears grew more poignant. At length a small Door, opposite to that by which He had entered the Hall, grated heavily upon its hinges. An Officer appeared, and was immediately followed by the beautiful Matilda. Her hair hung about her face wildly; Her cheeks were pale, and her eyes sunk and hollow. She threw a melancholy look upon Ambrosio: He replied by one of aversion and reproach. She was placed opposite to him. A Bell then sounded thrice. It was the signal for opening the Court, and the Inquisitors entered upon their office.

In these trials neither the accusation is mentioned, or the name of the Accuser. The Prisoners are only asked, whether they will confess: If they reply that having no crime they can make no confession, they are put to the torture without delay. This is repeated at intervals, either till the suspected avow themselves culpable, or the perseverance of the examinants is worn out and exhausted: But without a direct acknowledgment of their guilt, the Inquisition never pronounces the final doom of its Prisoners.

In general much time is suffered to elapse without their being questioned: But Ambrosio's trial had been hastened, on account of a solemn Auto da Fe which would take place in a few days, and in which the Inquisitors meant this distinguished Culprit to perform a part, and give a striking testimony of their vigilance.

The Abbot was not merely accused of rape and murder: The crime of Sorcery was laid to his charge, as well as to Matilda's. She had been seized as an Accomplice in Antonia's assassination. On searching her Cell, various suspicious books and instruments were found which justified the accusation brought against her. To criminate the Monk, the constellated Mirror was produced, which Matilda had accidentally left in his chamber. The strange figures engraved upon it caught the attention of Don Ramirez, while searching the Abbot's Cell: In consequence, He carried it away with him. It was shown to the Grand Inquisitor, who having considered it for some time, took off a small golden Cross which hung at his girdle, and laid it upon the Mirror. Instantly a loud noise was heard, resembling a clap of thunder, and the steel shivered into a thousand pieces. This circumstance confirmed the suspicion of the Monk's having dealt in Magic: It was even supposed that his former influence over the minds of the People was entirely to be ascribed to witchcraft.

Determined to make him confess not only the crimes which He had committed, but those also of which He was innocent, the Inquisitors began their examination. Though dreading the tortures, as He dreaded death still more which would consign him to eternal torments, the Abbot asserted his purity in a voice bold and resolute. Matilda followed his example, but spoke with fear and trembling. Having in vain exhorted him to confess, the Inquisitors ordered the Monk to be put to the question. The Decree was immediately executed. Ambrosio suffered the most excruciating pangs that ever were invented by human cruelty: Yet so dreadful is Death when guilt accompanies it, that He had sufficient fortitude to persist in his disavowal. His agonies were redoubled in consequence: Nor was He released till fainting from excess of pain, insensibility rescued him from the hands of his Tormentors.

Matilda was next ordered to the torture: But terrified by the sight of the Friar's sufferings, her courage totally deserted her. She sank upon her knees, acknowledged her corresponding with infernal Spirits, and that She had witnessed the Monk's assassination of Antonia: But as to the crime of Sorcery, She declared herself the sole criminal, and Ambrosio perfectly innocent. The latter assertion met with no credit. The Abbot had recovered his senses in time to hear the confession of his Accomplice: But He was too much enfeebled by what He had already undergone to be capable at that time of sustaining new torments.

He was commanded back to his Cell, but first informed that as soon as He had gained strength sufficient, He must prepare himself for a second examination. The Inquisitors hoped that He would then be less hardened and obstinate. To Matilda it was announced that She must expiate her crime in fire on the approaching Auto da Fe. All her tears and entreaties could procure no mitigation of her doom, and She was dragged by force from the Hall of Trial.

Returned to his dungeon, the sufferings of Ambrosio's body were far more supportable than those of his mind. His dislocated limbs, the nails torn from his hands and feet, and his fingers mashed and broken by the pressure of screws, were far surpassed in anguish by the agitation of his soul and vehemence of his terrors. He saw that, guilty or innocent, his Judges were bent upon condemning him: The remembrance of what his denial had already cost him terrified him at the idea of being again applied to the question, and almost engaged him to confess his crimes. Then again the consequences of his confession flashed before him, and rendered him once more irresolute. His death would be inevitable, and that a death the most dreadful: He had listened to Matilda's doom, and doubted not that a similar was reserved for him. He shuddered at the approaching Auto da Fe, at the idea of perishing in flames, and only escaping from indurable torments to pass into others more subtile and ever-lasting! With affright did He bend his mind's eye on the space beyond the grave; nor could hide from himself how justly he ought to dread Heaven's vengeance. In this Labyrinth of terrors, fain would He have taken his refuge in the gloom of Atheism: Fain would He have denied the soul's immortality; have persuaded himself that when his eyes once closed, they would never more open, and that the same moment would annihilate his soul and body. Even this resource was refused to him. To permit his being blind to the fallacy of this belief, his knowledge was too extensive, his understanding too solid and just. He could not help feeling the existence of a God.

Those truths, once his comfort, now presented themselves before him in the clearest light; But they only served to drive him to distraction. They destroyed his ill-grounded hopes of escaping punishment; and dispelled by the irresistible brightness of Truth and convinction, Philosophy's deceitful vapours faded away like a dream.

In anguish almost too great for mortal frame to bear, He expected the time when He was again to be examined. He busied himself in planning ineffectual schemes for escaping both present and future punishment. Of the first there was no possibility; Of the second Despair made him neglect the only means. While Reason forced him to acknowledge a God's existence, Conscience made him doubt the infinity of his goodness. He disbelieved that a Sinner like him could find mercy. He had not been deceived into error: Ignorance could furnish him with no excuse. He had seen vice in her true colours; Before He committed his crimes, He had computed every scruple of their weight; and yet he had committed them.

"Pardon?" He would cry in an access of phrenzy "Oh! there can be none for me!"

Persuaded of this, instead of humbling himself in penitence, of deploring his guilt, and employing his few remaining hours in deprecating Heaven's wrath, He abandoned himself to the transports of desperate rage; He sorrowed for the punishment of his crimes, not their commission; and exhaled his bosom's anguish in idle sighs, in vain lamentations, in blasphemy and despair. As the few beams of day which pierced through the bars of his prison window gradually disappeared, and their place was supplied by the pale and glimmering Lamp, He felt his terrors redouble, and his ideas become more gloomy, more solemn, more despondent. He dreaded the approach of sleep: No sooner did his eyes close, wearied with tears and watching, than the dreadful visions seemed to be realised on which his mind had dwelt during the day. He found himself in sulphurous realms and burning Caverns, surrounded by Fiends appointed his Tormentors, and who drove him through a variety of tortures, each of which was more dreadful than the former. Amidst these dismal scenes wandered the Ghosts of Elvira and her Daughter. They reproached him with their deaths, recounted his crimes to the Dæmons, and urged them to inflict torments of cruelty yet more refined. Such were the pictures which floated before his eyes in sleep: They vanished not till his repose was disturbed by excess of agony. Then would He start from the ground on which He had stretched himself, his brows running down with cold sweat, his eyes wild and phrenzied; and He only exchanged the terrible certainty for surmizes scarcely more supportable. He paced his dungeon with disordered steps; He gazed with terror upon the surrounding darkness, and often did He cry,

"Oh! fearful is night to the Guilty!"

The day of his second examination was at hand. He had been compelled to swallow cordials, whose virtues were calculated to restore his bodily strength, and enable him to support the question longer. On the night preceding this dreaded day, his fears for the morrow permitted him not to sleep. His terrors were so violent, as nearly to annihilate his mental powers. He sat like one stupefied near the Table on which his Lamp was burning dimly. Despair chained up his faculties in Idiotism, and He remained for some hours, unable to speak or move, or indeed to think.

"Look up, Ambrosio!" said a Voice in accents well-known to him—

The Monk started, and raised his melancholy eyes. Matilda stood before him. She had quitted her religious habit. She now wore a female dress, at once elegant and splendid: A profusion of diamonds blazed upon her robes, and her hair was confined by a coronet of Roses. In her right hand She held a small Book: A lively expression of pleasure beamed upon her countenance; But still it was mingled with a wild imperious majesty which inspired the Monk with awe, and represt in some measure his transports at seeing her.

"You here, Matilda?" He at length exclaimed; "How have you gained entrance? Where are your Chains? What means this magnificence, and the joy which sparkles in your eyes? Have our Judges relented? Is there a chance of my escaping? Answer me for pity, and tell me, what I have to hope, or fear."

"Ambrosio!" She replied with an air of commanding dignity; "I have baffled the Inquisition's fury. I am free: A few moments will place kingdoms between these dungeons and me. Yet I purchase my liberty at a dear, at a dreadful price! Dare you pay the same, Ambrosio? Dare you spring without fear over the bounds which separate Men from Angels?—You are silent.— You look upon me with eyes of suspicion and alarm—I read your thoughts and confess their justice. Yes, Ambrosio; I have sacrificed all for life and liberty. I am no longer a candidate for heaven! I have renounced God's service, and am enlisted beneath the banners of his Foes. The deed is past recall: Yet were it in my power to go back, I would not. Oh! my Friend, to expire in such torments! To die amidst curses and execrations! To bear the insults of an exasperated Mob! To be exposed to all the mortifications of shame and infamy! Who can reflect without horror on such a doom? Let me then exult in my exchange. I have sold distant and uncertain happiness for present and secure: I have preserved a life which otherwise I had lost in torture; and I have obtained the power of procuring every bliss which can make that life delicious! The Infernal Spirits obey me as their Sovereign: By their aid shall my days be past in every refinement of luxury and voluptuousness. I will enjoy unrestrained the gratification of my senses: Every passion shall be indulged, even to satiety; Then will I bid my Servants invent new pleasures, to revive and stimulate my glutted appetites! I go impatient to exercise my newly-gained dominion. I pant to be at liberty. Nothing should hold me one moment longer in this abhorred abode, but the hope of persuading you to follow my example. Ambrosio, I still love you: Our mutual guilt and danger have rendered you dearer to me than ever, and I would fain save you from impending destruction. Summon then your resolution to your aid; and renounce for immediate and certain benefits the hopes of a salvation, difficult to obtain, and perhaps altogether erroneous. Shake off the prejudice of vulgar souls; Abandon a God who has abandoned you, and raise yourself to the level of superior Beings!"

She paused for the Monk's reply: He shuddered, while He gave it.

"Matilda!" He said after a long silence in a low and unsteady voice; "What price gave you for liberty?"

She answered him firm and dauntless.

"Ambrosio, it was my Soul!"

"Wretched Woman, what have you done? Pass but a few years, and how dreadful will be your sufferings!"

"Weak Man, pass but this night, and how dreadful will be your own! Do you remember what you have already endured? Tomorrow you must bear torments doubly exquisite. Do you remember the horrors of a fiery punishment? In two days you must be led a Victim to the Stake! What then will become of you? Still dare you hope for pardon? Still are you beguiled with visions of salvation? Think upon your crimes! Think upon your lust, your perjury, inhumanity, and hypocrisy! Think upon the innocent blood which cries to the Throne of God for vengeance, and then hope for mercy! Then dream of heaven, and sigh for worlds of light, and realms of peace and pleasure! Absurd! Open your eyes, Ambrosio, and be prudent. Hell is your lot; You are doomed to eternal perdition; Nought lies beyond your grave but a gulph of devouring flames. And will you then speed towards that Hell? Will you clasp that perdition in your arms, ere 'tis needful? Will you plunge into those flames while you still have the power to shun them? 'Tis a Madman's action. No, no, Ambrosio: Let us for awhile fly from divine vengeance. Be advised by me; Purchase by one moment's courage the bliss of years; Enjoy the present, and forget that a future lags behind."

"Matilda, your counsels are dangerous: I dare not, I will not follow them. I must not give up my claim to salvation. Monstrous are my crimes; But God is merciful, and I will not despair of pardon."

"Is such your resolution? I have no more to say. I speed to joy and liberty, and abandon you to death and eternal torments."

"Yet stay one moment, Matilda! You command the infernal Dæmons:

You can force open these prison doors; You can release me from these chains which weigh me down. Save me, I conjure you, and bear me from these fearful abodes!"

"You ask the only boon beyond my power to bestow. I am forbidden to assist a Churchman and a Partizan of God: Renounce those titles, and command me."

"I will not sell my soul to perdition."

"Persist in your obstinacy, till you find yourself at the Stake: Then will you repent your error, and sigh for escape when the moment is gone by. I quit you. Yet ere the hour of death arrives should wisdom enlighten you, listen to the means of repairing your present fault. I leave with you this Book. Read the four first lines of the seventh page backwards: The Spirit whom you have already once beheld will immediately appear to you. If you are wise, we shall meet again: If not, farewell for ever!"

She let the Book fall upon the ground. A cloud of blue fire wrapped itself round her: She waved her hand to Ambrosio, and disappeared. The momentary glare which the flames poured through the dungeon, on dissipating suddenly, seemed to have increased its natural gloom. The solitary Lamp scarcely gave light sufficient to guide the Monk to a Chair. He threw himself into his seat, folded his arms, and leaning his head upon the table, sank into reflections perplexing and unconnected.

He was still in this attitude when the opening of the prison door rouzed him from his stupor. He was summoned to appear before the Grand Inquisitor. He rose, and followed his Gaoler with painful steps. He was led into the same Hall, placed before the same Examiners, and was again interrogated whether He would confess. He replied as before, that having no crimes, He could acknowledge none: But when the Executioners prepared to put him to the question, when He saw the engines of torture, and remembered the pangs which they had already inflicted, his resolution failed him entirely. Forgetting the consequences, and only anxious to escape the terrors of the present moment, He made an ample confession. He disclosed every circumstance of his guilt, and owned not merely the crimes with which He was charged, but those of which He had never been suspected. Being interrogated as to Matilda's flight which had created much confusion, He confessed that She had sold herself to Satan, and that She was indebted to Sorcery for her escape. He still assured his Judges that for his own part He had never entered into any compact with the infernal Spirits; But the threat of being tortured made him declare himself to be a Sorcerer, and Heretic, and whatever other title the Inquisitors chose to fix upon him. In consequence of this avowal, his sentence was immediately pronounced. He was ordered to prepare himself to perish in the Auto da Fe, which was to be solemnized at twelve o'clock that night. This hour was chosen from the idea that the horror of the flames being heightened by the gloom of midnight, the execution would have a greater effect upon the mind of the People.

Ambrosio rather dead than alive was left alone in his dungeon. The moment in which this terrible decree was pronounced had nearly proved that of his dissolution. He looked forward to the morrow with despair, and his terrors increased with the approach of midnight. Sometimes He was buried in gloomy silence: At others He raved with delirious passion, wrung his hands, and cursed the hour when He first beheld the light. In one of these moments his eye rested upon Matilda's mysterious gift. His transports of rage were instantly suspended. He looked earnestly at the Book; He took it up, but immediately threw it from him with horror. He walked rapidly up and down his dungeon: Then stopped, and again fixed his eyes on the spot where the Book had fallen. He reflected that here at least was a resource from the fate which He dreaded. He stooped, and took it up a second time.

He remained for some time trembling and irresolute: He longed to try the charm, yet feared its consequences. The recollection of his sentence at length fixed his indecision. He opened the Volume; but his agitation was so great that He at first sought in vain for the page mentioned by Matilda. Ashamed of himself, He called all his courage to his aid. He turned to the seventh leaf. He began to read it aloud; But his eyes frequently wandered from the Book, while He anxiously cast them round in search of the Spirit, whom He wished, yet dreaded to behold. Still He persisted in his design; and with a voice unassured and frequent interruptions, He contrived to finish the four first lines of the page.

They were in a language, whose import was totally unknown to him.

Scarce had He pronounced the last word when the effects of the charm were evident. A loud burst of Thunder was heard; The prison shook to its very foundations; A blaze of lightning flashed through the Cell; and in the next moment, borne upon sulphurous whirl-winds, Lucifer stood before him a second time. But He came not as when at Matilda's summons He borrowed the Seraph's form to deceive Ambrosio. He appeared in all that ugliness which since his fall from heaven had been his portion: His blasted limbs still bore marks of the Almighty's thunder: A swarthy darkness spread itself over his gigantic form: His hands and feet were armed with long Talons: Fury glared in his eyes, which might have struck the bravest heart with terror: Over his huge shoulders waved two enormous sable wings; and his hair was supplied by living snakes, which twined themselves round his brows with frightful hissings. In one hand He held a roll of parchment, and in the other an iron pen. Still the lightning flashed around him, and the Thunder with repeated bursts, seemed to announce the dissolution of Nature.

Terrified at an Apparition so different from what He had expected, Ambrosio remained gazing upon the Fiend, deprived of the power of utterance. The Thunder had ceased to roll: Universal silence reigned through the dungeon.

"For what am I summoned hither?" said the dæmon, in a voice which sulphurous fogs had damped to hoarseness.

At the sound Nature seemed to tremble: A violent earthquake rocked the ground, accompanied by a fresh burst of

Thunder, louder and more appalling than the first.

Ambrosio was long unable to answer the Dæmon's demand.

"I am condemned to die;" He said with a faint voice, his blood running cold, while He gazed upon his dreadful Visitor. "Save me! Bear me from hence!"

"Shall the reward of my services be paid me? Dare you embrace my cause? Will you be mine, body and soul? Are you prepared to renounce him who made you, and him who died for you? Answer but 'Yes' and Lucifer is your Slave."

"Will no less price content you? Can nothing satisfy you but my eternal ruin? Spirit, you ask too much. Yet convey me from this dungeon: Be my Servant for one hour, and I will be yours for a thousand years. Will not this offer suffice?"

"It will not. I must have your soul; must have it mine, and mine for ever."

"Insatiate Dæmon, I will not doom myself to endless torments. I will not give up my hopes of being one day pardoned."

"You will not? On what Chimaera rest then your hopes? Short-sighted Mortal! Miserable Wretch! Are you not guilty? Are you not infamous in the eyes of Men and Angels. Can such enormous sins be forgiven? Hope you to escape my power? Your fate is already pronounced. The Eternal has abandoned you; Mine you are marked in the book of destiny, and mine you must and shall be!"

"Fiend, 'tis false! Infinite is the Almighty's mercy, and the Penitent shall meet his forgiveness. My crimes are monstrous, but I will not despair of pardon: Haply, when they have received due chastisement...."

"Chastisement? Was Purgatory meant for guilt like yours? Hope you that your offences shall be bought off by prayers of superstitious dotards and droning Monks? Ambrosio, be wise! Mine you must be: You are doomed to flames, but may shun them for the present. Sign this parchment: I will bear you from hence, and you may pass your remaining years in bliss and liberty. Enjoy your existence: Indulge in every pleasure to which appetite may lead you: But from the moment that it quits your body, remember that your soul belongs to me, and that I will not be defrauded of my right."

The Monk was silent; But his looks declared that the Tempter's words were not thrown away. He reflected on the conditions proposed with horror: On the other hand, He believed himself doomed to perdition and that, by refusing the Dæmon's succour, He only hastened tortures which He never could escape. The Fiend saw that his resolution was shaken: He renewed his instances, and endeavoured to fix the Abbot's indecision. He described the agonies of death in the most terrific colours; and He worked so powerfully upon Ambrosio's despair and fears that He prevailed upon him to receive the Parchment. He then struck the iron Pen which He held into a vein of the Monk's left hand. It pierced deep, and was instantly filled with blood; Yet Ambrosio felt no pain from the wound. The Pen was put into his hand: It trembled. The Wretch placed the Parchment on the Table before him, and prepared to sign it. Suddenly He held his hand: He started away hastily, and threw the Pen upon the table.

"What am I doing?" He cried—Then turning to the Fiend with a desperate air, "Leave me! Begone! I will not sign the Parchment."

"Fool!" exclaimed the disappointed Dæmon, darting looks so furious as penetrated the Friar's soul with horror; "Thus am I trifled with? Go then! Rave in agony, expire in tortures, and then learn the extent of the Eternal's mercy! But beware how you make me again your mock! Call me no more till resolved to accept my offers! Summon me a second time to dismiss me thus idly, and these Talons shall rend you into a thousand pieces! Speak yet again; Will you sign the Parchment?"

"I will not! Leave me! Away!"

Instantly the Thunder was heard to roll horribly: Once more the earth trembled with violence: The Dungeon resounded with loud shrieks, and the Dæmon fled with blasphemy and curses.

At first, the Monk rejoiced at having resisted the Seducer's arts, and obtained a triumph over Mankind's Enemy: But as the hour of punishment drew near, his former terrors revived in his heart. Their momentary repose seemed to have given them fresh vigour. The nearer that the time approached, the more did He dread appearing before the Throne of God. He shuddered to think how soon He must be plunged into eternity; How soon meet the eyes of his Creator, whom He had so grievously offended. The Bell announced midnight: It was the signal for being led to the Stake! As He listened to the first stroke, the blood ceased to circulate in the Abbot's veins: He heard death

and torture murmured in each succeeding sound. He expected
to see the Archers entering his prison; and as the Bell forbore to
toll, he seized the magic volume in a fit of despair. He opened it,
turned hastily to the seventh page, and as if fearing to allow
himself a moment's thought ran over the fatal lines with
rapidity. Accompanied by his former terrors, Lucifer again
stood before the Trembler.

"You have summoned me," said the Fiend; "Are you
determined to be wise? Will you accept my conditions? You
know them already. Renounce your claim to salvation, make
over to me your soul, and I bear you from this dungeon
instantly. Yet is it time. Resolve, or it will be too late. Will you
sign the Parchment?"

"I must! — Fate urges me! I accept your conditions."

"Sign the Parchment!" replied the Dæmon in an exulting
tone.

The Contract and the bloody Pen still lay upon the Table.
Ambrosio drew near it. He prepared to sign his name. A
moment's reflection made him hesitate.

"Hark!" cried the Tempter; "They come! Be quick! Sign the
Parchment, and I bear you from hence this moment."

In effect, the Archers were heard approaching, appointed to
lead Ambrosio to the Stake. The sound encouraged the Monk in
his resolution.

"What is the import of this writing?" said He.

"It makes your soul over to me for ever, and without
reserve."

"What am I to receive in exchange?"

"My protection, and release from this dungeon. Sign it, and
this instant I bear you away."

Ambrosio took up the Pen; He set it to the Parchment. Again
his courage failed him: He felt a pang of terror at his heart, and
once more threw the Pen upon the Table.

"Weak and Puerile!" cried the exasperated Fiend: "Away
with this folly! Sign the writing this instant, or I sacrifice you to
my rage!"

At this moment the bolt of the outward Door was drawn back. The Prisoner heard the rattling of Chains; The heavy Bar fell; The Archers were on the point of entering. Worked up to phrenzy by the urgent danger, shrinking from the approach of death, terrified by the Dæmon's threats, and seeing no other means to escape destruction, the wretched Monk complied. He signed the fatal contract, and gave it hastily into the evil Spirit's hands, whose eyes, as He received the gift, glared with malicious rapture.

"Take it!" said the God-abandoned; "Now then save me! Snatch me from hence!"

"Hold! Do you freely and absolutely renounce your Creator and his Son?"

"I do! I do!"

"Do you make over your soul to me for ever?"

"For ever!"

"Without reserve or subterfuge? Without future appeal to the divine mercy?"

The last Chain fell from the door of the prison: The key was heard turning in the Lock: Already the iron door grated heavily upon its rusty hinges.

"I am yours for ever and irrevocably!" cried the Monk wild with terror: "I abandon all claim to salvation! I own no power but yours! Hark! Hark! They come! Oh! save me! Bear me away!"

"I have triumphed! You are mine past reprieve, and I fulfil my promise."

While He spoke, the Door unclosed. Instantly the Dæmon grasped one of Ambrosio's arms, spread his broad pinions, and sprang with him into the air. The roof opened as they soared upwards, and closed again when they had quitted the Dungeon.

In the meanwhile, the Gaoler was thrown into the utmost surprize by the disappearance of his Prisoner. Though neither He nor the Archers were in time to witness the Monk's escape, a sulphurous smell prevailing through the prison sufficiently informed them by whose aid He had been liberated. They hastened to make their report to the Grand Inquisitor. The story, how a Sorcerer had been carried away by the Devil, was soon noised about Madrid; and for some days the whole City was employed in discussing the subject. Gradually it ceased to be the topic of conversation: Other adventures arose whose novelty engaged universal attention; and Ambrosio was soon forgotten as totally, as if He never had existed. While this was passing, the Monk supported by his infernal guide, traversed the air with the rapidity of an arrow, and a few moments placed him upon a Precipice's brink, the steepest in Sierra Morena.

Though rescued from the Inquisition, Ambrosio as yet was insensible of the blessings of liberty. The damning contract weighed heavy upon his mind; and the scenes in which He had been a principal actor had left behind them such impressions as rendered his heart the seat of anarchy and confusion. The Objects now before his eyes, and which the full Moon sailing through clouds permitted him to examine, were ill-calculated to inspire that calm, of which He stood so much in need. The disorder of his imagination was increased by the wildness of the surrounding scenery; By the gloomy Caverns and steep rocks, rising above each other, and dividing the passing clouds; solitary clusters of Trees scattered here and there, among whose thick-twined branches the wind of night sighed hoarsely and mournfully; the shrill cry of mountain Eagles, who had built their nests among these lonely Desarts; the stunning roar of torrents, as swelled by late rains they rushed violently down tremendous precipices; and the dark waters of a silent sluggish stream which faintly reflected the moonbeams, and bathed the Rock's base on which Ambrosio stood. The Abbot cast round him a look of terror. His infernal Conductor was still by his side, and eyed him with a look of mingled malice, exultation, and contempt.

"Whither have you brought me?" said the Monk at length in an hollow trembling voice: "Why am I placed in this melancholy scene? Bear me from it quickly! Carry me to Matilda!"

The Fiend replied not, but continued to gaze upon him in silence.

Ambrosio could not sustain his glance; He turned away his eyes, while thus spoke the Dæmon:

"I have him then in my power! This model of piety! This being without reproach! This Mortal who placed his puny virtues on a level with those of Angels. He is mine! Irrevocably, eternally mine! Companions of my sufferings! Denizens of hell!

How grateful will be my present!"

He paused; then addressed himself to the Monk — —

"Carry you to Matilda?" He continued, repeating Ambrosio's words:

"Wretch! you shall soon be with her! You well deserve a place near her, for hell boasts no miscreant more guilty than yourself.

Hark, Ambrosio, while I unveil your crimes! You have shed the blood of two innocents; Antonia and Elvira perished by your hand. That Antonia whom you violated, was your Sister! That Elvira whom you murdered, gave you birth! Tremble, abandoned Hypocrite! Inhuman Parricide! Incestuous Ravisher! Tremble at the extent of your offences! And you it was who thought yourself proof against temptation, absolved from human frailties, and free from error and vice! Is pride then a virtue? Is inhumanity no fault? Know, vain Man! That I long have marked you for my prey: I watched the movements of your heart; I saw that you were virtuous from vanity, not principle, and I seized the fit moment of seduction. I observed your blind idolatry of the Madona's picture. I bad a subordinate but crafty spirit assume a similar form, and you eagerly yielded to the blandishments of Matilda. Your pride was gratified by her flattery; Your lust only needed an opportunity to break forth; You ran into the snare blindly, and scrupled not to commit a crime which you blamed in another with unfeeling severity. It was I who threw Matilda in your way; It was I who gave you entrance to Antonia's chamber; It was I who caused the dagger to be given you which pierced your Sister's bosom; and it was I who warned Elvira in dreams of your designs upon her Daughter, and thus, by preventing your profiting by her sleep, compelled you to add rape as well as incest to the catalogue of your crimes. Hear, hear, Ambrosio! Had you resisted me one minute longer, you had saved your body and soul. The guards whom you heard at your prison door came to signify your pardon. But I had already triumphed: My plots had already succeeded. Scarcely could I propose crimes so quick as you performed them. You are mine, and Heaven itself cannot rescue you from my power. Hope not that your penitence will make void our contract. Here is your bond signed with your blood; You have given up your claim to mercy, and nothing can restore to you the rights which you have foolishly resigned. Believe you that your secret thoughts escaped me? No, no, I read them all! You trusted that you should still have time for repentance. I saw your artifice, knew its falsity, and rejoiced in deceiving the deceiver! You are mine beyond reprieve: I burn to possess my right, and alive you quit not these mountains."

During the Dæmon's speech, Ambrosio had been stupefied by terror and surprize. This last declaration rouzed him.

"Not quit these mountains alive?" He exclaimed: "Perfidious, what mean you? Have you forgotten our contract?"

The Fiend answered by a malicious laugh:

"Our contract? Have I not performed my part? What more did I promise than to save you from your prison? Have I not done so? Are you not safe from the Inquisition — safe from all but from me? Fool that you were to confide yourself to a Devil! Why did you not stipulate for life, and power, and pleasure? Then all would have been granted: Now, your reflections come too late. Miscreant, prepare for death; You have not many hours to live!"

On hearing this sentence, dreadful were the feelings of the devoted Wretch! He sank upon his knees, and raised his hands towards heaven. The Fiend read his intention and prevented it —

"What?" He cried, darting at him a look of fury: "Dare you still implore the Eternal's mercy? Would you feign penitence, and again act an Hypocrite's part? Villain, resign your hopes of pardon. Thus I secure my prey!"

As he said this, darting his talons into the monk's shaven crown, he sprang with him from the rock. The caves and mountains rang with Ambrosio's shrieks. The dæmon continued to soar aloft, till reaching a dreadful height, He released the sufferer. Headlong fell the Monk through the airy waste; The sharp point of a rock received him; and He rolled from precipice to precipice, till bruised and mangled He rested on the river's banks. Life still existed in his miserable frame: He attempted in vain to raise himself; His broken and dislocated limbs refused to perform their office, nor was He able to quit the spot where He had first fallen. The Sun now rose above the horizon; Its scorching beams darted full upon the head of the expiring Sinner. Myriads of insects were called forth by the warmth; They drank the blood which trickled from Ambrosio's wounds; He had no power to drive them from him, and they fastened upon his sores, darted their stings into his body, covered him with their multitudes, and inflicted on him tortures the most exquisite and insupportable. The Eagles of the rock tore his flesh piecemeal, and dug out his eyeballs with their crooked beaks. A burning thirst tormented him; He heard the river's murmur as it rolled beside him, but strove in vain to drag himself towards the sound. Blind, maimed, helpless, and despairing, venting his rage in blasphemy and curses, execrating his existence, yet dreading the arrival of death destined to yield him up to greater torments, six miserable days did the Villain languish. On the Seventh a violent storm arose: The winds in fury rent up rocks and forests: The sky was now black with clouds, now sheeted with fire: The rain fell in torrents; It swelled the stream; The waves overflowed their banks; They reached the spot where Ambrosio lay, and when they abated carried with them into the river the corse of the despairing monk.

Haughty Lady, why shrunk you back when yon poor frail-one drew near? Was the air infected by her errors? Was your purity soiled by her passing breath? Ah! Lady, smooth that insulting brow: stifle the reproach just bursting from your scornful lip: wound not a soul, that bleeds already! She has suffered, suffers still. Her air is gay, but her heart is broken; her dress sparkles, but her bosom groans.

Lady, to look with mercy on the conduct of others, is a virtue no less than to look with severity on your own.

FINIS.

.

Milton Keynes UK
Ingram Content Group UK Ltd.
UKHW021939081024
449407UK00008B/156

9 781965 179055